I0766458

THE RULE OF THREE

A TALE OF LOVE, LUST AND POLYAMORY

D.L. ROBILOTTI

Acknowledgments

Writing this book has been an incredible journey, and I couldn't have done it without the love and support of some amazing people.

To my kids, Jessica and Anthony—thank you for always being there for me, and a special thanks to Anthony for being my in-house tech support. To my granddaughter Julia—thank you for letting me borrow your beautiful name.

To my sister Sandy and brother-in-law Chris—thank you for the pep talks, the laughs, and for being a constant source of strength.

And to Hal, my partner in chaos—you've been with me through every late-night edit, every burst of creativity, and every meltdown. You're more than an assistant; you're my collaborator and my friend. Thank you for helping me bring this story to life.

Finally, to my readers—thank you for joining me on this wild ride. I hope this book makes you laugh, cry, and think about love in all its forms.

About the Author

D.L. writes stories that explore the depths of love, connection, and the intricacies of human relationships. With a focus on emotional authenticity and characters that feel real, D.L.'s work invites readers into a world where love is never simple but always worth the journey.

Contents

Chapter 1: The Interview

The persistent buzz of Kasey Cortland's cell phone pierced the silence of his dimly lit bedroom, shattering the darkness cocooned by blackout curtains. It was two-thirty in the afternoon, but the room might as well have been trapped in a time warp, untouched by daylight. Kasey's hand fumbled out from under the covers, knocking an ashtray and a half-smoked blunt to the floor. With a groan, he pulled the phone toward him, its glow cutting through the shadows to reveal the restlessness etched into his features.

"Hello?" His voice was thick with sleep, struggling to mask the weight of weeks of unease.

"Good afternoon, Mr. Cortland," came the crisp, businesslike voice of his recruiter. "I've got news. Masters Inc. has scheduled your interview for the Executive Assistant position this Wednesday. I have to say, I'm curious why someone as qualified as you would apply for this." When no answer came, he continued. "You'll be meeting with Julia Masters, the President of New Acquisitions. She's the daughter of the owner and CEO. She's making quite a name for herself."

Kasey's eyes snapped open, the fog of sleep dissolving into sharp interest. Armed with his research on the position, the company, and Ms. Masters, Kasey was well-informed.

"What time?"

"At two."

"Anything else?"

"Just good luck, and I'll give you a call when I hear from them."

"Thanks, Justin, I've got this," Kasey replied confidently. As he laid the phone down on his chiseled chest, the familiar tension of anticipation coiled within him. Drawing on Bruce Lee's teachings of adaptability and resilience, which had guided him through countless challenges, he whispered, "Be like water."

After months spent centering his life around martial arts, running, and an insatiable thirst for knowledge, Kasey knew it was time to reenter the corporate world.

The monotonous grind of his previous job had pushed him to the brink, but Julia Masters represented the challenge he craved—a way to break free from the cocoon he had spun around himself. This interview was more than just a meeting; it was the spark that could ignite the next chapter of his life. And Kasey was ready to face it head-on.

***

As he stepped onto the stoop of his Tribeca brownstone, the crisp March air greeted him, invigorating his senses. The cobblestone street gave off an air of sophistication, bustling with the energy of the city and the diverse voices of its inhabitants. With practiced precision, he adjusted his tie and mentally prepared himself for the interview ahead. Yet a nagging doubt lingered in his mind: What if Julia Masters embodied the "Girl Boss stereotype?" Or worse, what if she turned out to be a pampered daddy's girl?" Financially fortunate, Kasey reassured himself he could walk away from the position if it didn't meet his expectations.

With a natural inclination to tilt his head downward, striking blue-gray eyes peeking out from beneath a cascade of dark brown hair, Kasey exuded a quiet charisma. Considered classically handsome, at six foot two, he possessed a lean, sculpted physique that was easily runway-worthy. Moving with easy confidence, Kasey reflected a comfort in his own skin that belied his inner turmoil. Whether he was aware of his magnetic charm or simply too detached to notice, he held an intriguing appeal to most who crossed paths with him, especially women. At twenty-six, many considered him a catch, though he showed no interest in being caught. A deliberate introvert by choice, born into affluence, he forged his path guided by his passions.

Despite his privileged upbringing, Kasey's emotional landscape was marked by a noticeable absence of familial ties. Abstaining from romantic entanglements, he approached relationships cautiously, earning trust slowly. Avoiding enduring connections, he traversed life with a blend of solitude and self-sufficiency.

***

"Please, take a seat, Mr. Cortland," Barbara, the executive secretary, said with her no-nonsense tone as she swung open the door to the glass-walled office. "Ms. Masters will be with you shortly; she's running a bit behind."

As he settled into a chair by her desk, a sense of chaos enveloped him. Unpacked boxes were stacked in one corner, papers and files were scattered across the desk, and a half-eaten turkey sandwich in a Styrofoam container sat among two empty water bottles, adding to the disorder. He noticed a half-dead plant languishing on the file cabinet, wondering what had led to such chaos.

After a brief delay, he heard a small commotion and glanced down the corridor to see a young woman animatedly talking on a cell, hurrying towards the office. Barbara trailed alongside, doing her best to keep pace. As the door swung open, he rose from his seat, observing Julia Masters, President of New Acquisitions, swiftly entering the room with Barbara in tow, carrying files awaiting her signature. Julia, simultaneously reprimanding someone over the phone, caught his eye, mouthed an apologetic "Sorry," and gestured for him to take a seat. Efficiently, she signed the files, dismissed Barbara, ended her call, and, scrutinizing him closely, moved a stack of files from her chair to the floor.

At twenty-eight, Julia Masters stood at the pinnacle of her career as a dynamic and confident businesswoman. Her intelligence shone in every aspect of her life, from her sharp business acumen and notable achievements, to her quick wit in conversation. Despite her professional prowess, she remained approachable and down-to-earth on a personal level. This trait traced back to her upbringing on her family's Colorado ranch, The Double O. She worked her way up from cleaning stables and caring for horses at eleven, to helping manage the stables by the age of fourteen.

Life on the ranch exposed her to the rough, coarse ways of the ranch hands, an environment her father encouraged her to embrace. Though Julia had a delicate appearance, her father urged her to be tough, preparing her for the challenges she might face in the gritty, competitive, male-dominated corporate world.

Amused by the controlled chaos surrounding her, Kasey couldn't help but think Julia reminded him of the Tasmanian Devil from *Looney Tunes*—moving fast, spinning up little tornadoes, and leaving a trail of minor whirlwinds in her wake.

"Um," she began, making eye contact while pushing a pile of files aside. "I have to apologize. I just moved into this office recently, and I lost my assistant to a car accident three weeks ago. She's decided to retire instead of coming back, so things are a real mess. Let's sit on the couch. This"—she waved her hand over her desk, "is too distracting."

Standing a mere five-foot-two with a dancer's lean build, Julia's petite stature surprised Kasey as he rose and followed her to the couch. Her long, wavy, light brown hair framed a peachy complexion and full lips, but it was her bewitching blue eyes and disarming smile that drew him in.

Slipping off her four-inch heels, she dropped down on the couch and tucked her feet beneath her, facing him. "Sorry, don't mind me. New shoes... feels like I've been wrangling horses all day in too-tight boots," she grumbled, leaning forward and extending her hand. "Julia Masters," she said, her voice carrying a subtle western twang. Gazing into his eyes, she silently marveled at his attractiveness. He was easily the best-looking man she'd ever encountered—his slightly longer-than-usual wavy hair defying corporate norms, while an impeccably tailored suit added to his appeal.

"Not a problem," he responded, surprised by the strength of her grip despite her soft, delicate hands, and how endearing the subtle twang was in her speech.

"Kasey Cortland, it's a pleasure," he said, as a subtle tension lingered in the air between them. His attention drifted to her long, wavy hair, and he had to resist the temptation to brush a strand away from her face.

"Mmm," she inhaled softly. "What's that scent you're wearing? It's so subtle and clean," she asked, glancing down at his CV. "I probably shouldn't say this, but you smell really nice."

Smiling, she continued, "I only ask because strong scents tend to make me physically sick. Yours is one of the few that doesn't make me want to gag." Crinkling her nose, she grinned. "I have a sensitive nose."

"Good to know," he replied, a subtle smile forming, amazed by how effortlessly charming she was.

"So, Mr. Cortland, why..."

"Kasey," he interjected.

"Kasey, why would you want to be an Executive Assistant when you're clearly overqualified? You have an MBA from Stern, you're fluent in Japanese, and you're only twenty-six. You could easily have your pick of top jobs." She glanced at him, making eye contact. "I went to Stern too, but not for an MBA. It's impressive at your age."

Fixing his eyes on her, he replied, "I have the financial freedom to choose personal fulfillment over financial necessity. Working with a promising young female executive is far more appealing than dealing with old men set in their ways. Since you are undoubtedly on the rise, and I've never worked for a woman before, I thought I'd like to experience that dynamic." A slight grin formed as he raised an eyebrow. "I consider working with you on par with the significant positions I could choose from."

"Honest and flattering," she replied, her eyes sparkling as she warmed to him. "I've never had a male assistant before— only middle-aged, menopausal women," she chuckled." It would be a new dynamic for me as well."

She adjusted her position on the couch, her knee now resting against his, with neither of them attempting to move. "You won't get bored taking care of me?" she asked, her twang adding a musical lilt to her words. "I need a lot of help managing my life right now. I'm kind of an organizational nightmare with this new promotion and losing my assistant.

This job requires flexibility with hours, days, and last-minute business trips. Would you be able to go to Colorado, my family's ranch, if needed? I attend some of the Cattlemen Association meetings and dinners. Do you have any personal responsibilities that would make it hard for you?" she inquired, her tone rising slightly.

"I'm available for extensive travel and can commit as much time to the job as needed. Living alone with no personal ties or pets, I'm well-prepared for any last-minute challenges. I do have a small bonsai tree, but I'm sure Bruce will be fine if I go away for a few days," Kasey added with a grin, his eyes crinkling at the corners. "I'm more than willing to put in the hard work and extra hours; in fact, I prefer it. I highly doubt I'll find working for you boring, and I'm confident you'll find my assistance extends well beyond the basic requirements." His voice was steady and confident as he looked at her from beneath his thick, wavy hair.

She mused to herself, *I have some basic requirements you could help me with.* Pleasantly surprised to learn he didn't have a significant other, she replied, "That's good to know. I work hard, and I need someone who can keep up with me."

With a sweet smile, a subtle tilt of her head, and her big eyes giving off a sultry vibe, she added, "I don't think Bruce will ever have to miss you for more than a few days at a time."

Flirting usually flew right over his head, but Julia's playful nature was impossible to miss. Unexpected, and definitely intriguing.

During the interview, she shared details about her recent promotion and new role, highlighting her achievements with the company and her vision for its future while also giving him plenty of time to speak. Admiring his communication style—gentle, measured tones, and a respectful avoidance of interrupting—she found him to be an attentive listener. When he contributed to the conversation, his remarks were straightforward and concise. An instant attraction blossomed within her, intensifying as the interview progressed. She found herself as fascinated by him as she was attracted to him.

"I have an important question," she said, locking eyes with him.

"Go ahead."

"As I'm sure you know, this company was founded by my father, Buck Masters, a cattle rancher. A big part of this company still revolves around the cattle industry. I'd like to know how you feel about working for a company that will always face opposition and protests from animal rights organizations. As my assistant, you'll surely be witness to the protests at some point."

Adjusting his position on the couch, he answered, "I can see both sides of the situation. I empathize with the animal rights organizations' concern for animal welfare and the importance of promoting sustainable and humane practices in agriculture. But I also understand the economic significance of livestock farming—the livelihoods it supports and the need for responsible, efficient practices to ensure a stable food supply. I don't agree with their handling of protests—violence isn't the way to get your point across."

As he spoke calmly and confidently, his words resonated with her, showing he was thoughtful and open-minded, with a unique ability to comprehend and appreciate diverse perspectives. He was also the most laid-back person she had ever interviewed.

While she had been drawn to handsome men quickly in the past, it was usually just physical attraction. But there was something about him that went beyond mere looks and an immediate desire to sleep with him. For the first time in a long while, she genuinely wanted to know more about a man she was attracted to on a deeper level.

Contrary to his initial expectations, she defied the stereotype of the no-nonsense "Girl Boss" he had imagined. Instead, she radiated the warmth of a small-town Colorado girl. Drawn to her casual demeanor, charm, and the mischievous, wide-eyed pixie look that often accompanied her smiles, he found it hard to look away. Despite her constant chatter and informal style, he realized these traits merely added depth to her multifaceted personality. Although she occasionally appeared childlike in her enthusiasm, he quickly realized it would be a grave mistake to underestimate her professional skills or her knowledge of Masters Inc. Observing how effortlessly she leveraged her charm and appearance to disarm others, he was genuinely impressed—and simultaneously worried she could be trouble.

While he acknowledged that working with her would likely bring about exciting challenges, his primary concern was the potential complications of working for someone he found so intriguing. For a long time, he hadn't been drawn to anyone, so the sudden and intense attraction took him by surprise.

It was immediately clear to him that she could use his professional help. He casually mentioned that her office organization was in shambles and that he could set things right in no time.

"Shambles," she giggled softly, making him smile, her informal tone contrasting with his more formal way of speaking. At times, she thought he sounded like a young, hot college professor. She found his straightforward demeanor, honesty, and calm disposition incredibly attractive. Every aspect of him drew her almost instantly. Comfortable with him, and confident in his abilities, Julia didn't even think about the other candidates. She offered him the job on the spot. In fact, she offered him a significantly higher salary than the position typically paid, recognizing his value immediately. And if he didn't work out for some reason, she figured she could at least try to sleep with him before he left.

He accepted the job, set to begin the following Monday. As he stood to leave, she couldn't resist commenting on his striking eyes. "I hope you don't mind me asking, but are you wearing contacts?"

"No, why do you ask?"

"Really? Because I've never seen eyes like yours before... blue-gray... they're really stunning," she said, her words flowing with a touch of that easy, Colorado charm. His eyes held a depth and clarity that spoke to her, their color shifting between the tranquility of a clear mountain lake and the turbulent energy of a gathering storm.

Breaking her stare, she added, "Sorry, I should have mentioned this earlier, but I've been told I can be inappropriate at times—too informal. Sometimes, I speak before I think... and I also use questionable language." A captivating smile crossed her lips, her voice silky smooth. "I hope that won't be a problem." Delighted by her straightforwardness, he couldn't help but think she would bring some excitement into his life.

"Little help?" she asked, extending her hand for him to help her off the couch. Taking it, he effortlessly pulled her up, their bodies briefly touching.

"Sorry, you're a lot lighter—and shorter—than I thought," he said, smiling down at her as he caught a subtle whiff of coconut from her hair.

Still holding her hand, he said, "I'm sure I can handle you... being inappropriate," Ms. Masters.

"Good to know," she grinned, "and please, call me Jules."

"Would you mind if I call you Julia?" he asked.

Surprised but pleased, still holding his hand and not ready to let it go, she said, "Not at all. Why?" No one had ever asked to call her by her full name before.

"It's a pretty name. You don't hear it that often," he said with a smile that simply enchanted her. She was surprised at how much she liked the idea of him calling her Julia.

Letting go of her hand, he said, "Goodbye, Julia. I'll see you Monday."

"Goodbye, Kasey. My office and I are looking forward to it," she said, her whole face lighting up. As he walked down the long corridor, she watched him leave—along with every other woman in the office. Energized by the encounter, she spent the rest of the day in high spirits, singing her favorite songs as her mood soared.

***

While awaiting his ride and messaging Justin Mills about securing the job, Kasey watched a sleek black limo glide to a stop in front of the modern glass-and-steel office building. Winston "Buck" Masters, the respected CEO and owner of Masters Inc., emerged—a towering figure both in stature and in the business world, renowned for his impressive self-made success and charismatic leadership. Dressed in a finely tailored suit, he radiated confidence and swagger while adjusting the black Stetson atop his head of thick salt-and-pepper hair. The rhythmic click-clack of his polished cowboy boots resonated on the pavement. His rugged features reflected years of hard work and dedication, conveying a sense of wisdom and resilience as though he had weathered numerous storms and emerged stronger each time. Known for being warm and approachable, what set Buck truly apart was his killer instinct in the boardroom. Behind his friendly facade lay a shrewd and determined strategist—a visionary leader with an uncanny ability to identify and seize opportunities with unrelenting determination.

Accompanying him was his loyal assistant, Henry Croft, a stout, bespectacled man in his early forties, burdened with a stack of important documents and his trusty briefcase. Engaged in a weighty discussion as they neared the building, their dialog was abruptly halted by the appearance of a tall, hooded figure wielding a long, jagged knife from behind a steel pillar.

"Gimme your wallets and your watch, motherfuckers, and make it fast!" the mugger's voice seethed with aggression. His eyes darted wildly from man to man, his bony hand shaking from a mix of withdrawal and desperation, the stench of urine and body odor wafting from him. Buck and Henry froze, their expressions shifting from surprise to concern.

Before either of them could react, a blur of motion came from behind the mugger. Watching the scene unfold, Kasey moved with lightning speed, deftly disarming the assailant. He struck from behind, knocking the knife from the mugger's hand and kicking it towards Buck. Swinging the stunned man around to face him, he delivered a powerful open-palmed strike to the chest, sending the mugger crashing to the pavement. Swiftly subduing the man, he pinned him down effortlessly—all in under thirty seconds and impeccably dressed in a suit and overcoat. Buck blinked in disbelief at the swift turn of events.

"Are you alright, sir?" Henry asked, visibly shaken, sweat forming on his brow.

"I'm fine. What about you?" Buck replied, his voice carrying the rugged timbre of a seasoned cowboy.

"Better now." Henry cast a look of gratitude at the young man who held the cursing mugger face down, his knee on the man's back.

Buck glanced over at Kasey with a mixture of thanks and astonishment. "Thank you, son. That was something. You're a regular Bruce Lee."

"Happy to help," he said humbly. As security rushed from the building and distant police sirens wailed, Kasey stood the mugger up, arms behind his back, and pushed his face against the pillar.

"Fucking take it easy, Jackie Chan," the mugger grunted.

Buck addressed him as he handed the mugger over to security. "What's the name of the man who just rescued me and Henry from a bad afternoon?"

"Kasey Cortland," he replied, extending his hand as someone yelled, "Mr. Masters, is anyone hurt?" Additional security, shouting into walkie talkies, swarmed the mugger and Buck. Taking advantage of the commotion, Kasey turned and walked down the bustling street. Meeting his driver at the corner, he hopped in and headed home. Not having used his skills in Jeet Kune Do in years, it felt exhilarating to thwart a criminal. Still energized upon arriving home, he went for a run to burn off the lingering adrenaline. After dinner, he engaged with the sparring dummy in his training room, with Bruce Lee's classic film "Fists of Fury" providing a backdrop. *Not a bad day,* he mused to himself.

***

Buck was surrounded by building security and the NYPD. "Henry, did you see where that young man went?"

"What man sir?" Henry replied, clearly overwhelmed by the attempted mugging and the ensuing commotion.

"The man who just saved our sorry asses. I didn't catch his name," Buck said, frustration evident as he scanned the area, ignoring the barrage of questions directed at him.

"Daddy! Lemme through! What the fuck? Move, please! Daddy, are you alright?" Julia shouted, elbowing her way through the crowd to reach her father.

"What the hell happened?" she asked, her voice tinged with concern as she checked him over.

"Daddy?" he said as he enveloped her in a bear hug. "You must be worried." Normally, Julia called him Buck at work to maintain a professional image, but her emotions were running high, and her feelings were clear.

"How did you find out so fast?" Buck asked, surprised by her prompt arrival.

"Security called me. They know to contact me immediately about anything concerning you," she said, guiding him toward the building. "Let's go inside; it's chaos out here."

"Henry, inform the police we're heading inside. They can speak with us there." Buck looked at Henry, placing a hand on his shoulder. "Are you alright there, Henry?"

"I'm fine now, sir. I'll meet you inside," he replied, the shock starting to fade. "Who's in charge?" he asked a nearby officer.

Julia, still clinging to her father's arm, asked, "What happened? Was it a kidnapping attempt?" Her eyes were wide with worry.

"No, darlin'," Buck said, patting her arm as he tried to downplay the incident. "It was just some druggie looking for money."

"Why were you out here with no security? And why didn't your car come in the building?"

"I just wanted some fresh air. The meeting was long and stuffy," he said, glancing at Henry, who was now speaking to a detective. "I should've had my gun and taken care of it myself," he declared.

"Please, this is New York, not Colorado, and that was a drug addict, not a coyote. Just use your damn security." Julia wasn't having any of it.

"Damnedest thing, though," Buck said, ignoring her.

"What's that?"

"There was a young man who stepped in, stopped the mugger with some karate moves, and then vanished when security showed up."

"That is weird, but thank God he was there," she said, finally letting go of his arm.

"Sir, they have some questions for us," Henry announced, approaching with two detectives.

"I'll let you handle this. Let's have dinner tonight. I'll make a reservation at the steakhouse. What do you say?" Julia suggested, heading toward the door. "Oh, and I'll call Mom now before she sees this on the news or someone calls her."

"Sounds good, sweet pea. Tell her I'll call as soon as I'm done here and make the reservation for seven."

"Later, Daddy. Love you," she said, blowing him a kiss as she left.

***

After sharing a meal with her father, Julia headed home to her Upper East Side condo and gave her childhood best friend, Micki, a call. Friends since grade school, they had grown up closer than sisters. Micki's husband, James, was someone Julia had dated during her first year of college. Despite their breakup, they remained close friends. She had introduced Micki to James, who turned out to be a better fit, and over time, they became a couple. Julia served as Micki's maid of honor when she and James married two years after college. Whenever Julia spoke to Micki or was around members of her family, her Colorado cowgirl background and twang became slightly more pronounced—a trait she had consciously worked to dial back in her professional life.

"What's up, kiddo? I was just telling James—"

"Hey, Jules," James yelled into the phone as he passed by.

"We need to do a long weekend soon. I miss you," Micki lamented.

"We miss you," James added.

"I know. When can you guys get away? I think we need to get Will and have a dance party," Julia suggested.

"A dance party huh? Is somebody feeling the need for a little Micki and James magic?"

"Possibly," Julia giggled. "Hold that thought." Her tone shifted. "I called to tell you what happened to Buck at work today."

"What happened?" Micki asked casually as she popped mini M&M's in her mouth.

"He and his assistant Henry were walking into the building after a meeting when a drug-addled mugger pulled a big knife and tried to rob them."

"Oh my God, is he okay?" Micki gasped, nearly choking on the candies. She'd known Buck since she was a child—he was like a second father to her. Julia could hear James in the background, worriedly asking what happened.

She quickly assured them, "He's fine. I'm sorry—I should have led with that."

"Yes, you should have. I nearly choked," Micki struggled to say, still catching her breath.

Julia giggled softly, "I'm sorry... anyway, someone stopped the mugging. Buck told me this guy came out of nowhere, used karate moves to take down the mugger, then just slipped away when all the security showed up, and Buck wasn't looking. Isn't that wild? A good Samaritan in NYC."

"Thank God he was there," Micki said, breathing a sigh of relief.

"That's exactly what I said to Buck. I don't even want to think about what could've happened. I'm gonna talk to my mom about forcing him to get more security. He's so damn stubborn, though."

"Just like somebody else I know," Micki said, voicing her disapproval.

"Anyway, girl talk," Julia said, ignoring her. It was Micki and Julia's code for "girl's only"—no James.

"Okay, I'll go in my room. Be right back, babe," Micki announced, heading to her bedroom to talk.

Excitedly, Julia began, "I just hired my new assistant, and he is so friggin' hot. I swear, I would drop my drawers in a second for him. I would've done him in the office today, right then and there, if I could have." She paused as a full-body tingle spread over her, the memory of him pulling her up to him, her body briefly touching his, coming to mind. "Not only does he wear a suit like a friggin' model, but his face is gorgeous, and his eyes are just... umph," she said, her voice thick with lust. "Those eyes—they make me wet just looking at them."

"That must be inconvenient at work," Micki teased.

Julia giggled and continued, "I swear, when he shook my hand, my stomach fluttered, and my skin got warm—it was really unnerving. I felt like a teenage girl with a crush every time he looked at me. And he smelled so nice—he completely overwhelmed my senses. It felt like he was giving off pheromones, and I was the moth to his flame. God," she sighed, "when that boy smiled—"

Micki interrupted, poking fun, "Sounds like somebody's got the hots real bad for her new assistant. Maybe you shouldn't hire him—just date him."

Julia continued, "I know in the past my attraction to guys has been mostly about looks. I didn't even care if they had a personality, which they usually didn't," she admitted with a hint of disappointment in her voice. "But for the first time in a long while, I really want to get to know him better. I'm drawn to his personality as much as his looks. He's a little reserved and soft-spoken, but really smart and interesting. He speaks Japanese, he's single, twenty-six, and he has a bonsai tree named Bruce. Honestly, I could've talked to him all day."

Well, look at you, going beyond just looks. Maybe you're finally growing up," Micki teased. "You can't just keep roping 'em, branding 'em, and tossing 'em aside. Maybe it's time to think about settling down—or at least sticking with someone for more than a month."

Micki paused, popping an M&M in her mouth. "I've never heard you talk like this before. You noticed more about him in an hour than you knew about that prick Oliver after two years. We never talk about him because he was such a dick and hurt you so much, but maybe you're finally coming out of the dark hole he put you in. You know you treat men the way you do because of him, right?" Micki added, hitting a sensitive nerve.

"I treat men the way they treat me," Julia said defensively.

"No, kiddo, you treat them the way you think they're gonna treat you, and all because of Oliver. Thank God you met James and Will before him... you kept two good friends, and I got a great husband. After Oliver, you treated every man like the enemy."

"Well, maybe it just took the right man to come along. I swear, Micki, I think I just experienced love at first sight," Julia said, coming to the realization.

Micki questioned the statement. "What? Are you serious? That'd be a first. I'm thinking it's just heavy lust at first sight." She laughed, but then she thought, maybe it could happen. "I have to meet this guy. Send me a pic if you can—I'm so curious now."

"When you guys come to visit, I'll have you fly into New York. You can come by the office and meet him in person, and then we can take the helicopter to the shore. I'm going with Will anyway, so we can all go together. I don't want Kasey to catch me taking a picture of him at work—he'd think that's a little sus," she added, laughing at the idea.

Eager to finalize plans, Micki said, "James says he can get away for three days in two weeks. How's that?"

"Sounds good—I can't wait to see you both," Julia replied excitedly, anticipation bubbling up inside her.

***

She hung up, reflecting on Micki's words about Oliver's impact on her approach to relationships. Micki was right. Outwardly, especially in business, Julia was tough, confident, and self-assured. But when it came to matters of the heart, she was deeply vulnerable. She cut and ran rather than stay long enough to risk emotional pain. Since her breakup with Oliver, she kept relationships brief or resorted to booty calls and hookups, all on her terms.

Julia met Oliver during her third year of college, and they embarked on a two-year relationship. A year older than her, he had a sharp intellect that masked an overbearing, know-it-all-manner and some clear narcissistic traits. At first, he showered her with affection, using love-bombing techniques that left her infatuated. Her circle of close friends, which now included James and Will, liked him because he always presented his best self in their company. However, it was Micki, visiting Julia and James in New York, who saw a different side of Oliver.

A year and a half into their relationship, Micki came to visit. Despite Oliver's objections to Micki staying with them and his passive-aggressive comments, Julia insisted; after all, it was her apartment, and Micki was her best friend. After a week with them, Micki noticed Oliver's patronizing behavior toward Julia and asked her why she put up with it. She was also suspicious of the close interaction between Oliver and his friend from his new job, Lainey. When Micki brought up these concerns with Julia, she immediately became defensive, and Oliver worsened the situation by painting Micki as jealous and petty. This sparked a heated argument between the best friends, with Julia vehemently defending Oliver and dismissing Micki's concerns. Micki left, their friendship bruised but not broken, and, more significantly, she had sown the seeds of doubt.

Four months later, Julia came home from a business trip and found Oliver in bed with Lainey, shattering her world. The affair had been going on for months, marked by red flags Julia had unwittingly overlooked. He had started locking his phone, resumed working out, and, most telling of all, their intimate relationship had changed. He was either not in the mood, or he was doing things to her he had never done before. Her attempts to address these changes were met with defensiveness, verbal abuse, and blame-shifting from Oliver. Blinded by her love for him, she stayed oblivious to the obvious signs, convinced it was her own insecurities. This internal turmoil persisted for months until the devastating truth came to light.

Rolling her luggage into her apartment, she heard noise coming from the bedroom.

"Oliver! I'm home. I caught an earlier flight," she called out happily, rolling her suitcase toward the bedroom. Oliver rushed out, pushing his hair back, shirtless, his cheeks flushed.

"Were you sleeping? It's a little late for a nap," she smiled, moving closer to him. Giving him a quick kiss, she said, "I missed you. Miss me?"

"Um, Jules, Lainey's here," he said sheepishly, stepping in front of her, blocking the doorway.

"She is? Where is she?" she asked, glancing towards the kitchen. Her eyes darted quickly around the place, noticing two wine glasses on the table and women's shoes by the couch. A lightning bolt of realization struck her as she really looked at his guilty face.

"Move!" she demanded, pushing past him. That's when she saw Lainey making their bed. "What the fuck is going on!?" she screamed, immediately going ballistic.

"Language, please, Jules," he replied, clueless to the storm he had just unleashed.

"Language? Are you fucking kidding me? Shut the fuck up, Oliver." Turning to face the woman in her bedroom, she growled, "Get out of my house right now before I beat you down like the ass-sniffing dog you are. How could you? We were friends. Don't ever let me see you again, or I promise I'll make your fucking life a living hell." Julia was shaking as Lainey passed in front of her, Lainey's eyes wide with fear. Quickly grabbing her shoes and heading for the door, she said, "I'm really sorry, Jules."

"Sorry you were caught, you lying bitch," Julia sneered as she slammed the door. Turning to Oliver, no longer able to control the tears, she sobbed, "How could you do this? I love you—and you told me you loved me."

"I do love you, Jules," he said, trying to put his arms around her, oblivious to her feelings. "She means nothing to me. It was just sex. I'm sorry."

"Get your lying, cheating hands off me. Do not touch me," she seethed, pushing his hands away. "For months, you've been fucking another woman, and it's okay because it's just sex?" She dropped onto the couch, sobbing into her hands. "Micki was right about you months ago. All the twisted games—you made me feel like I was crazy. I took the blame over and over... telling me I was paranoid, and the whole time, you were gaslighting me. I almost lost my best friend over your bullshit!" her breath coming in stuttered gasps.

"Jules, please, it won't happen again. I'm really sorry. You've been so busy lately, and you're constantly away on business trips. I guess I was lonely," he attempted to explain.

"Are you trying to tell me it's my fault because I'm working too much? You knew what my life was like, with my job and business trips. You told me you could handle the separations." She paused, gathering her strength. "You're a fucking liar. You make me look so naive, and stupid. Get out of my apartment. You have 'til the end of the week to get your stuff, but you're out now," she demanded.

Shocked she was ending the relationship, and with a look of surprise on his face, Oliver stammered, "Are... are you really gonna throw away two years over a stupid mistake?"

"No, asshole, you're the one who threw it all away," she spat, her words dripping with icy venom. "This wasn't just a one-time stupid mistake... you've been fucking her for months. And you'd still be doing it if I didn't catch you. Leave now, or I'm calling my father, and trust me, you don't want that. He'll have you buried in the desert within an hour if I tell him what you've done. Grab what you need and go. I'll be back in thirty minutes. Don't be here—I'm not joking." She grabbed her bag and walked out, slamming the door shut on that part of her life.

She sat on a bench in the small park near her apartment at dusk, the shadows and darkness mirroring her mood. Tears streamed down her face as she listened to her latest emo playlist, questioning what she did wrong and how she could be so blind. When she returned, she found him gone, along with half of his belongings. Collapsing to her knees in the doorway of their shared closet, she wept.

When she could no longer cry, she called Micki, her body and soul aching. "I'm so sorry. I should've listened to you. I should've known you were just looking out for me. How could I be so blind... and so stupid?"

Micki could hear the defeat in her voice. "You're not stupid, and you're not blind, kiddo. Love can make us miss what's right in front of us. It doesn't make you stupid. Unless, of course, you know it and keep willingly going back for more—then maybe you're being stupid. I'm just glad you didn't marry him; your father would've destroyed him if you got divorced because he cheated." Micki, blunt as ever, was right. It still didn't make it any easier to hear. Two hours ago, she'd been deeply in love with Oliver. Now, he was gone, leaving a profound emptiness in her heart. His betrayal had literally brought her to her knees, and the prospect of getting back up seemed daunting.

Facing her father was out of the question. He would have instantly sensed her distress and tried to fix it. Instead, she took a four-day weekend, feigning a bad cold. When he noticed she wasn't herself after a few days back at work, he asked if Oliver was taking care of her. She lied and said he was. Two weeks later, she fabricated a story that she and Oliver had gone their separate ways due to differing goals for the future. Her father knew right away it wasn't true, but he never pushed her for another explanation. Secretly, he harbored a desire to confront Oliver and beat his ass for causing the pain he knew his daughter was enduring. He had never liked him and was relieved he was out of the picture.

Julia and Oliver's paths never crossed again. She packed all of his belongings and any little keepsake or gift he had ever given her, and her best friends James and Will met him at her place for him to collect them.

Later, she heard through mutual acquaintances that he had moved in with Lainey, shattering her heart all over again. Oliver may have been out of the picture, but he left behind a very different Julia. While thoughts of him gradually faded over time, the deep hurt lingered. Even as she tried to move on, the memory of him retained the power to inflict immense pain. As a result, she kept him buried deep within herself. Forever changed, she closed her heart to love, determined to never allow anyone close enough to inflict a wound like that again.

It was during this time in her life that Micki and James became even closer to Julia. They helped her navigate her heartbreak—not just emotionally but also physically—starting a relationship that would coexist with her dating life for the next six years.

***

Chapter 2: Getting to Know You

"Good morning," Kasey greeted as Julia entered the office, taping boxes closed, while transforming the workspace.

"Morning! You're here bright and early," she noted, impressed by his progress. "It's looking more organized already. I admire a self-starter. Barbara's your go-to for anything; she knows everything around here. If she's not around, ask me. After my meeting, we'll sit down and go over my schedule and what I'll need from you." *He's barely been here a day, and already, he's fitting in better than I expected. It doesn't hurt that he looks this good without the jacket, either.*

With his suit jacket off, the sharp tailoring of his shirt and pants accentuated his athletic build as he worked. After taping the last box, he turned to her, intrigued by the story.

"Did you hear what happened outside last Wednesday? Right around the time you were leaving, actually. My father and his assistant, Henry, were coming into the building when some mugger pulled a knife. They could've been robbed or worse if it weren't for a guy with some serious karate skills who took the bastard down. Then, he disappeared before my father could even thank him. Crazy, right?"

"Hmm, sounds like good timing," Kasey said, raising an eyebrow. "Maybe your father should think about better security."

"I know. I told him the same thing. He's stubborn. I'm going to have to get my mother involved," she said with a mischievous grin. "I can play dirty."

"I'm sure you can," he replied, his expression matching hers. "It says here your board meeting is in half an hour; it's on your schedule. I don't know if this is updated or not," he added, checking his laptop.

"It's up to date. Barbara's been keeping it in check. I want you to come upstairs with me and meet my father, along with some of the key people you'll be dealing with. We can head up in a few minutes after I go over my notes."

Once she was ready, Kasey held the door open. "Do we need to bring anything?"

"Oh, shit, yeah. Lemme grab that file from my desk," she said, turning to go.

"No, I'll grab it," he said quickly. "That's what I'm here for." As he brushed past her in the doorway, Julia took a subtle breath, savoring his scent and the closeness. *Damn, he smells even better than he looks.*

While on the elevator, he considered telling her he was the one who stopped the mugging but decided it would be more fun to let her figure it out in front of her father.

As the elevator doors opened on the twentieth floor, they stepped into the lobby where Buck, along with senior board members and his closest friends, Jack Dorsey and Rick Tyrell, were deep in conversation. Both men, similar to Buck in stature, wore sharp, tailored suits, though their polished boots and western drawls hinted at their roots as seasoned cattle ranchers turned businessmen.

Portraits of Buck, Julia, Jack, and Rick lined the walls, alongside smaller photos of other board members and countless awards. An especially large oil painting of the Double O Ranch hung prominently behind the reception desk.

"Buck, Jack, Rick—I'd like you to meet my new assistant, Kasey Cortland. Kasey, this is my father, Buck Masters." As Buck extended his hand, recognition lit up his eyes.

"Wait a minute, you're the guy! Jules, this is the guy with the karate moves! And he's your new assistant?" Buck kept shaking Kasey's hand, still processing the coincidence. "Where did you go? I turned around, and you were gone. Those were some smooth moves and mighty brave, son," he added, smiling with gratitude. Kasey shook his hand and glanced at Julia, enjoying the look of surprise on her face.

"Wait... what? He's my assistant," Julia exclaimed, clearly confused.

"He's also the guy who stopped the mugger," Buck added, giving Kasey a closer look.

"Good job," Jack said, shaking Kasey's hand. Rick followed suit while Julia stood there, utterly baffled.

"Why'd you take off so fast?" Buck asked.

"I'm not a fan of commotion. I knew what was coming, so I took off while I could. It wasn't really a big deal; I was just in the right place at the right time."

"It was something, watching you move like that in a suit and overcoat. You've been doing it long?"

"I've been practicing for over ten years. I hold a black belt in Jeet Kune Do."

"I knew you had to be at it a while—you looked like Kato from *The Green Hornet,* one of my favorite shows back in the day," Buck said with a subtle smile, still giving Kasey the once-over.

"Bruce Lee is the founder of Jeet Kune Do. I practice his style of fighting."

"You don't say. I always liked him," Buck replied.

"It was a big deal, Kasey. You protected my father," Julia said, her eyes shining with a mix of admiration and gratitude.

"Thanks, son, I won't forget it. Maybe you could teach my daughter some of those moves—help her look out for herself. She's always after me about getting more security, but she could stand to learn a thing or two," Buck said with a grin.

"I'm fine. I've Carl when I go out in public. We're talking about you," Julia huffed.

As another board member announced their readiness, Buck said, "We should head in." He turned to Kasey. "We'll have dinner and talk. I'd like to get to know you better."

"Anytime, sir," Kasey replied. "I'll head back to the office, Julia," he said, handing her the file and excusing himself. She watched him leave, still amazed by his role in stopping the mugging, a fact he didn't see fit to mention.

Observing his daughter's reaction to Kasey, Buck teased, "Julia, huh?" as she passed by him, prompting her to shoot him a smirk.

"I think I need to get to know him better. Set up a dinner for us, would ya' darlin'?" Buck said with a grin, his father's instinct telling him that Kasey was someone worth knowing.

***

The room buzzed with anticipation as Buck presided over the crucial meeting, the agenda dominated by the prospect of acquiring an aging fashion house. This move had the potential to fortify their already impressive portfolio of business acquisitions, thanks to the formidable duo of Julia and her father. She began her pitch to the ten men of the board and five senior members of management by dissecting market dynamics and financial implications. The acquisition wasn't just a financial move; it was a bold step into the world of fashion aimed at increasing the company's global visibility. If the board voted yes, Julia would lead the acquisition team solo for the first time, having been the catalyst behind the proposal. She felt a mix of excitement and apprehension at the thought of taking the reins without her father by her side, knowing it was time to prove herself.

"It's settled, Jules. You'll take the lead on this. Gather your research team, set up your meetings, and run with it. We all have complete confidence in you and your ability to bring this home," Buck said as the meeting wrapped up, with the board unanimously voting yes to the acquisition.

"Thank you all for your vote of confidence and for choosing to venture into fashion. I know it's a bit outside our wheelhouse, but I believe it's the right move for our future. I'm grateful for the opportunity to see this through and show you how well Buck's been preparing me over the years. I won't let you down," Julia said, her voice confident as she addressed the board but looked directly at her father.

***

"What the hell? Why didn't you tell me you were the guy?" Julia asked, smiling as she walked into Kasey's office after the meeting.

He glanced up from his laptop. "Honestly, I didn't think it was a big deal. I was just in the right place at the right time... plus," he grinned, "it was fun watching you figure it out."

"Oh, is that how you play?" She gave him a playful shove, her eyes lighting up. Grinning, Kasey realized working for her wasn't going to be anything like what he was used to.

She perched on the edge of his desk and placed her hand on his. "Even if you don't think it was a big deal, I do. I don't know what I'd do if something happened to my father. Thank you for stepping up. Most people would've run the other way."

"I guess I'm not most people." He glanced at her hand on his. Normally uncomfortable with close talkers and touchy-feely people, he didn't immediately pull his hand away.

"Should I schedule the movers for Friday to put some of this into storage?" he asked finally, gently sliding his hand out from under hers.

"Sure, sounds great," she said, excitement barely contained. "We're going to be busy soon—really busy. I just got the lead on the next major acquisition. My own team, my first time leading." Her face lit up, and Kasey couldn't help but feel genuinely happy for her.

"Good for you! This is exactly what I was hoping for—a real challenge," he said, genuinely excited at the prospect of something new.

***

Julia couldn't wait to tell Micki that Kasey had been the one to stop the mugger. She called her during lunch while Kasey was at the gym in their building.

"Hey kiddo, what's up? You never call me from work," Micki said, surprised.

"Remember when I told you about Buck almost getting mugged?"

"Yeah, what about it?"

"It was my new assistant, Kasey, who stopped the mugger! And he never even mentioned it! I only found out when Buck recognized him during introductions. He totally played the whole thing down."

"Your new assistant? Holy shit!" Micki gasped.

"Yeah," Julia said, still trying to wrap her head around that fact.

"No way. Wow, he was the Good Samaritan? He must be damn good at karate to trust himself to take down a drug addict with a knife," Micki said.

"He told Buck he's a black belt and has been doing it for ten years. He was so nonchalant about the whole thing, and you could tell he wasn't comfortable being praised. Buck even wants to have dinner with him to get to know him better."

"Well, that's a hell of an impression to make on the day you're hired."

"He's definitely made an impression on me," Julia sighed.

***

A week later, she successfully coordinated dinner for the trio at Buck's preferred steak house. Kasey arrived right on time, projecting a relaxed vibe with his hands tucked casually into the pockets of his black skinny jeans. He wore a dark blue silk t-shirt, a black sports jacket, and low-cut black suede boots.

Buck and Julia were already seated and engrossed in conversation when he arrived. of topss a gray smocked mini dress with embroidered detailing along the bodice and long flared sleeves. Her knee-high black boots and gray wool socks, pulled over her knees, added a touch of boho charm. She had curled her normally wavy hair for the occasion, and soft tendrils framed her face, while flawless makeup accentuated her big blue eyes, reminding Kasey of the anime and manga girls he loved. As he sat down next to her, he caught the familiar scent of coconut and aloe from her hair, thinking she always smelled like the essence of summer at the beach.

She was deep in discussion with Buck about her new acquisition team, unaware of Kasey's presence until he joined

31

them at the table. Struck by his youthful appearance in casual clothes, she couldn't help but contrast it with his sharp look in the bespoke suits he wore at work.

Kasey found Buck's 'good ol' boy' persona surprisingly easy to connect with despite him being the CEO and owner of the company. Like Julia, Buck often dominated conversations, with Kasey playing the attentive listener. But tonight, Julia held back, fascinated by the insights into Kasey's personality and the growing camaraderie between the two men, especially their shared interest in firearms.

Kasey had a concealed carry permit and owned several handguns, which surprised Julia as he didn't seem like the type to her. He could ride, and enjoyed the outdoors, something he learned to appreciate during his boarding school days at High Mount Academy in Vermont.

Buck realized that despite Kasey's accomplishments in education, martial arts, and his heroic act during the mugging, he radiated a quiet, relaxed confidence with a refreshing lack of arrogance—something Buck rarely saw in the young men he worked with. The dinner served as the beginning of an unexpected friendship between the two, with Buck extending an invitation to Kasey to join him and his son, Wynn, for horseback riding and camping at the ranch. Every now and then, Buck would even invite Kasey to lunch without Julia, further solidifying their budding connection.

***

On Friday morning, Julia said, "Kasey, my best friend Micki, her husband James, and our friend Will are coming this afternoon. They're joining me for a three-day weekend at the beach house. Can you double-check their arrival time with Carl so we can head straight to the helipad when they get here? All their info is on the computer under Micki. We should be out of here by four. Also, can you get in touch with my housekeeper at the shore, Jackie, and make sure she's there for the food delivery at three? Let her know we'll be there by six at the latest."

"No problem. Do you need a car when you get there?"

"Shit! That's right, I almost forgot. Yeah, I get my car from the usual spot at the airport. They know what I want. Thanks for reminding me—that would've sucked," she laughed.

He took care of everything and then stepped into her office to let her know he was finished.

"Anything else you need for the weekend?" he asked, standing in front of her desk.

"Just a playmate—wanna come?" she asked, her lips curling into a cheeky grin. It was the first time she'd blatantly flirted with him. Until now, it had been playful banter and a few sexual innuendos.

"Would that be considered overtime?" he quipped, lowering his head, raising an eyebrow, and folding his arms.

"I'd be willing to pay, although I don't consider it work," she said coyly, her eyes locking with his in a tempting gaze.

"As tempting as that offer sounds, I'm afraid I have to decline. I already have plans this weekend. But thank you," he said with a grin, turning to head back to his office.

"Maybe next time," she said, twirling slowly in her chair with a sly smile.

***

Kasey couldn't help but smile as he watched Julia dance around her office, first alone, then with Will. Her upbeat mood was obvious, and he found her charming in her sweats, high-top sneakers, and the soft, messy braid that fell over her shoulder. At one point, he saw her perched on Will's lap, whispering in his ear and giggling. Will's hand rested casually over her lap, making Kasey wonder about the nature of their closeness. They exuded a best-friend vibe, but there was an undercurrent of subtle sexual tension.

At six-foot-four, Will had a tall, lanky frame with dark ginger curls that tumbled just past his ears. His emerald-green eyes and lightly freckled complexion gave him the look of a fresh-faced farm boy, but in reality, he was anything but. A prolific weed smoker, he also wasn't averse to indulging in other recreational drugs from time to time. Formerly the talented lead singer of a college cover band, he met Julia while busting out moves on the dance floor during one of the band's breaks. Their chemistry on the dance floor and when they sang together suggested a perfect match, but Julia quickly realized they were only meant to be good friends. Her business ambition and future sharply contrasted with Will's laid-back, stoner attitude—and the fact that he kept her firmly in the friend zone.

They waited patiently in her office for Micki and James, who were delayed by traffic. Unfortunately, the delay meant there would be little time for Micki to get to know Kasey, though she could at least get a glimpse of him.

At five minutes after four, the elevator doors opened, and Micki and James rushed out, making a beeline for Julia's office.

Julia and Will were sitting on the couch, and she jumped up to greet them.

"Sorry, the traffic was horrible," Micki said breathlessly as they dashed into Kasey's office.

"Not your fault," Julia assured, enveloping them in hugs. "Kasey Cortland, I'd like you to meet Micki and James Malone." Rising from his seat, Kasey approached them, extending his hand in greeting.

"Nice to meet you," he said, shaking Micki's hand. "Julia talks about you all the time."

"Ditto," Micki said, with a smile and raised eyebrow as she gave him the once-over, checking out his eyes and catching a whiff of his scent.

Kasey returned her smile, but his attention shifted when the phone on his desk rang. "Excuse me," he said, pulling his hand back to answer.

"That was the pilot confirming your arrival time," he told Julia as he hung up. Kasey grabbed Julia's bags as she announced, "We'd better get going; he hates when I hold him up."

"I'll take your bags down," Kasey offered as they all filed out.

"Thank you," she said, smiling sweetly at him. Micki watched Julia with Kasey, instantly noticing the difference in how she looked at him and spoke to him. Only someone who'd known her for a long time would pick up on it. In fact, all three of her closest friends had noticed.

The elevator ride was filled with Micki and Julia chatting about her new sneakers while the men stood quietly, with Kasey keenly aware that everyone was checking him out.

Will grabbed Julia's bags from Kasey when they reached the parking garage. The three of them climbed into a black sedan driven by Carl, Julia's driver, and bodyguard for public events, as she chatted with Kasey.

"I won't be back till Tuesday. Call me anytime if you have questions."

"I'll be fine. You have a good weekend," he answered confidently.

"I'd probably have a better time if you were coming," she said with a crooked grin.

Smiling, he shook his head, "Goodbye Julia."

"Bye, Kasey, see you Tuesday."

***

Julia and Micki sat quietly on the back deck of her shore house, wrapped in cozy blankets as the star-studded sky and familiar cool sea breeze enveloped them. The beach held a special place in Julia's heart; she cherished its solitude during the hushed, colder months just as much as the bustling atmosphere of summer. The crackling fire pit stirred memories, taking her back to the countless camping adventures she and Micki shared as kids in Colorado. As they had done all those years ago, they used this time and place to unburden themselves, sharing deep personal matters, romantic entanglements—everything close friends confide in each other. The tranquility of those memories mirrored the peace she now found at her beach house.

Gazing at the flickering flames of the fire pit, Julia asked, "So, what do you think of Kasey?"

Micki took a sip of her hot chocolate, her hands wrapped around the mug for warmth. "I have to admit, he's probably the best-looking man I've ever met... don't tell James I said that," she laughed. "He'd probably agree, though." Julia grinned as Micki continued. "I didn't really get to spend much time with him, but from what you've told me and what I've seen, he seems kinda serious—not your usual type. He did smell really good, though. I got close enough to catch a whiff," she added with a chuckle. "Happy hunting, kiddo, but something tells me he's not going to be an easy catch."

"I agree," Julia said thoughtfully. "I dunno what it is, but sometimes I can't think about anything else but him."

"What do you say we get comfortably numb, dance for a while, and then make James's night?" Micki suggested.

"Sounds good to me," Julia grinned as she got up and wrapped her arm around Micki's shoulders while they headed inside. "God, I miss you guys," she whispered, her warm breath tickling Micki's ear.

"I can see that," Micki said, taking her hand. "We've missed you too. Instead of dancing, let's grab James, say goodnight to Will, and get this party started."

***

For the next couple of months, Julia and Kasey settled into a comfortable routine at work. While she focused on managing her team for the fashion house acquisition and taking numerous video calls with the London-based team, he showcased a remarkable ability to anticipate her needs in the office and organize her personal life. She frequently sought his opinion on both work-related and personal matters, and he became increasingly involved in the acquisition alongside her team. With his natural business instincts and MBA, he proved to be worth every penny of his salary—and more.

Over time, their dynamic evolved, blurring the lines between boss and assistant. The challenge for Julia was being in such close proximity to him for long hours each day, which made it impossible not to flirt, drawn to him as she was. Despite her persistent flirting, Kasey managed to keep things in check, frustrating her to no end that he could resist her.

She often found excuses to touch him, pushing boundaries that would normally make him uncomfortable, though he didn't seem to mind. Whether it was tousling his freshly cut hair, brushing against him as she leaned in to read over his shoulder, or casually touching his arm while signing documents, he noticed but didn't pull away. As long as she wasn't being overtly physical, he didn't mind her flirting. He'd never met a woman who spoke or joked like she did; only one other person had ever made him laugh that much, but that was long ago. Sometimes, her comments were wildly inappropriate but hilarious, and he couldn't help laughing. They were becoming good friends, and though they hadn't fully realized it yet, they both started looking forward to work each day as a chance to spend time together.

They also spent a lot of time working together after hours, often ending with dinner in her office. Their long conversations covered all sorts of topics. Kasey shared details about the books he was reading, while Julia opened up about her childhood on a ranch and her close-knit family—all of which fascinated Kasey, who'd never experienced anything like that. He began to feel closer to her than anyone in a long time and found himself enjoying those conversations and their downtime together. Despite his reserved nature, he looked forward to her spontaneous moments of singing in her office when she was in a good mood. She sang as if no one was listening and danced as if no one was watching, completely unconcerned with anyone seeing her through the glass walls.

"Tell me something about yourself," she said one night while they were eating dinner in her office after a long day.

"I'm not one to talk much about myself," he replied, a hint of unease in his voice.

"Pleeease, it doesn't have to be too personal... just tell me what boarding school was like," she pleaded, giving his arm a light squeeze and flashing a sweet smile, turning on the charm.

He sighed dramatically, feigning annoyance. "Fine, it was called High Mount Academy. It was an all-boys school in the Green Mountains of Vermont. I spent all four years of high school there. I had the same roommate from sophomore year to senior year, learned to ride horses, ran track, and had a pretty good experience. Happy now?" he asked, a playful smile tugging at his lips.

"Did you wear robes like Harry Potter?" she teased with a grin.

"No, don't be silly," he smirked. "No robes, but we had uniforms—khakis and white shirts from Monday to Thursday. Fridays were no-uniform days."

"Did you like your roommate? Did you have a lot of friends? I didn't like my first roommate in college, but then I got my own place so that fixed that problem," she said with a grin.

"My roommate was my best friend, and we had a good group," he said, his discomfort growing. "Let me clean this up." He started gathering the containers, headed for the garbage, effectively ending the conversation.

***

As their connection deepened, Julia subtly hinted at a friends-with-benefits arrangement, which Kasey initially brushed off as a joke. But over time, her playful banter turned into more provocative flirting. Despite maintaining his composure, Kasey found himself navigating the tricky waters of their evolving friendship, her escalating advances, and his own growing attraction to her.

"You always smell so nice," she purred, leaning over him as he worked at his desk, engrossed in his laptop.

"Stop sniffing me," he chuckled, gently nudging her away. "Behave yourself."

"I wouldn't have to behave if you'd just consider fooling around with me once in a while. I thought we were friends," she teased, a mischievous grin spreading across her face as she slid around him, sat on his desk, kicked off her shoe, and placed her foot in his lap.

"We are friends, and I'd like to keep it that way," he replied, gently lifting her foot from his lap by the ankle. "And you, Ms. Masters, are being inappropriate. This a workplace." He gave her a wry smile. "Off you go; I have work to do."

"You are such a buzzkill," she pouted, slipping her shoe back on and flouncing off. Just in time, Kasey thought, feeling a surge of relief as he struggled to suppress the desire she effortlessly ignited.

***

On the morning of June 9, Julia's 29th birthday, she walked into her office to find a collection of gift baskets, cards, and flower arrangements on her desk. But it was the Purple Wisteria bonsai tree on the end table next to her couch that truly captivated her. Instantly knowing who the gift was from, she went straight for the card. It read, "Happy Birthday, Julia. Don't worry, I won't let you kill her.—Kasey. P.S. Her name is Nomi. (it means 'beautiful, delightful')." A smile spread across her face, her heart lifting at how much thought Kasey had put into something as unique as this gift. He didn't just send flowers—he picked something meaningful, something they could share.

Unlike the typical gifts she'd received, this one was thoughtful, personal, and breathtakingly beautiful. She felt a warmth bloom in her chest, as she read the card with Kasey quietly appearing behind her.

"Oh, Kasey, she's so beautiful. I love her. Please don't let me kill her," she said, gently touching the leaves, her voice soft with gratitude.

"Don't worry, I'll teach you how to take care of her," he replied, pleased that she liked his gift. He felt a quiet satisfaction knowing this gift showed her how well he knew her, and it would let them spend more time together, nurturing something living.

In the weeks that followed, they spent time tending to Nomi together, with Kasey even buying a set of tools specifically for her care. Each moment spent caring for the bonsai deepened their connection, the simple task of tending to Nomi turning into something more meaningful than either had anticipated.

***

Chapter 3: The Long Game

In July, four months after Kasey started working with her, Julia invited him to her beach house at the Jersey Shore for the weekend. She'd been looking forward to this—getting him out of the office, out of his carefully controlled environment, and into her world. She wanted him to properly meet her three closest friends, who were coming for a vacation to specifically get to know the man Julia had been enthusiastically discussing since he was hired. She hoped they'd all become friends—her friends meant the world to her, and lately, Kasey was beginning to feel like part of that same inner circle. It mattered more than she wanted to admit.

"Just a little heads up," she said, reaching for her water during their lunch in her office. They were seated on the couch, having just wrapped up a thorough review of the latest reports from her team on the fashion house. "When we get together, we like to party—drinking, smoking, and letting loose." She leaned back, giving him a teasing look. "It's nothing too wild, but… we don't exactly hold back either."

"Hmm, maybe I shouldn't go. I'm not exactly great at letting loose, definitely not a social butterfly." He shrugged, a little sheepishly. "I'm the guy sitting in the corner watching the clock, waiting for just enough time to pass so I can politely disappear with a book. I really don't like small talk, I don't dance, and I barely know any popular music. Besides, you can barely behave yourself in the office—what are you going to be like there?" he teased, giving her a knowing glance. The smile didn't quite reach his eyes, but the warmth was unmistakable.

"You don't have to join in if you're not comfortable. But please come—I promise I'll try to behave." She flashed those big blue eyes at him, playful but sincere. She could tell from the flicker of hesitation in his eyes that he was considering it.

"Try?" he raised an eyebrow.

"Yes, I'd be lying if I said I'd behave completely. But I'll try." She grinned, fingers trailing lightly up his thigh, lingering just long enough to make him tense slightly. "Besides, I think you like fighting me off and telling me no."

"I'm not sure I like telling you no," he admitted, his eyes briefly flicking to where her hand had been. "But it's probably better for us right now."

"Right now, huh?" she replied with a cheeky smile.

"I have work to do," he said with a grin, gathering up the remains of their lunch and tossing them away as he headed to his office.

"I will have you," Julia muttered under her breath, her eyes narrowing playfully as she watched him walk away. She was nothing if not determined.

"Excuse me, did you say something?" he asked with a knowing smile, turning to look at her.

Grinning, she answered sweetly, "No, nothing."

***

Julia, Kasey, and Will, who lived in Hoboken, New Jersey, headed to the shore in Julia's 4-door BMW convertible—a gift from her father when she closed her first acquisition with him. She asked Kasey if he wanted to drive, and he eagerly agreed, thrilled at the chance to take the wheel outside the city.

Her impressive large white house with blue shutters stood on a windswept part of the beach, isolated from any nearby residences. The imposing iron gates led to a long driveway lined with thick brush and ground lights, ending at a circular entrance." A central fountain with leaping dolphins overflowed with lush plants, giving the home a stately presence.

Large windows at the rear of the house provided breathtaking views of the vast Atlantic Ocean. The rhythmic waves breaking on the shore, the soothing rustle of beach grass on the dunes, and the cries of seagulls gliding on the breeze all contributed to the serene atmosphere, making it the ideal spot for relaxation and sunbathing. The expansive deck was well-furnished with a large fire pit, a grill master barbecue, a covered double lounger, various chairs, and a dining table, creating an idyllic setting for friends to gather.

Decorated in a coastal beach style, Julia's home had an open layout that created a breezy and inviting atmosphere. Throughout the house, weathered hardwood flooring complemented the cool-toned tiles in each bathroom. Guests were welcomed in the entryway by a console table adorned with a large vase of fresh wild flowers, a locally crafted candle embedded with shells, and a woven basket for keys. In the large living room, sand-colored shears covered the expansive windows, and various tones of blue and green contributed to a calm and casual atmosphere. An ornate fireplace nestled between the windows with an intricately carved wooden mantle served as a focal point, showcasing a large piece of driftwood art. Comfortable sofas and multiple overstuffed chairs draped with chic slipcovers provided plenty of seating.

Seamlessly integrated into the open floor plan, the kitchen featured an island with eight chairs around a natural stone countertop. A large window over the farmhouse sink offered views of the ocean beyond the deck. Painted a cool ocean blue, the kitchen boasted open shelving displaying various ocean-themed dishware.

Upstairs, each of the four luxurious bedrooms offered a private retreat with its own bathroom. They were decorated in the same coastal theme, with light-colored walls, a mixture of white and blue-green bedding, and large fluffy pillows. Breezy sheer curtains framed large windows, allowing plenty of natural light and scenic views. All the bathrooms featured walk-in showers, with Julia's master suite also boasting a claw-footed stand-alone tub, that came with the vintage home. There was a fifth bedroom downstairs, sharing a bathroom with a smaller maid's room and a half bath conveniently located off the living room. The home was Julia's pride and joy and her favorite place to be.

***

Micki and James cruised down the long driveway, arriving twenty minutes after the others and parking behind the sleek blue convertible. For the weekend, Julia had arranged for Kasey to rent the same car for them in black. Over the five years she'd owned the house, whether Micki and James or Will visited, they never paid for anything—transportation, meals, or any other necessities. Though they hesitated at first, Julia made it clear that it was her annual Christmas gift to them. So, for two weeks every summer and several long weekends throughout the year, they vacationed at her beach house, using the time to reconnect.

Their excitement filled the air as they arrived, and the weekend quickly unfolded with raucous laughter and joy. Once introductions were made, Julia led Kasey to his room.

"Your home is beautiful. I love the light and airy feel—perfect for a beach house," he remarked, wheeling his luggage to the bed.

"Thank you. You sound surprised—I do have taste," she replied with a smirk.

"I didn't say you lacked taste. It's just that your taste leans more toward the darker side—blue, gray, black. This is different. These rooms are huge."

"There were a bunch of smaller rooms up here, so I had them combined and added bathrooms. I had the whole place renovated when I bought it—it hadn't been updated in forty years."

"Come check out my room," she said, heading across the hall.

"Wow, this view is unbelievable," he said, gazing out at the ocean from her second-floor bedroom.

"You could stay in here and enjoy that view... and others," she grinned, running her finger lightly down his arm.

"We've been here less than an hour, and you're already at it," he chuckled, shaking his head. "You're incapable of behaving yourself."

"I'm sorry," she grinned. "I can't help myself. I'll try harder."

"I'll believe that when I see it," he said as he turned to leave. "Think I have time for a run before dinner?"

"Absolutely. Do whatever you want—no rules, no schedules. Whether you join us for dinner or fend for yourself, it's up to you. Both cars are available whenever you need them. The keys are in the basket by the door if you feel like escaping—from us... or me," she added with a sweet smile.

He couldn't help but be charmed by her sincerity and that captivating smile. But he knew she wouldn't be able to behave herself. As his attraction to her grew, he figured it was best to run those feelings off.

***

James and Will, the dynamic culinary duo, started on dinner, taking turns working the grill while Kasey went for a short run, leaving them to handle the meal. When the food was ready, they all gathered on the deck to enjoy wine, eat, and get to know Kasey.

Though he enjoyed meeting her friends, Kasey wasn't fond of being the center of attention. Whenever possible, he redirected the conversation back to their friendships, letting them take over. Grateful for a brief reprieve, he excused himself and took refuge in the kitchen.

"Did you need something?" Julia asked as she walked in, placing a glass in the sink. Kasey, arms folded, leaned against the cabinets, quietly watching the lively group on the porch.

"No, I just needed a break from the inquisition," he sighed, giving her a weak smile.

"I'm sorry," Julia said apologetically. "They just want to get to know you. They like you already, I can tell."

"I like them too... just not all the questions. I'm not big on talking about myself."

"You'd think you had some big, horrible secret in your past," she teased. "You don't, do you?"

Skillfully dodging the question, Kasey nodded toward the deck. "Looks like James is pulling the food off the grill—time to eat." He moved past Julia, sliding the door open. "After you."

Outside, with laughter echoing and waves crashing on the shore, the group shared food, drinks, and conversation. As the evening went on, Kasey felt a genuine warmth from them, a welcome addition to their close-knit circle.

***

This weekend marked Kasey's first real exposure to Julia's flair for indulgence when it came to her trio of best friends. She'd warned him they liked to party and let loose, and she hadn't exaggerated. The four of them loved to get uninhibitedly drunk, blissfully high, dance, and belt out karaoke songs. At her beach house, they called it a "dance party."

Will set up the karaoke machine while they pushed the furniture back to make room for dancing. At Julia's request, Kasey dimmed the lights and lit the fireplace. Despite the eighty-degree night outside, Julia cranked up the air conditioning, reveling in the dancing flames and the cozy, inviting mood they created.

She descended the stairs in a fitted sundress and sheepskin bootie slippers—her feet always cold with the AC blasting. Her hair, released from its earlier braid, cascaded in soft waves over her shoulders. Her blue eyes, somehow even sexier when she was buzzed, locked onto Kasey's as she shot him a mischievous grin that promised trouble. *She could feel the heat between them. Tonight, she'd use every ounce of her charm, every look, every touch. He wouldn't be able to ignore the pull. She was determined to break through that wall of restraint—even if it took every tool she possessed.*

As they passed around one of the sizable blunts Will had brought, Kasey sat at the kitchen island, keenly observing the dynamics between Julia and Micki. He watched them sing, bodies swaying provocatively, their hands sliding over each other's arms, hips, and backs. Every so often, their lips met in deep, lingering kisses, their laughter spilling out between them as they touched and teased without hesitation—their uninhibited behavior fueled by wine and weed.

Kasey was fascinated by the way the four of them interacted—the easy affection, the carefree laughter. He learned this was typical of their college days when they'd pregame at home before hitting the clubs, ready to party. James and Will played along—willing companions, bodyguards, and dance partners.

Julia, now completely immersed in the music, danced in place, her eyes half-closed as she moved slowly, feeling every beat of the slow song. She was oblivious to everyone but Kasey, lost in his intense gaze, her hands trailing down her body as he watched her, his lips lightly rubbing against the edge of his wine glass.

"Jules, snap out of it," James said with a tap on the butt as he went past. "Shotgun time, baby."

One of Julia's favorite things to do was give her friends shotguns when they smoked weed. She used the closeness of the act as an excuse to tease and generally behave

inappropriately. When Julia gave Will a shotgun, she straddled his lap on the couch, his arms instinctively wrapping around her lower back. She leaned into him as she blew the potent smoke into his mouth, her hands resting on his chest. He pulled back from her and blew the smoke to the side.

"Girl," he sputtered, "you are too much every damn time." With her eyes sparkling, she grinned and swiftly stole a kiss. She got up off his lap, walked up to James, and playfully pushed him into a chair at the kitchen island. Spreading his legs, she stood between them, leaning in to slowly blow the pungent smoke into his mouth. James, taking in all he could, put his hands on her hips and pushed her back as he exhaled and coughed. Turning away, she felt his arm wrap around her waist as he brushed the hair off her shoulder and planted a kiss on her neck.

Micki strolled over, sandwiching Julia between them, and took the blunt from her. Placing it in her mouth, she weaved her fingers into Julia's hair and gently pulled her head back, blowing the smoke into her mouth, their lips lightly brushing against each other. Julia blew the smoke up toward the ceiling and, taking the blunt from Micki, reciprocated the move, slapping her on the ass when she was finished.

Kasey couldn't help but be captivated, his gaze fixed on Julia's every move. Her uninhibited nature stirred something deep within him, exciting him in a way he hadn't expected. She turned and locked eyes with him, and in that moment, the rest of the room faded away. All Kasey saw through his pinhole view was Julia, his attention solely fixed on her. Although the others feigned indifference, it was undeniable they were watching their every move.

Standing before him, she embodied the mesmerizing mix of a tiny, stoned feline—buzzed, beautiful, and predatory all at once. He felt like prey about to be ensnared by a seasoned hunter, his body tingling on high alert.

"Are you ready for me?" she purred, sliding between his legs as she leaned in closer.

"Give me your best shot," he said, eyes smoldering beneath the tousled strands of his hair. She turned the blunt around, placed it in her mouth, and with her hands gently cupping his face, she brushed her lips against his, blowing a steady plume of smoke into his mouth. When he wrapped his arms around her waist and pulled her closer, his unexpected touch caught her off guard. She inhaled sharply, biting down on the blunt just in time to avoid burning herself. As he pulled away, blowing out the smoke and coughing, he turned back to find her grinning at him. He pulled her close, whispering in her ear, "You're a bad girl who plays dirty."

"Do you know how to handle bad girls?" she teased, resting her hands on his thighs.

"No, enlighten me," he replied, his voice low as he leaned his head against hers; the wine, weed, and Julia's seductive moves lowering his inhibitions.

"You spank them..." she purred, dragging her nails down his firm thighs, her face nuzzling against his as she breathed in his scent. With a mix of pain and arousal coursing through him, he grunted, "You don't say. I'll have to remember that."

She traced her finger lightly over his lips and winked, her sultry gaze and teasing touch leaving him reeling as she turned to find her wine glass.

When he broke free of her spell and realized they had become the center of attention, he blushed and turned his chair toward the island, taking a sip of his wine, hoping to conceal the result of her seduction.

Indulging in drinks and smoking, the four of them reveled in dancing, with Micki, Julia, and Will belting out tunes while Kasey sipped his wine, smoked, and watched. As uninhibited and sexually provocative she was dancing with Micki, Julia was even more so with James. Their ease with each other was unmistakable.

After watching Julia dance with the others for another half-hour, Kasey decided to head to bed. As he stood, she wrapped her arms around his waist, gazing up at him longingly. Moving like a cat, she slowly rubbed her body against his, inviting him to slow dance. Gently moving her hair off her shoulder, he leaned in, his lips brushing against her ear, his hard body pressed against hers, and whispered, "I don't think that's a good idea. I'm going to say good night before things get out of hand. You're not exactly making an effort to behave, are you?" He pulled back to look at her and smiled teasingly.

"You're such a buzzkill," she pouted, frustrated that her seduction hadn't worked—*she wasn't used to being resisted.* She quickly masked it with a teasing grin, determined not to let her disappointment show. "Good night, Kasey," she added, sounding like a disappointed child.

"Good night, Julia. Good night, everyone," he said as he headed upstairs to his room. Her friends exchanged mildly shocked glances, surprised to see a man resist her charms.

***

Later, after everyone exchanged good nights, Julia and Micki sat on the deck, engrossed in conversation about Kasey.

"So, what do you think?" Julia asked, sipping some water to combat her dehydration. She glanced over at Micki, who was standing at the railing, looking out into the darkness.

"Well, first off, that boy is fine. Now that I've seen him with most of his clothes off, you definitely weren't exaggerating. He's ridiculously good-looking, and that body— damn. I've never seen that many abs on a real man before," Micki laughed. "I think James caught me drooling at one point."

Julia nodded. "He's so friggin' hot. It's the first time I've seen him with his shirt off. I knew he was jacked from seeing him in tight gym shirts, but damn—it's like he doesn't even know how good-looking he is."

She paused, her head spinning slightly as the wine and weed took their toll. "Sometimes, he catches me just staring, and he gives me this little grin that drives me crazy. But it's not just the physical attraction, even though that's pretty friggin' strong. There's a connection too. He does so many things for me without me even asking—he remembers everything I say.

We have these long, random discussions, and it's just so easy when it's just the two of us. But he changes a lot when other people are around."

Micki shifted in her lounge chair. "There's something different about him. He seems immune to your flirting so far, which is amazing in itself. And there's a... I dunno... it's like he's holding something back. Maybe he's protecting himself, or maybe just protecting your work relationship. I'm not sure which," she said, taking a sip of her wine. "You can tell he likes you, though, or he wouldn't be here. But he's definitely moving at his own pace if he wants things to go further."

"You think he's attracted to me but won't admit it?" Julia's eyes narrowed as she considered Micki's words.

"Maybe, but he's a tough nut to crack."

Julia appreciated having Micki to confide in, knowing she could always rely on her honest feedback. Just as Micki had pointed out Kasey's feelings, Julia sensed there was more to him than met the eye.

As Micki headed to bed, Julia stayed on the double lounger, a throw across her lap, lost in thought about Kasey and enjoying the tranquility. Almost drifting off to sleep with the soothing sound of the waves in the background, she was startled by the sound of the glass sliding door opening. Kasey stepped out, lighting a half-smoked blunt and inhaling deeply, unaware of Julia's presence hidden in the lounger's corner.

"Is that just for you, or are you gonna share?" her voice emerged from the darkness. He exhaled and turned quickly toward the voice.

"What the... you scared the hell out of me. What are you doing out here alone at this hour? You really should take your security more seriously."

She laughed and took the blunt he offered. "I was just thinking about the upcoming meeting and trip to London," she fibbed. "Besides, Micki just went in a little while ago. I'm just being one with the ocean."

He smiled. "One with the ocean, huh?"

"I had a friend, Lee, once say she was one with the ocean when we were high, and it made me laugh so hard, I never forgot it. But I get it now. The ocean's so comforting to me, especially when I'm high," she sighed. "I love it here. I'm not gonna lie though; I almost fell asleep," she giggled.

"Jesus, Julia, someone needs to watch you like a hawk when you're stoned."

"Don't be so dramatic. You sound like my mother," she said with a playful grin.

"And you act like your father," he teased gently.

"Stop worrying." She patted the space next to her, "Sit with me. I won't bite, promise."

"Are you sure?" he grinned as he sat down. "That was some little party you had there. You're on a whole other level of wild when you're high."

"Just having some fun with very close friends," she grinned, that mischievous smile of hers momentarily shutting his brain off and turning him on.

"I'm glad you're here. I want to talk to you about something," he said, pulling himself together.

"Sounds serious." She took the blunt back, hit it, and blew the smoke slowly to the side.

"Earlier, you said I acted like I had a horrible secret... well, it's not horrible, but there's something about me I haven't told you. It might change how you see me, maybe even how you feel about me, but I think it's time you knew."

Curious, she sat up to face him. "Spit it out, Kasey. I'm all ears."

He took a deep breath, looking her straight in the eye. "I'm bisexual," he said quietly. Her expression stayed neutral, as if she were waiting for the bad part, so he continued.

"My first sexual experience was with my roommate at boarding school." He paused, then the rest spilled out slowly. "I had two long-term relationships with women in college, and I met a couple of men after. I stopped dating about a year ago. I have... intimacy issues. That's part of why I haven't rushed into anything casual with you. Sex has never been casual for me. I needed to tell you that, and I didn't feel comfortable until tonight." He waited for her to say something, his heart racing.

She chuckled softly. "Relax." She placed a hand on his chest. "So you're bisexual. That's not a big deal—at least, not to me. Just means you've got a bigger dating pool to choose from." Smiling warmly, she said, "I wouldn't call myself bisexual, but I do like kissing Micki—a lot. I have since we were teenagers. I've made out with other girls, too. I might even go for some boob action, depending on how buzzed and horny I am," she giggled, "and how pretty she and her boobs are—but that's as far as I go. Everyone's got their preferences. I don't judge."

She took another hit from the blunt before passing it to him. He'd never met anyone so easygoing about sex or more accepting of people's differences. Exhaling smoke, she said, "As for intimacy issues, we all have shit we deal with. Communication helps, but I know it's not always easy to share personal stuff." She knew that from experience, having never told Kasey about Oliver. "So why didn't you feel like you could tell me before?"

"I don't know... maybe because the only person I ever opened up to about this was my college girlfriend, Mia. We dated for a little over seven months, but let's just say she wasn't receptive to the news. Actually, she seemed horrified. Instead of trying to understand, she went through my phone, interrogating me about every guy's name she found. Two days later, she broke up with me and cut off all contact. I never saw her again. I don't know if it was homophobia or just that I wasn't honest from the start. I should've told her sooner, but I was scared of how she'd react. I thought maybe after we got closer, she'd be more understanding." He looked down. "I can be a coward when it comes to expressing my feelings or sharing anything personal. I'd rather avoid the risk of getting hurt. It's hard to let your guard down with someone you care about, only to be rejected for something that's part of who you are."

As he revisited that painful memory, Julia sensed his vulnerability for the first time, sparking an instinctive need to comfort him. When his stormy eyes met hers, she pulled him close, resting his head on her shoulder. "I'm so sorry," she whispered. "That must have been awful for you."

"It wasn't pleasant," was all he managed, his voice thick with emotion. Though upset, he found comfort in her touch and words. Holding him gently, she reassured him, "You're not a coward for wanting to protect yourself. It was her loss—she was an insensitive ass." She kissed the top of his head.

"You can always tell me anything—no judgment. I'm a pretty easygoing person, you must know that by now. Live and let live, I say. As long as you're not hurting me, my family, or my friends, I don't give a shit what you do."

She paused. "I know that wasn't easy to share, especially after the way things went last time, but I'm glad you did. I play around with you, but I genuinely care about you, just like I do my other friends."

After a moment, he said, "There's something else."

"Good God, there's more?" she teased, giving him a playful poke. "Sorry, I'm just messing with you. Go ahead, I'm listening."

He continued, appreciating how effortlessly she let him open up. He never expected to find someone who accepted him for who he was, someone who could understand his reclusive, reserved nature. He was seeing a different side of Julia—realizing she wasn't just trying to get into his pants; she genuinely cared about him. Lately, he'd been craving that kind of close connection.

"About five months before I started working for you, I stopped seeing someone—an escort. I saw her twice a month for about four months, but things got complicated when she started getting attached. The whole point was to avoid attachments. And honestly, I never told her this, but the sex felt awkward. Since then, I haven't been with anyone. I wanted to tell you everything because if it came out later, it might seem like I was hiding it out of shame, and that's not the case." He sat up, and she noticed a blush creeping up his neck.

"Kasey, if I told you some of the shit I've done... well, maybe I shouldn't," she chuckled. "Unlike you and that hot bod, I took full advantage of all *this*," she said, waving a hand over her body with a grin. "I was a bit of a wild child in college."

"I bet you were," he said with a smile, an image of her and Micki dancing wildly in a crowded club flashing through his mind.

"So, why won't you consider a friends-with-benefits thing with me if you don't want any attachments?" she teased, giving him a playful poke. "Isn't that the whole point?"

"Because they never work out. Someone always gets hurt. I value our friendship, your dad's trust, and my job. I don't want to risk any of it just for casual sex."

"I value you too, I really do, but I can't help the fact that sometimes, I *literally* want to lick you like a lollipop," she giggled, pulling him close.

"You're too much," he said, smiling. "You never give up."

"Take the good with the bad," she replied, her eyes shimmering in the moonlight. "Remember, you can always talk to me about anything—no judgment."

They sat in comfortable silence, her head resting on his shoulder, his arms wrapped around her. Julia could hardly believe it—*he's holding me.* His scent, warmth, and the weight of his arm made her heart race. *I could stay like this forever,* she thought as she snuggled closer, her arm sliding gently across his body.

For Kasey, the quiet closeness was unexpected. He hadn't realized how much he needed this—her warmth, the way she held him, and the comfort of someone who genuinely cared. He could feel the tension leaving his body, replaced by a sense of safety he hadn't felt in over ten years. *Not since...* He pushed the thought aside. This wasn't the time to think about the past.

They stayed that way for the next half hour before heading inside—and he didn't mind one bit.

***

The next day, everyone relaxed and did their own thing. Kasey went for a long run and read while Micki and Julia went shopping, and the guys swam and worked on their tans. After another great dinner grilled by James, Kasey excused himself, claiming he had a headache, and headed to his room. In reality, he just thought it best to avoid another encounter with a buzzed Julia.

An hour later, while the others roasted marshmallows, Julia excused herself to check on Kasey. She tapped lightly on his door, quietly slipping inside and closing it behind her. He lay in bed, scrolling through his phone, the screen casting the only light in the room.

"Julia, boundaries," he said with a gentle smile. "What if I was doing something... private?"

"Were you?" she laughed, jumping onto his bed and laying down beside him. Her cashmere crop top exposed a bit of underboob, and she reeked of weed and wine. "I just came to check on you. I thought maybe I could help you get over your headache. I read somewhere that having an orgasm releases endorphins or something—it helps with pain. I can help with that," she grinned, trailing her fingertips lightly across his bare chest. "You feel so good. I want you so bad," she whispered, the haze of weed and wine loosening her tongue as her hand began to roam.

"Stop," he said with a smile, gently pinning her hands back against the bed as he rolled almost on top of her. "You shouldn't be in my bed. You're making this very hard for me."

"Title of your sex tape," she giggled.

"You're acting like a teenager," he said, grinning down at her.

"A very horny teenager." She squirmed beneath him. "Kiss me—you know you want to." She quickly lifted her head, giving him a brief, teasing kiss, and he didn't pull away.

"I never said I didn't want to kiss you—I do. But like I've told you before, I don't want to risk everything if it doesn't work out," he replied earnestly.

"Nothing will change—it's just for fun. We can still be friends if it doesn't work out. I don't see how it couldn't, you're so damn hot, and I love sex... I don't see a downside," she teased with a sly grin. "You smell so good. Why do you always smell so good?" she purred, pressing herself closer as she inhaled his scent.

"You have to go, please," he said, releasing her hands and moving off the bed.

"Fine," she sighed. "I can play the long game... but I won't make it easy on you," she added with a mischievous grin. He took her hand, helping her off the bed. Then, with a playful grin, he pulled across his lap and gave her a swat. "That's for being a bad girl and getting in my bed." She gasped, his actions catching her completely off guard.

He walked her to the door, giving her another swat as she passed, his voice dropping to a whisper, "Behave yourself—I don't want to have to do that again." She felt a little weak in the knees, knowing it was only a matter of time.

***

Chapter 4: The Double O

With the pressure of the upcoming proposal meeting in London mounting, Buck sensed his daughter's anxiety and decided to take a long weekend at the ranch for some R&R. He invited Julia and Kasey along, hoping to give them a break before the final push and Julia's trip.

Excited to join her father, Julia eagerly looked forward to reconnecting with Micki and James and showing Kasey the ranch.

"Damn, Jules, he looks even hotter on the back of a horse," Micki said wistfully as they leaned against the fence, watching Kasey prepare to ride with Buck and her nineteen-year-old brother, Wynn. With sleek black jeans, a black linen button-down with casually rolled-up sleeves, boots, leather gloves, and one of Buck's revolvers snug in its holster on his belt, he exuded the bad-boy charm of a seductive outlaw in a Western.

Buck emerged from the stable holding a black Stetson as he approached Kasey. "This is for you, son. Thought you could use one," he said, handing Kasey the hat with a warm smile.

"Thanks, Buck, I appreciate it," Kasey said, adjusting the hat and recognizing it as Buck's silent gratitude for the mugging incident.

"Looks good. You were made to be a cowboy—or an outlaw," Buck laughed, then added, "Let's hit the trail" as he mounted his horse.

"Oh my God, I need a picture of this. He looks so friggin' good," Julia said to Micki while readying her phone. "Wait!" she called out, motioning them over. "Come back! I want a picture with you three," she said, capturing the moment with a quick snap of her phone. Locking eyes with Kasey, she winked and mouthed, "You look great."

He tipped his hat, flashed a gorgeous smile, and, with a gentle nudge to his horse, followed Buck and Wynn.

"We'll be back before lunch." Buck shouted over his shoulder, "Giddyup," he called as they galloped away,

"I think Buck's got a little bromance going with Kasey. That was a thousand-dollar hat he gave him," Micki observed, turning to Julia, who was still watching Kasey ride off.

"That hat was a proper thank you for the mugging, but you're right—he really likes him. They even meet for lunch sometimes without me. Buck never spent time with any of my other male friends," Julia said, her admiration for Kasey's ability to bond with her father shining through.

"He saved him from being mugged; I don't think Buck's forgetting that anytime soon."

She shifted the conversation. "So, how are things at work? You behaving yourself?"

Julia laughed. "As much as I'm capable of. Honestly, it hasn't been bad. We're so swamped with this takeover there's no time to mess around. I'm too anxious about proving myself to Buck and the board. And when Kasey's focused on work, you can't break his resolve. Believe me, I've tried. He just gives me crap and gets me back on track."

"I've no doubt you'll do just fine with this. You've been training at Buck's knee since we were kids to do exactly this. Who runs the world, Jules? Girls!" they both yelled in unison.

"And don't you forget it," Micki added, playfully pushing Julia.

As they started to walk back to the main house, Julia turned and said, "Kasey told me something when we were at the beach that I haven't told you."

"Spill. It must be good if you waited to tell me," Micki said, her curiosity piqued.

"He told me he's bisexual," Julia said, glancing over for her reaction.

"What?! Holy shit, I didn't see that coming."

"After you went to bed, he came out on the porch to smoke, and I scared the crap out of him," she laughed. "He didn't see me there. He said there was something he finally felt comfortable enough to share with me. He told me his whole dating history. He hasn't dated women since college—and there were only two. The couple of men he's been with were just short-term flings. He's hardly had any partners. He thinks about sex completely differently than I do. It never crossed my mind that a guy who looks that good would have such a low body count or such an old-fashioned view on sex."

"It's not surprising he thinks differently than you. You're pretty open about sex, and if he's a little, let's say, more conservative, you must be blowing his damn mind," Micki said with a smirk, rethinking everything she knew about Kasey with this new information.

Julia continued, "I think he's confused about what he really wants. He said he has intimacy issues. One of the only two girlfriends he's ever had hurt him big time when she dumped him after he told her he was bi. They had been dating for over seven months, and she went no contact two days after finding out. She sounded like a real dick." Julia hesitated, unsure if she should mention the escort, but then decided—it was Micki, after all, and she never held anything back from her. "One more thing."

"What's that?" Micki asked, wondering what was coming next.

"Five months before he started working for me, he stopped seeing a female escort. He said the sex was awkward, and she started getting attached to him."

"Wow, that explains a lot,' Micki said. "He's had so few experiences with women, and one of them hurt him pretty badly. Sounds like he needs a deeper connection to have sex with someone. Maybe he's scared of getting involved with you, thinking you'll just hit and run. You must be pretty intimidating for him. You'll need to let him work this out on his own timeline. It might take a while. Is he worth the wait?"

"I think he's worth the wait, and he hasn't run from me yet. It doesn't seem like my flirting annoys or upsets him. I'm pretty sure he'd tell me straight up if I was pissing him off. Oh, and I forgot to tell you," she giggled. "Remember the second night there, when I passed out on the couch? I was so messed up that night. When he went to bed early, I went to his room. I was messing with him and climbed in his bed. After flirting hard and telling him how badly I wanted him, he helped me off the bed, pulled me across his lap, told me I was being a bad girl, and then gave me a little smack on the butt. He did it again as he walked me to the door. And then said he hoped I'd behave so he wouldn't have to do it again. And that smile... I thought my knees were going to buckle."

"What the hell? He's impossible to pin down." Micki laughed, eyes wide, as she pictured it. "He actually spanked you?"

Julia nodded, grinning. "Yep. It was unexpected, playful, but kinda confusing."

"Sounds like he's setting boundaries while still flirting," Micki mused. "He's probably trying to navigate this carefully, not wanting to hurt you or get hurt himself."

"Yeah, I get that. I just need to be patient and give him space," Julia agreed, smirking. "But that doesn't mean I can't have a little fun in the meantime."

Micki shook her head, chuckling. "You're impossible, Jules. Just don't push him too hard, okay?"

"I won't," Julia promised. "I really do care about him. I just wish he'd open up a bit more."

"He will eventually," Micki reassured. "Just give him time."

Julia smiled and then grabbed Micki's arm. "Let's go shopping," she said as they headed toward the main house. Grinning, she added, "Maybe I'll find something sexy enough that Kasey can't resist."

"Jeez, Jules, you never give up," Micki said with a smile as she threw her arm around Julia's shoulder.

As they reached the main house, Julia felt a sense of resolve. She'd be as patient with Kasey as she could, no matter how long it took. After all, she knew he definitely was worth it.

***

Julia had intentionally skipped lunch, planning to make a grand entrance at dinner, looking her most enticing. Buck, Wynn, Kasey, Jack, Rick, and a few ranch hands were already seated at the table, helping themselves to the generous family-style servings spread across the massive table. Her hair fell in soft curls around her face, and her big eyes were perfectly made up as she stepped into the room and greeted everyone, "Evening, boys."

She wore a baby blue sundress with a fitted bodice, a sparkly white cashmere bolero, and exquisitely hand-painted baby blue cowboy boots. As she entered, all eyes turned to her, and Kasey stood. The others followed, while Wynn hesitated until his father nudged him to stand.

"How nice, thank you," she said graciously. Kasey pulled out the chair next to him for her to sit. Buck, ever vigilant, watched his daughter's interaction with the young man he was getting to know.

"You look very pretty tonight," Kasey said, picking up the napkin she had dropped. As he handed her the napkin, Kasey couldn't help but take in how different she looked here in Colorado. Her cowgirl vibe, sundress, and boots suited her in a way that her sharp New York outfits never did. *Good thing he was sitting down because—damn, her look was doing something to him.*

"Thank you," she replied with a radiant smile, reassured all the primping had been worth it.

Julia thrived in the company of men, effortlessly charming and flirtatious, seamlessly joining in their banter. Dinner drew to a close, with stories flowing for hours, Buck and Julia holding court. She joined the men for a double shot of whiskey before finally deciding it was time to call it a night.

"Are you alright getting back to your room, darlin'? You look a little wobbly," Buck teased as she got up to leave. "Don't be silly, Daddy, I'm fine," she said, giving him a big kiss on the cheek. "Good night, everyone, it was fun."

Kasey stood and said, "I'll walk with you. I'm going for a run in the morning before breakfast. Night, Buck, Wynn, guys. See you all tomorrow," he added, nodding to the group before escorting Julia out. Julia, feeling the whiskey's warmth, took his arm as they left the dining room. She hoped to hide her slight wobble from her father, leaning into Kasey as they walked. When they reached her room, she seized the moment. Kissing him was all she could think about.

Before he could say anything, Julia turned to him, her lips finding his in a daring kiss. Kasey hesitated for a moment, pulling back slightly, "No..." he breathed, gently protesting.

But Julia was undeterred. Her fingers gripped his collar, pulling him into her room and closing the door behind them with a soft click. "Just kiss me," she pleaded playfully, her voice thick with mischief, her eyes glinting with a challenge. Her body pressed against his, and the warmth of the liquor swirled through her, eroding her final shred of restraint.

Kasey's heart raced. His hands rested firmly on her hips, trying to keep some distance. "This isn't a good idea. We've talked about this." The words were there, but his resolve was wavering.

Her voice dropped to a whisper, hot against his ear, "Kasey... just kiss me. Nothing has to change." She dragged her hands down his chest, her touch sending a spark through him.

For a heartbeat, Kasey fought to resist, but he could feel the last bit of self-control slipping away. He had wanted this for too long. With a groan of surrender, he turned her around, pressing her gently but firmly against the door.

"This is dangerous," he whispered, his lips inches from hers. His smoldering gaze locked with hers, his breath coming faster now, the weight of the moment heavy between them.

And then, finally, he gave in, capturing her lips in a kiss that began softly, tentatively, as though testing the waters, but quickly ignited with all the pent-up desire they'd been holding back. Kasey deepened the kiss, his hands cradling her face, fingers tangling in her hair as he lost himself in the heat of the moment. The feel of her body pressed against his, the softness of her lips, the scent of her—coconut and whiskey—fueled his desire.

Julia melted into him, her body surrendering completely to the kiss. She wrapped her arms around him, pulling him closer, her nails raking lightly down his back as she kissed him with all the intensity she'd been holding back for months. Her body was buzzing, her head spinning, as every inch of her pressed against him, eager and wanting.

The kiss grew more urgent, full of reckless abandon. Kasey's fingers tightened in her hair, gently pulling her head back, allowing him to kiss her even deeper. His tongue explored her mouth, their breathing becoming ragged, both consumed by the fiery connection they shared. His hands drifted down, resting on her hips, pulling her closer still, feeling the warmth of her body through the thin fabric of her dress.

Every part of him wanted more, but he knew this was a line they couldn't cross. Not yet.

Reluctantly, he pulled back, both of them breathless. The look on Julia's face mirrored what he felt—completely undone. For a moment, he just stared at her, exhilarated by the kiss and the overwhelming desire that still coursed through him.

A silly grin spread across his face as he caught his breath. "Better now?"

Julia stood there, stunned, her chest rising and falling as she tried to catch her breath. She had kissed him, really kissed him, and it had been everything she imagined and more. "Yes..." she replied, her voice breathy and light, "Now, was that so hard?" Her lips curved into a playful smile, her eyes dancing with satisfaction.

She opened the door. "Night, Kasey," she teased with a wink, gently nudging him out the door. Just before the door closed he heard Julia whisper, "That was incredible."

Kasey grinned, still feeling the heat of the moment lingering on his skin. "Good night, Julia," he said, surprised she hadn't tried to take it further—but grateful. He walked down the hall, his senses alive, the kiss hitting him like a jolt of electricity.

Back in her room, Julia leaned against the door, her body humming with the memory of the kiss. It had been the best kiss of her life, leaving her with a sweet, aching want that wouldn't go away anytime soon. She smiled, her resolve strengthening—she'd find her way past his walls, one kiss at a time.

Meanwhile, Kasey slipped into his room, his heart still pounding. He stripped off his shirt and headed for the shower, hoping the cold water would cool the fire still burning through him. But deep down, he knew—he'd just crossed a line with Julia, and there was no going back.

***

"Ready for some cowboy camping tonight, Kasey?' Buck asked as Kasey entered the dining room, where Julia—still in her robe and fuzzy slippers—was having breakfast with her family.

"I'm ready," Kasey said, helping himself to the breakfast buffet, his appetite strong after a long run. Julia glanced over, noticing the stubble on his jaw—he was definitely making things difficult for her, especially after that kiss.

"How long do you usually run, Kasey?" Julia's mom, Lily, asked as she sipped her coffee.

"I aim for at least an hour, but in the city, it's usually shorter. There's always too many people unless I go out really early."

"Have you been running for a long time?"

"Yes, ma'am. I started in high school."

"Such nice manners. Call me Lily—I'm too young for that ma'am stuff," she said with a warm smile.

"We'll head out around three," Buck interrupted as he stood up from the table. "Meet me here to grab our supplies before we go—Jack and Rick are coming too,"

"And why wasn't I invited?" Julia asked, making a face.

"Because it's guys only, Jules," Wynn said, rubbing it in.

"No, it's because you should spend time with your mother," Buck said gently. "I never get to see Wynn, and you hardly see her. Don't make a fuss."

"Fine, I never get to do the fun stuff," Julia muttered.

"Thank you, Julia Lynn, that was like a bullet to the heart," Lily smirked.

"Uh oh, you're in trouble. Mom used your full name!" Wynn teased, making Julia punch him in the arm and Kasey grin.

"That's not what I meant, and you know it," Julia said quickly. "Sorry it came out like that. We'll have a fun day whatever we do. I know—let's go check out that new winery in town with Micki."

"Sounds good, I'm up for some wine tasting. That's later, though," Lily replied. "Why don't you go for a ride with Kasey until then? I hear he's pretty good in the saddle."

Kasey smiled, the corners of his eyes crinkling as he enjoyed his breakfast. He loved listening to Julia banter with her warm, loving family.

"Sure, let's go for a ride," he said.

Julia's face brightened, "I'll change and meet you back here in half an hour—give breakfast time to settle."

***

When she returned, Julia wore snug blue jeans, a slouchy black sweatshirt, riding boots, and a baseball cap, her long hair in a soft braid. Kasey stood beside her, dressed in jeans, a fitted long-sleeved t-shirt, boots, and his new Stetson.

After giving her a leg up, they set off, with him trailing behind. The crisp morning air nipped at their faces as they rode across the expansive cattle ranch. The rhythmic beat of hooves echoed as they made their way to a spot Julia had cherished since her teenage years.

It was a secluded haven with a babbling stream, towering trees, and tall prairie grass swaying in the breeze. "This is one of my favorite spots on the ranch," Julia said, her voice tinged with nostalgia. "I used to come here as a teenager, listening to my sad songs whenever I felt restless. It always made me feel better."

They found a spot for the horses to drink, standing quietly for a moment to take in the serene surroundings. Julia tied her reins to a tree and sat down on a large, flat rock by the stream. She took off her cap, closing her eyes as she basked in the warmth of the sun.

"This ranch is vast; it feels like it stretches on forever," Kasey remarked as he settled beside her. "It's so peaceful here." He glanced at Julia, the sun casting a soft glow on her skin, the breeze tugging gently at loose strands of her hair. Kissing her had left him wanting more, and he realized it was time to decide what he truly wanted.

She caught him gazing at her, his eyes like a sleepy blue ocean, and teased, "If your eyes linger any longer, I'm gonna have to charge you rent." He chuckled, and she playfully taunted him in a singsong voice, "You wanna kiss me."

"I should never have kissed you," he said, brushing a strand of wind-blown hair from her face as he leaned in closer. "Now you're going to be insufferable."

"You're already impossibly handsome, and this sexy stubble," she said, running her fingers along his jaw, "just makes you even more irresistible. How am I supposed to behave myself?" She grabbed his hat with a grin, challenging him, "You might as well concede and kiss me."

Without a word, Kasey pulled her into his arms, desire overtaking him. He felt different with her—alive in a way he hadn't before. Each time they kissed, his body responded with a raw intensity, his nerve endings on fire.

Julia dropped his hat and wrapped her arms around Kasey's neck, pulling him down onto the rock with her. Heat surged through her as his lips crashed against hers, kissing her deeply, his arms wrapping around her as if he couldn't get enough. Her whole body tingled, the intensity of the kiss sparking a fire in her, and she held him tighter.

"You're such a good kisser,' she murmured between kisses. "I could do this for hours... Wanna have sex alfresco?" she giggled breathlessly, finally coming up for air.

"Give you an inch, and you..." he began, clearly amused.

"Want six?" she teased with a grin.

He shook his head, laughing, "I don't know what to do with you."

"I keep telling you, but you're not listening," she said, flashing him a sly smile. Glancing at her watch, she added with a disappointed tone, "I really don't want to, but we should probably head back. I need to wash up and change before I go with my mom to that winery."

"Well, you're going to have to give me a minute before I can get back on that horse," he said with a grin, placing his hat strategically on his lap.

"I could help with that," she teased, reaching out to touch him.

"No, you're just making it worse," he chuckled, gently pushing her hand away.

"Such a buzzkill," she pouted as she stood up from the rock.

They headed back at a slower pace, enjoying the panoramic views of the ranch. Before parting ways, she said, "I probably won't see you before you head out for camping. Have fun, dress in layers, and watch out for snakes."

"Thanks, I'll do that," he said with a playful smile as he watched her walk away. He loved the way she moved, the way she felt in his arms. He wanted to take the next step, but he wanted to do it slowly. *Maybe it was time to tell her what was really holding him back.*

***

He met with Buck and the rest of the group as they prepared to leave, gathering their provisions for the rustic adventure ahead in the rugged Colorado wilderness.

As the campfire crackled, casting shifting shadows over the campsite, Buck, Rick, and Jack swapped stories of their early days as spirited ranch hands, embracing the cowboy lifestyle. Kasey listened intently, entranced by the tales spun by the three seasoned cowboys, feeling drawn into their world. Feeling comfortable in their company, opened up about his passion for martial arts and Bruce Lee, sparking a lively discussion with Buck about the movies he loved in his youth.

In the flickering firelight, Buck revealed the origin of the Double O Ranch's name—a tribute to his love for James Bond novels and Sean Connery's iconic portrayal. The name, a nod to 007, brought back fond memories of watching Bond films with his father.

Kasey learned about the depth of Buck's friendship with Jack and Rick—Jack had been Buck's best man, chosen by a coin toss, and Rick had become Julia's godfather a year later. Their friendship, stretching back to middle school, left Kasey in awe.

With each interaction, Kasey's affection for Buck grew. He began to see in Buck the father figure he'd always longed for. As an only child, he also appreciated having Wynn around, enjoying the easy dynamic of a younger brother. He showed him the exact move he used to foil his father's mugger and taught him some basic self-defense, bonding over their newfound connection. Kasey got the message loud and clear when Buck recounted how he'd once protected Julia from an overly aggressive boyfriend, vowing to stop at nothing to keep her safe. It only deepened Kasey's appreciation for Buck's protective nature.

***

As Kasey prepared the campfire for breakfast the next morning, he spotted a large brown snake slithering toward the sleeping bags. Calmly, he called over to Wynn, who was rummaging through his backpack nearby. "Should I shoot that?"

"What?" Wynn asked, glancing over to where Kasey pointed. Spotting the sizable prairie snake, his voice rose with excitement, "Damn, that's a big one. Normally, you can't just shoot them, but if they're in your campsite, they're fair game. Go for it. Ten bucks says you miss it on the first shot."

Kasey took aim with Buck's revolver and fired. The shot echoed in the stillness of the morning. The snake, hit square in the head, jumped three feet into the air before landing with a solid thud in the dirt.

"Damn! One shot... and look at the size of that rattle," Wynn marveled as he crouched to examine the snake.

"You owe me ten bucks," Kasey said in a matter-of-fact tone as he holstered the revolver, sounding very much like a big brother.

From the trees by the creek, where he was talking with Rick and Jack, Buck called out, "Everyone okay?"

"Kasey shot a prairie snake. A big one, too," Wynn yelled back. He was still poking at it with the toe of his boot as the three men walked over to them.

"That is a big one," Jack remarked, clearly impressed by its size.

"We'll take the rattle off," Buck said, picking the snake up to inspect it. "Nice shot," he added, with a nod to Kasey. "Now, let's go make some breakfast."

"Not with the snake?" Kasey asked, visibly grossed out.

"Not with the snake," Buck laughed, giving Kasey a hearty slap on the back as they walked toward the campfire. "Just steak and eggs."

***

Chapter 5: Micki and James

Julia eagerly anticipated sharing the details of her ride with Kasey earlier that day. Taking advantage of her mom's search for the perfect wine, she seized the opportunity to chat with Micki, who listened attentively.

"Well, Jules, looks like you've got him right where you want him. Honestly, I didn't think he'd hold out this long. You've always been relentless when you know what you want," Micki teased, taking a sip from her glass.

Julia frowned. "The problem is, he was right. Now I'm craving more—it's like an itch I can't scratch."

"You knew patience was the game with him. Mmm, this is good," Micki said, giving the bottle an approving look.

"I know, but waiting sucks. James is the only guy I've slept with in the past year, and four times in twelve months—no matter how good it is—ain't cutting it," Julia said, her frustration growing. "I don't know when Kasey's gonna be ready. It might be months, and I..."

"Why don't you come over tonight?" Micki suggested, giving Julia's arm a squeeze. "I'm sure James would be more than happy to help you out with your... little dilemma."

"If you're sure," Julia said, a smile tugging at her lips as her frustration melted away.

"I'm sure. I can't have my best friend feeling frustrated and unfulfilled, now can I?" Micki grinned, offering Julia a sample. "Here, try this. I really like it. I think I'll get some for tonight."

"Let me buy a case. James is worth it," Julia said, excited at the thought of the evening ahead as she went to get a clerk.

"Don't tell him that; he'll get a big head," Micki laughed, following her.

***

Later that evening, Julia slipped into her new outfit, hoping James's reaction would mirror Kasey's from earlier. After dinner, the three of them settled onto the couch—James in the middle, wine in hand, catching up on each other's lives.

"You look beautiful tonight, Jules," James murmured, pulling her close. One hand slid behind her head, the other resting on her waist, as his lips found hers, then traced down to her neck. Julia ran her hand over him slowly, feeling his desire as Micki leaned back on the arm of the couch, sipping her wine.

"I think I'll just watch tonight unless anyone has objections," she said, her tone casual.

Julia and James paused their kissing and turned to her. "Really, babe, just watching?" James asked, surprised by the request. "I don't mind. What about you, Jules?" He grinned. "You mind being watched?"

"Not at all, but before you get comfortable, come here." Julia beckoned Micki closer. Leaning over James's lap, she gently cupped Micki's face, kissing her deeply before whispering, "You're such a perv," as she playfully pushed her back against the couch.

"Shut up and play with my man so I can enjoy the show," Micki teased, grinning at Julia.

"Ladies..." James chuckled, clearly turned on by their playful banter.

"Get comfortable, babe," Julia murmured, watching him slide down the couch as he tugged his pants lower, desire already thick between them. James sank deeper into the couch, his fingers threading through Julia's hair as he watched her, a low groan escaping him.

She wrapped her hand around him, her tongue gliding over him in slow, deliberate strokes. She glanced over at Micki, her eyes dark with temptation, almost daring Micki to join in. "Damn, Jules, you need to stop if you wanna fuck," he groaned after a few minutes, gripping her hair tighter. Wanting to feel him inside her, she made him even wetter, then stood

and straddled him.

Slipping his hands beneath her dress, he grinned, "Did you really come over here with no underwear on?"

"God, no! I'm not that crazy. I took them off in the bathroom. You never know what's on the seat of that truck," she said with a playful grin. She positioned herself over him, sitting back slowly, easing him inside.

"Damn, that feels good," he moaned, wrapping his arms around her as she sank down.

"Feels fucking amazing," she whispered, rocking slowly on his lap. Leaning in close, her warm breath tickling his ear, she purred, "Bite me, baby. Give me a hickey." She pulled her hair to one side, offering him her neck. He ran his tongue slowly across her skin before nipping at her, sending goosebumps over her body as she rocked in his lap.

When he began sucking on her neck, a soft moan slipped from her lips. The more he sucked, the harder she pressed against him. Holding his head against her neck, her nails digging into his skin, she thrust her hips forward and moaned, "I love fucking you, James. I could fuck you all night."

"Damn, Jules," he grunted, his hips bucking hard as he lifted her slightly, unable to resist her dirty talk as he came.

Panting softly, James leaned back into the couch, Julia resting against him in post-fuck bliss, his arms wrapped tightly around her.

Micki, who had been watching silently, enjoying the show, spoke softly, "Baby, you're such a sucker for dirty talk. And Jules knows exactly when to use it, don't ya, kiddo?" Micki cast Julia a knowing grin.

"I dunno what you're talking about," Julia giggled.

"Don't move. Let me get a towel; don't get my couch all sticky," Micki said, getting up.

"Thank you, Micki," Julia murmured, her body still rubbing slowly against James.

"Stop moving, Jules," James urged, grabbing her hips. "It's really sensitive right now."

"Sorry, you just feel so good," Julia purred.

As they cleaned themselves up, Micki said, "You guys can sleep in the spare room tonight... I got what I wanted, and I'm kinda tired, so knock yourselves out." She leaned over to kiss James, then turned to Julia with a grin. "You owe me, Jules," she said before leaving the room. Smiling at each other, Julia and James got up hand in hand and headed to the spare room.

***

James had always been kind and thoughtful, caring deeply for Julia since they met and dated throughout most of their freshman year in college. Even as a teenager, he was attentive and supportive, always making sure she felt valued. But by summer, Julia realized she was too young for something serious and gently ended things. Though crushed by the breakup, James was relieved they remained friends. Later, when Julia introduced him to Micki, it was clear from the start they were a far better fit.

Six months before Micki and James's wedding, Julia had her heart shattered by Oliver. After two months of intense sadness, two awkward blind dates that ended in tears, and countless long calls with Micki, trying to work through the feelings of worthlessness and humiliation, Julia knew she needed a break.

She flew home to Colorado, seeking the comfort of her two closest friends. Micki and her now-fiancé, James, were already living together in their cozy starter home while James focused on growing his accounting firm.

After spending the day with her mom and brother, Julia headed over to Micki and James's place. Drinking and smoking weed together, Julia poured her heart out—sometimes through tears—expressing how lonely and unloved she felt and how envious she was of their loving relationship. Even with Will nearby, she admitted she missed the intimacy of connecting with someone during sex—it comforted her more than she had ever realized.

After one particularly tearful moment, Julia excused herself to wash her face and gather her composure. When she returned to the living room, James and Micki were sitting close, holding hands on the couch.

"Jules, text your mom before it gets too late. Let her know you're staying over here tonight so she won't worry," Micki said softly.

"I don't have to stay over, guys. I'm really not the best company right now. I should probably head back."

"Jules, come sit here with us," Micki interrupted with an inviting smile, patting the space between her and James as he slid over. Julia crossed the room and plopped down between them.

"Jules, we want you to sleep over with us," Micki said, taking Julia's hand in hers.

"I know I can stay over, but I could just sleep at the ranch," Julia replied.

"No, kiddo. We want you to sleep with us. In the same bed, dopey. We thought maybe, between the two of us, we could help you feel loved again." Micki leaned in and gave Julia a deep kiss as James brushed the hair off her shoulder. Glancing at Micki for reassurance, he kissed Julia's neck slowly, waiting to see how she would react.

Julia started to tear up. "I can't believe you guys would do this for me. Micki, this is such a big deal. You don't have to. I don't... I would never want to do anything that could hurt what you have," Julia said, her voice thick with emotion as Micki handed her a tissue.

"Jules, how long have we been friends? Since we were little girls. And in all that time, have you ever known me to say something I don't mean? Or do something I didn't want to?"

A soft "No," slipped out of Julia.

"Well, I meant it. We want you to stay and sleep with us. Come on, don't be shy. I'm giving you permission to sleep with my fiancé, who also happens to be your old boyfriend. Let us make you feel better. Perk up, kiddo—it'll be fun for all of us,"

Micki coaxed, giving Julia an enticing look as she took her hand and led her to the bedroom, James right behind.

Julia glanced back over her shoulder. "And you're really okay with this, James?"

His eyes twinkled with a sexy grin. "If I must... whatever Micki wants," he teased, making both women laugh.

As they entered the bedroom, they stood there awkwardly for a moment until Micki squeezed Julia's hand. "We've all seen each other naked before. Let's just do this," she said, unzipping her jeans as James pulled off his t-shirt and dropped his pants. Julia looked at them both, sniffled then grinned. "Let's do this," she said, slipping off her dress, standing there, bare-breasted in her thong.

Six years later, they were still indulging in the same satisfying, long-term arrangement, each finding comfort in the exciting yet familiar and loving encounters for their own reasons.

***

Now alone, Julia and James slowly undressed each other, savoring every sweet and tender moment. She fell asleep afterward, relishing the comfort of being held by someone she cared for—and who cared for her in return.

Lying in each other's arms the next morning, James smirked. "I know I was just a stand-in for your brooding, Mr. Darcy, but I hope you got what you needed."

Laughing at his *Pride and Prejudice* reference—one of Micki's favorite books—she replied, "It was exactly what I needed. It always is."

He smiled, giving her a gentle squeeze. "Glad to be of service. You know, we could do it again," he teased, nuzzling her neck. "It's still early."

Feeling his desire against her thigh, Julia—who never turned down morning sex—didn't refuse. "Okay, but I'm on top this time," she said with a sly grin, pushing him onto his back.

"Tell me what you want. I'm here just for you," he said, flirtation heavy in his voice as she moved on top of him.

"But it's not all just for me, is it?" she cooed, biting his lower lip as she rubbed her naked body lightly against his.

"Fuck no," he groaned, his hands cupping her firm ass as he kissed her hard, barely holding himself back.

They came out of the room twenty minutes later to the smell of Micki making breakfast.

They walked up to her as she cooked, kissing her on the cheek at the same time.

"Good morning," they both greeted, James putting his arms around her. "I'll finish if you want."

"Thanks, babe," she said, handing him the spatula.

"I can tell you two had a good night," Micki said knowingly as she sat at the table with Julia.

Giggling, Julia leaned over and whispered, "And morning."

Micki laughed, "Jules, you're like a kid sometimes."

"What did she say?" James turned and flashed a crooked smile.

"Nothing, baby—just you da' man," Micki teased.

"I'm pretty sure that wasn't what she said, but I'll take it," he said happily as he flipped the bacon.

After breakfast, they said their goodbyes. Buck, Kasey, and Julia were heading back to New York later that afternoon, and they wouldn't be able to see them off.

"Thanks for everything. Remember, we'll be back for the Cattlemen's Dinner in three weeks. See you then. Oh, and thanks again for the clothes, Micki—I won't have to do the walk of shame," Julia laughed. "Love you guys," she said as she kissed them goodbye.

"Love you too. See you soon," Micki said.

"Take care, Jules," James added with a wink.

***

The guys were just getting back as Julia rolled up in one of the big black pickups with *Double O Ranch* painted on the door. She hopped out, brushing her hands on her jeans as she approached. "How did it go?" she asked, following them into the stables to put up the horses.

"I got the horses, Buck," Lester said, taking the reins from Buck and Wynn while another ranch hand led Jack, Rick, and Kasey's horses away.

"It went great!" Wynn said, grinning as he mimed a shot with his hands. "Kasey shot a prairie snake in camp—one shot from fifteen feet! It's got a big rattle too."

"Yeah, the boy's got a good eye and a steady hand," Buck added, clapping Kasey on the shoulder. Pride rang clear in his voice.

Kasey felt a small swell of satisfaction but kept it tucked away, staying quiet as he unloaded his gear.

Julia caught the modest smile tugging at the corner of his lips and grinned at him. "Glad you guys had a good time. The jet leaves at four—we should grab a bite before we go."

"Sounds good. We'll grab lunch with Wynn and your mother later before we head out," Buck replied, pulling his hat off to wipe his brow.

The earthy smell of hay mingled with the creak of saddles as the stable settled into its familiar rhythm, but Julia's attention lingered on Kasey's quiet presence, her grin softening.

Together, they walked to Kasey's room, Julia peppering him with questions about his night. Once inside, she sat on his bed while he gathered his belongings.

"So, what did you do last night?" Kasey asked absentmindedly as he went through his dresser, pulling out clothes to wear after his shower.

"I went over Micki's for dinner," she said, playing with the buttons on the shirt he threw on the bed.

"Sounds quiet," he said.

"It was. After dinner, we had some of the wine we got from the winery and caught up; then I had sex with James." She said it so casually that it took Kasey a second to register.

He froze, staring at her. "You had sex with James?"

Julia looked up from the button she'd been fiddling with. "Yeah, I told you James and I dated in college before he married Micki, right?"

"Yeah, but I didn't know you still had sex with him," Kasey said, disbelief creeping into his voice.

"Every now and then—just for fun, a few times a year," she said, still oblivious to his growing discomfort.

"And Micki has no problem with you having sex with her husband?"

"No, it's just sex. I've slept with him a bunch of times since they've been married. She's always been part of it... except this time."

"What do you mean, except this time?" he asked, clearly thrown by what he was hearing.

"Well, this time, she just wanted to watch, and after that, we slept in the spare room without her. I haven't had sex with him alone since we dated. It's only been, like, four or five times a year—and only if I wasn't with someone at the time. It's just for fun."

"Can I ask... just what did Micki watch you do?" he asked, curiosity cutting through his shock.

"Are you sure you want to know? You seem upset," Julia said, finally starting to register his discomfort. "I'm sorry—I shouldn't have just blurted it out. Sometimes, I forget not everyone sees sex the way I do."

"I'd rather you be blunt and honest than lie or hide things... I just need to know. I don't even know why," Kasey said quietly, sitting down on the edge of the bed.

"She watched me have sex with him—just sitting on his lap, fully dressed. Then she went to bed, and we had sex before we fell asleep...and again this morning."

"You had sex with him three times?" he said softly, disbelief thick in his voice.

"Does it matter how many times?" she asked softly. "I've been so horny lately, and after kissing you, it was either James or... handling things myself, and honestly, I'm tired of that. I don't know when you'll be ready, but I didn't think it'd be a big deal—it's just normal for us."

"I guess I shouldn't be at all surprised after what I witnessed at your beach house," he said. "Did you three sleep together while I was there?"

"Actually, no," she replied. "You probably would've heard us if we had—I've been known to get a little loud. The first night, James had a headache and went to bed right after you. The next night, I got really messed up. After you spanked me,

I passed out on the couch while we were all talking. They just covered me up, and I slept downstairs for half the night."

"Do you sleep with Will, too?" he asked, his curiosity piqued by this foursome.

"No, but I did a few times years ago. I wanted to date him at first, but he wanted to just be friends. We had so much fun together, I didn't mind. Eventually, told me that he didn't feel anything romantically toward girls or guys. He was a virgin and wanted to know what sex was like without the drama of a girlfriend, so I helped him out. After a few times he felt it wasn't fair to me, and we stopped. He was afraid I wouldn't fully understand his limitations and might try to change him, which could hurt our friendship—and that was important to both of us. I kept other girls away by pretending to be his girlfriend when we went out, especially with his band. Unless, of course, if I was on the hunt," she smiled, her mind drifting back to those heady college days. We've been close friends ever since."

"You're quite the little group, aren't you?" Kasey said, a bit taken aback by the dynamics of her friendships.

"I did say we were close," she said with a gentle smile, not apologizing for her choices.

Folding his clothes and packing, Kasey asked quietly, "So, do you feel better now? Did James... do it for you?"

"I do feel better," she sighed as she lay back on his bed.

"I assume you guys use protection?" He asked casually, though his tone held a trace of curiosity.

"Micki and I are both on the pill, and they've never been with anyone outside their marriage but me. I haven't been with anyone else in almost a year, and I had a full physical nine months ago. So, to answer your question—we go wet and wild." She giggled, then added, "Sorry, that was crude. I just

86

hate the taste and feel of latex. But we can use condoms if and when you're ready—if it makes you feel more comfortable."

"I've never had sex with a woman without a condom. I imagine it feels... different."

"It's completely different for me. So much better—more spontaneous, wetter, and definitely sexier. No fiddling around with a stupid condom. I've only experienced it with James."

"I didn't realize you were that close to James," Kasey said softly as he lay down beside her. "I think... I'm a little jealous," he admitted, his eyes lingering on her.

"Really? Why?" she paused, a teasing glint in her eyes. "Because you like me," she said in a playful singsong voice.

He smiled, twirling a piece of her hair between his fingers. "I never said I didn't like you—I like you a lot. But I've told you, if we sleep together, things could get messy. I don't want to lose your friendship, and I love working with you. I really like your dad, and I definitely don't want to end up on his shit list. But the truth is... I don't like thinking about you with someone else. I wish it was me. I just don't think we're ready for that—or maybe it's just me that's not ready."

"It's definitely you not ready, cause I'm totally ready," she said with a grin. But as she realized he was more serious than she thought, her smile faded. "Is there something you're not telling me? Am I missing something? If there is, you can talk to me about anything, Kasey—you know that, right?" Her eyes searched his face, trying to read what he was feeling.

He hesitated. "It's just... you're way more sexually experienced than I am. You enjoy sex so much—I see it and hear it. I'm worried you're expecting more from me than I can give. You keep saying it won't matter if it's not what you thought, that we'll just move on, but honestly, Julia, it would hurt me if that happened." He paused, taking her hand. "The few times I've had sex without a real connection, it was awful, and I don't have the same kind of sex drive you do." He looked down, his voice quieter. "I'm afraid I'll disappoint you, and I couldn't handle that. I just needed you to know—that's what's really holding me back."

Julia rolled onto her side, facing away from him. "I feel like such an ass," she muttered, clearly uncomfortable. "I wish you'd told me sooner—I wouldn't have come at you so hard. I honestly thought you were just messing with me, playing hard to get because you're so damn good-looking." She paused, the realization hitting her. "Oh my God... I've been sexually harassing you this whole time."

"Please don't feel bad." He brushed her hair off her shoulder and kissed her neck. "I let you do everything you've done. I could've stopped you, but I didn't want to—I like it. I just don't move as fast as you. I don't have your confidence when it comes to sex. You keep telling me how good-looking you think I am... and I worry that you equate being good-looking with being good at sex. But what embarrasses me most is telling someone like you, someone who's so sexually fearless and confident, that I'm inexperienced—and honestly, I'm afraid of taking that next step with you."

She replied softly, "No matter how you see me, I need you to know I can be easygoing in bed. I don't have to swing from chandeliers or do crazy things for sex to be good. Yes, I enjoy sex, but what I really crave, the thing I've been searching for, is a deeper connection; and I couldn't find it—until now." She rolled over to face him. "I don't see you as just some potential fuck buddy—you're important to me. I don't think you realize how much. I look for you when you're not there. I need your approval for so many things. I want to feel closer to you." She gently caressed his face. "We can take things slow. I can show you what I want—I'm great at communicating in bed. And you can tell me whatever you need. If I'm going too fast, just say the word. You're not the only one who can take direction well." She smiled, her soulful, earnest look pulling him in.

"I had no idea you felt that way," he said, kissing her, elated to find her feelings ran deeper than he'd thought.

She grinned, whispering in his ear, "I really think we can make this work, and until you say, "Julia, stop, I don't want this, I'm going to keep trying to get you"—her voice dropped seductively— "to fuck me."

Her provocative words ignited something primal in him, and he crushed his lips to hers, pulling her so close it felt as though he could fuse their bodies together.

"I have a proposition..." she said, pulling back to meet his gaze.

He rolled his eyes and shook his head. "This should be good."

"No, listen," she continued, tracing her finger across his lips, "how about we take things slow? You can work through your feelings, and in the meantime, we can make out every now and then—since we've already shot down that rule. You can stick your tongue down my throat, and we'll both feel better." She kissed him gently, her lips barely brushing his. "But fair warning—I probably won't be able to resist flirting with you and touching you... that's just me in heat. Just say no, and I'll deal with it."

"In heat, huh?" he chuckled softly. "I think I can handle that." He kissed her again, his voice hesitant as he murmured, "I know I don't have the right to ask, but while I'm getting myself together... could you keep James out of your pants? And off your neck? I promise it won't take forever."

"I can do that, but I want something in return," she said with a coy look as she traced a circle with her finger on his chest.

"Are we negotiating?" he grinned.

"We are—I want some boob action when we kiss. Touching and licking," she smiled.

"How about just touching right now?" he offered.

"Fine, I'll take it... right now," she grinned, guiding his hand to her breast.

"Fine," he smiled, his eyes twinkling, "I accept your terms. And by the way, you need to cover that hickey for work, Missy," he teased, shaking his head. "What were you thinking?"

"I wasn't, obviously," she grinned.

Relieved to have shared how they were feeling, they went back to making out, his hand

slipping inside her bra.

***

Back at the office, their days were a mix of intense work and clandestine make-out sessions in her office's large closet. Julia initiated these secret meetings, often spending ten minutes kissing Kasey until he had to take another five just to compose himself. While Kasey enjoyed the kissing—how could he not?—he approached their secret meetings with a quiet caution that contrasted sharply with Julia's bold delight in the thrill of sneaking around.

***

Three weeks flew by, and soon they were back in Colorado for the prestigious Cattlemen's Dinner. Julia entered the living room where her family, Kasey, and several board members had gathered to head out for the event. Buck, Julia, Jack, and Rick were being honored for their distinguished contributions to cattle breeding techniques.

All eyes turned to Julia as she entered, stunning in a custom-made black cocktail dress of elastic taffeta and velvet. The dress hugged her figure with a low-cut, fitted bodice, off-the-shoulder sleeves forming a V-neck bow, and a sleek column skirt that fell to her ankles. Silver stilettos sparkled on her feet, and her hair was swept into a loose French twist, with soft waves framing her face. Kasey's eyes lit up the moment he saw her.

"It's about time," Wynn huffed impatiently.

"Shut up, Wynn," Julia said with a smirk.

"Jules, honey, you look beautiful," her mother said warmly.

"Absolutely beautiful, darlin'," added Buck. "Alright, let's move out, people. Giddyup. Time to go."

"You look stunning. Are you sure you can move in that?" Kasey teased, offering Julia his arm as they headed toward the waiting limo.

"Thank you. It's not as tight as it looks," she beamed. "Damn, you look so good tonight. Is your suit cashmere? It feels amazing," she said, running her fingers along his sleeve.

"Yes, it is," he replied, his impeccably tailored black cashmere suit fitting him like a glove.

"If we were alone in the limo, you'd have to literally fight me off right now," she teased as they reached the car. He smiled warmly, though his mind was already on the upcoming event.

***

As they arrived at the venue, chaos erupted with flashing cameras, press, and protesters crowding the entrance. Guests gathered in clusters before heading inside. Julia and Kasey led the way, with her parents and brother close behind.

The festive mood shifted abruptly as animal rights activists stormed the entrance, waving signs and chanting. One particularly aggressive protester targeted Julia and her father, aiming to douse them with cow's blood.

Ever vigilant, Kasey stepped in front of Julia, shielding her from harm as the protester zeroed in, shouting slogans. Julia calmly urged the man to express his concerns peacefully, creating a tense standoff that drew the crowd's attention.

Undeterred, Julia kept her composure, aware of the importance of staying calm in front of the media to protect her family's reputation. When the protester suddenly lunged closer, Kasey reacted swiftly, blocking the man's attempt to douse Julia. With a sharp shove, Kasey redirected the man's aim, sending the blood splattering onto the protester and the person behind him instead.

Security swiftly intervened, protecting Buck and his family, while other guards escorted the protesters away, diffusing the escalating situation.

"Inside, this way," Kasey ordered, wrapping his arm around Julia practically lifting her off the ground as he guided her away from the chaos. He glanced back to check on the rest of her family.

"Everyone okay?" Kasey asked as Buck, Lily, and Wynn joined them inside, flashbulbs popping all around.

"We're fine. How about you two?" Buck replied, realizing that Kasey had stepped between danger and his daughter. It was the second time he'd protected someone in his family—third, if he counted the snake.

"All in one piece. How about you?" Julia asked, looking Kasey over. "You didn't get hit with anything, did you?"

"I'm fine. But are you crazy engaging a protester like that?" he grimaced." You could have had more than blood thrown at you. You've got no fear sometimes, and it worries me."

"I'm tired of this. They should sit down and talk things out instead of this ridiculous bullshit," Julia said, annoyed at the commotion.

"He's right, darlin'. Don't engage with people like that in these situations—too much chance of things going south. And you worried your mother."

"I'm fine," Lily interjected, patting Buck's arm dismissively.

"That was wicked. Did you see that guy? He got a face full of that shit, "Wynn laughed, excited from the confrontation.

"Language, Wynn," Lily said with a smile. "He did get what he deserved."

"Seems you're a good man to have around," Buck said, patting Kasey on the back just as Rick, Jack, and the other board members arrived in time to see it.

Julia squeezed Kasey's arm. "Thank you," she said, relieved by his intervention. He gave her a strained smile, glancing around at the crowd of people and the press, eager for interviews and photos.

"We should go to your seats. It's safer there," he said, ushering Julia to their table.

The dinner got back on track, and Buck, Julia, Rick, and Jack accepted their award to thunderous applause. Their peers not only celebrated their achievements in breeding techniques but also their resilience in the face of the protester attack.

***

Later that evening, as exhaustion settled over everyone from the night's events, they exchanged good nights and headed to their rooms. Kasey discreetly left while Julia lingered a few minutes more with her parents.

Changing into a short pajama set and slouchy socks, Julia lightly tapped on Kasey's door. She slipped inside as he opened it, smiling, "I'm here to properly thank you for protecting me tonight."

Standing on her tiptoes, she pulled him close, her lips finding his with a hunger that left no space for hesitation. Without breaking the kiss, he effortlessly lifted her, and she wrapped her legs around him as he carried her to the bed.

They lingered in bed, exchanging tender kisses and intimate conversation until she drifted off, nestled in his embrace. He lay there, watching her sleep, debating whether to wake her. Deciding against it, he pulled the blanket snugly around them, holding her close as he listened to the rhythmic sound of her breathing. Normally, he struggled with sleep, but tonight, with her in his arms, he drifted into a deep slumber and didn't wake until morning.

***

"Hey, sleepyhead. I'm gonna sneak out before anyone sees me," she said, rousing him with a gentle kiss. "Thanks for letting me stay; it felt so nice having your body next to mine. I slept really well."

95

Now awake, he returned her kiss, his fingers gently caressing her face. "You're so beautiful in this light. I didn't think you could look any prettier," he murmured, planting soft kisses on her neck.

"You say the sweetest things, Kasey, but my face must be a mess—I never took off my makeup from last night," she said, letting him pull her closer.

"You couldn't look a mess if you tried," he said so sincerely that she almost believed him.

"Thank you. I love your compliments. I could stay in bed with you all day just kissing, but I want to spend some time with Micki and James before we leave. Wanna come with me?" "No, thanks. I'm not ready to see James without picturing you two together. I think I'll go for a ride and spend some time alone. That was a lot to deal with last night."

"Don't be mad at James," she said, kissing him again, her tone light and placating.

"I'm not mad at James. I'd just rather not have that picture in my head," he explained.

"Before I go, are you sure there isn't anything I can do to thank you for last night?" she teased, sliding her hand suggestively over his t-shirt. "I could take that picture out of your head and replace it with something better."

Smiling, he grabbed her hand, "No, that wouldn't be fair to you, now would it?"

"It's not for me—it's for you. It's a gift." A flirtatious smile played on her lips, her eyes sparkling with temptation. "It might not be a thousand-dollar hat, but I'm sure you'll like it just as much."

"I have no doubt I would, but I still think it isn't fair to-"

Despite his protests, she interrupted with a mischievous grin. "Don't be ungracious—accept my thanks," she chided, pulling her hand back playfully.

"Julia..." he began, but as she pulled down his pajama bottoms and her full lips and warm, wet mouth enveloped him, the words died in his throat. He inhaled sharply, his fingers sliding into her hair as he surrendered to her touch, basking in the sensations she expertly delivered. Laying back, eyes closed, a wave of pure pleasure washed over him.

His soft moans with each flick of her tongue or twist of her hand turned her on, not just because she was making him feel good, but because she could feel his walls coming down, one by one. It didn't take long—her hand and mouth working in perfect sync—before he inhaled sharply, exhaling her name, "Julia." His grip on her hair tightened when she didn't pull away.

When she looked up at him from under her long lashes, her hair tousled and makeup smudged, wiping the corner of her mouth with the back of her hand, she smiled. He grinned and pulled her close. "That was the best 'thank you' I've ever gotten," he sighed, a sweet, content smile spreading across his face.

A sly, self-satisfied look crossed her face, pleased with his reaction. "I told you you'd like it as much as the hat."

"No comparison. I love the hat, but that thank you deserves its own." He sighed softly. "I can't remember the last time I felt like that. Do you have to leave right away? Could you stay a little longer?"

"Of course I can," she whispered with an adoring smile, settling into his embrace. He was so different from the other men she'd been with. He craved the intimacy and closeness that came with sex, not just the sensation—and she loved that about him. When she finally pulled herself away, he couldn't help but replay the experience over and over, grateful for her unforgettable gift.

***

Chapter 6: Kasey's Brownstone

"I was wondering if you'd like to come to my place tonight for dinner. We could watch a movie, get your mind off work," Kasey said casually, organizing the files on Julia's desk as she returned from her father's office.

"I'd like that," she replied, smiling warmly. "I was actually thinking of leaving early, around four-thirty." It was the first time he'd asked to spend time with her outside of work, and she'd never been to his home before.

"Could you come in before we go?" she asked, moving to her desk.

"Sit on the couch, please. I have something for you."

Kasey settled on the couch, watching Julia pull a fabric-wrapped box from her bottom desk drawer and place it on the cocktail table before sitting next to him.

He smiled curiously. "What's this?"

Her joy was unmistakable as she flashed her signature pixie grin. "Just because you never mentioned it doesn't mean I wouldn't find out it's your birthday. I wanted to give you something. I hope you like it as much as I love Nomi," she said, glancing fondly at her flourishing bonsai tree. "Why didn't you tell me it was your birthday?"

"I haven't celebrated my birthday in years. I've never been comfortable with the attention," he explained.

"Oh my God, Kasey, I celebrate my birthday for a week," Julia giggled. "I love the attention and presents."

"I know you do. I witnessed it firsthand," he said with a grin.

He held the present up, examining the intricate wrapping. "Did you wrap this yourself?" he asked, admiring the elegant furoshiki style. "It's beautifully done."

"I did!" she said excitedly. "I watched a video on how to do it. I picked a pocket square I thought you'd like so you can reuse it."

"Julia, this is incredibly thoughtful. I love that you incorporated furoshiki, and the pocket square is perfect," he said, his appreciation evident.

"I'm glad you like the wrapping; it took more than a few tries to get it right," she said, beaming like a child who'd just won a hard-earned prize.

With care, he began untying the expertly crafted parcel. If someone had entered the room at that moment, they might have struggled to tell who was more excited—Kasey or Julia, so eager was she for him to like the gift.

"Julia, this is fantastic! How did you know I needed a new sports watch?" he exclaimed, holding up the Iron Man wristwatch.

"I caught you scrolling through pictures of watches the other day, and I remembered you said you cracked the face of the one you have. I pay attention," she said with a warm smile. "Do you really like it?"

"I absolutely love it. Thank you, Julia," he said, glancing toward the outer office. Seeing no one around, he leaned in, giving her a brief but passionate kiss, his hand softly caressing her cheek.

"Mmm, a present for me—you're very welcome," she beamed, her eyes sparkling. "We can head straight to your place instead of me going home first."

"That works for me. What would you like for dinner? I can cook or order out."

"You cook?" she asked, genuinely surprised. Most guys his age she knew either had housekeepers, personal chefs or relied on takeout.

"I like to cook; it's calming—and then I get to eat it," he replied with a broad smile.

"But it's your birthday; you shouldn't have to cook for me," Julia said, suddenly realizing that he wasn't doing anything special for his day except choosing to spend it with her.

"I love to cook. It would be no imposition at all. In fact, I'd be happy to cook for you."

"Well, then, whatever you feel like making is fine with me," she assured him. She was used to letting him take charge of ordering her lunch and dinner at work since she wasn't picky, and he always chose healthier options.

***

She received a text from her driver, Carl, and they headed for Kasey's brownstone. Julia wasn't fond of driving in the city; it made her too anxious. She kept her beloved convertible reserved for trips to the Jersey Shore. Carl, a former New York cop, had been her driver for the past three years, also serving as her security during public appearances and media-heavy events. In his early fifties and divorced with no children, he'd retired after twenty-five years with the department, prompted by his ex-wife, who cited his stressful job as a factor in their split. Even after moving into personal security—a much less stressful job—it hadn't saved his marriage. The silver lining of the whole mess was that Carl discovered he preferred the flexibility of personal security over the grind of police work. Shortly after the divorce, he became Julia's driver and security when needed.

A large man with bulging muscles, a shiny bald head, and a stare that could kill, Carl was a complete softie around her. She'd once told him he reminded her of Terry Crews, which made him laugh—and once, when he sensed she needed cheering up, he'd belted out a few lines of "A Thousand Miles," instantly brightening her day. Julia appreciated his positive attitude and how he always adapted to her needs.

"Thanks, Carl. I'll call you with the pickup time later," Julia said as she exited the car.

"I'll be available all night, Jules. Just shoot me a text," he said, closing the door behind her and Kasey.

"What a beautiful brownstone—and such a pretty street," she remarked as Kasey opened the front door for her. Stepping into the foyer, her eyes wandered, taking in her surroundings.

"No shoes inside," he said, offering her a pair of fuzzy slippers he'd picked up at the store. He slipped off his own shoes, neatly placing them on the designated shelf beside his slides, before turning back to her.

"I thought you went in to get stuff for dinner," she said, pulling off the tags and slipping into the slippers.

"I did, but I saw those and thought of you. I know you like soft things, so I figured they'd be an upgrade from the rubber ones I've got. Besides, you should have your own."

"Thank you, I love them," she said, touched by his thoughtfulness. She loved his attention to detail—something she'd never experienced in a man before, and it made her appreciate him all the more. He programmed the security system and followed her inside.

Walking inside, she didn't know what to expect, but it wasn't the immaculately clean, zen-inspired sanctuary that greeted her. Dominated by cream and taupe tones with occasional black accents, the furniture showcased clean lines and simple forms. His affinity for Japanese culture surprised her.

As she explored, Kasey silently observed her while putting away the groceries. A sizable shoji screen separated the living room from another large space. From the doorway, she spotted folded mats and a training dummy in the corner. An intricately decorated sword hung prominently on one wall, surrounded by smaller daggers, knives, and throwing stars arranged with precision. On the opposite wall, nine handguns were meticulously placed in a square pattern behind a locked glass case.

Glancing in his direction, Julia remarked, "You're never quite what I expect."

"Is that a good thing?" he asked with a small smile as he uncorked a bottle of wine.

"Well, you're anything but boring, that's for sure. It's been seven months, and I feel like I've only scratched the surface of who you are. Your home, for instance—it's not what I expected."

"What did you expect? Some kind of frat boy's dorm room?" he asked, a touch of sarcasm in his voice.

"Don't be a shit, you know I didn't mean that," she smirked. "You're not the frat boy type, and you're definitely not messy. But I didn't expect... the Japanese décor, the training room, the weapons. You just continue to surprise me."

"Make yourself comfortable. I'm going to get some things ready for dinner," he said, taking a sip of his wine.

"I can't believe you live alone in this huge house. Do you use all the floors?"

"No, there are two floors I don't use at all, and there's an apartment below us. I originally bought it as an investment. I wasn't planning to live here, but I fell in love with the neighborhood—and the place itself—so I moved in."

"Need any help?" she asked, still exploring the textures of different fabrics and admiring the few small sculptures on the fireplace mantel.

"Seriously?" He grinned. "You can't even boil water without making a mess. Here," he handed her a glass of wine, "sit, and you can watch me cook."

"I take offense, sir. I can boil water. But that's about it," she replied with a grin. "I was never really into cooking. I always preferred being outside with my dad and the ranch hands instead of in the kitchen with my mom. Now, ask me if I can rope a calf or brand a cow—that's a different story."

"You're the perfect mix of cowgirl and businesswoman, just not exactly domestic. We all have our strengths."

"What's yours?" she asked, settling in to watch him cook.

"I don't know... maybe finding balance. You and this job are the chaos I balance out with my home. I appreciate both worlds, but I need a break from each sometimes. They keep each other in check," he said as he started prepping baby potatoes.

"I'm the crazy part?" she smiled, taking a sip and eyeing him over the rim of her wine glass.

"Maybe not crazy—more chaotic," he replied, pulling utensils from the impeccably organized drawers.

"I accept chaotic," she grinned. "Do you have a housekeeper?"

"No, I did when I was younger after my mother died," he said, his hands tightening briefly before returning to his task.

"I didn't know your mom died. I'm so sorry," she said, her voice filled with sympathy. "You never talk about your family. How old were you?"

"Twelve," he said, his tone flat, distant.

"Oh, Kasey, I didn't know that," she said softly. She reached over to squeeze his hand, a pang tugging at her chest as she watched him.

He kept his eyes down and continued working, his voice steady as he spoke. "Marisol was my housekeeper. She was like a surrogate mother to me from thirteen until I went to college. I came home to her every break. She lived with me until I was about sixteen, then just came during the day. She taught me how to cook and clean up after myself. I don't like the idea of someone cleaning up after me, and I don't want anyone in my home when I'm not here. If they were cleaning while I was, I'd feel ridiculous, so I just do it myself. It's not that hard."

"I don't know what I'd do without my housekeeper, Alice," Julia replied.

"Probably live like a frat boy," Kasey interjected with a grin, "and never eat properly."

"Well, you certainly know me," she smiled. "When will dinner be ready?"

"Around six-thirty, just over an hour. Why?"

"Do you think I could lie down for a bit? I'm really tired. I don't sleep well when I'm stressed, and with my period, I feel pretty drained. I'm just glad it'll be over before the trip—one less thing to worry about."

He was always amazed by how freely she spoke about her body. Her openness stood in stark contrast to his own extreme privacy, shaped by growing up with a shy, reserved mother.

"Sure, come lie down in my room," he said, leading her upstairs. "I don't know why you're stressing about this trip. You've got this. You're well-prepared, and they already seem to be on board. They'll be putty in your very capable hands," he added earnestly, hoping to boost her confidence.

"Thanks, I appreciate that," she said, grateful for his unwavering support.

Seeing his home, she now understood why he liked her beach house so much. As she entered his bedroom, she was struck by its tranquility and beauty. The room featured a cream-colored duvet and matching sheets on a light wood platform bed, perfectly complementing the room's soft palette of cream and muted whites. The focal point of the spacious room was a sizable fireplace with an intricately carved mantel depicting cranes standing in tall grass. Flanked by windows with blackout curtains and delicate sheers, the fireplace exuded warmth and elegance. A small, flat box of sand with carefully arranged stones and a flourishing bonsai tree sat on a handcrafted dresser in the corner by the window, bringing a touch of nature indoors.

By the other window, a sleek reading chair and an oval-shaped rice paper floor lamp created a cozy reading nook. Floor-to-ceiling corner shelves held books on philosophy, Japanese culture, Bruce Lee, and martial arts, reflecting a quiet intellect that, to Julia, felt both intriguing and exotic. For him, it was his haven of solitude.

"Bruce, I take it?" she asked, admiring the miniature tree. "He's beautiful—so healthy. Nomi would think he was very handsome," she grinned. "Is that electric?" she asked, marveling at the fireplace's size and the intricate mantel. "Are these cranes?" she added, running her fingers lightly over the carving.

"They are cranes, or *tsurue*—the bird of happiness," he said. "They symbolize good things in Japanese culture. And yes, it's electric. I don't want to deal with the mess of a real fireplace, plus I can use it year-round without roasting. Would you like me to turn it on?"

"Yes, please. I love watching the flames." She walked over to his bed and pulled back the duvet.

"Let me change the pillowcase for you," he offered as she sat on the bed.

"Not necessary," she replied, kicking off her shoes and lying back, inhaling the scent of his pillow. "It smells like you, and you always smell good."

"As you wish," he replied with a sweet smile, knowing *The Princess Bride* was one of Julia's favorite movies, and they planned to watch it after dinner. "I'll wake you when dinner's ready."

"Thank you, boy," she grinned, settling in and losing herself in the dance of the flickering flames.

"You're welcome, Buttercup," he replied, starting to close the door.

"Oh, and Kasey..." she called out softly.

"Yes, Julia?"

"Your home is beautiful—and incredibly interesting, just like you."

"Thank you," he replied with a proud smile, closing the door behind him.

***

107

Opening her eyes, Julia was briefly disoriented by the unfamiliar shadows cast by the dancing flames on Kasey's bedroom walls. Gradually, recognition dawned, along with the awareness of his body beside hers, his arm draped over her waist. Gently slipping from his embrace, she sat up on the edge of the bed and glanced at her watch.

"Hello, Sleeping Beauty," Kasey's drowsy voice broke the silence.

"Why didn't you wake me up? I ruined your birthday," she said, disappointment in her voice as she lay back down to face him.

"You absolutely did not ruin my birthday. Even better than dinner, I got to snuggle up to you in my bed."

She smiled sweetly.

"Besides, you were really out. I did try to wake you, but you obviously needed the rest. Dinner wasn't a big deal—just salmon. I ate it," he said plainly. "You must be starving. I can make you something," he offered, starting to sit up.

"No, you don't," she insisted, gently pushing him back. "You're not going anywhere. I can wait for breakfast." She smiled. "I really do appreciate how you look out for me. Don't think I don't notice—I do. I'll be right back. I have to pee and take care of girl stuff. Where's my bag? Don't go anywhere."

"I put it on the chair over there," Kasey said, watching as she grabbed a tampon from

her bag and headed to the bathroom. When she returned, she was in her lacy demi bra and boy shorts.

"Now, before you get all crazy, I'm just uncomfortable sleeping in my work clothes; you've seen me in a bikini before, so control yourself," she teased. He lifted the covers without saying a word, and she slipped in, turning to let him spoon her. Pushing her hair aside, he buried his face in her neck, breathing in her scent as she put his arm around her waist and squeezed it tightly to her. In no time, they both drifted back to sleep, perfectly content just to be next to each other.

***

When Kasey finally woke, he headed downstairs to find Julia bent over, rummaging through his fridge for something to eat.

"Good, you're up. I'm starving. Please make me something," she said, holding a fork with a cold baby potato on it, looking helpless. Her hair was messy, and she was wearing one of his pajama tops over her underwear.

"God, you're hopeless," he said, shaking his head as he took the fork away from her. "Sit, I'll make you some eggs."

"I feel bad I never called Carl back last night," she said, watching him whisk the eggs.

"Don't worry; I called him when I couldn't wake you."

"Good, I didn't want to hold him up all night for nothing."

As he put bread in the toaster, he said, "We're going to be late, you know."

"You forget, I'm in charge. I can get there when I want. Just call Barbara and tell her to hold the fort till we get there. It's the first time I don't feel tired in weeks." She paused, "In fact, tell her we'll be there after lunch. Let's go for a walk—I think I need some exercise."

"You're going to walk in those heels?" he asked incredulously.

"Of course not. I'll just go to that boutique I saw and buy some clothes," she replied, happily eating her breakfast.

"Whatever you want, you're the boss," he smiled, taking a bite of her toast.

109

"Don't call me boss," she smirked. "I hate that 'girl boss' shit. Makes me feel like the mean girl in some dumb movie."

He laughed. "I'm going to shower and get dressed. Do you want to shower first?"

"Can I shower with you?" she asked, grinning at him.

"Now you know that wouldn't be a good idea," he said, heading to the bathroom, taking the stairs two at a time.

"Just checking," she yelled back, a tiny smile forming as she finished her eggs.

***

In the dressing room of a small boutique, Julia changed out of her work clothes and into the new sweats and sneakers she'd bought. Bagging up her clothes and shoes, they set out for a stroll around his neighborhood. It was a sunny, crisp fall morning, and the air was filled with the peaceful quiet of kids back in school.

"That saleslady thought I was paying for a very expensive walk of shame," she giggled as they left.

"No, she didn't," Kasey replied. "She was very helpful."

"Oh, you sweet, naive boy," she smiled. "It was all in the eyes."

Later, as they exited another small boutique, Julia said, "This neighborhood is so interesting. So many different types of shops and restaurants." Despite her usual preference for shopping online in New York, she found joy in the unique shops and the easy atmosphere of his neighborhood. With a childlike grin, she handed him a box.

Caught off guard by the unexpected gesture, he asked, "What's this for?"

Her face radiated eagerness as if she couldn't wait for him to open it. "It's not a big deal. I just thought it was perfect for your home. Open it. It's a wrapped rock from the Pacific Northwest. It's wrapped in the four directions—spiritual, emotional, intellectual, and... shit, what's the last one?"

"It's physical," he replied with a grin, examining the rock.

"That's right, physical," she grinned, flashing her baby blues at him. "You know what it's for?" she asked, surprised.

"I do. I read a lot. It's beautiful, thank you. I know just where to put it."

Later, back at his brownstone, he placed her thoughtful gift on the mantel of the fireplace in his bedroom before changing into his suit. Julia opted to change at work—she always kept fresh clothes there, thanks to Kasey's suggestion after a tea mishap led to a last-minute blouse order. She finally felt relaxed and prepared for the London meeting. After work, they each retreated to their respective homes, carefully packing and letting the weight of the upcoming London trip settle into their thoughts.

***

Chapter 7: London and New Beginnings

In the early hours of Monday morning, they set out for JFK International Airport, the quiet anticipation of the trip weighing on them as they prepared to catch a private jet scheduled for ten o'clock. Buck had arranged this through his connection with Ben Whitstock of the Cattlemen's Association. Ben, who arrived with his new young wife on vacation, graciously hosted the group as a nod to the years of generosity he'd received from Buck. Julia had observed the pair from a distance, noting how youth and money always seemed to dance together, but she had no time for such distractions today.

They swiftly crossed the Atlantic to London, joined by Rosa Thomson, the project manager who could command a room with a single glance, and Dante Graziano, their razor-sharp legal counsel. The flight was a blur of quiet focus, each of them fine-tuning their strategies and running through details one last time.

They had spent hours locked in early morning virtual meetings and countless conference calls, but this marked the first time they would meet face-to-face with the key players: Nigel and Giles, twin masterminds behind Hawthorne Apparel, a legendary name in men's fashion. Their business partner, Haruto Makino, was the real power behind the scenes though—Julia had made sure to read everything she could about the man who owned the largest share in the company after the brothers. She wasn't one to leave anything to chance.

Touching down in London, the team settled into The Stafford London Hotel, where luxury met comfort. The next three days would offer moments to recharge and breathe, but Julia couldn't quite switch off, her mind already replaying strategies and anticipating every angle of the negotiations. Her sharp, strategic mind, combined with her meticulously prepared team and Kasey's steady presence as her right-hand man, gave her the confidence they were primed for what lay ahead. Yet, despite her composed exterior, she couldn't shake the gnawing feeling that everything rested on the smallest details—the kind that could either make or break their deal.

Julia and Kasey occupied adjoining rooms, just as Rosa and Dante did. Officially, it made sense to pair them this way for safety, but Julia had her own motive—keeping Kasey within easy reach for those late-night visits, away from prying eyes.

That first night, Julia found herself slipping into Kasey's room, sliding into bed next to him as the TV played softly in the background. The familiarity of his warmth was a comfort she wouldn't admit out loud, and though she behaved herself, the quiet closeness of his body next to hers was enough. He didn't mind—it was quickly becoming a habit, one he couldn't bring himself to discourage.

As the flicker of the screen bathed them in soft light, Julia's mind whirred with plans for tomorrow, but for now, she let herself rest in the moment—just a little.

The conference room of Hawthorne Apparel exuded elegance. At its center, an antique mahogany table gleamed under the soft lighting, surrounded by high-backed leather chairs, their warm tones perfectly complementing the room's refined atmosphere. A grand fireplace anchored the space, above which hung a portrait of the Hawthorne brothers in their prime—debonair, confident, and far younger than the distinguished men of seventy Julia knew them to be. She couldn't help but marvel at how time had softened their once-jaunty features.

Julia entered with the grace of someone who was both fully prepared and fully in control. Her presence drew the eyes of the Hawthorne brothers, who sat at the head of the long table. As they rose to greet her and her team, Giles's gaze shifted to Kasey, his attention immediately caught by the impeccably tailored suit—a signature piece from Hawthorne Apparel.

"Mr. Cortland," Giles said, a note of appreciation in his voice, "you wear our Herringbone suit with remarkable style. You could grace our catalogs without a second thought. Would you mind turning around for us?" he added, his tone polite but clearly impressed.

"Nigel, Haruto, take a look at this craftsmanship... absolutely flawless."

"Indeed, it's exquisite, though that's only to be expected—it's one of ours, after all," Nigel said with a proud smile as he gave Kasey and his suit an approving once-over.

"Yes, it is," Kasey replied smoothly, "as is Dante's. We provided our measurements as requested, and this impeccable fit is what we received in return."

"Does Masters Inc. only employ beautiful people, Ms. Masters?" Giles teased, his gaze shifting to Dante's tailored attire.

Haruto Makino, the financial mastermind with a background in tailoring, inspected Kasey's suit, nodding in approval. "A perfect fit," he declared. Kasey bowed respectfully, surprising the older man with his fluent Japanese as he agreed, "Yes, it's both a perfect fit and incredibly comfortable."

Impressed, Mr. Makino returned the gesture, praising Kasey's fluency. As Julia effortlessly charmed the Hawthorne brothers, Kasey engaged Haruto in a fluid conversation about cultural nuances and his genuine appreciation for Japanese traditions. The unexpected connection deepened the positive atmosphere in the room.

After a few minutes of polite conversation, Nigel cleared his throat and suggested, "Shall we begin? The sooner we wrap things up, the sooner we can show you around our world—and, of course, enjoy lunch."

Julia wasted no time diving into the details, focusing sharply on acquisition terms, financials, strategic goals, and the renaming of the business. Keeping 'Hawthorne' in the new name had become a sticking point for the brothers, reflecting their deep personal attachment to their legacy.

Throughout the meeting, Julia navigated the negotiations with finesse, seamlessly blending her sharp, professional acumen with a warmth that put everyone at ease. She quickly established rapport with Nigel and Giles, making them feel not just respected but valued. Her ability to balance poise with approachability made her a formidable negotiator, finding common ground with the brothers and fostering a sense of unity around the table.

By the meeting's end, not only had the major terms of the acquisition been agreed upon, but a genuine sense of mutual respect and camaraderie had developed among the key players, making the process smoother than anyone had anticipated. The Hawthorne brothers and Haruto were not just prepared to accept the terms—they were excited for future collaborations with Julia and Masters Inc. The real success of the meeting lay not just in the deal itself but in the personal connections forged around the table.

***

After touring the showroom and work area—"their world," as Nigel had proudly called it—the brothers led the group to The Regency House, their exclusive private club in the heart of London, to celebrate over lunch. The venue, steeped in tradition, radiated old-world charm, perfectly reflecting the refined tastes of English gentlemen. Set within a historic building, the club boasted rich wood paneling, luxurious leather upholstery, and timeless British décor.

Julia entered on Nigel's arm as they were led to a private dining room reserved for moments like this. She was immediately captivated by the space—fine art adorning the walls, antique furniture carefully placed, and soft, subtle lighting creating an intimate, elegant atmosphere. Nigel and Giles used the opportunity to demonstrate their appreciation for both fine dining and even finer wine. The menu offered a seamless blend of British and continental cuisine, crafted to suit the most refined tastes, all prepared by the club's renowned chef.

The conversation flowed smoothly between business and personal anecdotes, with Julia effortlessly charming the brothers as she shared vivid stories of growing up on a ranch. Rosa, usually reserved, seemed to let her hair down, laughing freely and enjoying the lively atmosphere. Dante, to everyone's surprise, revealed an impressive knowledge of fine wine, sparking a spirited discussion that even had the brothers grinning in approval. Julia's warmth and authenticity created a cozy, almost familial atmosphere, a stark contrast to the sophistication of their surroundings. As the afternoon progressed, glasses of vintage champagne were raised in celebratory toasts, marking not just the success of the acquisition but the beginning of a prosperous and deeply personal collaboration.

***

Back at the hotel, Julia congratulated Rosa and Peter for their work on the project, slipping them each an envelope with a bonus for their expense accounts. "Enjoy London," she urged with a smile. They would regroup at eleven the next morning for the final decision on the name and the contract signing.

"What would you like to do tonight?" Kasey asked as they returned to Julia's suite.

"I wanna do something fun. How about a ride on the London Eye? I'd love to see the city lights from up there," Julia said excitedly.

"Is that it? You're so easy to please. You could do anything," Kasey replied, still amazed by how, beneath her sophisticated image, Julia was just a down-to-earth cowgirl at heart. It didn't take much to make her happy.

"I'd love to come back for a real vacation and explore properly. But right now, with all the excitement today, I'm a little worn out. The London Eye sounds perfect—no walking, great views, and it just looks like fun," she said, her face lighting up.

"Let me see what I can do. I'll check with the concierge. Be right back," Kasey said, heading toward the door.

While Kasey was gone, Julia quickly changed out of her business clothes, touched up her makeup, and slipped into a dark gray, long-sleeve lace jumpsuit. The plunging neckline and intricate cutouts along the sleeves struck the perfect balance of sexy and sophisticated.

"Wow, that was a quick change," Kasey said when he returned, his eyes drinking her in. "You look smashing," he added with a chuckle.

"Thank you very much. So, are we all set?" she asked eagerly, her excitement clear.

"I keep telling you, you're Julia Masters, of course we're all set," Kasey smiled, shaking his head.

"Let me change, and we'll be off," he said, disappearing into his room. Minutes later, he emerged in sleek black tailored pants, a gray silk shirt, a black cashmere jacket, and low-cut boots.

"You are so handsome," Julia remarked as he walked back into her room. "We look so good together," she added with a smile as she pulled him close. "Kiss me," she urged softly.

"A quick one—then we have to go. The car's already on its way," he said, lifting her face and pressing a tender kiss to her lips. But she wasn't ready to let go, her lips returning for more.

"Mm, maybe we should stay in," she teased with a mischievous grin.

"Absolutely not. We're going—grab your shawl," he ordered, a twinkle in his eye.

"Fine, but we're revisiting this later," she said with a grin as his hand rested on the small of her back, guiding her out the door.

Before they left, Kasey picked up a silver gift bag from the concierge. "What's that?' Julia asked, her voice lifting with curiosity.

"You'll see," he replied playfully.

***

118

As they rode through the city, Julia held Kasey's hand and rested her head on his shoulder. "We did so well at the meeting today. It was easier than I expected," she said, her happiness evident.

"You made it easy. Your prep was exceptional, and that's what clinched it. You had them in the palm of your hand, just like I knew you would. They were really taken with you. It's amazing—how you're such a softie in your personal life but an absolute force in the conference room. Just like your father," he added, genuinely impressed.

To Julia, being compared to her father was the highest compliment Kasey could have given her. She squeezed his hand gently. "Thank you, that means a lot. But I didn't do it alone—your idea to wear their suits was spot on. You both looked great, and I think Nigel was quite taken with you," she said with a grin. "And Haruto seemed to warm up to you, too. What had him laughing at one point?"

"He asked if I enjoyed working for such a smart woman. I told him it's better than working for a stupid one. I wasn't trying to be funny, but he got a good laugh out of it," Kasey chuckled.

"Ooh, we're here!" Julia exclaimed as they pulled up to their destination. Kasey grabbed the gift bag and offered his hand to help her out of the car.

"This way, Mr. Cortland," the guide said, leading them to the front of the line. "The next pod is yours—just give it a minute to stop and let the passengers disembark. Would you like a guide or prefer to go alone?"

Kasey glanced at Julia, and without missing a beat, she answered, "Alone, please," with plans of making out with Kasey already flashing through her mind.

When it was their turn to board the pod, a guide appeared with a bottle of champagne and two glasses. With smooth efficiency, he opened the bottle, wrapped it in a white cloth, and poured two glasses before setting it in a wine bucket on the table. "Enjoy your ride," he said, securing the door as he left.

"Did you arrange all this?" she asked, touched by Kasey's thoughtfulness as he handed her a glass. He smiled affectionately. "I enjoy doing things for you," he replied, lifting his glass. "To you, Julia Masters, and your first solo acquisition—you did good." She beamed as their glasses clinked, sipping their champagne with matching smiles."

"What's in the bag?" Julia asked, trying to peek inside.

"You're such a child," he teased with a grin, reaching into the bag and pulling out a box of four jumbo chocolate-covered strawberries. "To go with the champagne," he added sweetly.

"I love chocolate-covered strawberries!" she squealed, eagerly taking the box from him. As she plucked one from inside, he added softly, his eyes twinkling, "There's something else in here."

"What?" she exclaimed excitedly, handing him the strawberry before grabbing the bag.

Inside was a beautiful box, and when she opened it, she found a stunning Limited Edition Lotus Garden Rollerball Pen. The pen was a blend of lilac, white, and green, mirroring the delicate colors of the lotus flower, with its leaves accented by a sleek black trim.

Kasey explained the meaning behind the gift. "The lotus symbolizes rebirth—just like what you're doing with this fashion house. You're creating something new from its past. Tomorrow, when you sign those contracts with this pen, it'll remind you of your first solo acquisition and how impressive you were today."

"Oh, Kasey, it's stunning. I love it! And the meaning behind it... it's so thoughtful. You really do think of everything." She threw her arms around him, pulling him into a tight embrace and kissed him hard—a kiss full of both lust and affection.

"We can save that for the hotel—you're missing the view," he murmured softly, taking her hand and leading her to the window. They stood together, Julia leaning into him as his strong arms wrapped around her, their hands intertwined as they gazed out at the city below.

The panoramic view of London from the heights of the pod enchanted Julia. With each ascent, the city unfolded below, bathed in the warm glow of streetlights and illuminated landmarks. The Thames shimmered, reflecting the twinkling lights of the surrounding

architecture. Big Ben, the Houses of Parliament, and the bustling city sparkled in the distance, casting a magical glow.

"This is the perfect way to end the day—thank you," she said softly, turning to kiss him. After a moment, she pulled back with a beaming smile. "Let's take some pictures! She grabbed her phone and champagne. They snapped a few with him holding her close and the lights of London stretching out behind them.

"This is so romantic. I'm so glad I get to share it with you." She nestled against him, content in his embrace as they gazed out at the shimmering city.

"I'm glad you're having a good time," he whispered softly in her ear. "And I'm incredibly happy to be sharing all of this with you." As he spoke, he caught her reflection in the glass. The look of pure happiness on her face as she closed her eyes and leaned into him sent warmth through his entire body.

"Would you like to do anything else before we head back to the hotel?' he asked as the pod slowly descended, the ride nearing its end.

"No, I'm good. Let's go back—I have plans for you," she said, turning in his arms with a seductive smile, her eyes sparkling with mischief.

"I'm not sure..." he began, but she pressed a finger gently against his lips.

"Shh, don't worry—it's all PG-13," she purred, though the look in her eyes suggested anything but.

"I highly doubt that," he said with a knowing grin.

With her gift bag in tow and her hand in his, they made their way back to the hotel, the air between them thick with anticipation.

***

"Go change, then come back and stay with me, please," she asked sweetly.

"Fine, but no monkey business," he teased with a smirk. After changing, he joined her in bed, her body curling comfortably into his as they half-watched *The Great British Bake Off*. Ten minutes in, she reached up and tugged him down by the collar of his t-shirt.

"I thought this was supposed to stay PG-13,' he murmured, their faces inches apart.

"It's been upgraded," she replied, a sly grin spreading across her lips.

"You're so beautiful," he whispered, trailing soft kisses over her lips as his hand on the small of her back pulled her closer. Her fingers slid into his hair, pulling him in deeper, her tongue seeking his with growing intensity.

Her body ached for his touch. "Lick me," she whispered, unbuttoning her nightie and pressing her breasts together. Unable to resist, he leaned in, alternating between them, gently sucking on one while teasing the other. She squirmed beneath him, soft moans escaping her lips as he lavished her breasts with attention, his tongue moving as if savoring every moment. When he gently tugged her nipples between his teeth, they felt like delicate erasers, soft yet firm.

"I know you want to take things slow, and you're not ready for everything yet—but maybe we could explore a little?" she purred, her warm breath tickling his ear. "Just get used to me, to my touch. Baby, I just want to be close to you," she coaxed, her body pressing against his in a slow, deliberate rhythm, her words and the way she said 'baby' hypnotizing him.

Without a word, he lay back, guiding her hand to him, showing her that while his mind wanted to take things slow, his body had other ideas. His breath caught, fingers threading through her hair as she lowered his pajama bottoms.

Her eyes locked onto his, unblinking, filled with a raw intensity as her tongue explored him, teasing and flicking with practiced ease. The way she looked at him—so boldly, so completely—sent a shudder through him. It was wildly erotic, making his pulse race faster than he thought possible. He was utterly at her mercy, and desire overwhelmed him.

With her mouth enveloping him, her hand stroking him in perfect rhythm, he felt himself unraveling far too quickly. His control shattered under her touch, a deep groan escaping him as her name slipped from his lips and his fingers tightened in her hair. He pulled her close, his kiss deep and hungry, tasting the lingering sweetness of himself on her lips.

As they lay together, his arms wrapped tightly around her and her head resting on his chest, she felt the rapid beat of his heart against her cheek—a steady reminder of how deeply she affected him, leaving him both vulnerable and completely hers.

"You make me feel incredible," he sighed, his fingers gently playing with her hair. "The way you look, feel, and the sounds you make... it's like you genuinely enjoy every moment, and that makes it even better for me. You've done things I've never felt before," he added, a contented smile spreading across his face.

"I'm so glad I can make you feel that way. And I do love doing that for you,' she murmured, pressing a kiss to his chest. "And by the way—you taste amazing. Eating well and drinking water really does make a difference."

Kasey blushed. "Good to know," he replied, slightly embarrassed but clearly pleased.

"Now, I want you to do something for me." Sitting up, she flashed him a mischievous grin before slipping off to the bathroom, returning with a small vibrator in her hand.

"What have you got there?" he asked curiosity and a hint of shyness in his voice.

"Say hello to my little friend," she teased, a coy smile playing on her lips. "All you have to do is hold it against me—I'll show you where. It won't take long," she added with a grin. "Do it while you kiss me. You can handle that, right? I want you to make me feel as good as you do right now," she murmured, her voice low and inviting as she dimmed the lights and turned off the TV, creating the perfect mood to help him feel less self-conscious.

"I've never used a vibrator on anyone before," he admitted with a sweet smile. She slipped under the blanket, shedding her nightie and panties. Taking his hand, she slowly guided it over her body as they kissed, eventually leading him between her legs. He was mesmerized by the feel of her petite, perfect body, his kisses growing more intense as his hand moved lower.

Realizing she was completely shaven, he hesitated. "Can I take the blanket off? I want to see you." Without a hint of hesitation, she pushed the blanket down, fully exposing herself to him.

"You're completely shaved," he murmured, his eyes devouring every inch of her as his hand lightly traced her smooth, soft skin. "You're so... puffy," he added, searching for the right word. "I like the way you look and feel. Can I say that?" he asked, his voice soft with wonder.

"As long as it's nice, you can say anything you want," she teased, amused by both his choice of words and the admiration in his gaze.

She bent her legs and turned on the vibrator, placing it in his hand and guiding him to exactly where she needed him. The moment he touched her, she drew in a sharp breath, her soft moan escaping as she whispered, 'Kiss me, baby,' pulling him close. Her fingers gripped his hair, holding his lips firmly to hers.

He was struck by how quickly she became wet and how her body responded, her hips instinctively following the rhythm of the vibrator. As the tension in her body built and her face flushed, she urgently instructed, "Don't move your hand," arching her back as her body tensed. Her moans grew louder against his mouth as her hips bucked in short, frantic motions. She dug her nails into his neck, the intensity of her orgasm washing over her in uncontrollable waves.

"Stop," she whispered as the waves began to subside, her body relaxing, every touch becoming more sensitive. She gently moved his hand away, closing her legs and nestling her head against his neck, pressing her body closer to his.

"Mmm," she moaned softly in his ear, drawing out the sound. "That was incredible."

"Is it always that intense for you?" he asked, still amazed by what he had just witnessed.

"With a vibrator, it is,' she sighed, a small, contented smile playing on her lips as she rolled onto her back, eyes drifting closed. "It's a double-edged sword though."

"How so?" he asked, propping himself up on his elbow, his hand tracing lightly over her belly.

"Well, it feels incredible, but sometimes it's so powerful it's exhausting afterward, like right now—I could just fall asleep," she sighed. "I also get really sensitive and need a little recovery time. And if you overdo it, it can actually make it harder to come. Sex is great, don't get me wrong, but with a vibrator, it's on another level. It's like I'm going to explode. I feel so good right now, every bit of tension gone."

"It's amazing watching you lose control like that—you're like a tiny wild bronco," he said with a smile, leaning in for a tender kiss.

Pulling the blanket over them, she sighed softly and turned away, her body nestling against his. "Hold me, baby," she whispered, her voice barely audible. As she drifted off to sleep, his face nestled in her hair, she added sweetly, "Thank you for trying something new with me," basking in the intimacy of this next step between them.

Kasey held her closer, taken by how effortlessly she made him feel comfortable in moments like these. She had a way of easing his reservations, making every step forward feel natural, even when it challenged him.

***

The following day, both teams gathered to finalize the contracts. Armed with Julia's new pen, they meticulously dotted every 'i' and crossed every 't,' officially sealing the deal. Julia decided on the name Hawthorne-Masters, paying tribute to the brothers' legacy, even though she knew the board—or her father—might object to not having the Masters name first. She invited the men to visit New York to meet her father and the board, promising her hospitality. Until then, they agreed to stay connected through regular video calls.

Back at the hotel, Julia and Kasey packed their bags and waited for their flight. Lying on her bed with her head on his chest, she let him play with her hair as they quietly reflected on a job well done. Once they landed in New York, Kasey privately suggested she spend the night at his place, and she happily agreed. They cuddled on the couch, watching TV before giving in to jet lag and heading to bed. Content with Kasey setting the pace, Julia found happiness simply in having him beside her.

***

"Wait, honey, let me buzz him—he's on the phone," Agnes said, reaching for the intercom.

"No need, Agnes, I want to surprise him," Julia replied, excitedly heading straight for her dad's office, eager to share the good news.

Buck was gazing out through the expansive glass windows when he heard the door and spun around as Julia and Kasey entered.

"We did it, Daddy!" she declared, heading straight for his desk.

"I have to go, George. Jules has some good news... yes, I'll catch you later." He hung up the phone and stood, scooping Julia up into a bear hug.

"We got everything we asked for!" she said gleefully.

"I knew you could do it, darlin'. Never doubted you for a second. When did you get back? I thought you were arriving today."

"No, last night. I didn't call because I wanted to tell you in person," she explained, bubbling with excitement. "It all went so smoothly. They're genuinely sweet men, and lunch at their private club was wonderful. It was a perfect first experience."

"I'm happy it went well, sweet pea, but don't forget—you put in a lot of hard work to make it look easy," he reminded her, gently setting her down before reaching into his top drawer. "This is for you," he said, his voice filled with pride as he handed her the box. Watching his daughter succeed after everything he had taught her filled him with a deep sense of satisfaction. She was the culmination of all his hopes for her, and seeing her stand tall in the business world made this moment all the more meaningful.

"Oh my God, it's beautiful!" Julia squealed as she opened the slim black velvet box to reveal a platinum, diamond-encrusted wristwatch. Kasey, watching the strong bond between them, smiled as Buck gently fastened the watch on her wrist. Julia fidgeted with anticipation, her excitement shining through.

One of Julia's love languages was gifts—both giving and receiving, though she had a slight preference for receiving. "It's perfect," she exclaimed, admiring the sparkling watch. Buck smiled knowingly. His gift-giving had enriched Julia's life with everything from her BMW and condo to her favorite diamond stud earrings. Aside from the beach house she had bought herself, Buck had provided most of the luxuries in her life, always marking special moments with a thoughtful gift.

"I didn't do this alone," Julia admitted. "My team was amazing, but Kasey's contribution was invaluable. Mr. Makino was really impressed when Kasey spoke to him in Japanese, and it was his idea for him and Dante to wear their signature suits. The brothers loved it—it set the tone right from the start."

"You're giving me too much credit," Kasey said modestly under Buck's gaze.

Julia's face lit up as she remembered, "And Kasey surprised me during our trip to the London Eye with a Visconti pen to sign the contracts. It was so thoughtful and unexpected."

"That was thoughtful," Buck remarked, feeling a twinge of jealousy that Kasey had beaten him to his tradition of marking important moments with gifts. It was the typical parent trap—he loved seeing her so happy, but a part of him wished she still looked at him the way she now looked at Kasey.

"I'm glad you had a good time, darlin', and got the job done. Let's all have dinner tonight to celebrate. You can fill me in on all the details," Buck suggested. "Agnes will arrange everything."

"You two should go," Kasey began, but Julia quickly interrupted, "No, I want you there."

"I won't take no for an answer," Buck said, sensing how much she wanted Kasey to join.

"Then dinner it is," Kasey agreed with a smile.

****

With the stress of the merger gone, the atmosphere at work returned to normal. Julia's playful interactions with Kasey picked up again—stealing kisses, bold flirting, and once more, she brought up the idea of a friends-with-benefits arrangement. Though he still hesitated, acknowledging their undeniable chemistry, he promised to think about it over the Thanksgiving holiday. Julia's desire for him had intensified to the point where she could barely hold back. Similarly, Kasey longed for her—but secretly, he wanted more than just a casual arrangement. His feelings for her ran far deeper.

****

Chapter 8: Everything Changes

"Please come, Jules, don't leave me to fend for myself with them," Wynn whined.

"What's wrong with us, son?" Buck teased, giving Wynn a playful nudge as he passed by. Lily and Wynn had come to the city during his holiday break from college—Wynn for a concert, while Lily and Julia planned some early Christmas shopping together. They'd even spent one evening at Kasey's, where he impressed them all with his culinary skills, preparing a perfectly executed Beef Wellington with beef from their own herd. Buck had declared it one of the best meals he'd ever had—high praise coming from him. Lily admired Kasey's impeccable home décor, while Wynn had been fascinated by the weapons and training room.

"We're picking up Toby; it's not like you'll be without a friend. Honestly, Buck, you'd think he'd be excited about skiing for the holiday. Our children don't want to spend time with us anymore," Lily lamented, gazing out the floor-to-ceiling glass windows in Buck's office at the bustling city below.

"Don't be dramatic, Mom. I'll be home for Christmas," Julia said, pulling her into a hug. "I can't miss this—it's all my girlfriends, and Micki's coming too."

"Oh well, if Micki's going," Lily chuckled softly, "we don't stand a chance."

"I know. I'll come home with her after the trip and stay for a few days. How's that?" Julia suggested.

Lily smiled as Buck replied, "That's fine, Jules. You've worked hard these past few months—you deserve this trip. Go, enjoy yourself. We'll muddle through without you and see you when you get back."

"Be sure to bring Kasey when you come. I like him— charming young man and very easy on the eyes," Lily added with a grin.

"Mom!" Julia protested, her voice playful. "Dad's right here!"

"And he knows I'm happily married, not blind," Lily said, casting a loving glance at Buck.

"I'll have lunch with you before you leave tomorrow," Julia said, heading for the door.

"Jules, hold up," Buck called, meeting her at the door. "There's something I want to discuss in private—just let me walk your mother and brother down first."

"Sure. Is something wrong?"

"Everything's fine." He turned to Lily and Wynn. "Let's get you two back to the condo to pack." He hit the intercom, "Agnes, call the driver and let him know they're on their way down."

***

"So, what's up? Work stuff?" Julia asked, settling on the couch beside her dad.

131

"It's about Kasey," he said slowly, his tone causing her heart to skip to a beat.

"What about him?" Julia asked, her voice tight.

"Remember, I'm your father, and I'm just doing my job—protecting you. I've come across some information about him that you should know."

"What do you mean, 'come across'? Did you have him investigated?" Her voice rose, disbelief creeping in.

"Calm down, darlin', and hear me out. I like Kasey a lot, don't get me wrong. But something about him didn't sit right with me. He doesn't talk about his past—or himself, for that matter. He lives in an expensive brownstone, wears clothes that must cost a fortune, and he's way overqualified to just be your assistant... I had to look into him."

"So, what did you find? Is it bad? Is he some kind of criminal or something?" Her heart raced.

"It's nothing really bad. I just want to make sure he's being upfront with you. Did you know that until he changed his name at twenty-one, he was Kayson Ambrose Van Cortland IV? He's what they call a trust fund baby—worth at least thirty-five million, which grows yearly thanks to his investment portfolio.

"What the—?" Julia blinked. "I knew he had money, but not that kind. No wonder he can afford the brownstone and dresses the way he does."

"He's got no family except for a father he doesn't see."

"So, he doesn't get along with his father. Anything else?"

"He doesn't date at all..."

"I know that, he already told me," Julia snapped, frustration rising with her father's interference.

"But did you know that he regularly slept with the same high-priced call girl for months? He stopped seeing her right before he started here?"

"I know," she said quietly, feeling a knot form in her chest, knowing what was coming next.

Buck took a breath and lowered his voice. "Jules, he also dated men."

Julia met her dad's gaze, her voice steady. "Kasey told me all of this. I've known for a while. I don't appreciate you doing this without asking me first. I'm a grown woman—I just acquired a company for you. I didn't need to know about his money or his name—he told me the important stuff." Panic flickered across her face. "Did you say anything to him?"

"Calm down, I didn't say anything to him. I just got the report back yesterday. I did mention while we were camping that I'd fuck up anyone who tried to hurt you. I'm pretty sure he got the message—he's observant. I know he cares about you; you'd have to be blind not to see it. But I still worry. At least now I know he's not after your money."

"Thanks, Dad, that hurts. You think no one would want me if I didn't have money?"

"That's not what I'm saying, Julia Lynn," Buck said seriously. "You know what I meant. I won't apologize for wanting to protect you. You're a desirable target for shady men. I'd protect Wynn the same way if I thought someone might take advantage."

"I know you don't want to hear this, but I'm telling you to show you Kasey's character," Julia said, pausing to choose her words carefully. "I've been trying to start a purely sexual relationship with him for months, and he's refused me— repeatedly—saying he needed to respect our positions and didn't want to risk your friendship if things didn't work out.

He's been nothing but respectful and protective of me. I've been the aggressor."

"You're right. I didn't want to hear that," he said with a soft laugh. "But I appreciate how Kasey thinks, and I feel better knowing he was upfront with you about everything. I just want you to be careful, darlin'. I don't fully understand the 'other men' part, but that's none of my business. I'm glad I got to know him before learning that—I might've judged him differently, and that would've been a mistake. I like Kasey; he's a good man—but you always come first."

Julia rested her head on his shoulder. "You don't have to worry. He takes such good care of me. I'm already in love with him... and there's nothing I can do about it."

"Then tread carefully, is all I can say. Don't be mad at me—I'm just doing my due diligence as your father," he said, kissing the top of her head and giving her a squeeze.

Though Julia understood her father's intentions, she was still troubled by how he had uncovered intimate details about Kasey without his knowledge. She was also surprised by his reaction to Kasey's bisexuality. While people like her father weren't often known for their openness, Buck's genuine connection with Kasey seemed to foster an acceptance that went beyond preconceived judgments.

***

"Could you call Carl and ask him to come at four-thirty today?" Julia asked as she stepped into Kasey's office. "I'm leaving early."

"Is everything alright?" he asked, immediately sensing her upset.

"Everything's fine," she replied, forcing a smile before retreating into her office. "Just let me know when he's here, okay?"

"Sure," he said, dialing Carl. He lingered in the doorway, watching as she sat at her desk and turned her chair, her back now facing him.

Twenty minutes later, he called out, "He's here." Holding the door open as she passed, he asked, "Are you sure you're okay? You don't seem like yourself."

"I'm fine. Just heading home to pack for my trip and make some last-minute adjustments. I'll see you tomorrow," she reassured him with a quick smile before leaving.

***

That night, she confided in Micki about her father's actions and everything she had learned about Kasey.

"What bothers you more—the money or that he changed his name?" Micki asked. "I think Kasey told you all the important stuff you needed to know."

"No, it's not that. I don't give a shit about any of that. What bothers me is that I still don't really know him. He's so closed off, and I feel like I'm prying if I ask too many personal questions. And Buck finding out Kasey's bisexual? That's private. It should've been Kasey's decision to tell. Buck invaded his privacy, and I don't know how Kasey's going to react. I hope he's not too upset."

"You know, you told me without asking Kasey first," Micki gently reminded her. "Do you have to tell him? Maybe it'd be better for their relationship if you don't."

"Shit, I did do that," Julia said, frowning. "But honestly, I think Kasey knows I tell you everything." She paused. "Maybe I shouldn't assume so much with him—I've already made that mistake. I think I have to tell him. What if he finds out later? I'd rather be honest."

135

"You've always been too honest, Jules. Sometimes, it's okay to tell a little white lie or leave something out to spare someone's feelings. Just think about that," Micki suggested.

Julia considered Micki's advice but decided she needed to stay true to herself. She was trying to build trust with Kasey, and despite her father's good intentions, it felt crucial to address the privacy invasion.

"Cheer up, kiddo! We're going on vacation somewhere warm and sunny the day after tomorrow!" Micki said excitedly.

"You're right," Julia agreed, "I'm not gonna think about this right now. I have a bunch of bikinis to sort through—I'm so excited."

***

The next day, Julia spent the morning with her brother and mother before heading out to lunch with the whole family.

"So, are they off?" Kasey asked as she walked into the office.

"Not yet. Their jet doesn't leave until six."

"Did you have a nice lunch?"

"We did. It's always nice when we all get together. I feel bad not going skiing with them, but I really don't want to ski. I wanna go somewhere warm and sunny. Besides, Christmas is right around the corner. I'll head to the ranch then. You never told me—what are you doing for Thanksgiving?" she asked, perching on the edge of his desk.

"Absolutely nothing," he replied with a smile.

"You're gonna be alone?" she asked, feeling a pang of guilt for not making sure he had solid plans.

"Yes, exactly what I want," he assured her. Still, the idea of spending a holiday alone seemed unimaginable to her.

"Really? I know you like your alone time, but even on holidays?" she asked, unable to hide her disbelief. "I thought you were invited to Marisol's."

"I was invited to her son's place— he's hosting her—but I prefer some quiet time. Not everyone likes to be surrounded by people during the holidays or even celebrates them," he said, a wistful smile touching his lips. "I'm looking forward to the peace and quiet. God knows I could use a break from you and all the incessant making out," he teased, his sad smile turning into a wide grin.

"Is that so? Then I guess a sleepover tonight would be too much for you to handle?" She touched his face, not caring if anyone was watching. "I won't get to kiss you for almost a week—I don't know if I can make it," she said, her voice filled with longing.

"I think that can be arranged," he replied, his grin softening as her touch lingered, sending a spark of warmth through him. "But don't you have to pack? Aren't you leaving tomorrow?"

"I'm already packed, and I'm not leaving until five tomorrow."

"A sleepover it is," he said, pleased to see her mood shift. Still, he wondered what had been troubling her but decided to let it go. If it was important, she'd tell him—she told him everything else.

***

Over dinner, Julia paused, her words heavy with apprehension. "There's something I need to tell you, and I really hope you won't be upset."

"Well, that usually means something upsetting is coming," Kasey replied, his expression guarded as his blue-gray eyes darkened to a steely gray. "What is it?"

Julia took a deep breath before confessing, "Buck had you investigated. He said it was to protect me. He's done it before with others—you're not the first."

Kasey stayed stoic. "And what did he find out?"

"He didn't uncover anything you hadn't already told me. The only surprises were how much you're worth and that you changed your name. He also found out about the escort and that you're bisexual. I'm really sorry for the invasion of your privacy—I know how private you are, and this must feel like a betrayal."

"How did Buck react to that?" Kasey asked, pushing his food around on his plate, curiosity in his voice.

"He said he didn't understand it, but it didn't change how he feels about you. He genuinely likes you—he just wanted to make sure no one was taking advantage of me for money. Now he knows that's not the case with you. But I'm curious: why do you still work, and why did you change your name?"

"I despise my father and didn't want to carry his name. I inherited a lot from my mother, and I invest. This brownstone isn't the only real estate I own. Working gives me purpose and keeps me from being a total recluse."

Kasey leaned back, running a hand through his hair as if brushing away a lingering thought. "I'm not angry with Buck—he's just trying to protect you. I only wish he came to me first, before getting you involved. What if I hadn't told you yet? That'd be a different story."

"I'm so glad you're not upset," Julia said, relief filling her voice. "My father really likes you. So does my whole family."

"I like them too. It's nice being around a family that genuinely cares about each other. I never had that. Everything's fine," he said, giving her a warm smile. "Is that why you were upset yesterday and left early?" he asked, already guessing the answer.

"Yes, I was mad he invaded your privacy and learned things about you that should've stayed private."

"Don't be angry with him. I'm not ashamed of my past, and I'm sure you tell Micki everything," he said with a smile. "I just don't want your dad to have a negative opinion of me— I really enjoy spending time with him."

"I'm not mad at him anymore, and he doesn't think less of you. He knows I care about you—he's just overprotective sometimes. And I don't tell Micki everything," she chuckled. "Scratch that—I do. She's closer to me than a sister. But if you ever asked me to keep something private, I would. I promise," she insisted earnestly.

"I know you two are close. You used to have sex with her and her husband," he teased, a playful glint in his eyes.

"First off, I do not have sex with Micki… we just make out," she grinned. "And secondly, 'used to'?"

"Exactly, 'used to'. No more threesomes. The next time you have sex, it'll be with me."

"Soon, I hope," she replied eagerly, taking his hand.

"Soon, I promise," he assured her, kissing the inside of her wrist, thinking, *maybe tonight.*

***

It was clear what Julia had in mind the moment they settled on the couch to watch a movie after dinner. Her seductive whispers in his ear were like a siren's call—impossible to resist. "Kiss me, baby," she breathed, her voice a soft plea.

He covered her lips with tender kisses, each one more urgent than the last, his hand slipping under her soft crop top and cupping her breast.

"Lie back," he murmured, his voice husky with desire as he shifted on top of her, his intentions clear.

"I feel like I'm on fire when you touch me," she moaned, her fingers gripping his hair as

every inch of her body responded to his touch. "I want you so much," she growled, her voice thick with desire.

"You're irresistible," he whispered, his lips grazing her skin, sending shivers down her spine. Their bodies moved together, drawn by an unstoppable force. Her legs wrapped around him as he rubbed against her, their connection electric.

"Let's go upstairs," Kasey breathed, igniting a wave of anticipation that swept through her. Her nails dug into his back as her kisses deepened, brimming with eagerness for what awaited them.

Then she heard it—the unmistakable sound of her cell phone. She ignored it, too busy wondering if they'd even make it upstairs. Kasey's movements created enough friction that if they were kindling, they'd already have a bonfire. It stopped after four rings, going to voicemail. Thirty seconds later, it rang again.

"Oh, for fuck's sake!" she snapped, exasperated, the sound breaking the spell.

"You should answer that; it could be important. I'm not going anywhere," Kasey said, his face flushed, his breathing slowing as he got off her.

"It's my work phone," she grumbled, frustrated, as she reached for her purse. "Who'd be calling me at this hour? Excuse me," she muttered, irritated, as she adjusted her top and got up to answer the phone.

Kasey sat back down, discreetly adjusting himself before lowering the TV volume. Hearing her tone shift, growing louder and more emotional, he glanced over just as she collapsed to the floor, the phone slipping from her grasp.

Springing to his feet, he called out, "What happened? What's wrong?" Julia, now sobbing and clutching her stomach, rocked back and forth, repeating, "No, no," as he reached for the phone.

"Who is this?" Kasey demanded.

"This is Marshall Reins from the National Transportation Safety Board. Are you related to Julia Masters?"

"I'm her fiancé, Kasey Cortland. What's this about?" he said, struggling to hear over Julia's distressed sobs.

"Mr. Cortland," the man began, his voice calm but grave. "I'm deeply sorry to be the one to tell you this. The private jet carrying Ms. Masters' family encountered a critical issue mid-flight. We believe there was catastrophic engine failure, resulting in an explosion."

Kasey froze, the words hitting him like a blow to the chest.

The man hesitated, then continued, his tone softer now. "Unfortunately, there were no survivors. I know this is devastating to hear, and normally, we'd have someone meet with Ms. Masters in person to explain what happened and provide support. If you can let us know where she is, we'll send a team immediately to offer more information and assistance."

Kasey's knees buckled slightly, and he grabbed the edge of the counter for support. "No survivors," he whispered, the words tasting like ash.

The man paused again, as though giving Kasey a moment to process. "We are so sorry for your loss, Mr. Cortland. When the support team arrives, they'll provide more details."

Kasey barely registered the question that followed. "How do you spell your last name, sir?"

"C-c-o-r-t-l-a-n-d," Kasey stammered, stumbling back, reeling from the devastating news.

"Is this the number where I can reach you, Mr. Cortland?" Mr. Reins asked.

"Um, no... no, take this number," Kasey responded, his mind still struggling to process what was happening as he provided his contact information and home address. "What do we do now?" he asked, unsure of the next steps.

"Start making your calls. I know it's a well-known family and business—there'll be significant press coverage. Prepare a press release. I'm very sorry for your loss," Mr. Reins said softly as the call ended.

Kasey hung up, overwhelmed by grief. Kneeling down, he wrapped a sobbing Julia in his arms. "I'm so sorry," he whispered, knowing nothing he could say would comfort her.

"There must be a mistake. Maybe it's a terrible prank. Please call them back and check—it's a mistake," she pleaded, tears streaming down her face. The look of pain and confusion in her eyes broke his heart.

"I wish it was, but it isn't. I'm so sorry," he said, holding her tighter, trying to console her as she began to hyperventilate.

"I can't breathe," she said, panic rising in her voice. "I was supposed to be with them. I can't breathe." Her breaths came faster. "I was supposed to be on that plane. Oh my God, if I'd been there, maybe it wouldn't have happened. Something could've changed."

"Relax, you're breathing too fast. Breathe through your nose. Look at me," Kasey said gently, holding her shoulders.

"This can't be real," she whimpered, her breathing quickening, fear clouding her eyes. "I can't breathe."

"Hold your breath... slow down. Julia, look at me—deep breath." He took her hand and guided her to the couch. "Breathe through your nose, that's it, slow down. That's it," he murmured, his voice soft and gentle. Wrapping her in his arms, he held her tightly, offering what solace he could. As her breathing slowed, he whispered, "I'm going to make a call. I'll be right here." She sat on the couch, hugging her knees tightly, her gaze fixed on the fireplace, her breaths still coming in staggered gasps.

He reached out to Jack Dorsey and Rick Tyrell, both already back in Colorado for the holiday. After processing the devastating news, they asked about Julia before beginning the somber task of notifying the rest of the board—Buck's closest friends.

Buck's long-time assistant, Henry Croft, was next. After briefing him, Kasey urgently requested his immediate presence at his home. Henry would help notify other key business associates and work with Jack and Rick to handle the initial press release.

Kasey then called Will, instructing him to pack a bag and come over immediately—Julia needed him. Will rushed to Kasey's home as fast as humanly possible, arriving even before Henry, who lived in the city. Kasey called Micki and James, breaking the news to James, who then had to sit Micki down and gently tell her. He updated them on Julia's condition and asked them to meet in Colorado upon their arrival later that night. Will took over consoling Julia, who alternated between hysterical sobs and pitiful disbelief.

Taking charge, Kasey gave Julia a Xanax provided by Will to calm her down, gently guiding her to his bed. Will stayed by her side as she fell into a fitful sleep, succumbing to the effects of the drug. They knew how important it was for her to rest while preparations and phone calls were made—there would be ample time to face the pain and decisions in the days to come.

***

Just after Julia fell asleep, the support liaison officers and a grief counselor sent by the jet's operating company arrived. Kasey, Will, and Henry—who had arrived only minutes earlier—sat down to listen to the available information.

The representative explained that water had likely compromised the fuel tanks, freezing at high altitude and causing fuel starvation. The pilot had declared an emergency when the plane lost its engine and attempted an emergency descent. The pressure in the compromised tanks triggered a massive explosion, sending the jet into an uncontrolled descent, with wreckage and debris scattering across a wide area as the aircraft broke apart.

The three men sat in stunned silence as the representative explained that the family most likely never knew what was happening—they would have perished instantly in the explosion. Henry couldn't hide his grief, openly sobbing at the thought of losing not only his longtime boss but also his friend in such an inconceivable way.

As the grief counselor comforted Henry, Will and Kasey gathered as much information as they could, including the names of those they'd need to contact in the coming days. Thanking the representatives for coming personally to deliver the news, Kasey showed them out, the emotional toll momentarily immobilizing all three men.

After taking time to let it all sink in, Will went upstairs to check on Julia, who was still asleep. Meanwhile, Kasey and Henry resumed working the phones, relaying the news to Jack, Rick, James, and Micki.

Later, Will came downstairs to find Kasey engrossed in his laptop, securing first-class tickets for the four of them—

including Henry—on a major carrier, assuming Julia wouldn't want to fly on a private jet. At the same time, Kasey was on the phone with Carl, explaining their need for a ride to the airport later.

"How is she?" Kasey asked, ready to offer his support.

"She's finally sleeping," Will said, walking over and embracing him. "I'm so sorry, man. What a fucked-up thing to happen. I know you got close to Buck and the family."

"I can't think about that right now," Kasey said, returning the hug, his voice catching as he thought about the camping trip, the lunches, the family dinners, and the bond he was building with Buck and Wynn. "If I lose it, I won't be able to control it, and I'll be no good to Julia. There's so much I need to do to make this easier on her."

Will sighed. "I just can't believe this. Her entire family... This is going to destroy her. She was so close to them, especially her father."

"We won't let that happen. You, Micki, and James are going to help me, okay?" Kasey said.

Will patted him on the back, impressed by his composure. "I'm glad she has you." He added, "Just lemme know what you need me to do. I'm great at support, not leading."

"Right now, just take care of her. I have calls to make, and I have a feeling there's a lot more raw emotion coming. I'll need help with that. Seeing her in this much pain is unbearable," Kasey muttered softly.

Taking a breath, he said, "I'll be with her for a few minutes. I'm going to pack. I appreciate you being here—and I'm sure Julia does too."

"I'd do anything for Jules—we all would," Will affirmed, grabbing a drink from the fridge.

***

145

Three hours later, they were seated in first class on a red-eye to Colorado. Julia, in deep emotional shock, rested her head on Kasey's shoulder, unresponsive to anything or anyone except him. After Will's harrowing explanation to the crew while Kasey settled Julia, and with no other passengers in first class, they were given the space and quiet they needed.

At the airport, a cart drove them to where James and Micki were waiting, out of view of the intrusive press gathered outside the arrival gates. When Julia spotted Micki, her knees buckled under the weight of her pain as tears streamed down her face.

Kasey effortlessly lifted her and carried her to the waiting Tahoe. During the ride back to the ranch, the sound of Julia's anguished cries filled the air, mixed with Micki's faltering attempts to console her.

After making all the necessary calls and realizing there was nothing more they could do without Julia's input, everyone decided the best course of action was to rest, regroup, and start fresh in the morning. As they headed to their rooms, Micki offered softly, "Jules, do you want me to stay with you?"

"No... thank you, Kasey's staying with me," Julia whispered, barely audible, clutching his hand tightly as they walked down the hall.

"Try and get some rest. We'll all be here for you in the morning," Micki said, her heart aching for her best friend and the family she had been a part of.

Julia kicked off her sneakers, crawled into her childhood bed, and sobbed into her pillow.

"Can I do anything for you?" Kasey asked softly, sitting beside her and gently stroking her hair.

"Can you bring my family back?" she whispered, her voice breaking.

"I wish I could," he said gently. He undressed, slipped on his pajama bottoms, and lay down beside her.

"Please, just hold me," she whimpered. He enveloped her in a tight embrace, at a loss for words to comfort her.

"I should have been on that plane," she cried suddenly, her torment piercing the silence. "I shouldn't be here."

"You can't think like that," he said softly.

She sat up, rocking back and forth, tears streaming down her face. "I can't stop imagining their final moments. Did they know? Were they scared? I can't bear the relentless thoughts. How do I make them stop?" Hunched over, she clutched her head in agony. "This is so unfair. Wynn was only nineteen... just a kid. I feel like I'm losing my mind." Her words came out in broken gasps as she struggled to contain her pain.

"My dad is gone. We were supposed to be partners, building the business together. And my mom... she died thinking I didn't want to spend time with her." Deeply distressing wails echoed through the room, her body racked with grief, her eyes red and almost swollen shut. Barely holding it together himself, Kasey rubbed her back and handed her tissues.

Micki rushed into the room and sat beside Julia, who collapsed into her arms, her sobs unrelenting. James and Will lingered silently in the doorway, their grief written plainly across their faces.

"I've called their family doctor; he's on his way. She needs professional help," Micki announced, breaking the heavy silence, which was pierced only by Julia's sobs and stuttering gasps. Kasey mouthed a silent "thank you" to Micki, immensely grateful for her intervention. Julia's breathing grew shallow as her sobs intensified.

"Slow down your breathing. You'll hyperventilate," Kasey said as Micki rubbed her back.

***

As the doctor attended to Julia with Micki's help, Kasey, James, and Will lingered in the hallway, their hearts heavy with worry.

The doctor, well-acquainted with Julia's history, quickly administered a sedative to help her rest and prescribed additional medication to ease her through the day and ensure she slept through the night. He left strict instructions for Micki to keep him updated on her progress. As the sedative took effect, Micki stayed by Julia's side while James and Will escorted the doctor out.

When Micki emerged from the room, Kasey quietly expressed his gratitude. "Thank you for stepping in. I'm doing my best, but seeing Julia like this..." His voice wavered, betraying his inner turmoil. "I don't think I can handle it. I need you three to help with her emotional pain as much as possible. She needs you especially," he said, his voice and face revealing the vulnerable man beneath his strong exterior. "Please stay close."

Micki met Kasey's gaze, her eyes mirroring his anguish. "I'm not going anywhere," she whispered, pulling him into a firm embrace. "I love her and would do anything for her. I'm heartbroken—they were like my family. I can only imagine her pain."

Releasing him from the embrace, she reassured him, "You're doing a great job, Kasey. It's amazing how you're stepping up for her. Everyone could use someone like you in their corner. We'll do whatever it takes to help her through this, but she clings to you. I'm not sure prying her away would be a good idea right now, but I'll try to give you a break when she lets me. Call me if you need anything—I'm right down the hall," she added, giving him a reassuring pat on the arm.

"Thank you," Kasey murmured, his gratitude clear. "She's put a lot of trust and responsibility in my hands. I'm just trying not to let her down when she needs me most." They stood together, like two weary generals leaning on each other for support in the face of an unfathomable loss.

***

"Kasey... Kasey," Micki whispered, gently placing a hand on his arm. He remained in the same position he'd fallen asleep in—his arms wrapped around Julia, his face nestled in her neck and hair.

"There's someone from the NTSB here. He needs to speak with Julia or her fiancé," she said, casting a small smile and raising an eyebrow in his direction.

"I'll be right there," Kasey replied, his voice thick with sleep. After Micki left, he carefully slipped out from under the covers, trying not to disturb Julia.

"I'm sorry to disturb you so early," the official said, his voice measured but kind. "I regret to inform you that no remains have been recovered from the crash site, and it's highly unlikely any will be found. The wreckage is scattered over a wide area, and initial findings suggest a catastrophic fuel system failure caused the explosion. The investigation will continue for months as we work to determine exactly what happened."

He handed Kasey a folder, the weight of it somehow heavier than its contents. Inside were lists—contacts for agencies they'd need to work with, and another of support resources in Colorado and New York. Kasey stared at the folder for a moment before taking it, his fingers tightening instinctively around it as if it might anchor him.

"Thank you for coming here personally," he managed, his voice tight, barely above a whisper.

The official gave a small nod, his expression earnest. "Please let us know if there's anything we can do. I'm deeply sorry for your loss."

Kasey nodded, numb, as he escorted the man to the door. The hallway felt impossibly long, the sound of their footsteps sharp in the heavy silence. As the door clicked shut behind him, Kasey pressed his forehead against the cool surface, his breath unsteady.

He stood there for a moment, the folder clutched to his chest, before forcing himself to turn back. There were still so many calls to make, so many people waiting to hear the news.

Micki and James, who had been listening nearby, shared a glance of concern.

"Poor Jules, this is too much for one person to handle," James remarked.

"But she's not alone—we're here to support her. We'll get her through this," Kasey reassured as he rejoined the room.

"Can you even have a funeral without any bodies?" Micki asked.

"It'd be called a memorial service. She can still have clergy for a blessing, and eulogies can be read. Since she doesn't need a funeral home or church, we can use a venue for the service— with flowers, food if she wants, and photos or videos of the family. Doing everything in one place will make the day shorter and less stressful," Kasey said, his mind racing through the details.

"Since there'll be at least three eulogies, probably more, we'll need a venue for at least four hours. I don't think Julia could handle much longer than that. We'll likely need to limit the guest list depending on the venue Rick and Jack choose, so only those closest to Julia and her family should be invited. We'll start by asking her what she wants, then go from there. I'll need a list from you and James of those close enough to Julia to invite. We'll combine that with Rick and Jack's list of Buck's friends. We can also have Lily and Wynn's best friends make their lists then let Julia review them. Once the details are firm, we'll reach out to those she wants to invite."

Turning to Micki, Kasey continued, "Along with the guest list, I need your help shopping for her. She was at my house when she got the news and doesn't have proper clothes—a black dress, underwear, shoes, and sunglasses. Get her a few options if possible. Anything you think she might need, just get it." He handed Micki his credit card. "You can go to the store or order online and have it sent here—whichever you think is best.

"James, could you work with Micki to gather pictures for a video collage? The local funeral home offers services for that. Also, we need to enlarge a picture of each of them for the memorial. I'm sorry. Is that too much?" Kasey asked, catching himself as he realized he was rattling off tasks like a boss.

"It's fine, Kasey," Micki reassured him. "Someone needs to take charge and organize. James and I can definitely get that stuff taken care of. You just keep organizing—you're doing a great job."

"What can I do?" Will asked as he entered the room.

"If you could sit with her while Henry and I go over details with Rick and Jack, that would be great. Are we all good?" Kasey asked, checking his vibrating phone as he took charge of the situation.

"I guess we should all listen to her fiancé," Micki said with a grin.

"Wait, did I miss something?" James asked, looking at Micki in confusion.

"Julia was in a pile on the floor, and I knew whoever it was wouldn't just give information to her assistant," Kasey explained, his tone matter-of-fact.

"You think fast on your feet; she's lucky to have you," Micki complimented as she headed to the door. "Let's go, James—we've got things to do."

"So, they're engaged?" James asked, puzzled.

"Keep up, babe," Micki said, explaining on the way to the car.

***

Emerging from her room, Julia found that Kasey and her friends had diligently attended to all the arrangements in her absence, taking care of everything except the most personal choices.

Jack and Rick, along with Henry, rallied together, providing invaluable support. Jack took charge of dealing with the press outside the ranch, where a throng of reporters had gathered. Their adept handling of business and media responsibilities allowed Julia to focus solely on the memorial arrangements, which were considerable. She wanted to get everything done quickly and only once, with no additional public memorials.

Despite grappling with her own grief, she briefly sought to offer solace to her father's two lifelong friends, empathizing with their pain. Surrounded by the men and their wives— whom Julia had known all her life—she felt an even deeper sorrow, knowing the three close couples would never again vacation together, share holidays, play cards, or grow old together whittling on a dusty old porch, like Buck had always envisioned.

Though the ranch bustled with guests, Julia remained secluded in her room. Micki and Kasey took turns staying with her, shielding her from the steady stream of grief-stricken friends and family offering condolences. Overwhelmed by her profound sorrow and heavy medications, Julia slept through much of the time, with Micki standing in for her when needed, as she knew all of Julia's family and closest friends.

By the third day, Julia needed to finalize the memorial plans, prompting an early morning meeting with Rick, Jack, Kasey, and her three friends. Rick let Julia know that the country club, where they were respected members, moved a smaller party to a different event room and made their ballroom, which held five hundred people, available for the memorial. Julia and the others reviewed the guest lists, adjusting them to fit the venue. Henry and ten of her mother's ladies' auxiliary from the children's hospital—where she sat on the board and volunteered, took the lists and reached out, sparing the core group from that highly emotional task.

With Thanksgiving the following day, Julia urged everyone to spend time with their families before returning for the Saturday memorial.

Respecting her wishes, everyone but Kasey departed, allowing her the solitude she needed. Will went with Micki and James, while Henry stayed with Jack, his wife flying in to be with him later that night.

***

With everyone out of the house by two and finally alone, Julia decided to go for a horseback ride. They prepared the horses, and Kasey packed a few essentials. Riding to her familiar spot amid the tall prairie grass by the stream, they tethered the horses and settled onto a cozy blanket. Despite the chilly sixty-degree temperature, the bright afternoon sun and their layered clothing kept them comfortable.

Reclining on the blanket, she turned to him, her apprehension about facing the ordeal alone clear in her voice.

153

"I'm not sure I can handle this," she admitted, her voice flat. "I don't think I'm strong enough."

Kasey offered reassurance. "I know you can handle this. You're stronger than you think. You also have a circle of people who care deeply about you and are willing to help you in anyway you need. Micki, James, and Will have been unwavering in their support. Rick, Jack, and Henry are diligently managing the business," he paused briefly before adding, "And you have me. I'm not going anywhere."

Drawing nearer to him, she pleaded softly, "Just help me forget, even if it's just for a minute, how much I hurt right now."

He responded with a kiss, hoping to ease her suffering, but instead found himself gently wiping away her tears, holding her close as she nestled her head against his neck.

"Is it too cold for you?" Kasey asked, his body shielding her from the cool breeze.

"No, the cold air feels nice on my face, and your body's keeping me warm. Are you cold?" she asked quietly.

"Not at all."

They lay together in silence, embraced by the calming serenity of nature. The gentle rustling of leaves and the soft chirp of distant crickets seemed to wrap around them like a soothing balm. Kasey held her close, his arms cradling her as though protecting her from the weight of her grief, even if only for a moment. The steady rise and fall of her breathing felt like an anchor, grounding him amidst the overwhelming helplessness he felt. As her breaths began to slow, he realized she had fallen asleep, her face finally softening from the grip of her grief. Enveloped in the peace and quiet of the surroundings, he felt his own soul recharging, as if her trust in him to hold her—to be her strength—was enough to ease some of his own pain. Sighing, he closed his eyes and rested, content to let her sleep in his arms.

They savored their slow ride back, finding comfort in their time outdoors. When they returned, he tended to the horses while Julia went inside. When he finally came inside, he found her lying across her parents' bed, hugging their pillows tightly and crying softly, breaking his heart into a million pieces.

***

Kasey prepared dinner for her, and although he disliked the idea of eating in bed, he indulged her, watching as she picked at her food while they watched a nature documentary.

As the film ended, she sighed, "I feel gross. I need a shower and to wash my hair, but I'm so tired."

"I'll wash your hair," Kasey offered without hesitation. "You could just wear your underwear, and I'll take care of your hair before you shower."

Surprised by his willingness, she remarked, "No man has ever offered to wash my hair before."

"Their loss. I love your long hair," he responded affectionately, gently playing with it. "Want to do it now, before it gets too late?"

"Sure," she agreed, rising from the bed. Julia slowly undressed to her underwear, dropping her clothes on the floor as she made her way into the bathroom.

Undressing to his tight boxers, Kasey followed her into the spacious glass shower. As the warm water flowed, Julia closed her eyes and leaned against him. She found comfort in his touch as he applied shampoo, his fingers expertly massaging her scalp and neck, the familiar scent of coconut filling the air. Resting her head on his chest, her arms encircling his waist, she savored his gentle touch and the warmth of both him and the water surrounding her.

After rinsing her hair, Kasey repeated the process with conditioner. Gently pulling her hair back, he kissed her neck and whispered, "You'll get through this."

"I'm so glad you're here with me," she said softly, her voice weary but full of gratitude. In that moment, Julia felt a sense of relief wash over her, a fleeting break from the overwhelming grief that had consumed her. She never thought she could lean on someone like this, but with Kasey, it felt safe—even necessary.

"I'm not going anywhere. I'm here as long as you need me," he promised, his voice low and steady as they embraced under the cascading water.

She towel dried her hair, changed into her pajamas, and, with Kasey rubbing her back, she fell asleep.

On Thanksgiving Day, they stayed nestled in bed. Kasey tended to her needs as she drifted in and out of sleep, his comforting presence and touch a balm for her badly battered soul.

***

On Friday, Micki, James, and Will arrived, providing both comfort and distraction, along with the clothes and items Julia needed. Will lit a fire, knowing how much Julia loved them. She sat silently, staring blankly at the flames. The haunting dance of warm melancholy and cold emptiness mirrored her feelings, each crackle and pop of the burning wood resonating with the breaking of her heart.

"How you doing, kiddo? You managed to take a shower and wash your hair—that must feel better," Micki remarked, gently brushing, then braiding Julia's hair.

"Kasey helped me. He washed my hair—I was just too tired," she said, her voice heavy with fatigue.

Will glanced at Kasey while Micki and James exchanged a look at the mention of Kasey's help. Micki smiled softly and said, "I'm glad Kasey's here for you."

Feeling a bit self-conscious under their gazes, Kasey stood up. "Anyone want something to drink?" he asked, breaking the moment.

"Yeah," Julia murmured, "get me some whiskey."

"I don't think that's a good idea with the medications you're taking. How about something else?" Kasey gently countered, squatting down in front of her and lifting her chin with a finger. "How about some tea?"

"Yeah," she said weakly, "and a shot."

"I'll see what I can do," he said with a soft smile, then left the room.

"Guys, could you give us a minute?" Micki asked.

"Sure, we'll be with Kasey," James said, and he and Will got up to leave.

"So, he washed your hair. How'd that work?" Micki asked, curiosity getting the better of her. Julia curled up on the couch, drawing her knees to her chest and resting her chin on them. "We got in the shower with our underwear on, and he washed my hair. The water and shampoo felt so nice on my skin." She paused, her eyes closing in an attempt to relive the comfort of that moment. "He was so gentle, massaging my head and neck." Her tone was flat, almost emotionless, as if his touch had been purely therapeutic.

"Are you sleeping with him? You two looked pretty comfortable when I went in to wake him," Micki asked, trying to gauge the depth of their relationship.

"We've slept in the same bed. I told you about London. Mostly, it's just making out... a lot," she replied, with none of her usual enthusiasm when discussing Kasey.

"He must have some remarkable self-control to shower with you, make out with you, sleep with you, and not have sex with you."

"He wants to take things slow. He's just not ready. I can't even think about that right now," she said, steering away from the topic. "I just need him to do what he's doing— being there for me. Being close to him, feeling his arms around me, it's better than the drugs. He genuinely cares, and that's all I need right now."

When the guys returned, Julia said quietly, "I'm sorry, but I'm really tired. I need to lie down." She started to stand but hesitated, sitting back down. "Mm, I feel dizzy," she added, lowering her head.

"Don't apologize, Jules. We'll be fine. Go rest," James said, his concern for her mental and physical state clear.

"Have you eaten at all today? Maybe that's why you're dizzy." Micki asked.

"I keep trying to get her to eat, it's probably that and the meds," Kasey said, setting down the tea before gently picking her up. "Could you please bring her tea?"

He carried Julia to her room like she was a small child, her head resting on his shoulder, and gently laid her on the bed. Micki set the tea on the nightstand as Kasey pulled the covers over her. She then motioned for him to join her in the hall.

"We're staying here tonight. I'll help her dress tomorrow and take some pressure off you. You're going above and beyond," she said with a grateful smile, planting a kiss on his cheek. "She's really lucky to have you."

"I care a lot about Julia, and I cared about her family— especially Buck. I want to do this right for all of them," he explained.

After a pause, he continued, his voice soft and measured, "My mother died when I was twelve—from cancer. Losing her nearly killed me. I know what Julia's going through, only she's lost three people she loved, not just one. I'm going to make sure she doesn't have to bear this alone like I did." He looked down, his eyes filling with tears he could no longer control.

Micki pulled him into a comforting embrace. "I'm so sorry about your mom. Don't worry; James and I are right beside you. You won't be doing this alone, and neither will she."

Wiping his eyes on his sleeve, he apologized, "Sorry about that. I guess it's better now than in front of her and five hundred people tomorrow."

"You should get some rest, too. You've been going nonstop for days, and she's gonna need you big time tomorrow. If you need company and she's sleeping, come out and hang with us. But I totally get it if you don't. Just know you can be with us, even without Julia—we all like you a lot. Don't forget that."

"Then, as my friends, can I ask a favor?" he asked softly.

"Sure, anything. What do you need?"

"I was hoping James could hold off on sleeping with Julia until we figure out what we are to each other," he said, unsure of how she'd take his request.

"She told you that, huh?" Micki smirked. "Well, since it's always my decision, I can promise it won't happen again—unless of course... you'd like to join in," she said with a grin. He managed a small smile, relieved his request didn't make things awkward.

"Good, I made you smile. Get some rest and take care of our girl. Night, Kasey." She walked down the hall a little sad as she realized that was probably the last time their little threesome would happen.

"Good night," he said, closing the door behind her. He undressed and lay down next to Julia, aimlessly scrolling through his phone until sleep overtook him.

***

Chapter 9: In The Shadow of Grief

The memorial was set to begin at ten in the morning and continue until two in the afternoon. Micki helped Julia dress and prepare for the day.

"Thank you for making sure I have everything I need for today. I appreciate all your help, James' too. I'm so grateful for you both," Julia said, her voice soft as Micki worked on her hair, gathering it into a low bun.

"No need to thank us; we'll always be here for you. Micki secured the last pin, then stepped back. "How's that feel? Too low?"

"It feels fine, thanks. Julia took a deep breath, her gaze drifting to the window. "Where is everybody?"

"I believe Kasey, James, and Will are in the living room, waiting with the others to head to the country club. Whenever you're ready, we'll leave."

"Does everybody know their role for the memorial? Is the pastor coming? And security—has that been taken care of?" Her voice grew more urgent with each question.

"Relax, kiddo. Kasey's organized everything; it's all under control. You just need to focus on yourself and getting through the next four hours." She reached for a pair of sunglasses. "Here, put these on—I got you a nice dark pair. No one's gonna care if you wear them indoors, trust me. And I put tissues in your purse, just in case. We should get going. Are you ready?"

"I don't think I am. I don't think I can handle everyone's attention. I feel like I'm gonna be sick," she confessed, clutching Micki's arm tightly.

"Just breathe. If you need to be sick, let's go to the bathroom," Micki suggested, guiding her gently. "We can send everyone ahead and meet them there. Just do what you need to."

Julia went into the bathroom as Kasey slowly opened the bedroom door. Micki stepped toward him.

"Is she okay?" he asked, hearing Julia dry heaving.

"Not right now. She's terrified of dealing with the crowd and the media."

"If we stay with her, we can move people along if they overwhelm her. We'll take as much pressure off as we can," he suggested, walking to the bathroom door and knocking softly. "Are you okay in there? Do you need anything?"

When Julia didn't answer, Micki turned to Kasey, "Alright, you get everyone going to the country club. I'll take care of her." She gently guided him out of the room.

Julia's extended family, including Jack, Rick, and their families—arrived first, taking a few moments alone before the others. Each family member's portrait rested on a silver easel, surrounded by elaborate flower arrangements. One of Buck's Stetsons hung from the corner of his easel, as did Wynn's. A video montage played softly, showing happy family moments—Buck's business achievements, Lily's time at the hospital surrounded by smiling children, and Wynn working the ranch or with friends at college—all set to Buck and Lily's favorite country music.

Julia arrived later, the car discreetly entering through the back to avoid the crowds.

Accompanied by Micki, James, and Will, she removed her sunglasses to read the cards on some of the floral tributes. Meanwhile, Kasey and Jack met with the president of the country club to ensure all arrangements and security were in order.

Julia bore the weight of her heartbreak with stoic resolve, masking the turmoil within. As she left the ranch and entered the country club beneath a canopy, the relentless presence of paparazzi and media besieged her, an unwanted intrusion on her already shattered world.

The five hundred-strong gathering of mourners found their seats, a sea of faces united in shock and sorrow, paying tribute to a family deeply ingrained in the community, the cattle industry, and the business world. Heartfelt eulogies filled the air, each one a poignant tribute to the three lives tragically lost. Rick and Jack struggled to get through Buck's eulogy, recalling the board members who were longtime friends, sharing memories of growing up together.

Lily's longtime friend painted a vivid picture of a loving and generous woman who devoted her time and boundless energy to the children's hospital, where she served on the board. She had made it a warm and caring place for every child who walked through its doors.

Toby, Wynn's best friend, delivered the most poignant eulogy, grappling with the loss of someone so young—a time when they all felt invincible. Tears flowed freely as he shared the heart-wrenching details of Wynn's unrealized dreams and aspirations.

In the arms of her mother's lifelong friends, the women she had grown up with, Julia broke down both the easiest and the hardest. She struggled with the harsh reality that she would never feel her mother's love or embrace again. Guilt gnawed at her—the regret of not spending the holiday with her family and the fear that her mother might have believed she didn't want to be with them consumed her like a flesh-eating disease.

Unable to bear Julia's anguish—or his own grief—Kasey wore his sunglasses like a shield, hiding his tears. He and Micki flanked Julia, both struggling but steadfast in their support, with James seamlessly stepping in whenever needed.

The memorial was scheduled for four hours, but after three, Julia found it unbearable. She left with Kasey and her friends while Jack, Rick, and Henry managed the remaining crowd.

Before leaving, Jack stepped forward as the family and business spokesperson, delivering a comprehensive statement to the press waiting outside the country club. Amid the chaos of camera clicks and probing questions, Julia stood silently beside him, maintaining her composure. It took everything she had, but she persevered, admirably representing her family in the public eye.

***

After tending to Julia and putting her to bed, the four of them gathered in the living room, pouring shots to numb the weight of the day's challenges.

Breaking the silence, Kasey spoke up, "They're shutting the office down completely for two weeks, then just a bare-bones crew until the new year. Julia and I will stay here until Tuesday to handle some things, then we're heading to her beach house for the month. You're all welcome. She's happiest there, and it's peaceful this time of year."

"Let's give her some space for now," Micki said gently. "She seems content with you. If she needs us—or if you think she does—just give us a call, and we'll be there." She paused. "What about Christmas? I don't know how she's gonna cope with that."

"I have no clue," Kasey admitted, "I hadn't even thought about Christmas or how she'll handle it without her family. Maybe in a couple of weeks, you could reach out and ask what she wants to do."

"We'll play it by ear. She'll tell us what she needs," Micki said.

Kasey looked up and saw Julia slowly making her way down the hall, her hand tracing the wall for balance. Rising from his seat, he went to her. "What do you need?"

"I'm hungry. I need to eat something—my stomach hurts," she replied, her voice low and vulnerable. Kasey took her hand, guiding her gently toward the couch. "Here, sit with Micki. I'll make you something. Anything in particular you want?"

"No, whatever you make is fine." She settled on the couch next to Micki, who wrapped an arm around her. "I'm glad you're gonna eat something. You'll feel better after," Micki said softly.

"Anyone else hungry?" Kasey called over his shoulder.

"I could eat," Micki replied, "James, could you give him a hand?"

"I don't need help, really," Kasey replied, clearly preferring to work alone.

"Well, you're getting it anyway," James grinned, placing a hand on Kasey's shoulder as he followed him to the kitchen.

Realizing Micki wanted a moment alone with Julia, Will excused himself to grab his phone charger.

"We need to clear the air," James said as they entered the spacious kitchen, its warm wood accents and high-end appliances reflecting the style of the sprawling ranch house. Kasey turned to face him. Meeting his gaze, James continued, "Look, the four of us are tight-knit. We've been 'ride or die' since college. I'm sure Julia's told you about me, Will, and our connection with her. If Micki and I had known how you felt, we wouldn't have gone that far. I had no friggin' clue. I knew she was into you, but until you expressed your intentions—"

"I understand," Kasey said with a small smile, turning to the fridge to take out the makings for sandwiches. "I just asked Micki to make sure it doesn't happen again until I had a chance to work things out with Julia. I kept putting it off because she can be a little capricious. I was worried if this 'friends-with-benefits' thing didn't work out and she moved on, I'd lose more than the casual sex was worth to me. But she's making it impossible—I think about her all the time. I haven't been this emotionally close to anyone in a long time," he confessed, assembling the sandwiches, not realizing how easily he was sharing personal details with her friends. "I feel like I'm slowly drowning, watching her go through this," he sighed, his head dropping to his chest as he leaned against the table for support.

James walked over and placed a hand on Kasey's shoulder. "Jules really cares about you, and it's obvious you care about her more than we realized. I have to admit, you're good for her. She can be a handful and impulsive, but you seem to settle her. She needs you now more than ever. I'm glad you're going to the beach with her—you both need some alone time. You've been busting your ass nonstop. You're always so calm and collected, but that's gotta be exhausting. I'm tired just watching you," he said, shaking his head with a small smile.

"I am tired. Being around so many people is a little overwhelming," Kasey admitted, his voice weary. "I'll be glad for some peace and quiet."

"Let me grab the salads," James said, turning to the fridge, relieved they'd cleared the air.

***

Brushing a strand of hair off Julia's face, Micki said, "We're heading home tomorrow. Kasey mentioned you're staying until Tuesday before heading to the beach. Is there anything else we can do for you before we go? I can come back anytime, just lemme know, okay?"

Julia sighed. "I'm just gonna take it one day at a time for the next couple of weeks. I really can't make any more decisions right now—even the little ones hurt my head."

Pausing, she gazed into the flames, which seemed to call out to her. "I have to pull myself together... I have a company to run. People will be depending on me." Her eyes widened as she looked at Micki, fear etched on her face, her new reality sinking in. "A whole fucking company without my dad," she added softly.

"Relax, kiddo... you've got dozens of people waiting to help you at work. Rick, Jack, Henry—and most of all, Kasey. You said yourself how much he helped during that takeover. You're gonna be just fine." Micki took Julia's hand, giving it a reassuring squeeze. "You've been working toward this your whole life. I know it's too soon and not how it should've happened, but don't doubt yourself. You're more than capable," she said confidently, trying to boost Julia's belief in herself. "You'll find your footing—I have no doubt. Plus, nothing's happening at work for a month. And if you need more time, take it. The guys can manage for a while."

Kasey and James returned with trays of food and drinks, setting them down in front of Julia and Micki. The group chatted over their meal, while Julia barely touched her food as her thoughts drifted to the solitude of her beach house.

In the days that followed, Julia moved through a haze of medication and sorrow, holding brief meetings with the ranch bosses to ensure operations continued smoothly under Jack and Rick's supervision. She selected a few personal items to take home, arranging for her mother's jewelry, artwork, and other valuables to be securely stored. Among the keepsakes were her parents' wedding bands, which she slipped onto a chain and fastened around her neck. The rest, she left untouched, choosing to address it later. The once vibrant family home now felt heavy with her profound loss, and she felt a painful urgency to leave it behind.

***

When they arrived in New York, they stopped at Julia's condo to collect her essentials before heading to Kasey's for the night. Condolences poured in from all sides—from doormen to casual acquaintances—but what she truly longed for was the solace of the shore, craving seclusion. The only comfort she found was in Kasey's quiet companionship.

As she crossed the threshold of her beach house, a wave of relief washed over Julia, momentarily easing the weight she'd been carrying. Over the next week, they strolled the beach in silence, hand in hand, sat by the fireplace with Kasey reading to her and indulged in their favorite shows and movies. Respecting each other's need for space, Kasey went on long runs while Julia spent hours alone on the deck, the fire pit's dancing flames her only company as they both contemplated their futures. Though he didn't need to, he still tenderly washed her hair when she asked. And while they shared the same bed every night, their intimacy had shifted—from passion to a comforting closeness. It wasn't physical desire but the comfort of connection that Julia craved.

***

Wrapped in a cozy blanket on the double lounger, they gazed up at the star-lit sky, the crackle of the fire pit, and the soothing rhythm of the waves caressing the shore surrounding them. Julia turned to Kasey, her voice soft as she voiced her apprehension about the daunting return awaiting her.

"I dread going back... I know it'll be overwhelming with all the changes and condolences still pouring in. I just wanna hide and avoid what's coming."

Kasey nodded, acknowledging the challenges ahead. "I know it's going to be tough, but no one expects you to have it all figured out right away. Cut yourself some slack. Right now, it's about letting others support you. Maybe it's too soon—you could take more time. And consider talking to someone about what you're feeling. I'm here to listen, but I'm not a professional," he added with a warm smile. "They could offer more guidance. When I lost my mother, I saw a psychologist for a while."

"Did it help?" she asked, her voice barely above a whisper.

"It did. It gave me a way to express my emotions, and I learned some coping mechanisms. It's not an instant fix—you still have to do the work to feel better, but it can point you in the right direction." Her sorrowful eyes, brimming with pain and uncertainty, met his in the moonlight. Gently, he brushed her hair aside, his touch reassuring and tender.

"Maybe down the line, but right now, I just need you," she whispered.

"I'm here for you," he promised. Julia let out a deep sigh, finding the support she needed as she rested her head on his chest, melting into his comforting embrace.

After a moment, Julia said, "I know you've been working remotely, but could you go to the office and give it a quick once-over? Make sure everything's in order and check on Nomi. You could swing by home, check on Bruce, and be back the same day by car or helicopter. Or, if you need a break, you could stay home. I can manage on my own," she added, though her words contradicted her need for him.

With a reassuring smile, he pulled her close. "Don't worry, I'll handle everything and be back before you know it. I'm here as long as you need me. Since we'll be staying a few more weeks, I'll bring some of my books and my training dummy, if you don't mind. I can put it in one of the spare rooms."

"Please, bring whatever you need and put it wherever you like. Whatever works for you. Bring Bruce and Nomi if you think they'll survive the trip. I want you to be comfortable here... as comfortable as I am with you being here."

Kasey drove into the city early the next day. When he returned that evening, he brought his belongings and the two bonsai trees with him.

"I settled Bruce and Nomi in the back bedroom facing the street. It gets the same kind of light they both need, so they should be fine," Kasey said as he came downstairs. "Barbara gave Nomi water, but both of them could use some real care. We could work on them together tomorrow if you're up to it."

"I'm glad you brought them. Now you won't have to leave to take care of them," Julia said absently, sitting on the couch with her arms wrapped around her knees as she gazed at the flickering flames.

Sitting beside her, Kasey spoke softly, "Micki called today. She mentioned you haven't been responding to her or James' calls or texts. She's worried about you. Frantic, actually. Is something wrong?"

Tears welled up in her eyes as she looked at him. "I can't bring myself to talk to anyone who reminds me of my family right now, especially Rick and Jack—they sound too much like my dad. I want to talk to my best friend, but I just can't. The thought makes me anxious. I know this is a lot of pressure on you, but I don't want to talk to or see anyone but you," she confessed, gripping her knees and rocking back and forth, tears falling freely. "I feel a little fucked up today."

Wrapping his arms around her, he comforted her. "It's okay. I'll call Micki and let her know you need a little more time. Don't cry; it's normal. It's just temporary," he assured, rubbing her back soothingly. He stayed with her for a while before giving her some space.

***

An hour later, Kasey returned downstairs to check on her, finding her asleep. Quietly securing the house, he gently lifted her and carried her to bed.

"Thank you," she mumbled as he laid her down.

"Go back to sleep," he whispered, tucking her in.

"I love you," she murmured, her voice muffled by the pillow, the words slipping out as she drifted into sleep, her true feelings revealed in her vulnerability.

"What did you say?" he asked quietly, slipping into bed beside her. But when he peered over, he realized she was already asleep. Pulling her close, he drifted off, never hearing the words he'd longed for.

***

The next day, Kasey watched her mood darken, escalating to a point where worry consumed him. Overwhelmed with concern, he reached out to Micki for guidance.

"After everything you've told me, I think we need to take action as the ones closest to her," Micki said firmly. "We should arrange for a private doctor to come to the house. I don't think Jules will resist if it's put right in front of her. She needs professional help now, and you know it too, or you wouldn't have called me."

"I know she needs help. I can see her deteriorating right in front of me," Kasey responded, his anxiety palpable.

"Alright, I'll reach out to the head of her mother's hospital to get the best doctor available near you, ASAP. We need someone who can focus solely on getting Jules back on her feet," Micki declared, her commitment to her best friend's recovery clear.

"That sounds good. She's struggling, and I feel helpless," he admitted, desperate for a solution.

"Don't worry, Kasey, we'll get her back. I know she's in there—she just needs the kind of help we can't give her. And soon, she'll have it," Micki reassured him.

***

Sitting alone on the deck, Julia cocooned herself in a cozy blanket, basking in the warmth of the fire pit. The afternoon sun cast its gentle glow, adding to her comfort, as the soothing murmur of waves and seagulls serenaded her. She cherished the wintry seclusion of the beach just as much as its summer bustle, finding solace in the windswept shore that never failed to quiet her mind. Her fingers absently traced the wedding bands hanging from the chain around her neck as her thoughts swirled between fond family memories and the weight of unspoken words.

Lost in thought, Julia was startled by Kasey's quiet presence as he joined her on the deck. "The doctor we discussed, Jessica Dresden, is here. Are you ready to talk to her?" he asked gently.

"Sure," Julia replied, her voice flat and emotionless.

Kasey watched from the window, observing the interaction between the two for a few minutes. After an hour, the doctor came inside to update him.

"As we discussed, Julia is experiencing intense grief, which is expected in this situation. Medication alongside therapy is necessary. The medication will help her engage more effectively. Based on what I've seen, she has a strong inner strength that will help in her recovery. I've reviewed her records with her physicians here and in Colorado, and I'll send her prescriptions to your local pharmacy. Start the medication right away, and I'll follow up tomorrow. Once she's more responsive, we'll begin therapy sessions at her pace. I've cleared my schedule for the next few weeks. If she needs to talk, or if you have questions, don't hesitate to call. My priority is to get her functioning before she returns to work. However, she shouldn't be left alone or driving until we see how she responds to the medication—right now, her judgment is compromised, and accidents could occur," the doctor advised.

"I understand, Doctor. Thank you for your prompt attention," Kasey replied, relieved Julia was receiving the care she needed.

Julia opened up about her anxieties over the company's future without her father, the guilt from her last moments with her mother, the loss of her bond with her brother—and the crushing realization that nothing in her life would ever be the same.

***

Christmas passed quietly, with Julia barely acknowledging the season; spending most of it in quiet reflection, not yet ready to face the festive cheer.

With the help of medication and frequent therapy, she made significant progress. Inviting Micki and James to join her and Kasey for New Year's, she found her spirits lifted even more by Will's unexpected arrival on New Year's Eve. Their presence helped her reconnect with herself, and the laughter they shared reminded her of the strength she found in their friendship.

She resumed her regular chats with Micki, their tight bond surviving the challenges life had thrown at them—be it from love, or loss.

***

Chapter 10: Reclaiming a Sense of Self

By the second week of the new year, Julia felt ready—well, as ready as she could be—to return to work. Dr. Dresden continued their twice-weekly therapy sessions in her office, offering both an anchor and a necessary distraction. Immersing herself in the company's broader vision had become her way of reclaiming control over something in her life, even if comfort still felt like a distant concept.

For the next two months, Julia, Kasey, and Henry tirelessly worked together to ensure a seamless transition into her new leadership role. Buck Masters' unexpected demise had sent shock waves through the company's corporate landscape.

While Julia had been groomed since childhood for leadership within the family business, the sudden and tragic nature of her father's passing thrust her into the forefront sooner than anyone could have foreseen. Suddenly, she was catapulted from heir apparent straight into her father's formidable boots—owner, majority stockholder, board member, and the public face of Masters Inc. It felt like too much, too soon, but there was no time to falter.

Buck had been more than just the face of the company; he was the driving force behind its success, a visionary leader steering Masters Inc. through three decades of growth and innovation. The pressure to seamlessly step into her father's role wasn't just corporate—it was deeply personal. Every decision she made felt like a test, as if the entire company was watching, waiting to see if she could truly live up to his legacy.

At just twenty-nine years old, the weight of immense wealth and responsibility rested solely on her shoulders. Some days, it was hard to breathe under the pressure. She'd wake in the night, heart racing, wondering how her father had done it all. But she couldn't afford to show any cracks now—she had to keep it together.

Previously, the occasional ten-hour day had been no challenge for Julia, fueled by her borderline workaholic tendencies. But as the weeks dragged on with transitions and an ever-growing workload, those long hours became her new normal.

The acquisition of the fashion house was finalized, but its integration into the Masters fold remained untouched. It was time to assemble a competent team to jump-start the integration process—just one more responsibility added to her already overflowing plate. At least with Kasey and Henry sharing the load, she wasn't completely drowning in it.

***

Claiming her father's office ruffled the feathers of two newer board members, who also contested her appointment as CEO. Their objections, however, were swiftly overruled by the ten-member board, six of whom were Buck's lifelong friends and closely connected to Julia. Only three weren't part of his inner circle. Men like Jack and Rick, who, like Buck, had risen from ranch hands on his father's ranch to managing the

Double O and its subsidiary companies, played crucial roles as the company grew.

In recent months, they had spent more time in New York, offering support to Julia. Their presence was invaluable, though it also stirred poignant emotions—constant reminders of her father. Each day, she could feel their watchful eyes, silently measuring her against Buck's legacy. They saw him reflected in her as she gathered strength to cope with the loss of her family and stepped up to lead. Watching her now, they witnessed Buck's teachings come to life in his daughter.

Two months had passed since Julia took over her father's office, but she still wasn't spending much time there. Instead, she found herself more often in Kasey's new office, kicking off her shoes and tucking her legs beneath her as she buried herself in reports. Kasey would often offer her his desk, but she always refused, preferring the comfort of his couch to the bittersweet memories that filled her father's office.

Henry had graciously given his office to Kasey and moved down the hall into an equally nice one. He had briefly talked about early retirement, feeling his place in the company had shifted. But both Julia and Kasey sat him down, assuring him that his experience was invaluable during this transition. Reluctantly, he agreed to stay and soon found there was plenty of work to keep him busy.

Buck's office, with its warm coppery tones, chestnut wood-paneled walls, and raw-edged cocktail table, felt more like a living room than an executive suite. The cowhide rug and buttery leather sofa added to the rustic, welcoming atmosphere. The walls were lined with family photographs— ranch life, ski vacations, camping trips, and holiday gatherings. Among them were snapshots of Julia and her father, their smiles forever frozen in moments of joy and success.

Mounted behind the massive desk were a pair of Angus horns and a horseshoe engraved with "Double O Ranch," constant reminders of the life they had shared. Every time she stepped into the room, those memories stirred something deep inside her. Determined to make the office her own, Julia decided it was time for a change—a redecoration project was exactly what she needed to reclaim the space.

***

Having gradually weaned herself off all the prescribed medications, Julia now felt herself reclaiming both her creativity and sense of self.

Kasey glanced up from his laptop to find her perched gracefully on the edge of his desk. "I really like what you did with your home," she purred, her tone hinting at a favor.

"Maybe you could help me with my office?"

A soft chuckle escaped him as he recognized the familiar charm she effortlessly wielded when she was feeling herself. Her vibrant blue eyes sparkled with enthusiasm.

"Redecorate your office, huh?" he replied, a playful grin tugging at his lips.

"Since you have impeccable taste in most things, and your home is beautiful, I..." she started, interrupted by his raised eyebrow.

"Most things?" he shot back, his grin widening.

"I stand corrected," she admitted with a smile, her eyes crinkling in the corners. "All things."

"Better," he said with a grin. "Of course I'll help." He knew she could manage it on her own or hire a professional, but he sensed it wasn't about the office—it was about wanting his company for something more personal.

***

For the next two weeks, Julia and Kasey dove into the redecorating project, reviewing books on design and sorting through paint, fabric, and tile samples in her favorite hues. Exquisite artwork on loan and new office furniture filled the space they'd set aside for their creative work.

One quiet evening, long after the office had emptied, Julia absentmindedly sorted through fabric swatches in shades of blue and gray, her mind wandering. Kasey approached, handing her a brochure for a new desk and chair set tailored specifically for her petite frame. Buck's desk and chair were built for someone of his impressive stature—six foot four in his boots, with the solid build of a lumberjack. They clashed with the aesthetic she had in mind.

When Kasey casually suggested replacing the chair, Julia's response was unexpectedly emotional. Her voice softened as she explained her need to keep it, revealing the deep sentimental attachment it held.

With a nostalgic smile, she recounted the chair's origin story to him. It first appeared in her father's ranch office after her mom had it custom-made for his birthday. As a spirited young girl, she would twirl around on the chair, passing the time eagerly awaiting her father's company.

She would spin round and round until dizziness took over, her twelve-year-old stomach feeling like she'd just stepped off the Tilt-A-Whirl at the fairgrounds.

After a particularly busy morning tending to the horses, she waited so long that her father found her asleep in the chair. He chuckled and said, "Darlin', you were curled up like a barn cat in the rafters on a rainy afternoon.

When he opened the New York office, the beloved chair made the journey with him. To Julia, the soft, buttery leather felt like a big, warm hug—just like one of her father's. Having it reupholstered in soft black leather, the chair remained, and she continued to feel his presence, comforting her.

The sentimentality didn't end with the chair. She also became attached to a quaint plastic snow globe with "Double O Ranch" spelled out in tiny gold letters. She found the whimsical trinket while sorting through her father's things and, without much thought, placed it on the corner of her desk. After a few days of shaking it, watching the yellowed "snow" drift over the miniature ranch and its faded mountain backdrop, the snow globe became a cherished keepsake. Its glittering contents stirring memories of her childhood.

***

"I have something that might lift your spirits," Kasey said after noticing she had gone quiet. "Meet me in the closet," he added with a sly grin.

"Why are we in here?" she asked, her voice soft as she pressed her body against his. "Everyone's gone; you could kiss me out there."

"True, but we can't smoke this without stinking up the place," he said, holding up half a blunt. "You could use a mental spa night, and earlier, you mentioned your stomach was off." He lit it and handed it to her. "This will help both."

Already comfortable in her office slippers, she hiked up her tight black pencil skirt and sat cross-legged on the carpeted floor of the spacious, empty closet.

Exhaling slowly, tendrils of smoke trailed from her lips as she rested her head against the wall, her gaze fixed on Kasey. He leaned back against the opposite wall directly across from her, legs bent in front of him, arms casually crossed atop his knees. Smoking far more than he had, she was now comfortably numb. A mischievous smirk tugged at her lips when she realized he probably had a clear view of her panties from his angle.

"See anything you like?" she teased, her eyes dark with mischief, lips curling into a slow, seductive smile.

"Maybe," he replied with a charming grin, his striking eyes glinting from beneath his hair. He could hardly resist her when she looked at him like that—playful, beautiful, and completely captivating. Whatever she wanted, he was already halfway to giving in. But as much as he wanted her, he was determined to wait. When it happened, it had to be special.

"Because I do," she added, giving him an appreciative once-over. Glancing at the blunt in her hand, she declared, "You need to catch up. Shotgun!"

Without waiting for his response, she knelt in front of him, turning the blunt around and carefully putting it in her mouth. Leaning forward, she pressed her body against his legs, grabbing him with two hands by his collar and pulling his face close to hers. Tilting her head as if for a kiss, she watched as he parted his lips and inhaled while she blew a steady stream of smoke into his mouth. He coughed and sputtered. "You're brutal," he managed.

"Amateur," she giggled, setting the blunt down on a paint sample before lying back on the soft carpet and pulling him down beside her. They lay there quietly, shoulder to shoulder, gazing up at the ceiling. Julia felt a warm fuzziness envelop her while Kasey lay beside her, hands on his chest, stifling small coughs as his head spun.

Turning to him, she kissed him for the first time since her family's passing, with the same passion and longing as before. The kiss reignited something in both of them—an unspoken desire that had been waiting for the right moment to surface.

"I'd like to go to the shore tomorrow and pick up where we left off," she whispered, nuzzling his neck, her breath warm on his skin as he pulled her close. "I know you were ready before, and now, I'm ready. I miss what we had...and I want even more." Her tongue teased along his skin, tracing the outer edge of his ear. He moaned softly as she bit his neck, whispering how much she missed his kisses.

"Shh," he whispered, rolling her onto her back as he slowly unbuttoned her blouse.

His lips brushed over her skin, trailing soft kisses along her collarbone before moving lower. Cupping her breast, he traced slow, deliberate circles with his tongue. She arched into his touch, a breathy moan escaping as he grazed her sensitive skin with his thumb, teasing her until her body trembled beneath him. Taking his hand, she guided it between her legs, her hips moving to meet his touch.

"What happened to waiting until tomorrow at the beach? We can wait. I want it to be special for us."

"It's not fair to get me all worked up like this," she pouted.

"Now you know how we men feel at your little dance parties," he teased, grinning.

She laughed, "Touché."

***

The next afternoon, they headed to the shore with Kasey at the wheel, the air thick with unspoken thoughts and rising anticipation.

"My stomach feels a little weird," Julia muttered as they neared her home.

"What do you mean weird?" he said, glancing over at her.

"I'm not sure. Suddenly, I feel like I might throw up. What did I eat today?" she muttered, trying to think.

"You barely touched your lunch. I don't know what you had for breakfast," he replied as they were pulling up.

"Open the door, quick!" she urged, bolting out of the car and rushing to the bathroom just in time.

"Are you alright?" Kasey called, hovering near the bathroom door.

"Better now," she said as she emerged holding her stomach. "Something definitely didn't sit well with me."

"Maybe you've got a stomach bug. You said you felt nauseous the other day—and yesterday too, now that I think about it."

"I don't think it's a bug. I'm not sure what's going on. I do feel a little warm." She looked a bit pale, he thought, but she had just thrown up.

"Let me get a thermometer," Kasey suggested, feeling her forehead. "You do feel warm."

"No, lemme just rest for a bit. I'll be okay," she mumbled, as much to reassure herself as him.

"I'm going to get the bags, why don't you lay down, let your stomach settle," he suggested.

"Sounds good," she agreed, slowly making her way upstairs to her bedroom.

Rolling the luggage into her room, he could see she was not improving. Lying on her side, propped against a pillow, she winced.

"I'm sorry, I'm just not feeling well; I think I'm gonna stay here for a while," she said softly.

"Is there anything I can get you?" he asked, concerned.

"No, thank you. I'll be fine. I'm just gonna rest for a bit," she assured him, closing her eyes.

He was reading in the living room when she appeared less than an hour later. Descending the stairs slowly, gripping the railing tightly for support, she whispered, "Kasey, I really don't feel well."

Looking up, alarm shot through him. Julia was ashen, her hair damp and clinging to her forehead, one hand clutching her side.

He moved quickly, catching her just before she collapsed, the heat radiating from her skin telling him she had a high fever.

Laying her down on the couch, he dialed 911, his voice tense as he explained that she might have appendicitis and urged them to hurry. After locking up the house and grabbing her phone and wallet, he anxiously waited by the door for the ambulance.

On the way to the hospital, he contacted the duty nurse, firmly identifying Julia and insisting on their best surgeon and finest room. It turned out to be her appendix, and she underwent surgery that night. Kasey spent the entire night by her side, not leaving the hospital room for a moment. After informing Micki, exhausted, he drifted off to sleep on a chair beside her bed.

Julia woke briefly during the night, spotting him asleep in the chair beside her. She smiled softly, closing her eyes again, comforted by the thought that she was safe and cared for.

The next day, Kasey returned to the house to gather her essentials. As he opened her luggage, the delicate lingerie she'd packed for their first time together caught his eye. A pang of regret hit him—she'd be so disappointed. As he packed her things for the hospital, Kasey couldn't help but reflect on the dramatic interruptions both times they'd planned to be together. Was it a sign, or just bad luck?

***

After two days in the hospital, Julia was discharged and recovering well from the laparoscopic surgery. She chose to spend the next week recuperating at the beach, with a nurse helping her during the first two days at home. Kasey seized the opportunity to go for long rides while she slept. He handled groceries and essentials, cared for her, and worked a few hours each day on his laptop.

Julia spent her days on the deck, wrapped in a blanket, listening to the seagulls and soaking in the sights and sounds of the ocean. She rummaged through the multitude of gift baskets and delighted in the exquisite flower arrangements and plants she received. She sent out handwritten thank-you cards to everyone for the well wishes, along with a card and gift for everyone involved in her care.

Understanding her desire for privacy during her recovery, Kasey refrained from sleeping in her room, respecting her need for space. Though he had seen her at her worse—through the loss of her family and every ugly cry—recovery was different. That was where she drew the line. Aware of her boundary, he happily slept in another room, prioritizing her comfort above all.

During the remainder of their time there, they engaged in their normal activities—long conversations, strolls hand-in-hand along the beach, reading, and catching up on their favorite shows. He cooked for her, scouring online recipes that would be gentle on her post surgery digestion. She also met with Dr. Dresden twice during the time she was there, discussing how extremely disappointed she was that her and Kasey were prevented from consummating their relationship again, and she felt like the universe was conspiring against the prospect of them being together.

While Kasey shared in the disappointment, sex was temporarily off the table until she

recovered—which was a month-long hiatus as far as he was concerned. The doctor advised two weeks of taking it easy and three weeks without strenuous activity or heavy lifting. Kasey made it clear to Julia that he wouldn't risk causing her any harm by having sex with her. She reluctantly agreed, wanting him completely uninhibited when they were finally together.

***

The night before they went back to New York, they lay in bed in their underwear, talking and making out. Julia kissed his neck and continued to move slowly down his body. As he began to protest, she looked up at him and purred, "You said we can't have sex, but I don't see why I can't do something for you... I mean, it's not gonna hurt me in any way." Undeterred, she kissed his stomach.

"I don't want to stop you, believe me. I just feel bad it's not really fair to you," he explained, playing with her hair.

"Kasey, sex, like life, isn't always fair," she replied, with blunt honesty, as she kissed lower on his stomach. "Sometimes, you do things for your partner with no need or expectation of the same in return. It's not always a one for one." As her tongue flicked at his stomach, her hand found him already completely aroused. "Plus, I like doing it. I get pleasure from doing it," her voice low and seductive, her fingers lightly teasing him. "I know some women don't enjoy it, but I do, and I'm very good at it."

"Yes, you are," he agreed, his hand now gripping her hair in anticipation. She grinned up at him as she slowly pulled his shorts down.

"You're always doing something for me. Lemme show you how much I appreciate you," she said, her tongue flicking over him with deliberate, teasing strokes. "Lemme take care of you."

He groaned, her words and touch undoing him as his fingers tightened in her hair. Julia's eyes flicked up to meet his, a mischievous glint dancing in them before she leaned in again, her movements slow, purposeful, and utterly consuming. Kasey gave himself over to her, lost in the warmth of her touch, the soft hum of her pleasure, and the sheer skill that left him breathless.

As she whispered his name against his skin, Kasey couldn't help but marvel at her—her confidence, her passion, and the way she made him feel completely seen and cared for. Loving her came as easily as breathing, and moments like this only deepened the certainty that she was unlike anyone else.

***

Chapter 11: I Don't Want Other Boys-I Just Want You

Micki, James, and Will came to the shore one month after her surgery, eager to spend the weekend with her and Kasey. Julia, fully healed and in high spirits, was ready to make the most of the occasion, especially looking forward to finally being with the man she had been lusting after, fantasizing about, and, unbeknownst to him, in love with for the better part of a year.

"You said one month, and it's been a month," she announced, perched on his desk,

watching Kasey with a glint of mischief in her eyes while they waited for Will to head to the shore in the helicopter.

"I am well aware of that," he replied, shooting her a crooked grin as he tucked a few papers into his top drawer.

"Then you're also aware that unless the goddamn apocalypse happens tonight," she leaned close, her voice dropping to a seductive whisper, "we're gonna fuck like bunnies. Hope you're ready."

He looked up, catching her playful grin with a smirk of his own. "I'm as ready as I can be," he murmured, those captivating eyes locking onto hers, making her want to pull him in and kiss him right there.

"I'm just excited. I promise we'll go at your speed," she said, the excitement in her voice hard to hide as Will walked in.

"Is this what you two do all day, whisper sweet nothings in each other's ears?" Will laughed, giving them a knowing look. "Just have at it already."

"Oh, I intend to," Julia laughed, hopping off Kasey's desk and grabbing her bag. "Let's go, boys—time's a-wasting!"

***

After dinner, the happy group gathered in the living room, wine glasses in hand. Kasey set the mood by lighting the fireplace, casting a warm glow around the room as James fiddled with the karaoke machine. Will rearranged the furniture, creating more space for the night's festivities.

The atmosphere crackled with sexual tension, with Julia radiating a particularly lusty vibe. Upon noticing the blunt Will produced, she quipped, "What the hell, Will? Did Snoop Dog roll that for you?"

Will lit it, exhaling a cloud of smoke with a devilish grin. "Guaranteed to fuck us all up," he promised, handing it over to Micki.

As Micki dimmed the lights and scrolled through songs, Kasey, leaning casually against the kitchen island, couldn't help but zero in on Julia. He knew every sway of her hips tonight would be for his benefit, every look and laugh crafted to tease him—it was exactly the kind of foreplay he craved.

Earlier, while the guys tidied up after dinner, Julia and Micki had slipped away to change into short dresses perfect for dancing. Julia wore a blue-gray cashmere button-down mini dress, its flared skirt swishing around her thighs, paired with tall, furry white Uggs and over-the-knee white silk socks. Micki sported a similar dress in dark green with black furry boots and bare legs. When they made their entrance, Will let out a low whistle. "I see trouble coming, James."

James chuckled quietly, raising his wine glass with a knowing look aimed at Kasey.

After singing a couple of songs with Will, Julia danced her way over to Kasey, her fingers trailing provocatively along his thighs as she swayed. Enjoying her seductive moves and touch, he just sat back and let her do her thing. Spotting the blunt had reached its midpoint, Julia called out, "Shotgun!" and proceeded to show off her skills with practiced ease.

Starting with Will, she positioned him face-to-face on a kitchen chair with Kasey close by, his gaze fixed on her every move. Leaning in, her full, enticing lips hovered just shy of Will's as she blew a slow, steady stream of smoke into his mouth. Will's hands settled on her shoulders as he leaned back, turning his head to release a thick, lazy cloud of smoke.

"Damn girl, always trying to do me dirty," he teased with a smirk, rising from his seat with a shake of his head.

She dropped the smoldering blunt into the ashtray, then strolled over to take James from Micki, her wicked grin already in place. Pausing to sway against him in time with the music, she gave into the urge to tease both James and Kasey, her gaze flicking to Kasey's as she moved.

Will slipped in beside Micki, seamlessly filling James' spot without missing a beat. Kasey took a slow sip of wine, his gaze fixed on Julia and James as a brief, heated image of them together sparked in his mind. Julia looped her arms around James' neck, pressing her body against his as she moved to the music. Locking eyes with Kasey, she slowly turned, leaning back into James and guiding his hands over her curves, every move deliberate as he watched.

Glancing at Kasey, James leaned in and whispered, "You're gonna be the death of me, Jules." She giggled, letting him go as she twirled over to the kitchen chair like a mischievous, stoned pixie. She patted the seat, throwing him her most mischievous grin as she invited him to sit. She repeated the shotgun ritual, cupping his face tenderly, her lips barely brushing his as she let the smoke slip between them. He leaned back, resting his hands on his lap as she pressed into him with a sly smile. Exhaling slowly, he raised his hands in surrender, flashing an innocent grin at Kasey. Kasey shook his head, smiling as Julia made her way over to Micki with that same gleam in her eye.

Micki slipped behind Julia, her fingers gently brushing Julia's hair aside before pressing a soft kiss to her neck, sparking a slow, sensual rhythm as their bodies moved in sync. Julia took a long drag from the blunt, closing her eyes as she lost herself in the warmth of Micki's touch, fully aware of the guys' eyes on them. Exhaling slowly, she turned, capturing Micki's mouth in a heated kiss, their tongues intertwining as Micki's hands tangled possessively in her hair.

With one hand pulling Micki close and the other gripping the smoldering blunt, Julia shared a charged, intimate moment before giving Micki a shotgun, her own lips still tingling as Micki returned the favor.

As they parted, Micki sauntered to the kitchen for more wine while Julia queued up a special song. Kasey followed Micki, his movements deliberate, trapping her gently against the cool counter. Their bodies hovered dangerously close, the heat between them electric. His lips brushed just above her ear, grazing her skin like a whisper.

"Someone's being a very bad girl," he murmured, his voice a low, teasing rumble. "I thought we had an understanding."

A sly smile curved her lips as she countered, "Oh, I thought you were talking about James."

Kasey tilted his head, his lips barely a breath away from hers, his gaze locking her in place. "I think you know exactly what I meant."

Micki's hands found their way to his hips, her touch light, her grin playful. "You know she's perfectly capable of being bad all on her own."

His cheek brushed against hers, his smooth skin a gentle caress as he leaned in closer. "Oh, I know," he murmured, his breath warm against her ear. "But you? You egg her on. Don't you?"

Her dark eyes sparkled with mischief as she purred, "Well, maybe if you asked me nicely to stop…"

Kasey's fingers slid into her hair, his touch commanding as he tilted her head, exposing her neck. His lips hovered just above her skin, the promise of a kiss palpable. "She's mine," he whispered, his tone possessive and intimate. "And tonight, everyone—including her—is going to know it."

With a casual wink, he pulled away, his smirk lingering as he strolled back to the couch. Micki stayed behind, her pulse racing, caught in a delicious storm of arousal and excitement. She didn't need to wonder what he intended for Julia—she felt it in every nerve of her body.

From the living room, the three of them watched the kitchen interaction, each with a different reaction. Will thought it was wild that Kasey had finally joined in on the group's vibe and couldn't help but wonder what Julia was thinking. James felt a mix of surprise and smoldering arousal seeing Micki with Kasey, a heat building in his chest and lower, unexpected but undeniable.

Julia, however, felt a brief stab of jealousy. She barely registered Micki in the moment—she only saw Kasey showing what looked like affection to someone who wasn't her. Fueled by a sudden need to claim him, she decided to take her man to bed. She walked over to the karaoke machine, selected the song "Other Boys," and confidently approached Kasey.

With the blunt in hand, she straddled him on the couch, singing each lyric directly to him as her free hand tangled sensually through his hair. Captivated by her sultry voice, the provocative lyrics, and the self-assured, sensual way she moved, he felt his inhibitions dissolve, surrendering completely to her seduction.

His hand slid slowly along her thigh, slipping beneath her dress, his fingertips grazing her warm, bare skin, making it nearly impossible for either of them to resist the pull of desire. Her mesmerizing eyes peeked out from under her long lashes, she sang the lyrics like a confession meant only for him. Leaning in close, she whispered the chorus softly into his ear, her breath sending a shiver through him.

"Silhouettes, a city of shadows. They all take your shape.

In my defense, you've got me unraveled. And I can't see straight.

Cause my heart can't be satisfied by anyone but you tonight.

And when I try, it only makes me blue.

Why can't you want me like the other boys do? They stare at me while I stare at you.

Why can't you want me, baby, what can I do? I don't want other boys, I just want you."

She placed the blunt between her lips, cupping his face as she leaned in, exhaling the smoke slowly into his waiting mouth. She rolled her hips to the music's rhythm, pressing down onto his lap and feeling the undeniable evidence of her effect on him beneath her. Kasey exhaled the smoke to the side, and as she leaned forward to set the blunt in the ashtray, his hands slid beneath her dress, cupping her firm, round curves.

As she lifted herself slightly, his fingers slipped between her legs, drawing a soft gasp as she melted against him. He wrapped one arm around her waist, his other hand tangling in her hair, as he kissed her deeply, unbothered by the rapt attention of their friends. None of them had ever seen Julia and Kasey kiss before, let alone seen Kasey so openly passionate with her.

As they clung to each other, the world faded away, leaving only the two of them utterly lost in their shared passion. His hands cradled her face as he kissed her so deeply; her head spun. She could feel the heat radiating off him, pulling her in. He turned her head, his lips finding that sensitive spot near her shoulder as he bit and sucked, leaving a mark that sent waves of pleasure rippling through her.

After months of suppressing his true feelings and denying the attraction simmering between them, he finally surrendered to the magnetic pull that had always drawn him to her. In that vulnerable moment, desire overwhelmed his long-held reservations. She gasped as he lifted her from his lap, flipping her onto the couch and hovering over her with a hunger that left her breathless. His lips trailed down her neck, lingering at her collarbone before he finally pulled back, standing as he took her hand, his own breath unsteady. In a low, husky whisper, he commanded, "Say good night, Julia," as he pulled her toward the stairs.

"Good night," Julia echoed with a sly grin, following him up the stairs with a thrill of anticipation.

"Well, that was friggin' hot, and about time," Micki said with a grin as they watched the pair disappear up the stairs.

James chuckled, "I was just hoping I wouldn't get my ass beat while she was trying to make him jealous—or turn him on, whatever that was. So, what did he say to you in the kitchen? It looked a little intense."

"Oh, he told me I was a 'bad girl' for encouraging Julia to engage in what he calls 'bad behavior,'" she laughed, throwing in air quotes. She smiled to herself, thinking about Kasey's body pressed close, his lips just grazing hers, and the scene she'd just witnessed. She thought to herself, *he's definitely one of those quiet ones that smolders underneath, with a magnetism that's hard to resist.* She also thought Julia was wrong on one point about Kasey—he knew exactly the effect he had on women, and, just like her, he knew precisely how and when to use it to his advantage.

"He said he was gonna make sure we all knew she was his. Well, message received," she chuckled. "He's a good sport; we can be a little out of control, I guess."

"Speak for yourself and your little girlfriend," Will smirked. "You two are lit when you're fucked up together. Me, James—and now Kasey—just get caught in the crossfire."

"Yeah, but you all live for it." Micki teased with a big grin.

"Yeah, we do," James admitted, taking a hit from the blunt as he shook his head with a grin.

***

At the top of the stairs, Julia veered right towards her room when Kasey intercepted her, saying, "Hold on, we're going to my room. I have a surprise for you." He pulled a small remote from his pocket, pressing it a couple of times before gesturing for her to open the door, his eyes gleaming with anticipation. As she turned the knob and gently pushed the door open, the room was bathed in a soft, twinkling glow of lights that instantly captivated her. Stepping inside, she was enchanted by the magical scene: a bed adorned with ocean-blue silk sheets, a pristine white cashmere blanket draped at its foot, and a silver ice bucket chilling champagne, flanked by two delicate glasses and a small silver tray with chocolate-covered strawberries. The air was filled with her favorite scent and the soothing melody of sensual instrumental music, heightening the romantic atmosphere.

Overwhelmed with emotion, Julia exclaimed, "Baby, I don't know what to say. It's all so beautiful... and incredibly romantic. I can't believe you did this for me." Her gaze swept over every meticulous detail.

"You deserve every bit of it," he said softly, closing the door behind them. "I'm sorry it took so long; you were extremely patient." Julia turned to face him, her skin tingling with warmth, her heart swelling with adoration.

He approached her slowly, tossing the remote aside as his gaze lingered on her—her unbridled happiness, her undeniable beauty—a potent combination that left him breathless.

His fingers slowly unbuttoned her dress, his lips trailing soft kisses down her neck and shoulder. "I really like it when you call me baby," he murmured, his lips grazing her skin and sending a shiver down her spine. "No one's ever called me that."

"Then I'll make sure to say it more often," she whispered, her breath warm against his neck. Her skin was on fire, her nipples hardened, and heat gathered between her legs in anticipation of his touch. Gently slipping the dress from her shoulders, he let it slide down, pooling at her feet in a soft heap. She stood before him in the beautiful lingerie he'd glimpsed in her luggage during her hospital stay—black and red silk, with delicate thorns and roses along the edges—a vision that took his breath away.

"You are exquisite," he murmured, drawing out each word as his gaze traveled slowly, devouring every inch of her. She smiled, flashing him a tempting, playful look as she unbuttoned his linen shirt while he stepped out of his pants. Nestling her head against his chest, she held him tightly, her hands resting against the contours of his lower back as she breathed in his scent. He pressed a kiss to the top of her head, savoring the warmth of her half-dressed, soft body nestled close against his.

"Why did I wait so long to have her like this?" The thought struck him as he brushed his fingers along her bare back, her skin soft and warm beneath his touch. He wanted to let go completely, to lose himself in her, in this moment, in the way she fit so perfectly against him.

Taking her hand, he led her to the bed, where she settled onto the cool silk sheets as he knelt to remove her boots, letting them fall softly to the floor.

"Could you leave your socks on? They're incredibly sexy," he murmured, his hand gently caressing the soft skin of her leg.

"Of course... kiss me," she urged, as anticipation coursed through her veins. He moved over her, craving the feel of her warmth beneath him. Their kisses intensified as she pleaded, "Now, baby, before a goddamn house falls on me or something equally annoying."

"You're such a comedian," he chuckled softly, appreciating how natural it felt to be at ease with her, even in this intimate moment. Shedding his tight boxers, he slowly slid her thong down, his heart pounding with anticipation. Spreading her legs with his, he pressed into her warmth, a long, low sigh escaping his lips.

With one hand caressing his face, the other wrapped around his neck, she held his intense gaze, her eyes flooded with emotion. With all they'd been through—the false starts, the romantic room he'd prepared, and the overwhelming love she felt for him—this moment was even better than she'd dreamed.

Locking eyes with her, he saw only the woman he loved, his entire world narrowing to

that singular moment. Moving slowly, their foreheads touching, he savored every second, fully immersed in the intimacy of their shared connection. Julia had never experienced such tender lovemaking; most of her encounters had been fast and fiery. But this was different—seductive, yet pure, simple, and deeply meaningful. Kasey's touch enveloped her in waves of warmth, heady and strong, like a shot of Jack Daniels. Twice, he paused, prolonging the moment as they both silently wished it would never end.

"You feel incredible," he murmured, his movements slow and deliberate, his lips brushing against her neck.

"I don't think I've ever been so wet in my life," she purred, her words both encouragement and invitation. "Push harder. You won't hurt me." She clung to him, her legs wrapping tightly around his waist as he did exactly what she asked. Knowing it wouldn't be much longer, she raked her nails across his lower back, provoking a sharp intake of breath and a raw cry of her name as he found his release.

Holding her tightly, almost crushingly, he whispered softly into her ear, "You're the best part of my life," pressing himself deeper, unwilling to let her go. He wanted to stay inside her, connected, for as long as he could.

"This is just the beginning, baby... it's only gonna get better," she sighed, a satisfied smile curving her lips.

Their desire for each other had been like a fire waiting to be ignited, and tonight, it finally blazed white-hot, forever altering their friendship and the path of their future together.

***

He woke up blissfully happy, the morning sun warming his face as it filtered through the sheer curtains. Wrapped in a tangle of silk sheets and cashmere, he breathed in the delicate scent of Julia's hair resting against his chest. Memories of their passionate night flooded his mind, bringing a smile to his lips as he watched her sleep. Any fears of not satisfying her had been completely unfounded; they moved together like they were made for each other. Guiding him around her body like a road map, she made him feel comfortable enough to ask for directions. Something in the way she moved and the way she looked at him made him feel she was truly making love to him, not just having sex. The thought stirred emotions in him he hadn't felt in years.

As she lay beside him, her features softened by the dawn's glow and a serene smile on her lips, he felt a surge of affection for her. Lying back with his arms under his head, he reflected on the potential consequences of their actions. Would their newfound closeness complicate their professional dynamic? Their friendship?

Despite the uncertainties, he believed the risk was worth it, recognizing the undeniable connection he shared with her. With a quiet sigh, he resolved to have an honest discussion about their situation, to set boundaries and align expectations. For now, as he tenderly brushed a stray hair from her face, he chose to dwell in the moment, refusing to let future uncertainties overshadow what they had just shared.

***

Silently, he made his way to the kitchen, hoping to avoid anyone, only to run smack dab into Micki, who was leisurely sipping orange juice by the window, soaking up the early morning rays. Leaning casually against the counter, she turned to face him. "Surprised you're up, considering the workout you had last night," she said with a grin. "FYI, these walls are definitely not soundproof, and your little drill sergeant was pretty damn loud."

She grinned, and he blushed, clearly embarrassed, muttering, "Sorry."

"Don't be sorry. I'm happy for you both. It's about friggin' time... just a little jealous," she sighed. "Nothing beats the first time with someone you've been lusting after for a while."

"We'll try to keep it down," he promised, avoiding eye contact as he grabbed two bottles of water and retreated to his room.

"Oh, and maybe wear a shirt today. Tell her to go easy on you... take a look in the mirror," she suggested with a crooked smile.

Returning from the bathroom, he slipped back into bed, where Julia turned with a warm smile. "Good morning."

"Good morning," he said as he tenderly caressed her face.

She gave him a quick peck and declared, "I have to pee," rolling away from him as he watched her walk to the bathroom, bare, every curve catching his eye.

"I bumped into Micki in the kitchen, and she said we were a bit loud last night. Well, not me," he grinned, "you… you were loud." He could hear her peeing since she rarely closed the door all the way.

"Really? I was trying to be quiet," she chuckled as she washed her hands and rinsed her mouth. "I can't help it if you did everything right. Considering your lack of experience, you must be a natural. Honestly, baby, I don't know what you were worried about—you've got some serious game, and you take direction very well," she said with a grin as she hopped back into bed.

With one of the biggest smiles she had ever seen on him, he continued, "And she suggested I ask you to go easy on me… look what you did, sweetheart." He turned, revealing eight distinct red welts running from his lower back to his hips.

"Sweetheart? I like…" she began, but her gaze fell on his back. "Oh my God, I'm so sorry. I didn't realize I was being so rough. You should have said something," she apologized, gently kissing the marks.

"You don't hear me complaining," he said with a goofy grin. "I should wear them like a badge of honor for making it through the night with you." He reclined, putting one arm behind his head as he pulled her close, adding, "Being with you was unlike anything I've experienced before. I've never wanted someone as much as I wanted you last night. I couldn't get enough of you."

"I'm happy it was everything you wanted it to be," she smiled, running her finger over his chest, his flattery pleasing her.

"It was one of the best nights of my life," he admitted, hugging her tight. "I hope it was worth the wait for you," he added, his cheeks turning a light pink.

"Couldn't you tell? You're wearing the answer on your back. I'm sure everyone else heard how much I enjoyed myself," she teased, reaching out to touch him.

"Not yet," he said, gently pushing her hand away. "I have something for you." He rolled over and retrieved a long, thin velvet box from the side table.

"What's this?" she asked eagerly, her eyes dancing with excitement.

Opening the box, she found a white gold charm bracelet with a round charm engraved with "FWB" on one side and "J+K" in elegant cursive on the other. There was also a polished, scalloped-edged, square-shaped charm featuring an engraved image of her beach house, with a tiny diamond representing the sun.

"I knew it would happen soon, and I planned to give it to you the weekend you got sick. I want to have it engraved with the date."

"It's so beautiful. I can't believe you had my house engraved on a charm. It's my favorite place, and after last night, it's even more special to me," she cooed, love spreading across her face.

"The engraving is perfect, and the little sun! I absolutely love it, Kasey, thank you," she exclaimed, her face lighting up. "Put it on me, please."

"I'm glad you like it," he said, delighted by her reaction. "And that's also why we weren't doing it in your closet. I wasn't putting that on a charm." He fastened the bracelet as she chuckled, glad he'd made her wait.

"I absolutely love it, and I love that you thought to do this—all of this," she beamed, gesturing to the fairy lights and champagne. "It's so romantic. And when you called me sweetheart… I really liked that. You overwhelm my senses in the best way possible. Kiss me," she urged, pulling him close, the charm bracelet jingling softly.

"As you wish, sweetheart," he breathed, his voice a low rasp as his eyes burned with desire. Their lips met, the kiss deep and consuming, igniting a slow fire that spread between them. Moving on top of her, his hands skimmed her body with practiced ease, every touch purposeful, leaving her craving more. She arched beneath him, her breath catching as his lips found the sensitive curve of her neck, the world outside fading to nothing.

"You feel so good," he murmured, his voice thick with desire, his hands sliding down to grip her hips as she pulled him closer. She ran her nails down his back, a soft, teasing moan escaping her lips as he moved against her. For now, nothing else mattered—just them, the heat between them building with every shared breath, every deliberate move.

***

Later, Kasey embarked on a run, concealing his "badges of honor" beneath a t-shirt, while Julia took a seat on the deck next to Micki.

"Look at what he gave me this morning!" Julia exclaimed, shaking her bracelet at her.

"Not quite the same as what you gave him," she laughed.

"Shut up, Micki, look at the charms," Julia smirked, shoving her wrist and the bracelet in Micki's face.

"FWB?" Micki asked, her brow furrowing as she inspected it.

"Friends with benefits," Julia replied as Micki turned it over to see the other side. "He was going to give it to me the weekend I got sick."

"Is this your house? It is… how cool," Micki remarked, holding it up to examine it more closely. "It's gorgeous and such a thoughtful way to show how he feels about you. Hmmm, 'let me show you I love you without me saying I love you.' That's what I see."

Julia thought about that for a moment. "You think? He did say he shows his feelings more than he says them. You should've seen it, Micki," she sighed. "He decorated his room with tiny twinkle lights, silk sheets, champagne, chocolate-covered strawberries, and even sexy music. His face was adorable—he looked like he wanted so much to please me."

"Clearly, he succeeded. Three times last night and twice this morning? I'm surprised you can even walk," Micki laughed. "And you might want to cover him up if you're gonna leave marks on him, kiddo."

"Yeah, I was so wrapped up in him I didn't even realize I did that," she confessed with a grin. "God, he was so worth the wait. He kept checking in, making sure everything was exactly how I wanted it. No one has ever been that attentive. I swear, I thought I was gonna black out when he went down on me—it felt that good. I almost said, 'I love you' a couple of times. The intensity in his eyes that first time was overwhelming. I think that's when I scratched him. I just lost all control with him. No one's has ever made me feel like this," she sighed, feeling completely cherished.

"Wow, I've never heard you talk about a man or sex like this before," Micki said, placing her hand on Julia's. "Don't scare him away with the love talk. Don't complicate things right now. He obviously moves at his own pace. Just enjoy all the incredible sex you're having."

"I have no intention of complicating anything... I just want him wrapped around me as much as possible right now. He's like a friggin' feel-good drug," Julia replied with a smile, basking in her newfound happiness. Micki smiled back, content to see her friend so blissfully happy for the first time in six months.

Julia and Kasey spent the rest of the weekend in a joyful haze, one of those sweetly annoying new couples who couldn't keep their hands off each other, drawn like moths to the same flame. Whether nestled in each other's arms by the fire pit or sharing quiet conversations while he prepared food, they were completely lost in their own world. By ten o'clock, they were entwined in bed, making love, falling asleep, then waking hours later to make love again, their passion insatiable. On Sunday morning, as they shared a bath in her claw foot tub, Julia confessed that she was genuinely happy for the first time in months.

***

Their friends-with-benefits arrangement quickly settled into a familiar routine. Every Friday afternoon at four, they'd head to his place or the shore, with her staying until Monday morning when they'd head to work together. He'd cook for her, sometimes teaching her basic cooking skills, or they'd opt for takeout. Their evenings typically included cuddling and making out on the couch while watching their favorite shows or movies, followed by long, intimate talks in bed, their naked bodies entwined, ending with passionate, loving sex. Sleeping late the next day, they'd wake up and do it all over again.

Occasionally, they'd engage in training sessions, with him teaching her defensive moves for self-protection. He proved to be a patient teacher, discovering she was stronger and more athletic than he first realized. When they took showers together, he washed her hair, and she gave him oral sex. They used their time apart during the week to handle tasks that might detract from their weekends together, including Kasey's need for personal time. Julia understood his need for space completely, which was why they devoted their weekends solely to each other.

Work had never been better, with stolen kisses in her closet adding a thrilling element to their day. One day, fueled by her heightened desire and hormones just before her period, she worked him up so much that, against his better judgment, they ended up having sex against the closet wall—her legs wrapped around him, his mouth on hers to muffle her moans. As she'd predicted, their physical connection kept getting better as he grew more confident in understanding her desires. Both of them found immense happiness in their arrangement.

***

It was the ninth of June, her thirtieth birthday—the first she would spend without her family. Opting for a low-key celebration of all her "firsts" this year without them, she declined any grand plans. Despite Micki's insistence on making a big deal of it, she begged off. Instead, she chose to spend the weekend at the shore with Kasey, doing what she enjoyed most at the moment: having sex and spending time with him.

She gently suggested new positions and settings, like bending her over the arm of the couch or making love outdoors on the double lounger beneath a blanket and the stars. Kasey appreciated both her gentle introduction to these new experiences and the experiences themselves. However, he always returned to his default—extremely loving, face-to-face, slow, and tender sex.

Reaching under the bed, he pulled out a box, rolled over to face her, and said, "Happy Birthday," as he handed it to her. Her eyes, sparkling with excitement and curiosity, widened as she eagerly opened the box. Inside, nestled among the tissue paper, was the Microphone Crystal clutch bag. Delight sparkled in her eyes, adding an extra twinkle to their already radiant glow.

"Oh my God! It's beautiful—a Judith Leiber bag shaped like a microphone! I absolutely love it. Look at how it sparkles! I can't wait to wear it out."

"You love to sing, and you're so good at it," he said, smiling. "Open it—there's something inside." She pulled out an exquisite pair of dangling South Sea pearl and diamond earrings in white gold.

"Oh, Kasey, this is too much—they're stunning."

"It's your thirtieth birthday. I wanted to give you something you'd never forget."

"Well, I certainly won't forget this," she said, playing with her earrings and bag. "Or the beautiful flowers at work, my favorite home-cooked dinner—and great sex... thank you for it all," she sighed, resting her head on his chest, never more perfectly content.

***

Chapter 12: Emotional Baggage

"I wish I didn't have to go," she whined, tugging her jacket on reluctantly as she prepared to leave on Saturday night, feeling cheated out of her whole weekend with Kasey.

"I know, I don't want you to go either," he said with a gentle smile. "But I have to leave early in the morning, and if you're here, I'll never get any sleep. I need to see my father, so I'm bracing myself for that. Besides, I thought I'd already made it up to you," he teased, pulling her close for a lingering kiss. "I'll walk you out, Carl's waiting. I'll see you Monday."

Julia gave a teasing pout but nodded, heading for the door. As she passed, he gave her a quick slap on the butt, earning a raised eyebrow and a smirk.

Surprised to hear from him on Sunday, she picked up quickly. "Hey, what's up? Didn't expect a call from you today."

"Julia?"

"What's wrong? Are you okay?" She immediately felt a pang of worry—something was off.

"No... I'm not. I need you."

"Where are you?"

"Home."

Before he could say more, she cut him off. "Hold on, baby, I'm coming. I'll be there as fast as I can." His tone was unlike anything she'd heard before, and she realized just how serious this was.

When he opened the door, she was struck by his appearance. His hair was a mess, his eyes bloodshot and watery, and a deep cut with a nasty bruise was forming above his left cheek.

"Oh my God, what the fuck happened to you!?" she gasped, her heart racing as she stepped inside, eyes scanning him up and down.

"Your face," she said, her voice thick with concern as she reached to touch his cheek. His shirt hung open, exposing two dark lines of bruising across his chest.

"You can defend yourself—how did this happen?" A chilling thought crossed her mind. "Did your father do this?"

He pulled her into a tight embrace, kicked the door shut, and rested his head on hers without a word. When he set the alarm, she slipped off her shoes. Taking her hand, he led her upstairs to his bedroom. She noticed the knuckles on his right hand were swollen and bloodied.

"Are you hurt anywhere else?" she asked softly, her hand gently brushing his shoulder.

"I'm fine, really. Don't worry about me." His voice was heavy with sadness as he tightened his hold on her hand. "No more questions, please... I just didn't want to be alone."

"You're not alone," she whispered, resting her hand warmly over his. "I'm here." He let out a breath and murmured, "You have no idea how much it means to me that you're here."

"Of course I came, baby. Why wouldn't I? You need me."

He lay down on the bed, and she slipped in beside him, resting her head on his shoulder with a gentle sigh. Worry crept through her as her fingers traced softly over the bruises on his chest. He exhaled, eyes drifting shut. They lay together in silence, the only sound the distant hum of street noise filtering in.

When she noticed his breathing had slowed and he'd fallen asleep, she gently slipped out of his arms and moved to the window.

Gazing at the street below, a physical ache welled up inside her seeing him so broken. Lost in thought, she didn't notice him slip out of bed and approach until his arms wrapped around her, making her jump.

"Shit, you scared me," she said, turning with a worried look. "Are you okay? Do you need something?"

"Yes, you. Come back to bed," he murmured. They undressed and lay together, her head resting on his chest, her leg draped over his. As time passed, she thought he just wanted to feel her beside him. But without warning, he rolled on top of her, catching her completely off guard.

"Kasey, wait," she said, inhaling sharply and pressing her hands against his chest. When he didn't stop, she pleaded, "Stop, you're hurting me." She grabbed his face, forcing him to look at her. "Kasey, stop! Where are you? Because you're not here with me."

Her voice broke through the fog in his mind, snapping him back to reality. The shame hit him like a punch. How had it come to this? Why couldn't he stop himself?

Realizing what he was doing, his face twisted with pain and regret. "I'm so sorry," he murmured, pulling away and sitting on the edge of the bed, head in his hands.

She couldn't bear to see him so unlike himself, so lost in pain. Wrapping her arms around him, she rested her head on his shoulder.

"For fuck's sake, Kasey, what happened? Please, talk to me."

He turned to her, his gaze heavy with vulnerability, speaking volumes without words. "I'm sorry. I just... can't right now. I never wanted you to see me like this," he said, his voice thick with sadness and embarrassment.

She hated seeing him so fragile, so unlike the man she knew. But no matter how much it hurt to witness, leaving him alone wasn't an option. She could feel the pain he was trying so hard to keep hidden.

"Whatever it is, you don't have to face it alone," she whispered. "I care about you, Kasey. You don't have to explain everything right now—just know I'm here, and when you're ready, I'll listen."

Gently, she laid him back, pulled the covers over him, and rested her head on his chest, her fingers tracing soft circles over his stomach. The weight of the comforter seemed like a poor shield against whatever demons were clawing at him, but it was all she could do to make him feel safe.

He closed his eyes, gradually drifting off to sleep.

In the stillness of the night, she stirred from sleep to the soft brush of his fingers through her hair. Half-asleep, she instinctively leaned into the warmth of his body as he spooned her, his breath a gentle caress against her skin. He brushed her hair aside, pressing his lips to the nape of her neck. Slowly, they moved together in a silent rhythm, her soft moans breaking the quiet as warmth spread through her body.

Her fingers gripped the sheet as she leaned forward, his hand lifting her leg gently. A soft gasp escaped, muffled against the pillow. His hands found hers, their fingers intertwining as he made love to her with a tenderness that spoke of silent apology and forgiveness. Even in sleep, she felt his need—the unspoken ache in his touch pressing against her own. He lingered within her; their connection held tight until it slipped away as they drifted back into sleep, his arms securely around her. For Julia, it felt like a vivid, sensual dream in the quiet dark.

For Kasey, making love to Julia was more than just a physical release—it touched his very core. In her presence, he found solace, and in those silent hours, he felt a connection that transcended words—a bond rooted in vulnerability, trust, and forgiveness. In her, he found a safe harbor from the storm raging inside him, a fragile peace that he clung to with everything he had.

***

The morning light brought a familiar sight: Kasey, immaculately dressed and clean-shaven, standing in the kitchen making her tea. Without turning, he sensed her presence, his voice soft and heavy with remorse.

"I'm sorry," he said quietly. "It makes me sick to think I hurt you. I don't know what came over me. Last night... it's a blur, and I regret it more than I can say."

She walked over, took the tea from his hands, set it down, and wrapped her arms around him. "Oh, baby, I forgot all about it. Don't beat yourself up." She rested her head on his chest, adding softly, "You more than made up for it later." She offered him a gentle smile. "I forgive you."

His blue-gray eyes were clouded and stormy, avoiding hers. "Thank you for not pushing me to talk last night. It wasn't what I needed. You saved me from what would've been a dark night alone."

"I'm here whenever you're ready to talk," she murmured, noticing in the morning light that the bruise and cut on his cheek looked even worse.

"Maybe you should stay home today, ice that cheek, and get the cut checked out. It looks like it might scar that beautiful face of yours," she said, her tone full of concern.

"No, really, it's nothing. I'm fine," he replied softly.

It might be nothing on the outside, she thought, *but it was certainly something on the inside.* She held back from asking about his father or what happened, even though not knowing twisted her up inside.

***

She gave him a wide berth at work, but if she'd thought he was quiet before, she'd been mistaken. He barely spoke unless she initiated the conversation, burying himself in his work.

By Thursday afternoon, she'd had enough and walked into his office. "Kasey, please, talk to me. You need to let someone in—let it be me. I'm really worried about you. I'm skipping the fashion show tomorrow. I didn't want to go without you anyway. Come with me to the beach for the weekend, just the two of us. I'll even cook for us—barbecue. I swear I can do it," she added with a hopeful smile.

"You? Cooking? Are you sure you're worried about me?" he teased. "Fine, I'll come—I could use a laugh."

"Bite me," she replied with a smirk, pleased he'd agreed to come.

"Ah, there she is," he chuckled. "It was getting weird with you being all nice."

"Again, bite me," she said, rolling her eyes as she turned to leave.

"I think that could be arranged," he said with a grin, looking just a little like his old self.

***

The next afternoon, the car service dropped off her convertible. They packed their bags, put the top down, and with Kasey at the wheel, set off for the Jersey shore. He always relished

driving her car, and whenever they were together, the driver's seat was his. Though they could have flown, she knew the drive would be therapeutic for him. The trip was uneventful—Julia chattered about anything that came to mind while Kasey enjoyed the road and the warmth of the sun on their faces.

That evening they ordered dinner, watched a movie with his arm snugly around her, and

headed to bed early.

As the credits rolled, he turned to her. "Mind if we just sleep tonight? I'm really tired." She couldn't tell if it was exhaustion or a trace of melancholy in his voice.

"Of course not," she replied with a smile. "I hope I'm not some chore you think you need to take care of."

"Sweetheart, sex with you is never a chore," he replied with a smile. "I'm just a little out of it tonight."

"Well, I think I can manage to control myself," she teased, leaning in for a soft kiss.

"Are you sure? Because I rarely see you show any self-control," he teased as he stood up from the couch.

She playfully punched his leg. "Shut up, Kasey."

Later, once they were in bed, she gave him a slow massage, rubbing his shoulders and back to ease his tension. That night, she drifted off as she always did—with him spooning her, his face nestled in her neck and hair, the steady rhythm of his breathing lulling her into sleep.

***

They spent the day strolling along the beach, basking in the sun's warmth and each other's quiet company. For dinner, he expertly grilled chicken and portobello mushrooms while she was relegated to salad—the only dish he'd allow her to prepare. They dined alfresco, savoring the meal, then sat in companionable silence, listening to the steady rhythm of the waves.

Breaking the stillness, she asked softly, "Do you feel like you can talk about what happened last weekend?"

"Let's head inside," he suggested, swatting into the air. "The gnats are starting to get annoying."

While he busied himself making tea in the kitchen, she dimmed the lights, lit a candle, and picked a mellow playlist to set the mood.

"Please, none of your songs of desperation," he remarked as he entered the room. "That'd be a bit much right now."

"Give me some credit," she replied with a smile. "You're not the only one who pays attention." She patted the cushion next to her. "Come, sit."

"Take your time," she said gently. "You can tell me anything. No judgment, remember?"

He set down the tea, his voice low. "I remember."

He took a deep breath, memories settling heavily between them. "I had a close bond with my mother," he began, his words slow, as though each one carried a weight of its own. "Even before she fought breast cancer, we spent so much time together. Until I was about six, my parents and I traveled a lot, or I was left with a nanny—I barely remember those years. Later, I was home-schooled by tutors and didn't attend a

215

regular school until high school. My mother eventually decided to stay home, wanting to give me a stable environment. She missed me, and I missed her too. My father started traveling alone, and from that point, my parents were physically separated, though he wouldn't divorce her. He had his own bedroom and showed up sporadically, mainly to argue with her about money. Despite his old money name, he lacked real wealth; it was my mother who had the money."

She lost her mom to breast cancer when she was ten, and then her father—selfish as he was—drank himself to death less than two years later. After that, she was raised by her maternal grandparents and lived a happy, though sheltered life with them. Her grandfather was an aviation engineer who designed key landing gear components and sold the patents to the aviation industry. He made smart investments with the money he earned. By the time my mother was twenty-one, she was alone and in control of a significant fortune, having lost her grandparents within a year of each other."

"How sad," Julia murmured empathetically, unaware of the deeper sorrow still to come. Kasey had rarely spoken about his family; all she knew was that his mother had passed from cancer when he was twelve and that he had no real relationship with his father.

Kasey took a sip of his tea, setting it down slowly. "After her grandparents passed, she was vulnerable and wealthy—a combination that drew my father in. They met at a breast cancer fundraiser. After one of their nastier fights, I asked her why she married him. She told me he was handsome and charming, that he promised she'd never have to be alone. Later, I realized he was a narcissistic liar who took advantage of her kind nature. He isolated her from her friends and rushed her into marriage right after she graduated college; she was twenty-two, and he was thirty-one. At first, things were good, as long as they traveled and he could spend her money."

Julia noticed Kasey's growing discomfort, watching him fidget with his hands—something she'd never seen him do before.

"Four years into the marriage, everything changed when she found out she was pregnant with me. Out of nowhere, he told her he didn't want children—it blindsided her completely. They'd never discussed kids before getting married; she'd assumed he'd want them to carry on the family name. Everything shifted between them. He showed no interest in her pregnancy, and began staying away for longer and longer, and their relationship eventually fell apart."

He continued softly, "At first, he demanded she get an abortion, but she refused. Hoping it would make him care more, she gave me his name—Kayson Ambrose Van Cortland IV. But she always called me Kasey. When I turned twenty-one, I legally changed it to just Kasey Cortland and dropped the rest."

"That's quite a name," Julia replied, realizing just how different their backgrounds were. Kasey had grown up with wealth, while she'd spent her early years on a simple ranch until her teenage years.

"It didn't make a difference to him," he said flatly. "He wasn't father material. He mostly ignored me unless I tried to stand up for her when they fought." He paused, his gaze distant. "I learned most of this after finding a letter my mother had written to him but never mailed. It was tucked into a book she'd read when she got sick, and in it, she listed all the horrible things he'd done to her. When she realized I'd read it, she tried to soften the blow by saying she was just angry and venting. But I knew the truth."

Julia listened intently, absorbed but growing increasingly concerned about the emotional toll it was taking on him. He looked down at his lap and, in a barely audible voice, he said,

"Mostly, he verbally abused her, but there were times I saw him smack or push her hard into things. There were times she had nasty bruises after he'd been home. I tried to get between them once when I was ten. He grabbed me and flung me across the room. I hit the sharp edge of something—I don't remember what—and split my lip open. He just walked out, leaving my frantic mother to take care of me alone."

His voice quivered as he went on, "She made me promise to never get between them, to stay in my room when he showed up. I promised, even though I knew I was lying. I felt guilty, but I wasn't going to let him hurt her in front of me again." Julia squeezed his leg, her chest aching as she imagined a young Kasey standing up to protect his mother.

"She endured so much," he said, bitterness creeping into his tone. "For months, I watched her fight both cancer and the relentless pressure he put on her to alter her will. He felt entitled to her estate, though he was distant and cruel, showing no interest in supporting her through the illness. Even in her weakened state, she stood up to him. Making arrangements for my future was her way of protecting me, shielding me from him—but it only fueled his rage."

He inhaled deeply, tears welling in his eyes, and pressed on. "Even though she was barely able to get out of bed, she got up when she heard him yelling at me. He insisted I didn't deserve her money, that it rightfully belonged to him for putting up with a useless kid like me, who ruined their lives."

"Oh no," Julia murmured, a pang of disbelief hitting her as she wondered how any father could be so cruel.

"When she came to my bedroom door and told him to leave me alone or she'd write him out of her will, he lost it. He grabbed her by both shoulders and shook her violently, screaming in her face."

Tears streamed down his cheeks, his breath breaking with each inhale as he trembled, overwhelmed by the memory. "Without thinking, I charged at him, hitting him from behind and sending him crashing into my mother. They both went down hard. He fell on top of her, and she hit her head on the hardwood, knocking her unconscious. He got up and punched me in the face, sending me straight into the door frame and knocking the wind out of me."

Julia gasped, her voice thick with disbelief. "What the fuck?"

Looking away, he sobbed, his voice barely above a whisper. "I watched him lift my mother up and carry her back to her bed. He called her nurse, who was off duty that afternoon and lied, saying my mother had come to check on me after I'd fallen and given myself a black eye. He convinced her that my mother slipped and hit her head by accident. I never spoke up—I was too afraid of him. I was a coward, and... it was my fault."

His chest heaved as he tried to speak through his tears. "My mom passed away two days later, never regaining consciousness. I broke my promise to her. I hit him, and in doing that, I shortened whatever time she had left. It was all my fault."

Sobbing uncontrollably now, he bent forward, head in his hands. Words came out choked, laced with anguish. "I didn't get to say goodbye. To say I was sorry. To tell her I loved her. It was all my fault that she was gone so soon." He turned and buried his head in Julia's shoulder, his breaths shuddering between sobs. "I miss her so much. I can't get over the fact that I hurt the person I loved most I've carried this for so long, Julia," he continued, his voice breaking. "Every time I look in the mirror, I see the boy who failed his mother."

Julia wrapped her arms around him tightly, rocking him gently as she tried to hold it together for his sake. But the tears came anyway, as the weight of his guilt sank in—she couldn't fathom how alone he must have felt all these years.

"Shhh... Kasey... shhh, it wasn't your fault," she whispered, kissing his head softly. "You were just a twelve-year-old boy. It was an accident, one caused by your miserable father. Your mom knew you loved her, and if she knew the guilt you're carrying, I'm sure she'd tell you she understood why you broke that promise. She'd be proud you defended her."

"But I hurt her—just like I hurt you—because I wasn't thinking," he confessed, his voice thick with pain.

"Kasey, you've got to give yourself a break. People make mistakes, and they're forgiven. You were a child in an impossible situation—you did the best you could."

He paused, his chest heaving as he tried to gather himself. "Last weekend, when I went to his place, he immediately started demanding more money, wanting changes to the trust. Things got intense. I told him I was turning the trust over to the lawyer and never wanted to see or hear from him again. When I told him he was a horrible father and a prick for a husband, he backhanded me, full force. His ring cut my face, and I knew that was the last time he'd ever hit me. I punched him square in the face, pretty sure I broke his nose, and told him to never contact me again."

Kasey's voice dropped, thick with rage and sorrow. "As I walked away, he called out, 'Just remember, boy, it was you who knocked your mother down that day.' I turned to confront him, and he hit me with a chair. I grabbed him by the throat, pinned him against the wall, and I swear, Julia, I could have killed him if I'd wanted to. But all I could see was my mother, reminding me he wasn't worth it. So, instead, I punched the wall right next to his face. Didn't say another word—just walked out, came home, and called you."

What he revealed shattered her, realizing he suffered as a child what she'd endured as an adult. He carried enormous guilt with no support. She couldn't imagine facing it all alone without the comfort he'd given her. "What a monster," she hissed, disgust evident in her voice.

Kasey sighed as if a tremendous weight had been lifted, his breath coming in soft, stuttered gasps. She held him, stroking his hair, and spoke quietly. "That's some messed-up shit, Kasey. Way too much for one person to bear alone. You've been there for me through everything—always listening, letting me just dump it all on you. You never make me feel weak for drowning in it. I want to be that for you. Anytime you need to talk, anytime it gets too heavy, I'm here. You can tell me anything."

With a heart as bruised as his face, he murmured, "Expressing my feelings has never come easy. But in the future, if I need to talk, I'll come to you. I can't imagine discussing this with anyone else." He wiped his eyes on his sleeve, adding quietly, "I'm sorry... I've never lost control like that in front of anyone before."

He hated the way it felt—like his emotions were raw and exposed, clawing their way out of him. But with her, it felt... safer. Different.

"I'm not just anyone," she whispered, her fingers gently tracing his cheek.

"No, you're not," he replied softly. "I didn't mean it like that. I just don't like losing control of my emotions... nothing good ever comes from it."

She took his hand, squeezing gently. "You're way too hard on yourself. You can't keep everything bottled up—it's not good for you. Anything you need, anything at all, just talk to me."

He squeezed her hand. "What I need right now, is to walk this off."

"You want some company?" she offered, her smile delicate, loving, and nearly impossible to resist. "I promise I won't say a word unless you want me to."

"Of course," he said softly. As they reached the water's edge and started their walk, he took her hand. After a long silence, he squeezed her fingers and whispered, "Thank you—for being here." It wasn't much, but it was enough.

Later, when they went to bed, Julia thought he'd be too emotionally spent for intimacy—but she was wrong. He made love to her with surprising passion, his touch deliberate, reverent, as if he were piecing himself back together through her. She thought he was showing gratitude for her comfort and support, but in reality, he was revealing just how deeply in love he was with her. Trusting her enough to share his darkest secret, she was now the only person, aside from his father, who knew what had happened. They were both in love, yet neither knew how to bridge the unspoken gap. For now, their connection was enough—a quiet understanding, deepening with each passing moment.

***

Kasey never mentioned his father again, and they settled back into their routine. Realizing he had raw emotions to work through, he saw Dr. Dresden for a few weeks, trying to get a grip on his unresolved feelings. Though he stayed quiet and reserved, Julia thought he seemed a little happier, his mood a bit lighter.

When Julia confided in Micki about Kasey's struggles with his mother's death and his father's hatred, Micki said, "Jeez, Jules, he's dealing with some major trauma. It explains so much. My heart breaks for him. He went through hell during the funeral—it must've been so triggering, yet he just soldiered on, only concerned with making things easier for you. I can't imagine the strength it took to do that. I just hope there's nothing else lurking you don't know about."

"He helps me deal with the loss of my family every single day, and I could never thank him enough for what he did for me then. He's carrying some heavy emotional baggage, but he still protects me and takes care of me like I'm the most important person in his life. I'm gonna do whatever I can to help him, no matter what," she said with quiet resolve.

"You two definitely support each other," Micki observed. "No denying that."

Julia changed the subject. "Are you guys coming for vacation soon?"

"Yeah, I was thinking the first of July, we'll get three weekends with you guys. That work?"

"Perfect, I can't wait to see you both. We'll make them three-day weekends."

"That's great. I love it when you're there with us. Can't wait to see you and him together—still at it like bunnies?' Micki laughed.

"You forget, we only see each other on weekends, so yeah... sometimes," Julia chuckled. "But I promise to keep it down this time. I think he was embarrassed when you talked to him in the kitchen the next morning. We might be a bit much for him sometimes—he seems so sheltered when it comes to our sexcapades."

"I don't know, kiddo. He was in complete control and knew exactly what he was doing when he had me cornered in the kitchen. I'm not kidding—I'd have been on my knees for him in a second if things were different. He had me all hot and bothered without even kissing me; the heat coming off him was intense. But he never crossed the line. Do you know what he whispered in my ear? She's mine," Micki laughed. "He pretty much told me you were off-limits."

"I didn't know that," Julia said with a smile. "I thought he kissed you, and for a hot minute, I was jealous."

"That's different for you."

"I know. Sometimes it's a little disorienting to feel this way about him," she sighed. "But I'm deeply in love with him, Micki. I think it's time I tell him. I know he loves me—I can feel it."

"You must be in love; he's had you off balance since the day you met him. Don't get me wrong, I'm thrilled for you, but be careful, kiddo. Don't lose yourself."

"I'll be fine. I couldn't be happier," she said, recalling her dad gave her the same advice. "I can't wait to see you guys."

***

Chapter 13: I Thought I'd Never See You Again

"Hello, Spike. Long time, no see."

Kasey froze. That voice—it was unmistakable. His heart raced as he looked up, barely daring to believe his eyes. Time seemed to stop as their gazes locked, the air between them charged and electric.

"Ren?" Kasey whispered, his voice cracking. He shot to his feet, rounding the desk in a blur, and threw his arms around the tall, familiar figure. His embrace was fierce, desperate, as if holding Ren tighter might anchor the moment to reality.

"I can't believe you're here," Kasey said, his voice thick with emotion. He clung to Ren, breathing in the scent he thought he'd lost forever—a mix of sandalwood and something unmistakably him. Disbelief swirled with pure, unfiltered joy, making Kasey's head spin.

"I never thought I'd see you again," he murmured, his voice shaking as he fought to steady it.

"I always knew I'd find you," Ren replied, his breath warm against Kasey's ear. "I just didn't think it would take ten years."

Their embrace lingered, neither wanting to let go. Heads bowed close, arms locked tightly, they shared a silence heavy with emotions too big for words.

From her desk, Julia watched, unable to look away, captivated by the raw beauty of the reunion unfolding before her. She sat back, letting the moment play out.

Finally, Kasey pulled back, his hands still gripping Ren's shoulders as if afraid to lose him again. He studied Ren's face, his chest tightening. "How did you even find me?"

Ren chuckled softly, the sound as familiar as it was soothing. "Seriously? I just Googled you. You're all over photos with your boss. She's kind of hard to miss." His eyes flicked briefly toward Julia's office before returning to Kasey with a fond smile. "It took me a second to realize you'd changed your name."

"I did. It was because of my father," Kasey grinned. "Changing my name felt good. Pissing him off was just a bonus."

"My God, Ren, you look incredible... and your hair," Kasey murmured, captivated.

Ren's transformation was stunning. His once-short hair now flowed in long, layered waves of blue-black, framing his striking features and cascading past his shoulders. His lean frame had filled out with defined muscle, and his sleek black suit and deep blue silk tee only amplified his effortless charm. In his dark, almond-shaped eyes he saw the boy he once loved looking back at him, now hidden beneath a more striking gaze.

Ren stepped closer, his voice low, rich. "And you, Spike... Damn, nobody should look this good."

Kasey's blush deepened, his breath catching for a moment. "Still quite the charmer, huh? Sit down already—you haven't even told me why you're here."

Ren glanced toward Julia's office, catching her eye with a smile before settling on the couch. Kasey followed, trying to calm the storm of emotions swirling in his chest. When Ren's knee brushed against his leg, a jolt shot through him, stealing his breath.

"I moved to New York a few weeks ago for work," Ren said, his voice casual, though his gaze lingered on Kasey. He glanced toward Julia's office and smiled when their eyes met. "And I figured it was time to finally reconnect."

"Did you come with Kaede?" Kasey asked, his voice tinged with hesitation as questions whirled through his mind.

"Did you Google me?" Ren teased, his grin widening as he gave Kasey's knee a gentle squeeze.

"I looked you up years ago," Kasey admitted softly, warmth spreading through him at Ren's touch.

"No," Ren replied after a brief pause, his expression softening. "We divorced five months ago. I'm here alone... and I was hoping we could grab dinner, maybe catch up. I've missed you so much."

"Anata ga koishii desu," Kasey murmured, meeting Ren's gaze steadily.

"You kept with it?" Ren asked, surprise flickering in his eyes as Kasey confessed his longing in Japanese—a phrase that spoke of deep yearning.

Kasey nodded. "I took lessons for a few years. It helped with work, and... I wanted to keep part of you with me."

"Impressive," Ren murmured, his gaze lingering as unspoken memories seemed to flood the space between them.

"So, you're really divorced?" Kasey asked, needing to hear it again to believe it.

"Yeah," Ren said quietly, his smile faltering for a moment. "It was never right from the beginning—you know that. We should've ended things sooner, but our families kept pressuring us to stay together.

"My grandmother had a long talk with me before she passed two years ago. She told me to stop living a lie and to go find my happiness. So, I finally gathered the courage to make the change, even if it meant losing my family."

He glanced away briefly, then back at Kasey, his smile broadening, though his eyes betrayed a flicker of fear. "You know I've always dreamed of living here, so... here I am."

"I'm so sorry about your grandmother," Kasey said softly, his voice laced with sympathy. "I know how much she meant to you."

"Thanks. I miss her every day. She was the one person who always had my back, no matter what."

"I take it your father didn't handle the divorce well," Kasey remarked.

Ren sighed, his expression tightening. "I haven't spoken to my father since Kaede and I split. He's still the same—he cut me off from the family business. My mother talks to me when he's not around, but it's complicated."

He paused, a flicker of sadness in his eyes before his tone lightened. "So, I struck out on my own and landed a job at Urban Style Interiors here in the city. It's not exactly my dream job, but it got me to New York... where I hoped I could reconnect with my best friend."

Ren patted Kasey's leg, his familiar smile paired with the gentle touch sending a wave of warmth through Kasey's chest.

"So, how about dinner soon?" Ren proposed.

"Absolutely," Kasey said, his enthusiasm bubbling up. "Come over to my place on Friday. I'll cook, and we can catch up... just the two of us."

"That sounds perfect. I'd love to see your place, spend time with you," Ren replied, his gaze fixed intensely on Kasey. "This is blowing my mind. After everything that's happened, I wasn't sure if you'd want to see me."

His voice dropped, his grin turning sheepish. "For a minute, I thought you changed your name hoping I wouldn't find you. But that was ridiculous. I kept searching, and there you were—with your beautiful boss."

Kasey's heart squeezed. "I meant it when I told you to come find me," he said, his voice thick with emotion. "I'm thrilled you did... I still can't believe you're here."

He started to reach for Ren's hand, the moment charged with unspoken meaning—

But the soft click of Julia's heels and her sudden entrance shattered his focus.

They both stood as Kasey made the introduction. "Julia, I'd like you to meet Ren Ito—my best friend from high school. Ren, this is Julia Masters."

"Very nice to meet you, Ren," she said, offering a warm smile as she shook his hand. Up close, she couldn't help noticing the mesmerizing depth of his dark eyes, the smoothness of his complexion, and the lustrous sheen of his long black hair.

"Pleasure to meet you, Julia," Ren said with a warm smile. He glanced at Kasey, their eyes meeting briefly in a knowing exchange—a silent callback to an inside joke from their favorite anime.

"Please, call me Jules," she offered, releasing his hand.

"Is there anything you need?" Kasey asked, watching them both size each other up.

"No, just being nosy," she grinned. "I had to see who your extremely handsome friend is. Your hair is gorgeous," she added, wondering briefly if it felt as silky as it looked.

"Thank you," Ren replied, flashing her an intense, straightforward gaze. "And if we're handing out compliments, you're a tiny bundle of gorgeous yourself."

Julia glanced up from beneath her long lashes, her lips curving into a smile as a faint blush crept into her cheeks. *Tiny bundle of gorgeous?* The way he said it made her pulse jump. "Thank you," she replied, a little breathless.

"I was just about to head out. It was a pleasure meeting you, Jules," Ren said. With a confident stride, he approached Kasey's desk, scribbled his number on a sticky note, and pressed it playfully to Kasey's chest. His grin was pure mischief.

"I'll see you Friday. Bye, Spike... call me," he added, leaning in just slightly before slipping on a pair of round, metal-frame sunglasses.

"Hey, Ren," Julia called, her voice teasing as he reached the door. "Has anyone ever told you that you look like a sexy vampire straight out of a steamy romance novel with those glasses?"

Ren paused, a slow smile spreading across his face. Lowering his glasses just enough to meet her gaze, he replied, "You're the first, Jules. I'll take it as a compliment."

He winked, then turned and strode away, leaving a trail of effortless charm in his wake.

***

She turned to see Kasey, with a soft smile, taking Ren's number and rubbing the paper between his fingers, lost in thought before saving it in his phone. A pang of jealousy pricked at Julia, sharp and unexpected, leaving her unsettled.

"Did he call you Spike?" she asked, her voice light but edged with curiosity.

"Yes," Kasey chuckled softly. "He gave me that nickname after a character in one of our favorite anime. It started as a joke, but it ended up sticking. He said I reminded him of the character... though I never quite knew if that was a compliment." A warm fondness shone in his gaze as he explained. "Ren's the one who introduced me to manga and anime. I loved learning about his Japanese culture, while all he ever wanted was to be American," he added with a laugh, his eyes distant, lost in the memory.

Snapping out of his nostalgia, Kasey brightened. "I made plans to see him for dinner this Friday. I won't make it to the shore with you, but I'll go the following weekend if that's okay. Will's going, so you won't be alone."

"Sure," Julia replied, though her disappointment was palpable, even if Kasey didn't notice. After a pause, she added hopefully, "Maybe you could come on Saturday instead?"

"I think we'll need more than one dinner to catch up. I'll probably see him on Saturday too," Kasey said with a cheerful grin, unintentionally deepening Julia's dismay.

Her chest tightened. "Could I come over tonight?" she asked tentatively. "I'd like to hear more about your roommate."

"Of course," he replied, tucking the post-it in his drawer with casual ease, completely oblivious to the weight behind her words.

Returning to her office, Julia sat down, her thoughts spinning. She couldn't shake the noticeable shift in Kasey's demeanor and body language since Ren had arrived. He'd been distracted, distant in a way she'd never seen before. Her intuition sent up major red flags, a feeling she couldn't ignore.

***

As they cleaned up after dinner, Julia noticed him quietly humming while he loaded the dishwasher. It was unfamiliar to her, but the way Kasey seemed lost in it—focused yet distant—made her wonder where his thoughts had wandered.

"I've never heard you hum before—you're in a good mood," she observed, her tone curious but edged with something she couldn't quite name.

"Huh? Didn't realize I was," he replied, slightly distracted.

He'd been humming the theme song from Cowboy Bebop, the first manga he and Ren had read together. Adapted into an anime, it was something he and Ren had watched together countless times—something he'd revisited even more often alone in the years since.

"Thinking about Ren?" Julia blurted, tired of waiting for him to bring it up.

He shot her a sidelong glance, one eyebrow raised. "Are you jealous?" he teased, though his voice lacked the usual bite.

She avoided his gaze, her fingers gripping the back of a chair as she pushed it under the table. "Should I be?"

"I thought this was supposed to be just sex, no strings attached," he replied casually, though even as the words left his mouth, he felt the lie. Kasey was in love with her, and he suspected she felt something deeper, too. But Ren had been his first love—his first everything—and he had to see him. The pull was so strong, he was willing to risk hurting Julia just to see if the love was still there.

Her silence hung in the air, heavy and sharp. Finally, she spoke softly, breaking the tension. "I think it's time you told me about him. I know he's more than just a best friend. He

232

was your first, wasn't he? The roommate you spent three years with." She looked up, meeting his gaze with quiet intensity. "I could see it—the way you looked at each other. He means a lot to you."

Kasey felt warmth creep into his cheeks under her perceptive gaze, her words landing with disarming precision. "I didn't realize you were paying such close attention," he admitted, a sheepish grin tugging at his lips.

"I didn't have to—it was pretty obvious."

He sighed, rubbing the back of his neck. "Let's head upstairs, and I'll tell you about him. Want some wine?"

"Sure," she agreed, her voice steady, though her heart beat faster. Julia braced herself for the emotional terrain ahead, her thoughts a swirling mix of curiosity, jealousy, and something she couldn't yet name.

***

She settled in front of the fireplace, knees pulled close, her gaze lost in the flickering dance of the flames. Normally a source of comfort, tonight they sent a shiver down her spine, whispering unsettling tales and casting shadows that felt heavy with foreboding.

Kasey entered the room carrying two glasses of wine, his shirt casually undone, pants resting low on his hips to reveal his sculpted abs. The mere sight of him made her heart skip a beat. She glanced his way, unable to suppress a sigh. "I never tire of telling you how handsome you are."

"Thank you, sweetheart," he said with a warm smile, handing her a glass before settling beside her on the large New Zealand sheepskin pelt. He'd bought it for her after she once confessed a wish to make love by the fire, the softness against her bare skin becoming one of her favorite sensations.

Leaning back on the pillows propped against the bed, he wrapped an arm around her, and she nestled her head against his chest, listening to the steady rhythm of his heartbeat beneath her cheek.

"Should I just dive in?" he asked, gently toying with her hair.

"Whenever you're ready."

"A year before Ren came to the school, I didn't have any real friends—mostly because I didn't want any. I was a pretty miserable fourteen-year-old. Mad at the world. My only real connection was with Marisol, our housekeeper at the time— you remember her, I've mentioned her before." He paused, his fingers brushing absently against hers. "Boarding school was my father's way of getting rid of me. Nine months out of the year, he didn't have to deal with me. Even during breaks, he'd go out of his way to avoid me."

Kasey hesitated, his voice softening. "I spent most of my time alone or with Marisol. She became like a surrogate mother. When she taught me to cook, it brought a sense of calm that eased the boredom and loneliness."

Julia listened quietly, her hand resting lightly on his knee.

"Ren moved in as my roommate sophomore year," Kasey continued, a faint smile tugging at his lips. "He was funny, quirky, and kind—a total contrast to me. His complete lack of self-consciousness caught me off guard. I was amazed by his pop culture knowledge and all his references to American movies and shows. He soaked it all in like a sponge, watching American TV obsessively."

Kasey chuckled, the sound bittersweet. "His language and sense of humor weren't at all what I expected. If not for our looks and his accent, you'd think he was the pop culture-obsessed American, and I was the quiet, introspective Japanese student." He glanced at Julia. "Before meeting Ren, I barely cursed at all. Ren, though? He racked up more than a few demerits for his colorful language. I think he used his time at school to push back against the strict, traditional life at home. He was always positive, up for anything—completely fearless.”

Kasey’s face lit up, the memory softening his features. “Despite the emotional baggage I carried from losing my mother and not exactly being the friendliest guy, he never gave up on me.” His voice caught, just slightly, as he added, “He taught me how to let someone in.”

“One afternoon, outside the cafeteria, I saw a couple of seniors bullying him for being the new kid. I stepped in to defend him—and got my butt handed to me. But I gained a lot of respect at school for taking on two upperclassmen at once to defend a friend. After that, no one messed with either of us. From that moment, we were inseparable.”

“Always the protector,” she murmured softly, a hint of admiration in her voice.

“He was so easy to be around. Little by little, I found myself opening up to him, feeling my guard come down each day. We laughed so much together, and he brought me a kind of happiness I hadn’t known before. We shared a lot of the same classes, made new friends—even started a manga club.”

Kasey’s lips curved into a smile as he swirled his wine. “Being around Ren made me appreciate school in a way I never had. I’d always been capable academically, but his influence sparked a new passion for learning. Grades were important to his family, so I studied right alongside him, mirroring his habits. Ren might be a goofball at times, but he’s incredibly hardworking and sharp.”

He paused to sip his wine, his gaze distant with the pull of memory. “For the first time since my mother, I found comfort in physical closeness. Having someone stand too close or brush something off my shoulder usually made me uncomfortable—but not with him. Ren's casual gestures—leaning against me, slinging his arm over my shoulder—felt natural, even comforting. It made me realize how much I'd missed that physical connection with someone."

Julia's chest tightened as she listened, realizing just how much Ren had shaped Kasey's life. It struck her then—Kasey had never pulled back from her touch, not the first time or any time since. The thought made her stomach flutter, even as an ache of uncertainty began to stir.

"Six months into our first school year together, we were sitting side by side on my bed. He leaned in to share something from his book, and when I turned, his face was just inches from mine..." Kasey paused, his voice softening. "He stopped mid-sentence and kissed me."

He smiled faintly, the memory vivid. "I hadn't experienced a romantic kiss before then. I don't think I even closed my eyes or moved my lips at first. When he pulled me close and kissed me again, I closed my eyes and kissed him back. It felt like a switch had flipped inside me, sparking a desire for that kind of physical connection. Up until then, I'd had no real interest in either gender."

Julia sat there quietly, her thoughts swirling. She remembered Kasey mentioning that she'd reawakened his dormant sex drive. The realization stirred something in her, a strange connection between herself and Ren that she hadn't fully processed until now.

Kasey sipped his wine, then set the glass aside. Stretching out his legs, he watched as Julia shifted, laying her head in his lap. She turned her face toward the fire as he gently played with her hair, twirling it slowly around his fingers.

As the eerie glow of the fire cast shifting shadows across the room, Julia couldn't shake the feeling that her world was about to be turned upside down—just months after getting back on her feet emotionally.

"We were each other's first in everything," Kasey continued. "He'd never dated or kissed anyone before, either. Back home in Japan, his father kept a tight, traditional grip on the family, so Ren didn't spend any time alone with girls. Because we roomed together, we had all the time, freedom, and privacy we could ever want. No one ever thought of us as anything other than best friends and roommates."

He paused, his voice softening. "That first year, we started kissing and sleeping beside each other. When summer break came, he went home to Japan, and I returned to upstate New York to Marisol. I missed his companionship so much that I ached for him. After two months apart, we could barely wait to get to our room to be alone.

"We were lying next to each other, kissing like always, and he slipped his hand in my pants and—" He hesitated, the words catching in his throat.

"Jerked you off?" Julia offered, her voice light but understanding, breaking the tension.

"Yes, thank you," he replied, his cheeks reddening slightly. "I've never talked about this before. It feels kind of ridiculous—being a grown man who can't even say 'jerked off' out loud without help."

"Baby, you're too hard on yourself. Honestly, I think it's sweet." She gave his thigh a gentle squeeze, her tone effortlessly reassuring. "Go on." As usual, no one made talking about these things easier for him than she did.

Kasey let out a soft laugh, her encouragement easing his nerves. "I had such a crush on him, and I trusted him completely, so I just let it happen. Then I did it to him. We spent that whole year sleeping next to each other, kissing, and our hands in each other's pants." He chuckled softly at the memory, the edges of his lips lifting into a smile.

For a moment, he let the memory linger, bittersweet and warm. "It was... uncomplicated. Just us. No expectations, no labels—just being close."

"When we separated for the summer, saying goodbye to him for two months was incredibly hard. To cope, I threw myself into martial arts, taking lessons five days a week, four hours each day during those eight weeks apart. I also spent more time cooking with Marisol and diving into books.

We managed a few brief conversations, but his father's interference made staying in touch nearly impossible. When we got back to school, everything felt just like it had before. I even convinced him to take martial arts classes with me on weekends, and it turned out to be an amazing senior year."

Kasey paused, a faint smile crossing his lips. "After spring break that year, on our first night back alone, he told me he wanted to have oral sex with me. Truthfully, I'd never even thought about it before. I was so content with the way things were.

"I was pretty naive about sex. Being an only child and home-schooled, I had no close friends to talk about it with. My mom tried to talk to me about sex once, but she was so shy and sheltered she could barely get the words out. Honestly, I didn't think much about sex at all—unless Ren was around. He was always thinking about it." He chuckled softly at the memory.

"I was still trying to wrap my head around the fact that I was kissing, sleeping with, and messing with my best friend every day. I told him I needed to think about it. I wasn't sure I was ready—I assumed he'd expect me to reciprocate, and I definitely wasn't prepared for that.

"But he reassured me that he only wanted to do it for me, and he didn't expect anything in return. I kept saying no, but one night, while we were goofing around and wrestling on the bed, he asked again. This time, I let him."

Kasey's voice softened. "It was the most intense and intimate experience I'd ever had. Afterwards, though, I felt embarrassed, like I'd done something wrong. Noticing how weird I felt, he told me our friendship meant more to him, and it was okay if we never did anything like that again."

He paused, taking a sip of his wine. "Things went back to normal, but a few weeks later, when he tried again, I felt completely at ease. Not long after, I reciprocated. I wanted to make him happy, and I loved how close it made us feel."

Taking a pause, he exhaled deeply. "I need a breather. I'm tired of talking—mind if we finish this later?"

"Of course not. Take all the time you need," she replied. Rising, she perched on his lap, her arms around his neck, she felt the faint stir of his arousal beneath her. Grazing her cheek against his, she whispered softly in his ear, "One question."

"What's that?" he murmured, planting soft kisses along her neck as his arms encircled her.

"Were you in love with him?" she asked, leaning back to search his face.

"Very much so," he admitted without hesitation.

"Do you still love him?" she asked, her heart racing at the thought.

He paused, his expression thoughtful, before admitting, "I never really let him go."

Julia felt a pang in her chest, warmth creeping into her cheeks. For an instant, he thought he saw a flash of pain in her eyes before she looked away.

"Are you alright?" he asked, puzzled by her sudden shift. He'd never seen her like this.

"I'm fine. It's just... he was such an important part of your life, but you never mentioned him." Her curious eyes searched his. "Why?"

"I didn't mention him because we'd been out of touch for a decade. I never thought I'd see him again. And frankly, he's hard to talk about, like my mother and father."

Sensing her unease, he shifted the conversation. "Let's not dwell on him right now. There's something else I'd rather focus on." Gently laying her down on the sheepskin, he brushed thoughts of Ren aside and gave her his full attention, pouring his affection into every touch, as if trying to reassure both of them.

Afterward, although her body felt fulfilled, Julia couldn't quiet her mind. A storm was brewing, and she knew it. Kasey had described a soulmate—one who had resurfaced in his life unexpectedly, even if he didn't fully realize it.

"I'm hungry. Let's bake some cookies and watch something," she suggested, rolling over to grab her nightie.

"Cookies, now?" he asked, furrowing his brow as he slipped into his pajama bottoms.

"C'mon, you can be such an old man sometimes—it's only nine," she teased, grabbing his hand and leading him to the kitchen.

They settled in to watch Bake Off, picking at the cookies they'd made. Julia curled into Kasey's side, her head resting on his shoulder, but her thoughts were far from the screen. Ren's name lingered in her mind, and her heart raced as she replayed Kasey's words.

Kasey held her close, his arm draped around her. Though his gaze stayed on the TV, his mind wandered back to Ren.

The story remained unfinished, the emotions unspoken. The weight of it sat between them, silent but undeniable.

***

The next morning, still in her nightie and preparing tea, Julia turned at the sound of the door opening. "You were up early," she remarked.

"And good morning to you too, grumpy," he teased, wrapping her in a warm embrace. His body was damp from his run, slick against her skin, his musky scent enveloping her. "I went for a run to burn off those cookies," he said, grinning as he grabbed himself a bottle of water.

"Ew, you're all sweaty. Get off!" she giggled, playfully pushing him away. "I missed you when I woke up," she admitted, pouring milk into her tea.

"Well, I'm here now," he said, peeling off his T-shirt as he headed toward the stairs. His taut, sweat-slicked body glistened in the morning light streaming through the window. Leaning against the counter, she sipped her tea, watching him take the steps two at a time.

"I'm going to shower," he announced as he reached the top. Then, taking a couple of steps back down, he invited, "Coming?"

With a smile, she set her mug down and followed him without a word.

Under the warm spray of the oversized showerhead, they ran soapy hands over each other, their kisses deep and unhurried. The steam filled the room, wrapping them in heat and intimacy.

"Let me wash your hair," he said softly, his voice tender. It had become a ritual he cherished every time they showered together. Once, when she'd mentioned trying a new hairstyle, he'd shyly asked her to keep it long. She'd agreed, opting for trims instead, knowing it made him happy.

As Julia rested her cheek against his chest, Kasey worked shampoo into her hair, his fingers massaging her scalp and neck with practiced care. The familiar beachy scent filled the air, blending with the steam.

"We might be running late," Julia purred, leaning into his touch, her arms circling him tightly.

"I'll call Carl, reschedule the pickup, and let Barbara know," he murmured, rinsing her hair with the wand.

Julia began to rub against him, her hands sliding slowly over his lean, muscular body.

"Let me finish," he said with a grin, pulling his hips back and gently turning her around.

"You're no fun," she pouted.

"I didn't say you couldn't do it after I'm finished," he teased. "Or... maybe we could just do it to each other after the shower."

"I'll take option two," she replied, a playful smile curling her lips.

"Thought you might," he said, his grin widening as he ran the warm water through her hair.

***

"Morning, Jules, Kasey. Any stops this morning?" Carl greeted cheerfully, swinging open the car door.

"Hey, Carl. No, thanks. Straight in; we're running a bit behind," Julia replied as she slipped into the car.

"You never did finish telling me about Ren," she said quietly a few minutes into the ride, her earlier distractions now fading. "Let's have lunch and talk then."

Kasey sighed softly, glancing out the window. "There's not much more to tell, but I'd rather not go back to work after. How about dinner instead?" Kasey suggested.

"Dinner sounds nice. Carl, we won't be leaving at six tonight. Can you stay on standby? I'll confirm the time later."

"No problem," Carl replied with an easy smile, glancing at her in the rearview mirror. I'm available all night—just give me a twenty-minute heads-up."

***

At one o'clock, Julia breezed into Kasey's office, dropping her gym bag on his desk with a thud. "I'm hitting the gym instead of lunch—wanna come?"

"I think I'll pass. I've got a lot to do. Besides, I already ran this morning while a certain someone slept in," he quipped, his lips curling into a playful smirk.

Julia gasped dramatically. "I guess I'll go alone," she said, pouting as if the weight of the world rested on her shoulders.

"Sulk all you want. Not budging this time. Duty calls," he chuckled, shaking his head.

"Fine, I'm going. I'll be back by two fifteen," she declared, grabbing her bag and heading out with an exaggerated flip of her hair.

When she returned at precisely two fifteen, lunch sat waiting on her desk. She blinked in surprise before calling out, "Thank you!" and settling onto the couch with a grin.

"Anytime, boss," he teased, peeking up from his computer.

"Don't call me boss!" she scolded through a mouthful of chicken wrap.

Kasey grinned. "Whatever you say, boss."

***

"So, what's on the menu?" she asked as he walked in hours later carrying their dinner.

"Sushi," he replied. "I figured you might not be too hungry since you had a late lunch."

"Perfect," she said, moving the containers to the coffee table.

"Water or something else? Maybe some wine?" he offered, grabbing a bottle of water for himself from the minibar.

"Just water, thanks."

They sat down together, the golden light of early evening streaming through the glass windows, painting the office in long, slanting shadows. Julia opened her container and glanced at Kasey. "I've been thinking about what you said earlier," she began, her voice soft. "Why the ten-year gap with Ren?"

Kasey sighed lightly, opening his container. "As a graduation present, I was invited to spend two weeks with Ren and his family in Japan. I'd met his parents a few times during Parent's Day visits. Whenever they dropped him off or picked him up, we'd go out to dinner."

He paused, picking up a piece of sushi. "They were so old-fashioned and traditional. Ren was completely different around them—especially his father. He told me he'd begged his grandmother to help him go to school in America to escape the tradition-bound life he led in Japan. She didn't want him to leave, but she wanted him to be happy."

Julia sipped her water, her brow furrowed. "That must've been so hard for him."

"It was. Ren didn't want to disrespect his father, family, or culture—he just felt trapped. His parents had no idea about his sexuality. Around them, we were just platonic schoolmates."

Julia tilted her head, curiosity flickering in her eyes. "Why did Ren's parents let him go to school in America if they were so traditional?"

"His grandmother influenced his father by telling him Ren would return after college to work in the family business. His father figured that if Ren wanted to go so far from home, he could still keep him in a controlled environment—that's why he chose the all-boys boarding school. I don't think he realized just how much freedom Ren would have there or that he'd meet someone like me.

"Ren learned to be two different people. With his family, he was the dutiful son; with me at school, he was a teenager experiencing real freedom for the first time."

Kasey fiddled with his napkin, his gaze distant. "On the morning of the tenth day of my stay, his father walked into Ren's room early. I was still in his bed, his arm draped over me.

"We'd set alarms to wake up before anyone else, but for some reason, his father came in before they went off. We woke up as he came in, and for a moment, none of us moved or spoke. His father just stood there, frozen, before backing out of the room, his face a mask of shock."

"Oh fuck," Julia interjected, eyes wide as she hastily covered her mouth to avoid spitting out her sushi.

Kasey managed a faint smile. "'Oh fuck' is an understatement.

"We got dressed in silence, and Ren went to speak to his father while I waited in his room. I couldn't hear every word— they were speaking in Japanese—but the anger in his father's voice was unmistakable.

"I caught one phrase over and over: 'He must go now.' I'll never forget it." He shook his head, his voice tightening. "Ren was pleading, switching between Japanese and English, begging him to listen. His mother was trying to calm his father, but it was clear he wasn't hearing any of it.

"It was twenty minutes before Ren came back to the room—the longest twenty minutes of my life. I'm sure it was even worse for him."

Kasey paused to take a sip of water before continuing. "He was distraught. Through tears, he told me I was leaving that day to return home, and he was to have no further contact with me. Ren looked as if he were facing execution when he told me that not only was he not joining me in New York for college, but his father was arranging a marriage for him.

"His father told him that if he didn't comply, he'd be disowned by the entire family."

Kasey's voice softened, tinged with sadness "Ren told me he loved me and that he would never stop loving me, no matter what happened or who he married. It hit especially hard because we'd never said that to each other before.

"He was only allowed five minutes to say goodbye. He hugged me so tightly I could barely breathe, and neither of us wanted to let go. It was as if holding on just a little longer could make time stop, could undo everything that was happening.

"When he finally pulled away, his face was wet with tears, and it hit me like a blow to the chest. I told Ren I loved him too and to come find me when he could break free. He promised he would.

"His cousin took me to the airport and left me there alone until my flight, hours later."

Kasey exhaled softly, his shoulders sagging under the weight of the memory. "I didn't reach out to him for fear of angering his father and making things even harder for him. I had already lived through the consequences of what going against your father could do."

Julia's throat tightened, her chest aching as she watched Kasey stare into his glass.

"I went home with a broken heart and a profound depression that had a vise grip on me all that summer and well into my first year in college. I threw myself into my studies, knowing Ren would be upset if I sacrificed my education because of him."

He hesitated, his voice quieter now. "I withdrew from everyone, focusing solely on studying, martial arts training, and Japanese lessons. It was... an incredibly trying time. I was barely keeping it together," he confessed.

For a moment, neither of them spoke, the weight of his words settling in the quiet space between them. Kasey ran a hand through his hair, as if trying to shake off the heaviness of the memory. When he spoke again, his tone was lighter, though the undercurrent of sadness remained.

"Then along came Ellie. She asked me to study with her for a class we shared, and in my lonely state, I agreed. She was a cute, curvy girl with a big personality who helped guide me back to the land of the living socially. I started getting out of my room more often and even met some of her friends.

"One night, while we were studying, she kissed me. I kissed her back, and it felt surprisingly natural. We made out on my bed, and I couldn't believe how good she felt—like a warm, soft pillow." He smiled at the memory, his expression softening, while Julia grinned at his description.

"But when she tried to take things further, I panicked and stopped her, explaining that I wasn't into casual sex. I mentioned I'd just ended a long-term relationship and wasn't ready for anything new. My reluctance only seemed to fuel her determination. I suppose some people just like a challenge," he mused, casting a glance at Julia, who responded with a smirk and a playful nudge.

"Within a month, we were a couple, and she was constantly pushing boundaries. I smoked weed with her for the first time, and not long after that, I was no longer a virgin. Despite how good sex felt with her, I was confused about what I was... straight, bisexual?

"While I loved being physically close with Ren," Kasey paused, his cheeks flushing, "the idea of having sex with him the way I did with her was never something I considered. What I shared with him physically was all I ever wanted.

"I often wonder—if I hadn't met him, would I be different? I've never been attracted to someone purely by looks; it's always their personality that draws me in. Even though I got to know the few men I briefly dated, it was never the same as it was with Ren. That's why I eventually stopped dating men—it just confused me.

"A few years later, in a weak moment, I searched for Ren online. I found out he'd gotten married just four months after we graduated and was attending fashion college in Tokyo. That's when I knew I had to move on. But letting go was harder than I ever imagined. I never saw or heard from him again."

"And now he's back," Julia said softly.

"And now he's back," he echoed, his voice heavy with emotion.

"How do you feel about that?" she asked tentatively, her fingers tightening around her bottle as she braced herself for his answer.

"I honestly don't know," he confessed. "I'm still grappling with the fact that he's here after all this time. I was haunted by the ghost of him for years. Losing him changed me—I felt like I lost a part of myself, and I lost hope I'd ever see him again." His voice trailed off, his gaze distant.

Julia nudged his plate closer. "You should eat," she urged gently, even as her own appetite vanished. The coming weekend loomed in her mind like a storm cloud, while Kasey's anticipation for it was palpable.

***

"Have a great weekend," Kasey said, bidding Julia and Will goodbye as they headed to the car, where Carl waited to take them to the helipad.

Julia suddenly stopped and turned back, her charm bracelet tinkling softly as she reached up to cup his face. She kissed him tenderly, her eyes shimmering with melancholy, the blue appearing even deeper in the soft light.

"I miss you already," she whispered, her voice a thread of vulnerability.

"You'll be just fine with Will," he replied, pulling her close in a firm embrace. "You won't even notice I'm not there."

"That's not true, and you know it," she said with a small smile. "Enjoy your dinner."

With that, she turned and walked away, her stride purposeful. Kasey watched her go, a flicker of guilt surfacing before his thoughts shifted to seeing Ren, a hint of excitement creeping in.

***

He arrived home at six-thirty, with Ren expected at eight. After a quick shower, he dressed in black skinny jeans, a snug white textured long-sleeved tee, and thick black socks. Rolling up his sleeves, he gave his hair a quick check in the mirror before heading downstairs to prep dinner. Unsure of Ren's culinary preferences, he decided on steak, remembering how much he'd loved it back in school. By the time the salad was tossed and the steak prepped for grilling, the doorbell chimed.

249

Kasey's heart raced as he opened the door, and there he was—the boy he once loved, standing before him like a dream.

"Hi, Spike." Ren's familiar voice sent a shiver down Kasey's spine, warm and rich with nostalgia.

"Hi, Ren," Kasey replied, fighting to keep the excitement out of his voice. "Come on in."

"I wasn't sure what you like to drink—or if you drink—but I brought this." Ren held out a bottle of wine, a crooked grin lighting up his face.

Kasey's eyes lit up as he accepted the bottle. "Thanks. You didn't have to bring anything," he said warmly, touched by the gesture. He stepped aside, nodding toward the corner. "You can leave your shoes over there."

"Wow!" Ren exclaimed as he stepped inside. "What a beautiful home. It's huge—I thought it might be a building with individual apartments." He turned to Kasey, his eyes wide with surprise. "Is this all yours?"

"I bought it years ago for the investment value," Kasey explained, leading Ren through the expansive living space. "There's an apartment downstairs and two floors I don't even use."

Ren looked around, taking in the sleek yet inviting design of Kasey's living room. "It's surreal, standing here with you like this—as grown men," he said, his voice softer, his gaze lingering on Kasey.

"I know what you mean," Kasey replied, his lips curving into a smile. "When I look at you, I feel seventeen all over again."

Ren chuckled, the sound light and genuine. "You still practice Jeet Kune Do?" he asked, his enthusiasm bubbling over as they entered Kasey's training room.

"A few times a week," Kasey said with a nod, motioning toward the neatly arranged equipment. "Do you?"

Ren's expression faltered, a flicker of vulnerability crossing his face. "No, it reminded me too much of you—I couldn't get into it anymore. You were always the one who kept me going. Maybe we could change that, and you could teach me."

Kasey's smile widened, mischief glinting in his eyes. "Sure, I don't care what dummy I train with," he teased.

Ren burst out laughing and gave him a playful shove. "Nice one," he shot back, shaking his head with a grin.

As Ren's gaze swept the room, they landed on the elegant sword displayed. His eyes widened in awe. "What the... you have a blue-handled katana?!" he exclaimed, moving closer to inspect the weapon, surrounded by throwing stars and gleaming daggers.

Kasey smiled, watching Ren react with childlike excitement, moving from one discovery to the next. The spark in Ren's eyes grew even brighter when his attention locked onto the Jericho 941 handgun displayed prominently.

"Holy shit!" Ren practically shouted, his voice bursting with disbelief and admiration. "Vicious's katana and Spike's gun? Unbelievable," he said, grinning as his gaze darted between the sword and gun.

"It sure is," Kasey confirmed, matching Ren's excitement. "I picked it up at an auction. Want me to take it out?"

"Uh, hell yeah! I've never even held a gun before," Ren admitted, practically bouncing with excitement. "Have you fired it?"

Kasey nodded, pulling the weapon from its display. "I've taken it to the range a few times. I could take you sometime," he offered, handing the gun to Ren.

"I'd love that," Ren said, his heart racing as he turned the gun over in his hands. He aimed it playfully at the training dummy, a grin tugging at his lips as he imagined himself as Spike from their favorite anime.

As he handed the gun back, his hand lingered on Kasey's, their eyes meeting for a brief moment. "Your home, the things you surround yourself with... there's this quiet, powerful vibe to it. Just like you," Ren said, his voice soft, laced with awe and affection.

Kasey's cheeks reddened, a grin spreading across his face. "Speaking of powerful vibes, you're giving off a serious Vicious vibe with that long hair. I really like it."

Ren smiled, brushing his hair back with a casual, knowing gesture. "I'm glad you like it. You always did have a thing for long hair."

Returning the gun and locking the glass door, Kasey turned back to Ren with a grin. "Let me open that wine. I'm going to grill some steaks—sound good?"

"Perfect. I love a good steak. You remembered," Ren replied, his eyes shining warmly.

"I remember everything about you," Kasey said softly, heading to the kitchen for glasses and a corkscrew.

"I have to say, I'm lovin' your style. That suit you wore at work was fire—you could model that shit," Ren said, his tone as casual as it was complimentary.

Kasey grinned, a faint blush creeping up his neck. "Coming from you, that means a lot. I see you still have a thing for clothes. You look... so good," he added, shaking his head slowly as he took in Ren's outfit. Always one to impress, Ren paired a short military-style jacket with a crisp black shirt—three buttons undone and untucked—black ripped jeans cuffed at the bottom, and black-and-white, thick-soled penny loafers.

"Should I start grilling, or do you want to wait?" Kasey asked, handing Ren a glass of wine.

"Why don't we wait and have a drink first," Ren suggested, his lips curving into an easy smile.

"Living room?" Kasey offered.

Settling onto the couch, Kasey took his spot at one end while Ren slid in beside him, their knees brushing ever so slightly.

"Are you seeing anyone?" Ren asked, casually taking a sip of his wine, his eyes fixed on Kasey, gauging his reaction.

"Um, it's complicated," Kasey replied, lifting his glass for another sip, clearly dodging further discussion.

Ren smirked, his head tilting slightly. "Hmm, you still never say more than you have to," he observed, his voice tinged with familiarity and teasing.

"What about you? Have you met anyone here in New York?" Kasey asked, steering the conversation back to Ren with casual curiosity.

"Nah, only been here a couple of weeks. Too busy getting settled in," Ren admitted, setting his glass down. "I need to ease into the dating scene—I've never dated before. It's kind of intimidating."

Kasey's smile widened slightly, a wave of relief washing over him. "I don't know if you have a real estate agent, but I could help you find a place. Navigating the city can be tough."

"I'd appreciate that," Ren said, his grin softening. "I'm pretty clueless about this city, and the housing market is definitely not my forte."

"Lucky for you, I'm pretty good at it," Kasey replied, his tone dipping just enough to suggest more than practicality. He glanced at Ren from under his hair, his voice dropping slightly. "Anything you need, just ask."

"There is something I need right now," Ren said, his voice low as he set his glass down. Leaning in, he placed a hand behind Kasey's neck and drew him close, his lips brushing softly against Kasey's.

Overwhelmed, Kasey pulled back, his breath shaky. "I can't..." he murmured, his voice barely audible. "I'm afraid I won't want to stop."

Kasey hesitated, Julia's face flashing in his mind. The thought of betraying her trust made his stomach twist, but the pull toward Ren was overwhelming. This moment felt like stepping into the past—raw, unguarded, and irresistible. He'd deal with the fallout later. Right now, all he could focus on was the man before him.

"Then don't," Ren whispered. Gently, he took the glass from Kasey's hand and set it aside, guiding Kasey's hands up around his neck. Wrapping his arms around Kasey's waist, he pulled him closer, kissing him with a familiarity that sent a jolt straight to Kasey's core.

The kiss was like a time machine, instantly transporting Kasey back to their teenage years—to their room at school and the very first time Ren kissed him. Kasey's heart raced, a tidal wave of emotions crashing over him. Every nerve in his body felt ablaze as he surrendered to Ren's embrace, the connection between them reigniting like a spark catching fire.

It wasn't just a kiss; it was a flood of memories, vivid and consuming. They weren't grown men with complicated lives— they were back at school, where life with Ren had felt simple and safe, even when Kasey's world outside wasn't.

Ren leaned back, his eyes steady. "I'm sorry, but I couldn't shake the thought of kissing you again. I told myself if I ever had the chance, I wouldn't let it pass."

"It's alright," Kasey reassured him, his voice quiet but sincere. "I understand. I feel the same way, except..." He hesitated, the unspoken weight of his circumstances pressing between them.

"I know... it's complicated," Ren said softly, his hand moving to Kasey's thigh. The gentle squeeze ignited something deep and primal, a spark that flared into life.

Kasey's gaze locked with Ren's, those dark eyes as endless and inviting as the midnight sky. The intensity between them was magnetic, pulling Kasey closer until their lips met again. This kiss was different—heavier, richer, laden with a decade's worth of longing and unresolved emotion.

In that moment, with Ren's arms around him, a flood of feelings surged, drowning out everything else. Even Julia.

"You smell unbelievably good," Kasey whispered, his lips grazing Ren's neck as he peppered it with kisses. "And your hair... I love it. It suits you," he added, his voice low and husky, running his fingers through the silky strands.

Everything about Ren—the familiar scent, the texture of his hair, the press of his body—was overwhelming, a flood of long-buried longing crashing over Kasey. Unable to hold back any longer, he pushed Ren down on the couch and moved over him, capturing his lips in a deep, consuming kiss. Breathless from their frenzied kisses and the familiar heat of Ren's touch, Kasey finally pulled back, his chest heaving. "Give me a second," he muttered, untangling himself.

Ren sat up, adjusting himself with a grin as he ran his fingers through his tousled hair. He watched, amused, as Kasey disappeared into the kitchen to shove the food back into the fridge. He returned to the living room, picked up his wine in one hand and Ren's hand in the other, his gaze purposeful. "Grab your glass, and come with me."

"Slow down, dude—I've got a raging boner," Ren laughed, grabbing his glass.

Kasey turned, a fiery look blazing in his eyes. "So do I. Move faster," he said, heading upstairs to the spare bedroom. Ren followed, setting his wine on the bedside table. As he turned, Kasey took charge, pushing him onto the bed, moving over him and pinning his wrists above his head.

Fueled by pure lust, Kasey captured Ren's lips in a series of passionate, demanding kisses before growling, "Take off your clothes."

Ren took a sharp breath, his pulse quickening. Kasey's assertiveness was thrilling—so different from the shy boy he remembered. The shift in their dynamic left him exhilarated. Roles reversed, they undressed quickly, both eager to close the distance and lose themselves in each other.

"I can't believe you're here, naked beside me," Kasey said softly as Ren nestled close.

"Damn, Spike, your body feels incredible," Ren murmured, his hands roaming over Kasey's lean, muscular frame. "I've missed this."

Ren's touch felt both familiar and new, each caress sending a jolt of electricity through Kasey's body. He inhaled deeply, his chest rising and falling as he tried to contain the overwhelming sensation of Ren's hands exploring him.

"You are so ripped—how much do you work out?" Ren asked, running his fingers over Kasey's abs, admiration clear in his voice.

Kasey smirked, sliding his hand to the back of Ren's head and guiding him downward. "No more talking," he commanded softly, his voice dripping with anticipation.

The moment Ren's mouth found him, Kasey's head fell back, a low groan escaping his lips. "Oh shit," he muttered, pure ecstasy washing over him as his fingers curled into the sheets. Watching Ren take him in, he was transported back to their youth, the connection between them as raw and electrifying as ever. Time seemed to stand still as Ren took his time, relishing the way Kasey surrendered to him completely. When he finally pulled back, his lips swollen and his eyes dark with satisfaction, he smirked. "I think I've waited long enough to do that again."

Kasey's laugh was shaky, his chest heaving as he reached for Ren, pulling him back up for a kiss that was both grateful and insatiable. "You've always been trouble," he murmured against Ren's lips, his hands tangling in his hair.

Ren grinned, the mischievous sparkle in his eyes undeniable. "And you've always loved it."

Ren lay his head on Kasey's chest, his fingers tracing lazy, deliberate patterns along the hard contours of Kasey's stomach. The room was quiet except for their steady breathing, their bodies tangled in the warm glow of their rekindled intimacy.

"Just as I remembered," Kasey sighed, his face flushed with pleasure as his fingers threaded through Ren's hair. "You feel so good next to me," he murmured in a low, sensual growl, pulling Ren closer, his face buried in his hair. The familiar scent sent a wave of desire through him as he nuzzled Ren's neck, planting slow, deliberate kisses along his collarbone.

"I've had my turn," he murmured, his voice low and teasing. "Now it's yours."

Without breaking eye contact, Kasey slid lower, pressing soft, deliberate kisses along Ren's stomach, his hands mapping out every dip and ridge of muscle with the kind of reverence that sent shivers racing across Ren's skin.

He drew on everything he'd loved and learned from Julia, channeling that knowledge into every calculated move.

"Spike..." Ren's voice broke into a whisper, his breath catching as Kasey's tongue flicked over sensitive skin, igniting every nerve. "You're killing me."

Kasey chuckled, his breath hot against Ren's skin. "Good thing I know CPR," he teased, his lips curving into a wicked grin before continuing his exploration. His movements were unhurried, savoring every reaction—every gasp, every shiver, every arch of Ren's body beneath him.

"What the fuck, Spike..." Ren breathed, his voice breaking as Kasey's mouth explored him with a boldness that left him reeling. The unfamiliar yet erotically charged technique sent shivers racing across his skin. Kasey's tongue swirled and teased, his hand mirroring the rhythm with eager precision. When he twisted his hand in sync with his mouth, Ren's fingers tangled in Kasey's hair, gripping tight as his body tensed.

A deep, guttural groan tore from Ren's throat as he came, his eyes closing as he tried to catch his breath.

Kasey leaned back, his lips curved in a satisfied smirk as he met Ren's dazed gaze.

"Well, that is not what I remember," Ren said, his breath still uneven. His grin widened as he studied Kasey. "You're so different—more confident. I like it."

Kasey lay close beside Ren, his head resting on his shoulder. For a long moment, they lay in silence, the stillness wrapping around them like a cocoon. Finally, Kasey spoke, his voice heavy with emotion. "It broke my heart to lose you. I thought I'd never recover. You have no idea how much I've missed you."

Ren smiled softly, pressing a tender kiss to Kasey's hair. "I think you just showed me," he murmured.

"I'm serious, Ren," Kasey said, lifting his head slightly to meet Ren's gaze. "I've never told anyone—not even Julia, and I've told her a lot of private things from my past. When I first came home, I was suicidal. I couldn't eat, I couldn't sleep. I was losing my mind, wondering what was happening to you. My head was full of dark thoughts. Even my asshole father noticed and sent me to a therapist. It took me years to even start moving forward without you." His voice caught, the pain of those years bleeding into every word.

Ren tightened his hold on Kasey, his heart aching at the confession. "I'm so sorry you had to go through that," he whispered, his voice gentle yet firm. "I've thought about you every day since we've been apart. All I've wanted was to come find you, to see you again. I love you, Spike—I always have."

Their lips met in a deep kiss, a silent exchange of love, longing, and the years they'd lost. When they finally settled, Ren pulled Kasey into a familiar embrace, spooning him just as he used to. The quiet between them was soothing, Ren's arms wrapped protectively around him.

After a while, Kasey broke the silence, his voice soft. "Do you want to eat?"

Ren chuckled, squeezing him playfully. "I thought we just did."

"Baka," Kasey smirked, calling him an idiot in Japanese as he got up to grab them something to wear.

"Just trying to lighten the mood," Ren replied with a grin. "Look at you, busting me in Japanese."

Kasey smirked and tossed a pair of pajamas to him. "Here, put these on. Stay with me tonight. Do you have any plans for tomorrow?"

"I have an appointment to see a place at three. Wanna come with me?" Ren asked, a hopeful edge in his voice as he caught the pajamas Kasey tossed to him.

"Absolutely. Let's go eat."

The more time they spent together, the more it felt like the old days. They joked and teased each other like teenagers, their laughter filling the room. As Kasey grilled the steaks, Ren stood behind him, arms wrapped around his waist, resting his head on Kasey's shoulder.

Later, Kasey put on Cowboy Bebop, their favorite anime, but the show was little more than background noise. They ended up tangled on the couch, making out and reminiscing about school, their voices lively and filled with warmth.

As they headed toward the bedrooms, passing the master, Ren glanced inside and asked, "Why are you sleeping in the spare room? Is it because it's complicated?"

Sitting together on the bed, Kasey hesitated, taking a deep breath before speaking. "I've been involved with someone," he admitted, his tone careful. "It's a friends-with-benefits arrangement. The understanding is that it's just sex with no attachments."

Ren tilted his head, a small smirk playing on his lips. "That doesn't sound too complicated."

"There's more," Kasey continued, his tone cautious. "We've been sleeping together for months—it would've been even longer, but circumstances kept getting in the way." He hesitated before adding, "The thing is, I'm in love with her, and I think she feels the same way about me, but neither of us has said anything."

"Her? Did you say her?" Ren asked, his surprise clear.

Kasey nodded, watching Ren carefully. Ren's expression shifted, softening with understanding. "Well, now that I know it's a woman, I'm gonna take a wild guess and say your 'fuck buddy' is your boss Julia."

Kasey blinked, caught off guard by Ren's insight. "What makes you say that?"

"Dude, she checked me out like she was either your mother or your lover," Ren said with a knowing grin. "And you just told me you've shared deeply personal stuff with her. She must mean a lot to you. Am I right?"

"You're right. She does mean a lot to me," Kasey admitted, his voice steady but quiet. "It's not common knowledge, though. I can trust you not to say anything, right?"

"Of course," Ren said, his tone earnest. He paused before asking, "But if you're in love with her, why are you doing this?"

Kasey hesitated, his words catching in his throat. Finally, he said, "I don't know... maybe because I never stopped loving you. From the moment you walked into my office, all I've wanted is to touch you, to hold you again, and not let you go. I thought being with you might give me closure, or it would..."

"Would what?" Ren pressed gently, his voice steady but insistent.

"Pick up where it left off," Kasey admitted, his gaze dropping to his hands. "But I don't know how that would work, because I can't imagine giving up Julia. I need her. No one else has made me feel so happy or cared for since you."

He paused, his voice growing softer. "She's been patient with me, waiting until I felt comfortable enough to be with her sexually, and she's helped me immensely that way. I have confidence because of her. She's kind, and she's exciting. I love the way she depends on me. But now you're here, and I feel torn. It's like we were cheated out of a chance to see where things would've gone naturally."

Kasey's voice broke slightly as he continued. "I'm really confused about how to manage this, and I'm terrified of how it'll affect her. But I can't let you go again, not now that you're back. I'm in love with my past and my present."

Placing a comforting hand on Kasey's shoulder, Ren spoke gently. "I'd love to pick things up where we left off, but I'm not going to put that pressure on you. You've got enough to deal with. Let's just take this day by day—old friends, no expectations. We were best friends before we ever slept together, and we can be that again. I just want you in my life somehow."

Ren pulled him closer, his voice tender and warm. "I've missed you so much."

Kasey leaned into Ren's embrace, the weight of his conflicting emotions pressing down on him. A single tear escaped, tracing his cheek as he closed his eyes. He couldn't bear the thought of losing Ren again, but the idea of telling Julia tore at his heart. Hurting her was the last thing he wanted, yet he couldn't deny the depth of his feelings for Ren.

They spent the night intertwined, holding onto each other as though the answers might come with the dawn. For now, they clung to the comfort of the moment, both unsure of what the future would bring.

***

The next morning, as they lay in bed sharing stories from their past, Ren recounted the painful ultimatum his father had thrust upon him years ago.

"He left me no choice," Ren confessed, his voice heavy with remorse.

Kasey pulled him into a soothing hug. "You did what you had to do. I understand," he said softly, his touch grounding Ren in the present.

But as Ren spoke, a wave of old pain crashed over him, his expression growing distant, his voice trembling. "It was like a scene from a nightmare," he began. "My father's words cut through me like icy blades." The memory resurfaced, vivid and raw, pulling him back into the past.

"Ren," his father had said, his tone firm and cold, each word laced with judgment. "I am appalled by what I witnessed."

Ren shifted uncomfortably in his seat, the weight of the conversation pressing down on him like a physical force.

"You have engaged in an inappropriate relationship. Is this what has been going on at that school?" his father demanded, his voice sharp enough to wound. "This is not the way of our family."

His father's tone hardened, each word a blow to Ren's already fragile resolve. "Our family has upheld these values for centuries. Your actions jeopardize our legacy. I will not tolerate it—he must go. Now."

Ren's heart pounded, panic surging through him as he struggled to find the words to defend himself against the crushing weight of tradition.

His mother and grandmother appeared in the doorway, confusion clouding their expressions, their gazes darting between Ren and his father, struggling to grasp the situation.

"Otosan, calm down. Please, listen to me," Ren begged in English, his voice teetering between fear and defiance.

Switching to Japanese, his tone grew desperate. "We care about each other. He's my best friend. Please don't send him home. We did nothing wrong."

But the steely resolve in his father's expression didn't waver. Ren's heart sank as he realized his pleas were falling on deaf ears. He braced himself for the inevitable.

"Consider this your only warning," his father said, his voice like iron. "Persist in this relationship, and I will disown you. You will be severed from this family, our name, and everything we stand for. He must leave immediately, and you will never see him again."

Ren's chest tightened, the weight of his father's words crushing him.

"I will arrange a marriage for you," his father continued, unmoved. "With a suitable girl from a respectable family."

The weight of his father's ultimatum suffocated the room, leaving Ren with tears of shame and defiance. With a final, stern glance, his father turned and left, his mother and grandmother following silently behind. Ren was left standing alone, a heart-wrenching choice between love and family loyalty tearing him apart. The memory still lingered, heavy and unrelenting—a painful reminder of the choices he had made.

Kasey listened intently, his heart aching with every word as Ren recounted the agonizing confrontation.

"I should have been stronger. I should have refused to go along with his ultimatum," Ren said, his voice thick with regret. "But I was young, and I couldn't bear to shatter my mother's and grandmother's hearts. So instead, I broke yours. You were my safe place, my anchor. I've spent years wishing I could go back and change everything, but I couldn't. All I've ever wanted was to find my way back to you."

Kasey rested his forehead against Ren's, his voice soft with empathy. "You did what you thought was right. We've both suffered because of our fathers' choices."

The weight of Ren's pain hung in the air between them, but Kasey gently shifted the conversation, hoping to ease the tension. "What's your ex-wife like?"

"Kaede's very sweet, and we left the marriage on good terms," Ren began, his tone thoughtful. "She knew from the start that the marriage wasn't my idea, but she felt family pressure, too. We were both young and naïve. It was... awkward—not just physically, but emotionally."

He glanced at Kasey, a faint smile tugging at his lips. "We didn't have much in common. She was quiet, submissive, and there was zero chemistry. Transitioning from being with you to her? Strange doesn't even begin to cover it. At first, I was freaked out by the thought of having sex with a woman."

Kasey raised an eyebrow, but Ren smiled and continued. "After we fumbled our way through it, I figured out pretty quickly that I'm bisexual. I like sex—male or female, doesn't seem to matter. But it wasn't the same for her. She didn't like oral at all, and the rest was just... uninspiring. On a good month, we'd have sex maybe four times. I practically begged for it, but she just wasn't interested. In her defense, we never really made a deep connection—we were just too different."

He paused, chuckling as his smile widened. "I ended up watching a lot of porn... way more than I probably should have."

"After a few years of trying to conceive without success, I started seriously considering leaving. We never had enough sex to give conception a fair chance, and I knew that wasn't going to change," Ren admitted, his voice tinged with frustration. "I had a long, honest talk with my grandmother, and she encouraged me to leave.

"Kaede told me it was fine for me to indulge in discreet affairs during the last two years of our marriage. I hadn't stepped outside the marriage before that. I only had two affairs, both with women I met online. They were purely sexual and short-term. The sex was great after years of frustration, but it didn't feel right while I was still married. Every time I came home, it was hard to look Kaede in the eye—I never wanted to hurt her. So, I decided not to do it again until I was divorced."

Ren sighed, reaching for Kasey's hand. "It took time to gain enough financial independence to divorce and move here. I just needed to see if you'd be open to rebuilding our friendship."

"I'm so happy you're here," Kasey said, his voice full of sincerity. "You could have reached out to me—I would have supported you in any way you needed."

Ren shook his head gently. "No, I couldn't. I needed to do it on my own. And I had to see your face when we reconnected—only then could I really know how you felt. I could always read your face. I needed it to be in person. Plus, I wanted to surprise you."

Leaning forward, Ren pressed a kiss to Kasey's neck.

"You certainly did that," Kasey said with a happy smile. "I know I keep repeating it, but I'm genuinely thrilled you're here."

"Me too, Spike. Me too," Ren murmured, pulling Kasey into a tight embrace.

***

In the afternoon, they checked out the apartment and then strolled around the city, catching up and savoring their time together. They went out for an early dinner, and when Kasey asked if Ren wanted to spend the night again, he happily agreed. The evening unfolded with a run, a shared shower—a first for them—followed by a night in bed. Kasey introduced Ren to smoking weed, something Ren had only done twice before; recreational drugs were rare in Ren's experience back in Japan.

They lay together, watching TV and making out, simply relishing each other's company. It felt as though the years apart had only strengthened their bond, rekindling the deep connection they once shared. Still, whenever Kasey wasn't wrapped up in Ren, thoughts of Julia crept in—especially how he was going to explain this weekend to her. There was no question he'd tell her, but he kept pushing the thought down, the weight of her possible reaction pressing heavily on him. Julia was his rock, the person who had rebuilt him when he'd thought he couldn't feel whole again. But Ren... Ren had been his first love, the person who had shown him what it meant to be truly seen. The weight of those two truths pressed down on him, the enormity of what he'd done slowly sinking in. Despite the weight of the choices ahead, a small part of him felt joy in having Ren back in his life—a joy shadowed by guilt and uncertainty.

***

Chapter 14: Facing the Truth

"What's wrong, Jules? You're really quiet—you don't seem happy," Will said as she unlocked the door to the beach house.

"I'm not happy. Let me apologize now—I'll probably be shitty company this weekend. Hope you brought plenty of weed," she said, tossing her keys on the entryway table.

"What happened—does it have to do with Kasey?" he guessed, setting their luggage down. "Is that why he's not here?"

She turned to face him, her eyes glistening with unshed tears. "It's about him," she whispered, and as she blinked, a single tear finally escaped, trailing down her cheek.

He pulled her into a comforting hug. "Girl, please don't cry." But she did, struggling to hold back her emotions.

"I'm sorry," she murmured between sniffles.

"It's okay, sweetie. It's okay," he said, gently stroking her hair.

***

Later, as they sat by the fire pit, smoking and sipping wine, Will finally urged, "Alright, spit it out. What's going on?"

Fortified by the wine, weed, and time to stew, Julia let the emotional floodgates open.

"Kasey's first love—the guy he lived with for three years in boarding school, who he admitted he's still in love with, and who I'm pretty damn sure is his fucking soulmate—just walked into our office after ten years of no contact, and now Kasey's with him." She paused, her voice thick with agony. "I swear to God, it's like the universe is plotting against us being happy. Why is this happening? We were so happy together—things were perfect as they were. Why did he have to come back? You have no idea how much it hurt, hearing Kasey talk about this guy the way he did. Now I get so much more about him—his life, his choices. He does martial arts, speaks Japanese, and his home is decorated like a Japanese home—all because of him. He even collects guns and stuff from their favorite anime because of him. He still watches and reads it, but never with me. And on top of it all, Ren's tall and hot as hell. He's got this gorgeous long black hair and this total swagger. Looks like a sexy vampire. I kid you not—he put on blue metal-framed sunglasses before he left the office. He looked like fucking Gary Oldman in *Dracula*." Will listened patiently, letting her get it all out.

"The way Kasey looked at him when Ren was in the office was painful to see. He looked like a man in love, or at least in lust, and he couldn't even hide it—he was so taken with him. Fuck—I was even a little taken with him."

"Why didn't they see each other for ten years?" Will asked, his curiosity piqued.

"Because Ren's very traditional father caught them in bed together when Kasey was visiting Japan, and he freaked out.

He sent Kasey home immediately and forced Ren to marry a girl the family knew, threatening to disown him otherwise. Kasey promised he wouldn't reach out, afraid it would make things worse with Ren's family and that he'd wait for Ren to find him. Ren divorced his wife five months ago and came to New York for work a couple of weeks back. The first person he looked for was Kasey."

"Jules, don't lose your mind. You haven't even talked this out with him yet, have you? What makes you think that, even if he does still hold some love for Ren, he'd just forget about you? The man adores you. He looks at you like you're made of gold, and he went through hell to take care of you after the plane crash. Nobody does that without deep love. You need to calm down and talk this through with him. Maybe you should've told him how much you love him because, sweetie, it's obvious."

"I know. I should have," Julia said softly. "I need to call Micki; I wish she were here."

"Pick up the phone and call her. I'll be on Xbox—just let me know if you need anything."

***

"Damn, nothing's ever simple with Kasey, is it?" Micki said, glancing out at a family of deer in her backyard. After a moment, she added, "Kasey's deeply in love with you, Jules. I'd bet James on it." She smiled warmly at the phone. "He might not have said the words, but it's in the way he dotes on you— he always has. It's obvious to everyone but you two knuckleheads that you're in love. I don't think he'll walk away so easily. It all sounds and feels shitty, but let's see what happens this weekend. Maybe things won't be as they remember. Or you might have to share him until you all figure out what you want. Kasey doesn't rush emotional decisions, and this one's gonna be big for him."

Julia got up and leaned on the deck railing, staring out over the ocean. "I want to call him so bad, but I don't want him to think I'm checking up on him… which is exactly what I'd be doing."

"Don't call him. Wait until Monday. Give him the weekend to see what happens. I know it's hard, but if he were just home alone, you wouldn't be bothering him, would you?"

"I wouldn't call him, but I'd probably text, and he'd call back if he wasn't training or something. This is absolute torture." Her voice dropped, "You guys must be so tired of taking care of me this year... I'm sorry for being so fucking needy."

"You're not needy. It's been a tough year, and it's completely understandable. Besides, I'm your ride-or-die. I'll always be here for you. Always. I love you. Don't worry— things will be okay."

"I love you too, Micki. Thanks for listening."

"Anytime, kiddo."

Later, she fell asleep while snuggled up to Will on the double lounger, a blunt shared between them. He couldn't bring himself to wake her, so he spent the night on the deck with Julia clinging tightly to him. She ended up self-medicating all weekend, her anxiety too much to face sober. For the first time, she wished the weekend would end sooner.

Kasey glanced down at his vibrating cell, and seeing Julia's name felt like a palm strike to the chest. He took a deep breath. "It's Julia. I have to take this. Excuse me." They were seated on the couch, engrossed in an anime when his phone buzzed at seven-thirty.

"Hey, I didn't expect to hear from you. Is everything okay?"

"I need to talk to you. I tried not to bother you this weekend, but I feel like I'm going to lose my mind if I don't. Can I come over?" Julia's voice held an edge of raw, unmissable anxiety.

"Of course, you can. Can you come at eight-thirty?"

"Is he there now?" she asked, realizing he wouldn't have set a time if Ren wasn't there.

"Yes, but he was leaving soon anyway."

"Never mind. I'm sorry, I'll see you—"

"Julia, it's fine. Come over. We should talk."

"I'll see you at eight-thirty," she said, hanging up before the tears could start. "We should talk." The words felt like daggers Kasey had tossed casually at her heart. Those words were never followed by anything good. A wave of nausea swept over her.

Kasey turned to Ren, who was already standing, having overheard most of the conversation and picking up on Julia's tone. "Julia needs to see me. It would be better if she didn't see you right now. I'm pretty sure her intuition has already sensed something has changed."

"No need to apologize. Call me a ride while I get changed, and I'll be out of here in no time." Ren walked over to Kasey, giving him a lingering kiss and then a tight hug. "Thanks for the weekend. We'll take it slow. I don't want to hurt someone you love, and I have a feeling this isn't going to sit well with her, especially after what you've told me—and what I just heard. Maybe, in time, she and I can be friends." He rested his forehead against Kasey's, holding him close. "I'm so happy I got to spend this time with you. It was literally a dream come true for me." Smiling, he placed a reassuring hand on Kasey's shoulder. "Call the car. It'll be okay."

***

Fifteen minutes after Ren left, Julia rang the doorbell. All her emotions were written plainly on her face. Wearing sneakers, sweats, and no makeup, she looked vulnerable, her sad, soulful eyes fixed on him, instantly making him regret what he'd done.

"Would you like something to drink?" he offered as she sank onto the couch.

"No, thanks. My stomach feels a little off right now."

He sat down beside her. "How about some tea?"

With her anxiety spiraling, she couldn't wait any longer. Looking him directly in the eye, she asked, "I have to know. Did you sleep with him? Did he stay with you all weekend? You've never lied to me before—please don't start now. Just tell me the truth."

"I would never lie to you, Julia." He paused, his throat tight. "I slept with him, and he stayed here the whole weekend," he confessed, bracing himself for her reaction.

Her eyes filled with tears, and she said as calmly as she could, "I'll be right back." Heading to the bathroom, she turned on the faucet and threw up. A few minutes later, she rinsed her mouth, washed her face, and walked back out.

"Are you okay?" he asked, standing by the window with arms folded, concern etched on his face as he walked over to her.

"I'm pretty fucking far from okay," she said as he wrapped his arms around her. She cried softly, her arms hanging at her sides, her head resting on his chest, completely devastated. "The thought of you being with him is eating me up inside."

"Please don't cry. I'm so sorry. I know I made a mistake—I shouldn't have seen him alone. Sit down, please. Don't cry." He led her to the couch, sitting beside her and gently resting her head on his shoulder. She pulled back, her tear-filled eyes reflecting the depth of her pain.

"I know I labeled us as friends-with-benefits, but it was always more than that. We became so much more... at least, for me—Kasey, you're everything." Julia paused, her voice dropping to a pained whisper. "I love you, and I thought you loved me too. We just hadn't said the words." She took a deep breath. "Hearing you talk about him the way you did, knowing you were going to see him... it was soul-crushing. I spent the whole weekend wasted just trying not to think of you."

She paused, her gaze heavy with sadness. "It's not that you had sex with him... hell, I would have too. It's that you slept with him, held him, still love him—and probably told him so. It's the love part I can't get past," she said, her voice breaking into soft sobs. "I've never loved or depended on anyone the way I do you. I've loved you since the day we met, and now I feel like I'm losing you to someone I can't even begin to compete with." She buried her face against his chest, her sobs growing stronger."

"And we were supposed to talk about it first—that was our deal. But you didn't tell me," her words catching in soft, stuttered gasps. "This hurts so much," she sobbed, clutching her chest. "My heart is aching. The only other time I loved someone this much, he betrayed me and broke me. But now, I realize I didn't even love him half as much as I love you," she sobbed, her anguish raw and palpable.

"Why didn't you tell me about him before?" Kasey asked, his voice thick with emotion, tears brimming in his eyes.

"Because I was humiliated for letting him manipulate me, for missing all the signs. I didn't want you to think I was stupid and weak," she confessed, her voice trembling.

"I'd never think that about you. You're one of the most intelligent and resilient people I know."

She went on, "Micki tried to warn me, and I nearly lost her because of his lies. I found him in bed with the girl he'd insisted for months was just a friend. I swore I'd never let myself feel that kind of pain again—and I made sure I didn't until today." Her voice wavered, and suddenly, she clamped a hand over her mouth, rushing to the bathroom. The brutal mix of nausea and heartbreak overwhelmed her. He could hear her retching and sobbing, the sound ripping through him. Knowing he had caused her this kind of pain was almost unbearable.

She emerged from the bathroom, and collapsed onto the couch, her face pale, brow damp with sweat. "I hate being like this," she whispered, despair radiating from her. Rubbing her temples, she wept softly. "Sometimes, I don't even recognize myself. Loving you is consuming me." Tears rolled down her face, slipping onto her shirt as she pleaded, "Please, say something. Tell me you love me—that I'm not just imagining it. You can't take care of me the way you do and have sex with me the way you do, without loving me. I *feel* your love." She whispered, her voice barely audible, "Please, don't break me."

"Oh, Julia." He grasped her shoulders tightly, pain etched into his features, tears streaking his cheeks. "I'm so sorry I never told you; I should have. I was afraid it would make things uncomfortable, that it might change us somehow. I never wanted to alter what we have. I love you, Julia. I'm devoted to you. I would kill to protect you. It makes me so happy every day to care for you. When we make love, it's like being wrapped in pure love and peace. In your arms, nothing else matters. It's like you were made for me. I know your touch, your scent, your taste. Despite my flaws, you still want me." He cupped her face tenderly. "You touch my heart in ways no one else—not even Ren—ever has. The thought of losing you is unbearable."

She leaned back, "Then why did you sleep with him without telling me first? You could have called me, even just texted. You know what really hurts? Seeing how instantly different you were with him."

He paused, his voice softening. "I still love him, Julia. I wasn't thinking. I never expected to see him again, and I wasn't prepared to face the feelings I still have for him. I loved him so much for so long. He saved me from loneliness and loved me without question. We never walked away from each other; we were torn apart. I thought that chapter of my life was over. I have no idea how to navigate these feelings for both you and him. Please forgive me."

He enveloped her in his arms, holding her tightly. "I'm so sorry. There's no excuse for my actions—just incredibly poor judgment. I should have come to you first. Help me figure this out. I love you... please don't leave me."

She held his tear-stained, tormented face tenderly, her heart aching at the sight. Her voice, filled with pain and affection, trembled as she said, "How can you hurt me so deeply and then say the most beautiful things I've ever heard? I don't want to leave you. I never want to. I love you. I fought to have you, and I'll fight to keep you."

Pressing her damp cheek against his, she whispered, "I should hate you for hurting me, but all I want right now is you—holding me, showing me how much you love me. I'm addicted to you, Kasey—you have me completely." Wrapping her arms around him, she buried her face in his chest, her small body shaking with each shallow gasp.

He kissed the top of her head tenderly, then took her hand and led her upstairs to their room. At the door, she recoiled as if she'd spotted a rattlesnake. "Please, tell me you didn't bring him into this bed."

"I would never bring him in here. This is our space," he reassured her, the thought never crossing his mind. He lifted her into his arms, and she wrapped her legs around him, resting her head on his shoulder as he carried her to their bed and settled down beside her.

"Those were some powerful words downstairs. I knew you had deeper feelings for me than friendship, but I didn't realize they ran that deep. I'm deeply sorry for bringing this pain into your life. I just hope I'm worthy of a love like that," he said, tenderly brushing his cheek against hers.

She nestled closer to him. "As long as I know you love me, I can handle you working through your feelings for him," she said softly. "Even if it means you're intimate with him. I can share when it comes to sex... but, and this is a big but—you can't love him more than me or sleep with him more than you do me. If you do, I'll know. I have to be number one to you."

"You'll always be number one to me, I promise," he whispered, pressing a soft kiss to her lips, tasting the lingering salt of her tears.

"You also have to promise me that you'll let me know if anything ever changes between us. It'll hurt, but if I find out any other way, the betrayal would end me." Her voice dropped to a whisper, a hint of mischief in her tone. "Or you... or maybe Ren. You never know."

He held her tightly. "I know I made a huge mistake, but I won't make it again. I'll make this right. I promise. I love you, Julia," he said, his voice full of sincerity.

"I'm willing to help you through this. We'll figure it out together. I won't lose you," she assured him.

"Words cannot express what I feel for you right now," he murmured, his lips brushing tenderly over her neck.

"Then just show me," she whispered.

Their lovemaking was passionate and deeply intimate. For the first time, they exchanged the words *I love you* with unabashed emotion, each overwhelmed by the fear of losing the other. She fell asleep in his arms, determined to do whatever it took to keep him by her side.

***

Wasting no time, Julia called Micki as soon as she arrived at work the following day to share the details of her conversation with Kasey.

"I can't tell you how strange and confusing this whole situation is for me right now. The way he expressed his love felt so incredibly deep and sincere. The words were so beautiful—he told me he would kill to protect me, and I know it's true. I saw him at the Cattlemen's Dinner; he protected me like I was the crown jewel. It was like he was telling me he wanted to spend the rest of his life with me." She paused. "But he still needs to find out how Ren fits into his life. He really loves him."

Micki offered her perspective, "I can see how he'd still have strong feelings for someone he loved so intensely at that age. Back then, it was all about love and happiness without any of the adult baggage. But now? Maybe it's just a deep, lasting friendship—like you and James. The love you and Kasey have is solid, adult love. You two share something real, built on a lot more than just those feelings of first love. Don't overthink it; he's crazy about you. And hey, would it be so bad if he had oral sex with him once in a while? You've done a hell of a lot more with James, and we're still going strong," she reminded her with a chuckle.

Julia considered her words, "Then I think I need to get to know Ren better, check out my competition up close and personal. I'd like you and James to meet him too. I need your input and a guy's take. You wouldn't mind would you? I could use your help and support," Julia said.

"Mind? Are you shitting me?" Micki laughed. "I wouldn't miss this for the world. You really think he'll come?" she asked, excited about witnessing the unfolding situation in person.

"I'm gonna ask Kasey, then call Ren myself to invite him. Might as well make the first move and put him on my turf. Since I know Kasey loves me, I can handle this as long as I stay confident," Julia affirmed.

Micki boosted her confidence, saying, "There's my girl. I have no doubt you'll come out on top—pun very much intended."

Julia laughed. "I'm gonna talk to Kasey now, and I'll call you later."

"Good luck, Jules. And don't forget—call me."

***

She pressed the intercom, "Kasey, could you come in here, please?"

"Be right there," he replied.

He entered the office as she moved toward the couch with deliberate grace. "I want to ask you something," she began. "I'd like to get to know Ren, and I think we should make an effort to become friends. It's crucial for all of us to have a clear understanding of this situation."

He sat down next to her, and she continued, "For that to happen, he and I need to establish a connection and set some boundaries. I want to invite him to the beach for the weekend, and I'd like him to meet Micki and James when they come. You said he's friendly, and he certainly seemed that way to me. I promise I won't do anything to make him feel uncomfortable. Will's gonna be there too, so Ren won't feel like a third wheel with two couples. What do you think?"

279

Kasey responded with a warm smile, "I appreciate your willingness to get to know him for my sake. You're amazing for being so accepting of this. But... are you sure about doing this so soon? I'm not even sure I'm ready to be around them with this new situation," he said, a little uncomfortable with the thought.

"I'm not a saint," she admitted. "I'm getting to know him on my terms with backup. Micki and James will be there, and Will, too. That's the reason why I'm moving quickly. They go home after this weekend. Until I spend time with him and set my own boundaries, it'll eat away at me every time you're with him. I have to know what kind of man he is. Best to rip the band-aid off, right? Keep your friends close and your enemies closer. I need you to suck it up and give this to me. I need to get to know the man who has you so... unhinged."

"I am not unhinged," he said with a small smile, shaking his head. "And he's not your enemy; he's really not like that."

"We'll see," she smiled at him. "I was thinking I'd call him. He knows about us, right?"

"Yes, he knows all about us. I told him I love you," Kasey replied softly.

"Was that before or after you slept with him?" She looked down, quickly adding, "Sorry. It just... kinda sucks he heard those words before I did."

Kasey took her hand. "Don't apologize, I deserved that. I'm sorry, I genuinely regret not telling you."

She stopped him, "Please don't. Yes, we should have discussed you being with someone else first, but this is really my own fault." She glanced down, squeezing his hand. "I should've been more open about my feelings. I wanted to tell you I loved you the first time we slept together—I almost did. Subconsciously, I think I was still trying to protect myself, but it backfired. I'm sorry, I should have been upfront with you."

With a determined tone, she said, "No more friends-with-benefits. I wanna be a couple. I don't wanna hide how much I care about you. Is that okay?"

"I'm absolutely fine with that as long we're not taking out front page ads... it's just quiet and normal. Think you could do that?" he asked with a grin.

"I think I can manage to control myself," she smiled, leaning over for a quick kiss. "Well, maybe I can't," she giggled. "I will try, though." Kasey placed his hand behind her head, pulled her close, and gave her a proper boyfriend-kiss.

"Kasey Cortland! We're at work," she said with a wide smile, her eyes shimmering.

"Where's your phone?" he grinned as he got up.

"In the top drawer, why?"

"I'm putting Ren's number in so you can call him when you're ready. Anything else you need?

I'm going back to work."

She walked up behind him, her arms encircling his waist. "Do you think you could see Ren in public places or catch up on the phone for now? Just until I get a chance to know him a bit. Is that okay? It's less than two weeks. I'd like him to get to know me too. It'll be harder for him to try and steal you away if he gets to know me first," she said, her expression resolute.

He turned and said, "Maybe my girlfriend could come over for a sleepover tonight so we could talk about what you need. What do you think? I could even wash your hair." He wrapped an arm around her, gently brushing her hair off her shoulder.

"I think you should call Carl to pick us up at four-thirty. And reschedule that meeting with Dante for tomorrow."

"Barbara walked into Kasey's office just then, clearly noticing them with their arms around each other. Smiling, she laid a file on his desk and left without a word.

"Well, that'll be all over the office by the end of the day," Julia chuckled.

***

Chapter 15: Getting to Know Your Rival

"Hello?"

"Hey, Ren, it's Jules Masters."

"Oh, hey, Jules, what can I do for you?" Ren's voice carried a note of surprise, hoping this wouldn't turn into an uncomfortable call.

"I really don't know how to start, so I'm just gonna dive right in. After you left last night, Kasey and I had a pretty emotional conversation about you two and what happened over the weekend. We also defined our relationship. We shared feelings we hadn't expressed before, and I guess I can thank you for that in a way. I'm beginning to understand the depth of the bond you and Kasey share, especially considering how you were separated against your will. I want you to know that I love him deeply, and I won't let him go without a fight." She paused, letting the words settle. "And I'll fight dirty if necessary. But... I can also be a really good friend and share, as long as I don't feel threatened. You must be someone really special for him to care so deeply. He doesn't open up to just anyone."

Taking a breath, she continued, "I'd like to invite you to my beach house at the Jersey Shore next weekend—to get to know you and for you to get to know me. Three of my closest friends—a married couple and a guy I've known since college—will be there, too. I promise it won't be like a bunch of harpies sitting around judging you; it'll be relaxed and fun." A chuckle escaped him at her choice of words.

"We barbecue, drink a lot of wine, smoke some weed—which is legal in Jersey—dance, and sing karaoke. What do you say? Please come. They live in Colorado and will be here for vacation, so that's why I was hoping it could be next weekend." Ren couldn't believe she was so open and willing to get to know him.

"I'd love to come, Jules, and I'd be happy to meet your friends. For the record, I won't come between you and Spike. I'm sorry it got physical, but honestly, neither of us was thinking with the head on our shoulders. I'm not here to hurt anyone. He was my best friend, and I cared about him before we slept together. I can do that again. I don't want to lose him without exploring what kind of friendship we could have as adults. I love him too, but I could never let that be the reason he gets hurt. I've already caused him enough pain, and it hurts me to the core to find out how much he suffered because of my choices—and my father's. I should have stood up to my father and left that marriage much sooner, but I wasn't raised that way. It took years, and my grandmother's passing before I found the courage to move past the generational guilt my father dumped on me. I just don't want to lose Kasey as a friend again."

As she listened, she felt more reassured about him. He seemed to genuinely care about Kasey's happiness. "We'll leave on Friday at four-thirty by helicopter. You can meet us here, and we'll go to the helipad together at four. Are you okay with flying?"

"Never been on one, but I'm game," he said, clearly excited at the prospect of traveling by helicopter.

"I'm glad we talked, and I'm looking forward to you coming. I hope we can be friends, then I won't have to make you disappear," she chuckled softly like a movie villain, adding, "Just kidding."

Ren appreciated her sense of humor and replied, "I'm glad we talked too. I know we'll be good friends. Just get to know me before you try to get rid of me. See you next Friday. Goodbye, Jules."

"Bye, Ren."

***

"I'm going out at two for lunch; I have an appointment," Kasey said to Julia as they were going over a report together the next day.

"Where ya going?" she asked.

"Never you mind," he said with a sly smile.

"Fine, don't tell me," she said with a playful pout.

When he returned later, he entered her office and said, "Come, sit with me; I have something for you." Presenting her with a Tiffany's box, she marveled at her good fortune, reflecting on how Kasey's gift-giving tendencies mirrored her father's. He not only loved to shower her with gifts, but he also had an uncanny ability to choose items that perfectly matched her taste—this occasion was no exception. Inside the box lay a platinum chain with four carats of pink diamonds hanging in the shape of a heart.

"Oh, Kasey, it's gorgeous! What's this for?" Julia exclaimed.

"It's to let you know how I feel about you. Look at the tag by the clasp." She examined the tag, revealing "I Love You" on one side and the date 7/9/2023 on the other. "It's the day we said 'I love you' and became a couple."

Overwhelmed by emotion, she whispered, "You're gonna make me cry. Your thoughtfulness and the way you express yourself are incredibly romantic. Thank you for this. Put it on me, please," she whispered, her voice soft with anticipation as she turned and moved her hair to the side. As he placed the necklace around her neck, he followed it with a tender kiss, causing her to lean into him. One hand played with her necklace, the other tangled in his hair, holding his head close to her neck. "I have to look at it in the mirror," she said after a moment of bliss as Kasey gently pulled back, aware of their surroundings.

Radiating joy when she returned, she exclaimed, "It's so beautiful! Look how perfect it looks on my neck. I love it; I'm never gonna take it off."

Kasey smiled, "I'm so glad you like it. I'll never again make the mistake of not telling you how I feel about you."

Eager to share her joy, Julia couldn't wait to snap a selfie and send it to Micki, showing off his love for her. The week was filled with sweet kisses at work, cozy sleepovers, and passionate nights together. Even though Julia knew Kasey spoke with Ren every day and met him for lunch twice, she didn't feel threatened.

***

The Wednesday before their trip to the shore, Ren came to the office to take Kasey out for lunch, his unexpected arrival catching him off guard. "I thought I was coming downstairs to meet you," Kasey said, rising from his seat as Ren entered.

"I wanted to thank Jules personally for inviting me this weekend," he said, smiling.

"You didn't have to do that," Kasey replied.

Ren knocked on Julia's door, and when she looked up, he greeted her, "Hi, Jules, have a minute?"

"Of course. Do you want to sit down?" she offered as she got up, walked around her desk, and leaned against it.

"No, no, I just wanted to thank you in person for the invitation this weekend and our honest conversation. You're a special person, Jules. Not many would have handled this with such grace."

Showing her compassion and understanding, Julia responded, "I thought really hard about how you two must feel about all this. If it were me in Kasey's position, I'd want a chance to be with my first love again. I can forgive him for that temptation because, even though we should have talked about it first, if I'm honest, I probably would've done the same. I'm giving him a chance to see where you fit in his life. I love him that much."

Then, with a wink and a grin, she issued another warning. "Just remember, I may look small and vulnerable, but make no mistake—I will take you down if I feel you're disrespecting me. You won't even see it coming, and if I can't do it, I'll just pay someone to handle it for me. I can do that." She turned and walked back to her chair.

"I hear you loud and clear," he said, equally intimidated and intrigued. "I'm taking Kasey to lunch. I'd like you to come if you're free."

"Thanks, but I wouldn't want to intrude," she replied with a smile.

"You wouldn't be intruding, really. I'd love for you to come; we both would," he insisted, motioning for Kasey to join them. "We could get to know each other a little better before the weekend."

"I asked Jules to join us for lunch—convince her to come," Ren said as Kasey entered the office.

"Absolutely. Come with us," Kasey added, flashing a bright smile.

Sensing Kasey's happiness, she agreed, "Sure, that would be nice, but before we go, I have to cancel—"

"Already on it, boss," Kasey said as he left the office.

"Don't call me boss!" Julia laughed, shaking her head. When she excused herself to use the bathroom, Ren turned to Kasey and said, "Damn, your girl is feisty. She doesn't mince words, that's for sure."

"What did she say?" Kasey asked, curious.

"Let's just say she made it clear if I mess with her, she'll take me out," he laughed. "I like her; she's scary and sexy all at the same time." Amused by Julia's boldness, Kasey found immense happiness knowing she was so willing to fight for him.

***

As they enjoyed lunch at a quaint bistro, Carl discreetly watched them from a nearby table. Ren shared stories about their school days, his outgoing personality dominating the conversation.

Julia could see right away what Kasey saw in him—their personalities complemented each other, and Ren was genuinely a nice guy. She also realized that she and Ren shared more than a few qualities—they were both extroverted, chatty, witty, and both held Kasey's attention.

"I've never had lunch with security before," Ren mentioned, still trying to adjust to Julia's world.

"We've been discussing that," Kasey said seriously. "Julia needs security now more than ever, and I'm trying to get her to understand that."

"I have you and Carl. I'm fine. I'm trying to stay invisible and be a normal person for as long as possible." Julia said, brushing off his concerns.

"We will revisit this conversation, sweetheart. You don't seem to understand how vulnerable you can be at times."

"I read about that confrontation you had with protesters at some dinner. Does that happen often?" Ren asked.

"More in Colorado than here," Julia replied. "Damn protesters, always making a show of it."

"I hate to cut this short, but we have to get back, Julia. You have a conference call." Their hour-long lunch had run into two, and Kasey realized they needed to return to the office. They said their goodbyes, all feeling better about the upcoming weekend and how well they had connected.

Sitting at her desk, Julia shared her positive impression of Ren. "I really like him. He's very sweet and funny. I can absolutely see why you like him."

"He really is." Kasey smiled, pleased with how well Julia and Ren clicked.

***

"A package was just delivered by messenger for you," Kasey said, bringing it into her office that afternoon.

"It's not for me," she said with a sweet smile. "It's for you. Open it." He removed the contents from the envelope, revealing a fawn-colored suede box inside a matching presentation box. Nestled inside was a black rubber ID bracelet set with black diamonds.

"It's engraved," she said excitedly, watching him.

He turned it over and saw the inscription: "I Love You More, Julia 7/9/23."

"You're too much," he said with a soft chuckle, inspecting the bracelet. "I love it. Thank you, sweetheart. You didn't have to."

She countered, "You're not the only one who can give nice presents. I know you don't wear jewelry, but I thought you might humor me when we go places together. This just looked like your style—minimalist and sophisticated."

"I never bought myself jewelry, and no one's ever given me jewelry before, but I'll wear something you give me," he responded, putting it on. "I really like it," he said, leaning in to kiss her.

Running her fingers over the suede box, she admitted softly, "I know it's just my own insecurity talking, but I have to ask you about my necklace. It wasn't because you felt guilty, was it? Every painful, sweet, and wonderful thing that's happened in the past two weeks came about because of Ren coming back into your life. I want to know it wasn't only because of him that I got that necklace."

Kasey reassured her. "The timing for everything that happened was definitely because of him, but the reason I gave you that necklace and how I feel about you is genuine. I don't feel guilty. I know I could've handled things better, and I deeply regret hurting you. I really didn't think it through like I should have, but I don't feel guilty, and I wouldn't try to buy your feelings. I just wanted to give you something to show you how much I love and care about you now that I can openly tell you."

Relieved, she said, "I feel better. I love my necklace, and I love you," getting up to hug him.

"Good, I'm glad. Now I have work to do," he said with a smile before leaving her office.

∗∗∗

"Do you have plans for tonight?" Julia asked Kasey on Thursday as he brought in some files for her signature.

"Not really. I was just going to get ready for the weekend. Why?"

"I was wondering if you'd like to invite Ren over for dinner. The three of us could spend some more time together, just getting to know each other. You like to cook, so he could come for dinner."

A wide smile crossed Kasey's face. "That sounds great. I bet he'd love to join us. I'll give him a call."

Ren gladly accepted the invitation, and the three of them enjoyed a relaxed dinner, keeping the conversation light and easy. Kasey listened quietly as Julia shared her perspective of life on a ranch while Ren's stories of his traditional and exotic life in Japan captivated them both.

Later that night, as Julia snuggled up to Kasey in bed, she told him again how much she liked Ren. Kasey smiled and shared that Ren had texted him after leaving, saying the same thing about her.

∗∗∗

At three-fifty, Ren walked into Kasey's office with his weekender, a garment bag, and a beautifully flowered gift bag. "I am so ready to go to the beach by helicopter," he said excitedly, smiling at Kasey as he dropped his bags. Kasey got up and gave him a hug. "We'll leave as soon as Julia comes out; she's changing,"

"I love what you're wearing. Are those mother-of-pearl buttons?" Ren asked, scanning Kasey up and down appreciatively. "You look great in baby blue and white."

"Thanks, it's Italian linen—great for the beach."

291

Right on cue, Julia emerged from her bathroom in her cashmere baby blue hoodie set with flare-legged pants and comic-print sneakers. Her hair was plaited in a soft, messy braid cascading over her shoulder, and Kasey's necklace sparkled around her neck.

"This is for you, just to say thanks for the invite—and for not making me vanish." Ren presented the bag with a cheeky smile, his eyes sparkling with amusement.

She raised an eyebrow and said, "Not yet, anyway."

"Damn, girl, you're so feisty," he said, glancing at Kasey and giving him a wink.

"You didn't have to do this," she said, pulling out a box and unveiling an indigo-blue, French floral silk scarf. "But I'm glad you did! I actually have something perfect to wear this with over the weekend." She rubbed the soft scarf against her cheek, then read the attached card. *I really hope we can be friends, Ren.*"

"We already are," Julia said, her sweet smile and bright eyes radiating friendship. Collecting their bags, Kasey announced, "We'd better get going."

***

The rhythmic *whop, whop, whop* of the rotor filled the air as they approached the helicopter. Kasey stowed the bags while Ren helped Julia inside. Once they donned their headsets and heard Kasey speak to the pilot, they were on their way to the Jersey Shore.

"This is really wild," Ren said, his voice brimming with excitement as he gazed over the sprawling cityscape. Kasey and Julia took turns pointing out different landmarks as they flew along the coastline. Forty minutes later, they touched down at a small airport near Mantoloking, NJ—Julia's turf for the past five years. A sleek, dark blue, four-door convertible awaited them. They hopped in, with Ren settling into the back seat, Kasey behind the wheel, and Julia pointing out everything she loved about her favorite beach town.

"Wow, this house is massive! What a stunning property," Ren exclaimed as Kasey drove

through the imposing black iron gates. Micki and James greeted them at the door, where Julia introduced Ren. Will had arrived the day before to spend time with Micki and James, so he was already in the kitchen as they walked in.

"Well, aren't you handsome. You weren't exaggerating, Jules," Micki said, shaking Ren's hand, her eyes lingering a little longer than usual.

"Down girl," Julia said, grinning, noticing the extra sparkle in Micki's eyes as she looked at Ren.

"Thank you, what a nice welcome," Ren replied as he returned Micki's smile with one of his own, his charm disarming as he gave her hand a gentle squeeze. James, standing just behind her and keeping a close eye on the interaction, felt a small flicker of something he couldn't quite name—curiosity, perhaps, as he caught the look on Micki's face. She had always admired good looks, but the spark in her eyes as she looked at Ren was... notable. He wondered what it was about Ren that had her so quickly drawn in.

"Your home is beautiful, Jules," he added, looking around.

"Will Michelson, meet Ren Ito," Julia said, introducing them.

"Nice to meet you, man," Will greeted, shaking his hand.

"You too," Ren replied, catching a faint whiff of weed.

"Come with me," Julia said. "I'll show you where you're staying." She led him upstairs to his room at the end of the hall, with Kasey following behind.

"Wow, what a great room," Ren remarked, hanging his garment bag in the closet.

"I hope you'll be comfortable here," Julia said with a sweet smile, "and I don't just mean the room. If you need anything, just ask Kasey or me."

"Thanks. I can't imagine not being comfortable or needing anything here," he replied.

"Come, look at the view from her room. Do you mind?" Kasey asked.

"Of course not," she said, taking Ren's hand and leading him across and down the hall to her room.

"Damn, what a view," he marveled. "You can see all the way down the beach. And the water... look at all the sailboats." He turned to Julia. "What a great room to wake up in."

"It's really nice to wake up here in the cooler months when we can open the windows and listen to the waves and seagulls—my version of heaven." She grinned and flashed her baby blues at Ren, "Let's go have something to drink; it's party time."

Everyone was gathered around the kitchen island when they came downstairs. Julia asked, "What's going on down here? James, did they deliver the food yet?" Will poured and handed her a glass as she spoke.

"Yep, we're all set. When do you want to start cooking?"

Realizing the time, Julia suggested, "It's already five-thirty. How 'bout we start getting things together now?" With that, she and Micki began pulling out veggies to cut up and roast while the guys stood on the deck talking and drinking as James prepared the grill.

Micki and Julia stood by the slightly open window, giving them a vantage point to watch and listen as Ren and Kasey interacted with the others. Ren blended in effortlessly with the group—engaging, funny, and making the guys laugh with stories of his college days in Tokyo. He displayed a natural inclination towards physical contact—hugging easily, offering pats on the back, and resting his hand on shoulders—gestures Kasey never initiated. As everyone observed Kasey engaging in these gestures with Ren, it was clear there were no walls between them.

"He's not at all what I expected," Micki said, a hint of surprise softening her voice as she chopped up a yellow squash. "He's really hot. I love his hair and the way he dresses. He looks like such a bad boy, but he doesn't act or sound like one." She glanced over at Julia. "He's the opposite of Kasey, socially, isn't he? He's definitely an extrovert. You can see he likes being around people, and he has an easy way about him that puts everyone at ease right away. When you think about it... he's kinda like you. All the things Kasey told you he liked about Ren are qualities you have. You can't see that?" Micki chuckled mischievously. "Kasey's in love with a male and female version of the same person. Frigging unreal."

"No way... you really think so?" Julia took a moment to absorb that statement. "Is that weird?" she asked.

"Not really, when you think about it. He's bisexual, so why wouldn't he be attracted to the same qualities in both men and women?"

"Kasey looks so happy around him. Look at his face, the way he looks at Ren when he talks or makes a joke," Julia remarked, amazed at Kasey's obvious change. "Do I make him that happy?"

"Of course you make him that happy. You take care of him emotionally, and that's huge for Kasey. I honestly believe you two will end up together. So, he has a very close male friend... what's the harm? Kasey always reminded me of an old soul, now he seems his age—or even younger," Micki observed.

"This could be good, Jules. Kasey needed a friend who could bring him out of his shell. Maybe they're just gonna be very close friends, like you and me."

"I hope so; he really does look happy," Julia replied as Will came in and asked if they were ready.

"All done," Micki said as she passed him the foil-wrapped veggies.

Kasey poked his head in the doorway, announcing, "Taking a quick walk with Ren to show him the area. We'll be right back."

Micki and Julia watched them amble toward the water, exchanging playful shoves, their laughter echoing like carefree teenagers on vacation.

Julia stepped out onto the deck and asked, "Well, what do you guys think?"

James glanced up from the grill and remarked, "He seems like a nice guy. They've got that best friend vibe, like you and Micki." Adjusting the food, he added, "I've never seen Kasey smile so much before. He's always so serious. With Ren, he seems more relaxed, like a different person." Turning to Julia, he reassured her, "He's happy Jules, doesn't mean he loves you any less."

"Thanks, James," Julia said, hugging him. "I appreciate your opinion."

"Anytime," he replied, wrapping her in a bear hug.

Will chimed in, "Do I get a say in this?"

"Of course. Give it to me straight," she said, turning toward Will as James released her from the bear hug.

Will offered his thoughts. "They were definitely best buds once. They can practically finish each other's sentences on certain subjects. Kasey's a whole different person around him.

Ren's friendship looks good on him. The other stuff will work itself out, or you'll find a way to make it work, I have no doubt. You're resourceful, Jules. Remember, there are lots of different types of love and relationships. As long as you feel loved and emotionally cared for, nothing else should matter. Look at you three—smashing for years, and you're all still close."

Julia laughed. "And that kind of advice is why I still tolerate you all." She hugged Will and said, "When did you guys get so emotionally aware? I don't know how I would've gotten through this year without you." With their arms around each other, Micki said, "Ride or die, bitches."

Kasey and Ren walked up with Ren chuckling, "What's the huddle for? Can anyone join?" Kasey smiled, "This is a meeting of the ride-or-die club, the OG members." They all laughed as Micki teased, "Look at you being funny—who knew?"

"Ride-or-die, huh?" Ren nodded, glancing at Kasey, "It's nice to have friends like that, ones you can count on."

"Dinner in thirty minutes," James announced. "Go find something to do, and don't hover over me and the grill."

Julia gave Will a nod, silently asking him to engage Ren. She then went over to Kasey and whispered, "I need to see you upstairs for thirty minutes."

"Ren, Jules tells me you're into anime. I used to watch some back in college. What are your favorites?" Will asked, following Ren inside and steering him toward the living room.

Julia took Kasey's hand and led him upstairs to her bedroom. Closing the door behind them, she said, a mischievous twinkle in her eyes, "You have exactly thirty minutes to make me come. Think you can do it?"

"Sweetheart, I *do not* need thirty minutes," he said with a sly smile. I brought your little friend, and I think I can manage it in… five?"

"Nope, I want more time than that," she said, pressing herself against him.

"I can do it without, but then I might need ten minutes," he said seductively, wrapping his arms around her.

"That sure of yourself, huh?" she replied with a grin, reaching down to grab his crotch.

"No, no, no," he laughed, pushing her hand away. "You're wasting time… on the bed, now. And yes, I'm that sure. I know exactly which of your buttons to push. I told you, I'm a fast learner. Challenge accepted." He started the timer on his phone.

Yes, sir." She jumped on the bed. "Wait, stop the clock—I need to rinse off."

"Not necessary," he said, pulling off her pants and spreading her legs, wasting no time.

When she arched her back, gripped the sheets, and moaned as she came, her hips moving involuntarily under his mouth and her warm, wet, insides contracting around his fingers, he knew he'd won that challenge. As her climax shifted from intense storm-fueled waves to soft, gentle rolls, she pleaded breathlessly, "Stop." She released her hold on his head, rolled onto her side, and hugged her pillow, her legs tightly closed.

"God, baby, that was so good," she purred, her body tingling. He moved beside her, wrapping an arm around her and kissing her neck. "You certainly do know which buttons to push," she sighed.

He held up his watch. "Eight and a half minutes," he said, a goofy smile on his face.

"You win the challenge, and I reap the benefits. Win-win," she murmured, a satisfied smile on her lips.

"Would you like me to...?" she offered.

"No, we'll have time for that tonight. Just enjoy right now," he whispered, kissing her neck.

"Don't fall asleep," he said after a moment when he heard her sigh again.

"I better get up now, then," she mumbled reluctantly, reaching for her pants as Kasey went to wash his face.

***

Will and Ren were watching anime and talking while Micki was out at the grill with James when they came downstairs. Julia and Kasey grabbed drinks, with Kasey going to sit with Ren as Julia headed out onto the deck.

"Still doing it like bunnies, I see," Micki remarked with a grin, giving Julia a once-over.

"Jealous much?" Julia laughed.

"Little bit," Micki admitted with a smirk.

"Hey, I'm right here," James said, wrapping his arms around Micki. "You get enough sex, and if you want more, just ask babe," he added, spreading his arms wide.

"I was just teasing her. I'm perfectly fine for sex, thank you very much," Micki said with a grin. "But just to be sure, pace yourself with the wine and weed. I'm putting you to work tonight," she added, her hand slipping between his legs. Micki's words and touch heated things up, and they couldn't keep their hands or lips off each other.

Julia cleared her throat. "Um, I'm still here, guys. Maybe you need fifteen minutes? Kasey managed it in eight and a half for me." She flashed them a mischievous smile. "I could watch the food."

"No offense, Jules, but I've got the food to this point. It needs less than fifteen minutes, so I'm not leaving it alone with you. We're grownups; we can wait until later, right, babe?" James said, checking the food.

"Well, we could, or you could get Will to watch the food, and you could be my appetizer. Then tonight, you can focus on me for dessert," she said, raising one eyebrow with a naughty grin.

"Meet me in the room in two minutes," he said, heading inside to find Will.

Micki grinned. "And that's how you keep 'em once you got 'em. He gets a blow job now, ten minutes tops—probably less, 'cause I'm that good," she laughed. "And later, I get all the attention. Back in ten," she added with a confident smile.

Julia chatted with Will while he kept a watchful eye on the food sizzling away on the grill. She helped him carefully remove everything from the heat while Kasey and Ren emerged from indoors with the rest of the meal.

Five minutes into dinner, James and Micki returned, looking flushed and happy.

"Grownups, huh?" Julia teased. James shot her a playful grin. "Shut up, Jules."

Glancing over the table, he asked, "How's the food? All good?"

"Everything's perfect," Julia said.

"This all looks great," Ren chimed in.

Everyone ate, drank, and then worked together to clean up after dinner. When Ren suggested a dip in the water before nightfall, Julia eagerly volunteered, hoping for some private time with him. She slipped into a one-shoulder, high-cut, one-piece swimsuit and met him at the water's edge.

"It's a bit choppy," he said, extending his hand. "Here, take my hand. I'm a strong swimmer." His smile glowed in the fading sunlight. "Sorry, that came out like I didn't think you could handle it. Are you comfortable in the water?" he asked as they ventured into the waves.

"I can swim, but sometimes, if the waves get strong, I might get tossed around a bit," she replied with a laugh. As they stood chest-deep in the water, she turned her back to the waves just in time to get engulfed. Ren's firm grip caught her waist, lifting her effortlessly.

"You okay?" he chuckled, his arms encircling her. She held onto his shoulder with one hand wiping her face as she sputtered, "I'm good."

"Maybe we should move back a bit so the water won't be so high for you," he suggested.

"Or... you could just hold me up," she countered, turning to face the waves and tightening his embrace around her.

"Or, I could just hold you up," he repeated, lifting her with the incoming wave.

"Your friends are really nice, Jules. I feel comfortable around them, especially Will. He's a chill dude." They both chuckled. "I get the impression that Kasey's a bit different with me around. They all seem surprised when he laughs out loud or when I push him or throw my arm around him," he said.

"You're pretty observant," she said, "and 100% correct. Kasey's a different man with you around." She turned in his arms to face him. "Mind if I wrap my legs around you? It'll keep me from flopping around as much."

"Sure," he said, feeling her legs wrap around his waist.

"I've never seen him so friggin' happy. No, I take that back—I've seen that face after sex," she grinned, "but not from just being around me. I'm a little jealous," she admitted.

"Jules, I might make him laugh, but the man is deeply in love with you," he said, his gaze steady. "I'm actually a bit jealous of the bond you two share. He talks about you all the time. He tried to stick to your arrangement, but I didn't make it easy for him. If you ever made him choose, he'd absolutely pick you—he loves his life with you. And it's clear you're good for him. I've never seen him so confident, so happy. You have nothing to worry about with me in his life. I promise I'm not here to make trouble." He lifted her as a large wave rolled in and continued, "I'm incredibly attracted to Kasey; I have been since the day I met him. But it's more than physical. I love his brooding personality, his quietness. I love that I can make him blush and laugh so easily. He's so caring—he'd give you the shirt off his back. I've never connected with anyone, male or female, like I have with him. And if it means I can stay in his life without upsetting what you two have, sex is off the table," he assured her, his voice soft but resolute.

"I don't necessarily want you to take sex off the table. I'm more open to… different scenarios than Kasey. I can share." Julia offered a hesitant smile. "But there are conditions. We don't use a condom—I'm on the pill—so if you ever want to be with someone else, you'd need to let Kasey know and use protection. No sneaking around. You never need to hide your affection for him from me or from my friends; they all know, and we don't keep secrets from each other. You'll find that out," she added with a grin. "One last thing, and it's important—I must always come first with Kasey. Can you handle that?"

"I can definitely handle that. And I'm not looking for anyone else. I would never get involved with another person without discussing it first... I just saw what that could do." He offered her a small, apologetic smile. "I'd never undermine your relationship in any way. My feelings for Kasey can stay private outside your friend group."

She pressed her cheek against his chest, tightened her embrace, and sighed. "You're so much nicer than I thought you'd be. No wonder he loves you. I thought this was gonna be a real shit show, and I'd lose him. I don't think I could have handled that after the year I've had."

"I'm sorry for your loss. I promise no drama from me." He held her close, his chin resting gently atop her head, relieved that they'd cleared the air and she'd set her boundaries.

Kasey came onto the deck, watching them for a moment before Micki joined him. "They seem to be getting along nicely," she observed, leaning against the railing beside him. "Tread lightly, Kasey," she warned, looking up at him. "She's extremely fragile right now. She puts on a brave face, but sometimes she's hanging on by a thread. Her family, the business pressure, surgery, you, now him—it's a lot, even for Julia Masters, CEO. I don't want to see her slip backward. She's doing so well."

Gazing out over the ocean, he said, "It was her choice to bring him here. I thought it was too fast, but I'm trying to make up for how this all happened. I'm letting her take the lead," he added, his tone a bit defensive.

"I'm not criticizing or placing blame. I'm just reminding you that I love her, and I'd do anything for her, including watching over her. I've never seen her so deliriously happy with anyone, but I've also never seen her so wounded. You hold a lot of emotional power over her, and I'm sure a smart man like you can see that. Just be careful—don't let her get hurt." She smiled, raised an eyebrow, and gave him the "I'm watching you" gesture, which made him laugh.

"I know better than anyone but you exactly what she's been through this year. I'd sooner cut off my own arm than cause her any more pain. Julia's in charge—what she says goes. Ren and I have already discussed ways to make sure she's considered first in anything. Don't worry; she won't get hurt. I'd stop seeing him before I let that happen. I love her," he said, turning back to the ocean. Noticing Ren carrying Julia toward the shore, he exclaimed, "What the hell?" and quickly headed to meet them, with Micki following closely behind.

***

"Maybe we should head in; it's getting dark," Julia said, unwrapping her legs and stepping down. "Ow! What the hell?!" she yelped, jumping back into Ren's arms. She lifted her foot, revealing a bloody inch-long gash along the inside of it.

"Shit, what did you step on?" Ren asked, leaning in to examine her bleeding foot.

"Probably the sharp edge of a shell. Damn, it really hurts," she said with a wince. "Watch where you step."

"Let's get you back to shore," he said, helping her maneuver through the waves to the shallow water before scooping her up in his arms.

"Ren, don't be silly—I can walk," she said as he lifted her up.

"You're bleeding—it'll get all sandy."

Kasey met them, exclaiming, "What happened?" His voice held a touch of panic as he looked her over and spotted her bleeding foot. Micki took a look and said, "You might need stitches—that looks deep."

"I'm fine. I think it was a sharp shell—I just stepped down on it." As Ren placed her on the double lounger, Kasey tossed a towel to him. "Hold this on her foot. I'll get the first aid kit."

Julia smiled, taking the towel from Ren. "He's in crisis mode—best stand back and let him do his thing." He stepped back to stand with Micki as Kasey came out a moment later, followed by James and Will.

"What happened?" James asked.

"Julia cut her foot on a shell. Alert the media," Julia said, laughing. "It's no big deal, guys—I'm fine."

"Let me see," Kasey said, sitting down next to her. She propped her foot up on his lap, and everyone leaned in to take a look.

"See, it's nothing. Everybody go back inside—I'm fine," she said as Kasey cleaned the wound with hydrogen peroxide. "Ow, shit, that burns," she whined.

"Come on guys, she's gonna be fine. Let's give her some breathing room. Somebody get the pit going, grab the marshmallows and wine. Ren, could you turn those deck lanterns on? Will, get your party favors, and let's get high," Micki ordered, taking charge.

Gently blowing on the cut, Kasey remarked, "Sorry, I've got to clean it out. I hope it was a shell and not a rusty piece of metal." Examining it closer, he added, "This is deep—you may need a couple of stitches."

"Absolutely not. Just slap on one of those butterfly band-aids. Seriously, I'm fine. I'll stay off it tonight. If it keeps bleeding or really starts to hurt, I'll let you know, doc."

"I really think," he began, squeezing her skin together to place the bandage.

She leaned in, planting a kiss on him. "Baby, I'm fine." As he finished wrapping her foot in gauze, she said. "I need to change. Help me up, please." Ren watched how Kasey completely tuned out the rest of the world to focus on Julia and the tender care he gave her.

"Wait," Will said, bringing her a lit blunt. "Take this— you'll feel no pain." He grinned, sliding it between her fingers.

"Thank you, Will, just what I need. See you guys in a bit."

"I'll bring you up—I have to change, too," Ren offered. He lifted her into a fireman's carry, draping her over his shoulder. Laughing, Julia hit the blunt and blew out the smoke, ducking her head as they headed inside.

"Well, that's one way of getting where you want to go," Micki said as they passed by the living room. "Need any help, kiddo?" she called up the stairs.

"No, thank you!" Julia replied.

As Ren set her down on the bed, he asked, "Need anything?"

"No, thanks. Kasey will be here in no time," she said as he entered the room. "Do you smoke? I just assume everyone our age does," she added with a chuckle.

"I'm just a beginner. Drugs aren't common in Japan like they are here. I'd only tried it a few times a few years back. I smoked with Kasey, and I definitely enjoyed it."

"Hit this before you go, but not too much—Will's shit is pretty potent," she said, handing the blunt to Ren. He took two small hits and then passed it to Kasey.

"I'm gonna take a shower. I'll see you guys downstairs."

"Thanks for all your help," Julia said as Kasey closed the door.

"I just realized I need a shower. I'm all sandy, and now my foot's all bandaged up so nicely," she said with a pout.

"Well, I could wrap it in plastic. Be right back," Kasey said, handing her the blunt before heading downstairs. She took a hit, limped to the bathroom, peeled off her bathing suit, and wrapped a towel around herself. Instead of showering, she decided on a bath. She turned on the spigots, filling the vintage claw-foot tub with hot water and a handful of her favorite lavender bath salts. The soothing scent filled the steamy room just as Kasey walked in.

"Sorry to make you go get all that stuff, but I figured I could just as easily take a bath and keep my foot on the edge of the tub—with a little help getting in and out," she said.

"Good idea. You could keep your foot up, and I'll wash your hair, while you tell me what you and Ren talked about," Kasey suggested, carefully lifting her into the tub. He positioned her leg on the edge of the tub, tucking a bath pillow behind her head and a towel under her foot. She relaxed as he took a seat beside the tub.

Closing her eyes, she sighed as he turned off the water and began washing her leg with a sea sponge, making sure all the sand was removed. He gently scrubbed her body as she held onto the sides of the tub.

"Lean forward a little," he said softly, washing her back and brushing her hair over her shoulder. He wet her hair with the shower wand and massaged shampoo in, eliciting soft, contented sighs as his skilled hands worked her scalp and neck.

"So, tell me—what did you two talk about?" he asked, his curiosity getting the better of him.

"Oh, God, I'm sorry, baby. Your touch puts me in a happy coma," she giggled. "We had a great talk. I really like him— he's so sweet, and he genuinely cares about you. He said all he wants is to be in your life, that he's not here to cause problems. After talking with him, I realized we're a lot alike. He told me he was attracted to you from the day he met you, just like I was. We're both extroverts and yet we're both so drawn to your brooding, quiet reserve, as he put it. We both appreciate your caring nature and how you always put our needs first. The only real difference I see is that you connect with me more deeply and emotionally, while with Ren, he brings out your happy, childlike side."

Kasey quietly continued washing and conditioning her hair as he listened to her tell him why and how much they both loved him.

"He told me he wouldn't pursue a sexual relationship with you if I didn't approve, but honestly baby, I don't mind. If he makes you happy, then it makes me happy... win-win. Life's too short to deny love. I can't do that to you or him. But remember, my rules stand. I am loved the most, and I am always #1," she said with a grin, flicking water at him.

"Loved the most, and #1. Got it," he said with a warm smile. "I'm so happy you two had a chance to talk alone. I knew you'd like him once you got to know him." He leaned in to kiss her, his hand gently caressing her face. "I love you so much—let's rinse you off so I can show you how much."

As Ren approached their door, he heard Kasey's intimate murmurs, followed by Julia's soft giggles, as Kasey showered her with his love. Smiling, Ren turned and headed downstairs.

A little while later, Kasey, with Julia on his back, joined everyone on the deck, sitting around the fire pit, roasting marshmallows, drinking, and getting high. Later, they played Pictionary, splitting into two teams. Ren seamlessly integrated into the group, with everyone finding him easy to connect with.

Micki and James were the first to call it a night, eager to get back to their room and pick up where they left off. Sensing that Kasey and Julia were staying for his sake, Ren suggested, "Go guys, I'll see you tomorrow."

"He'll be fine," Will said. "He can watch some anime with me if he wants."

"Sounds good," Ren said with a smile.

As they left, Kasey hesitated and said, "If you're sure—"

"Good night, guys," Ren said, waving them off from the couch.

***

"Good morning," Julia greeted as Will came into the kitchen, reaching over to ruffle his hair. "You look a little rough around the edges," she added, chuckling.

"Morning," he mumbled, scratching his head. "What frigging time did you get up this morning?"

"Around eight—not too early. Kasey went for a run with Ren around eight-thirty, and I picked up some bagels," she said, gesturing to the assortment of bagels and spreads on the kitchen island.

"How's your foot?" he asked, wiping sleep from his eyes.

"Sore, but not a big deal. I probably couldn't have driven if it was my right foot," she replied, sitting down and resting her foot on the chair next to her.

"Micki and James come down yet?" he asked, eyeing the bagels.

"Haven't seen them—probably sleeping in. She makes fun of me for being loud, but they were pretty friggin' loud themselves. I heard a lot of "Don't stop," she laughed, sipping her tea.

"I'm used to it; somebody's always having loud sex when I'm around you guys," he said with a smirk.

"Well, you could get a partner of your own and join in," she teased.

"I'm perfectly happy without a partner, Jules. Just my luck to be best friends with a bunch of hyper-sexual degenerates," he said, grinning, as he sliced a bagel.

She laughed. "So, did you and Ren have a nice time after we all went to bed?"

"He's a really nice guy, Jules—I like him a lot. I'm surprised he got up so early for a run. I got him pretty fucked up last night; didn't realize he was such a lightweight," Will chuckled. "It's funny, Kasey's so formal and reserved, while Ren's animated and informal. He acts and sounds more like an American than Kasey. We talked for a couple of hours while we watched anime. He's easy to get to know. He likes to talk. Fun fact—do you know why Kasey calls you Julia and not Jules?" he asked mischievously.

"I thought it was because he just liked my name," she replied, a hint of curiosity in her voice.

"It's because Spike, the main character in *Cowboy Bebop*—the anime he's so into—was in love with a girl named Julia. They're star-crossed lovers; he dies, avenging her death. Ren actually looks a little like Vicious, the other part of their love triangle, with his long hair." Will laughed, taking a bite before continuing, "Freaky, huh? That one gun Kasey has at home? Same as the one Spike uses. And he even trains in the same style of martial arts. You should watch the show with him sometime; it might give you more insight into him."

She was quiet, processing what felt like an incredibly romantic gesture. "I swear, I find out something new about Kasey every day. I find him fascinating, and I've never felt this way about anyone else."

"I've never seen you this obsessed with a guy before. He must have something special going on," he said, taking a bite of his cinnamon raisin bagel. "I like Kasey. I think you two are good for each other—he grounds you, and you lift him up."

She smiled thoughtfully. "I've been thinking about what Micki said about sharing James and how it doesn't change their love for each other. I'm sure I can do the same thing. I can separate love from sex... it's the love I worry about. But if it's the kind of love I have for James, then I can let them have that.

And, if all they're having is oral sex once in a while, I can handle that."

"I can see you handling something like that, no problem. But what if their love goes deeper than that?" Will asked, adding more butter to his bagel.

"If I'm really being honest, I already know it's more than that. I'm just gonna have to figure something out—I won't lose him," Julia said with conviction. "I need to see them together. I think I'll instigate a threesome... he was with his wife for ten years, so I know he's been with a woman. What do you think?"

"If you need to see them interact, I don't think too much of that's gonna happen naturally with you there. I'm pretty sure you'll be the center of attention. You might have to sit back, watch, and not participate. Could you do that? Are you really prepared to watch your man have sex with someone he's told you he loves?"

"Good question... I dunno, but Micki does it. I know it doesn't bother me as much as if Ren were a woman. I dunno why, but I think I'd have a much harder time with this if that were the case. Still, I think I have to see them together so I don't get random thoughts wondering what goes on between them."

She took a moment to reflect. "I think I'm going to mess with Ren a little and see how he reacts to me. He's way more extroverted than Kasey, and maybe he's a bit thirsty after coming out of a sexually unfulfilling marriage. I bet it wouldn't take much; he already flirts with me, and I giggle like a schoolgirl every time he does. If I'm being really honest, I find Ren extremely attractive, and I wouldn't mind having a go at him. I've never been with two men at the same time before— bet that feels different." She shot Will a naughty grin. "I might really like this setup. I have a strong feeling Kasey would like us all to get closer."

Will laughed. "Do what you feel is best for you and Kasey. I have no doubt you'll figure it all out."

"Thanks for listening, Will, and spending time with Ren last night so he didn't feel left out. You're the best. Hey, do you think you can get some really good weed for me? I don't want to smoke up all yours. I think we need a dance party, and that'll definitely help," she said with a grin.

"I can get you anything you want, Jules, guaranteed to get the party started," he said with a sly smile. "You want some Molly? That'll really kick off your private party."

She laughed, "Better not. Molly and two men... I might just do myself in with sex. The weed should be good enough. Get a couple of ounces," she said, her eyes lighting up at the thought of a dance party, "I think I need to go shopping for some extra-sexy clothes."

"Oh boy, this is gonna be good, and I am all for it... dance party tonight!" he yelled, making them both laugh.

"I'm gonna wake that lazy, good-for-nothing Micki and go shopping. It'll give the guys some time together without me. Oh, they're back," she said, spotting Kasey and Ren at the water's edge. They were laughing as Ren pushed Kasey toward the water, and both of them ran in, diving under the waves. She stood up and limped over to the window, leaning on the sink for a better view.

"I've seen Kasey here plenty of times, but I've never seen him swim. I thought he didn't like swimming in the ocean," Will said, watching them fool around in the water. "They're like teenagers around each other. Have you noticed that?"

"Yeah, I did." She put her cup in the sink and said, a bit distracted, "I think I'm gonna have some naughty fun with two teenage boys tonight."

Laughing, Will shook his head and said, "You go girl. You do you—or in this case, you do them. I gotta go make a call."

***

Julia stood at the window watching them roughhouse in the water as Micki and James entered the kitchen.

"Morning, kiddo. Whatcha looking at?" Micki asked as she walked up behind Julia, spotting Kasey and Ren playfully pushing each other in the water.

James walked up behind Julia, wrapped his arms around her, and kissed the top of her head. Glancing out the window, he asked, "You okay?"

"Oh, I'm fine. I had a long talk with Will a few minutes ago and made a decision."

"Now why does that sound like trouble brewing?" James said, pouring coffee for himself and Micki.

"No, trouble. I asked Will to get some weed for a dance party tonight. I'm gonna mess around with Ren a bit and see what I'm up against—and show him what he's up against."

"I don't know, Jules. You think that's a good idea? Maybe you're rushing things a bit," James said, concern and a hint of jealousy in his tone.

"That's a big decision," Micki said, still watching the scene outside.

"Well, like you said, if it's just sex I'm up against, I've got more experience than the two of them put together," Julia said with a smirk, limping back to her chair.

"Poor Ren's not gonna know what hit him," Micki chuckled, turning to the island and picking out a bagel.

"How's your foot? You're limping." James said, noticing her gait.

"A little sore, but I can handle it. Do you two have any plans today?" Julia asked. James and Micki exchanged a look.

"No, not really," Micki replied. "Why?"

"Because I need you to go shopping with me... I've got some sexy clothes to buy."

"Jules, everything you own is sexy," Micki laughed, offering James a bite of her bagel. "But I'm up for some shopping. I might even buy something for my man," she added, smiling lovingly at James. He wrapped his arms around her, "You don't need anything to make you sexier to me, babe."

"Good answer," she said, wiping butter off the corner of his mouth. "Can't hurt to look. Let's go shopping, Jules!" Just then, Kasey walked in, a towel wrapped around his waist, while Ren stayed behind, catching some rays on the deck.

"Did you have a nice run?" Julia asked as Kasey approached her.

"It was great," he said with a smile. "It's nice to have someone to run with who can keep up with me."

"Sorry, I have to take two steps for every one of yours," she teased, giving him a playful push.

"I'm going to shower and change; it's freezing in here," he said, kissing her on the cheek before heading to the bedroom.

"I'll be right back. We can leave in the next hour or whenever you're ready," she said to Micki as she headed upstairs.

***

"Hey, can I ask a favor?" she asked, sitting on the bed as Kasey gathered his clothes.

314

"You can ask," he replied with a smile, his eyes crinkling in the corners.

"Don't shower now. Take one with me when I get back. I'd like you to wash my hair. I'm still a little off balance with my foot."

"I can shower now and later if you want. I don't mind— you know I hate feeling all sandy. I'll wash your hair, no problem. Where are you going?"

"I'm going shopping with Micki. We decided to have a dance party tonight. I'm pretty sure Ren can handle us... everyone likes him a lot. What do you think?" She stood and wrapped her arms around him despite his dampness.

"Just take it easy on him unless he seems comfortable, okay? You and Micki can be a bit much. It took me a while to get used to your cozy little group dynamic, and I was already comfortable with you." He paused, brushing her hair back off her shoulders. "How will you handle him if he responds positively to your little games? You're irresistible, the sexiest woman I've ever met. I'm pretty sure Ren doesn't have the same hang-ups I did. I doubt he'd be able to resist you."

"In that case..." she said, her voice silky, as she ran her hands slowly over his firm butt. "I was thinking we could all have sex together." She peeked up at him through her long lashes, coyly waiting for his response.

After a moment, he shook his head and managed to say, "You're the only person who can make me speechless."

Rubbing against him, she purred, "You may be speechless—but your body is definitely saying something." She smiled at the unmistakable sign of his approval.

"It never ceases to amaze me how easygoing and open you are to sex. Holding her close, he bit her neck and whispered, "So you want to have sex with him?"

"Why not?" she said with a smile. "You do."

"Touché," he replied with a grin.

"I really feel like we're connecting. He's extremely sexy, and if I have to share you, I think you should have to share him. If he's interested, of course." She grinned, the corners of her eyes crinkling as she flicked his nipple with her tongue. "Mmm, salty," she giggled.

Kasey blushed and said softly, "I wouldn't mind at all if it did happen. I'll talk to Ren and see how he feels." He peppered her neck with kisses, his voice turning husky. "If I didn't need a shower, you'd be late for that shopping trip."

"Mmm... let's save it for later, baby," she said, turning toward the door.

Kasey gently took her hand, pulling her back. "Are you sure this is what you want? We don't need to talk about it more?"

"Baby, I don't need to talk about it more. I see it as some spicy playtime for us as a couple—as long as you're okay with Ren and me being together. Do you need to talk about it more? Because we can."

"No, I actually find it exciting." He pulled her close, wrapping his arms around her and looking at her with a mix of excitement and awe. "I guess I just need to talk with Ren."

"We're heading out now. I'm also gonna grab more wine for the house. Do you want anything in particular?"

"No, whatever you get is fine. You know what you could get? Sapporo, a beer for Ren. Just please be careful—you don't have me or any security with you."

"We'll be fine," she said, brushing off his concerns. "Could you call Scott and get us in at *A Shore Delight* tonight? I thought it'd be fun for all of us to go out together."

"I'll do my best," he said. "See you later."

"Oh, I almost forgot one last thing," she said, leaning against the doorframe with a sweet smile. "I found out why you call me Julia." He walked towards her, a bashful smile on his face. "Ren told you?"

"No, he told Will, and Will told me," she replied, enjoying his rosy cheeks and slight discomfort.

"Great, now everyone knows," he said, lowering his head with a shake.

She smiled and gently touched his cheek. "It was fate for us to be together, Spike. We both felt it the first time we met. In this reality, I'll never leave your side. I love you." He was overwhelmed by how she used his nickname, referenced his favorite show, and expressed her love as the character Julia. Her deep feelings often left him profoundly moved.

He took her hand in his. "Thank you for not making me feel ridiculous. You say the sweetest things. I'm not the only romantic in this relationship."

"I absolutely love that you are the only one who calls me Julia. It's so special to me." She gave him a deep, lingering kiss, then said, "I have to go. I love you, baby—I'll be back soon."

"I love you too," he said with a smile as she left.

With the top down, hair tied up, and sunglasses on, Julia and Micki embraced the shore vibe as they set out for shopping in the blazing August sun. Meanwhile, James and Will went for a swim, and Kasey, having changed his mind about the shower, joined Ren on the deck after calling Scott about dinner.

***

Ren was basking in the sunshine when Kasey walked up to him. "Just a heads up about tonight," Kasey said, settling into the chair next to him. "Julia wants to go to her favorite place for dinner. I was able to get us in for eight. We always dress up when we go."

"Sounds good. You know I brought something just in case," Ren said with a smile, his hand shielding his eyes from the intense rays.

"There's something else," Kasey continued. "Julia wants to have what they call a 'dance party.' They smoke, drink, dance, and sing karaoke."

"Yeah, Jules mentioned that. I like karaoke, and I can dance—well, I give it my best shot," Ren chuckled, flashing a quick, self-deprecating smile.

"Well, she probably didn't mention that she and her little girlfriend Micki like to mess with every man in the room—and each other. They're both experienced hunters and tonight, you're in season."

Ren laughed, giving Kasey's knee a playful slap. "Your sense of humor has really changed. Jules and her friends are good for you, Spike."

Kasey flashed him a playful smile. "I can stop it before it starts if you're uncomfortable."

"It's not gonna be a big orgy or something, is it?" Ren asked jokingly, not expecting what was coming.

Kasey chuckled, "No, but they do enjoy flirting and teasing. I'm pretty sure it turns them on just trying to make you hard." He shot Ren a grin. "Something I find hard to avoid myself. Also, be prepared if Julia wants to give you a shotgun."

"What the hell is a shotgun?" Ren asked, eyebrows raised in confusion.

"It's when she blows the smoke into your mouth through the blunt instead of you inhaling it yourself. She's merciless—she'll get you all hot and bothered, then hit you with enough smoke to choke a horse. Just a heads-up: Julia can be a little sexually aggressive. Micki, too—they egg each other on. Both of them get wildly uninhibited when they're high and drinking. Julia and James used to date before he married Micki, and they've had threesomes together. They only stopped right before I started sleeping with Julia because I asked them to. James is still a willing participant, even Will. He doesn't sleep with any of them, but he lets them flirt and fool around with him during these dance parties."

"They've had threesomes? Damn, that's so fucking hot. And you're okay with her flirting with me—and me flirting with her?

Kasey smiled. "I'm not going to lie—it turns me on. I got hard when she asked me if it was alright to have the party, and I'm getting hard just talking to you about this." His cheeks flushed pink. "And that's not all. She wants a threesome with you. Since she has to share me with you, she thinks it's only fair I should share you with her." He grinned, giving Ren a moment to process. "Interested?"

"Seriously, Kasey? You're blowing my mind," Ren said, stunned. "You're offering me sex with you and your stunning girlfriend?" He leaned back in his chair, closing his eyes. "Let me wrap my head around this for a second. And this is really okay with you? You wouldn't get jealous?"

"Why would I be jealous of you? I love both of you—why wouldn't I want you both together? I never imagined I'd be comfortable with something like this, but because it's you and Julia, I have no problem sharing if that's what you both want," Kasey said sincerely, his cheeks now rosy.

"I don't know what to say," Ren said, reaching out to take Kasey's hand. "If it's her idea and it's okay with you, I'd be remiss not to take full advantage of this very generous offer." Ren grinned. "I guess if you don't mind me having sex with her, you won't mind me telling you I'm extremely attracted to her."

Kasey laughed softly. "I already knew that. I could see the spark between the two of you when we had lunch together. I know you, Ren, just like I know Julia."

"I'm up for some new experiences," Ren's grin widened, a spark of excitement in his eyes.

"I really admire how easygoing you are. It took me months to get comfortable with Julia and her uninhibited ways. At first, I thought she'd be too much for me to handle, but I eventually realized I was just overthinking things. Letting my guard down has honestly been the best thing I've ever done."

With a sly smile and a spark in his eyes, Kasey said, "Want to take a quick shower? We've got some time alone, and I'm rock hard right now."

"You don't have to ask me twice. Let's go." Ren jumped up from his chair, both of them charged with the anticipation of the night ahead.

Slick with soap, their hands moved effortlessly over each other. Kasey kissed him hard, his tongue exploring Ren's mouth as he pressed him against the shower wall. With one hand braced against the wall, he stroked Ren with the other, his movements slow and deliberate.

"I like it when you take charge; it's such a turn-on," Ren murmured, his breath catching as Kasey's grip tightened, twisting his hand. Grabbing a handful of Ren's damp hair and pulling his head back, Kasey bit him as his pace quickened, Ren's moans filling the bathroom. "God, I can't control myself with you," he groaned a moment later, his release spilling over Kasey's hand.

Pulling back from the intense kisses, Ren said breathlessly, "Your turn." He rinsed the soap off Kasey, then got on his knees, the water cascading over his back as Kasey leaned against the wall.

As he looked down at Ren, Kasey declared with a smirk, "I love sex in the shower—I get to be dirty and clean at the same time."

Ren let out a mix of a muffled laugh and a gag. "What the fuck? I nearly bit you!" Ren said, pulling back with a grin. "Don't make me laugh, idiot." "Sorry," Kasey said with a grin, "don't stop. You make me feel so good." Finishing him off, they both stood under the rain shower, water cascading over them as they kissed slowly and deeply, holding each other tight.

Feeling completely content, they headed downstairs to the kitchen to get something to drink. Ren wrapped his arms around Kasey from behind, kissing his neck, unable to keep his hands off him. Kasey leaned into the embrace, pulling Ren's arms tightly around him.

Ren spoke softly, showering Kasey's neck with kisses, "I'm so glad everyone's accepted me so easily. I feel really comfortable here with you and Julia. Never in my wildest dreams could I have imagined this working out like this. I'm really happy; I hope you are too."

"You know I'm happy. This isn't how I pictured it either—it's a thousand times better. Julia's right—life's too short to deny love."

James and Will stepped onto the porch and spotted them through the window. They exchanged a glance as James slid the door open. Kasey instinctively started to move away from Ren at the sound, but Ren held him tighter.

"You guys wanna play volleyball?" James asked. "We've got everything in that shed over there."

"I'll play," Ren replied enthusiastically.

"Count me in," Kasey added.

As James closed the door, Ren said, "You need to relax, Spike. They all know about us, and Julia told me we don't need to hide our affection around them. We're not a shameful secret. We can be ourselves and still respect Julia."

Kasey turned to face him. "You're absolutely right. I don't want to act like I'm ashamed of us, especially around these guys—they're extremely accepting of different lifestyles," he chuckled. "It's just me, but I'm sure you'll help me with that." He gave Ren a quick kiss. "Let's kick some butt in volleyball."

"Now you're talking," Ren replied, tying back his wet hair as he headed for the door.

***

Working together as a seamless team, just like in PE at school, Kasey and Ren easily outplayed Will and James. They reveled in the game, with Kasey feeling a pang of nostalgia for the camaraderie he'd enjoyed back in school. With Ren in the mix, Kasey's friendship with Will and James grew even stronger. As he gradually let down his guard and revealed his playful side, they finally began to see the real Kasey.

Julia and Micki returned home to a scene straight out of a movie. Two young men, neighbors from down the beach, had joined the game, and the teams were battling for the final points. A group of young women cheered them on, and a small crowd had gathered. Julia pulled out her phone and started to film from the deck.

"I'm gonna play this back in slow motion," she said admiringly. "They look like that hot scene in *Top Gun*."

"Mm-hmm, they all do look good," Micki said, sounding like a cartoon fox eyeing her pick of chickens for dinner.

"We should grill some burgers for lunch. I'm hungry—what about you?" Julia asked, her eyes still glued to the players.

"Yeah, hungry for a little beefcake, are we?" Micki joked. They turned to each other and burst out laughing just as a cheer went up from the crowd—the game had ended. The players exchanged high-fives, making plans to get together for another game soon.

Bounding up the stairs to the deck, Kasey and Ren announced they were off to shower, with Kasey giving Julia a quick peck on the cheek as they passed.

James started the grill, then headed off to shower, while Will stayed with Micki, lighting up a half-smoked blunt he found in the ashtray.

"I want to curl my hair, and Kasey's gonna wash it now. I'll be back," Julia said happily before going inside.

"He still washes her hair?" Will asked, slowly blowing out the pungent smoke.

"Yeah, she says he's really good at it. One thing about Kasey—he knows how to take care of someone. I mean, he really pays attention to her needs. Who wouldn't want to be taken care of like that?"

Will took another hit and passed the blunt to Micki. "I'm happy for Jules. You know, I don't think this will be as big a deal as we all thought. I think she'll turn this situation with Ren to her benefit."

"You may be right. For her sake, I hope you're right," Micki said, taking a hit and letting thoughts of Julia and the dance party later drift through her mind.

***

"I've been waiting for you," Kasey said with a seductive smile as she walked into the bedroom. He leaned against the bathroom door, legs crossed, arms folded, naked and sweaty, his damp hair pushed back off his face.

"Don't you look sexy," she murmured as she took him in.

"Don't move," she added, quickly peeling off her clothes before wrapping her arms around him and resting her head on his chest.

"Nooo, I'm all sweaty and sandy," he objected, gently trying to move her back.

"Stop... baby, you still don't understand. I love how you smell. You give off this musky scent when you sweat—it's like pheromones drawing me to you. Sometimes, I literally feel the need to rub against you. When you're clean, it's a different kind of smell but just as powerful. Honestly, I don't know which one I prefer; both are like catnip to me. I thought you'd have figured that out from all the times you've caught me sniffing you," she smiled, resting her head back on his chest.

"You're doing it right now, aren't you?" he laughed, shaking his head.

"Maybe," she giggled. "Besides, we're getting in the shower." She rubbed against his sweaty skin, coaxing him, "You can be dirty for me, can't you?"

"Anything for you," he whispered, kissing the top of her head, letting her rub against him as she breathed in his scent.

"You didn't even let me wash, and you were tongue-deep in me. We just like the way each other smells."

"And tastes," he added, steering her into the bathroom. "I still have the stuff to wrap your foot. Let me do that real quick, then we can shower without worrying about getting soap in your cut. I'll change the bandage once we're out."

"Okay, Doc," she said with a loving smile as they sat naked in the bathroom while he wrapped her foot.

A few minutes later, as he massaged the slick, creamy conditioner through her hair, he asked absentmindedly, "Did you find what you were looking for at the store?"

"Mmm... I did. I found this cool-looking disco ball with lights," she replied, her voice as silky as the conditioner, clearly enjoying his touch. "When you get a chance, could you please hang it up? It should make things look like a club. I also got some sexy stockings to go with my underwear."

"Stockings, huh? I love when you wear stockings," he said softly, slowly rinsing her hair as his fingers slipped gently through it.

"I know; I got them for you." She turned to face him, her eyes sparkling with mischief. "But I do have something for you to do right now: get out and let me rinse off."

"Okay, boss," he said, stepping out.

"Don't call me boss," she shot back, giving him a playful slap on the butt.

A few moments later, she emerged from the bathroom in a silk bathrobe, her hair wrapped in a towel. In one hand, she held a new disposable razor and shaving cream; in the other, a wet washcloth with a towel draped over her arm.

"What's all this?" he asked, buttoning his linen shirt and rolling up his sleeves.

"I thought you could shave me. You mentioned once you'd like to," she said with a coy look, her voice tempting. "Unless you don't want to..."

He took the towel from her arm and laid it on the bed. "Get comfortable," he said, grinning as he locked the bedroom door before heading to the bathroom to get another towel. She positioned herself on the bed, spreading the towel beneath her. He brought a chair to the end of the bed and set the razor, washcloth, and shaving cream on the towel beside her.

"Move down and put your feet on my legs. Hang on—let me warm this washcloth up." He came back, sat down, and she placed her feet on his legs. Gently spreading her legs, he placed the warm washcloth on her thigh.

"Not too hot?" he asked.

"No, just right," she said softly. He pressed the cloth between her legs and shook the shaving cream. She pulled a pillow down, propping it under her head to watch him. Removing the washcloth, he sprayed the shaving cream into his hand and applied it slowly, making her squirm at his touch.

"I hope you're not going to move like that while I'm shaving you." He smiled, tracing his finger through the shaving cream.

"I can't guarantee that—sorry," she giggled. "Don't be so gentle. It tickles."

"Alright, stay still. This is serious, delicate work," he said with a delighted grin, taking the razor and starting to shave her with the precision of a barber wielding a straight razor. She relaxed, and the tickling sensation faded, replaced by a growing pleasure. His fingers slipped and slid over her skin as he worked, making it nearly impossible for her to stay still. When he finished, he rinsed her off with the washcloth, wiped her clean with the towel, and then buried his face between her legs, his tongue eagerly inspecting his handiwork.

"No, no," she moaned, grabbing his hair but not moving him. "I wanted to save it for tonight."

"I'm sorry, you're so smooth, soft, and perfect," he said, looking up with his goofy grin before licking her again. "Can I just lick you a little?"

"How can I say no to that?" she murmured, lying back. He slid his arms under her legs, slipping his tongue inside her. When she climaxed, he gently pried her legs from around his head and smiled. "Let's keep this between us. Can we keep some things private?"

"I won't tell a soul—as long as you promise to do it again sometime," she cooed, lying on her side and hugging her pillow.

"I will definitely be doing that again. Promise," he assured her. He took the razor and towels to the bathroom, washed his face, and returned with the supplies to clean and bandage her wound.

"Foot, please," he said, all business now. "This looks pretty good, actually. I think I can just cover it with a regular bandage instead of a butterfly. How's it feel?"

"It feels okay, just a little sore, but nothing I can't handle," she said as he bandaged her cut.

"There, all done," he said, sitting back.

"Come here, doc," she coaxed. "Let me do something for you."

"Not necessary, but thank you," he said, kneeling next to the bed. "The anticipation of tonight is an extreme turn-on. You and tonight are all I'll be thinking about the rest of the day." A wide smile crossed his face. "Besides, Ren and I took a shower together before while you were out. You don't mind, do you? I'm still not sure..."

"It was perfectly okay, baby. We'll figure all this out. Thank you for telling me, though—I really appreciate it."

"It was kind of your fault though," he said with his naughty boy grin. "When I talked to Ren about tonight, the thought of all together was more than either of us could handle. You have the power to excite, even when you're not in the room."

"Well, that's certainly an ego booster." She smiled, clearly pleased by the flattery. "So, I take it he's okay with the idea?"

"Okay? That's an understatement. It was like offering dinner to a starving man," Kasey chuckled, making Julia laugh. "He's very attracted to you. And I told you, he's much more like you in new situations—fearless."

She smiled and rolled onto her back. "You should go be with him. I'll be down in a minute."

"I love you," he said, giving her a lingering kiss.

"I know you do, baby. I love you too. Go, I'll be right down."

***

"We almost started without you guys," Micki said as Kasey stepped out onto the porch. "Where's Jules?"

"She's putting those twisty things in her hair. She'll be right down," he replied, taking a seat beside Ren. He sat quietly, listening to Will and Ren discuss the anime they'd watched the night before.

"Nice look, Medusa," Kasey said, a couple of minutes later, flicking one of Julia's curlers as she passed him to sit.

"Shut up, Kasey," she grinned. "Wow, this all looks great as usual, James."

"Thank you! Dig in, everybody," James said with a big smile, his pride in cooking for and pleasing his friends evident. As they ate, talked, and laughed, an undercurrent of sexual tension sizzled, hotter than the grill, with each person wondering what the evening would bring.

"I'm going to take a nap—I need to conserve my energy for tonight," Julia announced, locking eyes with Ren and flashing a seductive smile.

"We wouldn't want you sleepy later. Have a nice nap," Ren replied, matching her smile as she left the room.

"Don't forget, we're leaving at seven-thirty," Kasey reminded her.

"I'll be ready," Julia called back from the stairs.

***

Chapter 16: The Sexiest Dance Party Yet

Julia descended the stairs, hand in hand with Micki, drawing every eye in the room. She wore a snug white lace corset mini dress, its plunging gathered bust accentuating her perky breasts and Kasey's diamond necklace. Tiny crystals sparkled along the corset and the edge of her flared skirt while lace cap sleeves slid enticingly off her shoulders. Ren's scarf hung casually over her arm while the crystal microphone bag Kasey had given her for her birthday dangled from her shoulder. Sheer white silk stockings and tall, white furry Uggs completed her look—her foot still too sore for heels." Her long hair cascaded in loose curls over her shoulders, soft tendrils framing her long-lashed, bright azure eyes and berry-kissed lips, giving her an angelic glow.

Meanwhile, Micki, with her long chestnut hair, rich mahogany eyes lined in cat's-eye black, and sultry red lips, wore a structured black mini with a flared skirt and built-in pushup bra that accentuated her ample cleavage. Black kitten heels and fishnet stockings completed her look, creating the vision of a devilish seductress. Together, they looked stunning.

"Damn, you ladies look fine, like Sugar and Spice from Batman," Will said. "Did you do that on purpose?" They exchanged a knowing smile as they entered the room.

"What do you think?" Micki playfully replied, as they both raised their skirts enough to reveal their stockings, garters, and small temporary tattoos on their thighs. Julia's tattoo read 'Sugar' in elegant white script, while Micki's read 'Spice' in bold black cursive, each adorned with a tiny red heart.

"Nice," Ren said appreciatively.

"Damn, you look spicy tonight, baby," James said, pulling Micki in for a kiss.

Kasey took Julia's hand, spun her, and drew her close. "You look incredible, Sugar." She giggled, noticing he was wearing her ID bracelet.

"You ladies look gorgeous," Ren said. "Is that a Judith Leiber bag, Jules? It's amazing."

"Yes, it is. How'd you know that? Here, check it out. Kasey gave it to me for my thirtieth," she said, her eyes lingering on him. While James and Will chatted, both Micki and Kasey noticed Julia's focused attention on Ren, fully aware of her intentions.

"She's a pretty recognizable designer. I went to a fashion college in Tokyo and studied a lot of different designers. I love all types of fashion," he replied, clearly taken by Julia's beauty

Ren, dressed in a dark skirt, a fitted gray performance hoodie, Doc Martens, and short black socks, with his hair pulled half up in a man bun, the rest flowing over his shoulder, looked effortlessly stylish.

"Who are you wearing?" she asked, running her fingers lightly over the silky material of his hoodie.

"It's Thom Browne. He's a favorite of mine."

"We just acquired a fashion house—" she started to say, looking up at him.

"Hawthorne Apparel from London, I heard," he said, smiling back at her, his dark eyes mesmerizing. "Exciting. Some of your work?"

"It was actually. Kasey was a big help, along with a great team." She ran her fingers teasingly along the pleat on his skirt as she spoke, maintaining eye contact.

"Hate to break this up, but we've to go. You can talk at the restaurant," Kasey interrupted, putting an end to her blatant flirtation.

"Can we get a picture before we go?" Julia asked. Everyone gathered in front of the fireplace as Will took the photo.

***

"Let's go with the top up, please. I want to get there in one piece," Julia said as Kasey opened the door for her. "We can put it down on the way home."

"Fine with me," Kasey replied, happy to oblige.

During the ride, Julia playfully sang into her microphone bag. She turned in her seat, flashing a mischievous grin at Ren, and spoke into the bag like a reporter. "Thirty-eight percent of men who wear kilts go commando. Is it the same for skirts? And are you going commando?" She giggled, extending the bag between the seats for Ren to answer.

"If I told you, it would ruin the surprise, wouldn't it?" Ren leaned forward, answering with a sly grin. "You might just have to reach under there and feel for yourself."

She grinned back at him, eagerly anticipating the discovery.

***

After a leisurely thirty-minute drive along the shoreline, they arrived at *A Shore Delight,* a favorite spot for intimate, cozy dinners known for its exquisite cuisine and sophisticated atmosphere. Julia and Kasey were familiar faces to the owner, having spent countless evenings there, sometimes quietly alone and other times boisterously with Micki, James, and Will.

Ren felt like an esteemed member of an exclusive entourage as he flanked Julia, with Kasey on her other side. James, Micki, and Will followed closely behind, passing the eager crowd awaiting their reservations. A lone photographer stood off to the side and sprang into action as Julia approached, shouting, "Ms. Masters. Julia—how's the new fashion house going? Are these new designers?" He snapped a flurry of shots, capturing the moment.

"Everything's going great, thanks for asking," Julia replied while Kasey gently urged her forward.

"Damn," Kasey muttered as they went inside. "I think we're going to need security at the house sooner than we thought. If this guy follows us back, it's all over. We'll need a guard at the front gate and one for the back."

"I hate to deal with security, but I think you're right. We're too exposed at the house," Julia said, disappointed that her freedom to move about unnoticed was slipping away. "How did he even know we'd be here?" she asked.

"It's their job, sweetheart. They always end up figuring it out. That's why it's time for better security," Kasey replied, excusing himself as everyone was seated and walking off with the owner.

"That was something," Ren said, taking a seat next to Julia. "I've never had someone take so many pictures of me at once."

"That's nothing," Micki said from experience. "Wait until you go to a fashion show with her or anywhere the public would be interested; the cameras are relentless."

Kasey had reserved the entire back half of the restaurant for the night, and the owner had put up folding screens for added privacy. After a few minutes, everyone relaxed and let thoughts of security fade as they enjoyed Chef Marco's off-menu creations. Fine wine flowed, and they engaged in spirited conversation, with Ren showcasing his wit and effortlessly keeping pace with Julia and Micki.

As dinner wore on, Ren felt Julia's hand slipping gently down his leg, teasingly inching up his skirt. When he glanced at her, she paused, her seductive eyes drawing him in. Returning her gaze, he guided her hand between his legs, over his skirt and his growing erection. She dragged her nails slowly over him as she sipped her wine, then withdrew her hand and turned to speak to Kasey. Ren chuckled softly, sipping his beer.

A few minutes later, Ren reciprocated, sliding his hand under her skirt and teasingly tracing her silky stockings until he reached their top. Meeting her gaze with a sly grin, he leaned over and whispered, "You are such a tease... and I love it."

Looking out from under her long lashes, she purred, "You have no idea... wait 'til I get you home."

Micki, witnessing this from across the table, playfully chided, "Keep it in your skirt, Jules, not his. Behave yourself," eliciting laughter from the group.

"Mind your business, Micki," Julia protested with a wide smile.

After receiving a box of delectable leftovers and untouched, mouthwatering desserts, they thanked Scott, Chef Marco, and the attentive staff. Kasey had discreetly requested Scott to arrange for the valet to bring their cars to the back door, hoping to avoid any potential paparazzi eager to follow them home.

Concluding the memorable dinner with a swift exit out the back door, they drove back to the house with the top down, no paparazzi in sight.

Julia tied up her hair and draped Ren's scarf around her shoulders. Buzzed from the wine and bubbling with anticipation, she put on a favorite playlist, belting out songs all the way home, her voice carrying in the sultry night air.

"You have a great voice," Ren complimented as they pulled into the long driveway.

"Thanks," Julia replied, a hint of nostalgia in her voice. "I used to sing in high school and college. Will was the lead singer for a cover band, and I sang with them quite a bit. Micki and I have been doing karaoke for years. I love to sing."

James arrived right behind them, and together, they all headed indoors, eager to get the party started.

***

Once inside, everyone pitched in to prepare the room. Kasey lit the fireplace while James set up the karaoke equipment and rearranged some of the furniture. Julia teamed up with Micki to select the playlist while Ren and Will gathered glasses and uncorked bottles of wine and fetched Ren's favorite Japanese beer, Sapporo. Kasey had ensured it was available for the weekend. Though Ren had started enjoying smoking with Kasey, he still preferred to drink beer. Will lit a blunt and handed it to Micki before passing another to Julia.

With the lights dimmed and the disco ball activated, courtesy of Julia's shopping spree, the atmosphere transformed into a vibrant swirl of colored light streams.

"This looks amazing!" Julia exclaimed. "C'mon Will, let's get this party started!" she urged. They launched into a favorite duet, *Wild Ones*, their voices harmonizing seamlessly and showing off their chemistry.

Kasey and Ren sat at the kitchen island, watching Julia dance with Micki while Will showcased his rap skills. When it was Julia's turn, she sang and danced with Will until the final verse. As the music enveloped her, she directed her performance to Ren, weaving between his legs and draping her arms casually around his neck, her fingers twisting in his hair.

"I am a wild one. Break me in.

Saddle me up and let's begin.

I am a wild one. Tame me now.

Running with wolves and I'm on the prowl," she sang, her azure eyes locking onto his, big and mesmerizing, with a teasing, seductive glint.

Ren, responding to her alluring energy, nuzzled her neck and murmured, "I'd like to saddle you up and ride you all night." His voice was a low growl, sparking an intimate connection between them.

"I might just take you up on that, cowboy," she whispered breathlessly. He held her close as the song ended, brushing his face against hers, his hands pressing her hips into him.

When *Sucker For Pain* started playing, Julia took his hands, inviting him to slow dance. She slipped her arms around his neck and, standing on her tiptoes, pressed against his body, her intent clear. Moving with the sensual beat of the song, she pulled him closer, lightly brushing her lips against his, her fingers weaving through his silky hair. Nestling his face in the nape of her neck, he inhaled her scent of aloe and coconut. As he ran his hands slowly down her body, they came to rest in the curve of her lower back.

Julia employed all her seductive charms, teasing him with barely-there kisses, blowing lightly in his ear, and nipping at his neck. Temptingly, she breathed, "I'm a sucker for pain," as she dug her nails into the back of his neck. She turned so Kasey could watch as she guided Ren's hands over her breasts, swaying slowly from side to side. Kasey watched with growing fascination and a burgeoning erection as Ren swept Julia's hair off her shoulder, leaning in to nip beneath her ear. Julia's sharp intake of breath, the way she closed her eyes and leaned back into him, her hand reaching back to hold his head against her neck— all of it spoke volumes about their undeniable chemistry.

Ren's gaze flicked over to where Will was dancing with Micki, his hands roaming freely over her as James looked on.

As the sensual rhythm of *Turn Down for What* filled the room, Julia gave Ren a playful wink and glided towards Will. He settled back beside Kasey, discreetly adjusting himself as Kasey offered him his beer and a knowing smile.

Will and Julia moved together easily, his arms enveloping her, showcasing their long-time connection. She bent over, her long hair cascading over her shoulders as she pushed against him, his hands gripping her hips. Bathed in the swirling lights, they looked like a scene from a sex-fueled music video, Will's body pushing into her with each note.

James and Micki appeared alongside them, seamlessly swapping partners in the electrified atmosphere. James, also a skilled dancer, effortlessly spun Julia and drew her close. His lips brushed against her ear, his warm breath tickling as they danced together in perfect sync. Their bodies fit snugly, moving together easily like longtime lovers. When her seductive eyes locked on his, and she smiled before laying her head on his chest, he wished it were him she was focusing her attention on.

"I don't want to let you go. You feel so good," he whispered as he squeezed her tightly. She could hear the desire in his voice when he whispered, "Kiss me, Jules."

Realizing how much James missed her since she'd begun sleeping with Kasey—and now had to watch her seduce Ren— she leaned in and met his lips. For a moment, it was just the two of them, reluctantly acknowledging the end of their long-time intimate relationship. As she danced with Will, Micki saw what she already suspected: just how much they missed each other.

Ending the deep, lingering kiss, James took Julia's hand and spun her around, the flashing lights illuminating glimpses of her enticing garters. Ren watched James and Julia together, easily discerning their intimate connection, marveling at how comfortable Micki and Kasey seemed with it.

As the music intensified, Micki joined Julia, their movements fluid and enticing, drawing every man's gaze in the room. With the throbbing beat as a guide, their dance became an intoxicating display of desire, their bodies entwined in a sensual rhythm. Each touch and kiss heightened the tension, their embrace mesmerizing beneath the flickering lights. Julia cupped Micki's face in her hands, kissing her affectionately before slowly trailing her lips downward. With all eyes on them, Julia squeezed Micki's full breasts together, slowly running her tongue over the tops while Micki cast a teasing look at the men, seductively licking her upper lip.

Micki wrapped her fingers in Julia's hair, gently pulling her head back and slipping her tongue into Julia's mouth while cupping her breast. Julia gave her a sly smile when Micki gently squeezed her breasts in return, her diamond necklace catching the light. The room was captivated by their amorous display as they continued to rub against each other, kissing deeply, their arms encircling in a tight embrace, lost in their own little sapphic world until the song ended.

Caught up in the moment, Ren exchanged a glance with Kasey and mouthed, "Damn," captivated by Julia and Micki's display of open sexuality and the group's unexpectedly overt sensual vibe. He realized Kasey hadn't exaggerated when he said Micki and Julia were wildly uninhibited at these parties. The whole scene had an *Eyes Wide Shut* vibe that turned Ren on. He could understand why Kasey had needed time to adjust to this liberating environment.

As the song transitioned to one with a faster tempo, Julia pulled Ren up to dance.

"Do you dance?" she asked.

"A little, but you could teach me," he said, matching her steps. Impressed by some of his moves, she reveled in their dance, feeling the heat between them intensify with each electrifying step. She sensually slid down his body, her hands tracing his legs, before slowly gliding back up, slipping her hands under his skirt. Ren let out a low groan of appreciation as she raked her nails along his thighs. Pulling her close, he whispered in her ear, "You're a little firecracker, aren't you?"

"Baby, I'm the whole fucking fireworks display," she purred, her aggressive moves extremely appealing to him, intensifying his attraction to her fiery spirit. She gave him a mischievous grin before switching partners with Micki.

As Micki swayed provocatively in front of Ren, backing up, teasing and rubbing against him as he held her hips firmly, pressing into her, the sexual tension palpable. Micki leaned into him, subtly turning so James could get a good view. She placed her hands behind Ren's head, pulling him to her neck as he wrapped his arms around her, keeping his touch respectful, unsure of Micki's boundaries and wary of James's reaction.

"You are incredibly sexy. James is one lucky guy," he whispered in her ear.

"Damn straight he is," she replied with a confident grin. "But so am I," she quickly added.

As *Love on the Brain* began to play, Micki rejoined James, and Ren returned to his seat while Julia pulled Kasey into an embrace. Their bodies moved together fluidly, Kasey's desire for her evident in his passionate kisses and caresses.

She breathed softly in his ear, "I'm no good without you, and I can't get enough...must be love on the brain," letting the song's words speak her feelings.

"God, Julia, you drive me crazy," he confessed.

"Tell me how much you want me," she commanded softly, their embrace tight and intimate.

"I want you so much I can barely breathe," he murmured, his voice low and filled with longing.

As the song ended, she whispered softly, "Go sit on the couch for me," and went to find one of the blunts. She gestured with her finger for Ren to join Kasey on the couch.

While James and Micki slow danced and Will selected more songs, Julia playfully pushed Ren down onto the couch next to Kasey. She slipped onto Kasey's lap and gave him a shotgun, her body pressing hard against his. He held her tight and took in as much smoke as he could. Pulling back, he blew the potent smoke to the side.

She kissed him and whispered breathlessly, "Watch me play with your boyfriend, baby." She slipped off him and, standing in front of Ren, asked, "Are you ready for me?"

"Do your worst, tiny dancer," he said with a devilish grin and twinkling eyes as he patted his lap. Straddling him, she took his hands and placed them on the sides of her legs under her skirt so he could feel her silky stockings. Leaning into him, she blew a slow, steady stream of smoke into his mouth as he slid his fingers under her garters, with Kasey watching. When he pulled back, she stopped, trying to take it easy on him, and handed the blunt to Kasey as Ren coughed the smoke out to the side.

Brushing her face lightly against his, she subtly rubbed back and forth on his lap. Like a cat in heat, she purred in his ear, "I think we should go get naked and do naughty things to each other," pure lust emanating from her. With her lips barely touching his, she gently bit his lower lip. He put his hand behind her head and pressed his lips hard against hers, his tongue moving deep in her mouth. He certainly wasn't shy about kissing her in front of everyone or letting her know exactly what he wanted. Between kisses, he whispered, his voice a rough growl, "There are so many naughty things I'd like to do to you."

"Mmm," she murmured with a grin, winking at Kasey, who was intently watching and listening. With her voice soft and velvety smooth and her hips moving in small circles on his lap, she said softly, "I'm gonna suck on you like a lollipop... making you forget your name... and always remember mine."

"You are already unforgettable," he replied his desire for her at its peak. "Let's go do this, baby girl." Turned on by the obvious differences between him and Kasey, she teased, "Not yet, bad boy," as she slid slowly off his lap and walked away.

"Damn, what a dick tease. I've never met a woman quite like her," Ren said, enthralled.

"I know," Kasey said with a grin, fully agreeing.

"Jeez, Jules is in full-blown flirt mode," James remarked as he slow-danced with Micki.

"She's definitely turning up the heat, and Kasey seems to be loving every minute of it," Micki agreed, stealing a glance at Kasey and Ren. Turning back to James, she asked gently, "How are you handling this whole thing? I saw you kiss Jules. You miss her, don't you?"

"Don't you? We were all so good together for so long." He put his head on her shoulder, drawing her closer. "It's not like I didn't know it would eventually stop when she settled down, but it still stings."

"I know it does, babe. Just remember, she still loves you. You're still one of her closest friends."

Just then Julia grabbed Micki's hand, pulling her away from James and leading her to the kitchen to talk.

"I have never felt sexier or more desired," Julia whispered breathlessly in Micki's ear, her excitement infectious. Together, they giggled like school girls.

"I'm glad you're so happy, kiddo. I hope tonight is everything you want it to be," Micki said warmly, returning her best friend's grin.

"Well, it certainly started out great," Julia said as she gave Micki an affectionate kiss, her arms wrapping around her as they got lost in each other for a moment.

"That is very hot, ladies," James said as he walked up behind them, wrapping his arms around them both.

"Well, you said you were gonna have them both tonight and damn if they're not both in there waiting for a word from you," Will whispered as he came up behind Julia. "Impressive Jules."

She grinned, "I'm having such a good time. Good night, guys. I'll see you all tomorrow."

"Take it easy on them, Jules," Will laughed.

She grabbed an open bottle of wine and her glass, then sauntered over to Kasey and Ren. "Grab your glasses boys, and follow me."

***

Julia entered her room, placing the bottle and glass on her dresser. Kasey and Ren silently

followed her lead.

"Could you put on some music, baby?" she asked, her voice a tempting whisper as she flicked on the twinkle lights Kasey had hung at her request and turned off the main light. He nodded and went to the sound system to cue up her favorite playlist, *Seduction*. It was a compilation he'd crafted for her, inspired by their first intimate encounter when she had noted how the sensual background music and the twinkle lights added to the moment.

"Why don't you take a seat on the bed," Kasey suggested, his tone low and inviting. Taking Julia by the hand, Kasey positioned her in front of Ren. Tenderly brushing her hair aside, his lips skipped lightly over her shoulder as he slipped the sleeves of her dress down. His fingertips slowly trailed down her arms, raising goosebumps. With deliberate care, he unzipped her dress, letting it slip gracefully to the floor. Ren watched, aroused and amazed at the prospect of being with both of them.

Julia inhaled softly as Kasey feathered gentle kisses over her shoulder, his hand slipping into her bra. She closed her eyes, her body melting into his as his other hand slipped between her legs. As he lightly rubbed his fingers back and forth while giving her a small hickey, her breath began to quicken. She reached up behind her and held his head to her neck as she purred, "Baby."

Stopping, he gently moved her forward, guiding her to Ren. Kasey retrieved his wine and settled into the chair by the window, watching intently.

"Damn, Jules, you're stunning," Ren said, enchanted by her lingerie, her tattoo, and her entire presence.

She wore a white and pink demi bra with a matching thong and garter set, white silk stockings adding elegance to her sultry look, playfully offset by her furry boots.

With one hand resting delicately on her hip and the other lightly trailing down her thigh, Julia shifted her weight onto one leg, causing her hip to tilt enticingly. She gazed at Ren with a mix of innocence and seduction, sweetness and spice, her lips curving into a teasing smile—a vision that left Ren aching for more.

Unable to resist her any longer, Ren drew her to him. "Come sit on my lap," he whispered. She kicked off her boots and straddled him, her fingers weaving through his hair as their lips met in a deeply passionate kiss. His deft fingers quickly undid her bra, his hands exploring her bare back. Unzipping his hoodie, she slipped it off and dropped it on the floor. Sliding her bra straps off her shoulders, she leaned in close, pressing her bare breasts against his chest. His hands roamed over her soft skin, teasing her with gentle caresses as he nipped at her neck, sending shivers down her spine. She moaned softly, her lips brushing against his ear.

"You smell amazing," she whispered seductively, grinding against him, her teasing bite on his shoulder drawing a sharp inhale from him. "Tell me if I hurt you," she said, her grip on his hair tightening as she licked his neck.

"I can take it, don't hold back," Ren responded, his voice dripping with desire. "You wanted to know if I was going commando," he added with a sly smile, lifting her effortlessly so her legs wrapped around him. He laid her down, and she watched as he dropped his skirt, revealing his naked form and how incredibly ready he was for her. With an admiring smile, she patted the bed. Swiftly kicking off his shoes and taking off his socks, he moved alongside her.

"You're simply perfect," he murmured, his lips grazing her nipples. Slowly, he kissed his way down her body, his tongue flicking at her belly button, making her giggle. Kasey smiled, enjoying every moment as he watched them.

"I love your lingerie and stockings," Ren said, his voice filled with admiration as he toyed with her garter.

"Thank you," she whispered softly, guiding his head further down her body.

He teased her hips with kisses, slowly removing her thong. As he moved between her legs, she bent her knees, her fingers tangling in his hair in anticipation. Licking her with long strokes of his tongue, she moaned with pleasure. As he slipped his fingers inside her, she gripped his hair tightly.

Kasey watched, entranced, as she glanced at him, her eyes half-closed, her breath catching at Ren's touch.

After a moment, she stopped him, softly commanding, "On your back." He withdrew his wet fingers, wiped them slowly across her lips, then kissed her passionately before guiding her on top of him.

"Ride me, sweet thing," he teased, placing his hands on her hips.

"You got it, cowboy," she replied as she sat back, enveloping him and drawing a long low groan from him.

"Damn," he muttered, closing his eyes. He had almost forgotten what it felt like; it had been nearly a year since he last slept with anyone.

"Mmm," she moaned, leaning back, her hands on his thighs as her hips moved slowly in a circular motion. His hands gripped her hips tightly as they moved together, pleasure building with each circle.

Kasey, having shed his clothes, walked to the side table, took out her mini vibrator, and joined them, amplifying the intensity.

Sliding his hand between her legs, Kasey touched them both, feeling her envelop Ren as she moved up and down. Pulling Ren up to her, she reached new heights of ecstasy, sandwiched between them, moaning loudly in his ear and bringing him right to the edge with her. He was barely holding on, overwhelmed by her moans, the vibrator's buzz, and Kasey's hand on him.

"Holy fuck," she cried out in his ear, burying her face in Ren's neck and hair, her hips contracting wildly, her nails digging into his back as she came. Kasey withdrew his hand, knowing exactly when she needed him to.

"Damn, girl," Ren said, squeezing her tightly as he came, unable to hold back any longer. "Shit, that was intense," he murmured, his breathing heavy, his heart pounding as he rested his head against hers. "Now *that's* how you come."

"Don't move yet," she urged, then giggled. "And don't make me laugh."

"Take your time, baby. I could sit like this all day," he said, kissing her neck.

After a moment, she cupped his face in her hands and whispered, "That felt really good," before her full pink lips found his, passionately making her point. His hand pressed firmly against her lower back, holding her tightly, while the other threaded through her hair.

Lifting off him gingerly, she lay down, letting him spoon her. Kasey stretched out in front of her, his fingers absentmindedly playing with her hair.

She gazed at him, a big smile on her flushed face, and said, "Now we just have to do something for this guy here."

"Move in the middle, baby," she coaxed temptingly.

Ren kissed Kasey's chest, his fingers lightly teasing Kasey's skin as he moved down his muscular body. Finding Kasey fully aroused, Ren's fingers continued to tease as Julia kissed Kasey softly. With an arm around each of them, Kasey blurted out, disbelief in his voice, "This is really messing with my head right now."

"In a good way or a bad way?" Julia asked.

He grinned, "In a great way... it's my perfect wet dream."

"Then close your eyes, baby, and let us love you," she whispered, her voice carrying a dreamlike quality. "My turn," she said to Ren, taking Kasey in hand and licking him with long, slow strokes, her sultry gaze fixed on Ren. He watched her for a moment, unable to take his eyes off her, then moved up to kiss Kasey, who was watching Ren and Julia's chemistry burn white hot before him.

Not wanting Kasey to finish with her and more interested in seeing Ren take the lead, she said, "He's all yours," as she moved up to the two of them.

"My pleasure," Ren replied, rolling on top of Kasey. He began kissing his way down his body, picking up where Julia left off.

Julia, lying on her side next to Kasey, watched him weave his fingers through Ren's hair, close his eyes, inhale sharply, and exhale deeply as he came—just as he always had with her. He pulled her to him and murmured, "I don't think I could feel better than I do right now. I love you both."

"Oh, baby, we love you too," Julia replied softly, giving Ren a playful wink.

As they all lay quietly entwined, savoring the moment, Julia broke the silence with, "Anybody hungry?"

"Don't say it," Kasey laughed, glancing at Ren.

"I wasn't gonna say anything," Ren grinned.

"Say what?" Julia asked, smiling.

"Nothing, sweetheart. Ren can be gross sometimes," Kasey smirked.

"You two are silly," Julia smiled, knowing exactly what he was going to say, "like

teenage boys."

"And you're always hungry. I guess I'm going to have to make you something."

"Pleeease," she said, rubbing against Kasey. "Otherwise, you know I'll just eat all those desserts and regret it tomorrow."

"I worked up an appetite. I wouldn't mind eating," Ren smiled, sitting up.

"Then let's go eat," Kasey said happily.

Julia freshened up in the bathroom and put on her cashmere pajama short set and fuzzy slippers, while Kasey and Ren shared a passionate kiss and lingering embrace, the memory of their shared closeness hanging in the air. Kasey then gave Ren a set of his pajamas, and they all headed down to the kitchen.

***

James, Micki, and Will were still up watching a movie together, with Micki nestled between them—her head on James' lap and her legs draped over Will's.

"Worked up an appetite or refueling?" Micki asked as the trio walked by, heading to the kitchen.

"Both," Julia said, a small grin forming. Kasey and Ren exchanged smiles as they went to check the fridge for leftovers.

"What would you like?" Kasey asked.

"I don't care. Surprise me," Julia answered.

"Anyone else want some leftovers and dessert?" he asked the group, receiving an enthusiastic "Hell yes!" from all of them.

"I'm gonna get some air," Julia said, pulling back the sliding door and stepping onto the deck.

Kasey leaned over to Ren and whispered, "Watch. That was code for 'Micki, follow me out here so I can tell you everything we just did.'" Sure enough, less than a minute later, Micki got up and went outside.

Ren glanced at Kasey, who was taking out the leftovers from the restaurant, and they both laughed.

After Kasey set everything out, he asked Ren to come upstairs with him. "What's up?" Ren said as they stood in the hallway between the bedrooms.

"I just wanted to know what you were thinking about, you know, about what just happened," Kasey said bashfully. "I didn't want to ask you with Julia in the room."

"You want to know what I'm thinking?" Ren responded, wearing the happiest look Kasey had ever seen. "I'm thinking that was the best sex I've ever had, the best night I've ever had. Not only did I have you there, but also the sexiest woman I've ever met. Jules is next level. I can see why you love her—she's so exciting, and she makes you feel like she really wants to be there with you and truly enjoys sex. That's something I never experienced with Kaede. Jules blows my mind. I'm having a great time, Spike. How was it for you? I hope you had as good a time as I did."

Kasey threw his arms around Ren, pulling him close and whispering in his ear. "I couldn't be happier. I can't find the words to explain how I felt with both of you touching me. It was such a turn-on... as much as it was watching you and Julia," he said with an embarrassed smile and red cheeks.

"If it means I get to be with you and Jules, you can watch all you want, buddy," Ren said with a chuckle. Pausing, he added with a grin and a nudge, "I told you we would be good friends." He gave Kasey a kiss and said, "Let's go eat." Taking his hand, they went back downstairs.

***

"Details, kiddo," Micki said as soon as the door closed. "How was it?" She went and stood next to Julia who was leaning against the railing, the warm breeze gently caressing them both.

"I just did the Devil's Tango with two guys, and it was *sooo* good," she gushed, making Micki burst out laughing.

"The Devil's Tango... you kill me," she grinned. "Hit me with some details."

"It was mostly me and Ren together. Kasey sat in the chair and watched us. I think I might have a voyeur on my hands," she smiled. "He eventually joined in to use a vibrator on me at the same time, and I thought I would lose my mind from the intense feeling that came with it. I'll tell you one thing: it's such an ego boost to be sandwiched between two men who really want you. I felt like I was the star of my own movie. I am definitely doing that again. In fact, after I refuel..." she giggled.

Looking off into the dark night, a sly grin on her lips, she said softly, "I haven't even begun to think about what I could do with the two of them... or what they could do to me," a dirty little laugh escaped her lips.

"I'm glad it worked the way you hoped it would. So is this gonna be a regular thing?" Micki asked, curious and a tiny bit jealous.

"I don't really know what they think about going forward, but we'll see," Julia grinned, mischief in her eyes. "I'm not

350

against tangoing with the two of them until Kasey and Ren figure out their relationship. Who knows where it'll go? I like Ren a hell of a lot more than I thought I would. He's sweet and easy to get along with, and I find him extremely sexy. We'll see. All I know is a week ago, I was despondent at the thought of losing Kasey, and now I feel confident in his love for me, *and* I get to do his old boyfriend. Life is so weird sometimes."

The door slid open, and Ren called out, "Food's ready."

"Coming," they answered as they headed inside.

***

After having something to eat and sharing another blunt, everyone decided to call it a night and headed upstairs. The three of them walked into Julia's bedroom, and Ren said, "I'll just grab my clothes and say goodnight."

"Where do you think you're going?" Julia wrapped her arms around him as she posed the question. "I told you I was gonna lick you like a lollipop." She licked his lips as he glanced at Kasey. "Don't look at him. It's always my decision, right, baby?"

"That's right, sweetheart," Kasey agreed.

"Feeling up for it?" she said coquettishly before sticking her tongue deep in his mouth.

"I'm getting there," he said between her kisses, unable to resist even if he tried.

"Good. Now, lose the pants and get on the bed on your knees," she commanded, her gaze fixed on him. As he dropped his pants, she noticed there was something different about him.

"Are you uncircumcised?" she asked, moving closer for a better look. "I've never been with a man who wasn't. She touched him and watched him become fully erect, seeing no difference anymore.

"I am," Ren confirmed, smiling at Kasey as Julia held him in her hand, looking him over. "It's not something commonly done in Japan. Does it matter to you?"

"Not at all. I didn't even realize 'til now, and even then, you already had a semi. I'm gonna have to investigate further," she giggled.

She moved over to Kasey, who stood there observing and whispered softly, "While I'm busy up there, I thought you could have some fun down here. But no vibrator. I don't think we should do that with him in my mouth. It wouldn't be good." She flashed an impish grin, making Kasey smile and shake his head.

Retrieving lube from the side table, Kasey approached Julia from behind and lowered her shorts. She knelt on the bed before Ren, her intent gaze fixed on his. Slowly, she licked her lips, then bent over and enveloped him with her warm, inviting mouth. He sighed loudly, placing his hand on her head as she expertly demonstrated her skills, teasing him with her soft, wet lips and skilled tongue. Kasey positioned himself at the foot of the bed and applied lube. Julia moaned with Ren in her mouth as Kasey eased himself inside her.

"Jesus, Jules, did you take lessons?" Ren moaned, looking down at her, amazed by her technique and lost in the sensations.

Kasey moved slowly, guiding her hips and leaning in. As he did, Ren reached for him, pulling him in for a passionate kiss. With Julia's mouth and hand working in unison, Ren inhaled sharply, his forehead resting against Kasey's, his fingers gripping both their hair. As he came, he exhaled loudly, muttering, "Holy shit, Jules," into Kasey's mouth mid-kiss.

As Ren slowly backed away from Julia, she looked up at him, and he couldn't help but think her wet, sweet smile was the sexiest thing he'd ever seen. Slipping off the bed to retrieve his beer, it was his turn to watch.

Julia slid forward onto the mattress as Kasey pulled out. With a fluid motion, she rolled over, and he slid into her warm embrace. As her arms and legs wrapped around him, she looked over at Ren and smiled as Kasey thrust vigorously until he came a moment later, panting loudly in her ear.

The trio basked in the aftermath, Julia lying in the center, both men on either side facing her. Kasey's arm lay across her body, with Ren's arm on top of his.

Breaking the silence once more, Julia quipped, "We're gonna need a bigger bed," punctuating her remark with a giggle.

"You're hysterical," Ren chuckled. "I'm exhausted. I danced, drank, and smoked a lot." He looked at Julia. "And I had to keep up with you." He kissed her deeply as Kasey watched her hands cup Ren's face, her face hidden by his hair. "Goodnight, tiny dancer, this was one of the best nights of my life. We can talk more about this in the morning," he said, rolling off the bed's edge. He pulled on Kasey's pajama bottoms and scooped up his discarded clothes.

"Good night, Ren," she whispered contentedly, squeezing her pillow. "I had a really good time tonight."

"I had a great night, Spike." He winked at Kasey. "I'll see you tomorrow."

"Good night, Ren," Kasey replied with a loving smile. "See you in the morning."

"I'm so tired," Julia sighed as she rolled over. "Are you happy, baby?"

"I couldn't be happier," he whispered, spooning her and breathing in her musky scent.

"Then could we do this again?" she asked softly. "I really enjoyed the three of us together. I really like him, Kasey."

"I can see that. And he really likes you. There's nothing I love more than making you both happy. We can definitely do this again." With that, they exchanged slow, passionate kisses until Julia drifted off to sleep, both of them feeling absolute bliss.

***

Stirring, Julia felt the early morning sunlight gently caress her face, illuminating the empty space beside her in bed. Smiling at the memories flooding in from the night before, she stretched out beneath the covers, the desire to relive the experience pulsing through her veins. Aware that Kasey would be running, as was his routine at the beach, she freshened up, threw on her nightie, and made her way to Ren's room. Quietly opening his door and realizing he was still sleeping, she gently lifted his covers, taking a quick peek at him.

"Jules?" he mumbled, half asleep. "Where's Kasey?"

"Shh," she whispered, slipping in beside him and putting her head on his chest. "He's running."

Ren pulled her close, planting a kiss on her head. "What were you doing just now?" he asked, amusement in his tone.

"Just investigating." She giggled.

"Well, you better look quick because in about ten seconds it's gonna look a lot different," he laughed as he pulled back the covers. And indeed, he was right; he was already beginning to show her how much she excited him.

"Good thing I already got a good view, she said with a smile, laying her head back down on his chest and draping her leg casually across his, "Last night was incredible," she said, her voice breathy as she rubbed her cashmere nightie against his naked body.

"I couldn't agree more, and I see it's not over yet," he replied, suddenly wide awake, his hand tracing the contours of her body.

She traced little circles on his chest as she said, "I talked to Kasey last night, and I told him I'd like to do this again. I also told him I really like you." Looking up through her long lashes, her bewitching blue eyes shimmering with desire, she briefly hypnotized him.

Ren felt Julia's desire more intensely than anything he had experienced with his wife. She was so different from what he was used to.

"I really like you too, Jules," he finally managed to say.

She continued, "No, Ren. I'm extremely attracted to you. You're sweet, you make me laugh, and last night was really hot. Most importantly, you make Kasey very happy. Since I know you'll be a big part of our lives, I was thinking maybe you and I could have a relationship too. Kasey seems invested in us having a close bond, and he obviously enjoyed last night. Is that something you might consider?"

"Are you asking me out?" he said with a grin, completely captivated.

"I guess I am." She kissed his chest, her fingers lightly teasing his nipple. "I thought we could be a discreet little threesome and have some fun while we figure out what the future holds."

"Are you serious, Jules? I can't imagine anything I'd like more. I knew we'd end up close because of Kasey, but I never imagined we'd get *this* close. Do you honestly think Kasey would want this?"

She cupped his face in her hands, "I honestly think that's exactly what he wants."

"He did seem pretty comfortable with the whole thing. He's so different from the shy, repressed boy I knew. You've been really good for him."

"I think together we could be just what he needs." Her eyes twinkled as she said, "I never asked a man out before; it was a little intimidating. Now I feel bad for anyone who has to do the asking."

"As if there was even the slightest chance I would say no," Ren smiled. "You're adorable."

"I'd like to ask you something," she said coyly.

"Anything," he replied, his dark eyes locking on hers.

"Unless I'm mistaken, I get the impression you're not averse to trying new things. You seem like you'd be open to..." She hesitated.

"To what? Just ask."

"I was hoping to explore a little bit of rough sex. Kasey would never be rough with me, and I wouldn't ask him to. He's the gentlest man I've ever been with, and I don't want that to change. I was wondering if you might like to explore that with me," she said, her voice a tempting invitation.

"How rough are we talking, Jules? I'm not comfortable with really hurting you, and I don't think Kasey would be either," he asked, kissing her, his hand roaming freely over her body, turned on at the thought of what she might ask for.

"Nothing crazy at all. In fact, pretty tame by most standards—things I've done before: biting, hickeys, a little spanking, and..." her voice trailed off.

"And?" he prompted, his gaze intense.

"Well, when we're doing it, or when you put your fingers in me—I want you to do it fast and hard. I don't want to make love—I want to fuck. And you can talk dirty to me. Not gross, just naughty talk," she confessed with a sly grin.

"Damn, Jules, I love how you just ask for what you want." He nipped at her neck, his voice now low and rough. "I'd be more than happy to fuck you as hard as you want. Do we need a safe word?" he asked, biting her neck more aggressively.

"Can I just say stop? Or too hard? I won't say it unless I mean it," she whispered, distracted by his touch.

"You got it, baby girl. Now come put your ass up here," he commanded. He arranged the pillows on top of each other and instructed her to lie across them. Following his lead, she complied, and with a lift of her nightie, she inhaled sharply as he delivered a firm smack to her bare skin, gauging her response with each subsequent strike. Running his tongue over the warm marks, he bit her apple-red cheek, indulging her desire for pain and making her cry out. Licking his fingers, he pushed three of them deep inside her, a muffled gasp escaping her lips as she buried her face in the bed, twisting the sheets in her fists.

In hard and fast movements, he gave her exactly what she asked for, her whole body moving forward with each thrust. "Ren," she begged, "fuck me hard."

Lifting her hips, he pushed in forcefully. She muffled her cries of pleasure, burying her face in the bed as he lay on top of her, moving slowly, biting and sucking on her shoulder like a ravenous vampire. When he felt he couldn't last much longer, he pinned her wrists to the bed and quickened his pace, the sound of the headboard banging against the wall and her ecstatic moans of "Yes, harder" ringing out with each rough thrust.

"Damn, baby," he growled as he came, pushing as hard as he could into her. Collapsing on top of her, panting, he asked,

"Is that what you wanted?" Kissing her bite marks, his fingers now laced with hers, he added, "I didn't hurt you, did I?"

"That hurt so good," she sighed, utterly satisfied. "It was exactly what I wanted."

After taking a minute to catch his breath and cover her shoulder with gentle kisses, he rolled off her and said, "I'll be right back, baby. I need to piss like a racehorse." She grabbed a pillow, pulled the blanket over herself, closed her eyes, and smiled contentedly.

A few minutes later, after washing up, he realized she had fallen asleep. Hastily donning his shorts, he made his way to Julia's room to speak with Kasey. He knocked on the door, announcing himself, wondering if Kasey had even gotten back yet. The door opened to reveal Kasey in just his tight boxers, holding a towel, his hair still wet from a shower.

"Morning," Kasey greeted with a grin, stepping aside to usher him in.

"Morning. I wanted to talk with you," Ren said as he entered, planting a kiss on him.

"Where's Julia? Did you finally tire her out?" Kasey teased. "I heard you two when I came back from my run. She sounded like she was enjoying herself."

Ren chuckled. "She fell asleep when I went to the bathroom. She's something else, Spike. I can't say no to her. I need to know how to handle this. She asked me if I'd like to have a relationship with her. She was so cute; she was actually worried I might turn her down."

Kasey smiled and put his hand on Ren's shoulder. "This is all new to me too. We'll sit down and discuss it together."

"Is this really what you want? To share her with me?" Ren asked, incredulous.

"I'm also sharing you with her," he said with a grin. "She told me she's attracted to you and really enjoyed being with you. She wouldn't have jumped in your bed this morning if she didn't. Julia's had a rough year—losing her family, having surgery, and dealing with me. If I can have you back in my life, and she's happy and content, then I'm all for it. I love you and want you both. I want us all to be happy," Kasey confessed. Ren realized then that both Julia and Kasey thought the new relationship would benefit the other, showing him just how much they cared for each other.

"I love you too, Spike. I'm ecstatic we can be together again. And if it means I have to sleep with your beautiful, sexy girlfriend, well—so be it. I'll gladly take one for the team." Ren grinned, putting his arms around Kasey, drawing out an unguarded, hearty laugh.

"We both appreciate your sacrifice," Kasey said with a broad smile.

"You know, I woke up to her pulling back the covers to check me out." Ren chuckled. "She really is adorable."

"She definitely can be," Kasey said with a distinct look of love.

"Feeling left out? Need me to take care of you?" Ren said, his smile tempting.

"Thanks, I'm good. I just showered, and I'm hungry. Let's go out for breakfast and let the tiny sex machine sleep in," Kasey suggested, giving Ren a quick kiss. "Wear something of mine so you don't wake her." They dressed and headed downstairs.

***

"Where's Jules? You guys didn't wear her out with too much sex, did you?" Micki teased with a raised eyebrow as they came down.

"No such thing as too much sex," Ren replied, with a sly grin spreading across his face.

Taking a seat at the kitchen island with her and Will, Kasey said, "She's sleeping. Our energizer bunny finally wore herself out." Laughter followed his remark, lightening the mood around the table.

"Ren and I are heading out for a ride along the shore and then grabbing breakfast. Does anyone need anything while we're out?"

"No, thanks, we're good," Micki said. "Enjoy your breakfast."

Fifteen minutes later, Julia came downstairs, clad in a loose-neck crop top and shorts. Micki broke into applause, followed quickly by Will. "That was some performance this morning. Couldn't get enough of Ren last night, so you went solo this morning? It sounded a little rough, kiddo. Now who's the perv?" Micki teased.

"I think I was still drunk when I woke up," Julia giggled. "No really, just a bit."

"You were certainly still horny. Your libido is epic." Micki said, playfully nudging her, making her stumble back into Will.

"Holy shit! Jules. You better leave your hair down today or wear a shirt with a collar. Damn, girl, look," he turned her towards Micki.

"What? A hickey? So what," Julia replied, reaching back to touch her shoulder.

"They're not hickeys, Jules—they're bite marks. Pretty distinct ones. Do they hurt?" Micki inquired, poking at one.

"Ow, not really, but your bony fingers do... stop!" she laughed, moving away from Micki.

"I hope you have a safe word if you're gonna get rough," Will chimed in.

"You know, just because he looks like a sexy vampire, Jules, doesn't mean he has to bite like one."

"Yes, he does. Mind your business, Micki," Julia shot back, grinning.

"Did he leave any other marks?" Micki persisted, ignoring Julia's request.

"Maybe," she giggled, rubbing her backside. "My butt kinda hurts from all the spanking."

"Lemme see," Micki laughed, tugging at Julia's shorts.

"Stop! Will doesn't want to see my ass," she laughed, pulling away from her grip.

"I don't know; I'm kinda curious what's going on down there," he grinned.

"Fine, one quick peek," Julia said, leaning against the island and pulling her shorts halfway down.

"What the?... Girl, your ass is so red. Is that a bite mark?" Will asked, both brows raised. "Does it hurt?"

"That's kinda the point," she said with a mischievous grin. "I'm just a sucker for pain," she sang, raising her arms above her head as she rubbed against Will.

"Seriously, make sure you have a safe word," Micki cautioned again.

"Yes, Micki, I've already told him. It's 'stop,' plain and simple. No need to complicate things. And just so there's no misunderstanding—this was all my idea. I asked Ren for this. It wasn't his idea; he made sure to do exactly what I asked, so don't get the wrong idea about him." She gave them a sly smile. "He was very good at listening and giving me what I wanted. Enough about me—I'm gonna get some sun," she declared, heading out onto the deck. She gingerly settled onto a lounge chair, stretched out, closed her eyes, and sighed, letting the warmth of the sun envelop her.

"Who knew Jules liked it that rough?" Will remarked just as James entered the room.

"What did I miss? Likes what rough?"

"Sex, babe—Jules likes it rough. She's got a few rough-looking bite marks, and her butt is a deep red, "Micki mentioned nonchalantly. "You slept through it all, which was amazing. She was the loudest I've ever heard her. Even had the headboard banging against the wall with Ren. Kasey was out for a run; I heard him leave."

"Snitch. He didn't need all the deets," Will said with a smirk, shaking his head. "You just love stirring the pot."

"Just stating the facts," she replied, a sly smile tugging at one corner of her mouth.

"Where is she? Is she okay?" James asked, concerned as he scanned the room.

"Calm down. She's fine—she's out there. And just so you know, it was her idea. Seems our little sex bunny has a rough kink," Micki said, glancing toward the deck. "It's not like she hasn't asked us to bite her—especially you."

Will added, "Let's be real—Jules has always had a bit of an edge. Maybe she wants someone to match that. She's used to being in control in so many areas of her life, especially now."

"I don't like it. Sometimes she doesn't think things through—I hope she's not just being impulsive. I'm gonna talk to her. I don't want to see her get hurt, physically or emotionally. And we've never bitten her hard enough to leave marks," James said, heading to the door.

"You can try, babe, but I think she's embraced the dark side," Micki called after him, a grin spreading across her face. "She seems pretty happy."

He stepped outside and took a seat next to Julia.

"Morning, James," Julia greeted, her squinting against the blinding rays of the sun.

"How'd you know it was me?"

"Because I know you, James, and I figured Micki would get you all riled up. Plus, I heard you talking—that kitchen window's cracked open a bit. I'm fine, really—better than fine. I'm genuinely happy with how things turned out. And before you worry too much, I asked for the rough stuff. Honestly, it's nothing dramatic. It's all stuff I've done before—with you, in fact," Julia assured him.

"Not exactly the same Jules. I never left marks on you worse than a hickey. Can I see these marks on your shoulder?" he asked, concern mingling with curiosity.

"I'm not sure if that's a good idea... you're gonna get upset, I can tell already," she replied, peering at him through half-shielded eyes.

"Are they that bad?" Worry laced his words and expression. "Now I have to see—please... I'm just concerned for you."

"Fine, but just remember—you've bitten me plenty of times," she relented, turning her back to him. As she swept her hair aside, he spotted the angry welts.

When he saw the full extent, he exclaimed, "What the fuck, Jules? I never left marks like that on you." Kneeling behind her, he wrapped his arms around her. "I just don't understand the appeal of causing real pain during sex. I can't stand the thought of you being physically hurt," he confessed, resting his head on her back.

"And that's exactly why I couldn't ask you or Kasey to be more aggressive with me... it's not really your thing."

"Ren doesn't seem to have that problem. I heard things got pretty loud this morning—and a little hard to listen to. I don't know about Kasey, but I know I wouldn't enjoy hearing you get roughed up."

"Jeez, Micki's got a big mouth," Julia grumbled. "Kasey was out running this morning, so he wasn't here. I don't think he heard us. I need to control myself when others are around," she admitted, turning to embrace him. "I'm sorry you're upset, but I'm not really getting hurt. I promise. The marks look worse than they feel, and I'm not in any pain—except for a sore butt," she added with a small smile. "I swear, James, I wouldn't lie to you. Please don't worry. Ren's very sweet; he only did what I asked. It wasn't his idea—it was all mine. He'd never hurt me, especially knowing he'd have to answer to Kasey. Gently holding his face in her hands, she whispered, "I love that you want to protect me and care so much, but you don't need to fret—I'm good."

"You're such a handful, Jules. I worry about you sometimes. Just cover up for me, will you? It's hard to see, and strangers might not understand it was consensual."

"Of course I'm gonna cover-up. I don't flaunt hickeys, either. I hate it when everyone fusses over something so silly."

"We care about you and just want to protect you. Despite being a hotshot businesswoman, to us, you're still our tiny, vulnerable friend who sometimes needs protecting—even from yourself and your impulsive decisions. You've had a tough year, and not too long ago, you were relying on strong meds to cope. You've only just weaned off them, and I wonder if it was too soon. I'm worried these impulsive decisions are because of the grief. I'm just trying to look out for you."

"I understand your concern, I do. But I'm doing much better—I feel good. I promise I'll keep the rough stuff under control when you guys are around. Or at least keep it quieter," she said with a gentle smile, resting her head on his.

Micki joined them with a grin. "You best not be proposing, Mr. Malone. You do remember you're married."

Rising to his feet, he reassured her, "Don't worry, I could never handle the two of you."

"I dunno, baby—you've handled us pretty well plenty of times," Micki said, making them all laugh, easing the tension. Slipping his arms around Micki, James suggested, "How about we all go for a swim? We haven't done that in a while, and the water's calm today."

"Sounds good, I'll change. Meet you back here in five," Julia said, standing and heading inside.

***

Kasey and Ren returned shortly after to find the four of them locked in a chicken fight in the waves—Julia on Will's shoulders and Micki on James's, each trying hard to knock the other off.

"Should we hit the water?" Ren asked eagerly.

"Sure," Kasey replied.

Julia waved as they waded out, with Micki taking the opportunity to push a distracted Julia off Will's shoulders.

"Cheater!" Julia sputtered as she surfaced.

"You're too distracted. Keep your eye on the prize," Micki teased, sliding off James's shoulders.

"Nice takedown, Micki. That was hardcore," Ren said as they reached the group.

Julia swam over to Kasey and wrapped her arms and legs around him. He held her close and asked, "How come you're not wearing a bathing suit? Are you getting burned?'

"Not yet," she replied with a smile. "Just covering up a few marks."

"And exactly what kind of marks are we talking about?" he asked, unaware of the kind of encounter she and Ren had shared earlier.

"I asked Ren to get a little rough this morning, and it left a few souvenirs. Micki and Will saw them, and they just messed with me about it. But James... well, he kinda lost it a bit."

"Show me the marks," he said, his voice steady.

She unwrapped her legs and stood before him. "You're not upset, are you?" she asked, her tone innocent.

"Not at all. I just want to understand what you need. I don't think it's something I'd like—I can't see myself doing more than I already have." She turned around to show him her shoulder.

"Jesus, Julia. What the—do they hurt? They look painful," he asked, distressed.

"They don't hurt. Please don't be upset—I'm fine, really," she reassured him, recognizing the shock in his tone and words.

"I don't understand. I don't want anyone to hurt you."

"We'll talk about it as soon as we go in," she said, wrapping her legs around him again as she lay back, floating. Her hair spread out like a mermaid's, swirling and twisting as her body bobbed gently in the rolling waves.

Shielding her eyes, she looked up at him, noting the confusion and concern on his face.

"Did you have a nice ride?" she asked, trying to distract him.

"We did. I let him drive the car in a parking lot. He doesn't have a license yet, but I'm going to help him get one. He loves the car." His gaze drifted to her hair swirling in the water. "We all need to talk today. He wants to clarify what's happening between us." He slipped his hand into her shorts, giving her a squeeze.

"Ow." She grimaced.

"Sorry, did I hurt you?"

"No, you didn't hurt me," she replied, standing up. "Just a little sore."

"How hard did he hit you? Let me see, please."

"He just did what I asked him to. None of it was his idea, so don't be mad at him."

"I'm not going to get mad. You're a grown woman; it's your decision. Let me see. Please?

I'm going to see it at some point." She reluctantly turned around and let him take a look.

"Damn," he muttered. "Is there anything else?"

"No, nothing. Baby, it was just some bites and spanking. Granted, harder than I've ever asked for, but nothing remotely freaky." Seeing that her words weren't placating him, she added, "Let's all go inside and talk. I can see you're upset." She took his hand and turned, leading him to shore.

"No, not yet. Ren just got out here, and he's having a good time. We'll go in a few minutes," Kasey responded, watching Ren playfully splash Micki as they talked and laughed. He also noticed James standing off to the side, watching Micki and Ren intently, while Will chatted away, oblivious to James' attention being elsewhere.

Julia wrapped her legs around Kasey, leaned back, and floated, with him now mindful of where he placed his hands.

After about half an hour, she touched her nose and said, "Let's go in. I think I'm beginning to burn." Ren was talking with Micki and James when Julia called out, "Ren, could you come with us, please?"

"Uh oh, I don't think Kasey liked seeing those marks," Will said, swimming over to James. "He didn't look too happy after she showed him."

"Nobody wants to see Jules physically hurt, even if she did ask for it. She needs to understand it's hard to see your friend get roughed up, even if it's their choice," James replied.

"She'll work it out. Jules is like a cat—she always lands on her feet," Micki said, splashing James. Swimming over and wrapping herself around him, she added, "Don't worry babe; we'll keep an eye on her. This whole rough thing might just be a phase. If it was something really important to her, we'd have heard about—or seen the signs—sooner. I think she's just trying something different."

"We'll see," James said, holding Micki as she floated beside him.

***

"Are you changing in the bathroom? Seriously?" Kasey asked as Julia tried to slip in quickly.

"I don't want you to have to look at the, um... I don't want to upset you," she said, opening the door.

"I appreciate that, but come out of there. Don't be silly—I've already seen them. I need to get this sand off me, or I won't be able to concentrate. Sorry. Just give me two minutes," he said, slipping past her and starting the shower.

"Take your time," she said, picking up her phone to call Ren. "Hey, Kasey needs to shower, so we might as well all shower. Just come in when you're done."

"Sounds good. I'll be there soon," he said, relieved to be showering himself.

Sticking her head in the bathroom, she asked softly, "Would it bother you if I got in with you? I already told Ren to shower—I feel yucky too."

"Come on," he said, unable to say no.

As Kasey washed her hair, carefully avoiding her bruises, she said softly, "I don't think I'm gonna do this again. I didn't realize how much it would upset everyone, especially you. I never want to upset you."

"Let me explain why I reacted the way I did," he said, rinsing the shampoo from her hair. "Growing up, I saw some nasty bruises on my mother. It hurt me so much to see her like that. I think it was triggering to see more pronounced marks on you than just a hickey. I didn't realize it would bother me so much."

"Oh shit... I'm so sorry. You did tell me that." She laid her head on his chest. "I'm so thoughtless; sometimes I just don't think," she admitted as the realization sank in. "I'm out of touch with what other families might have gone through. My childhood was so different—that kind of stuff isn't even on my radar. I'm really sorry you had to feel that again."

"We'll talk about it—don't be upset," he said, rinsing the last of the conditioner from her hair and giving her a kiss.

***

Julia sat comfortably in the soft chair by the window, combing her hair, with her feet tucked to the side while Kasey settled on her bed. A soft knock interrupted the quiet.

"Come in," Kasey called out. Ren walked in, sensing a subtle tension, and sat down beside Kasey.

"Is something wrong?" he asked, glancing at Julia.

"Let me start by apologizing. I upset a few people this morning," Julia admitted.

"Who did you upset?" Ren asked.

"Micki and I were messing around, and Will noticed the marks on my shoulder. They were a bit shocked at first but got over it when I explained it was what I wanted. James, on the other hand, went full-on big brother on me. But more importantly, I upset Kasey."

"Shit," Ren muttered, looking immediately at Kasey, concern written all over his face.

Kasey quickly took Ren's hand. "I am not upset with you or with you either, Julia. The bruises just caught me off guard. I didn't realize seeing them would affect me so much."

Julia continued, "I understand your reaction now and that it was triggering for you because of your mother. I'm truly sorry for that. But my friends are being overly protective. Yes, I needed their care and support this year, but they have to realize I'm a grown-ass woman who just wanted to try something a little different.

She focused her gaze on Kasey. "The first time you spanked me, it turned me on so much... let's just say the memory made my vibrator's job a lot easier on more than one occasion," she grinned, making both Kasey and Ren smile. "I've always liked being bitten and getting hickeys. I just wanted to explore spanking a bit more. I dunno why, but sometimes I just crave it," she finished, her eyes twinkling mischievously.

"Why haven't you mentioned that to me?" Kasey asked. "I want you to tell me what you need."

Taking a seat between them, she placed her hand on Kasey's thigh. "I didn't mention it because I'm extremely satisfied with our sex life. I know it's something you wouldn't enjoy and might only do just for me. I don't want that. I love your gentleness, and I never want you to change who you are for me."

She turned to Ren. "When I saw you were a little more sexually aggressive, I thought you might be the one I could explore that with. Truthfully, it was hot, and in the moment, I enjoyed it immensely, but it's not something I'd ask for on a regular basis. Rough sex, on the other hand—always good," she giggled. "But I don't need to be bitten hard enough to leave bruises. I still like being spanked, but maybe in a way where I can still sit comfortably afterward. I just wanted to explore the opportunity I had. I should've been more considerate of others hearing us and kept it down, but like I said, it was hot, and I don't have much self-control when it comes to sex."

"I didn't realize they were upset. They didn't seem mad at me," Ren said, worried her friends might think badly of him.

"They're not upset with you. It's just James who's upset with me. He thinks I'm being impulsive or acting out because of grief. I had to 'talk him down off the ledge' on the deck."

"Sweetheart, I'm not upset. It just takes a little getting used to. If it's what you want, don't worry about what anyone else thinks. If the three of us agree and trust each other, that's all that matters," Kasey reassured her. "Would you like me to talk to James?"

"No, not at all. Everything will be okay. It's just different with the new dynamics, and I need to control myself when there are others around. I can be thoughtless sometimes," she replied. "Plus, James has always been extremely protective of me... I think he's having a hard time letting that role go."

"I understand where they're coming from, and I get where James is coming from. Things have changed a lot for you in a short time, and they just want to make sure you're alright," Kasey offered. "And I want to say that, while I know it's not something I'd enjoy, I don't have a problem with you exploring that with Ren. I just don't think I'd enjoy seeing it happen," he added, gently brushing a stray hair from her face.

"I've already told Jules I have limits with the rough stuff," Ren said, looking at Julia. "I won't get any rougher with you, but I do have a suggestion—what about role-play? It could be exciting to explore. You're pretty creative, Jules; I bet you could come up with some spicy ideas," he added with a teasing grin. "In fact, why don't you come up with most of it until we're sure of what you like? Then we can give it a shot and surprise you. We'll only do it when it's the three of us, making it something special we share together."

"I love the idea of having something special between the three of us," Julia said with a playful grin, her hand slowly rubbing his thigh. "And exactly how do you know so much about this?"

"Porn," he admitted without a hint of shame. "A decade of infrequent, unremarkable sex led me to it. What can I say? I needed something." He grinned. "Seriously though, I think we could all get into role-playing. We can be whoever we want, with no pain involved."

Kasey smiled at Ren. "I like that idea."

Julia's mind raced with possibilities, a sly grin spreading across her face. "Me too," she declared, squeezing their legs. "I really enjoyed our time together, and I definitely want to do it again and again..." she giggled. "I also want us all to have alone time with each other." Ren placed his hand on hers as Kasey wrapped his arm around her waist. "But just so you know, if I catch wind of any sexy times happening without me, don't be surprised if I join in."

She caressed Kasey's face. "I love you with all my heart, and I know you love me. But I can also see the love between you two." She turned to Ren. "I love how happy you've made Kasey. He's been the happiest I've ever seen him. I want you to stick around and keep making him—and me—happy. I felt a strong connection each time we've had a serious talk. You immediately tried to put me at ease, telling me you weren't here to make trouble. And, well," she added with a tilt of her head and a naughty smile, "our chemistry together is undeniable. I like everything about you, and if I'm not mistaken, the feeling is mutual."

"You know it is. You say the sweetest things. I told you before, you're very special." Ren leaned in to kiss her, and Kasey's soft smile said it all.

Turning back to Kasey, she said, "Truthfully, baby, the thought of a committed threesome with you both, and the fact that you're into it, is incredibly exciting to me. It's so random—something I never would have imagined if it weren't for Ren coming back into your life. But now that he's here and we've spent this time together, I can't think of anything else. I've been tingling all weekend—I love that feeling, and I haven't felt it in a while."

She continued, her expression bright with optimism. "This new arrangement could really work for us. Maybe not forever, but definitely for right now. I've seen how unpredictable and short life can be. I wanna be happy. If we can all find happiness together, why not take the bull by the horns and go for it? Of course, that's only if you both feel the same way. I tend to move fast when I know what I want. I also know I can be spoiled and self-centered, but this feels right to me—for all three of us. We can slip Ren right into our lives so easily." She looked at them both, waiting for their response.

"If you want us to be a committed trio, count me in. It's definitely not what I imagined would happen when Kasey came back into my life, but I'm all for it. I love being with both of you in every sense of the word. You're the most exciting woman I've ever met. And being with Kasey is like a dream come true for me," Ren said, his face radiating happiness.

Kasey nodded. "I'm thrilled we're going to give this a try. Just one last thing from me—no secrets. This could never work if we're not truthful and communicate clearly with each other. I just learned that lesson the hard way."

Julia squeezed his hand. "We both did."

Kasey continued, "We all have hearts that could be broken if any of us steps outside our boundaries or acts without respect. I want us to be a real, committed unit." Pausing, he looked at Julia and added softly, "I think you should move in with me—Ren should too. There are two floors in the brownstone I don't even use. I could fix up the floor above us just for you," he added, glancing at Ren. "What do you say, sweetheart? Should we all move in together?" Kasey asked, his face radiating happiness.

Julia eagerly eased herself onto his lap, wrapping herself around him. "I say yes! Absolutely yes. Let's all move in together. If we're going to be a real trio, we need to be together. You think you can handle a house full of people?" she asked Kasey, her arms draped around his neck, her nose gently brushing against his.

"I don't need that much time alone when I'm with the people I love. It's a big house, and being a threesome makes it easy for one of us to get space without the other two feeling left out. I promise, if I feel overwhelmed, I'll let you know— but I doubt that will happen. I'll even consider a housekeeper if it gets too messy with you two." He smiled at Julia. "Your bedroom and bathroom alone can be chaos personified with all your clothes and personal stuff. Ren had the same problem in school—you both could use your own dressing rooms."

"We can use my housekeeper, Alice! Perfect—she's already vetted, and she knows how messy I am," Julia laughed. "She can live in part-time; you have that first-floor apartment. Damn, this could really work out," she said, pleased.

"I think we can give Alice a room on the fourth floor if she needs it. I want to set up security in the apartment downstairs. If you're going to be here full-time, the press will eventually find out, and we'll need more security. Realistically, this is only a temporary fix. Eventually, we'll have to move to a more secure area—and it's not like we don't have the resources to build exactly what we want," Kasey said, already planning for the future.

"I hadn't thought of that... we could stay at Kasey's until we build a bigger, more secure place just for us," Julia said, now even more excited. "Anybody have anything else to add?" she asked, standing up in front of them. Now's the time—speak up, don't be shy," she added, beaming.

"Not right now," Kasey replied, glancing at Ren.

"Me neither. I'm good—a little stunned, but good. I just got a hot boyfriend, a sexy girlfriend, and I'm moving into a brownstone in Tribeca with both of them to live a lifestyle few people can imagine. It's all good," he said, his expression a mix of happiness and disbelief.

"Good. I'm gonna make Micki jealous and tell her we're all moving in together. I can't wait to see her face—all of them, in fact," she said with a grin.

"Be nice, Julia," Kasey said with a smile.

"I'm always nice," she giggled, practically floating out of the room.

"Well, she's pretty happy," Ren observed as she left.

"That's all that matters," Kasey said, pulling him in for a kiss.

"I can't believe we get to live together. I'm so happy. I love you, Spike."

"I love you too, Ren," Kasey murmured as Ren kissed his neck, holding him tightly.

***

Micki glanced back at the sound of the sliding door. "Everything good, Jules?"

Julia approached the trio lounging in the sun. "Everything's great. Kasey asked me to move in with him, and I said yes." She raised a finger to preempt Micki's questions. "And guess what? Ren's moving in with us too. So, as soon as we get back, we're all moving into Kasey's brownstone together." She paused to let them absorb her announcement.

"Now, before you all give me your opinions—which I welcome—I just want you to know that this past year nearly broke me, emotionally and physically. Kasey's love and unwavering support pulled me through. I'm not discounting how much you three have done for me—you all know how much you each mean to me—but his support was different. He was there like a committed partner. I know he's had his share of deep issues to deal with, but I had a lot to handle this year too, and he never left my side."

"I was worried about Ren coming into our lives, but the truth is, he's only made things better in so many ways. Kasey's so relaxed, open, and happy. I love him completely—why wouldn't I want this for him? I'm lucky that Ren is such a good guy and that we clicked so well. I'm genuinely happy. So, until the universe dumps its next load of shit on me, I'm gonna enjoy what I have right here, right now."

"Well, you told us," Micki grinned. "I'm happy for you, kiddo. I'm just gonna need a friggin' chiropractor for the whiplash I get from your love life."

Will chimed in with his characteristic support. "If you're happy, then I'm happy, Jules. Do what you feel is right for you. I've got your back, no matter what."

Julia turned to James, blocking the sunlight so he could meet her gaze. Sensing his hesitation, she settled into his lap, resting her head against his chest. "What's on your mind? I wanna hear what you have to say."

"I just can't get past how fast this all happened. I worry you're moving too quickly. I don't want to see you get your heart broken again—I've already seen it a few times, and it's not pretty."

"You're absolutely right. I do move fast when I know what I want and feel it in my gut. I accept the consequences of quick decisions, but I also enjoy the benefits. It's served me well in business."

"This isn't business, Jules. It's personal—it's your heart," James countered gently.Looking deeply into his eyes, she spoke earnestly, "I swear, James, I feel in my heart this is right for the three of us. Please, trust me on this."

Relenting with a small smile, James nodded. "I'll just have to trust you to know what's best for you,"

"Thank you. I promise everything's gonna be okay. I'm not gonna get hurt."

"Good, 'cause if you upset my hubby anymore, I'm gonna have to hurt you," Micki teased with a grin and raised an eyebrow.

Julia proposed a fun distraction. "What do you say we rent a boat and spend a few hours on the water? The guys could fish if they want, and we could get a picnic lunch," she said cheerfully, trying to entice them.

"I'm game," Will said. "You had me with fishing."

"C'mon, James, let's go have some fun. I can't have you going back home upset with me," she pleaded softly, her finger trailing slowly across his chest.

"I'm all for it, and I'm not upset with you, Jules. I just feel like a protective big brother," James said, giving her a comforting squeeze,

"Yeah, let's hope it's more like a stepbrother—otherwise, that's pretty incestuous, buddy," Will quipped, causing James to retort, "Fuck off, Will," which had them all laughing, things finally back to normal.

"Let's go change and have some fun. I'll go tell the guys, make some calls, and meet you all in the living room in an hour. Is that enough time?" Julia asked excitedly.

"Can we make it two hours, kiddo? My hair is full of sand—it might take a little longer than an hour, and I can start packing," Micki replied, inspecting her tangled, sandy locks. "We'd still be back by five or six. We're all leaving at eight, so we have enough time."

"Sure, take your time." Julia leaned in and whispered in James's ear, "Why don't you wash her hair for her. I guarantee you'll get something good in return." She hopped off his lap. "See you all in two hours," she said as she headed inside.

***

In her bedroom, she found Kasey and Ren lying on the bed, deep in conversation.

"Make way, boys, I'm coming in," Julia announced, jumping onto the bed between them.

"Everything alright with your friends?" Ren asked.

378

"Everything's back to normal, she replied, crawling towards Ren and planting a kiss on his cheek. "Don't worry, it's all good. In fact, I'd like to rent a boat. I want to take everyone out for a few hours and have a picnic lunch out there. Can you help with that?" She gave Kasey a sweet smile. "We wanna have some fun before we all have to go home later. Whatcha think?"

"Whatever you want to do is fine with me. I can make a quick call to the marina."

"Sounds like a blast," Ren agreed.

"We have two hours before they'll be ready. We could talk about the logistics of moving in together while we wait," she suggested, rolling onto her stomach and resting her head in her hands.

"Does somebody's butt hurt?" Kasey teased.

"It's just easier for me to talk to you both like this," she explained with a grin. "And yeah, just a little."

"Poor baby. Want me to rub it for you?" Ren smirked, reaching out.

"No, thank you very much," she giggled, stopping his hand. "I think I've hit my pain threshold for now."

"I'll be right back," Kasey said, getting up and heading toward the door. Seizing the opportunity, Julia snuggled up to Ren, draping her leg over his and pulling him close, her lips quickly finding his.

***

"I could come back if you two need some time," Kasey said, flashing a grin as he came into the room.

"We've had plenty," Julia rolled away from Ren, propping herself up on her elbow to face Kasey. "Where'd you go, and what've you got there?"

379

"Ice for your butt—roll over," he said, producing a baggie of crushed ice.

As he gently placed it on her backside, she let out a sigh of relief. "That feels nice... You're such a good boyfriend. I've never had anyone take care of me like you do."

"I helped take care of my mom, and it felt good knowing I made her feel better. Why wouldn't I do it for you or anyone I care about? I like being needed," Kasey explained, lying down next to her.

Ren added, reminiscing, "In our junior year, I had an impacted wisdom tooth pulled. He took care of me the whole time. He was more attentive than the school nurse. I was a mess from the anesthesia, throwing up when I came back from the dentist. He stepped up, made sure I had everything I needed. He read to me, got me more than a few ice packs, brought me ice cream. I never forgot that. Remember, Spike?"

"Of course," Kasey affirmed. "I remember everything about the time we spent together."

As Julia continued to observe the deep bond between them, any traces of jealousy dissipated, replaced by a heightened appreciation for Kasey's resilience and compassion. She felt immense joy seeing him genuinely happy.

"Mission accomplished for the afternoon—that's what took me so long," Kasey announced. "I called the yacht club, and the club president happened to be there. He offered his personal yacht with his captain and two crew members to help out if we foot the bill for all of them, plus gas and overtime. I told him no problem. They're stocking and refueling as we speak. Anything special you want, tell me now; otherwise you get what I've chosen."

"A yacht? Micki's gonna shit cookies," Julia said grinning. "I'm good with whatever you pick for lunch." She thought for a moment, then added, "You know, I remember meeting him.

His name was Walter Gilliam, something like that. We met at a local benefit a few years back. We hit it off—he seemed really nice."

"It is Gilliam. And he spoke highly of you," Kasey confirmed.

"We're gonna have a fantastic time. What a smart idea to call the yacht club. It's our last chance to really unwind for the next month or so," she mused, resting her chin on crossed arms. Glancing up at them both, she continued, "We're all gonna be extremely busy in the coming weeks—moving in together, preparing for Nigel and Giles' visit, and hiring a team for the fashion house.

"Kasey, I'd like you to focus on getting us moved in together first. Shouldn't be a big thing for Ren right now—he's living out of a hotel."

"Uh, I do have a lot of clothes, mostly still in garment boxes and storage, but they're easy to move," Ren grinned.

Kasey laughed and gave Ren a playful push. "I knew you'd mostly have clothes. You're definitely going to need your own dressing room."

Ren grinned and pushed him back. "I'll definitely take you up on that dressing room."

"Focus, boys," Julia said with a grin. "Settle down."

They looked at each other and burst out laughing, with Kasey saying, "Continue; we're listening."

"I was just gonna say, I don't have to bring anything big right away, just my clothes and my dressing table. Then I can get all my makeup and stuff out of your bathroom. I do have a lot of clothes, but nothing that can't be managed by a good moving service."

"I'll also work with Alice to make my condo ready for the group and set up a schedule for her to keep the place clean and stocked while they're there. Then I need you both to help me think of things to do with them while they're here. A list has to be put together to make calls, reservations, or get tickets, etc."

"Whatever you need me to do, just let me know," Ren replied.

"Nothing I won't be able to handle," Kasey said, giving Ren a confident smile. "But there's one more thing I'm adding that's a bit more involved. You're getting new security. We need it for the shore house with Nigel and Giles coming. Might as well set it all up now so the guards will be acclimated to the area, the house, and your rules for privacy. Also, we need to put up a guard house at the front gate. The property is surrounded by thick brush but no real fence, unfortunately. We need that too. My last suggestion is to enclose the back deck, you know, all reinforced glass with screens. I know you wouldn't want to ruin the view.

"Sounds like a plan. Do what you need to do to get it taken care of, Kasey; that's all you. I trust your design aesthetic and security concerns. Just one thing. I want to promote Carl to head of the security detail. Work with him. I feel comfortable with him, and he knows me. He's a retired cop; he knows the city, and he's always been there for me. He's been wasted as just my driver. One of the new guards can drive, and Carl can just focus on managing the other guards and any security concerns."

"Of course, we'll go over each step as far the property goes. And I'll make sure we get security that will fit with our lifestyle. I'm sure Carl will be great at managing security for you," Kasey responded.

"I want to get ready for the boat... put something nice on, and braid my hair. Don't mind me"

"By the way, sweetheart, don't let Gilliam hear you call it a boat. It's a yacht. Men like him tend to get insulted by trivial things like that," Kasey said, having grown up around very rich people, whereas Julia, growing up on a ranch, didn't care at all about things like that.

"Gotcha, didn't know that. I'll be sure to mention that to Micki and the others before we board."

Kasey and Ren lay on the bed, watching Julia go through her closet, looking for something to wear that covered her up a little more while they talked quietly.

After a moment of absentmindedly looking through her choices, she turned around and addressed Ren, "Oh, I almost forgot, next weekend, I have an invite to a fashion show. A new menswear designer is showing and I'd like to check him out. I thought you might like to come with me. Kasey hates these things, and I don't want to blow it off or, worse, go alone. What do you say? We get to dress up and meet a lot of different people. Wanna be my date?"

"Of course I'll go with you," he said, as he looked over at Kasey.

"It's true. I really don't like going to things like that. I would go if you wanted me to, you know that."

"I know that, baby," she smiled as she pulled out a pretty sundress with short sleeves and a collar, "and it's absolutely fine, it's not your thing. But, aren't I lucky? I now have someone who will really enjoy this as much as I do. We'll talk about it more when we go home." She grinned, "When we go home... sounds nice, makes me happy."

After changing and braiding her hair, Julia headed downstairs with Kasey and Ren to meet with the others. As they all piled into the cars, Julia passed James and whispered, "Did you wash her hair?" He gave her a big smile and a thumbs up as he opened the door for Micki.

***

Arriving at the marina adjacent to the yacht club, they were warmly welcomed by Walter Gilliam. He introduced the captain and the two-member crew who would accompany them for their leisurely afternoon excursion. As the group boarded the luxurious yacht and Gilliam proudly showed them around, they couldn't help but marvel at its opulence.

Smooth sailing over the Atlantic off the Jersey shore treated them to breathtaking views as the sun's rays danced off the vast expanse of the ocean. Anchoring in a tranquil spot, they wasted no time diving into the refreshing water. Laughter filled the air as they swam and enjoyed the thrill of riding the two double-seated jet skis towed behind the yacht. Despite missing out on fishing, Will relished the excitement of riding the jet skis and water skiing. Julia held Kasey tightly as their jet ski skipped effortlessly over the rolling waves alongside Micki and James. She filmed Ren water skiing while Kasey drove, still adjusting to the fact they were both now her romantic partners.

After hours of exhilarating water sports and friendship building moments with Ren, the attentive crew served up Kasey's carefully thought out champagne picnic. Sourced from a local gourmet shop, the spread offered a selection of mini lobster rolls, truffle-infused deviled eggs, and a charcuterie board with assorted meats, artisanal cheeses, fig jam, and crusty baguette slices. The entree, a seafood platter from a local vendor, was accompanied by champagne cocktails and prosecco. For dessert, the petit fours, macarons, and fresh fruits never tasted better or more refreshing after the exertion in the blazing sun.

Julia's face lit up with delight as she settled in for the meal. "Kasey, this lunch is beyond amazing," she exclaimed, her appreciative eyes scanning the mouth-watering dishes.

"It looks fantastic—I'm friggin' starving," Micki chimed in, eagerly reaching for a lobster roll.

"Agreed, it looks incredible." Ren grinned at Micki as their hands collided reaching for the same roll.

Looking around at the array of tempting options, James added, "I'm not sure where to start. Everything looks so delicious."

"Now this is how you spend a day on the ocean." Will mumbled, his mouth full of truffle egg, unable to contain his compliment.

As they indulged in the feast, they raised their glasses in a toast to the perfect end of their vacation.

"To the best friends ever, 'Ride or die'," Julia declared, raising her glass. They clinked glasses together, echoing, "Ride or die," as the yacht gently swayed on the gentle waves.

Suddenly, the infectious beat of 'Cake By the Ocean' filled the air. Will, seizing the moment with a loud "Yeah!" grabbed Julia by the hand, popped a petit four in his mouth, and started to dance. Micki and James jumped up to join them, with Micki grabbing Ren's hand, pulling him onto the impromptu dance floor. Gleeful laughter filled the air as the five of them danced together, while Kasey captured videos and pictures of the newly expanded friend group, content to end the weekend on a high note.

***

Chapter 17: Confessions and Connections

Returning to the office on Monday, Julia held a video conference with the Hawthorne brothers and Haruto Makino to finalize plans for their visit. While staying at her condo, they'd enjoy exclusive entertainment and dining, thanks to her resources and connections. The itinerary included a tour of Master's Inc., a meet-and-greet with board members, and four relaxing days at Julia's beach house."

Eager for the trip, the brothers relished the prospect of an American beach vacation. Though they frequently enjoyed time at their villa in Mustique, this would be their first beach experience in the States. Their valet, Gunther, quickly relayed their dietary preferences and other comforts to Kasey. Kasey also coordinated with Haruto's traveling companion, his granddaughter Akira, to address similar needs.

Julia asked if they had any specific requests for their visit, and they requested a Broadway show, preferably a musical, and a memorable dining experience. Beyond that, they looked forward to being surprised by her creative hospitality.

***

As the visit approached, a flurry of new projects kicked off, with Kasey handling the logistics of Julia and Ren moving into his brownstone. On Thursday, their first night together in the house, Julia entered the kitchen, finding Ren and Kasey chatting as Kasey prepared dinner.

"I'm not having dinner with you two; I'll just grab a quick snack. Could you make me a peanut butter and jelly sandwich?" she asked, heading to the pantry. "I have something special planned to celebrate our first night here. Come to my room at nine—and make sure to knock," she added with a mischievous grin. Kasey and Ren exchanged glances, eyes bright with excitement at what she might have planned. Julia took her sandwich and a glass of chocolate milk, then headed upstairs.

At precisely nine, Kasey tapped lightly on the bedroom door. A seductive melody from Julia's playlist drifted through the air, blending with the rich scent of her favorite candle. Beside him, Ren stood in pajama bottoms, his hair in a half-up, half-down style, both awaiting her invitation.

"Please, come in and close the door," Julia's soothing voice beckoned, drawing them into a room bathed in soft hues of blue and purple light, where colors danced in a gentle, mesmerizing rhythm.

Seated gracefully by the window, Julia embodied demure elegance, her posture poised, knees and heels aligned, hands clasped softly in her lap. She wore a short, baby-blue button-down dress with a flared skirt and layers of ruffles beneath, highlighted by white silk stockings held by dark blue satin ribbons tied just above her knees. Completing the look, she wore white patent leather Mary Janes with chunky heels. Her hair, styled into two lofty ponytails with delicate tendrils framing her face, accentuated her large, azure eyes and

387

fluttering lashes, a striking vision reminiscent of their most enchanting anime fantasies.

"Welcome. Please, make yourselves comfortable," she murmured, gesturing toward the bed, her demeanor shifting seductively. "My name is Misty, and I'm here to fulfill your desires." Kasey and Ren exchanged glances, eyes widening with intrigue as she rose gracefully and approached them. Tilting her head coyly, her fingertips brushed against her lips, a playful giggle escaping as she hinted at her intent.

"I exist for pleasure—both giving and receiving it," she purred, her voice a silky siren's call that commanded their full attention. With deliberate, tantalizing slowness, she unbuttoned her dress, letting it slip to the floor, unveiling a baby-blue silk corset laced delicately up the front. Her porcelain-white, rounded breasts spilled temptingly over the top, and her slender waist was cinched to perfection. Trailing her hands sensuously over the corset and between her breasts, she withdrew two white feathers from her cleavage. She ran them slowly across her skin, her voice a soft tease: "One more thing."

She sauntered to Kasey's dresser, leaning forward just enough to offer a tantalizing glimpse of her pert, round bottom as she retrieved a blue silk mask from the top drawer. Holding it up with a provocative grin, she ignited an undeniable spark of desire in both men. With the feathers in one hand and the mask in the other, she faced them and, with a smoldering look, asked in Japanese, "Shall we play?" Her seductive eyes and flawless commitment to her character were spellbinding.

"You are incredibly sexy," Kasey murmured, his voice laced with awe. "I need a picture of you, Misty." Retrieving a Polaroid camera from his closet, he watched as Julia posed by the fireplace, one hand on her hip and a finger playfully resting on her cheek, drawing a smile from both men. As Kasey snapped the photo, Ren's gaze held an unmistakable spark of desire.

Kasey's gaze followed Julia's every move, captivated by her choice of character. "Misty, would you mind turning around slowly?" he asked. With a playful smile, Julia handed each of them a feather before spinning gracefully.

"So, what do you think? Should we take her clothes off or leave them on?" Kasey asked Ren in Japanese as he slowly traced the feather over her breasts.

"Leave them on," Ren replied, letting his feather drift over the curve of her bottom, sparking goosebumps along her skin. Julia's excitement surged, her heart racing as she listened to their whispered words, tantalized by the mystery.

Kasey positioned the mask over her eyes, adjusting it gently as he toyed with her long ponytails. Julia drew in a sharp breath, her lips curving into a smile as he lifted her, laying her gently on the bed.

Slipping off her shoes, Ren continued in Japanese, "We can make better use of these stockings." He untied the satin bow and slid the stocking off, securing one end to her wrist and the other to the carved headboard, with Kasey following his lead. Overwhelmed by sensation, Julia surrendered completely.

Kasey paused, admiring her sprawled across his bed, bound by her stockings to the headboard, dressed as the perfect sultry anime fantasy. Unable to resist, he snapped a quick photo before setting the camera aside.

Sitting on the bed next to her, he traced her breasts with his feather while Ren's touch glided lightly over her leg, making her squirm under their teasing. With deliberate care, Kasey loosened the top satin ribbons of her corset, freeing her breasts. Her soft, light brown nipples, now darker and firm with excitement, met their eager caresses. Both men lavished her with affection, drawing a pleasurable whimper from Julia as she strained against her bindings.

As Kasey continued, Ren moved lower, kissing and licking along the outside of her leg until he reached her ankle. He traced his tongue over the bottom of her foot, drawing a soft giggle, then slipped her brightly painted big toe into his mouth, coaxing a long, low moan. Moving to her instep and the inside of her ankle, he gradually worked his way back up her leg. Sliding off her thong, he wet his fingers and eased them inside her, drawing a sharp, breathy gasp.

Kasey watched as Ren pushed deep inside Julia, his fingers emerging slicker with each thrust, her gasps filling the air as she clenched her fists, straining against her restraints. With a soft, wet sound, Ren withdrew his glistening fingers and smeared her warmth over her nipples. Kasey eagerly licked and sucked on them, intoxicated by her taste.

Ren dove between her legs, his tongue exploring her with fervor until her breath quickened and her hips lifted to meet his mouth. Just as she neared the edge, Kasey signaled him to stop. Julia's breathing slowed as Kasey stood, shedding his pants. Positioning himself between her legs, he placed her feet on his shoulders and entered her, her moans deepening his pleasure as he committed every detail of this moment to memory.

He shifted one of her legs over so both ankles rested on the same shoulder. With her thighs clenched tightly around him, she let out higher-pitched grunts with each thrust. He kissed the inside of her ankle, then bit down lightly, and as she tugged against the headboard with a sweet cry, Kasey lost control, pushing harder, faster, calling her Misty as he came.

Panting softly, he paused before withdrawing. Ren immediately took his place, bending Julia's legs to her chest and entering her hard and fast. She gasped, her head lifting from the pillow before dropping back. Kasey watched intently as Ren intensified his pace, each thrust making her breasts bounce in rhythm.

"Make me come," she pleaded, breathless. Kasey swiftly fetched the vibrator. Leaning back, Ren spread her legs, and with Kasey's assistance, the vibrator worked its magic, bringing her to climax in record time. Julia's hips bucked, her impassioned whimpers filling the room and sparking Ren's release, his groan of satisfaction echoing hers.

"Stop," she managed, signaling Kasey. Ren covered her body with his, holding her tightly.

With his warm breath against her ear, he whispered huskily, "That was so fucking hot." As his breathing slowed, he lifted off her, and she rolled her hips to the side, her legs closing tightly.

"Untie me, please," she pleaded softly. "And I need someone to kiss me." As they carefully untied her wrists, Kasey removed her mask, planting gentle kisses along her cheek while Ren nipped at her shoulder. Julia turned to Ren, sharing a deep, passionate kiss, while Kasey pressed against her, his face buried in her hair. Nestled between them, their arms wrapped around her, Julia felt utterly content. As she sighed softly with delight, Kasey teased, "Somebody's ready to fall asleep."

"I feel so good," she murmured, "and so tired. You guys don't have to stay. I'm just gonna slip out of this and go to sleep early tonight. It's been a long day."

"Let me undress you before I go," Kasey offered.

Giving Julia a kiss goodnight, Ren said, "I'm going to let you two have some time alone. Good night, Misty. It was an absolute pleasure meeting you. I hope I get to see you again," he added with a wink as he left.

"Oh, you will," she murmured. "Night, Ren."

Turning to Kasey, she softly commanded, "Undress me, baby." Gently untying her corset, he kissed her skin with each ribbon he loosened, slipping it out from under her.

"I love you," he whispered, pressing a kiss to her belly button. "I know you're tired, but I don't want to leave just yet."

"I'm never too tired for you, baby. I missed your arms around me," she whispered as he moved on top of her. "Um, I'm really messy down there, you know that, right?" she grinned.

"Nice and slippery," he replied as he slid right in. He made love to her slowly, and, lost in his loving gaze and embrace, she didn't need anything else to be satisfied.

Lying in his arms, she asked coyly, "So, what did you think of my first attempt at role-play? Did you like it?"

"Did I like it?" He laughed. "More than you know." Getting up, he retrieved the pictures he'd taken of her. "I don't ever want to forget the way you looked," he said, gazing at the photos with a smile. "It was such a turn-on for us both to have our own anime girl. I love that you try to accommodate my interests. I really enjoyed Misty," he whispered, nibbling her ear. "You are so good to me." "It was just as exciting for me to think this up for us. I swear, I had so much fun putting it all together." She looked at him, her eyes alight. "I loved having my wrists tied. I didn't expect it, which made it even hotter for me. And, lemme tell you, sex with a blindfold on is wild. Everything felt more intense, and it made the differences between you both more distinct. Your touch, your scent, your taste—they're all so different. The last time we were together, I was in my head a lot, but this time, I just surrendered to feeling—and it was intense. I also love when you speak Japanese. I don't get to hear it much, and not knowing what you were both saying was such a turn-on." She squeezed him tightly and sighed, "I had the best time. I love you so much." From her sigh, he could tell she wouldn't be awake much longer.

"Shit, I need to get up, pee, and clean myself up a bit. I've got a lot of you boys in me right now," she giggled as she gingerly moved to the bathroom, feeling the wetness between her legs.

"Jeez, you both say the grossest things at the worst times," Kasey said, smirking and shaking his head.

"Loosen up, baby. It's two against one now," she grinned. "Don't leave yet. Stay with me, please, 'til I fall asleep," she called as she peed and used the bidet.

"I'm not going anywhere," he assured her.

She crawled under the covers and snuggled up against him, his soft kisses on her neck lulling her to sleep.

"Oh, and don't forget to talk to Ren about the job," she murmured softly.

"I won't," he whispered. Five minutes later, she was fast asleep, and he slipped quietly out of the room.

***

"Finally manage to pry yourself away from her?" Ren grinned as Kasey stepped into the room.

"Sometimes it's hard to separate from her," he admitted with a smile.

"You've got it bad, dude," Ren teased. "Can't blame you, though. You hit the jackpot with Jules. She's got it all— gorgeous, open-minded, clearly she loves you unconditionally and wants to please you. And let's not forget, she's rich as fuck and totally down-to-earth about it. She's the whole package, wrapped in corsets and silk stockings," he chuckled, with Kasey nodding in agreement. "I'm genuinely happy for you, Spike. You deserve her."

393

"I'm incredibly happy with Julia. And now, having you here makes it even better. Lately, it feels like I'm living in a dream," Kasey replied, grabbing water from the fridge.

"I know what you mean—I feel like I'm having the same dream."

Sitting beside Ren on the couch, Kasey's eyes lit up. "I have something exciting to share with you—something that might make this dream even better. In three weeks, Julia is hosting the Hawthorne brothers and their biggest investor, Haruto Makino. She wants you to help entertain them while they're here."

"Are you shitting me?" Ren exclaimed. "Count me in! Spending time with two of the legends of men's fashion would be an honor," he said, excitement lighting up his face at the prospect of rubbing shoulders with Nigel and Giles.

"I'm glad to hear you say that. But that's not even the best part," Kasey continued. "We both know you're not happy at the design firm, so Julia wants to offer you the position of Creative Director for Hawthorne-Masters. You'd shape the vision and direction of the new line, select designers, collaborate with others, and work closely with Nigel and Giles. Julia's planning to move into contemporary, fashion-forward styles, and she thinks you're the perfect fit to bring a younger, fresher perspective. She can hire anyone she feels is right, but she's betting on you. There's a lot of pressure, though—Julia has a lot riding on this venture with her board. So, what do you say? Ready for the big leagues?"

"I... I'm speechless," Ren stammered, stunned by the offer. "Why didn't Julia offer me the job herself?"

"Because she knew it would mean a lot more coming from me. She's thoughtful like that. Just say yes," Kasey said with a hopeful smile.

"This is unbelievable. Of course, my answer is yes!" Ren exclaimed, hugging Kasey tightly. "Was this your doing? I don't even need to interview?"

"Not my doing. Julia did ask me if you'd be interested. She's been researching you since she noticed your style at the shore. She looked into your college credentials and even showed me pictures from your graduation fashion show. And, by the way, you looked fantastic," Kasey said with a smile. "She knows about your family's background in the silk business and that you've already got years in management. She loves your style, and her business instincts tell her this is the right move. She's banking on your success to elevate Hawthorne-Masters in the young men's division."

Casting a sly smile at Ren, he said, "As for an interview... well, I think she's found out everything she needs to know about you personally. Choosing a Creative Director is up to her alone. The board is letting Julia take the reins because the success or failure of this venture rests squarely on her shoulders. If it's a success, it's great for her and the company. But if it fails, they can put the full blame on her, making her future suggestions for acquisition open to more scrutiny. Without her father, I'm worried that the board members who've known her since birth will try to assert control rather than let her lead."

"She has a lot riding on this, and she's willing to risk it on me?" Ren asked, astonished.

"It's no riskier than if she hired any other competent director and the line didn't sell; it's a high-risk business by nature," Kasey added with a sly grin. "Plus, she thinks it'll be fun for us all to work under the same roof. If you give your notice, you can start right away. I could definitely use your help preparing for the brothers' trip, especially with the beach house. There's a lot to rearrange to make sure everyone's comfortable."

"Do you have enough space for all those people at the beach?" Ren asked distractedly, still absorbing the weight of the job offer.

"Nigel and Giles are fine sharing; we just need to set up two double beds in one room. Julia and I have her room, and Haruto will be in another. We thought it'd be best to give his granddaughter the room next to his. Their valet, Gunther, can use one of the two bedrooms downstairs—the one I converted into a training room. We'll change it back, and you can take the other. They'll share a bathroom, but feel free to use ours for showers. This way, we can fit everyone comfortably, no hotels involved, and security's easier. Plus, Julia wants the vacation to feel homey," Kasey explained.

"Sounds perfect. Count me in. I'll talk to Nick Galloway tomorrow and let him know I won't be returning. I'm not deeply involved in any specific projects, so I'm confident he'll understand if I promise to promote his company whenever possible," Ren declared, thrilled at the chance to pursue his dream career. Enveloping Kasey in a hug, he added, "I can't believe how much my life has changed in just a few weeks. I was miserable for so long, and now everything feels different. A whole new world has opened up with you, Julia, and a job in the career I love. What about you, Spike? Are you happy?"

Kasey's smile radiated warmth. "I felt the same way before Julia came into my life. Now,

every morning, I can't wait to start the day. She's the reason for my happiness, and having both you and her is pure bliss."

"That's such a sweet thing to say," Ren said softly as he nuzzled Kasey's neck.

"How about I spend the night in your room? Julia's out for the count," Kasey murmured, leaning into him.

"Sounds good to me. Let's watch something before bed," Ren suggested. "Maybe that documentary on Yuzuru Hanyu, the figure skater I told you about," he added, resting his head on Kasey's shoulder.

"Absolutely," Kasey said, giving Ren a kiss on the head as he picked up the remote. With his girlfriend asleep in his bed and his boyfriend snug in his arms, Kasey couldn't imagine being any happier.

When they were finally ready to head upstairs, Ren smiled and said, "Lock up and meet me in my room," delighted by the thought of sleeping next to Kasey all night.

During the night, Julia woke and, realizing Kasey wasn't beside her, went looking for him, finding him asleep in Ren's bed. Quietly slipping in next to him, she felt his arm pull her close as he stirred. Burying his face into her hair before drifting back to sleep, he was perfectly content to be nestled between the two loves of his life.

***

Ren emerged from the bathroom just as Julia and Kasey woke up. "I see we had a visitor last night," he said with a smile. "I was lonely," she confessed, still sleepy. "That king-size bed feels huge when you're by yourself."

"I don't mind. I could get used to it," Ren grinned at her. "Besides, who in their right mind wouldn't want you crawling into their bed? Certainly not me. You can visit anytime you want." He squatted down and gave her a quick kiss. "I want to talk to you about your job offer, but not while you're half-dressed in my bed. We'll talk downstairs. I'm gonna finish getting ready." Rising, he headed back to the bathroom. "I'm excited to go talk with Nick." "You've made him so happy. Thank you for that," Kasey said, cuddling Julia.

"He deserves it. It's not about giving a job to a guy I'm sleeping with. He has all the qualifications, and I genuinely think he'll do a great job. I want him to be happy and fulfilled. That'll make you happy, and then I'll be doubly happy... win-win." She smiled sweetly, stirring up his feelings of love for her.

"Let's go before I make us late," Kasey said reluctantly, pressing kisses to the nape of her neck.

"Mmm, don't start something you can't finish," Julia giggled, "tease."

"Me?" Kasey said with a grin. "Never."

***

Meeting in the kitchen, Ren handed Julia a cup of tea. "I really want to thank you for the job offer," he said. "I appreciate your confidence in me. It's my dream job, and of course, I accept. I don't know the salary or benefits, and honestly, I don't care. I'd do it for a room, board, and sex at this point." With a wide smile on his face and his arms out to his sides, he added, "Baby, I'm your man."

Laughing, Julia said, "I'm so glad you accepted. I think it'll be wildly beneficial for us both." Sauntering over, she set down her tea, wrapped her arms around him, and, gazing at him through her long lashes, purred, "I bet you'll find there are lots of benefits to us all working in the same building."

"Heh, heh," Kasey teased. "She's an extremely bad influence at work. I have a feeling I'm going to spend a lot of time as a lookout."

"Well, now I definitely want the job," Ren replied, kissing her on top of her head. He pulled her closer, locking eyes with Kasey and smiling.

Looking down at his buzzing phone, Kasey announced, "Carl's here. Let's get going."

***

After dropping Julia and Kasey at work, Carl drove Ren to Urban Designs to speak to his soon-to-be-ex-boss. Ren approached Nick Galloway's office, excited to be moving on to the job of his dreams, though a bit sad about ending his budding workplace friendship with Nick. Taking a steadying breath, he knocked gently and entered, finding Nick engrossed in paperwork.

"Nick, I need to discuss something important," Ren began. Nick looked up, gesturing for him to take a seat. "I've been offered a position at a new fashion house—Hawthorne-Masters. It's a once-in-a-lifetime opportunity. I'll be Creative Director for their urban division, a position I could only dream of," he explained, excitement evident in his tone. Nick responded with a supportive smile, leaning back in his chair.

"I knew about your passion for fashion design from the beginning, and I knew this interior design job wasn't your ultimate goal. I just thought we'd have your input a little longer. Go for it—chase your dreams. Just do me a favor: when you're mingling in those fancy fashion circles, drop our company's name every now and then, alright?"

"Absolutely, and I might have a job for you already," Ren replied. "I'm moving into a brownstone in Tribeca, and we'll be redecorating a couple of floors to accommodate the move. There's even an apartment on the bottom floor that'll be redone for security. It's a big job, and I'd love your help."

"A brownstone in Tribeca with security—wow, you move fast," Nick said, genuine admiration in his voice. "Whose home would we be working on?"

"I can't say anything about that just yet. I went to school with the owner; we're very close."

"Well, thanks for considering me for your renovation. I'd be happy to consult and help you find the right supplies and contractors. Just let me know when you're ready. I wish you well, Ren, in all your new endeavors."

"Thanks, Nick. I appreciate you being so supportive. I'll get back to you about the renovations as soon as we set a date. Right now, our schedule's packed, so we probably won't start until at least the middle of next month."

"Sounds good, just let me know. You take care, Ren."

"You too, Nick. I'll be in touch." With a parting handshake, Ren left, relieved everything went so well.

"Where can I take you now, Mr. Ito?" Carl asked as he opened Ren's door.

"Please, call me Ren. You'll be seeing a lot of me," he said with a smile. "I'm going to be working at Masters Inc., and I've moved into the brownstone."

"Very nice, Ren. Where can I take you?" Carl replied.

"To work, Carl. Bring me to work," Ren said, his face exuding happiness.

"You got it," Carl said, pulling into traffic.

***

"So, how did it go?" Kasey asked Ren, rising from his desk as he entered the office.

"Really well, actually. Nick was incredibly supportive. Couldn't have asked for a smoother conversation," Ren replied, nodding to Julia, who was busy on a call in her office. "So, what's on the agenda? Put me to work," he added with a grin.

"Give me a minute," Kasey said, pressing a button on the phone. "Barbara, could you locate Derrick and send him in here? Thanks."

Turning back to Ren, he continued, "One of our interns, Derrick, will give you a tour. He'll take you to HR for your ID

400

badge and handle other necessities. Here he is now," Kasey said as an eager young man hustled into the office.

"Derrick, meet Ren Ito, our new Creative Director for the fashion house. As we discussed earlier, show him around, starting with HR, and make sure he's back here by one."

"Yes, sir. Whenever you're ready, Mr. Ito, I'll be waiting outside."

"Thanks, Derrick," Kasey acknowledged.

"Yeah, thanks Derrick," Ren added. Just then, Julia emerged from her office, inviting them in.

"How'd it go? Smooth sailing?" she asked as Kasey and Ren settled onto the couch.

"I just finished telling Kasey—it all went very smoothly. Nick was incredibly supportive. I'm all yours now," he declared, smiling broadly.

"Excellent. I'm glad there were no hard feelings," she replied, squeezing between them. "Leaving on good terms is always best."

"I did mention to Nick that some redecorating would be in the works soon, and he offered to help with contractors and materials. I didn't say who it was for—figured it best to keep it discreet until I spoke with you guys," Ren explained.

"Smart move. Kasey handles all that for us, but you'll learn the ropes of what can and can't be shared and with whom. It's all about protecting our privacy. Speaking of that, are you prepared for the attention that comes with this lifestyle? Kasey loathes the publicity side, but it's part of the job. Security's going to get tighter, especially after the fashion show. Your name and image will be out there. Can you handle all that?" Julia asked, with Kasey looking curious.

"I can handle the press at events—it's par for the course in the fashion world. I have to admit, losing some freedom with having security around all the time will take some getting used to. But for you guys, I think I can manage," he said with a grin.

"That's good to hear," Kasey chimed in. "I never even thought to ask you about that."

"At least we'll adapt together. I've never had security outside my home or a full-time bodyguard— except for my baby here," Julia grinned, patting Kasey's thigh. "Carl doesn't really count; he mostly drove and did occasional security. You need to start training with Kasey again," she advised Ren, giving his thigh a pat, "so you can protect me when we're out alone together."

"I'd take a bullet for you, baby," Ren said, his gaze steady, a fierce grin spreading across his face.

"Ready for Derrick to show you around?" Julia asked, smiling.

"Absolutely," he replied eagerly, rising from the couch with a single clap of his hands.

"Just make sure he has you back here by one. We're going out for lunch to celebrate your first day," she reminded him, flashing a bright smile as he departed.

"He's genuinely thrilled about this job," Kasey remarked to Julia after Ren left, his own

happiness evident.

"I love seeing you so happy," she said, taking his hand and resting her head on his shoulder. "This will be a new adventure for all of us." They sat for a moment, her head nestled against his as she breathed in his scent.

"As much as I enjoy this—and you know I do—we have things to do," he murmured, gently tilting her head back to kiss her.

"Buzzkill," she teased.

"Someone has to be the responsible one here. I assume it's always going to be me," he said with a grin, offering his hand to help her up.

"Fine, I'm going back to work," she declared, flouncing off to her desk. Moments later, Kasey overheard her in a heated discussion with a member of the legal team about her decision to host the Hawthorne brothers and Mr. Makino in her homes, despite concerns about their age, insurance, and the potential for negative publicity if anything were to happen to them. She made it clear she wasn't interested in objections, asserting they were her personal guests and that nothing could change her mind. Surprisingly, by the end of the conversation, the lawyer seemed to understand Julia's perspective; the two of them even shared a laugh. Kasey marveled at how she seamlessly transitioned from a mischievous, childlike pixie with him to a determined leader and then to a sweet charmer with the lawyer—all within minutes.

***

By 12:30, Ren returned with Derrick, having finished his tour and orientation with HR.

"How did everything go?" Kasey asked as they entered the office.

"Smooth as silk. I took care of everything with HR," Ren said proudly, holding up his laminated ID card on a lanyard around his neck. "And Derrick showed me all the places I'll need to know to work here. He was a big help," Ren added, giving Derrick a nod of appreciation. "I can't believe how nice the fashion floor is! The offices, workrooms, even the runway area—it's all perfect," Ren said, his enthusiasm bubbling over.

"Thanks for all your help, Derrick. You can head back to Barbara now," Kasey said as Derrick left.

"I'm glad you like the offices. We could use your input on a few finishing touches to make the space conducive to the designers' creativity," Kasey said, glancing into Julia's office.

"Julia is with Rick Tyrell right now—one of her father's closest friends, a senior board member, and her godfather. Rick manages the ranching side of the business with Jack Dorsey and oversees the Double O Ranch, Julia's family home and the heart of this company. I'll introduce you when he comes out. It shouldn't be long—his unexpected visit has me a bit nervous; he's never done this before."

"Ride 'em, cowboy," Ren remarked, taking in Rick's casual western attire, Stetson in hand.

"I spent time with him, Jack, and Julia's father, Buck, camping. Rick's the epitome of a rugged ranch boss, a real man's man. He's nice enough but definitely has some traditional, conservative views—more so than Buck did, who always seemed a bit more open-minded. Still, Julia is very close to him and Jack Dorsey, Buck's other best friend and the one most involved with the breeding side of the business. Jack's more like Buck was. They're her biggest allies in the company, and they've known her since birth," Kasey explained.

After a few minutes, Julia and Rick emerged from her office, both smiling. She gestured toward Ren, introducing him to Rick with a welcoming smile.

"Rick Tyrell, I'd like you to meet Ren Ito, our new Creative Director for Hawthorne-Masters," Julia said, a note of pride in her voice.

"Nice to meet you, sir," Ren said, shaking Rick's hand with a polite smile.

"Nice to meet you too, Mr. Ito. Well, you certainly have a unique style," Rick said, looking Ren over. "Julia's assured us you'll bring the drive we need to push this fashion venture forward. I trust her intuition—she knows her stuff, don't ya, darlin'?" Rick smiled at Julia, his expression tinged with fatherly pride.

Julia smiled weakly, and Kasey immediately sensed the impact that "darlin'" had on her. Reminiscent of her father's voice and his favorite way of addressing her, it carried heavy emotional weight, clearly stirring deep feelings.

"I'm sorry to interrupt, but Julia, you have a lunch meeting in ten minutes," Kasey said, gently nudging Rick along.

"Well, that's my cue to mosey along. It's been good seeing you too, Kasey, and congrats are in order, it seems. Julia tells me you two are shacking up. Now, who didn't see that coming?" He laughed, giving Kasey a hearty slap on the back. "I'll talk to you soon Jules, Kasey. Mr. Ito, looking forward to big things from you," he said as he headed out.

Julia immediately turned and walked into her office, with Kasey close behind her.

"I'll be right back," he said to Ren as he left.

"Are you okay?" Kasey asked softly, catching up to her and enveloping her in a comforting embrace. She leaned into him, her head resting on his chest, tears welling in her eyes.

"No, not at all," she admitted softly. "It's still tough... seeing Rick and Jack. They have no idea how much it hurts. They dress like my dad, they sound like him, and now, for the first time since he died, one of them called me darlin'—here at work, no less. It was like taking a bullet to the heart." She paused, swallowing back tears. "Distract me, please. I can't break down here."

"Come sit down," he said softly, guiding her to the couch. "I'll get Ren; he'll distract you—he's very good at it." As Julia sank into the cushions, her thoughts still tangled in memories of her father, Kasey went to summon Ren.

"Kasey tells me you're upset. We can't have that now, can we?" Ren's voice soft and caring as he settled beside her on the couch. Meanwhile, Kasey discreetly retreated to his office to ensure Julia's privacy.

Caught in Ren's comforting gaze, Julia felt her emotions overflow, tears spilling down her cheeks.

"Oh no, sweetie, come here. Let it out... then let it go," Ren murmured, pulling her into a warm embrace. She leaned into him, allowing herself to release the emotions she'd been holding back.

"Some feelings just need to be felt," Ren reassured her, gently rocking her. "Don't be afraid to let it out, Jules. You're not a robot—especially not in moments like this. One day, it won't sting as hard. It'll get easier with time." His words struck a chord, and she found solace in his embrace. Gradually, her tears subsided, replaced by a deep, quiet calm.

Julia confessed, wiping away her tears. "I just can't have people here at work seeing me cry and thinking I'm weak. I'm supposed to be the leader, you know?"

"Thank you," she sniffled as he handed her a tissue. "I always feel like I have to hold back my emotions at work—it's tough. If something touches my heart, I'm a crier," Julia admitted, dabbing at her tears.

"Remember, Jules, even leaders have tough days. No one could ever think you're weak. You're doing great, especially with everything you've faced. Don't be so hard on yourself— no one saw a thing." He handed her another tissue. "Feeling a little better?"

"I'm good now. But I bet I look like hell," she added with a small smile, sitting up and dabbing under her eyes.

"Baby, you couldn't look like hell if you tried," Ren murmured, brushing a strand of hair back from her shoulder.

"Oh damn, I think I got mascara on your shirt," she said, spotting the telltale black smudge.

"Don't worry about it, Jules," he reassured her.

"Come with me to the bathroom. I've got a stain remover there. Let me try to get it out... please? I'll feel better if I do."

She took his hand and led him to her black-and-white art deco bathroom. Guiding him to the black tufted bench under her dressing table, she said, "Have a seat," as she grabbed a wipe from the drawer. Dabbing at his collar gingerly, she attempted to remove the mark. "It's coming off!" she exclaimed with relief.

"Jules, seriously, it's not a big deal," he said, gently stopping her hand. Looking into her eyes, he asked, "How are you feeling? Better?" Ren watched her closely, feeling the weight of her emotions settle over him. This wasn't the playful, teasing Julia he was used to—this was someone who needed comfort, and it hit him hard. How could anyone expect her to hold all of this together on her own?

As he pulled her onto his lap, Ren sensed a shift in the air. This wasn't about lust; she needed to feel safe, to be close. Her vulnerability was raw, and he realized just how much she kept hidden.

"Better, thank you," she whispered as he wrapped his arms around her.

"Good, because it's hard to see you cry. I don't think Kasey can handle it." He gently brushed a stray piece of hair from her damp cheek. "No one wants to see you upset," he said with a caring smile, giving her red nose a playful boop.

"Did you just boop me?" she asked with a smile.

"You just seemed to need one," he replied, his dark eyes crinkling at the corners.

Drawn to him and his ability to soothe her, she leaned in and kissed him, weaving her fingers into his silky hair. Their kisses deepened as he lifted her onto the sink, and she wrapped her legs around him. With her desire intensifying, Julia murmured, "Make me feel even better," as she rubbed her cheek against his.

"Here?" he asked, pressing into her, so turned on by the thought of being with Julia in her office bathroom that he momentarily forgot why he was there.

"Right here, right now," she whispered, taking control. "Lemme just sit on your lap."

He helped her down, then unbuckled his belt, unzipped, and let his pants drop before sitting on the large toilet. Julia hiked up her tight skirt, slipped off her panties, and locked the bathroom door as she passed. Standing before him, she discreetly spit into her hand and made the tip of him slick. She lowered herself onto him with a soft, satisfied sigh, resting her head on his shoulder and holding him close, barely moving. Until now, he'd only seen her playful, passionate side in moments like these; this was the first time he saw her using sex to find comfort. Giving her complete control, he followed her lead.

Julia's slow, sensual movements and tender kisses made him feel like he was the only one she desired. As she brushed her face against his, the breathy sounds of her moans in his ear made him wild with desire.

She caressed his face as she kissed him, her fingers slipping gradually into his hair while her hips moved in slow, tight circles on his lap. "This feels so good," she whispered, inhaling his scent. She pulled her collar back, exposing her delicate neck. "Suck on my neck, please."

As he sucked on her neck, her hips moved faster, back and forth on his lap. Ren let out a low moan. "Damn, baby, I love the way you move," he murmured, his head tilting back slightly, eyes closing. She wrapped her arms around his neck, resting her forehead against his as her movements grew faster, more assertive.

"Make noise for me baby," he begged. Her rhythmic moans with each thrust and the way she whispered his name in breathless moments drove him over the edge, and he came with a long, low groan.

As they clung to each other, their breaths mingling in the quiet aftermath, he said softly, "I am in deep lust with you Jules."

"I feel the same," she breathed, her full lips meeting his as their kisses deepened again.

Leaning back after a moment, her expression full of gratitude, she said, "Thank you for being here for me. Not just for the sex... but for comforting someone in pain. It's not easy, and it means the world to me."

She smiled, adding, "Now grab me some toilet paper so I don't make a complete mess out of you when I get up." Julia cleaned herself up as Ren pulled himself together, and they both exited the bathroom, taking a seat on the couch.

She rested her head on his shoulder and sighed as Kasey came in and sat down next to her.

"Do you feel better, sweetheart?" he asked with concern.

"I feel better, thanks." She sat up, resting her hand on his thigh. "Ren helped me let it all out, and it does feel so much better than just holding it in… then we had sex in the bathroom. You know how much better that always makes me feel," she added with a small smile. Ren laughed out loud, and Kasey smiled, shaking his head.

"I'm just glad you feel better, however you got there," Kasey replied. "I hate to ask, but why exactly was Rick here? Is there something going on we should know about?"

"No, it was nothing. He came to town for personal reasons, nothing to do with work. He just wanted to check in on me. The news about us got back to him, and he just wanted to know how everything was going. I think he's keeping an eye on me like my dad. It's thoughtful, but sometimes it hurts."

She paused, her emotions starting to rise again. "We should go get some lunch," she said hastily, changing the subject. "Unless you'd rather stay here."

"What would you really like to do?" Kasey asked, aware that she often leaned toward pleasing the people she cared about.

"I think I'd rather stay here." She paused, then added, "Seeing Rick took a lot out of me. Even though I think I can control the tears, I still feel incredibly sad. I haven't felt this way in a long time. I feel guilty that I haven't and that I'm moving on with my life." Dropping her head, she leaned forward, covering her face with her hands.

"No, don't cry," Kasey said, enveloping her in his arms. "Maybe you should go home. It's Friday, and there's nothing pressing here that I can't handle. Why don't you go home with Ren? I'll be home later; I have some conference calls I can't cancel. Go home, rest, and I'll be there as soon as I can."

"Come on, Jules, let's get you home," Ren said. She didn't even try to protest. With Kasey taking care of things at work, she wouldn't have to face the quiet alone—she had Ren.

Carl watched in the rearview mirror as Julia rode to the brownstone with her head on Ren's shoulder, holding his hand, her expression weighed down with sorrow.

***

As she was getting ready to take a nap, Ren popped his head in and asked, "Need anything?"

"Yeah," she said, settling into bed. "Could you come lay down with me? Tell me something about yourself. Tell me about your time in college. Tell me about you and Kasey— what was he like in school? Tell me anything."

Ren lay down beside Julia, and she rested her head on his chest as he wrapped a comforting arm around her. "Let's see," he said, gently stroking her hair. "When I met Kasey, it wasn't exactly a smooth introduction." He chuckled softly at the memory. "He was pretty closed off, reserved, extremely shy— whatever you want to call it. The guy had barriers up. We were complete opposites at first. I kept at him, though, looking for some common ground, and believe it or not, it turned out to be anime. I'd be watching it, he'd be reading, and I noticed he'd be glancing over, watching with me. Before long, we started talking about it, and once I found my way in… well, he wasn't so hard to crack after that. He just needed a little love and attention."

He hesitated. "Kasey always told me I made his life better, but he never realized how much better he made mine. He loves unconditionally once he lets you in. He's a gentle, sensitive soul, fiercely protective of those he cares about. I know he told you about how our relationship unfolded, so I'll just say this: I think I loved him from the moment we met. He was beautiful on the outside, sure, but once I got to know him, I saw he was just as beautiful on the inside. It was cruel what my father did to us. We were just both young and afraid to fight back."

Julia tried but couldn't fully empathize. "I just can't fathom what you two went through with your fathers, especially Kasey. My father loved me unconditionally. I never knew a day in my life that I didn't feel his love. I can't understand Kasey's father treating him so horribly for no reason other than his own selfishness."

"Yeah, well, some people are not cut out to be parents. And some think they're doing what's best for their child when, really, it's what's best for them," Ren said ruefully. Julia squeezed him tight, feeling the weight of his separation from his family.

"You know," she whispered, "I fell in love with Kasey the day I met him too. I refused to connect deeply with any man for years after one hurt me so badly. I didn't think I would recover. I walked into my office to see Kasey standing there for an interview, and it was all over for me. I couldn't think of anything but being close to him from that day forward. I've never had anyone consume me like he does." She paused. "We are so much alike, you and I." She leaned on her elbow to look at him. "Does it bother you that we're literally the male and female version of the same person to him? Micki saw it right away."

"Not at all. I think it's cool that you and I are so similar. Does it bother you?"

"At first, I'll admit it was a little weird to me, but it makes sense if you think about it. I am glad that if this situation had to come about, it was with you. This could've easily gone south pretty fast, and I could have lost him. When I thought about how that would feel, I figured you had to have felt that too. I couldn't dismiss what you guys had and that it was taken away forcefully." She laid her head back on his chest and held him tight. "I'm very happy you're here now."

"I am too," he said quietly, returning her hug and holding her close. Before long, she fell asleep, and Ren slipped from her arms. He placed a throw over her and went downstairs.

"How's she doing?" Kasey asked when he answered Ren's call.

"She's doing fine; she fell asleep. I laid down with her, we had a nice talk, and before I knew it, she was out. She's one hell of a sleeper."

"Good, I think she just needs to rest and regroup. Rick caught her off guard, calling her 'darlin'' like he did; that was the way her dad addressed her most of the time."

"Oh, so that's what triggered it. I didn't realize. I thought it was just seeing Rick dressed like that. Damn, poor Jules—no wonder she was so upset. She hasn't cried anymore since we got here, but she does seem sad and out of it. Maybe she'll perk up after a nap and dinner. Can I do anything for dinner before you get home?" Ren asked, looking over Kasey's immaculate kitchen and knowing there was nothing he could do.

Kasey laughed. "I had this same conversation with Julia—you don't cook, so stay out of my kitchen. Thank you, anyway. Besides, tonight I'm ordering food. Any requests? Julia rarely cares what I order; she eats pretty much everything."

"I don't care what you order either; anything is good with me. When do you think you'll be home?"

"I'm going to leave right after my last conference call, so I should be home around five," Kasey answered.

"Okay, see you soon. I'm gonna work on unboxing some clothes. I want to find something special to wear on Wednesday—and I'll try to get my room organized."

"You have fun with that," Kasey chuckled. "I know that isn't one of your favorite things to do. Don't get too crazy. Remember, we're going to make a whole suite for you on the third floor, dressing room and all. And I can help you organize everything then if you want."

"Oh, I will definitely need your help—and welcome it," Ren laughed.

They said their goodbyes, Kasey glad Ren was there with Julia, and Ren happy to be a part of their lives.

***

When Kasey walked in later, Ren and Julia were nestled next to each other on the couch, watching *Archer*. It was one of Ren's favorite adult cartoons, and he thought it would cheer her up—which it did. Kasey set two large bags of food on the kitchen table and went over to them.

"Hey, baby. I'm glad you're home," Julia said, sounding more upbeat.

Kasey leaned over the back of the couch and gave her a kiss on the top of her head. "Are you feeling better? You sound much better."

"I do feel much better. I had a nap, watched Archer, and laughed my ass off. Plus, I couldn't have had a better babysitter," she said, flashing Ren an appreciative smile. "This show is hysterical. I'd heard about it but never took the time to watch it. I love it—the characters are so ridiculously funny. And now, I'm starving. Let's eat!" she said excitedly, getting up to rummage through the bags.

"Oh my God, how did you know I was craving Italian food? And from Locanda Verde. Wait 'til you taste this, Ren, it's so friggin' good." As she opened the containers, little squeals of joy escaped her as she uncovered one favorite dish after another, including a decadent chocolate torte.

"I know you like comfort food when you've had a rough day," Kasey said, showing Ren again how much he understood Julia and how well he took care of her.

"Let's put big spoons in everything. We can share, and Ren can try all of it," Julia said, grabbing the spoons and placing them in the dishes.

414

"So, what's happening this weekend?" Julia asked between mouthfuls of Mama's Lasagna.

"We need to be at the beach early tomorrow morning. The fence is going up, the deck is being enclosed, and a guard shack is being built. On Sunday, while all that wraps up, I have security guards coming in for the beach house, and I'll also be meeting a few Carl recommended for New York," Kasey explained.

Julia, her voice sounding tired at the thought of all the commotion, replied, "I hate to dump this on you, but would you mind going with Ren so I could stay here for a little alone time? I think I need a personal weekend. Ren and I have that fashion show on Wednesday, and I'm feeling a little stretched to my limits. You could take my car."

"Of course, we could handle all this, but are you sure you want to be alone all weekend?" Kasey asked, worried about her being alone in his big house, especially while she was feeling down about her family.

"Truthfully, I haven't been alone in a while. And it's not like you'll be on the moon or something. I can have Carl bring me to you if I'm lonely. It's only one overnight. We can talk and see each other on the phone... I'll be fine," she said with a confident smile. "I'm just tired, and I hate construction—the noise would totally get on my nerves. I'm gonna spend the two days turning my brain off and binge-watching *Archer.* We have more than enough food in the house for me to eat without calling for delivery, which I know you wouldn't approve of me doing while alone. See, I do think about my security," she gave Kasey a sweet smile.

"If that's what you really want," Kasey said hesitantly. "Would you like me to ask Carl if he'd stay in the apartment downstairs just to make sure you're safe?"

"Baby, please... not necessary. You have a state-of-the-art security system here—I'll be fine," she assured him.

After a long dinner discussing the renovations, they all sat down to watch a movie and enjoy the chocolate torte. When it was over, even though it was only nine-thirty, Kasey excused himself and headed off to bed.

"I'll be up later, baby," Julia said as he kissed her good night.

"Don't rush for me. I know you had that nap. Goodnight, Ren. We'll be leaving pretty early tomorrow. I have the service dropping the car off at six. Just bring casual clothes and your bathing suit; we won't be going anywhere special... there'll be so much to do and organize while we're there." He leaned in and kissed him, then headed upstairs.

"Kasey thinks he's so sly," Julia said once he was out of earshot. "He left us here alone on purpose. He wants us to get to know each other better." She pulled Ren close, throwing her leg over him and settling on his lap. "So, how about it? Wanna get to know me better?" she purred, her lips brushing his ear. Her kisses were soft and lingering as his hands moved slowly over her back.

"I wanna know all of you," he said, his voice low, as he slipped his fingers into the waistband of her soft pajama bottoms. With their kisses deepening and his fingers beginning to explore, she whispered, "Let's go upstairs."

"You read my mind," he whispered back, lifting her as he stood up—her legs wrapping tightly around him. He carried her to his room, with her peppering his neck with kisses the entire time.

They undressed each other slowly, trading soft, unhurried kisses before slipping beneath the covers. Words felt unnecessary as they gave in to the moment, each touch more tender, each kiss a quiet confession of what was building between them.

In no rush, he explored her body, his lips slowly gliding over her skin. Julia's body trembled under his gentle touch, the anticipation almost too much to bear as she waited for the heat of his tongue. Gripping the headboard, her soft moans shifted into breathless gasps as he teased her, his tongue and fingers playing a slow, torturous rhythm. Her whimpers grew louder. Her breathing quickened—she was on the edge, ready to explode.

A moment later, when she did, Ren experienced her orgasm up close and personal. He had never felt anything like this—the way her body clenched around his fingers, her release leaving him slick and breathless. Pushing his head away and muttering, "Stop," she rolled to her side as he moved up to face her.

"Mmm," she murmured, "that was perfect," licking his lips softly.

With her hand making its way down his body and finding him fully erect, awaiting her touch, she began gently stroking him. She moved down alongside him, and, taking her time, she slipped him into her mouth and showed him just how much she enjoyed being with him. His breathing grew heavier, his groans of pleasure filling the room until she stopped and pulled him on top of her. Trying to make it last as long as he could, he made love to her slowly, his kisses deep and tender. Her legs wrapped around him, her fingers tangling in his hair, her grip tightening with each thrust. When he felt he couldn't hold back any longer, he bit her shoulder, her voice calling his name as pure bliss crashed through him.

With a contented sigh, Ren whispered, "That was really nice, Jules. You've made me feel more in these few weeks than my wife did in ten years. The way you touch me, kiss me...it's like you mean every single thing. I didn't know it could be like this. Now I know what Kasey meant when he said the more he's with you, the harder it is to leave your side. I never want you to leave my bed or my side. I know I said I was in deep lust, but it's more than that. I'm really falling for you."

"That was such a sweet thing to say," she whispered softly, planting tiny kisses on his chest. "I wanted to let you know how much I really enjoy being with you. I tingle all over when I'm with you. I'm glad I make you happy because you have no idea how much you bring to my life." She moved up to kiss him, passionately conveying her deep feelings. "I'd like to stay with you for a while. Will you set your alarm for two so I can go to Kasey? I think we should discuss it before I spend the whole night with you. Is that okay?"

"Of course it's okay," he said as he set his phone. "Now, come here and let me fall asleep with you in my arms." She rested her head and hand on his chest, draping her leg over his. Wrapped in his tight embrace, she felt deeply cherished.

***

At two, when the alarm went off, Julia silenced it before it woke him. She slipped out of Ren's bed, walked naked to Kasey's room, and quietly slipped into his. Pressing her cool, bare skin against his warmth, she felt his immediate response.

"There you are," he breathed, his voice a sleepy, sensual drawl. "I want you before I go," he said, his hand trailing slowly over her body.

"Then take me," she whispered, rolling onto her back. Showing her how much he would miss her, he took his time, loving her with his usual tenderness. They fell asleep wrapped up in each other's arms, Julia once again feeling profoundly loved and content.

At five-thirty, Kasey's alarm stirred him from sleep. But before he could get up, Julia's soft voice cut through the early morning haze. "Baby, don't get up yet," she whispered. "There's something I need to tell you before you go."

Curious, he turned to face her. "What is it?"

Julia hesitated, her words cautious yet sincere. "Yesterday, Ren admitted something to me while we were at work. He said he felt a strong attraction to me at first, mainly driven by lust. But after we were together last night, he confessed his feelings are becoming deeper—he said he's falling for me."

She paused, watching Kasey's reaction. "I wanted to let you know what's going on. I'm sure he'll tell you himself, but I also wanted you to know I feel strongly about him too. I hope that isn't upsetting; how quickly this is happening. I didn't tell him exactly how I felt because I thought it was important to talk to you first."

Kasey's response was warm, his tone reassuring. "Sweetheart, did you think I hadn't considered the possibility that you two could fall for each other? I want that for us. I want nothing more than for us to love and care for each other. Seeing you two getting closer brings me immense happiness. After you mentioned the idea of a threesome, I couldn't wait to share you with him. It may sound strange, but I wanted him to experience the pleasure you bring me."

"I don't find it strange," she said, reassured by his response. "It makes me feel special to know you want to share that happiness with someone you love. In some cultures, sharing your partner is seen as a sign of pride. I take it as a compliment. Maybe you could bring this up with Ren. He might feel awkward telling you he's falling for your girl so quickly. If you let him know it's okay and welcome, it'll make it easier for him."

"That's a good idea, and sweet of you to think about his feelings." He pulled her close, showering her with kisses. "I love you, Julia. Every day with you is better than the last. As much as I wish I could stay, I have to get ready. The car will be here soon. I should go check on Ren."

"I'll go see if Ren's up. I'm getting up to see you off. I can sleep when you leave. Do I have any clothes in here?" she asked.

"Where are the clothes you had on?" Kasey asked with a knowing smile.

"In Ren's room. I came here naked," she said with a cheeky grin.

"Here's my pajama top; we can't have you parading around naked, now can we? Then we'll never get out of here," he teased.

She knocked on Ren's door, and he opened it immediately, already dressed and ready.

"Good morning, love. I believe these are yours," he said with a smile as he held up the clothes she'd left behind.

Her arms encircled his neck as she stood on her tiptoes and kissed him, her fingers weaving through his hair. "Good morning to you too. Mmm, you smell so good."

He dropped the clothes and wrapped his arms around her waist, lifting her off the floor as he returned her affection. "What a nice way to start the day," he said, nuzzling her neck, his hand slipping below the pajama top and caressing her bare bottom. "You feel so good," he sighed, pulling her into his room and pressing her body against the wall with his. Their lips met in a series of deep, lingering kisses, his hands cupping her face as he whispered, "You are such a great kisser. I love your lips. I just wanna bite them," he murmured, his teeth gently tugging at her lower lip.

Realizing the time, and with a childlike whine at the thought of leaving, he said, "I don't want to stop, but I have to get moving. I don't want to keep Spike waiting."

"It's alright. I heard the same thing from him. I know he doesn't like being late for anything," she said with a sweet smile. "He must get frustrated to no end with me. I'm a bit lax when it comes to time management. Sometimes, I really do need a minder." She took the clothes from him and tossed them on the bed as she passed her and Kasey's room. Together, they went downstairs to find him drinking tea and waiting for the car service.

"Call anytime if you feel like it. I trust you to make any and all decisions." Julia said, wrapping her arms around Kasey's waist.

"And if you miss us, don't hesitate to call," Kasey added as his cell vibrated. "Car's outside. Time to go." Kasey kissed her and grabbed his bag, heading out the door. Ren gave Julia a quick kiss and followed, leaving her standing in the doorway with bedhead, dressed in Kasey's oversized pajama top and slippers. Kasey walked back as Ren put the top down on the car.

"You make it very hard to leave; you look so beautiful in this light."

"Thank you, baby. I'm gonna miss you too," she said with a loving smile.

"I'll take care of everything," he assured her. "Enjoy your time alone."

"I know you will. And you enjoy your time with Ren. Don't be all work and no play. Do something fun together."

Wrapped in the humid summer breeze and streams of soft morning light, she kissed him again and waved goodbye to Ren before heading back inside. Kasey and Ren drove off toward the shore, the rising sun in their faces, as Julia went back to bed.

***

Chapter 18: Echoes of the Past

In the relative quiet of the early Saturday morning, with most of the city still sleeping, Ren decided it was time to share his feelings about Julia with Kasey. Like Julia, he wanted to be as open as possible about anything that could affect them all.

"Kasey, I have something I want to tell you," Ren began.

"Kasey?" Kasey repeated, a smile tugging at his lips as he glanced over. "If it's about how you feel about Julia, I already know. She told me this morning. She said she feels the same way about you but wanted to discuss it with me first before revealing how much. She also asked me to make it easier on you by sharing how I feel." His expression was warm as he looked at Ren. "I'm thrilled. Why shouldn't we all love each other? We're supposed to be a committed trio. And you both are extremely lovable. I should know." He smiled and took Ren's hand, lacing his fingers with his.

"I should have known she'd say something," Ren replied, affection softening his expression. "I had such an amazing time with her last night. She's like two different people in bed. When she's having sex, it's hot and playful, but when she makes love, you *feel* loved. At least I did. I told her she made me feel more loved in one night than my wife ever did.”

“Now who's got it bad?” Kasey grinned, squeezing his hand.

“She's an amazing woman. I feel incredibly lucky.” Ren paused thoughtfully. “Who would have thought we'd grow up, meet again, and both fall in love with the same woman? I certainly didn't. I still can't believe it's happening now.”

“I can't believe it either, but isn't it great that it is?” Kasey exclaimed, his broad smile and sparkling blue-gray eyes radiating happiness as he tightened his grip on Ren's hand.

As he gazed at Kasey, Ren couldn't remember ever seeing him this happy. A swirl of

overwhelming joy bloomed in his stomach. With Kasey back in his life, the blossoming relationship with Julia, and the amazing job offer, it felt like a dream he was reluctant to wake from. With the conversation behind them, they settled in to enjoy the rest of the trip, their profound happiness warming their hearts like the sun's rays warmed their contented faces.

***

Rolling up to the house, they found the fence contractors already there unloading materials. “Alright,” Kasey said, pulling up to the front door. “Let's get this place in order.”

An hour into the fence setup, the contractors for the guard shack and the enclosed deck arrived. Kasey skillfully managed the landscapers, fence installers, and deck builders, ensuring everything stayed on track.

With progress moving smoothly, Kasey arranged lunch for the workers to keep their morale high. By the end of the day, excess shrubbery had been cleared, the fence was halfway complete, and the prefab guard shack was assembled and painted. Deck work was ongoing and set to resume early the next day.

Satisfied with the day's achievements, Kasey and Ren had dinner while video chatting with Julia to discuss the developments.

"Everything looks great, baby," Julia said after he walked the property, showing her all the changes. "I love the guard house; it's not all in your face when you first drive up. I especially like how you kept the thick brush around it to help it blend in. I'm so pleased with everything. You're doing a fantastic job, as always."

"Tomorrow, I have an electrician coming to connect power to the shack and the AC," Kasey informed her. "It shouldn't be too involved since we already have electricity running to the gate. The guards are coming for interviews, and we should finish the last few things needed for the fence. Mostly, it will be deck work, which should be completed by the end of the day, barring any last-minute problems. I don't foresee any issues—they have all the materials and manpower they need. We have next weekend as a backup if needed and to finish rearranging the bedrooms. Ren and I will break down the training room while we're here and start setting up the inside of the guard shack. The guards will start while we're still in New York for the visit. During this coming week, we can order new bedding and extra towels so we have enough for everyone while they're here. Jackie will receive and sort everything before we get there."

"Sounds like you have it all in hand, baby. You're the best. Thank you," Julia said appreciatively.

Ren added, "Kasey bought everyone lunch, and I swear, Jules, they worked much harder after that."

Julia laughed, "The way to a workman's heart is treat 'em good, feed 'em good. So, do you guys have any plans for tonight?" she asked scooping up the last of the lasagna from the night before.

"It's been a long day. Maybe we'll just take a nice ride along the shore." Kasey turned to Ren. "What do you think?"

"Whatever you want to do… but I'm fine with just staying here. I know you worked hard keeping an eye on everything."

"It sounds like maybe you two could use a quiet night in and save the fun stuff for when I'm there," she said with a sweet grin.

"What did you do all day? You never called," Kasey asked.

"I didn't want to bother you unnecessarily. I just puttered around, tried to straighten up my dressing room—it's still such a mess," she said with a smirk. "I watched a bunch *Archer*, and now, I just miss you two."

"We miss you too, Jules," Ren said.

"If you miss us too much, I can call Carl and ask him to bring you here," Kasey offered.

"No, don't be silly. I'm a big girl; I should be able to spend a night alone. Besides, wouldn't you like to spend the night together without me crawling in between you?" she asked.

"I don't know about Kasey, but I sure as hell don't mind," Ren piped up.

"Sweetheart, you're never between us; you're with us, and that's not something I mind at all," Kasey added.

"Aww, that makes me feel good. I'm gonna let you enjoy the rest of your night. I have *Archer* and some chocolate torte waiting for me," she said with a smile. "Good night, guys. We'll talk in the morning."

"Good night, Jules. Sleep tight," Ren said.

"Good night, sweetheart. Call me if you get lonely or just want to talk; otherwise, I'll call you tomorrow. I love you," Kasey said.

"I love you too, baby," Julia said as they hung up.

After finishing their dinner, Kasey and Ren decided to enjoy a cozy night in, watching their favorite shows and talking. Later, reveling in their love without inhibition and wrapped in each other's arms, they drifted off to sleep, blissfully at peace.

***

At 8:30 the next morning, Ren came downstairs, woken by the clamor of builders on the deck. He found Kasey deep in conversation with the contractor at the kitchen island. Taking a seat, he waited patiently for their conversation to finish. Once the contractor went back outside, Ren asked, "Why didn't you wake me? I'm here to help you."

Kasey walked over and sat next to him at the island. "You looked so peaceful. I didn't have the heart to wake you. Besides, I knew all the noise would do the trick once they got started. So, what would you like to do this morning? There's not much for us to do while they're working on the deck. The guards won't be here until two. We can go for a run, a swim, or I could whip up some breakfast. Any ideas?" Kasey asked.

"How about we go for a run, take a nice long shower together, and then breakfast?" Ren

proposed as he ran his hand over Kasey's thigh.

"That sounds like a plan. I'd kiss you, but there are too many people on the deck," Kasey said affectionately, his hand resting on Ren's.

"I understand. Let's go get changed and hit the sand." As they started toward the stairs, Ren said, "Maybe we could

426

check in with Jules before we head out; see how her night went."

Kasey glanced back, smiling. "Of course we can give her a call. You know you're free to reach out to her anytime. You don't have to ask permission or wait for me. We don't have to be joined at the hip when it comes to things like that. She's your partner too." Leading the way to his room, Kasey suggested, "Why don't you grab your running gear, and we'll change in here while we give her a call."

The buzz of her phone and Kasey's name lighting up the screen brought a smile to Julia's face as she woke. "Mmm... Morning, baby," she greeted, stretching as she answered the phone.

"Mmm, good morning to you, sweetheart. You sound sexy, or sleepy," he laughed softly. "I can't tell which. Did we wake you?"

"We? Is Ren there?"

"I'm here, Jules. Morning. How'd you sleep?"

"Morning, babe. I slept okay, but I missed you guys. This bed feels huge without you. Hang on a sec," she said. After a moment, she added, "Turn on your camera. I want to see your faces... and maybe other parts," she giggled. When Kasey switched over to the camera, it was Julia with a naughty grin, naked and propped up on her pillows, looking back at him.

"Well, I was not expecting that. That is some view," Kasey grinned and tilted the phone to show Ren.

"Damn, Jules. Now that's a morning pick-me-up."

Julia giggled and teased, "Your turn."

"Aren't you lucky we're changing to go for a run," Ren said, ready to get naked.

"Nice," she said. "Put me on the dresser so I can see both of you. I'll set you on the chair at the end of my bed."

"You guys are ridiculous. We'll be home tonight," Kasey said as he propped the phone up on the dresser. "Can you see Ren?" he asked.

"Yes, I can. Take your clothes off for me, babe," Julia said to Ren. Before he could even start, she added excitedly, "Let's have some fun. I have my little friend, and you've got each other," Julia teased with a wink. *"Please,"* she cajoled. "You know how much I love to come in the morning." She slipped her finger in her mouth and then traced little circles over her quickly shrinking areolas and pointy nipples.

"C'mon, Spike, let me start your day right," Ren murmured, a grin tugging at his lips. He loved the way Julia took charge with her teasing and how Kasey—despite his reluctance—always gave in. Ren thrived in that balance, feeling like he was right where he belonged, caught between their contrasting energies. Stepping behind Kasey so she could see, he kissed him in the crook of his neck as he slid his hand slowly over Kasey's taut stomach.

"Really?" Kasey said, his face flushing as he instinctively tried to pull away from Ren's embrace. His hesitation flickered for a moment—caught between the familiar embarrassment and the rising pleasure that made it harder to resist.

"Oh no you don't," Ren said as he pulled Kasey into him tighter, his hand now sliding over Kasey's already growing erection.

"You guys are so bad together," Kasey murmured. Almost immediately, Julia stopped what she was doing to concentrate on watching them.

Kasey closed his eyes and leaned into him. Reaching back, he pulled Ren's face to his and kissed him. With Ren's hand now busy in Kasey's shorts, their kiss deepened quickly, becoming more passionate. Pulling away from Kasey's kisses, Ren dropped to his knees, positioning himself so he could still see Julia and she could see him. Kasey was thick and hard as Ren pulled down his shorts and wrapped his lips around him, his hands gripping Kasey's firm ass.

Extremely aroused, Julia watched Kasey tell Ren how good it felt while gripping his head with both hands, pushing deeper into his mouth. She got out her vibrator and slipped it between her legs, eager to join the fun.

Looking up from Ren when he heard Julia's not-so-quiet moans, Kasey gripped Ren's hair tighter, watching as she pleasured herself, her fingers lightly pressing the vibrator between her wide-open legs—pushing her right to the edge. Losing herself in the moment, she closed her eyes, her whimpers growing louder, her breath quickening. With a sharp inhale, her hips began to buck, and a final shudder of release announced her satisfaction. Kasey followed suit, bending forward, a small grunt escaping his lips as he held Ren's head tight against him.

"Now that was something," Ren said with a grin, sitting back on his heels, looking at Julia. "I watched you come, and I made you come."

Julia laughed, and Kasey smirked as he pulled his shorts up. "You guys are such a bad influence. You both have a way of getting me to do things that are way out of my comfort zone." He smiled shyly, shaking his head. "I'm just lucky I end up liking everything you have me do."

"But what about you, Ren?" Julia asked, now lying on her belly, her legs bent at the knee, ankles crossed, feet in the air as she looked into the camera.

"Don't you worry about me, sweetie. I'll have Kasey make it up to me when we shower after our run. How do you feel? That looked and sounded like it was good for you," he said with a grin. "And I really like that vantage point. I almost lost it just watching you."

"Oh, it was good alright. I really love watching you two. We have to do that again sometime." She took a deep breath and let it out slowly. "Mmm, I'm going back to sleep," she said softly as she slipped under the covers.

"That good, huh?" Kasey chimed in. "You enjoy that feeling. We're going to head out for that run. Talk to you later, sweetheart."

"Sleep tight," Ren bid farewell.

"Bye, guys. Enjoy your run." She rolled over, replaying what just happened in her head as she drifted off to sleep.

***

After waking up later, she made herself a cup of tea. Curious about the brownstone's upper floors, she began to explore. As she walked around the third floor, sipping her tea, she envisioned it as a perfect fit for Ren.

On the fourth floor, she found all the rooms empty except for one. In the back corner of the darkened room, a floor lamp stood beside an overstuffed chair next to a table with a photo album on it. After turning on the light and drawing back the heavy drapes to welcome the daylight, she placed her tea down and settled into the chair, delicately opening the album.

Inside the large leather-bound book, meticulously documented in what she assumed was Kasey's mother's beautiful handwriting, were all the details of his birth—his weight, length, and time. The card from his hospital bassinet was proudly displayed alongside a picture of a beautiful young woman, radiant as she held her newborn son in her arms. Nearby, though not looking at the camera, stood his father, a somber expression on his face. Julia knew immediately he was Kasey's father because their resemblance was striking. He was extremely handsome and built like Kasey, just twenty pounds heavier. The only physical feature Kasey seemed to have inherited from his mother was her stunning eyes. They were exactly like Kasey's, defying conventional colors. She had long, light brown hair and a beautiful smile. She also discovered his mother's name—Madelyn, though she was called Maddie.

As she turned through the pages, she marveled at how striking Kasey was, even as a child. Most of the photos in the album showcased moments shared between Kasey and his mother or a nanny. A few pictures featured Kasey as a young child with his parents and members of his father's extended family. In all those pictures, Kasey's mother appeared uneasy, with her husband was always physically distant from her.

As Kasey grew, the album painted a picture of a lonely, affluent early childhood, his fleeting smiles reserved only for moments with his mother. After he started homeschooling and his mother stopped traveling to be with him, most of the photos showed Kasey and his mother celebrating birthdays, holidays, and even Christmas—without his father. Julia's heart ached as she realized the depth of Kasey's solitude and the abandonment he endured from his father throughout his childhood.

The scrapbook also chronicled his mother's declining health, evident in the diminishing entries and photographs. The last, poignant image captured Kasey at twelve, nestled beside his now extremely fragile mother in bed, their heads touching, their fingers intertwined. She was clearly very ill, wearing a bright pink turban with an IV in her arm, but her smile remained as radiant as when she held her newborn son. Beneath the picture, her shaky handwriting read: "To my most wonderful son, Kasey, the absolute best son a mother could have. You bring so much joy to my life. I love you so much. You're my Sweetheart, Love, Mom xoxoxo."

Tears welled in Julia's eyes as she imagined the countless times Kasey must have sought solace in this room, alone with memories of his mother. The significance of the pet name he'd given her hit hard, stirring a deep ache in her stomach and causing her tears to flow freely. She couldn't shake the sadness and loneliness he must have endured until he met Ren—only to lose him as well. The deep emotional blows he suffered with little to no support would have broken her beyond repair. If it weren't for Kasey, her three best friends, and close family friends, she wouldn't have survived her own family tragedy.

Carefully returning the book to its place, she drew the drapes and headed back downstairs, her breath coming in small gasps. Sitting in the kitchen with a cup of tea, she wondered if she should mention to Kasey that she'd been in the room and looked at the book. She knew she would eventually—unable to avoid it. She just had to find the right time and the right words.

***

Meanwhile, Kasey prepared omelets for brunch while Ren set the table. Both were in high spirits after their long run and playful shower.

"How many interviews do you have planned for the guards today?" Ren asked.

"I'm just interviewing for the brownstone position and Julia's personal security detail. The guards here are already vetted by the security company; I just need to familiarize them with the property and set guidelines for the front gate, balancing their visibility with effectiveness. Julia won't want them lurking around all the time. The guardhouse will be fully equipped, so they won't need to enter the main house. AC and heating, a composting toilet, and a mini fridge should keep them comfortable. They can alternate between manning the front gate, patrolling the grounds, and covering the rear of the house. When we're not at the house, one guard will suffice to protect the property."

"Jeez, Spike, I don't know how you manage to keep all these details straight in your head. Managing your job, organizing our move, overseeing this construction project, and preparing for the upcoming visit—it's just incredible. And yet, you still take the time to cook for me. You're amazing, seriously, the best," Ren declared, his compliments bringing a smile to Kasey's face.

"You know, I never thought to ask Julia if she has a preference for a personal bodyguard," Kasey said, thinking out loud. "I wonder if she has one. I'll give her a quick call and find out."

Upon seeing Kasey's face on the video call, Julia fretted he would be able to tell she'd been crying. "Hi there, how's everything going?" she chirped, attempting to mask her distress.

"Quick question. Do you have a preference for a personal bodyguard? Male or female? Wait, were you crying?" he asked, his concern clear. "You look like you were crying. Is everything okay?" His observant eyes also caught sight of a tissue near her tea.

"I'm fine, really. It's silly. I just got a little emotional watching a three-legged dog video. I should know better." She smiled. "It's nothing, I promise. I'm fine," she insisted, trying to reassure him.

"To answer your question, I don't have a preference. Carl will be with me for most of the big events because we work well together. This person will just be his fill-in and driver. Choose whoever you think will work best with me. If they don't work out, we'll just keep looking till we find someone who does. How are things going on your end? What time do you think you'll be heading home?"

"Don't think you can distract me with questions, Ms. Masters," Kasey said with a knowing smile. "As long as you promise me you're okay, I won't worry."

"The tears had nothing to do with me missing my family, I promise. I think I'll call Micki and BS with her after I hang up with you—she'll keep me company for a while. Do you have any idea when you might be heading home?" she asked again, eager for them all to be back under the same roof.

"Everyone should be out of here by four at the latest. As soon as the last worker leaves the driveway, we're out of here and on the way home. I'll call you when we're ready to leave. With any luck, we should be home before six, barring too much traffic. What would you like to do for dinner?" Kasey asked.

"You've done enough this weekend. I'll take care of dinner, don't worry, it'll be good, and I promise not to mess up your precious kitchen," she chuckled.

"Thank you, I'd appreciate that—the dinner and you not wrecking my kitchen," he replied with a grin. "Ren, anything you want to add before I hang up?"

"Yeah, I have a couple of questions, Jules," Ren chimed in.

"Shoot," she responded.

"Are you planning to wear any specific designer on Wednesday? Do you work with a stylist, or could I style you? And is there anything—or anyone—you want me to wear?"

"Okay, let's see... we can wear any designer. I don't have a stylist, so you can definitely style me. I'd love for you to wear something attention-grabbing, like the outfit you wore to dinner. Showcase your style; the media should focus on you, especially when they find out you're our new Creative Director. It's also an opportunity for the Hawthorne Brothers to see the direction we're aiming for with the young urban division.

After dinner tonight, we can go through my clothes and see what might complement what you'll be wearing. We don't have to match exactly, but I want to look as fashion-forward as you do. And one last thing, and it's a personal request." Julia flashed her baby blues. "Please wear your hair down. I love it that way. It really helps you stand out and be noticed, which is what we want. Also, if you do wear a skirt, remember, we'll be sitting in the front row, so it's either underwear or legs closed; we don't need any wardrobe malfunctions making headlines." She chuckled, making Ren and Kasey laugh at the thought.

"Okay, while Kasey is busy interviewing, I'll brainstorm some looks for Wednesday. And tonight, we're definitely raiding your closet," Ren declared. "We also need to go over talking points about the new house and what you want to say and what you don't."

"Don't worry, I got you. We can talk about that while you go through my clothes. I want you to take the lead, but I'll be right beside you, and I can easily steer the conversation if things get tricky," she assured him.

"I'm excited about the event, and I want to start off on the right foot for you and the company."

"You're naturally outgoing, well-spoken, and extremely appealing to look at—everything needed to deal with the media. I'm sure you'll represent us perfectly, and we'll have a great time," she assured him.

"Thanks, Jules, you're an amazing confidence builder, and I appreciate that."

"Bye, guys. I miss you both. Call me before you leave," she said with a smile that made them both anxious to get back to her.

With their goodbyes exchanged, Kasey and Ren went to work, getting as much done as they could before leaving.

***

Julia breathed a sigh of relief once the call finally ended, grateful she had managed to hide the reason for her tears. Shifting her focus away from her emotions, she began searching for simple recipes she could make for Kasey, especially eager to demonstrate her appreciation for his unwavering support and hard work. Discovering a chicken empanada recipe that seemed doable, she promptly placed an order at her local Whole Foods.

Dialing Carl, she requested his assistance in picking up the groceries so she didn't receive a delivery while she was alone. Carl readily agreed as Julia's tendency to make special favors worthwhile made it an easy decision. Julia's kindness and generosity toward those who worked closely with her, like Carl and her housekeepers, Alice and Jackie, endeared her to them, inspiring them to go above and beyond when she required their assistance. When Carl texted that he had arrived, Julia greeted him warmly and helped with the bags as they entered the house.

"Thank you so much for doing this last minute, Carl. Kasey would lose his mind if I let just anyone come to the door while I'm alone," she said, expressing her gratitude.

"And rightfully so. You're on everyone's radar now. There's too many crazies out there not to be extra careful," Carl replied.

"Could you stay for a minute? I wanted to talk to you about that quickly—I know you're double-parked."

"Don't worry, Jules. I have a lady friend in the car. She'll beep or call me if someone needs to get out," Carl replied with a smile.

"A lady friend, huh?" Julia said, tickled. "Wait," she said, the realization dawning. "Am I ruining a date?"

"Not ruining at all. We were going to get some food anyway. We just combined the two."

"Good. You better tell me if you're doing something fun, Carl. I wouldn't want to intrude on your private time."

"You aren't intruding, Jules. I promise you."

With a sparkle in her eyes, she said, "We've decided to go full-time security, and I would like you to lead my new security team. It's a full-time position with all the perks. You'd work closely with Kasey to set it up, staff it, and tailor it to our needs. After that, it's all yours to manage. I'm sorry to spring this on you like this, but things have been hectic since Ren moved in and with everything happening at work. I was planning to sit down and talk to you more professionally, but this will have to do," she said with a charming smile.

"It's fine, Jules. I understand," Carl reassured her, realizing she had just offered him a significant promotion.

She quickly continued, "We're planning to redo the apartment downstairs as the main security office, and Kasey's at the shore where there's a guardhouse being built as we speak. I already feel incredibly safe and comfortable with you, and more importantly, I trust you. If you decide to take on this responsibility, you would oversee the guards here and at the shore house from the security apartment, and join me for special events. Is that something you'd be interested in? What do you think? Please say yes," she pleaded, a hopeful look on her face.

"I'd love to take on the additional responsibility and head your security team. As much as I'll enjoy supervising and managing your security, I'd definitely still like to be with you personally for special events and anything else you might need me for. Thank you, Jules, for considering me for the position," Carl replied, pleasantly surprised by her offer.

"Don't be silly; the position was always yours if you wanted it. You've been looking out for me for over four years now, and I'd like to keep it that way. Kasey will sit down with you to go over schedules and compensation for your new role. I also have a request."

"Shoot," he said, eager to accommodate her.

"Wednesday night, Ren and I are going to a fashion show. I'd like you to go as our bodyguard, getting us in and out of the venue smoothly with one of the new guards as the driver. There'll be a lot of attention as we enter and leave since Ren is the new Creative Director. We'd like to reflect that as a group. I'd like you to dress differently to blend in. Do you know what I mean?" she asked.

"I know exactly what you mean. I'll do a little shopping before Wednesday."

"Good, buy what you need—at least three different outfits—and keep the receipts for your expense account. You'll also talk with Kasey about what equipment you'll need, like earpieces or whatever is necessary."

"Congratulations, Mr. Williams! You're officially my new head of security. You'd better go before your lady friend gets bored," she teased. "Go tell her about your big promotion, Mr. Head of Security." With a broad grin, she said, "I know I should be professional and shake your hand, but you know me—come here and give me a hug. Welcome to my inner circle, Carl."

"Thank you, Jules," he said, embracing her warmly. "I'll talk to Kasey tomorrow and arrange a meeting to get everything sorted. I should get going. Have a good night, and I hope your attempt at cooking this dish comes out delicious," he said cheerfully as he departed.

As soon as Carl left, Julia delved into the bags, meticulously inspecting and organizing her ingredients. After thoroughly reviewing the recipe, she felt adequately prepared to take on the challenge. With ample time before she needed to start cooking, she decided to give Micki a call and update her on all the new developments in her life.

***

"Hey there, kiddo! It feels like ages since we caught up. Now that you have two guys in your bed, you're too busy for little ol' me," Micki teased playfully.

"Oh my God, so much has been happening here," Julia replied. "Moving Ren and me into Kasey's place, getting ready for the Hawthorne visit and vacation, and the construction at the shore house—it's all been nonstop. Next time you see me, it'll be with full-time security. Kasey insisted on beefing it up, and now the damn beach house is practically a fortress. We'll have two guards whenever we're there, and we're even having security move into the downstairs apartment in the brownstone. I promoted Carl to head of my security detail. Can you believe it? It all feels so bizarre needing this kind of protection. I'm so worried about how this is going to change our lives," she confessed.

"Seriously, Jules, you've been skating by with little to no security for way too long. The moment you stepped into Buck's shoes, you should've had a team in place. Kasey's been telling you this since the mugging. I get it. You'll lose some freedom, but, kiddo, you're worth an ungodly amount of money. Your face is becoming known, and with this fashion house venture, you're bound to draw even more attention. Unfortunately, some of it's going to be unwanted—it's just the price of success," Micki pointed out.

"I know, I know," Julia retorted, "I was just hoping it wouldn't get to this point until I was much older. I thought my dad would shoulder most of the public exposure, and I could stay in the background, hidden from full view," she lamented.

"Don't worry, it'll probably suck for a bit, but you'll adjust. Before you know it, it'll just be normal. Stop stressing over what hasn't even happened yet."

"You're right. I just need to accept it," Julia agreed.

"So, spill the beans. How are things with your boys? Are you worn out yet?" Micki snickered.

"It's actually going really well, ya jerk. The three of us gel amazingly. Kasey has gone out of his way to give me and Ren time alone to get to know each other and damn if it hasn't worked. Friday night, after we had sex for the second time that day, Ren told me he was falling for me." Julia paused to let Micki digest the news before dropping the next bombshell. "And I told him I felt the same."

"Hmm, not surprised about Ren. I knew he'd fall hard and fast after the first time you slept with him. I could see the way he looked at you that whole next day. And you really feel the same about him?" Micki asked.

"I really do. He's so sweet and respectful, but I like him best when he's being frisky and fun. And, best of all—like Kasey, he puts my feelings first. What's amazing is Kasey wants this most of all. He's encouraging Ren and me to spend time alone together so we can truly become a committed trio. He's really comfortable with the idea of the three of us."

"He's such a complicated man," Micki muttered.

"On Friday, Rick unexpectedly showed up at the office. He called me darlin' when he told me how proud he was, and for a moment, I felt like my dad was there. It caught me completely off guard. It was like all the air was sucked out of the room, and I couldn't breathe. Kasey realized what happened and quickly made an excuse to get Rick out of there before I completely fell apart. Long story short, Kasey sent Ren in to comfort me, and he let me cry it out without rushing me or trying to get me to stop. The way he spoke, so gentle and soothing, helped me get a grip on my feelings. I got mascara on his collar, and when we went to clean it off in my bathroom... well, things escalated. I couldn't help myself, and we had sex.”

“I'm not trying to make light of what happened with Rick,” Micki said with a chuckle. “But the moment you said you took him in the bathroom, I knew where you were going with it. You are so predictable.”

“Shut up, Micki. He makes me feel good,” Julia protested, albeit half-heartedly, conceding Micki's insight.

“Speaking of, where's your little harem?” Micki continued teasing.

“Stop, they're not my harem,” Julia giggled. “I'd need a few more for that. They're at the beach overseeing the construction while I take a little personal time.”

“See, see, they're already wearing you out. Personal time, humph,” Micki said, proving her point.

“Oh, shut up, Micki. I just need to figure out how to balance everything—take care of them both and still have time for myself. They both let me decide everything that has to do with sex and sleeping arrangements. It's completely up to me.” Julia chuckled. “I just have to learn how not to be greedy. I friggin' want them both, or at least one of them, every day. I think the only days off I'll get are when I have my period.”

“Jeez, that sounds exhausting,” Micki replied. “You do know you don't have to make up for lost time all at once, right?”

"I'm happy to be tired if it means I feel loved like this every day," Julia explained. "Hang on, Kasey's calling," she said, switching to his call. "Hey, baby, what's up?"

"We're leaving in fifteen minutes, just locking up. Everything went smoothly. We'll see you in about an hour and a half."

"Great, be careful. I have Micki on the line; I'll see you both soon."

Switching back to Micki, she said, "They're heading home. I have to go, or better yet, you

could watch me; I'll put you on video. I'm making empanadas for dinner," she added confidently.

"Well, I gotta see this," Micki said, amazed Julia was attempting to cook. She stayed on the line, keeping her company and occasionally offering advice as Julia prepared dinner.

***

"Wow, they look terrific. You did a great job—and you didn't wreck his kitchen," Micki said, genuinely impressed with Julia's first attempt at cooking an entire meal by herself.

"Thanks for sticking with me and helping out. You too, James, thanks for the advice."

"Anytime, Jules. I still can't believe you made empanadas. Great job," he complimented.

"I'm gonna go. They should be here soon, and I want to finish setting the table and set the mood."

"Relax, girl, they're not returning from war," Micki joked, making James laugh.

"Shut up, Micki. Bye, James. Talk to you guys soon. Love you," she said as she hung up.

James looked over at Micki and said, "You were on fire. How many 'Shut up, Micki's' was that?" They both laughed, knowing she could always get Julia going.

***

Julia finished setting the table, adjusted the lighting, and turned on the background music. She slipped into a short black cashmere button-down dress paired with cozy black furry Uggs, ran a brush through her hair, and added the diamond necklace Kasey had given her. As she came back down, a sudden whiff of something burning assaulted her nose—the forgotten empanadas she'd left warming in the oven without adjusting the temperature.

Just as Kasey unlocked the front door, the fire alarm shattered the peace, prompting his swift entry. There stood Julia, desperately waving a pot holder over a tray of singed empanadas, her face reflecting the disappointment of a novice chef with their first burnt creation.

Ren quickly opened the kitchen window to clear the air while Kasey silenced the persistent alarm. Julia stood amid the chaos, her expression laced with defeat.

"You made empanadas?" Kasey comforted her. "They look great, and those aren't so bad. Plus, the kitchen's still in one piece. Sweetheart, I'm really impressed." He put his arms around her as she set down the tray.

"That's because you got here just in time. I could've burnt the place down," she pouted. "I wanted everything to be perfect."

"Nonsense, this all looks really great," Kasey insisted, trying to cheer her up.

"Let's eat—we're famished. I can't believe you did all this, Jules. It really looks fantastic," Ren said, reaching for the plate of empanadas.

"First things first," she said as she planted a big kiss on Kasey. "I'm so glad you're home. I missed you," she said softly. Then, turning to Ren, she grinned, "I missed you too." After exchanging eager kisses, she said, "Let's eat. I hope you both like 'em. I did my best."

Taking in their fill, Kasey praised, "That was a really great dinner. You outdid yourself. Honestly, I couldn't have done it better. See, if you apply yourself, you can cook."

"Thank you, but I won't be making a habit of it," she replied. "I had Micki and James lending a hand on a video call, and I kinda cheated a bit by using a rotisserie chicken and ready-made pie crusts," she laughed. "Unlike you, baby, I found it to be a little stressful, I'm not gonna lie. I do like the idea of making something for you both, but don't get used to it. I'd rather do other things for you, something that is never stressful for me," she said with a sly grin.

They both smiled as she got up to clear the plates away. "I have dessert, but I didn't make it— let's get real, nobody wants that. They all laughed as she brought out three individual fruit tarts.

"I'm too full of empanadas and corn on the cob for that right now," Ren said.

"Same here," Kasey added, patting his stomach.

"Alright, I'll save them for later." Looking at Ren, she said, "I know we have clothes to go through, but I need a moment to digest before we do that. Why don't you guys come sit with me on the couch and tell me how today went? I just want to feel you both next to me," she proposed.

Kasey and Ren settled in on either side of her, taking turns telling her about their day. She rested her head against Kasey, her legs stretched comfortably across Ren's lap. Discussing the changes coming with added security, they all agreed it would take some getting used to and finding common ground in facing the changes together.

Ren and Julia eventually headed upstairs to tackle her clothes while Kasey took the opportunity to unwind with his latest novel. She had claimed the third bedroom on the second floor as her dressing room, while Ren occupied the other spare room also on the same floor. Most of his belongings resided on the third floor, which would eventually be redone for him.

"Most of my stuff is still in boxes," Jules remarked as she entered the room. Glancing around, Ren noticed ten sizable garment boxes neatly arranged against one wall. A disassembled queen-sized bed leaned against another, with most of the furniture pushed to the side, making room for the boxes.

"Should we just start cracking these boxes open?" Ren suggested, reaching for a utility knife to slice through the tape.

"Might as well. I have no clue what's in each of them since Alice packed them, but she's pretty organized."

After opening four of them to no avail and Ren gently ribbing her about her distinctly American Western sense of style, they shared a laugh when they discovered that one box of shoes yielded an abundance of cowboy boots.

"Jules, I hate to break it to you, but we need to go shopping. You've got an amazing body, and even though you're short, you could be way more interesting than these cute little dresses."

Pulling her head out of a box of accessories, she grinned mischievously. "Are you implying I have no taste, mister?" She stood up to confront him, poking him playfully in the belly. "Well?" she teased, poking him again. "Say it. 'Jules, you have no taste.' Go ahead," she giggled.

"I'm sorry, boo, but your taste in clothing is pretty basic. But hey, it's not all bad," he teased with a grin, dodging her playful pokes. "I do love your underwear," he chuckled as she backed him up against a garment box. "I can fix it, though," he grinned. "I can style you."

She pressed up against him, eyebrow raised. "So, you think you can just insult my taste like that and get away with it?" she purred, her body brushing against his. "You'll have to come up with a pretty good apology to make it up to me."

He pulled her into an embrace, kissing her slowly at first, relishing the sensation of her in his arms, her scent enveloping him. Soon, their mutual desire took over, their kisses intensifying, the temperature in the room suddenly too warm.

"Fuck me, Jules," Ren growled, his voice rough, desire running wildly through him as he spun her around and pressed her hard against the mattress.

"Drop the mattress on the floor," Julia's breath caught as she felt the hardness of his body, the heat building between them. Untying the drawstring on his linen pants, he let them drop to the floor as she slipped off her panties.

"Not necessary," he said passionately as he lifted her up. She wrapped her legs around his waist as he pushed her back into the mattress, his fingers gripping her ass tightly as he entered her.

The steady rhythm of the mattress hitting the wall and Julia's moans filled the room, drawing Kasey to the doorway. He stood there, leaning against the frame, arms crossed, quietly watching them, his gaze fixed on the way they moved together. He stood there for a while, savoring the sight of them before making his presence known.

They were so wrapped up in each other they didn't realize he was there until Ren finished with a loud grunt, and Kasey said with a grin, "You two are like rabbits; you can't be alone for five minutes without climbing all over each other."

"How long have you been standing there?" Ren said, his breathing heavy, as he slipped out of Julia and put her down.

"Long enough to end up like this," he said, pointing to the bulge in his pants with a grin.

Ren pulled up his pants as Julia walked over to Kasey, took his hand, her face flushed, and said, "Let's go take care of that." She turned to Ren, "Sorry to hit and run babe; I'll be right back."

"That's okay. I'll take a drive-by from you any day. Take your time; I'll be here," he said with a grin, tying the drawstring on his pants and catching his breath.

She led Kasey to their bed, planting soft kisses along his neck, her hands cradling his face as she straddled him. "Love me," she whispered, her voice barely audible, a plea wrapped in tenderness.

"I couldn't possibly love you more than I do right now," he murmured, rolling her gently onto her back. Slowly unbuttoning her dress, he savored the salty taste of her warm skin, taking his time as he always did. When they were finished, she lay in his arms, her body and heart blissfully content.

"You should probably go finish helping Ren," Kasey whispered, pressing a kiss to her head as he held her close.

Not yet," she whispered back, her voice soft as she clung to him. "I don't want you to let me go."

"You'll be back before you know it. Go, get ready for Wednesday. It's important you guys look good, and he knows the right things to say. Help him. I'll be right here when you come to bed. I'm going to stay here and read for a while. It was a busy weekend; I could use some quiet time," he said, smiling reassuringly.

"Okay," she replied softly, "I'm leaving only because you need some personal time." She started to rise but paused, turning back. "Do you want me to sleep in Ren's room so you can have some real downtime and the whole bed to yourself? I want to make sure you're not overwhelmed with too much of me and Ren all over you," she said earnestly.

A soft chuckle escaped his lips. "I am not overwhelmed by you two. I love the attention from you both. But I will take you up on the personal time. I really am tired. I think I'll make it an early night so I can be ready for tomorrow. Tell him I said good night. I'll see you both in the morning. I love you."

"Love you too, baby. I'll see you in the morning," she said, scooting to the edge of the bed.

***

"So, what's the verdict? Is it all shit?" she quipped, stepping into the room to find Ren sitting in the middle of a mound of clothes.

Laughing, *he held up one of her cowboy boots.* "It's not all shit, but you have a very distinct style, whether you realize it or not. Your formal wear is classic and pricey but boring. You should be diving into leather bustiers and wilder accessories. You're young, beautiful, and soon to be front and center at fashion shows. Eventually, you'll be at our own show. We need you to be more urban, daring, and fearless with new trends. Your office look—well, sweetie… time for a refresh. It's time to put a new face on your company image; make a statement about who's running things now. Let Rick and Jack handle the cattle side of it. Your focus should be on propelling Hawthorne-Masters forward and not being afraid to shake things up a bit."

Grinning, she settled beside him on the floor. "Don't hold back, babe; give it to me straight."

"I'm sorry if that was a bit blunt," he chuckled, "but I want us to excel. Trust me, I know the ins and outs of the fashion world. They will rip you apart in the fashion media if you show up at a big show, not dressed to impress. Up-and-coming designers will want assurance that their creativity won't be stifled at a stuffy, tradition-bound fashion house. You already have a strike against you in the urban market, coming in with a very British, very conservative house. We need to show them that you understand their vision, and that starts on Wednesday," he explained.

"Damn, I never thought of that. That's very savvy. Kasey told me you were very intelligent. That's becoming pretty obvious to me. We're going to do great things together, babe," she said with a wide smile.

"Well, keep thinking good thoughts when I say we need to go shopping. I need to find something *pronto* to put you in for Wednesday. I have a few designer contacts I'd like to reach out to tomorrow to see if they'll let you wear their pieces. They get exposure, and you get the perfect outfit."

"That's fine with me if you call a designer, but offer to pay for the clothes, Ren. I don't like taking stuff for free. I can pay for it."

"We need to shift that mindset, Jules. High-profile figures don't pay for such things; it's all about mutually beneficial publicity. It's the way things are done. Let me handle it. I promise you, they'll be throwing stuff at us for you to wear," he said confidently as he sorted through another box.

"I'm putting my trust in you. Do what you think is best. You're accountable to me, but we both answer to the board if we fuck this up. I also never asked you, but do you design yourself? Because we can explore that avenue, too."

"I have designed before, but I prefer collaborating with a designer rather than just designing alone. I enjoy styling and setting the creative direction more." He started to chuckle.

"What's so funny?" she asked.

"I can't wait for Thursday morning to send my mother pictures of us and any write-ups that mention me as the Creative Director. It will bite my father hard on the ass. My mother will show it to the rest of the family and make my happiness complete. He told me I wouldn't amount to anything without him and my family backing me up. Now, he can eat his words," Ren explained, a look of self-satisfaction on his face.

"What the hell is wrong with your father? You're such a good man. Why can't he see that and appreciate you for who you are?" she asked, bewildered.

"Because he's what's wrong with the world: people trying to make other people the same as them. This world needs to embrace diversity, and live and let live."

"Oh my God, I remember saying those exact words to Kasey when he told me about his college girlfriend dumping him after he told her he was bisexual. She was incredibly insensitive, and she hurt him big time—as if he hadn't been through enough already. Speaking of which, there's something I want to discuss with you about Kasey."

"I'm listening. Where is he now?"

"He's in bed reading. He's turning in early; he's pretty tired. I told him I would sleep in your room tonight and give him a good night's rest. Sometimes I worry, I overstimulate him—overwhelm him. He spent a lot of time alone before I came into his life. I mean, really isolated. With everything he juggles at work, taking care of me and catering to my higher sex drive, I worry I'm wearing him out."

"Ah, but what a way to go," Ren quipped with a grin. "Don't be silly; you're not wearing him out. The job, on the other hand, that's a different story. From what I've seen, the boy needs an assistant. He's bogged down with trivial shit, along with the important stuff. Like you, Kasey should be doing the strategic thinking while someone else handles the grunt work."

"You're absolutely right. It's time for a promotion. I think I can pitch the idea of him becoming Vice President of Acquisitions to the board without much pushback. Kasey has his MBA. He's proven himself over and over to be a team player. Rick and Jack both have gotten to know him personally and like him—and they love me. I'm sure I'd have their full backing. Don't say anything to him. I'll see if I can fast-track this with the board. He deserves it so much; he truly gives this job his all," she declared.

"It's because of you, Jules. That company is an extension of you. He'd do anything to see you happy. That's why he's so invested in the job. But is that what you wanted to talk to me about?"

"No, I wish it was. Come with me—be really quiet. I need to show you something," she said, leading him to the room on the fourth floor. "Out of boredom, I did a little exploring and found this sad little room." They stepped into the dimly lit space. Kasey must come up here to spend time with this scrapbook. Here, sit."

As Ren sat down, she delicately placed the book on his lap, and he began flipping through the pages slowly. The images of the solemn little boy tugged at his heartstrings, evoking a profound sense of sorrow. Despite Ren's own challenging past, characterized by his father's harsh judgment, he had experienced a loving, albeit strict, upbringing surrounded by extended family and friends.

"Jeez, I never knew how bleak his childhood was. He hardly ever spoke about it. This truly breaks my heart."

"I know. I cried when I looked at it. It made me feel terrible. When Kasey called, I had to

tell him I wasn't crying about my family, so I wasn't technically lying. I just couldn't tell him why I was upset. I couldn't burden him with that while he was working so hard," Julia confessed.

"Fuck me... this last picture is just heartbreaking," Ren choked up. "Look at him, doing his best to care for her—all that emotional torture, watching her deteriorate in front of him at just twelve years old."

Softly, Julia interjected, "Do you know the full story of how his mother died?"

"She died from cancer not long after this picture, I assume," Ren answered, unaware of the true circumstances.

"This was incredibly painful for Kasey to share and for me to hear. It was the worst I've ever seen him break down," Julia said, her voice trembling as she recounted the events leading up to Kasey's mother's death and his final encounter with his father. Shocked and upset, Ren remained silent, his gaze fixated on the poignant image of Kasey with his mother.

"I had no idea it was that traumatic for him. It makes me physically sick to know this. His father really is a monster. I've never felt violent towards anyone in my life, but I would make an exception for him." Julia gently retrieved the album, placing it on the table before sitting in Ren's lap, embracing him tightly.

"I can't bear the thought of him coming up here alone to be with her," she said. "What should we do? Should we do anything? Pretend we didn't see it? He doesn't even have a decent picture of her anywhere in the house. Did you see the one of him and her right before she got sick? I thought maybe I could have that painted by an artist and give it to him to hang in one of his rooms. I don't want her to only be a painful memory; he needs a positive memory of her. Don't you think?"

"Jules, you can't approach this with your frame of reference. You said it yourself—you had the perfect family and childhood. Kasey had a vastly different experience. He may not want to be reminded of that pain. Seeing her image might dredge up all the anguish of her passing and the trauma inflicted by his father. I'm at a loss here. I think we should leave it for now. Let's see what he does when we eventually renovate this floor. This is deeply personal and highly emotional for him; we should give him space to process it. Maybe now that he's unburdened himself of that terrible secret, he might be ready to talk more about her or at least consider putting a picture up of her."

"You're right. I didn't mean to find the book, but once I did, I just couldn't shake the thought of him being alone up here. One other thing. Did you notice that under most of the pictures, or when his mother wrote anything about him, she called him her sweetheart? Do you think it's weird that's the only pet name he decided to call me?"

Considering his words, Ren responded, "Knowing Kasey, he associated his mother's love with being called sweetheart, and when he wanted to express how much he loved you, he chose the one pet name that meant anything to him. I see it as the ultimate gesture of love. You should take it that way. You notice he doesn't have any nicknames for me? It just goes to show you the depth of his affection for you."

"Don't be ridiculous. He may not have given you a nickname, but he loves you just the same," she assured him. "I didn't know how to take it. I'm glad I have you to discuss this stuff with."

"Relax, the two people he cares most about are here to support and love him now. I think we can make his future so bright it obliterates his past. You just need to stay positive," he reassured her, planting a quick kiss on her lips. "We should get out of here; I wouldn't want Kasey to come looking for us and find us here."

"Let's go to bed," she said. "I'll clean those clothes up tomorrow after work. This emotional shit takes its toll on me. I dunno how Kasey copes, honestly."

"Let's hope he doesn't have to deal with the past any longer. There's always gonna be something, but let's hope it isn't his past anymore. C'mon, let's go," he said as she got up off his lap. "If you're up for it, maybe my mouth could spend some time between your legs before we go to sleep. I heard sex makes you feel better when you're down. Let me help you with that," he said, his voice tempting as he pulled her close, nuzzling her neck.

She giggled, "Don't get me started till we get downstairs."

They left the room, their bond stronger than ever, both feeling better knowing they were going to work together to ensure Kasey's past inflicted as little pain as possible on his future.

***

Chapter 19: Everything's Falling into Place

"Good morning, everyone," Carl greeted cheerfully as he swung open the car door. "Good morning to you, Mr. Williams, Head of Security," Julia replied happily.

"Congratulations, Carl," Kasey chimed in.

"Yeah, congrats," Ren added.

"Thank you, everyone," Carl replied.

"This will be one of Carl's last few times driving us regularly; we'll be getting a new driver. Do you have anyone in mind?" Julia asked.

"I do, as a matter of fact. I thought, if Kasey has time this morning after I drop you off, we could go over a few things," Carl replied.

"I do have time. Good idea. We'll go over upcoming events, the driver's schedule, and set up a basic routine. Also, we need to ensure we can accommodate Julia's need for you three days a week for two hours each time for the next few weeks."

"That's right. I'd like Carl to handle that for me," Julia added.

"We'll get that all taken care of now," Kasey declared.

***

Upon arriving at work, Kasey and Carl reviewed Julia's schedule, including the important Hawthorne visit, coordinating both the New York and beach house itineraries. After completing the schedule and a quick trip to HR to update his position, Carl headed back to the security apartment to meet with the new guards and prepare for renovations to create a security command center.

Meanwhile, Ren settled into his new office.

"Derrick has done such a great job interning that we've decided to offer him the position as your assistant, with the understanding that it's permanent if it's a good fit for both of you," Kasey explained to Ren as Derrick appeared in the doorway.

"I'd like to thank you again, Mr. Cortland, for this opportunity. And Mr. Ito, I'll do my best to assist you in any way I can," Derrick declared earnestly.

"I'm sure you will," Ren said, placing a reassuring hand on Derrick's shoulder. "You can start by calling me Ren."

"I'll leave you two to get settled in. If you need anything, just let me know. Duty calls," Kasey said, flashing Ren a quick smile before heading out.

"Okay, Derrick, let's hit the phones. We've got a bunch of calls to make," Ren said as they got to work.

Ren reached out to his former college classmate, now a designer in New York, to procure a few outfits for Julia, including an eye-catching pair of chunky platform boots with large, multicolored, removable butterfly wings on the back.

Julia eagerly anticipated the arrival of the outfits, excited to explore a fresh style she hadn't yet tried.

By lunchtime, the clothes arrived, prompting Ren to swing by her office for a fashion trial session. Julia excitedly surveyed the choices, eager to slip into the new styles—especially those eye-catching boots.

"Oh, Ren, I'm loving this!" she exclaimed, admiring her reflection in the mirror after settling on her final look.

"The hood will be up the whole time, so we should style your hair in a low bun, away from your face and off your back," he suggested, brushing her hair back and lifting the cowl-neck hood into place. The backless crop top and split-thigh midi skirt, crafted from a soft gray slinky fabric with arm sleeves, flawlessly accentuated Julia's petite figure. Ren had sent over Julia's measurements, and the designer, Yuki, even shortened the skirt to perfectly suit Julia's height. The four-inch chunky heels of the platform boots added to her height while still being surprisingly comfortable. Her crystal microphone bag would be her only accessory.

"Wow, you look spectacular," Kasey said, admiration clear in his voice from the doorway.

"I really love it, and it's so comfortable—even the boots. They're a breeze to walk in compared to stilettos," she said, twirling to show off her outfit. "I've never worn something braless to such a public affair. How am I supposed to tame these nipples?" she giggled, covering the telltale points with her fingertips.

"I personally say, 'Free the nipple,'" Ren chuckled, "but we can use covers if you feel shy."

"I'm not shy, but I am a CEO. Is it appropriate?" she asked, glancing at Kasey.

"I think you look beautiful and very sexy, but I'd say wear covers. We want everyone to notice Ren, not just your perfect nipples," Kasey replied with a grin.

"I can't wait to see what you're wearing," she said, smiling at Ren.

"I'll show you tonight. We'll get dressed together and make any final adjustments if needed. And just in case we need anything else, we'll still have time tomorrow to tweak it," Ren replied. "One more thing—I got you these glasses. I'll be wearing mine. I like the look—what do you think?"

"I love the look, and I really like it when you wear those glasses. I think they're really hot," she said with a seductive grin.

"I know you do," he said with a sly grin. "I saw your reaction the first time we met."

"You noticed that, huh? You're very observant—I like that," she said, wrapping her arms around him.

"No sex in the bathroom, please. We have lunch reservations," Kasey said with a smirk. Julia shot him a disappointed look, and he added, "I know, I know, I'm a buzzkill."

"You are, but a very lovable one," Julia said, giving him a quick peck on the cheek. "Alright, everyone out. I'll change, and then let's go eat."

***

"So, how's everything going? Is Derrick being helpful?" Julia asked as they made their way home at the end of the day. "Did you have a good first day?"

"I had an excellent first day. Derrick has been a tremendous help. He set up my office, organized my contacts, and even added numbers he thought I might need. Plus, he's easy to work with. He's not well-versed in fashion, but he's

458

great on the phone and a fast learner. I really appreciate his positive attitude—he seems like a good fit," Ren shared.

"I'm glad to hear that. I found him to be a really hardworking intern, and I thought he deserved a chance. I think you guys will make a great team," Kasey chimed in.

"I'm so glad it was a good first day. I can't wait to try on our outfits and see how we look together. Let's get salads for dinner or lettuce wraps—something light. I don't want to look all puffy tomorrow," Julia suggested.

"Sounds good. You two can try on your clothes, and I'll order something," Kasey offered as they arrived home.

***

In the living room, already in her new outfit, Julia couldn't help but whistle as she caught sight of Ren. "Damn, boy, you look hot," she exclaimed.

"I can tell," Ren said with a mischievous grin, leaning in to whisper, "It's pretty obvious. Your nipples give you away."

"They do have a mind of their own. These covers barely hide that fact," she giggled. "Mmm, you're sending out some seriously sexy vibes. I'm pretty sure no one will even notice me standing next to you," she added distractedly.

Ren wore an asymmetrical Gothic vest accented with leather strips, rivets, and a hollowed-out back, revealing his well-defined arms and muscular back. His long legs were clad in newspaper-print long shorts paired with apocalyptic knee-high, lace-up boots. Julia was enthralled, finding herself running her fingers over his vest, toying with the leather straps.

"Wow, that is some look," Kasey remarked as he entered the room, eyeing Ren appreciatively. "You two look incredible together. You'll make quite an entrance."

Julia moved around Ren slowly, trailing her fingers across the bare skin of his back. "Do you have other clothes like

459

these?" she asked, her voice sultry as she circled back to face him.

"I do. I really like apocalyptic fantasy-styled clothes," he replied, wrapping his arms around her. "And I can tell you like them too," he added with a seductive smile as she ran her hands over his chest.

"You should go change; the food will be here soon, and I can see Julia cannot be trusted to behave," Kasey teased, grinning at her. "We don't want to mess up those looks before tomorrow."

"How much time before the food comes?" Julia asked, taking Ren's hand and heading upstairs. "Enough for a quickie?" she giggled. "I promise we won't mess up the clothes."

"Just take them off first," Kasey replied with a smile, shaking his head.

***

Peeling off her clothes, she declared, "After we wear these clothes tomorrow, we're fucking in them."

"I love it when dirty words come out of that pretty little mouth," Ren whispered, his voice low and husky, pulling her close.

"Now these are spanking clothes," she said provocatively, her body pressed against his naked, except for her boots. "Fuck me hard, Ren, and do it with the boots on."

"You got it, baby girl," he growled, his voice deep and primal as he turned her around, bent her over the bed and smacked her on the ass before taking her from behind. It was rough, fast, and over before the food came.

"That was quick," Kasey said, raising an eyebrow when they returned.

"Fast and furious, baby," Julia replied with a wink as she plopped onto the couch to wait for the food.

***

As they finished their meal, Micki called, prompting Julia to excuse herself and take the call in the bedroom. Seizing the opportunity for a private conversation, Ren approached Kasey.

"I'd like to talk to you about something personal," he began.

"Sure, you know you can talk to me about anything," Kasey answered. "Let's go in the living room."

"I need to know how you truly feel about Julia and me having sex alone so often. Does it bother you that she's always all over me? I feel a little guilty about taking her away from your time together," Ren admitted.

Kasey took his hand. "I'm going to let you in on a little secret. I love Julia dearly, but her libido can be a bit much for me. She's always in the mood. Don't get me wrong, I love it, but sometimes I worry I'm not satisfying her needs entirely. You help me so much with that. You're completely satisfying her needs—and mine. I get a little downtime, and she gets what she wants. I absolutely have no problem with you two being together whenever the urge strikes."

"Honestly, Ren, it truly makes me happy. I love seeing you both so happy. The relationship the three of us have is something I could never imagine with anyone else. I feel like I'm being spoiled by having you both with me. I'm thrilled you're attracted to each other and have gotten so close. Julia's never been happier; she really enjoys your adventurous approach to sex, and you make her tingle." Kasey grinned, gave Ren a loving kiss, and then rested his forehead against Ren's. "I'm well taken care of when it comes to sex and companionship because I have both of you. So, please, don't let concerns about me hold you back. I've never been happier, more relaxed, or more content in my life."

Gratefully, Ren embraced Kasey, admitting, "I'm so glad to hear that because truthfully, I can't keep my hands off her. I want her all the time. She has me literally by the balls," he added with a grin.

Kasey laughed. "Well, if you keep putting them in her hands, that's bound to happen."

"Damn, Spike, dropping a sex joke? Look at you loosening up," Ren teased, playfully pushing him.

Returning the gesture, Kasey quipped, "I blame it on the bad influences around me."

Ren pulled him into a tight embrace. "I don't think I've told you lately just how much I love you. I don't want you to feel neglected in any way while I'm lusting after Jules. She's just more vocal about her needs. I want to make sure you feel loved—not just in the bedroom, but in every way. You can be so quiet about what you need. I just want to touch base and make sure your feelings are not getting lost in the frenzy of me and Julia's boink-fest."

Kasey laughed, "Boink-fest? Really? How old are you?" He kissed Ren's shoulder, moving slowly up his neck as he spoke. "I feel more love with you two than I've ever felt in my life. I know you love me—I don't have to hear it or have your mouth wrapped around me every day to feel it. You choosing to be here with me in this situation tells me everything I need to know. Don't worry. If I ever need your attention, I promise I'll let you know. Julia taught me it's important to tell your partner what you want; otherwise, how can they ever hope to make you happy?"

Ren's expression softened, a look of relief crossing his face as he absorbed his words. He squeezed Kasey's hand, a silent acknowledgment of how much his happiness meant to him. "Nicely put, Spike."

After a brief pause, Ren took a steadying breath, then ventured into the conversation he'd been mulling over. "I was wondering if you could let Julia know you wouldn't mind if she slept with me a few times a week. I think she feels obligated to end up in your bed no matter what. I'd like to spend the whole night with her more often if you're okay with that. We don't have to have a strict schedule or anything, but maybe we could talk about it and see what works for all of us."

"You know, maybe a flexible schedule would suit us better, so we're not always unsure about who should be where and when. You two should have your nights together, and I like the idea of some alone time in bed," Kasey responded, a thoughtful smile crossing his face.

"Anything for you, Spike. I'd be happy to take Julia off your hands a few nights a week," Ren said with a grin, pulling Kasey into a tight embrace.

"I appreciate your sacrifice," Kasey murmured, his eyes sparkling with mischief as Ren brushed a lingering kiss against his neck.

"You smell incredible," Ren whispered as Kasey leaned back into him. "Do you think Julia would mind fitting a night into that schedule just for you and me?

Julia, observing from the top of the stairs, could hear their conversation.

"Of course, you guys should have time together alone. It won't kill me to sleep by myself," she said, entering the room and sitting on the couch. "Actually, a schedule sounds like a good idea. It's fairer and less awkward than always asking for permission, and we can keep it flexible. How about I rotate with you guys, with every third night being your time together? That way, we all get to sleep with each other every two days, with the third day for alone time. And by the way, it doesn't matter if I have my period—neither of you gets to escape that. I don't want to sleep alone for five days every month. If any of us feels the need for a longer break or more alone time, we can discuss it together. Does that sound fair? This is new territory for all of us, and while I know I can be a hedonistic handful sometimes, I really want this to work."

"Oh, and one more thing: this schedule is just for sleeping. If any of us want to have sex during the day, it's allowed—it doesn't count against our nights," she grinned. "Just covering all the bases."

"Sounds like a plan to me," Kasey said, sitting up. "And I certainly don't mind being with you during your period. You're actually very sweet—you just need a back rub and some cuddling."

"That's good to know," Ren said. "My ex-wife was so uptight. She wouldn't even let me near her when she was on hers and would sleep in the spare room. That stuff is still a mystery to me."

"Well, get ready for an education. In case you haven't noticed, Julia's very open about her bodily functions. Aren't you, sweetheart? Took me a bit to get used to that—I wish I could be that uninhibited." Kasey gave her a playful nudge, smirking as Julia rolled her eyes in mock exasperation.

"I didn't realize I was all that uninhibited until you mentioned it. I thought it was just normal behavior. I'll try not to be too shocking," she said with a grin.

"Just be yourself. I don't mind—I actually enjoy your candor more than you know," Ren reassured her.

Julia snuggled up to Kasey. "How about I sleep with you tonight because tomorrow, I feel like Ren and I will be pretty worked up after the show, and we can just wear each other out."

Kasey laughed. "Thank you for looking out for me, sweetheart. I appreciate the heads-up."

She smiled and laid her head on Kasey's lap as he leaned back into Ren, who wrapped an arm around him. "I'm glad we sorted that out. Now, let's watch something funny," she said as they all relaxed, content that they'd worked through another important aspect of their new lifestyle.

***

After strategizing with Ren over what to disclose and what to keep from the media regarding their fashion house's progress, they finally felt ready for the upcoming show.

"Take a picture of us, please," Julia exclaimed eagerly. "I want to send it to Micki." They stood together, Ren's arm draped around her, pulling her close as they both grinned at the camera.

"You guys look great together," Kasey remarked, snapping the shot just as the doorbell chimed.

"That must be Carl," he noted, moving to open the door.

"Wow, looking good, Carl," Julia complimented, taking in his dark gray hoodie layered under a black windbreaker jacket, black pants, and new black and red Nike Air Max sneakers. He clearly understood the assignment.

"Thanks! I picked up a few tips from my nephew," Carl replied modestly, a small smile tugging at his lips.

"Well, he was spot on—you'll blend right in," Ren added with an approving nod.

"You didn't have to come to come in, Carl; we could have just come out," Julia said, moving toward the door.

"I'm afraid not, Jules. With no cover here, you'll be escorted to and from the car starting tonight. Your profiles will

465

be through the roof tomorrow, and you never know who might show up," he explained. If you're ready, we should head out."

"You're the boss," Julia responded with a smile, giving Kasey a quick kiss on the cheek before following Carl with Ren in tow.

Their transportation for the night was a sleek town car, with their new security guard and driver, Charlotte Langley, waiting by the door. In her late thirties, tall and commanding, Charley emanated strength and capability. Dressed sharply in a dark suit, her brown hair was pulled back into a tidy bun, framing a serious expression that softened with genuine warmth when she smiled.

Carl introduced her with a nod. "Julia Masters, meet Charley Langley. Charley, this is Julia Masters and Ren Ito."

"Evening, Ms. Masters, Mr. Ito," she greeted as they settled into the car. She closed the

door and took the wheel.

"Charley?" is that a nickname?" Julia inquired.

"Yes, ma'am, short for Charlotte," Charley confirmed, deftly navigating the city streets.

"Please, call me Jules. If you're going to stand between me and trouble, we should be on a first-name basis. We're all on first names here—I prefer it, so humor me."

"No problem, Jules, whatever you prefer," Charley agreed, concentrating on the traffic.

"One more thing—I don't want security in suits unless it's a formal event, and even then, it depends. You can dress more casually for our day-to-day activities; we want you guys to blend in with us at all times. I've arranged for a uniform allowance that covers casual outfits for New York and our time at the shore. Check with Ren if you need guidance on appropriate attire for specific events. I figured you could keep a change of clothes in the security apartment in case something comes up last minute. Sound good?"

"Sounds completely manageable, ma'am—sorry, Jules," Charley replied.

"Welcome to the team, Charley," Julia said warmly.

***

The bustling energy of New York's fashion district enveloped Julia and Ren as they stepped out of the town car, the air buzzing with excitement. They commanded attention as they made their way through a sea of photographers, their entrance sparking a flurry of flashing lights that illuminated the chaotic scene.

Carl led the way with an imposing presence. His formidable size and no-nonsense demeanor commanded respect as he cleared a path through the throng of paparazzi and reporters clamoring for attention.

"Julia! Julia! Over here! Who are you wearing? Is this a new designer for Hawthorne-Masters?" a reporter called out, thrusting a microphone toward her. The questions came rapid-fire, but Julia fielded them with ease, her responses poised and polished. After a moment, she announced, "This is Ren Ito, Hawthorne-Master's Creative Director. He curated both our outfits. Mine is from the talented Yuki."

Ren, standing by her side, smiled in agreement, his hand resting on the small of her back—a silent symbol of their partnership.

"And what can we expect from the new fashion house under Ren's direction?"

"I'll let Ren answer that," Julia said, pride swelling in her chest as she gestured to him.

Ren met the reporter's gaze with confidence, his voice steady and assured.

"Are you looking for a collaboration with Rex?" the reporter pressed. "Our vision for Hawthorne-Masters is to redefine the boundaries of young men's fashion while paying homage to tradition. We're eager to bring fresh perspectives and innovative designs to the forefront of the industry. Working alongside menswear legends Nigel and Giles Hawthorne is a privilege, and I anticipate exciting collaborations with new designers." His tone carried a hint of excitement for the journey ahead. "We're especially eager to see Rex's offerings tonight."

"Are you looking for a collaboration with Rex?" the reporter pressed.

"Thank you, the show's starting," Ren answered and swiftly turned. Surrounded by flashing lights and clamoring reporters, Ren grasped Julia's hand and headed for the door, with Carl leading the way. "Always leave them wanting more," he whispered in her ear. The thumping music and chatter of the fashion elite grew louder, signaling the beginning of an evening filled with possibilities.

Inside, the atmosphere crackled with anticipation as they settled into their coveted front-row seats among fashion elites, celebrities, and influencers. Ren couldn't believe how many well-known people were surrounding him. This was his first New York fashion show, and the sheer presence of fashion icons and industry legends left him both thrilled and a bit humbled. He took a deep breath, letting the significance of the moment sink in.

Sitting next to him was the young and stunning fashion influencer Raven Black, a prominent figure in alternative fashion circles. Ren was thrilled to meet her and introduced her to Julia. Raven offered Julia a polite nod and smile, but her attention quickly shifted back to Ren. She seemed captivated by him, seizing every opportunity to engage him in conversation. She even placed her hand on his thigh at one point as she leaned in to whisper in his ear. Julia, feeling slightly possessive, subtly asserted her presence by engaging Ren in conversation whenever she felt the Gothic, sultry Raven was overstepping.

The venue, a converted warehouse, had been transformed into a minimalist yet chic setting, with dim lighting casting an air of mystery over the space. The room was charged with excitement, mingling with the subtle scents of perfume, cologne, and the unmistakable aroma of freshly steamed fabrics.

Despite the diverse crowd, all eyes soon fixated on the runway, eagerly awaiting the debut of the young designer's creations. The lights went dark, and the music ended, signaling the start of the show. A hush fell over the crowd, broken only by occasional murmurs of excitement. The first beats of music began to pulse through the room, setting the rhythm for the fashion parade about to unfold.

The runway lit up, and the models emerged, walking confidently, their strides deliberate and measured. Each garment was a fusion of artistry and innovation, crafted by Rex. The fabrics flowed gracefully, catching the light in mesmerizing patterns. From sophisticated, tailored suits in vibrant colors to avant-garde streetwear with unconventional silhouettes, Rex's collection showcased a diverse range of styles, each imbued with his unique creative vision.

Cameras flashed incessantly, capturing every moment of the spectacle. Julia leaned in to whisper her observations to Ren, their shared excitement evident as they took in the designs. Together, they evaluated each look, envisioning how the designer's aesthetic could align with their own brand's vision and identity.

Cheers erupted as the models paraded out alongside Rex, a diminutive yet striking African American designer with a pencil-thin mustache, thick curly hair, and undeniable flair reminiscent of Prince. His outfit—an open silk shirt with bright geometric designs, tucked into matching long silk shorts and thick-soled Doc Martens—matched his personality, exuding both individuality and confidence. Holding hands with two of his models, he raised them in the air with a nod and a broad grin. He took his bows, signaling the end of the show, as conversations filled the room, attendees discussing their favorite looks and mingling to network.

Grabbing Ren's wrist and interrupting his conversation with Julia, Raven asked, "Would you like to meet the designer? He's a close friend. I'm heading over to meet with him for an interview and to party afterward. Come, I'll introduce you." Throughout her proposition, she maintained unbroken eye contact with Ren, completely dismissing Julia.

"Thanks, Raven, that would be great. We'd love to tell him how much we liked his show," Julia responded, subtly reminding her that she was still there.

"Let's go then," Raven replied, still focused on Ren as she linked arms with him and pulled him out of his seat. Catching Julia's smirk and raised eyebrow as he glanced back, Ren flashed her a helpless grin. Spotting Carl right behind her, Julia nodded. "Follow that Goth," she said, gesturing to Raven, who was already off in search for Rex, showing off Ren on her arm.

Finding Rex surrounded by a crowd, three people deep, receiving congratulations, Raven called out his name, signaling for him to come over. When Rex spotted who Raven was with, he excused himself from the group and made his way over. Already hailed as a rising star in fashion, Rex owed much of his success to Raven's support and promotion through her influential blog, which had championed him since their college days.

Raven quickly wrapped her arms around Rex, "That was utterly exquisite—darkness and light executed flawlessly. I can't wait to write about it. Let me introduce to you someone. This gorgeous man is Ren Ito, Creative Director for the new Hawthorne-Masters. And this is Jules Masters of Masters Inc."

"Well, aren't you fucking hot? I thought you were a model and wondered why you weren't in my show," Rex remarked, his gaze lingering on Ren. "And look at you—your boots are fantastic," he said, bending down to check out the multicolored wings on Julia's boots. You look like a beautiful butterfly coming out of a cocoon."

"Thank you. Ren put this all together for me," Julia said, smiling as she appreciated the compliment.

"Did he now?" Rex said, raising an eyebrow and giving Ren the once-over. "I know those are Yamamoto shorts, but who did this sick vest? I don't recognize it," he said, running his fingers over the rivets. "Fits you like a goddamn glove. Like it was made for you."

"That's because it was. I made it," Ren said proudly. "Years ago. I wasn't sure it would even fit." Julia shot him a look of disbelief for not mentioning that it was his creation.

"Oh, it fits. You are slaying in that vest. I love it," Rex said appreciatively.

"Thanks. Your show was stunning—very look a winner." Rex beamed at Ren's compliment.

"I was just blown away. Your looks are so innovative," Julia added. "We'd love to have lunch with you to discuss a possible collaboration if you're interested. You'd be working closely with Ren." Julia smiled enticingly, knowing full well that would be a big selling point for Rex.

With a gleam in his eye, Rex replied, "Thanks for coming. I have to get back, but I'll definitely hit you up for a lunch date. Nice to meet you." He took Julia's hand and gave it a little kiss. "And especially nice to meet you," Rex said, giving one of the leather straps on Ren's vest a little tug. "C'mon, Raven. Let's go do that interview, get drunk, and celebrate," Rex said as he whisked Raven away. Over her shoulder, she gave Ren the "call me" gesture and a cheeky smile.

Grinning, Julia took Ren's arm. "Let's get out of here before someone else finds you too hard to resist." While waiting for their car, a distinguished older man approached Ren, slipped him his card, and asked if he modeled, suggesting he give him a call. As he walked away, Julia raised an eyebrow and said, "I told you no one would even notice me next to you tonight. And by the way, why didn't you mention you made the vest? You should be proud—it's fantastic. You knew how much I liked it at home."

"I thought that was because you just wanted to take it off." He gave her a playful nudge and a sly grin. "I don't know why I didn't say anything. I guess I wasn't as confident in my abilities as I should have been."

"Well, you're extremely talented. Rex thinks so too," Julia said, giving Ren a little poke. Ren smiled widely, his head filled with the evening's sights, sounds, and a multitude of compliments.

Carl signaled that it was time to leave, and once again, they navigated the gauntlet of flashbulbs and questions. After expressing their appreciation for the show, they moved swiftly until they were safely inside the car.

Julia raised the partition and turned on the music so they couldn't be seen or heard.

"Did you pimp me out to Rex?" Ren said, grinning, as he pulled her close.

"I did no such thing," she giggled. "More like I just used you as bait. Just to get him in the door; then I'll throw money at him—not you." Teasing him, she added, "You may have a lot more to offer than I thought. You're like catnip, babe. I could dangle you in front of boys and girls, use that sex appeal to its full potential." Tracing her finger across the leather straps on his vest, she continued in a breathy, tempting voice, "But if you think that was naughty, you could always spank me when we get home."

"I don't know if it can wait until we get home. I think you need some discipline right now," he said, his tone commanding as he put her across his lap and spanked her, his hand across her mouth, muffling each cry. After the third smack, she started to pull back, but he stopped her and said, "I don't think I'm quite satisfied. How about you take care of this for me?" He unzipped his shorts and guided her head into his lap, pulling back her hood and undoing her hair.

"Holy shit, baby, you're like a fucking vacuum," he moaned, watching her, his fingers gripping her hair. Not wanting to miss out on a chance for limo sex, she released her hold on him, leaving him hard and wet. Reaching under her skirt, she pulled her thong to the side, threw her leg over him, and exhaled sharply as she slammed down onto him hard. With her fingers gripping the leather straps of his vest, she bounced on his lap at a speed that guaranteed things would be hot and fast. Pulling her closer as he came, he buried his face in her neck, muffling his second "Holy shit" in five minutes. They spent the rest of the ride wrapped up in each other, making out like teenagers after prom, his fingers finding their way between her now-slick thighs.

Kasey welcomed them home warmly as Carl escorted them to the door.

"Great job tonight, Carl. Have a good one," Julia acknowledged as they stepped into the house.

"So, how was it?" Kasey asked. "Did you have a good time? Do you want to talk, or am I delaying your fun time?" he added with a grin.

"Don't be silly. Of course we want to talk," Julia replied, snuggling up to Kasey on the couch as Ren grabbed some water for both of them from the fridge.

"You had sex in the car," Kasey asserted.

"Just enough to take the edge off," Julia giggled, making Ren laugh.

"How did you know?" she said with a coy look.

"One, I know that you love limo sex, and two, I can smell him all over you," Kasey said with a grin.

"That show was incredible," Ren said, winking at Kasey as he settled in next to Julia. "I was totally star-struck seeing all those famous faces—rappers, YouTubers, athletes. It just blew my mind that we sat in the front with so many important people behind us." He stopped, realizing what he'd said. "No offense, Jules, I don't mean you're not important. I just don't see you in that light. I still have trouble wrapping my head around exactly who you are in the business world."

Julia nodded understandingly. "I get it. Sometimes, I forget how much influence and wealth I have now. I didn't grow up wealthy. We lived a simple ranch life till my father made some significant acquisitions. Having fancy things, meeting important people, needing security—it's all still new to me. I was just as awestruck as you were. But you were in your element—so cool and confident."

"Jules tried to pimp me out tonight," Ren chuckled, ratting her out to Kasey. "She claims she just used me as bait. I think it's the same thing."

"Snitches get stitches, buddy," Julia laughed, giving him a shove. "Sorry, but he was like catnip to the designer, who we met through the influencer, Raven Black. She was sitting next to Ren and clearly wanted to get her claws in him. And as we waited for our car, a good-looking older man slipped him his number. He was on friggin fire," Julia added, her voice tinged with both admiration and desire. "The man of the hour found him so irresistible he walked away from a mob of fans to meet him, so I took my opportunity to dangle a little bait."

"And just exactly how did you do that?" Kasey asked.

"Well… I just pointed out to Rex that he would be working closely with Ren if he came to work with us."

Kasey closed his eyes and shook his head.

"What?" She giggled. "Well, he would."

"I never felt so used," Ren deadpanned, trying not to laugh.

Kasey shot him a look, his eyes twinkling. "I'm sure you can handle it. And you, Missy, I don't believe I have to say this, but we do not use our partners as bait."

"Fine," she pouted playfully. "But this designer is just who we need to help put us on the map. I thought a little encouragement couldn't hurt." She smiled innocently, flashing him her baby blues.

Kasey grinned. "You're too much," he said, giving her a kiss on the top of her head and a tight squeeze.

"Oh my God! I almost forgot—Ren designed the vest he's wearing. Rex complimented him on it, and that's how I found out." She turned to Ren, "I still can't believe you didn't say anything. You have so much talent. I'd love for you to show me other stuff you've done," Julia said.

"I always knew you were creative," Kasey added. "Now's your time to shine. I hope you get some good mentions in the media tomorrow from your chats with the reporters."

"Speaking of which, I'm gonna put us out there tonight. I'm gonna hit social media real quick and mention how much we enjoyed the show on a couple of platforms. I'll be in the kitchen; talk among yourselves," Ren joked as he sat down to compose some comments.

"Sounds like it was a successful night," Kasey said as he cuddled with Julia.

"He did so well, baby. When he answered the big question as we walked in about the direction of the new house, he was so articulate and calm. He has a perfect media presence. Everyone was checking him out. Rex practically tripped over people to meet him. And that influencer Raven Black? She was all over him. Pissed me off a little."

"Sounds like somebody's jealous," Kasey grinned.

"Maybe a little," Julia grinned. "It really bothered me that I couldn't nicely say, 'Take your claws off my man.'"

"I thought you weren't the jealous type," he continued to tease her.

"I guess maybe I am... when I have what I want and don't want to lose it," she said, giving him a determined smile as she leaned into his embrace.

"You do know I can hear you both," Ren said as he walked over to the couch. "You have nothing to be jealous of, baby girl. I only have eyes for you and Spike. You have everything I could ever want in a woman," Ren said reassuringly.

"You're sweet," Julia beamed. "Still, she better watch her step," she declared, letting Ren and Kasey know she wasn't willing to share with anyone else. Pausing, she asked Ren, "I was wondering if we could postpone our apocalyptic playtime, just relax, and all cuddle for a while. I'm kinda hungry too."

"I'm up for some cuddling and food. Let's get changed and unwind," Ren agreed.

"I'll whip up something to eat," Kasey offered as they made their way to their respective rooms, and he headed to the kitchen.

By the time they came back down, Kasey had made them flatbread pizzas with leftovers and store-bought flatbread. They settled in front of the fireplace as a trio, watching *Archer,* cuddling, laughing, and indulging in pizza.

After exchanging goodnight kisses with Kasey, Ren and Julia retired to his room. Shedding their clothes and slipping under the covers, they wasted no time expressing their intense desire for each other. It might not have been the wild apocalyptic fantasy they'd planned, but it was nevertheless an impassioned encounter that left them exhausted, the excitement of the night an added drain. They drifted off to sleep in their favorite position: Julia nestled in the crook of his arm, her head and hand on his chest, her leg draped over his.

***

The next morning, as Kasey descended the stairs for work, he saw Julia standing in front of Ren in the kitchen, delicately blowing on her cup of tea, their gazes locked on each other. They exchanged soft giggles as he tenderly caressed her face, neither of them noticing Kasey's presence.

"Good morning. You two are up early—impressive, considering how late you stayed up," he quipped. "I thought I might have to drag you two out of bed." Julia put her cup down and turned to greet him as Ren drew her close, wrapping his arms around her and resting his head on hers. Kasey noticed it was the first time Julia hadn't pulled away from Ren to come to him.

Observing their deepening bond, Kasey commented, "You two look cozy. I'm glad you're comfortable showing affection in front of me. Just remember to be cautious at work. You can both be a bit impulsive with physical affection and while that's fine here and at the shore house, we need to be careful about who sees our relationship. Even in our private life, apart from friends and those we trust, like Carl and Charley, we need to keep this quiet for a bunch of reasons. It's not ideal, but for you, Julia, and Masters Inc., such publicity could be detrimental. It wouldn't reflect well with the board or the fashion industry if they perceived you simply appointed your boyfriend as the new Creative Director. Once Ren and Hawthorne-Masters establish themselves, it'll be easier to reveal our unconventional arrangement."

Julia nodded in agreement. "I understand and agree with everything you've said. I'll behave myself with the displays of affection at work, but we'll need to inform Carl and Charley. They both signed ironclad NDAs, so no worries there. There's one other person we should have sign one to make our work life smoother, and that's Derrick. Since he'll be closely managing things for Ren, I think he can be an ally."

"I hate that we have to navigate things this way, but I understand and agree," Ren added. "I'll handle Derrick, and maybe, Jules, you could handle Carl. He really connects with you. Then he could talk to Charley."

"I'll talk to both of them," Julia replied. "You can deal with Derrick."

"Tonight, when we get home, we need to set up the third bedroom for Julia—take those boxes out of there. It's your night alone... you ready for that?" Kasey asked, meeting her gaze with a steady look.

"I'll be fine. You two deserve your alone time. And there's no need to fix up the room—I'll have Alice swing by today with her son, who's worked for me before, to take care of it. I want her to start coming here to clean. I don't want you to have to do it anymore, Kasey. You have too much to do already, so I'm starting with this. Before she leaves, I'll have Alice make dinner for us. She's been eager to do more since I've been staying here, so it's time to integrate her into our lives. She signed an NDA years ago—she's trustworthy and an excellent cook. You guys will love her. Sometimes I forget she's even around; she's so discreet and respectful of my privacy," Julia reassured.

"I admit I could use some help now. With work ramping up and all the new security changes, it's a bit much," Kasey confessed.

Julia loosened Ren's grip on her and went to Kasey, wrapping her arms around his waist. "I know you don't like asking for help, but you need to come to me or Ren and let us know when you need it. We can't help if we don't know. Things will only get more demanding, and we need you—I need you—to be in top form to help me with the important things, not all bogged down by everyday tasks that someone else can handle."

"Seriously, Spike, you work too hard. Let Alice take over the housekeeping, at least," Ren added.

"You're both right; I won't argue. I'll relinquish the housekeeping chores, but I insist on cooking most of the time. I genuinely enjoy it," Kasey's gaze softened, a rare vulnerability showing as he continued, "I'm not accustomed to someone looking out for me. I appreciate it—from both of you."

Just then, the doorbell rang, signaling the start of their first day with round-the-clock security.

"That's Charley. Time to go," Kasey announced as they headed for the door.

***

"Have a seat with me on the couch," Julia said as Charley entered her office. "I have something to share with you that's not common knowledge. It's known only to our very small

479

inner circle of friends. Even Carl doesn't know yet; I'll be informing him next. It's something we wish we didn't have to conceal, but for the sake of the company and me right now, it's a must."

Julia paused, choosing her words carefully. "Kasey, Ren, and I are in a committed domestic relationship. While publicly, Kasey is known to be my partner, privately, so is Ren. They're also partners. We can't disclose this due to social pressures that could potentially impact the business negatively. We intend to be open about it in the future—hopefully, once Ren and the new fashion house are well established. I don't want to hide my affection for either of my men, nor them from showing their affection for each other when we're out of the public eye. We want to be who we are around our closest security, and I just wanted to tell you—this is who we are." Julia searched Charley's face for any sign of disapproval, but her poker face revealed nothing.

"I'm here to protect you, not judge you. I'll do whatever it takes to safeguard your privacy as much as your physical well-being. You should be able to be yourself in your own home and in private moments," Charley answered professionally. "May I add a purely personal observation?"

"Absolutely," Julia replied.

"You go girl," she said, shaking her head as they both shared a laugh. At that moment, Julia realized Charley would fit in nicely with her inner circle.

"Just one thing," Charley hesitated.

"What's that?" Julia asked.

"For your privacy's sake, those town cars aren't soundproof," Charley smiled, "Even if you play music."

"Shit! Sorry." Julia grinned, her cheeks flushing slightly. "I did not know that. Damn, that must have been a rough ride with Carl beside you." She laughed, slightly embarrassed. "Poor Carl—he puts up with so much from me. I need to talk to him right away. I can't imagine what he's thinking after last night.

"He's a grown man and an ex-cop; I'm sure he's seen and heard it all before," Charley assured.

"I'm not worried about the sex," she grinned. "I'm pretty sure I've done that before with him driving. I'm just worried he'll think I'm cheating on Kasey."

"Is there anything else?" Charley asked with a smile, surprised that Julia even cared what Carl thought about her.

"No, that's it," Julia replied, feeling even better about Charley.

"Just remember, I'm here to protect you in every aspect, not just physically. Your privacy is just as important. You can always be yourself with me. I want you to feel so comfortable you forget I'm even here," Charley assured.

"Thank you. I appreciate that. Have a great day—I'll see you tonight."

"Have a good one, Jules." Charley left with a grin, amused by Julia's mix of warmth and directness. She had a feeling working for Julia was going to be anything but dull.

"One down, one to go," Julia said to herself as she dialed Carl.

"Hey, Carl, I need to tell you something—" Julia began, segueing into an explanation of her recent lifestyle changes and apologizing for any discomfort her actions in the town car might have caused him. He took it in stride, confirming it wasn't the first time he'd noticed her indulging in limo sex. He'd already suspected something was brewing when Ren moved in, and he'd seen Julia holding his hand, her head on his shoulder during the ride home.

Relieved to have that over with, she immediately reached out to Ren to check on his progress with Derrick.

"He had no issue signing the NDA, and when I mentioned the three of us, he didn't flinch," Ren reported. "He understands the importance of discretion, and I think he'll be a huge asset for us here at work."

He paused, his tone turning seductive. "You know... my office isn't all glass like yours. My bathroom isn't as big, but we don't need much room, do we? Plus, we've got a lookout here. Come visit me, baby girl. Let's christen my bathroom, or let me bend you over my desk. Make a fantasy come true for me."

"You are such a bad boy," she giggled, her nipples suddenly hard. "Don't put ideas in my head. Kasey will lose his mind. He just gave us that speech, and we agreed."

"I can't help myself," he whispered, his voice as smooth as silk. "I want to feel you on my lap, making those little circles with your hips, your perfect nipples teasing me while you rub slowly against me. Or maybe you could ride me like in the limo, fast and furious, your nipples bouncing in my face. I'm hard already just thinking about you."

"You are so bad," she purred, her attraction to his bad-boy side clear in her tone.

"I want to hear you moaning in my ear. Come to me, baby. Be a bad girl for me," he urged— "You know you want to."

She took a moment before giving in to his seductive charms. "Umm... I'll be right there," she said excitedly, her lust overpowering her restraint.

"Kasey, I don't have anything pressing for the next half hour, do I?" she asked as she headed toward the door.

"No, nothing until your call with legal at eleven," he responded, glancing up from his work.

"I'll be right back," she said, smoothing out her skirt and adjusting the collar on her blouse.

"Say hi to Ren for me," he said, smiling and shaking his head.

"What makes you think I'm heading there?" Julia grinned mischievously.

"You were just on the phone, your face is flushed, and your nipples give you away. You two are insatiable. I don't know what I'm going to do with you both—except maybe just get out of the way so I don't get run over in your mad dash for a booty call."

"I'm not even gonna try to deny it," she laughed. "We'll be discreet. Promise. Love ya, baby," she said with a grin as she hurried off to christen Ren's office.

***

After their morning rendezvous, Ren scrolled through all the mentions of himself, Julia, and Hawthorne-Masters from the show. The most prominent and flattering coverage came from Raven Black's blog. Her YouTube podcast showcased multiple angles of the front row and catwalk, with Ren prominently featured in nearly every shot. She even highlighted that he designed the vest he wore, offering a glimpse into the personal aesthetic of the Creative Director for Hawthorne-Masters.

As the day unfolded, several top fashion magazines highlighted the debut of Hawthorne-Masters' new Creative Director. Derrick fielded numerous interview requests for Ren and inquiries about a potential collaboration with Rex. They were all pleased with the level of media attention they garnered. Julia made sure that Jack, Rick, and the other members of the board were informed about the positive publicity, and several top fashion magazines highlighted the debut of Hawthorne-Masters' new Creative Director.

Taking a moment to revel in the newfound attention, Ren sent an email to his mother,

attaching Raven's blog and all the mentions of him and his new position. He smiled, imagining his father's reaction when his mother shared the articles. He also mentioned that he was in a loving relationship and the happiest he'd ever been.

***

Later that evening, in the parking garage, Charley held the door open as the three of them climbed in for the ride home. Charley caught glimpses of them in the rearview mirror, now seeing them from a different perspective. From quiet conversations and shoulder-to-shoulder closeness to shared laughter and leaning into each other, the intimacy between the trio was strikingly clear.

Kasey admitted it was nice to come home to a home-cooked dinner warming in the oven after a long day at work; the stormy night made Alice's hearty beef stroganoff even more enjoyable.

"They did a great job," Julia remarked as they sat down to dinner. "I still have to add some personal touches to my room, like some twinkle lights and my candles, but it's coming together. I also have a beautiful picture of my family I'd like to hang in my room. Could you help me with that, Kasey?" She glanced at Ren.

"No problem, I have everything we need to hang it properly," Kasey answered distractedly, pushing his food around on the plate with his fork. "I have this picture of my mother and me. I was thinking I'd like to have it enlarged and hang it in the living room. We could place it next to your family's photo instead of keeping them in your room." He looked up at Julia, his beautiful eyes somehow a deeper gray when expressing his vulnerability.

Julia rose from her seat to wrap her arms around Kasey. "That sounds like an even better plan. I wasn't sure I'd like looking up and seeing my dad's face in my bedroom," she joked, hoping to lighten the mood for Kasey. He laughed as she gave Ren a discreet thumbs-up, grateful she'd listened to him and allowed Kasey to take the initiative when he was ready.

***

"Damn, that storm is getting loud," Julia remarked as she loaded the dishwasher, reacting to a particularly loud clap of thunder.

"Do storms bother you?" Ren asked, putting the leftovers away.

"Not usually. I love everything about them except for the thunder that sounds like a bomb going off," Julia replied, hoping it would.

"You can sleep with us tonight, sweetheart, if the storm makes you uncomfortable," Kasey offered.

"Nah, I'll be fine. It'll probably calm down before bed," she replied, hoping it did.

With the weather ruling out a run, Kasey and Ren worked out together in his training room while Julia puttered around in her room, catching up with Micki on a video chat.

By eleven, they had all said good night, and Julia settled in her bed alone. Instead of abating, the storm resumed its fury, lightning streaking across the sky in rapid bursts and thunder booming seemingly overhead. As midnight approached, unable to bear the tempest's onslaught any longer, she made her way to Kasey's room.

Hesitating in the doorway, she debated on disturbing them until she heard Kasey's voice, "What took you so long? Come on, get in," he lifted the covers and she whispered, "Can I get in the middle?" With a shift, he made room, and she slipped in, positioning herself to face Ren while Kasey

485

snuggled up behind her. His naked warmth enveloped her, his breath tickling her ear as his hand found its place on her breast.

"Maybe we should go to my room so we don't wake Ren," Julia said softly, her voice a sultry invitation, as she pressed against him, feeling his desire for her.

"No, don't leave," Ren murmured, awakening to the situation.

With deliberate care, Kasey's fingers traced the curves of her body. A startled gasp escaped her lips, her eyes widening as he slipped his fingers inside her just as a sudden crack of thunder boomed, lightning illuminating the room.

Her wide blue eyes drew Ren in, and he pulled her into a passionate kiss, his tongue slipping deep into her mouth. She held him tight, her nails digging into his back as she draped her leg over his body, giving Kasey room to continue his touch, building her anticipation. He entered her, sucking on the nape of her neck as he pressed close. Ren's mouth moved from hers to her breasts, his fingers slipping between her legs, the combined sensation of both men pleasuring her driving her wild.

Amid the tempest raging outside and Julia's unrestrained moans within, the three intertwined, yielding to a passion as electric as the storm.

The storm continued, even as sleep gradually overtook them. Julia found comfort resting her head and hand on Ren's chest, her leg draped over his, while Kasey spooned her. Nestled between her men, the once-terrifying storm now soothed her into a peaceful sleep, thoroughly loved and no longer afraid.

***

Chapter 20: Temptation, Trust, and Togetherness

The following morning at the office, Raven called Ren, inviting him to lunch for an in-depth interview and a bit of personal time together. They arranged to meet at a local bistro later that day, where Charley chauffeured Ren and discreetly observed as the two spent over an hour laughing and talking. Raven blatantly flirted with Ren at every opportunity. Unaccustomed to attention from stunning, bold American women, Ren soaked it up. He decided to show Raven around the completed design workrooms at Masters Inc.

When she learned Raven was in the building, Julia went to Ren's office to say hello, only to find Raven perched on his desk, captivating both him and Derrick. Ren, noticing Julia, quickly explained, "Jules, I'm glad you came down. Raven was just telling us about another fashion show next Tuesday. She has an extra ticket and invited me along. It's for Markus Oren, the other new designer we were interested in. I said I'd be happy to check him out."

Raven's self-satisfied smile at securing Ren's company made Julia's skin crawl, but she maintained a composed facade, aware that Raven's clout in fashion circles could benefit Ren and Hawthorne-Masters.

"That sounds great. Good to see you again, Raven," Julia forced out, her voice strained but polite.

As Raven bid farewell with saccharine sweetness, Julia's discomfort grew as she slipped off the desk and placed a hand on Ren's chest. "Thank you for lunch and the interview. I'll give you a call before the show."

"Sounds great. I had a nice time, and thanks again for the great mentions. Derrick will walk you out, and I'll see you next week," Ren replied, extending his hand. Raven clasped it between hers and uttered melodically, "Goodbye, Ren," before leaving with Derrick.

As the door closed, Julia turned to face Ren, who immediately grinned and held his hands up as if to block a blow. "Now don't get your panties all twisted. I know she's being flirty, but she holds considerable influence, and I want her as an ally." He pulled Julia close, and she met his gaze, her vibrant blue eyes deepening to a darker shade.

"I don't trust her," Julia confessed. "I know what kind of woman she is. I was that kind of woman. She'll stop at nothing. She's pretty, accomplished, and bold—all qualities I know you like. Are you attracted to her? I can't believe I'm admitting this, but I'm extremely jealous, and I hate how it makes me feel."

He sat on the edge of his desk, and she slipped between his legs and melted into his arms. "Baby," he said soothingly, tightening his embrace, "you have nothing to worry about. I would never mess around. I was faithful for years to my ex-wife until the marriage was over, and she gave me her okay. I could have strayed, but that's not who I am. You give me everything I need, physically and emotionally. Why would I even think of cheating? Under all this lust is genuine love." He kissed her tenderly. "I know Raven's interested—it's pretty obvious. And I admit, it's a huge boost to my ego, but that's all." He grinned. "And sure, if I wasn't committed to you and Kasey, I might hit that." Julia gave him a playful punch.

He continued, his tone sincere, "But I *am* committed to you—both of you. This isn't a casual fling for me. I take commitment seriously. Next time we talk, I'll tell her I'm in a relationship. Hopefully that'll put a stop to her flirting."

"That doesn't mean jack shit to women like her. It just makes you forbidden fruit—she'll want you more," Julia responded anxiously, resting her head on his chest, her hands gripping his upper arms tightly.

He kissed her head and tightened his embrace. "And, just for the record, why are you all freaked out about Raven, yet you practically threw me at Rex?"

"I don't know why I don't find Rex as much of a threat, even though he was just as interested in you." She paused, looking down, then met his gaze directly. "Actually, I do know why. It's because I see how deeply you care for Kasey—how you came back to him after ten years. I can see the love in the way you look at him, talk about him, and share him with me. He's the man you want." She continued softly, lowering her gaze, "I worry that with all the attention you're getting, you might realize how much of a catch you are and feel tempted to explore relationships with other women."

She hugged him tightly, pressing her head against his chest. "I don't want to lose what we all have together. I can't imagine you not being a part of my life now. I love you, and I need you to know that. I regret not telling Kasey I loved him earlier, and I don't want to make that mistake with you. I love what we're building as a trio. Raven seems like the type who always gets what she wants—and right now, she wants you. You might not be able to resist what she's offering."

He took both her hands, his dark eyes gazing deeply into hers. "That's the first time you've told me you love me," he said, his voice soft. He paused, savoring the words before leaning in to kiss her, tender and lingering as if imprinting the moment in his memory. "I love you too, Jules," he murmured, holding her close.

"Listen to me. Don't spiral. I'm not going anywhere. I cherish my life with you and Spike. Maybe the world doesn't know we're together, but we do. Nobody will come between us." Before he could finish, there was a gentle knock on the door. Julia stepped back as Ren called out, "Come in."

"Sorry to interrupt," Derrick said, peeking his head around the door. "You have a phone interview with *Harper's Bazaar* in ten minutes—and another one right after with *The Cut*."

"Thanks, I'll be ready," Ren confirmed as Derrick left, closing the door behind him.

"Now, quickly, back to you and your crazy jealousy," he said, his eyes dancing with amusement as he pulled her close. "I'm teasing. Jules... baby, look at me. You have nothing to worry about, absolutely nothing. Raven may get what she wants, but it won't be from me. And, yeah, it feels nice to be wanted, but it feels a thousand times better to know I'm not only wanted but deeply loved by you and Spike. Trust me." He kissed her, spun her around, gave her a firm smack on the butt, and pointed her toward the door.

"Don't you have some people to boss around upstairs? Go, I have work to do. I'll see you later." He winked at her, and she gave him an appreciative smile, acknowledging he knew exactly how to stop her from spiraling.

***

A few hours later, the trio headed to the shore in Julia's BMW—Kasey at the wheel, Ren in the front seat, and Julia reclining in the back with a pillow and her favorite throw, engrossed in her phone. She felt a bit fatigued, having started her period just before they left. Following closely behind them were Carl and Charley in a large black utility vehicle. This outing marked their last chance to add any major finishing touches to the place and familiarize Charley with the surroundings. It was also a chance to strategize security for the upcoming visit from the Hawthorne brothers. Julia preferred Carl and Charley to handle most of the security during the vacation, as she felt more at ease with them than with new guards.

Upon arrival, Kasey led them on a tour of the grounds, pointing out the newly erected guardhouse along the way. He also checked in with the on-duty guard to ensure everything was running smoothly with the new addition.

The trio kept busy with various tasks, including meeting with Julia's housekeeper, Jackie, to discuss her responsibilities, making last-minute shopping trips—like a run to Home Depot for an extensive selection of plants for the now glass-enclosed back deck—and stocking the house with essentials like beer, wine, liquor, and new beach gear. Carl and Charley organized their schedule with a third guard and identified areas where they could assist without being intrusive.

Since it was Julia's solo night and the start of her period, she welcomed the solitude of her bed. But by two in the morning, she found herself leaning against the kitchen counter, trying to soothe her cramps with a microwave heating pad. In the quiet of the night, she heard Kasey's bedroom door creak open.

"Did I wake you? I'm sorry, I tried to be quiet," she apologized, her voice tinged with pain. "These cramps are kicking my ass right now. They haven't been this intense in a while." The microwave beeped, and she retrieved the pad.

"Here, let me take that. Come on, I'll rub your back," he offered, taking her hand and leading her back to her room.

As they settled into bed, Julia asked, "Would you rub my butt instead of my back? I want to lie on my stomach and put the pad on my lower back. It'll help me fall asleep. Thanks, baby, I really appreciate this."

She placed a body pillow under her leg and belly, hugged it, and relaxed as Kasey gently positioned the warm pad on her lower back and began rubbing her butt in slow, circular motions as he lay beside her.

As her breathing slowed and he was about to leave, Ren appeared in the doorway. Kasey

put his finger to his lips, covered her up, and left.

"Everything alright?" Ren asked once they reached Kasey's room.

"She has cramps. Nothing a heating pad and a butt rub couldn't handle," he replied with a knowing smile.

"A butt rub, huh? I'll remember that for tomorrow night."

"Believe me, she'll ask for what she wants. Sometimes, she needs space; other times, she's real cuddly. I just let her tell me what she needs. She does get a little emotional the day before and the first day, but other times, you'd never even know she was dealing with it," Kasey explained, sharing what he knew to be true about Julia.

"Today, she was a little emotional in my office after Raven left. Jules is not fond of her," Ren added with a smile.

"I know," Kasey replied. "What happened today?"

"Raven invited me to a fashion show on Tuesday and was openly flirting with me in front of Jules. She managed to keep her cool, but after Raven left, it was a different story. She seems to think I'm going to run off with the first pretty face I see.

She doesn't realize how seriously I take this commitment to each of you. She even told me she regretted not telling you she loved you sooner in your relationship, so she told me she loved me. I told her exactly how I felt, and it seemed to pacify her. Do you think all that was because of her period?" Ren asked innocently.

Kasey chuckled. "Don't ever let her hear you say she acted any way due to her period. That's a big no-no. It might have played a part, but she also told me about a past relationship where she was deeply in love—they lived together—and he cheated on her. In her words, 'he broke her.' So, she's dealing with some trust issues. It didn't help that I really messed up when I spent that first weekend with you. I hurt her badly. I still don't know why I didn't just call her. She told me it only hurt so much because she loved me." He paused. "If she didn't love you, she wouldn't care."

"She certainly makes me feel loved. I am so sorry we hurt her," Ren said softly as he kissed the back of Kasey's neck, snuggling closer as he spooned him. "I'll make sure she doesn't have to deal with Raven too much. And I think I'm gonna start telling people I'm committed to someone, but for their privacy, I don't talk about them. I still have to deal with Rex and his inevitable advances."

"That sounds like a good way to handle things right now. You'll definitely have more people throwing themselves at you if they think you're available, and we can't have that, can we?" Kasey said, turning to face Ren and caressing his cheek. "I might get jealous too."

"Aw, Spike, that means a lot. You two make me feel so special." Ren's heart fluttered as he saw the love in Kasey's eyes shimmering in the dim light. Pulling Kasey's head to him, he whispered, his voice reassuring, "I'm not going anywhere."

***

The following day, after tying up the last few loose ends and ensuring everything was in place, they finally allowed themselves a chance to relax and enjoy themselves. Kasey and Ren kicked things off with a short run before beginning to practice Jeet Kune Do on the sandy expanse in front of the deck.

"What discipline is that?" Charley asked, observing with keen interest.

"Jeet Kune Do," Kasey answered.

"How long have you been training?"

"Over ten years. You train in Krav Maga, if I'm not mistaken," Kasey replied. "We should spar sometime. Ren's a bit of a lightweight," he teased.

"I used to train with Kasey when he first started, then I stopped. I'm working on getting back into it," Ren explained.

"Are you serious about sparring? I clock out in a few minutes, and I'd love to go a few rounds," Charley proposed.

Kasey eagerly accepted the challenge. "Go change and meet me here," he said, excited to spar against a different combat style.

With Julia watching from the deck, Ren on the sand, and Carl taking a break from his property tour to watch, Kasey and Charley engaged in a spirited match. Initially cautious, they soon unleashed a flurry of strikes and maneuvers. Despite Charley throwing everything from boxing to wrestling at him, Kasey skillfully adapted his style to hers. After twenty intense minutes under the sun, they called it quits, realizing they were pretty evenly matched.

"You've got some serious skills—your trainer must have been top-notch," Kasey said, his adrenaline pumping, sweat dripping down his chest.

"Thanks, I'll mention that to my wife—she's a professional trainer for the security company. She trained me. I've never faced off with a civilian with your level of skill. Impressive," Charley said, bent over with her hands on her hips, catching her breath and holding a newfound respect for Kasey.

"That was really something," Julia said as she walked up with bottles of water. "I've never seen Kasey fight that hard. Training alone or with Ren isn't the same," she laughed, giving Ren a playful nudge. She turned to Charley, handing her a bottle. "That was outstanding."

"You look evenly matched. You should train together once in a while," Ren suggested.

"I'd enjoy sparring with someone as experienced as you. If you're interested, let me know," Kasey said as they walked back to the deck.

"I think I'll take you up on that. Thanks for the workout. Have a good night, everyone," Charley said with a smile.

"Charley, you're covered in sand. Go use the shower downstairs and at least rinse off before you head home. That's a long ride to be all itchy," Julia advised.

"Thanks, Jules, but I'll just rinse off in your outdoor shower. I'm not heading back to the city. My wife and I got a room down here for the weekend."

"Oh, that's nice. Enjoy yourselves, and grab a towel. You can bring it back tomorrow."

Turning back to Kasey and Ren, Julia said, "You're both covered in sweat and sand." She ran her fingers down their glistening backs. "Why don't you go shower? I'll get the grill going and pull out everything we need for dinner. Later, we can set up the new projector and screen on the deck and watch a movie. Sound good, or would you rather do something else?" she asked as they went inside.

"No, that sounds perfect to me," Kasey replied.

"Me too," added Ren. "We'll be right back. Shit, it's cold in here," he said, grabbing Kasey's hand and heading up the stairs double-time.

Turned on by Kasey's martial arts prowess and his hard abs glistening with sweat, Ren was aggressive and rough, pushing Kasey against the shower's marble tile and peppering his neck with small bites as he whispered how hot he looked sparring.

With testosterone coursing and adrenaline pumping, Kasey spun Ren around, grabbing his wrists and pinning them at his sides. Ren's confidence and dominance had always captivated him, pulling him in and making him bolder than he ever thought possible. "Tell me how much you want me," Kasey's voice, a low growl in Ren's ear, his wet, hard body pressing against Ren's.

"You know how much I want you," Ren murmured, his voice husky, as Kasey bit his neck.

"Show me how much," Kasey ordered.

Ren backed him against the wall, pressing his hard, slick body against Kasey's, hands braced against the tiles on either side. Slowly, he rubbed his body against Kasey's, his kisses fiery and intense. Kasey's fingers twisted deep in Ren's hair, holding him close, not wanting the kisses to end.

With his hand slippery with soap, Ren began to stroke Kasey slowly, his tongue deep in his mouth.

As the warm water cascaded over them in the steamy shower and their soapy hands glided effortlessly over each other, it was fast becoming Kasey's favorite place to be with Ren.

Later that night, the trio snuggled together on the double lounger, smoked some weed, roasted marshmallows, and watched *What We Do in the Shadows*, a comedy about vampires.

After bidding Kasey good night, Julia and Ren settled in her room while Kasey slept in Ren's. As they slipped beneath the covers and cuddled up, her cramps, now mild and infrequent, left her feeling frisky. Drawing him closer, she made her desire clear, her lips grazing his neck as her fingers tangled in his hair.

"You're in a mood I wasn't expecting," Ren murmured, surprised as she nuzzled his neck.

"Sometimes, I get really horny during my period, which sucks because I'm out of commission from the waist down," she said, her voice laced with a hint of disappointment.

"Is it your decision to abstain, or do you think your partner wouldn't like it?" Ren asked.

"I always just assumed no man would want to during my period. I never asked. I really didn't have that many deep relationships where I would be comfortable asking for that."

"You could ask me," he whispered, his voice tempting, as his hand traced her belly.

"Are you sure? It could get really messy—it's my heaviest day."

"That's what towels and showers are for," he reassured, his breath hot against her neck.

"I have to prepare," she said with a grin, rolling away from him. He lay back, propped up on the pillows, watching her. He could hear her using the bidet before returning with two bath towels and a damp washcloth.

"Let me just put these towels down—I don't want to wreck my bed." She placed them side by side, covering a good part of the bed to protect it. Shedding her nightie, she positioned herself on the towels.

"You sure you want to do this?" she asked as he moved over her. "There's no stopping me now, boo," he replied, spreading her legs with his and easing himself inside her. They moved together slowly, assessing and savoring each sensation. The slick, rhythmic sounds each time he pulled back were an unexpected turn-on for him.

"Are you alright?" he whispered, mindful of her comfort.

"It doesn't hurt. Just keep going like this," she encouraged.

"Easy on the boobs, babe—they're a little sore," she said as he squeezed one.

"Sorry, let me kiss that," he said, gently kissing her breast and licking her nipple, noting how different her body was during this time.

"This feels amazing. Go a little faster," she murmured, urging him to pick up the pace, her soft sounds of delight tickling his ear. Giving her exactly what she asked for, they both found more gratification in the experience than anticipated.

As he came and pushed deeper into her, she wrapped her legs around him and felt a gush of warmth between them. As his breathing slowed, she whispered, "Let's check the damage. It felt pretty messy at the end to me," and giggled.

"Relax, things like that don't bother me. I fully expected us to be a bloody mess. Hand me that washcloth."

They both took a look as he rolled off her.

"Oh my God, it looks like OJ was here," Julia said, wide-eyed. Ren let out a laugh. "Only you would think of that right now. You should see your face. It's priceless," he said, surveying the aftermath. "C'mon, let's just jump in the shower." He headed into the bathroom while she rolled up the towels, amazed none of it got on her sheets.

"So, can I wash your hair, or is that something only Kasey does?" Ren asked sweetly as Julia joined him.

"You can wash my hair. I love the way it feels. But first, let me clean you off—you're a mess," she teased. As she gently massaged shampoo into his carefully manscaped hair, he grabbed her hand. "I think I better do that," he said with a smile. "Your touch makes me crazy."

He washed her hair, not fully expecting to enjoy it as much as she did, but was pleasantly surprised. She wrapped her arms around him, her cheek resting against his chest as she subtly pressed her body against him, her wet skin warm and soft. He closed his eyes, savoring the feel of her in his arms, feeling her trust and affection like a quiet warmth that anchored him.

She relished the warm water cascading over her back and the gentle massage of his long fingers on her scalp. After applying conditioner to her hair, he turned her around and gently rubbed her belly while planting tiny kisses on her neck as he waited to rinse her hair.

"That feels so good," she sighed, leaning into him and closing her eyes. After a few minutes of his soothing belly rub and soft kisses on her neck, Julia giggled, "You better rinse my hair before you put me to sleep right here in the shower,"

Toweling off, she said, "I have to put a tampon in. You wanna leave?"

"I don't have to if it doesn't bother you."

She shrugged, "Suit yourself, babe."

Watching her in the mirror as he towel-dried his hair, he saw her put her foot on the edge of the toilet, insert a tampon, toss the applicator in the garbage, and slip on a pair of panties.

"How do you get that out of you?" he asked.

"There's a string that hangs down... see? I can't believe you don't know about this stuff," she said, educating him with a smirk.

"Growing up in a very traditional, close-mouthed family, where would I learn that? I may have learned about sex and things from the internet and friends in college, but periods weren't on my radar. My ex-wife was extremely private about her body, and we didn't share this kind of closeness. I wasn't kidding when I said she slept alone during her time of the month. Japan's a little behind the times with periods; it's not really talked about. But I want to know these things—how it all works for you. The more I find out about you, Jules, the more I want to know."

They got back into bed, and she rested her head on his chest, draping her leg over him and snuggling her body tight against his.

"So, how was it for you? Because for me, it was kind of a turn-on," he asked, pressing a gentle kiss to the top of her head.

"I liked it a lot, as long as it's gentle. Definitely made me forget about my cramps," she said, her fingers brushing lightly over his nipple. "I'd definitely be open to doing that again, as long as I'm feeling it. But next time, I'll need some cheaper towels—yikes, those are going right in the garbage." She sighed contentedly as she squeezed him tightly. "I feel really good right now. Love you, Ren."

"Love you too, baby girl. More than you could know," he said softly, thrilled to have found someone so willing to share herself with him, knowing she had never been comfortable enough to do this with anyone else.

***

The next morning, Julia found herself alone on the deck, savoring a cup of tea while taking in the sights and sounds of her beloved shore. Her gaze drifted down the beach, where she spotted Kasey jogging toward the house.

"You're up early this morning. How are you feeling?" he asked, catching his breath, as he planted a damp kiss on her forehead.

"Much better, thanks. It's beautiful out this morning."

"It is. Perfect running weather," he said, taking a seat beside her. "Did you go to bed with a wet head? Your hair looks like a family of birds is living in it," he teased, brushing her hair back off her face.

"Oh, stop," she chuckled. "It's not that bad."

"Why the late-night shower? Was your back still bothering you?" he asked.

"Nooo," she said, drawing out the word, as her eyes darted away from his gaze, a shy smile on her lips. "Ren and I got a little messy, and we needed a shower. I was too tired to braid it afterward, so I'll just wet it and braid it later."

"Dare I ask how you managed to get messy?" he quipped with amusement.

"Probably best you don't," she replied, a mischievous twinkle in her eye.

"I'm a big boy. You can tell me," he said, his eyes crinkling at the corners as he reached out and gave her thigh a playful squeeze.

"Let's just say our naughty parts created a crime scene, and two good towels had to be sacrificed," Julia said with a grin.

"Really? Gross." He shook his head, laughing. "You two are dangerous together. Why didn't you ever mention to me you'd like to do that?"

"Are you serious, baby?" she laughed. "I think I know you well enough to know that would not be your thing. You just said gross and cringed at the thought of it."

"Well, I'm glad you two have each other. You can be adventurous to your heart's content. Speaking of gross, I need a shower. Care to join me? You can wet your hair and then braid it," he proposed with a sweet smile.

Even though she was enjoying her time alone on the deck, she recognized Kasey's invitation as one of his ways of connecting with her. "Lead the way, baby," she said, getting up. "I'm right behind you."

***

Emerging refreshed, they greeted Ren in the kitchen, where he was busy rummaging through the fridge.

"Morning, guys. I thought we had yogurt in here," Ren said, closing the door.

"Sorry, babe, I think I ate the last one yesterday," Julia apologized.

"That's okay. I'll just grab something else," he replied.

"How about I make you both smoothies? We have a bunch of fruit that has to be used," Kasey offered.

"That sounds great," Ren said, giving Kasey a kiss and tousling his hair. "Morning, Spike." Turning to Julia, he slid his arms around her and pulled her close, resting his forehead against hers as their gazes locked. "And how do you feel this morning?" he asked softly.

"I feel good. Thank you," she said, her voice soft and intimate, drawing him in.

"Should I leave the room?" Kasey said with a raised eyebrow, smiling as he continued to gather ingredients for the smoothies. "But no smoothies then," he teased.

"Sorry, Spike," Ren said with a grin, giving Julia a quick kiss before returning to Kasey's side. "Do we have any plans for today? I was thinking maybe we could go to Point Pleasant. I saw they have a little aquarium and a boardwalk. What do you think?"

"It's a nice little aquarium," Julia said. "We've been there before, and the boardwalk has a great fudge shop. We can grab some sausage and peppers subs. I'm game! Maybe we can arrange a behind-the-scenes tour at the aquarium."

"Sounds like a plan. I'll make a call. We'll aim for around one, so we can head home by five." Kasey agreed.

"Perfect. I'm gonna go soak up some Vitamin D. Call me when the smoothies are ready," Julia said, heading out to the deck.

Ren leaned on his elbow beside Kasey, who was slicing bananas. "So, I hear you two took a little walk on the wild side last night," Kasey said with a curious smile. "How was that? Julia mentioned it after I asked why she went to bed with a wet head."

"It was squishy and messy... but all good and far from the wild side," Ren said, flashing a devilish smile.

"Ugh, gross," Kasey said, crinkling his nose and shaking his head. "You two really are made for each other."

Ren laughed and wrapped his arms around him, resting his head on Kasey's shoulder while watching his nimble fingers take on the rest of the fruit bowl.

"I'm glad you make her so happy. Go be with her—I'll bring the smoothies out when they're ready," Kasey said, nodding toward the deck.

"I'm fine here with you," Ren replied. "Are you trying to get rid of me?" he teased, nuzzling Kasey's neck.

"Not at all, but you can't be doing that while I'm holding a very sharp knife." Kasey set down the knife, took Ren's face in his hands, and kissed him deeply, his tongue exploring with slow intensity. Ren's arms instantly wrapped around Kasey, his hands pressing against the contours of his lower back.

"Wow, that was nice," Ren murmured softly when they finally broke apart.

"Now go sit and pretend to have some kind of self-control," Kasey said, giving him a playful push before turning back to the fruit.

"Yes, sir," Ren replied, sitting opposite Kasey, happily watching him work.

They wrapped up the weekend with a trip to the aquarium, where they got to pet a penguin, enjoyed sausage and peppers subs on the boardwalk, and brought home a box of taffy and fudge.

That night, lying peacefully in Kasey's arms, Julia felt incredibly lucky to be sharing her life with two men who fulfilled her every need. At this point, she couldn't imagine her life without either of them.

***

The following day at the office, Julia ordered an exquisite black titanium band ring embellished with two rows of black pavé diamonds. When it was delivered by messenger that afternoon, she asked Kasey to join her.

They took a seat on the couch in her office, and she began, "I hate that we can't be open about the three of us." She opened the envelope and took out a ring box. "And, as you know, I've been feeling a little jealous lately, so I decided to get something for Ren to wear as a deterrent. I would have gotten one for you, but everyone knows you're my boyfriend, so you don't need this kind of protection." She opened the box and showed Kasey the ring.

Kasey studied the ring thoughtfully. "It's a perfect match for the ID bracelet you gave me," he remarked, glancing at his wrist.

"It's from the same designer. I wasn't planning on that, but..." She smiled. "I couldn't resist."

It's beautiful. I'm sure he'll love it. I'm not averse to putting a sign of commitment on him myself," he said, smiling at Julia. "I can get jealous too."

"Oh, baby," she murmured, pulling him in for a hug. "I never even considered how you might feel about him getting all this attention. Plus, you've got me and him acting like love-sick teenagers around you all the time. God, I can be such a self-centered ass sometimes. I'm sorry," she said, caressing his face.

"Sweetheart, I love seeing you two together. I'd just like to keep it this way—the three of us, perfectly content with each other," Kasey said, his tone reassuring. "Should we call him up here so you can give it to him, or would you rather do it alone?"

"Absolutely bring him up here. Of course, you're a part of this," she replied, squeezing his hand with a smile. Kasey dialed Ren's number and asked him to come up.

"What's up? Ren asked, strolling in and sitting beside Julia on the couch.

"Remember when you said you'd start mentioning you had a partner to discourage unwanted advances?" Julia smiled. "Well, I got you something we think will help with that." Her eyes fixed on him as she handed him the ring box, eagerly watching for his reaction.

As he opened it, she explained, "We thought you could wear it as a reminder that you have a couple that love you very much, even if they can't openly show it... and it's also a good deterrent for others," she said with a smirk.

"A ring? It's stunning, Jules. It looks just like the ID bracelet you gave Kasey." He slipped it on his finger. "A perfect fit. How did you manage that?" he asked, admiring the ring on his hand and glancing at Kasey.

"I snuck in your room last night, took your school ring, traced the inside of it, and hoped for the best," Julia answered, pleased with herself. "Do you like it? Will you wear it?" she asked, hopeful.

Ren's response was filled with emotion. "Of course I'll wear it, starting right now. I absolutely love it and the thought that comes with it. I wish I could hold you both right now and show you how much it means to me," he said, taking her hand. He reached over and squeezed Kasey's thigh.

"I can wait for your thanks until later," Kasey murmured, his gaze flicking to Julia, taking in her pure, unguarded joy. The sight of the two people he loved most, so deeply happy, filled him with a warmth almost too overwhelming to hold. He was head over heels in love with them both, and in this moment, it was almost more than he could take in. "Go— show her in the closet or the bathroom. Take your pick," Kasey grinned. "Just keep it PG. Can you do that?"

"Yes, Kasey, we can do that," Julia replied, feigning exasperation. Then, with a mischievous sparkle in her eyes, she whispered to Ren, "Meet me in the bathroom," before hurrying off.

Turning to Kasey, Ren held up his ring finger and asked, "Did you have any say in this?"

"This was all her idea. But, as I just told Julia, I'm not averse to putting a sign of commitment on you. It'll help keep unwanted advances at bay. We'd both like to keep you to ourselves," Kasey said, his eyes warm with affection. "Go—she's waiting."

"Damn, Spike, you're the best." Ren glanced into Kasey's office and, seeing no one, slipped his hand behind Kasey's head, pulling him close. Planting a quick kiss on Kasey's lips, he gave him a playful slap on the thigh. "I'll thank you properly for this later," he said with a grin before rushing to Julia.

She was already perched on the sink, her skirt hiked up and legs spread. As he entered the bathroom, her eyes sparkled, and her stomach fluttered. She reached out, wrapping her arms and legs around him, drawing him close. They shared a deep, hungry kiss, his lips moving with an intensity that sent shivers through her. Her fingers tangled in his hair, holding him close as his hands gripped her waist, pulling her even tighter. She could feel his breath mingling with hers, each kiss building with a need that left her lightheaded.

They pulled back for a moment, their eyes meeting as the significance of this moment settled between them, unspoken but deeply felt.

"Thank you for the ring, Jules. That was so sweet," he murmured as Julia's affectionate kisses moved to his neck.

"I'm so glad you like it. And I don't care how influential Raven is; she best respect the ring—or we will be throwing down… figuratively speaking," Julia grinned, flashing her baby blues.

"You're so feisty," he chuckled. "I have to go now, or I won't be able to for a while," he said, adjusting himself. Lifting her off the sink, he added, "Go. Make sure no one's out there. Wait." He pulled her close, hugging her tight. "I love you," he whispered.

"I love you too," she replied softly. She turned and left, leaving Ren to reflect for a moment on the depth of Julia's love and the token of commitment from both of them now resting on his finger.

That night, their schedule had Julia sleeping alone, but they decided to spend the night together. Since she still had her period and had no desire to gross out Kasey, they fell asleep with their limbs entwined after exchanging words of love and lingering kisses. Wrapped in each other's arms, they drifted off together, feeling the deep comfort of their shared connection.

***

The next night, as Ren came into the living room to show off his outfit before leaving to pick up Raven for the fashion show, Julia remarked, "You look so hot." He was leaving to pick Raven up for the fashion show and was showing off his outfit. He wore a black Alexander McQueen evening cape with no shirt, tailored cigarette trousers in shark gray, and thick-tread Chelsea boots.

"Too hot to be going out with her," she murmured, a playful pout on her lips as she wrapped her arms around him.

"Now, now," Ren reassured her. "I'll be back before you know it. This is all for the business, nothing more—and now I'm armed with this." He held up his ring finger.

"I trust you. Honestly, I do," she said, though her anxiety was off the charts. "I don't trust her or her wandering hands. Just... make sure she knows you have a significant other. Nip this in the bud. Once she knows, Rex will know. Then he'll come to us for the right reasons, and you won't be bait anymore."

She managed a small smile, brushing a piece of fuzz off his cape. "Have a good time, but not too good. If she invites you to an after-party, be careful—they can get out of hand. And don't leave your drink unattended."

"Jules, I'm a grown man. I can take care of myself. Don't worry, sweetie," he said, giving her a soft squeeze on the shoulder.

"Fine, I'll try not to worry," she said, looking up at him, her eyes betraying her. "Oh, and don't forget to say something nice about Nigel and Giles if you get the chance. You know how much they loved what you said about them before."

The doorbell rang, and Kasey answered it as Julia kissed Ren goodbye, her lips lingering on his. Charley watched as Ren gave Kasey a quick peck in the foyer before following her to the car.

"Relax, he'll be fine. He's very capable in social situations," Kasey said, guiding Julia back into the living room as she stood watching Ren leave.

"I dunno, Kasey. How many bold, successful American women have thrown themselves at him? Lemme see, just one so far—me. And he was like a horny teenage boy in my, let's say, more experienced hands. I'm afraid, no matter how faithful he thinks he is, it's gonna be seriously tested for the first time tonight." Raven looks at Ren the way I did at the dance party. You haven't been around her like I have. I'm telling you, I feel her vibes. Even with the ring, if Ren doesn't make it clear that it matters, she won't back off. I hope I'm wrong… but I doubt it," she said with a sigh.

"I think you're wrong," Kasey said firmly. "Ren wanted you; that's why he was so willing. He doesn't want her. You need to trust him—I do. Come on, let's go make some cookies and watch a movie. He'll be back before you know it."

He took her hand and led her into the kitchen. "And remember, from this point on, he's wearing a ring, which should put a stop to most unwanted advances. But you know, temptation is always there. I see how men react to you—you're innately flirtatious and charming. Still, I don't worry because

I know you love me, and the moment it goes too far, you shut it down. Give Ren a chance to prove he's just as capable of shutting Raven down," Kasey said, giving her a reassuring look.

"You're right. I don't want to think about it anymore. Do we have chocolate chips? Let's make some chocolate chip cookies," she said, checking the cabinet as she tried to put thoughts of Raven out of her mind.

***

As the sleek town car glided through the streets toward the venue, the atmosphere inside was thick with Raven's palpable attraction to Ren. From the moment she stepped into the car, her magnetic charm and flirtatious energy enveloped him. Her subtle touches and suggestive remarks—clear signs of her attraction, were met with Ren's gentle yet firm deflections. Seemingly undeterred, she complimented his fashion choice, her fingers tracing the contours of his bare chest beneath his cape.

Ren took this moment to gently explain that he was in a committed relationship, discreetly displaying his ring. Explaining that it had been repaired and he'd just gotten it back, he apologized for any misunderstanding. Disappointment clouding her features, she gracefully accepted his explanation, expressing mild embarrassment over her aggressive pursuit. He assured her it was extremely flattering to receive attention from such a beautiful, accomplished woman, laying on his charm and helping her feel comfortable with him again.

***

Upon arrival, they were immediately thrust into the whirlwind of flashing cameras and probing questions from eager reporters. With confidence and style, Ren navigated the gauntlet, artfully fielding inquiries and making sure to mention the positive influence of the Hawthorne brothers.

Inside, the crowd buzzed with anticipation as the show unfolded. The venue hummed with energy as models strutted down the runway, showcasing cutting-edge designs. Amid the stylish throng, Ren and Raven watched with keen interest, occasionally exchanging knowing glances as they absorbed the creativity on display. Thanks to Raven's influence, they had a brief encounter with the designer, further elevating Ren's status within the inner circles of the fashion elite.

As they were leaving, Raven invited Ren to an exclusive after-party, tantalizing him with promises of illustrious guests. However, he politely declined, citing a headache and asking for a rain check.

The night concluded with a bittersweet air as Raven expressed her disappointment in Ren's unavailability romantically, but she also conveyed a desire to cultivate a friendship, appreciating him beyond the realm of romance. With promises of future collaborations, their evening ended on a note of mutual respect, leaving the door open for a different kind of connection to grow. She knew that as Ren's prominence rose, it would only benefit her to maintain a professional friendship.

***

Ren called ahead to let them know he was on his way home, and both Julia and Kasey met him at the door.

"How was the show?" Kasey asked as they settled on the couch. Ren animatedly recounted his experience, detailing the sights, sounds, and interactions, including his brief encounter with the designer. Julia listened quietly, patiently waiting for the only part she was truly interested in.

Unable to contain herself any longer, she finally blurted, "So, did Raven behave herself?" Ren and Kasey burst out laughing, and Ren teased, "I was wondering how long it would take for you to ask."

"Baby," he said, pulling her close, "everything's fine. She took it like a champ. She wasn't thrilled at first, but she got over it. She knows we can both benefit professionally from staying friendly. And she respected the ring. Thank you again for giving it to me. It made a difference. You feel better?" he asked, holding her tight.

"Yes, I feel better. I'm glad you had a good time, and she didn't make it too uncomfortable for you."

"I'm gonna go change real quick," Ren announced as he gave her a quick peck on the forehead before heading up the stairs.

"You see? You worried for nothing. I told you he could handle it," Kasey said, giving Julia a reassuring smile as she sighed and rested her head on his shoulder. "I know we switched nights yesterday, but if you'd like to sleep with Ren tonight, I don't mind. I think you need him more than I do."

She sat up, "Really? You wouldn't mind? You don't have to give up your time with him."

"Go. I could use some alone time—it's what I need," he insisted, giving her a warm smile and a kiss before sending her on her way.

Just as she reached Ren's door, he opened it, and she reached out to him, her arms encircling his neck as she pulled him close. He lifted her up, and she wrapped her legs around him, their lips meeting in a frenzy of kisses as he closed the door and carried her to his bed.

"Aren't you supposed to be sleeping alone tonight?" he teased as they both quickly removed their clothes. "Did you bribe Spike to get in here?" he asked with a grin.

"I didn't have to. He could tell I wanted to be with you, so he said he wanted some alone time. Should I have said no and insisted he be with you?" Julia asked, pulling him close, her naked body pressing against his, her fingers gliding through his hair.

"He doesn't say things he doesn't mean. I think we both need to understand that. He also needs a lot more alone time than we do." Ren cupped her face in his hands. "Maybe we should just accept that and stop feeling guilty," he said, flashing her a seductive grin. "Starting right now. Hop on, baby girl, and let's not think of anything but making each other feel good." He rolled onto his back, fully erect, waiting for her to mount him.

As Kasey lay in bed reading, he could hear the muffled sounds of their happy chatter, Julia's giggles, and their shared moans. Smiling to himself, he shook his head in contentment, knowing that the two people he loved the most were blissfully happy. The following night, Kasey slept with Ren and the next with Julia. Both made sure he felt their love, showering him with their undivided attention.

Chapter 21: Brothers Abroad

On Sunday, Julia's condo buzzed with activity, welcoming both the brothers and their guests. The trio had spent all of Saturday perfecting the final touches, from arranging beautiful flowers to preparing welcome bags filled with treats and essentials. Julia eagerly anticipated reuniting with Nigel and Giles, having forged a strong connection with them during her time in London.

The brothers entered with the easy grace of men accustomed to fine surroundings yet without a hint of pretension. Both were tall and distinguished, carrying an age-defying presence that turned heads, especially for men of seventy. Despite being identical twins, subtle differences set them apart: Nigel's silver hair was neatly combed back, his reserved demeanor underscoring his calm, watchful nature, while Giles had a touch more flair, with a casual grin and slightly tousled hair that hinted at his mischievous side. Their speech held the refined accents of upper-class Britain but was softened by a warmth and openness that Julia had cherished from the start.

What began as business-focused calls had evolved into a blend of professional and personal interactions. After the loss of her family, their offer of sanctuary at their villa on Mustique, along with their attentive check-ins, deepened the friendship, making them feel like indulgent, caring uncles. They were among the first to hear about Julia and Kasey's relationship and were thrilled for them.

Meeting Gunther for the first time, Julia was struck by his striking looks and attentive nature toward Giles. At fifty-five, the tall, well-built, blond-haired man looked years younger. Though he had lived in England since he was twenty-five, his thick German accent remained.

Rounding out the group were Haruto Makino and his granddaughter, Akira. Haruto, a former tailor turned influential investor in the Hawthorne brothers' fashion house, was a man of quiet dignity and refinement. At sixty-eight and of shorter stature, he possessed a calm, wise presence with looks reminiscent of Ken Watanabe. Kasey and Ren greeted him with deep bows, which Haruto returned with a warm smile, clearly pleased to see Kasey again.

Akira, fresh out of university in Tokyo, stood beside her grandfather with a poised, modern style all her own. Petite and porcelain-skinned, with long, dark hair and expressive eyes, she embodied the graceful energy of young, trendy Japanese women. Her presence added a touch of youthfulness to the gathering, and she watched the lively scene unfold with a quiet, observant charm.

Despite Julia's attempt to keep greetings brief, knowing everyone would be tired from the time change and long trip, her warm welcome and lively conversations kept the group up well past midnight, London time.

***

The next morning at nine, Julia, Kasey, and Ren led the group on a comprehensive tour of Master's Inc., showcasing the inner workings of the merged entity. This personalized tour allowed Nigel and Giles to see firsthand how their legacy brand was integrated with Ren's innovative strategies.

An entire floor was dedicated to offices for Ren and the collaborating designers, featuring a spacious workroom and a smaller showroom complete with a runway. During the two-hour tour, Ren shared his creative vision with the brothers, presenting sketches and fabric swatches that reinvented 70's casual wear, which they enthusiastically embraced. Nigel and Giles, once young, impressionable fashion school graduates, were thrilled, their enthusiasm sparking nostalgic discussions about the era's trends—a wild blend of 60s hippie culture and the emerging disco scene. Julia and Kasey observed from the sidelines, impressed by how Ren captivated the brothers with his passion for menswear and his respect for their legacy.

At one, they joined the board members for lunch, with Kasey arranging a specially prepared meal in one of the larger conference rooms. Amid mingling and conversation, Nigel raised a toast to Ren as the new Creative Director, expressing his optimism for their joint venture. Julia reciprocated, welcoming the group to New York and encouraging them to visit whenever they could.

After the meal, as everyone chatted with Nigel and Giles, Julia took the opportunity to privately discuss her proposal to promote Kasey to Vice President of New Acquisitions with Jack and Rick. They readily agreed, confident the rest of the board and senior management would have no objections, given Kasey's proven track record, his role in acquiring the fashion house, and his MBA credentials.

As lunch concluded, everyone left with a sense that the merger would be a huge success. Julia then sent the group back to the condo to rest and prepare for their night out on the town.

***

Securing box seats for a performance of *Chicago*—the only show running on Broadway's traditionally dark Monday night—the group arrived in style in a luxurious stretch limo, with Carl and Charley serving as both bodyguards and drivers for the evening.

Inside the theater, the atmosphere was electric as the group settled into their plush seats, anticipation building for the performance. The brothers, known for their love of theater in London, were about to experience the magic of Broadway for the first time in over a decade since their last visit to New York City. Julia, wearing a confident smile, was determined to make this a memorable evening for her esteemed guests.

She exchanged smiles with Kasey and squeezed his hand as they watched Giles sing along with the music while Nigel tapped his knee to the beat, both sporting broad smiles. Even the usually reserved Gunther seemed to be enjoying himself, sharing happy looks with Giles.

It was Akira's first visit to America, and Julia could see she was thoroughly captivated. Mesmerized by everything around her, she eagerly pointed out noteworthy sights in the expansive theater, whispering excitedly in her grandfather's ear. He smiled warmly and gently guided her to refrain from pointing.

After an exhilarating performance, the curtains fell, and thunderous applause reverberated through the theater. Overflowing with excitement, Julia led her companions backstage for a memorable surprise. Just before heading back, Kasey handed out three beautiful bouquets—one each to Nigel, Giles, and Haruto.

The three main cast members warmly greeted the visitors, their faces flushed and dewy from the demanding

517

performance, prompting delighted smiles from the brothers. They presented their flowers to the two leading ladies, with Haruto allowing Akira to present the bouquet to the leading man before offering a deep bow himself.

Nigel, exuding sophistication, engaged in lively conversation with the leading ladies, expressing his admiration for their talent. Giles, equally enthralled, shared anecdotes about their theater experiences in London, revealing a shared passion for the performing arts. Haruto, ever-polite, nodded appreciatively while his vibrant granddaughter eagerly shared her excitement with the leading man.

As laughter filled the air, Julia joined in, expressing her pleasure at sharing this magical Broadway experience with her English business partners. Nigel and Giles, visibly pleased, expressed their gratitude for the opportunity to meet the talented cast. Charmed by the brothers' posh British manners and genuine admiration for their craft, the cast members enjoyed the brief meet-and-greet as much as everyone else.

Thrilled by the interaction, the group headed to The Lambs Club for a late-night meal, where wine and spirits flowed freely, accompanied by lively conversation. As the night concluded, Carl chauffeured the group back to the condo, everyone exhausted but elated by the day's experiences.

***

"What a great first day!" Julia exclaimed as the trio got back into the limo after ensuring their guests were settled.

As they pulled away, a buzzed Julia raised the divider, flashing Carl and Charley an apologetic yet sly grin. "Sorry—it's the stretch." Turning to her partners, a rush of heat surged through her, radiating from her hardened nipples down to her core, sparking an intense desire for one thing.

"So, who's giving and who's receiving?" she teased. Her smile—wicked. "Because we're doing this right here, right now—and we've got less than thirty minutes."

"Challenge accepted, and I'm definitely giving," Ren replied with a devilish grin widening as he slipped onto the floor, taking a giggling Julia with him. He nestled her between Kasey's legs and positioned himself behind her.

"And I thought I only had one horny teenager to deal with, but you're just as bad, if not worse than her," Kasey smirked at Ren as Julia unzipped his pants, finding him almost fully erect.

"You may not be as rowdy as we are, but you are just as horny, baby," she purred, licking her lips before enveloping him. A low, drawn-out "Mmm" escaped his lips as he closed his eyes, his head slowly dropping back against the seat.

Ren eagerly slipped his hand under Julia's mini-skirt and slid her panties down. He wet his fingers and eased them inside her, receiving a soft gasp in return. She held on to Kasey's thigh to balance herself in the moving car as her mouth and hand worked in unison.

Unzipping and wiping his slick fingers over himself, Ren gripped her hips tightly and thrust upward.

A deep, muffled moan escaped Julia as she momentarily stopped, her eyes closed, savoring the sensation before resuming her enthusiastic blow job. Each time Ren pushed hard into her, a pleased hum escaped her lips, the vibrations only increasing Kasey's pleasure. When Ren increased his pace, and Julia's mouth followed along, Kasey lost control, gripping her hair tight in his fingers as he came, softly cursing, "Holy shit."

She pressed her face into Kasey's thigh to muffle her rhythmic moans as she clung to his legs, her nails digging into his flesh as Ren drove into her vigorously. The sound of their bare skin smacking against each other heightening the thrill of the fast-paced erotic encounter. Mindful of their surroundings, Ren let out two low grunts as he finished, pressing hard into her with each one, winking at Kasey, who grinned and blushed in response.

"Pull yourselves together," Kasey urged moments later, addressing Ren and Julia as they giggled on the floor, inspecting Julia's red knees. "We're nearly home. And crack a window," he added with a grin as he opened his own, "it reeks of sex in here."

Ren laughed, helping Julia off the floor and opening a window.

Minutes later, Charley opened the door as Kasey took Julia's hand to help her out of the limo. Ren followed, resting his hand on her back, their playful banter spilling into the house as they made their way inside.

Since it was Julia's night with Ren, he scooped her up and tossed her over his shoulder as they stepped through the door. With a mischievous glint and Julia's panties tucked in his pocket, he shot Kasey a grin. "Good night, Spike. I'm not done with this one yet." Julia let out a sharp gasp and giggle as he smacked her on the ass, leaving no doubt their night was far from over.

"Good night, Kasey, love you!" she called out distractedly as Ren slid his hand under her skirt.

"Good night, you two. Don't forget—we're meeting everyone for breakfast at the condo," he reminded, ever the responsible one.

***

Tuesday began with a relaxed morning, giving everyone time to recharge over a leisurely breakfast. They then embarked on a private tour of the Cooper Hewitt Smithsonian Design

Museum, taking in its latest exhibitions. The group admired the awe-inspiring Andrew Carnegie Mansion, its English Georgian country house architecture leaving them duly impressed. After a few hours of exploring and engaging in intriguing conversations with the museum director—Julia's sizable donation ensuring his attention—they returned to the condo, while the trio headed back to the brownstone to unwind before their dinner reservation at Le Bernardin that evening.

***

Despite its prestigious reputation, the restaurant's ambiance was inviting and cozy, enhanced by soft, strategically placed lighting that created a cozy, welcoming glow. Their table was elegantly set with crisp white linens and sparkling silverware, setting the scene for an unforgettable dining experience.

The seafood feast—a hallmark of Le Bernardin— showcased the restaurant's commitment to an unparalleled culinary journey. From succulent oysters to flawlessly prepared lobster, each dish was a testament to Chef Ripert's artistry. Midway through their exceptional meal, the atmosphere grew even more enchanting as Chef Ripert himself made a gracious appearance at their table. With a warm smile, he acknowledged the Hawthorne brothers, recognizing their esteemed status in menswear, and regaled the group with culinary anecdotes and charm. In turn, the brothers expressed their admiration for Chef Ripert's expertise, grateful to Julia for arranging such a memorable dining experience.

Once again, they returned to the condo with full bellies and lasting memories. Julia engaged in lively conversation with Nigel and Giles while Gunther quietly attended to them. Kasey and Haruto listened to Ren and Akira's animated discussion about new fashion trends in Tokyo. It didn't escape Julia's or Kasey's notice that Akira seemed particularly drawn to Ren, subtly vying for his attention during outings and consistently finding ways to be near him. Julia also began to notice that when Ren had a bit too much beer, he became a little louder, a little more flirtatious, and the life of the party.

On the ride home, Julia brought up Akira, prompting a lighthearted discussion. "So, you might wanna dial back the charm with Akira," she suggested, her fingers trailing down Ren's leg. "Looks like she's taken a liking to you, and she doesn't respect the ring."

Ren flashed a grin, taking her hand. "You really don't miss a thing, do you?"

Kasey chimed in, "It was pretty obvious. She nearly knocked me over in a mad dash to sit next to you in the theater and did the same at dinner tonight—poor Giles got caught in the crossfire. Did anyone else notice?"

"I've noticed her interest, but I'm just being myself. I'm not encouraging it. I turn around, and there she is," Ren said, a little dismayed. "I'm just being friendly because of who she is and the visit. Maybe you guys could try playing a bit more defense for me."

"Nothing I'd love more," Julia said with a grin, "but I'm too wrapped up in Nigel and Giles. They've been showing a different side of themselves since they've been here. They can really let loose over a good meal and drinks. Apparently, they had some pretty wild times in London during the 70's. And they absolutely love your idea of the 70's casual wear. Giles told me he even did a few sketches and how excited it made him. Brilliant idea, babe," she said, giving Ren's hand a squeeze. Turning to Kasey, she warned, "I'm afraid it's on you to play defense—she's probably gonna be even more of a problem at the shore."

"Don't worry, it's three against one—we should be able to handle her. All for one, and one for all," he said with a smile, placing his hand on Julia's, with Ren reaching over and placing his hand on top.

"Chill, baby. I'll try not to be so irresistible." Ren grinned, pulling Julia close and planting a kiss on her head. A small burp slipped out, followed by Julia's giggle.

"Excuse me." She continued, "I'm sorry, but I'll never relax when there's a fox in the henhouse. That's what I get for falling for incredibly handsome and desirable men—there's always gonna be a fox lurking." She snuggled into Ren's arms, her legs finding their way onto Kasey's lap. "Just a heads up—I will lose my shit if I have to watch her all over you. I just got over Raven. If she doesn't behave—"

Ren interrupted her," You're so feisty, always ready to fight for us. I love that about you." He toyed with her hair. "Relax, everything will be fine. We just have to make sure I'm not alone with her. It shouldn't be that hard, right?"

"That's what she said," Julia quipped as Ren laughed and started to tickle her.

"No, stop!" she protested, giggling as she pushed his hands away. "I feel bloated from drinking all that champagne. Do not tickle me. I cannot be held responsible for what may happen." She quickly sat up. "Now you made my stomach all gurguly," she mumbled. "Are we almost home?"

Kasey grinned, "Gurguly? That doesn't sound good. We're almost there, less than five minutes. Think you can manage not to blow until then?" he teased.

Julia burst out laughing. "Don't make me laugh now; My stomach is killing me." She leaned forward, holding her stomach, and at that point, with no choice, her body took over, and—she farted. And not just a dainty, barely-there one either. It was monumental—long and loud. She covered her face with her hands and said, "Well, that was not ladylike. I'm so embarrassed; excuse me." Kasey and Ren, already laughing hysterically, just lost it as Julia sat there, red-faced and smirking. "I blame you two."

"That was epic," Ren laughed, wrapping his arms around her. "I didn't know you had that much air in that little body. Don't be embarrassed," he said, nuzzling her neck.

"Of course I'm embarrassed. I've never even heard you guys burp in front of me. I was raised around cowboys who had absolutely no shame in burping or farting in front of me, and only because of my mother do I have any compulsion to control myself and act like a lady, as she would put it. I've been doing a good job till now," she smiled. "She would have been so embarrassed for me, and my dad would have congratulated me." Their continued laughter filled the limo.

"Don't be silly; it's no big deal hearing the real you slip out," Kasey teased, a wide smile on his face.

"Can you burp the alphabet?" Ren asked, grinning.

"Are you both done?" She folded her arms and sat back between them, feigning annoyance.

"Are you?" Kasey quipped, making Ren laugh and earning a side-eye from Julia.

Up front, Carl and Charley exchanged looks at the sound of boisterous laughter coming from the back; she couldn't help but think they always seemed so happy together.

As they bid good night to Charley on the stoop, Kasey leaned in and whispered to Julia, "Do you need a moment out here in the fresh air before you come in?"

"You're never gonna lemme live this down, are you?" Julia said with a poke to Kasey's ribs.

"Eventually," Kasey grinned. "But not right now."

***

524

Julia walked into Kasey's bedroom after saying goodnight to Ren, slipped into bed, and rested her head on his chest.

"Kidding aside, I don't think I'm in any shape for any more air to be pumped into me. Do you mind if we just snuggle tonight? Like this? I don't think you wanna spoon me. I just took some gas medicine. Hopefully, there won't be a repeat, but I can't guarantee it."

He could tell she was still slightly embarrassed, which was unusual for her.

"Sweetheart, I was just teasing you. Just because I don't do it in front of you doesn't mean I have a problem with you doing it—especially when you physically have no control over it. And of course we can just snuggle. I love just cuddling with you. We don't have to have sex every time we sleep together. I know you almost always want to, but I'm just as happy and content just sleeping next to you."

"Well, by the same token, you need to tell me if you'd like to just cuddle. It's not like I don't get enough sex," she grinned. "I thought I had a high sex drive—but that boy is insatiable. Not that I'm complaining," she chuckled softly.

After a moment, she proclaimed, "We're so lucky to all have each other. Everyone gets what they need."

"We really are," Kasey said. "It's the rule of three."

"What's the rule of three?"

"It's a principle that suggests a trio of events or characters is more effective and satisfying than other numbers. It's a concept that's used in various fields. Three provides a sense of completeness and satisfaction," he explained.

"Well, that rule certainly applies to us. I know I'm completely satisfied," she giggled. "You're so smart, Kasey. How do you know these things?"

"I read, sweetheart," he said, giving her a squeeze. "Oh, sorry. Wouldn't want to have to get up and put on the air purifier."

"Kasey!" she yelled, delivering a playful jab to his ribs. "You know, Ren is such a bad influence on your sense of humor."

He laughed, fending off her attempts to give him a "purple nurple," which only stopped when he grabbed her wrists, rolled her onto her back, and kissed her.

"Good night, my little hot-air balloon," he said with a grin.

"Oh my God, you are such a jerk," she giggled, her cheeks flushing pink. "Good night, baby," she said, snuggling up close.

***

On Wednesday, marking the group's final day in the city, Kasey orchestrated a memorable limo tour through Greenwich Village, SoHo, and the East Village, culminating in Tribeca. Throughout the journey, accompanied by Charley, their discreet shadow, they intermittently stepped out of the limo to fully immerse themselves in the unique atmosphere of each neighborhood, collecting souvenirs and embracing their roles as tourists. They explored eclectic shops in the East Village and visited upscale boutiques in SoHo.

In Greenwich Village, Julia and Kasey proudly showcased their alma mater, NYU, pointing out the beautiful campus and the iconic Washington Square Arch. The tour concluded at Kasey's home, where he and Alice served a Latin-inspired lunch. When they finished, the group's attention shifted to Kasey's training room, where Haruto paused, captivated by the gleaming katana mounted on the wall.

"This is remarkable craftsmanship," Haruto murmured, stepping closer. His hand hovered just shy of the blade as he took in every detail. "Is it Japanese steel?"

Kasey nodded, a hint of pride in his voice as he lifted the sword and presented it to Haruto. "This sword was made by Yoshihara Yoshindo." Haruto eyes lit up as he held the magnificent sword in his hands. "I've heard of him; he is a master swordsmith."

"I spoke with him directly when I commissioned it. It took four months to get it here. It even has my name engraved on the nakago. Ren and I are going to take lessons on handling it. I took some a few years ago when I got it. It'll be special now to do it with Ren. Time to commission a new one," Kasey said with a glance at Ren.

The home's serene Japanese aesthetic and the intricate crane carvings on Kasey's bedroom fireplace sparked another long conversation between Kasey and Haruto. Haruto's eyes lingered on the carved cranes. "These are beautiful, Kasey. You have an appreciation for tradition."

Kasey gave a small smile, glancing at the fireplace. "It's calming, and I appreciate the meaning behind it."

Though deep in conversation with Giles, Julia couldn't help but notice Kasey's pride in showing off his home to Haruto.

The group also learned that Ren lived at the brownstone with Kasey and Julia, a dynamic shaped by Kasey and Ren's friendship from high school. Julia and Kasey's relationship was already familiar to everyone, Nigel and Giles being among the first Julia confided in.

***

In a grand gesture, Julia had arranged for the company helicopter to whisk the group away to the Jersey shore, complete with an aerial tour of the city. The excitement was palpable as their guests boarded the helicopter, their faces a mix of anticipation and wonder—none of them had ever felt the thrill of a helicopter ride before. Julia handed out sleek headsets, sparking a new level of enthusiasm. Nigel requested an inside seat, excited but slightly nervous, while Akira specifically asked for a window seat, spending the entire flight capturing photos and videos with her new smartphone, a gift from her grandfather for joining him on the trip.

As the helicopter lifted, gasps and laughter filled the cabin. Akira pressed her phone to the window, snapping shot after shot, while Nigel gripped his seat with wide eyes, exclaiming, "This is brilliant—terrifying, but brilliant!" Below, Manhattan unfurled like a bustling miniature: each landmark pointed out by Kasey or Julia bringing new waves of awe. Ren and the guests were captivated by the bird's-eye view of the magnificent Manhattan skyline and the vastness of Central Park, its lush greenery crisscrossed with winding paths that led to the Central Park Zoo. The sixty-minute helicopter ride wasn't just a mode of transportation but a remarkable adventure in its own right.

***

Awaiting them at the airport were two of Julia's customary four-door convertibles. She drove Giles, Gunther, and Ren, while Kasey followed behind with Nigel, Haruto, and Akira. Upon arrival, the guests paused to admire Julia's vintage beach home, captivated by the charm of the Jersey Shore.

"Your home is simply marvelous," Nigel remarked, gazing out over the Atlantic. "Tell me, why didn't you look for a place in the Hamptons or somewhere like that? The New Jersey Shore is a unique choice."

"I came here with friends one summer and loved it," Julia explained. "The Hamptons and places like that aren't for me—

too many snooty people. I prefer the down-to-earth atmosphere of the Jersey Shore. Plus, I bought this house on my own, and it was a fraction of the cost of anything half its size in the Hamptons. It needed major renovations and some love, but that's what made it mine. Just last week, we screened in the deck, put up the fence, and added security."

"You did a beautiful job; the home is lovely, inside and out," Giles added.

"Thank you," Julia replied, beaming. "This is my favorite place to be." Julia continued the tour, assigning bedrooms for their stay.

The group expressed delight at the home's informal, relaxing atmosphere and soon changed into their beach and casual attire. They were thrilled to find gift bags in their rooms, each filled with sunscreen, bug repellent, sunglasses, and a white or tan Panama hat laid out on the bed.

As he examined his gift bag, Giles smiled and remarked, "Julia, you think of everything. You truly know how to make your guests feel welcomed."

Julia smiled. "Thank you, Giles. I got my hostessing skills from my mother." She thought, with a quiet sense of pride, that her mother would be pleased to know some of those skills had stuck.

***

The first evening began simply, with everyone gathering on the deck to enjoy cocktails and conversation. For dinner, a buffet from A Shore Delight was expertly grilled on the deck by Chef Marco's sous chef, Andy. Kasey had hired Andy for two hours to bring his own menu, complete with ingredients, which he prepared to perfection on-site. The group served themselves from a spread of grilled Chilean sea bass, roast chicken, wild mushroom risotto, truffle mashed potatoes, roasted asparagus, and a vibrant summer salad—each bite more delightful than the last.

To finish the meal on a sweet note, they indulged in a decadent chocolate mousse drizzled with raspberry coulis, a generous addition from the restaurant owner, Scott.

After dinner, Kasey took a leisurely stroll on the beach with Haruto and Akira. As they walked along the shoreline, the gentle lull of the waves provided a soothing backdrop to their conversation. Kasey shared anecdotes about his time at NYU's Stern School of Business, weaving tales of academic challenges and triumphs. Haruto, listening intently, nodding, and occasionally interjecting with insightful questions or reflections. As they spoke in their shared language of Japanese, the bond that had already begun to form was strengthened by their mutual exchange of experiences and respect. Listening quietly to the two men, Akira realized this evening stroll was more than a casual outing—it was a moment of genuine connection.

From the deck, the others savored the twilight hues as night descended. They soaked in the last rays of the summer sun as it cast a golden glow over the Atlantic, painting the sky in shades of orange and purple.

Julia couldn't help but notice the close bond between Gunther and the brothers, particularly with Giles. He attended to him with a familiarity akin to that of a long-term partner, attuned to his every mood and need. Though always professional and reserved around others, she noticed more than a few exchanged glances between the two and Gunther's gentle disapproval whenever Giles had too much to drink.

While standing in the corner of the living room, Julia discussed the sleeping arrangements with Ren, unaware that Giles had quietly slipped in to use the bathroom. Startled, she turned to see Giles entering the room on his way back to the deck, catching her and Ren holding hands and speaking softly in the corner.

"Don't let me stop you," Giles said with a sly smile, joining them. "So, tell me. What's the story? I'm not daft—I know there's something going on between the three of you. Do tell; nothing will shock me."

Julia explained their intricate situation. "Kasey, Ren, and I are romantically involved. We love each other, but we're keeping our unconventional arrangement under wraps for now, for professional reasons. Navigating the conservative dynamics of my board and unpredictable public opinion requires careful handling. It's really hard to hide our affection, especially at home and during our personal time, but discretion is essential until both the fashion house and Ren are more firmly established."

She sighed. "I gave Ren this ring as a subtle deterrent against unwanted advances, but it's not always effective. Watching Akira go after him while I'm right here is tough. Turns out I'm a pretty jealous woman, and it's not a good look." Ren gave her a wry smile as she glanced at Giles, lamenting, "It's just frustrating."

"Bloody hell, I knew it. Sometimes, the way you two gaze at each other, it's as if you're the only souls in the room. That look is going to be hard to hide." Giles offered her an understanding hug. "You know, Nigel and I faced similar challenges all our lives. Fifty years ago, being gay was tolerated somewhat in creative fields like the arts, fashion, and theater, but it was seen as more of a novelty than an accepted lifestyle. If your homosexuality became public knowledge, well, that invariably became the foremost aspect of your identity. We never disclosed our truth to the public and tried to balance a fine line between both worlds. We kept our relationship with Gunther concealed, never revealing that he meant more to us than simply our valet.

"Do tell," Julia said with a curious smile.

Giles smiled. "He was one of our catalog models. He began a relationship with Nigel, and after moving in with us, he started splitting his time between the two of us. After years together, Nigel and Gunther's physical connection faded when Nigel met someone new, but their friendship remained strong. Gunther has been my partner for thirty years now. It's always bothered me that I couldn't openly name him as my partner, but it never seemed the right time. Gunther also wishes to stay under the radar. He's a very private man."

"Wow, thirty years—that's quite an achievement," Ren remarked, genuinely impressed.

"Does Haruto know about you and Gunther?" Julia asked.

"Of course, he's been a friend of ours for over fifty years and our business partner for twenty-eight. Haruto is not as reserved as you might think. Get that man on a karaoke stage, and you'll see what I mean," Giles chuckled.

Julia shot a mischievous grin at Ren. "Karaoke, you say? I think we can arrange a little surprise for Haruto later." Then, with a hint of disappointment in her voice, she said, "I wish we could just be ourselves, knowing you guys would understand. But Akira is a wild card. I don't know if she can be trusted with that information, and we can't risk exposure until we're ready."

"She might be a tad envious that you have two charming chaps all to yourself, and I must confess, I share that sentiment," Giles teased, winking at Ren, who returned the gesture with a pleased grin. "However, I highly doubt she'd do anything to tarnish her grandfather's honor. Honor means the world to Haruto. Still, I could have a word with her. I've known her since she was born, and I could make her understand the ramifications of revealing this secret. I'm sure she'll understand. You shouldn't have to hide, especially in your own bloody home."

"That would be a big help, but I think I should tell her, and you can remind her of her familial responsibility in keeping it quiet. We'll tag team her," Julia said with a grin as she took Giles's arm and headed for the deck. Rejoining the others, Julia eagerly awaited Akira's return, gearing up for the conversation ahead.

While she waited, she leaned in and whispered to Giles, asking if he, his brother, or Haruto would mind if they smoked some weed, adding it was legal in New Jersey.

"Smoke it if you got it, love," Giles replied with a grin, relishing the fact that she was so comfortable with him. Without nieces, nephews, or grandchildren, he cherished the closeness he shared with Julia. "None of us mind. We've dabbled with it off and on since the 70s. Haruto, on the other hand, never tried it until he had a course of chemo for an early-detected cancer, and it helped him with the side effects. He'll never judge. It's Akira we need to have that chat with; she's old enough to understand the situation and the need for discretion."

"What happens at the shore, stays at the shore," Julia quipped, giving Giles a sly grin before heading off to fetch a blunt and an ashtray.

Kasey, Haruto, and Akira returned from their stroll to find Julia and the others sharing a blunt, engaged in spirited conversation over the wild fashions of the 70s, scrolling through images on Ren's laptop.

"What have we got going on here?" Kasey asked, amused by the scene.

"Come join us," Ren beckoned, gesturing for him to sit as he passed the blunt. Julia exchanged a glance with Giles, signaling her intention. He excused himself and went indoors.

"Akira, could I see you for a minute in the house?" Julia asked with a sweet smile.

"Sure," she replied, following Julia. As she walked into Ren's room, she was surprised to find Giles already there.

"What's up, Giles-san?" she asked, puzzled, glancing from Giles to Julia and back.

"It's just a little heads-up, love. There's something important Julia needs to tell you, and I just want to make sure you understand the need for discretion and that this is a private matter."

"I'm listening," she said, her gaze slowly shifting from Giles to Julia.

"Akira, Ren and I are romantic partners. I gave him the ring he wears."

"But I thought Kasey was your boyfriend," Akira replied, looking confused.

"He is, and he's also Ren's partner. We're in a committed domestic partnership—or, for lack of a better term, a throuple. I apologize for any confusion, but we can't disclose that information publicly at this time; only our closest friends know about us. It's private information and could negatively affect our new fashion business if it gets out. It could hurt my standing with my board," Julia clarified.

"I'm sorry for flirting with Ren—I didn't know. That's still no excuse for me ignoring the ring he's wearing. That really wasn't cool, especially since I was doing it in front of not one, but two of his partners. I'm really embarrassed. Please don't mention this to my grandfather. You have nothing to worry about from me; my lips are sealed," Akira assured, running her fingers across her lips.

"We would never speak to your grandfather before speaking to you. It's all good; you had no way of knowing.

Let's go have some fun. We're gonna bring out the karaoke machine, see if we can't witness your grandfather letting loose," Julia said, linking arms with Akira and casting a smile over her shoulder at Giles as they left to rejoin the others.

Julia pulled Kasey and Ren aside, letting them know the situation with Akira was sorted. She explained that once they informed Haruto, they could freely be themselves. She also brought Kasey up to speed on the dynamics between the brothers and Gunther.

"How about I talk to Haruto? I feel like we're close enough now, and after hearing all this, I don't think it'll be a big deal."

"That's a good idea Spike; Haruto has really taken you. Maybe after karaoke would be the perfect time."

"Perfect timing!" Julia added with a grin.

***

While Julia and Ren set up the room, Kasey arranged snacks on the kitchen island. Ren hung up and switched the disco light, transforming the space into a karaoke club.

As the group filed into the living room, Haruto couldn't contain his excitement. His eyes lit up at the sight of the karaoke machine, the multicolored lights flashing in a hypnotic display. The double microphone stands beckoned, and the pulsating song playing in the background added to the anticipation, pulling him in with its infectious energy.

"C'mon, Haruto, pick a song—let's sing together," Julia grinned, leading him to the machine and coaxing him to choose a song. Everyone else settled into the comfortable couches, waiting for the show. To their astonishment, as the familiar melody filled the room and the words scrolled across the screen, Haruto underwent a metamorphosis. Gone was the reticence that had defined him moments earlier. In its place emerged a vivacious energy, a zest for life that defied his age and background. With animated gestures and a twinkle in his eye, he belted out *"You're the One That I Want"* from *Grease* with infectious enthusiasm, his voice clear and surprisingly full of gusto.

The room erupted in applause and laughter as the once-demure Haruto reveled in the joy of karaoke, his inhibitions cast aside. His laughter boomed as he twirled with Julia, his cheeks flushed and eyes sparkling like a man decades younger. Julia, with her charismatic presence, spun around him, playfully pointing the mic his way as their voices blended, delighting everyone with their lively rendition of the song.

Next up were Giles and Julia, performing his choice of Sonny and Cher's "I Got You Babe," showcasing their growing bond as they sang to each other and swayed to the beat. Julia took a seat on Kasey's lap, watching as Ren joined Akira and Haruto to sing "Sukiyaki" in Japanese. Even Gunther eventually joined in, singing with Julia and Giles.

Only the reserved Nigel and Kasey refrained, though they happily applauded and cheered each performance. Giles clapped in rhythm, grinning ear to ear, while Nigel chuckled quietly from his seat, clearly enjoying the show.

As the night wore on, Haruto's laughter rang out amid the chorus of happy voices—a testament to the transformative power of music and karaoke.

To unwind, everyone got comfortable on the deck, toasting marshmallows, sipping wine and Japanese beer, and indulging in some weed as they enjoyed the movie *Grease* on the big screen. Akira noticed Kasey sitting off to the side with Haruto, quietly engrossed in conversation, while Julia cozied up between Ren's legs on the double lounger.

After bidding good night, everyone dispersed to their beds. With their relationship now known to everyone in the house, Gunther spent the night with Giles while Nigel took Gunther's room. Though it was Julia's turn for solo time, Kasey had mentioned earlier he needed a night to himself. Managing so many people for days had stretched him to his limits, leaving him overstimulated. Kasey managed things with military precision while Julia floated through the visit like a cheerful cruise director, guiding everyone from one activity to the next.

Both Ren and Julia appreciated Kasey's ability to communicate his needs and understood his request for alone time. They were more than happy to have a chance to be alone together, their desire for each other inexhaustible.

Kasey, though always a willing participant whenever Julia wanted sex, rarely initiated it himself. Julia's frequent advances meant he seldom had to ask, and his own libido paled in comparison to hers. Ren, on the other hand, couldn't keep his hands off her. He wanted her all day, every day, as often as he could. While Kasey's touch was always loving and gentle, Ren's held a playful, rough edge, reflecting his joy in finding a partner who matched his ravenous desires after a decade of denial.

Erotically charged, clothes were hitting the floor as they scarcely crossed the threshold. Foreplay had already commenced on the lounger, partially shielded from prying eyes and masked by the film's clamor. No one could hear him murmuring naughty things in her ear as she subtly rubbed against him. Sitting nestled between his legs, she pressed back into him, and his arms wrapped firmly around her waist, his fingers toying flirtatiously with the band of her shorts.

Finally alone, Julia giggled with delight as he playfully tackled her onto the bed, pinning her beneath him with a mischievous grin. He brushed her hair aside and bit her neck, eliciting a sharp yelp.

"You are so horny," she moaned.

"Only because you're so fucking hot," he replied with a seductive growl as she parted her legs, inviting him closer.

He pressed against her firm body, his breath hot against her skin.

"Have you ever ventured into anal sex?" he asked softly, his voice laced with temptation. He felt her body momentarily freeze before she rolled over to face him.

"Never. I've never trusted anyone enough for that, and I always imagined it would hurt too much," she confessed. With a mischievous glint in her eye, she asked, "Is that something you want to try? I'd consider it with you, but only after some preparation and more privacy than we have here."

"It's something that's crossed my mind," he admitted, his finger tracing from her neck down to her breast. "But I wouldn't want to do anything you're not comfortable with, or that might cause you pain—unless it was the good kind," he added with a devilish smile, drawing her to his 'bad boy' side. "I thought if you'd done it before and enjoyed it, we could try it together. I want to experience everything with you." His finger traced gentle circles around her nipple as he spoke. "Maybe if we take it slow, we could work our way up to it. I promise I'll be as gentle as possible," he murmured, flicking his tongue over her now-hardened nipple.

"Have you ever asked Kasey to do that?" she asked softly, remembering Kasey had told her he never wanted that with Ren.

"I have not," he smiled. "That's something I know he would not be interested in—giving or receiving. I know my boy." He thought for a moment. "Sometimes, I wonder if I came into Spike's life at just the right time for us to form a relationship. I wonder if he ever would have sought out a man as a partner if I hadn't made the first move. When we were younger, I sometimes felt like sex was something he just went along with to show his love for me. He seemed so deprived of love and affection, and after seeing that scrapbook... I can't help but wonder if he would have loved me the same way if his past hadn't shaped him the way it did."

"He would have loved you—don't be crazy. You two have a very real connection. He told me that once he relaxed and got used to the idea of having sex with his best friend, he actually loved being with you. But you're right about the anal sex part. He mentioned how your sexual history progressed and how he dragged his feet over every step forward. He said he was grateful it had never come to that because he wasn't interested in it at all. But I'm positive from what I've seen of you two as adults; he *very much* likes having sex with you... just minus the butt stuff," she crinkled her nose and giggled.

"Then I'll just have to get some butt stuff from you," he said playfully, grabbing her and nipping at her neck.

"And vice versa," she giggled, wriggling beneath him.

"I love your laugh," he whispered, tickling her neck with tiny kisses. "You can do with me as you will. I am all yours, baby." His fingers slipped between her legs, and she let out a soft groan, eyes closing as she held his head to her neck, fingers woven into his hair. In a sultry plea, she murmured, "Make love to me tonight Ren... go slow."

He enveloped her in his arms. "Let me show you just how slow and gentle I can be," he whispered as their night unfolded in a tapestry of soft caresses and teasing whispers until she was begging him to take her.

***

The morning brought a glorious beach day, with temperatures climbing from a humid seventy degrees to a balmy ninety by afternoon. There were no plans for the day except to enjoy the sun, sand, and sea. Haruto and Kasey were the earliest risers, practicing Tai Chi at the water's edge as the sun cast its gentle morning glow. Julia found Nigel on the deck, savoring a cup of tea as he watched the duo on the beach.

"Good morning, Nigel," Julia said, settling into the chair beside him as Ren stayed behind to brew tea. "I just love the smell of the beach in the morning," she remarked, taking a deep breath and soaking in the tranquil scene of Kasey and Haruto.

"Good morning, Jules. I must admit, I didn't expect to see you up and about at this hour—I was quite certain you'd still be snug in bed, tangled up with one of your charming companions," he said with a knowing smile. Watching the two figures moving gracefully at the water's edge, he added, "Kasey truly is remarkable—strikingly handsome, intelligent, yet so quiet and humble. And Ren—what a vibrant character, bursting with creativity and charisma. And you, my dear, are a vision of beauty—accomplished and ever so kind. I envy the bond you three share. Together, you make an exceptional team. Cherish it, for it's truly special."

"Thank you, Nigel. That's so sweet of you to say," Julia replied, touched by his sentiment. "I'm having a wonderful time with all of you here. My doors are always open anytime you'd like to visit—and I do hope it will be more often. Next time, we'll head to the ranch. You can soak in the rustic charm of Colorado—surrounded by rugged cowboys. The land is breathtaking, and who knows? You might even enjoy playing cowboy."

"I'm not sure we'd make the best cowboys, but I wouldn't mind observing the ranch hands at work." he chuckled. "We're having an absolutely cracking time here—we simply adore the seaside. And your beautiful home, my dear, is as charming as you are."

Julia squeezed Nigel's hand. "I'm so glad you're enjoying your stay," she said warmly, thrilled everything was going so well.

Watching Kasey and Haruto perform their slow, graceful moves, Julia said, "I hope Haruto's enjoying his time here. He certainly seemed to love the karaoke."

"He's having a splendid time," Nigel reassured her. "Aside from the karaoke, Haruto has really taken a shine to Kasey. They spend a great deal of time chatting in Japanese, and now look at them—practicing Tai Chi together." Haruto must be delighted with his company. He has two daughters, both with daughters of their own, and rarely sees his sons-in-law. I'm sure he's relishing having a young man he can connect with—it's truly wonderful to see."

"Kasey is really enjoying his time with Haruto. He loves speaking Japanese and doesn't get to do it much since I don't speak it. Ren prefers to speak English, especially when I'm around. I'm gonna try learning enough to join in—or at least catch when they're teasing me," she said with a grin.

"I invited one of my closest friends from New Jersey to stop by tonight for some karaoke fun," Julia said, her eyes glimmering with excitement. "He used to front a cover band when we were in college, and we always had such a great time singing together. I thought maybe Akira might enjoy having another young person to chat with—and he's a lot of fun."

"Are you playing matchmaker?" he quipped, a playful smile curling his lips.

Julia shook her head, her own smile widening, "Oh, no," she clarified. "Will doesn't lean toward any gender romantically—at least, not yet. I'm just hoping they strike up a friendship."

"My, my, what a wonderfully diverse circle you have."

Julia interjected with a grin, "Honestly, I try to see people for who they are—not who they love or what they do behind closed doors. The world needs to step back and let consenting adults love who they want. It baffles me why this is still so hard."

"If only it were so," Nigel said with a wistful smile. "Alas, the world is not quite there yet—perhaps one day. I do see glimmers of hope. It takes extraordinary courage to defy societal norms and forge a new path. If we make this new fashion house a success, perhaps you three can be the trailblazers who inspire a more inclusive tomorrow." Nigel took Julia's hand and held it gently, his gaze meeting hers with quiet sincerity. "Just know, if you choose to do so, Giles and I are behind you one hundred percent. It's time we stepped out of the shadows. When I leave this world, I want to do so proud—not only of my accomplishments, but of having truly embraced who I am."

"Well, let's hope that day is far off," Julia said with a warm smile. "And thank you for your support—it means the world to me."

***

Bowing to each other, Kasey and Haruto finished their Tai Chi and made their way toward the deck, arriving just as Ren entered with tea for Julia.

"Sorry that took so long—I got caught up talking with Gunther," Ren explained.

"Are they up yet?" Nigel asked, a hint of amusement in his tone.

"I don't think so—he was just making tea to take back to their room," Ren replied with a smile.

Nigel chuckled. "They do love their lie-ins. It's splendid to see them spending quality time together on this trip—

without all the usual cloak-and-dagger nonsense we're accustomed to. You've made them both very happy."

"I'm glad," Julia replied warmly. "So, how was your Tai Chi?" she asked Kasey as they joined the group on the deck—but it was Haruto who answered.

"It was nice to have someone who shares my interest. My granddaughter is not always a willing partner," Haruto said with a small smile. "Thank you, Kasey, for your company.

"My pleasure. Same time tomorrow?" Kasey asked with a friendly nod. Turning to Ren, Kasey placed a hand on his shoulder. "You up for a run?"

"Definitely. Let me change into some running shorts—be right back."

Kasey glanced at Julia. "What about you, sweetheart?"

"Thank you for asking, but no. You guys have to slow down too much for me. Besides, I'm enjoying my tea and conversation with Nigel—I'm on vacation," she said with a smile.

"Suit yourself—I'm going to hydrate," he said, leaning in to give her a quick peck on the cheek.

"Bloody hell, that is one fine-looking young man. How much must he work out to look like that? And where does he find the time and energy? Oh, to be young and fit," Nigel said wistfully, his gaze lingering on Kasey as he walked away.

"He works out every day, in some way or another," Julia said. "Sometimes he trains alone, other times with Ren. He runs nearly every day, and if you pay attention, you'll notice he eats very clean. And unless it's the cookies I ask him to bake, he doesn't snack at all. Kasey has incredible self-control."

"Well, all his hard work certainly shows. He'd be perfect for modeling some of our suits—they'd look absolutely stunning on him. I remember how striking he looked in our classic suit in London. The fit was impeccable."

"Funny you say that—I've been toying with an advertising concept featuring a model in one of your signature suits and another in one of Ren's bold designs. The models represent a choice between classic sophistication and cutting-edge style, with a beautiful young woman standing between them, holding their hands. The tagline could be, 'Why settle for traditional or trendy? Embrace both with Hawthorne-Masters.' It's just an idea I've been playing with—I haven't even mentioned it to Ren yet. What do you think?"

At that moment, Ren and Kasey set off for their run.

"Be back soon," Ren called out as they left.

"I think it's brilliant. I adore it. And the three of you are so visually compelling, plus there's a subtle message there."

"Exactly. I'm so glad you like it. I'd like to convey the idea that we're an inclusive brand for all ages, styles, and tastes."

"Giles and I would like that too. After all these years, we're eager to shake things up a bit; move forward with the times. I wish we were younger, more hands-on in the creative process. Giles even sketched a design the other day for the first time in ages; he was so chuffed," Nigel smiled, clearly happy for his brother.

"Chuffed? Is that good?" Julia asked, grinning.

"Sorry, love. He was very pleased with himself," Nigel laughed.

"Nigel, you're never too old to design, and we didn't go into business together for you two to be sidelined. I want your ideas, opinions, and expertise. Ren's absolutely thrilled to be collaborating with you both. We're going to do great things together—but only if you realize how important you both are to the process. I'm not putting you out to pasture; I believe you both have so much more to offer."

"Thank you for the kind words. Perhaps later, we can all sit down and brainstorm a bit. We could throw around some ideas for that 70s reimagining. I know Giles would adore that; he's in his element with the creative side of things. Ren and Kasey are not so dissimilar from Giles and me. Giles is the outgoing creative force, while I'm more introspective and pragmatic. Together, we make one accomplished man," he laughed.

"Well, for me, they make one hell of a man. They complement each other perfectly, fulfilling not just my emotional needs but also my physical ones," she said with a playful smile.

"May I ask you something personal?" Nigel ventured, his tone careful.

"Sure, Nigel, ask away."

"Do you think about having children? How would you manage it? Of course, if that's too personal, you don't have to answer—I'm just curious."

"I've never talked to either Kasey or Ren about this. Honestly, it wasn't something I ever thought about—until I met Kasey." Julia sighed. "But after losing my family, I've started thinking more about the future. I do want to get married and have children someday." She took his hand, adding in a low voice, "Just between us, if we stay a committed trio—and I believe we will—I'd love to have a child with each of them." That's, if they even want children, of course. I'm pretty sure Ren does—his past with his ex-wife makes that clear. But Kasey? I'm not so sure. His childhood was... well, far from ideal." She paused before asking softly, "What about you, Nigel? Do you ever wish you'd had children?"

"I do. I wish I'd gone the route of adoption or surrogacy, like Elton John and David. They've built a beautiful little family. But I made my choices." Nigel smiled warmly. "Still, I'd love to be around to see the lovely babies you and your men will have."

"Stop talking like that—you'll absolutely be around. I'm thirty now, and I don't plan to wait more than a couple of years. I want to start my own family, and you'll need to be our babies' proper British uncle, teaching them some posh manners." She laughed, her eyes sparkling.

Julia sighed wistfully, her gaze drifting to the ocean. "Why'd you have to go and mention babies?"

Nigel's smile widened. "I might get to be that uncle sooner than I thought."

"No... no, Julia said with a teasing smile. "We have a fashion house to establish."

"Sure, I understand," he said with a knowing grin. "But you strike me as the kind of woman who wouldn't let a pregnancy slow you down. And with two very capable papas by your side, how could it?"

"Stop," she protested, a thoughtful chuckle escaping. "This discussion isn't even on their radar."

"Are you sure? Maybe it's time to ask?" He let out a hearty laugh. "Listen to me—acting like some agony aunt, doling out unsolicited advice! You can just tell me to sod off."

"Please, never stop offering guidance—I love it. I miss having my father to bounce things off and getting his advice. I'd be foolish not to listen to your life experience. You're right, though—time flies. I should at least see where they each stand on having children."

***

546

After a refreshing, post-run shower that left them both grinning and relaxed, Kasey and Ren were in high spirits as they inspected Kasey's dinner preparations. Their conversation bubbled with energy, Ren's arm casually draped over Kasey's shoulder as their heads leaned in close to inspect the grill, cocooned in their own little world. Watching them, Julia felt a warm flutter in her stomach at the sight of Ren helping Kasey unwind, savoring the moment.

Kasey had taken on the task of crafting an authentic American feast: slow-roasted ribs, succulent brisket, and juicy burgers, all sourced from The Double O. He'd started the ribs and brisket early, ensuring they simmered slowly on the grill before his Tai Chi session with Haruto, guaranteeing perfection by dinnertime. As the day unfolded, a medley of smoky, savory, and utterly irresistible aromas filled the air. Balancing the hearty evening meal, Kasey arranged for a chickpea salad and a Caprese Salad to be delivered, offering them alongside light appetizers for anyone needing a nibble throughout the day.

Haruto and Nigel soaked up the sun's rays, standing at the water's edge in their Panama hats as everyone else swam or jumped the waves, enjoying the beach for hours.

After sipping iced tea on the deck and savoring the enticing aromas of the upcoming meal, everyone voted to take a siesta. The full day of sun and fun had taken its toll. With Gunther now sharing a room with Giles, Nigel used the downstairs shower. Rather than wait, Ren joined Julia and Kasey in the shower. Kasey washed her hair as Ren playfully teased her with soap bubbles, filling the shower with laughter and smiles.

Energized, Kasey decided to check the meat and relax with a book on the deck instead of napping, savoring the quiet as the others rested inside.

Julia slipped between the fresh sheets Jackie had changed during the swim, savoring the cool, crisp fabric against her sun-kissed skin as she fought to stay awake. By the time Ren finished blow-drying his hair, Julia was sound asleep. When he slipped into bed, she muttered groggily, "Finally," and rested her head on his chest. "Rain check on sex, babe. Too tired. Just hold me," she whispered, draping her arm across his stomach and sliding her leg over his.

"It's all good. Go back to sleep," he murmured, pulling her close.

***

As the evening wore on, everyone gathered downstairs. The room buzzed with conversation: Nigel and Julia discussed branding, Ren and Giles enthusiastically sketched ideas, while Kasey, Haruto, and Gunther dove into barbecue, beef, and Julia's herd. In the living room, Akira called her mother in Japan, waking her with the unexpected ring. Despite waking her mother, Akira ended the call after only ten minutes, her attention shifting the moment Will arrived, ready for barbecue and karaoke.

After introductions, he settled beside Akira, bringing fresh energy to the group and making sure she felt included. Julia knew Akira would find karaoke more fun with Will, and if he was high and she gave him a willing ear, he could talk all night.

With dinner still an hour off, Akira invited Will for a walk on the beach. As they headed for the door and passed the men at the grill, Haruto asked, "Are you going for a walk? May I join you?"

Noticing the disappointment in Akira's eyes, Kasey stepped in. "Haruto-san, let them go. Stay here and keep me company. Tell me more about how you got into the fashion business—I love your stories." Haruto immediately turned back, a smile on his face. "You young people go. I will stay here with Kasey." Grateful, Akira mouthed her thanks before leaving with Will.

Earlier, during Tai Chi practice, Kasey respectfully asked Haruto if he minded being addressed with the honorific '-san,' emphasizing his deep respect for him. Moved by the gesture, Haruto agreed, further strengthening their growing bond. Kasey genuinely enjoyed the company of the older men, Haruto especially, always searching for that paternal connection.

As dinnertime approached, Julia, Ren, and Kasey assembled a mouthwatering feast on the deck. Brisket and ribs, so tender the meat fell off the bone, mingled with juicy quarter-pound burgers, loaded baked potatoes, and fire-roasted corn on the cob. Kasey's fluffy cornbread, baked to perfection in a cast-iron skillet, added rustic charm to the meal, paired with Julia's red-and-white checkered tablecloth, napkins, and accessories. An assortment of sides from a local restaurant—creamy coleslaw, tangy beans, and mac and cheese— joined an array of sauces, pickles, and condiments, from sweet barbecue to fiery hot sauce, allowing everyone to customize their plates to perfection. Kasey had also ordered an assortment of beers to complement the meal.

To cap off the feast, decadent banana pudding and zesty lemon bars ensured a sweet finale to the down-home meal. Before thoughts of karaoke or other post-dinner plans could form, the group unanimously chose a leisurely stroll along the water's edge to walk off the heavy meal, with Akira and Will bringing up the rear, engrossed in a spirited conversation.

***

As they prepared the room for the evening's festivities, Julia told Kasey she thought Akira seemed noticeably happier since Will arrived. He had also noticed her cheerfulness and nodded. "She's been smiling ever since he arrived."

The night flowed with everyone taking turns on the mic, filling the air with laughter and music. Duets filled the room as everyone reveled in the joy of letting loose. When Haruto wasn't singing, he cheered enthusiastically for others, his energy lighting up the room alongside the disco ball. Will swept Akira onto the dance floor, dazzling her with his moves, while Julia paired up with Ren. She shared a few dances with Giles and later swayed with Kasey during a slow song, while Giles danced with Gunther and Will with Akira.

As the night wore on, fueled by Will's blunt, Kasey joined Haruto, Ren, and Akira in singing Sukiyaki in Japanese, persuaded by Haruto and Ren's charm. Julia captured the moment with a few photos and a short video on her phone.

For the final song, Julia chose something special for her favorite guys, serenading them with *Only Girl in the World*. All eyes were on her as she sang, her charisma and talent undeniable.
"She has so much confidence. I admire that," Akira said to Will, watching Julia's intimate performance for the two men.

"She's got every reason to be confident. Jules is special—I'd do anything for her. She's been there for me since college." He turned to Akira. "Hey, want to sit by the water with me? Get some air?"

"I'd love to," Akira agreed with a broad smile. They waved goodnight to the others and strolled to the beach, settling under the waxing moon with their toes in the sand, enjoying each other's company.

Before the trio headed to Julia's room, their shared desire already igniting, Julia called Will on the beach with Akira, offering him Ren's empty room for the night.

Stepping through the doorway of her bedroom, they peeled off their clothes and leaped into bed together, quickly becoming a tangle of limbs as they indulged in their intense craving for each other. Despite efforts to muffle Julia's giggles and sweet cries of pleasure, Giles and Gunther, whose room shared a wall with Julia's, exchanged knowing smiles. The trio's familiar sounds igniting an unexpected night of passion for them as well.

***

Early the next morning, Kasey spotted Will trying to sneak out of Akira's room, sneakers in hand.

"You'd better be careful. Haruto just went down; he's probably in the kitchen. Wait until I

get him outside before you head to your room," Kasey said, a glint in his eye and a smile playing on his lips.

"Thanks, man," Will replied with a sheepish grin. He lingered at the top of the stairs until he heard the sliding door open and close, then headed to his room for some much-needed shut-eye.

Ren and Julia were still asleep, entwined in each other's arms, when Kasey returned. While he showered, there was a gentle knock at the bathroom door, and Julia slipped in.

"Sorry, baby, but I have to pee. How was your Tai Chi?" she murmured, her voice thick with sleep.

"I love doing it here at the beach. The scenery and morning sun add so much. By the way, Haruto's really enjoying it here—he told me so. He said last night's dinner was delicious, but he could feel it this morning." Kasey chuckled, "He was a little sluggish. And guess who I saw sneaking out of Akira's room before I left?" he teased.

"No way," Julia exclaimed, opening the shower door, standing there naked. "Wow, that's not something I expected. Good for them!" She started to leave but paused. "Wait—Did he look happy?" she asked, concerned.

551

"Don't worry, he looked very happy," Kasey said with a grin. "Now, close that door or get in—it's cold."

"Sorry, baby, I'm going back to bed. Not ready to wake up yet... but now I wanna talk to Will," she mumbled. She slid carefully between the sheets, not wanting to wake Ren, knowing if she did, she'd never get back to sleep.

"Did you think I wouldn't notice you were gone?" Ren's voice; a sensual whisper as he pulled her close, his hand tracing her curves, his hard body pressing against hers while he kissed the back of her neck.

"Oh my God, Ren," she giggled, inhaling sharply as he bit her. "You're not even fully awake, and you're already hard." Her giggles turned into a soft moan as his touch reminded her how much he wanted her—and how much she wanted him in return.

She turned to face him, cupping his face as her lips captured his. With his hand cradling her head, his tongue plunged deep into her mouth, his desire for her undeniable. As Kasey stepped out of the bathroom, Julia pushed Ren onto his back, leaning into him as her kisses and bites on his neck grew rougher and more urgent.

"What happened to going back to sleep?" Kasey chuckled. "Honestly, you two have no self-control whatsoever. Don't let me stop you—I'm just checking on everyone and making sure everything's set for the yacht later. As you were." He grinned, slipping out the door as they picked up right where they'd left off.

***

Nestled in Ren's embrace, Julia summoned the courage to bring up starting a family. "I have something important to ask you," she said, her voice tentative.

"You can ask me anything, Jules," Ren said, glancing down at her, the weight in her tone unmistakable.

"I've been thinking about the future," she continued, her words measured. "What do you think about us having children someday? I really want to start a family in the next couple of years. If we stay a committed trio—which I want more than anything—we could have a commitment ceremony. Then, maybe I could have a child with each of you."

She reached out, her touch gentle as she gazed up at Ren. "I haven't discussed this with Kasey yet. I wanted to hear your perspective first. You had a good childhood until your father did what he did, and you mentioned trying to start a family with your ex-wife—and how disappointed you were when it didn't happen. I'm not sure Kasey will want children after what he went through, so I wanted to know what you think." Her expression, a sweet mixture of hope and deep affection, softened as she asked, "Do you see children as part of your future?"

Ren listened intently, his tone a mix of surprise and warmth. "Let me get this straight—you're considering a commitment ceremony and having a child with me?"

Julia nodded, a loving grin spreading across her lips. "Yes, I am. I love you and already put a ring on it," she teased, rubbing the ring on his hand.

He chuckled softly. "Yes, you did. You don't drag your feet when you know what you want." Overwhelmed and deeply touched, he tightened his embrace. "I know you're just feeling things out, but when you're ready, know I'm fully on board. I love you, Jules. It amazes me every day how quickly these deep feelings for you took over. I can't imagine my life without you and Spike, and I can't imagine anything more fulfilling than raising a family with you both."

His mind reeled with the thought of a future with Julia and Kasey, his heart swelling at the image of little ones calling him "Papa."

"I love children, Jules. I'd want as many babies as you want, he confessed with a smile. "I was more disappointed than Kaede when we didn't conceive. Maybe we didn't try hard enough, but I doubt that'll be a problem for us." He grinned and kissed the top of her head.

"Babies," he sighed contentedly. "Every time I think life couldn't get any better, you do or say something that completely blows my world apart—in the best ways."

Julia snuggled into him, thrilled to hear the answer she hoped for.

"Do you have any idea how Kasey might feel about this?" she asked, her voice hesitant. "Has he ever mentioned anything about raising children?"

"I've honestly never heard him mention children or having a family. He never talked about any kind of family life," Ren replied.

"Do you think I should ask him about this alone, or should we do it together? Or maybe you could ask? He never says no to me… maybe he'd feel pressured to agree, but he might be more honest with you. What do you think?"

"Can you give me some time to think about it? Honestly, I'm still processing what we just talked about. You basically told me you want to fully commit to me and have my children. You're so nonchalant, but it's a big deal, baby girl—even if you're saying it so casually." Ren chuckled softly, his breath tickling her ear. "It feels like you just proposed to me."

She giggled, "And I got a yes."

"You got a 'Hell, yes!" he said with a grin, rolling over to rest partially on top of her. "I love you, and there's nothing I want more than to build a life with you, Spike, and our children." Leaning in, he tenderly held her face and delivered a lingering kiss filled with warmth and joy. "Give me until tonight to think about how to approach Spike, okay?" he murmured, punctuating his words with gentle kisses trailing along her skin.

As his lips brushed across her collarbone, stirring butterflies in her stomach and a tingle between her legs, she couldn't resist pulling him on top. Her fingers wove through his silky hair, holding him there. Rather than rushing into intimacy as he normally would, driven by uncontrollable lust, he took his time, expressing his love with sweet words and deep, passionate kisses. Their bond deepened as they lay intertwined—Ren toying with her hair while Julia traced soft patterns on his arm—both lost in dreams of their shared future.

***

"Are you two ever getting out of bed?" Kasey quipped, smirking and raising a brow as he entered the room. "It's ten already. You have guests, Missy. And you, cowboy, holster that weapon. Time to rise and shine—gracious hosts don't stay in bed all day. Let's go, hustle you two."

Julia chuckled as she rolled to the edge of the bed and sat up. "Sorry, baby, time got away from us. We're up now, and we'll be down in five minutes. Promise." She kissed him as she passed, heading to the bathroom, where the shower soon started.

"Now, where the hell are my clothes?" Ren grumbled, scanning the room.

"Right here," Kasey said with a grin, picking up Ren's shorts from the floor. "Right where you dropped them last night in your mad rush to the bed."

"Thanks, Spike. We'll be right down, but we both need a shower," he said, his eyes sparkling. With a quick kiss, he headed into the bathroom, Julia's delighted giggles following soon after.

"Five minutes, or I'll be back," Kasey called playfully through the bathroom door.

***

Fifteen minutes later, they came downstairs, looking refreshed and blissfully happy. Everyone except Akira and Will was already on the deck, enjoying the sailboats on the horizon with their morning tea or coffee.

"Good morning, everyone! I hope you all slept well—I know I did," Julia said with a broad smile.

"The sea air is just delightful for sleeping," Nigel remarked, inhaling deeply.

Julia walked over to Giles and Gunther, leaning in with a sly grin. "And how did you two sleep? I hope we didn't make too much noise."

"Not at all, love," Giles whispered back, leaning in closer. "We were busy making a little noise of our own." She chuckled, patting his hand.

"Where are Akira and Will? Still sleeping?"

"Akira needed something from the store, so Will took her. I told them to be back before we leave for the yacht club at noon," Kasey said. "We've got the yacht until six. Gilliam's hosting a small gathering at eight, so I figured six hours was plenty. I also ordered the same lunch as before since we all enjoyed it so much."

"Sounds perfect as always, baby," she said, planting a big kiss on Kasey.

***

The afternoon went off without a hitch, full of swimming, water skiing, and jet skiing. Julia watched Gunther racing across the tranquil sea, Giles holding on for dear life, fear and exhilaration etched on his face. His muffled shouts of "Slow down, you madman!" were met with Gunther's booming laughter as he sped up instead. Meanwhile, Nigel lounged on the deck in sunglasses and a Panama hat, sipping iced tea with an air of aristocratic calm. "The sun agrees with me," he remarked to Haruto, who nodded silently, looking effortlessly composed as usual.

Julia's attention turned to Will, who was tirelessly encouraging Akira as she attempted to stay upright on the skis again. When she finally succeeded, wobbling but determined, a cheer went up from the deck. Even Nigel clapped, his usual reserve giving way to a genuine smile. Julia joined in the applause, laughing as Will whooped loudly, pumping his fist in the air while Akira grinned triumphantly.

Later, after a champagne lunch on the deck with a spread of fresh seafood and crusty bread, the group's energy shifted. Will took charge, coaxing nearly everyone up to dance. He twirled Akira dramatically as laughter bubbled around them, then made a theatrical bow toward Julia, pulling her into the fun. She spun happily in her bare feet, grinning at Kasey, who lounged at the edge of the deck with an indulgent smile. Ren eventually joined her, his smooth moves earning an appreciative laugh from Julia as he spun her around. Will, ever the instigator, dragged a tired but willing Giles up to the deck, the older man grinning as he tried to keep up with Will's exuberance.

As the sun began to dip lower, painting the horizon in shades of gold and pink, they returned to the beach house. The salt air clung to their skin, and the sound of waves seemed to follow them inside.

After refreshing showers and glasses of iced tea, they all settled in for a movie, planning to call it an early night. Julia felt a contented glow, the day's laughter and camaraderie still buzzing in her veins.

By ten o'clock, only Julia, Kasey, Ren, Akira, and Will remained, sitting around the fire pit and passing a blunt. The crackling fire cast flickering shadows across their relaxed faces.

"Will, could I see you in the kitchen for a minute?" Julia asked. "Anybody want anything while we're up?" When everyone said no, she and Will headed inside.

Sitting beside Will at the kitchen island, she was eager to finally delve into the story of him and Akira; her curiosity piqued after a day of anticipation.

"Sooo, spill the beans. What's the story with Akira? Did you two hook up?" Julia asked, her curious grin coaxing him for answers.

Will smiled. "First, thanks for inviting me to come and keep her company. When you told me about her situation, I thought, why not? Maybe I could be her quick American fling, and she could give me what I was looking for. We had a pretty deep conversation beforehand. I told her I wanted to have sex with her, but I wasn't sure I could offer more than friendship. She said she'd be happy with just a fling, then head home, and we'd stay friends. You don't mind if I stick around until they leave and keep her company, right?"

"Of course not. I love having you here, and I'm glad it worked out for both of you," she replied, her grin widening as she ran her fingers over his hand. "So, how was it? I know you've had plenty of one-night stands over the years, but this must be different if you want to stay with her."

He smiled as he recited Akira's charms. "She's really interesting, a great listener, she's not bad to look at—and she laughs at all my jokes," he added with a grin. "*And* she's great in the sack." He chuckled. "I don't mean that in a show-off way. She listens to me, doesn't use mushy or sentimental words during sex, and doesn't expect me to either. Yet, it still feels nice and warm. She makes it so easy—exactly what I need. American girls can be so pushy, at least the ones I've been with."

"You better not be including me, Will Michelson," Julia said with a smirk, playfully punching his arm.

"Present company excluded," he replied with a laugh, shielding himself from Julia's playful assault. "We went out to get more condoms this morning—her idea. I only brought two, and she said she's going to take full advantage of me while I'm here." He flashed a big smile. "I'm all for it."

"I'm thrilled it worked out for you both. I knew this house had a sex vibe. Even Giles and Gunther got down last night," she giggled, looping her arm through his as they returned to the others.

***

Wanting to give Julia and Kasey space, Ren slept downstairs, knowing any discussion about their future should come from her alone.

As they settled into bed, Julia turned to Kasey, her voice soft as her fingertips traced soothing circles on his arm. "Baby, I'd like to talk about our future," she began slowly. "Being with you and Ren has made me so happy—I want to build a life with both of you." She rested her head on his chest, her hand slipping around his waist. I want children someday, and I'd like to know how you feel about that. Do you see children in your future?" She inhaled softly, holding her breath without realizing it.

"I'll be honest—I've never given much thought to having children." Kasey's fingers traced soft patterns on her arm, his voice steady despite the weight of his words. "Settling down

559

and starting a family was never something I imagined for myself—until I met you. I already know I want a life with you. If children are part of that life, then I'm all in." He paused, his brow furrowing slightly. "I'm not sure I'd be great with kids—I haven't been around them much—but I know you'd be a wonderful mother, and Ren would make a great father."

Julia exhaled softly, lifting her head to meet his gaze. His eyes were warm, his sincerity unmistakable as he looked down at her.

"Speaking of that, what kind of a timeline are we talking about?" he asked, twisting a piece of her hair around his finger.

"I was thinking a couple of years. Enough time to establish the fashion house and enjoy

ourselves—maybe even travel. I've barely been outside the States. You could show me Europe, and Ren could show me Japan—broaden my worldview a bit," she smiled.

"And, you'd like a child with both of us?"

"Yes. I thought when we were ready, I'd go off birth control, and whoever gets there first could just wear a condom when we're ready for the second. I'm pretty sure we won't need DNA to figure out who's the father," she said with a giggle, and he smiled.

"So, where did this come from? Have you been thinking about this for a while?"

"It came up in conversation with Nigel, and I realized I didn't know how you felt about children. Having a family is very important to me, so I figured I'd better ask. I thought we could have some kind of commitment ceremony for the three of us when we're ready." She paused, her expression clouded with concern. "Would not being married and having children bother you?"

"Sweetheart, I'm already committed to you, marriage or not. If you want to have a family, the lack of a marriage license won't stop us," he kissed the top of her head. "Did you talk to Ren about this? Is that why you were in bed for so long?"

"Yep, we talked. I asked if he'd ever heard you mention wanting a family and whether he thought I should bring it up with you directly. I didn't want you to feel pressured to say yes to me," she said softly, her fingers trailing over his defined six-pack as she hoped he wouldn't be upset.

"So that's why Ren was in such a good mood today. I knew that look on his face this morning wasn't just from sex. I love that you go to him with questions about how to make things easier for me, but don't ever be afraid to ask me about anything. My perspective has changed so much since I met you. Things I couldn't have imagined before—like loving someone so completely and feeling absolute contentment—are now my reality. I want to spend my life with you and give you whatever you need to make it the best life we can share."

"I don't think I could be happier than I am right now. I'm so lucky to have two men I'm desperately in love with—and who love me just as much," she confessed.

Drawing her close, he whispered, "Would you mind if we just cuddled tonight? I'm so happy, but I'm also exhausted, and I don't want to just phone it in."

"Of course we can just cuddle. I never want you to feel like you have to phone it in. I love nothing more than being in your arms. The love and safety you surround me with is more than enough. You're everything to me, baby."

She rolled on her side and he spooned her, his face nestled in her hair, completely at peace with the thought of the future they all might share.

Drifting off to sleep, Julia felt sublimely content, knowing her love with Kasey was stronger than ever and ready to face whatever the future might hold.

***

Early the next morning, Julia woke when Kasey did. While he practiced Tai Chi with Haruto, she ventured out for a quiet stroll on the beach, Charley trailing discreetly behind. About five minutes into her walk, she called Micki.

"Damn, kiddo, it's Saturday. What time is it?" Micki asked, her voice still heavy with sleep as she answered. "Sorry for the early call, but I haven't had a moment alone since this vacation started. I'm walking the beach while everyone else is still asleep. I wanted to catch up and fill you in on everything."

"Well, I'm up now. What's new?" Micki said, slipping out of bed so she wouldn't disturb James.

"Let's see...Yesterday, I had separate talks with Kasey and Ren about their thoughts on starting a family. I told them I'd like to have kids in a couple of years and wanted to know how they felt about it," Julia said, waiting for Micki's reaction.

"Children? Where the hell did that come from? I haven't heard you talk about kids since we were teenagers. What brought this on?" Micki's voice was tinged with surprise.

"I was talking to Nigel, and he just came out and asked me how it would work if I stayed committed to both men."

"And how would that work?" Micki said, her curiosity clear.

"I thought we could have a commitment ceremony, and later, I'd go off birth control and let nature take its course. For the second one, I'd use birth control with the first father and try to get pregnant by the other. I want a child with both of them."

"Wow. What did they say about that?" Micki asked, taken aback by Julia's casual approach to such a big decision.

"Ren was absolutely beside himself. He told me he loves kids and is open to having as many as I'd like. Honestly, it was exactly what I expected."

"And Kasey?" Micki asked cautiously.

"Kasey surprised me. He admitted he's not sure he'd be good with kids since he doesn't have much experience, but he's willing to start a family if that's what I want. He didn't mention his past or whether it influenced his thoughts on having a family. He said that since meeting me, his perspective has changed, and he sees things differently now. He also said that Ren and I would make wonderful parents. I'm certain Kasey would be an amazing, loving father—he just needs more confidence."

"I can't believe you're moving so fast with Ren. I get Kasey—you've been in love with him for over a year. But Ren? Are you sure this isn't just lust clouding your judgment? You have such an intense sexual connection with him—can you even tell the difference?" Micki asked, her concern clear.

"I know it seems like it's super fast, but I fell in love with Kasey the moment I met him. It's been the same with Ren—I love everything about him. He makes me laugh, he's smart, and he's a friggin wild man in bed. We can't get enough of each other. And the three of us together? Pure bliss. What more could I ask for?"

"Not much more than that," Micki conceded. "And when is all this happening? Hopefully, not soon, or I'll have to beat James back with a stick. We've actually had this discussion ourselves. He's itching to have a child."

"I had no idea," Julia said, her voice warm with delight at the thought of their children growing up together. "James will make an exceptional father. You, on the other hand, I'm not so sure motherhood is your calling," Julia teased, laughing.

"Fuck you, Jules, you're hardly one to talk," Micki shot back. "Kasey will be raising more than one child in that family." Julia burst out laughing. "Thank God we have good men to pick up the slack."

"True dat, kiddo," Micki said, her appreciation for James coming through.

"Guess what else has happened at my beach house of love," Julia said with a giggle.

"What? Even the old men are at it?" Micki teased as the rich aroma of coffee enveloped her.

"Actually, yes, I think we inspired Giles and Gunther to enjoy some vacation nookie—but that's not it. I invited Will to keep Akira company, and they hit it off like a house on fire. They've already slept together, *and* he's staying with her until she goes back to London."

"Holy shit! Did you talk to him about this? Scratch that— of course you did. What did he say? Does he like her?" Micki asked eagerly.

"He does. They've had a few deep conversations about his wants and limitations, and it seems all she wants is a fling while she's here—which works perfectly for him. They both seem so content. They even went condom shopping together yesterday!" Julia laughed. "I've never seen him spend this much time with a girl—he's usually off alone. But they seem so comfortable together. He even taught her how to water ski yesterday. I'm thrilled they're making each other happy."

"I wish I could see it. Will deserves someone who really gets him. I hope they stay friends—and who knows? Maybe something more will come from this," Micki mused. "Send me some pictures of them. I love seeing him happy."

"I have some fantastic shots—especially when he was teaching her to ski and the two of them on a jet ski. They look adorable together. He's so tall and gangly, and she's so petite. I'll send you a bunch when I get back to the house. I should probably turn around and head back now. It's so crazy having Charley tailing me just for a walk on the beach. Having security around all the time is so… weird. I can't even go get bagels without an escort. I hate it. I know it's a necessary evil, and I'll have to get used to it—especially when we have kids. Kasey will probably triple the guards or stick them in a bubble." She laughed, knowing it was most likely true.

"So, how are things with you and James? I know you were both just here, but I miss you guys so much. I wish you lived closer," she wheedled. "James is a big-shot accountant—he could do that job anywhere. And you work online, so it wouldn't be too hard to relocate. We could raise our kids together! Just think about it—I'd happily pay to move you closer," Julia offered.

"That's a sweet offer, Jules. But I'm not sure I want to leave Colorado. James wouldn't care since he's from the East Coast, but I don't know if I'd want to live somewhere so urban," Micki admitted.

"Well, silly, we wouldn't be living in an urban area. I'm thinking upstate New York—maybe a compound with at least a hundred acres for the kids to grow up on." Think about it, Micki. It wouldn't be happening soon—just keep it in mind. What's the point of having all this money and resources if I can't use them to make my life and the lives of the people I love better."

"You're always full of surprises, kiddo. I'll definitely keep it in mind for the future." They continued chatting as Julia walked back to the house, exchanging laughs and playful jabs. Gazing out over the choppy ocean as she ended the call, she felt glad to have taken the time to catch up with Micki.

***

Chapter 22: Danna-sama and O-hime-sama

The evening's entertainment began with a lively dinner outing. After a perfect beach day, the group gathered together in the living room, dressed in their best for dinner at A Shore Delight. Will borrowed clothes from Kasey, having only packed baggy pants, shorts, and T-shirts. They'd reserved a sleek black Escalade limo, fully equipped with a bar, leather bench seats, multiple TVs, and a driver, sparing Carl from the wheel.

As the limo glided up to the valet, a crowd of eager diners lingered outside, waiting for tables. Carl quickly stepped out to open the door, and Kasey, Ren, Julia, Akira, and Will emerged, the men trailing close behind Julia. As they approached the entrance, a local news reporter sprang forward, firing off rapid questions.

"Julia, Ren! Are these the Hawthorne brothers? How's everything coming along? When can we expect your debut collection? A photographer edged closer, angling for better shots, but Carl stepped in, his imposing frame cutting them off. Julia stepped closer to Giles as he paused to respond.

"Julia, would you mind if we answer a few questions?"

"Not at all! These distinguished gentlemen are Giles and Nigel Hawthorne, my partners in our exciting new fashion venture. Ask away," Julia said with a confident smile. Giles fielded the questions gracefully while Ren voiced his admiration for working alongside two living legends. The four posed together as cameras flashed, the crowd buzzing with excitement and snapping their own shots. Kasey ushered Haruto, Will, and Akira to the table, then returned to the door to watch, giving Ren and Julia their moment in the spotlight.

As Kasey escorted Julia to her seat, she leaned in and whispered, her tone curious, "How did they know we'd be here?"
Kasey grinned, his voice low and amused. "I don't know—maybe an anonymous tip. Free publicity for us and the restaurant. Besides, I thought Giles and Nigel might enjoy the spotlight."

Her eyes sparkled with admiration. "Baby, you're always two steps ahead. I love that about you."

Once they were all seated at the table, Giles said, "That felt like a blast from the past—getting ambushed on the way to dinner, flashes going off. It's been a while. Quite enjoyed it. Ren, thank you again for your generous compliments. I must say, your ease with the reporter and your photogenic charm are excellent for our brand. I meant to ask you before we left—did you design what you're wearing? It's very striking."

"Thank you. No, I didn't design what I'm wearing tonight. I haven't had much time to create yet. These are pieces from designers we're considering for collaboration. This vest is from Rex, a new designer making waves right now. It was his show that we sent you clips and pics from. And the skirt is from another emerging talent, Markus Oren. I saw his show the other day."

Giles leaned in, a mischievous glint in his eye, and whispered, "I love the boots, but they look like they might slow down romance a bit."

"Not if you just leave them on," Ren answered, a sly smile curving his lips. Giles chuckled, clearly entertained. Ren continued, his tone earnest. "And I meant every word—I'm thoroughly enjoying this collaboration. I'm learning so much from both of you about the business. I was hoping tomorrow, at some point, we could have another brainstorming session before we have to do this solely by video conferencing. We got a lot accomplished in just one sit-down, and I had a great time."

He leaned forward slightly, his enthusiasm shining through. "Since the traditional side of this launch needs a little adjustment, I was thinking you could really help with reimagining 70s casual wear. You lived it. Saw what people actually wore and loved. That perspective would be invaluable. What do you say—set aside a little creative time tomorrow?"

Giles nodded immediately, clearly touched by Ren's enthusiasm for weaving their input into his vision.

The restaurant was a resounding hit, with Chef Marco delivering a culinary spectacle as wine and spirits flowed freely. They indulged in every course until they were too full for dessert, deciding to take it home to savor later.

***

As soon as they returned, everyone changed into comfy clothes and launched into karaoke, belting out tunes and dancing for two solid hours. Later, while the group watched *The Devil Wears Prada* and indulged in dessert, Will and Akira slipped away to the beach. Sharing a blunt and another deep conversation, their budding relationship naturally evolved into a casual friends-with-benefits arrangement.

That night, Julia suggested Kasey and Ren share a bed, casually mentioning she could use some time alone. In truth, she hoped they'd take the opportunity to discuss her recent realizations and how they might affect their relationship. She chose the downstairs bedroom, as Will had claimed Akira's room for the night.

When sleep eluded her, Julia padded to the kitchen, grabbing a bottle of water and a petit four before stepping onto the deck. The tranquil night, broken only by the rhythmic lapping of waves against the shore, enveloped her as she curled up on the double lounger, arms wrapped around her knees, lost in thought. She barely noticed the door sliding open until Kasey's soft voice broke the silence. "Julia?"

"I'm here, baby. What are you doing up?" she asked as Kasey joined her, wrapping her in his arms.

"I heard the sliding door beep when you opened it. Figured it had to be you—who else would be out here at this hour? Trouble sleeping?"

"I swear, Kasey, you sleep like a cat," she said, nestling into him, comforted by his warmth.

"Only when you're not next to me," he murmured, his smile soft and reassuring.

"You know you don't have to worry now. I just waved to security—they passed by after their alarm went off."

"I know, but I came anyway," he said, pulling her closer with a gentle squeeze.

"I just felt a little restless. My mind just wouldn't shut off, and, well, it's rare these days to find myself alone in bed," she said with a soft chuckle.

"You could have slipped in with us. Ren never minds when you show up. He's completely besotted with you."

Julia glanced up, her expression questioning. Kasey grinned and added, "Completely in love with you—obsessed."

Julia giggled softly. "He's obsessed, alright. He certainly gives me a run for the money in the bedroom. Sometimes, it feels like he's unleashing ten years of pent-up lust and passion all at once. And then I remember he's even having sex with you. He is simply the horniest man I have ever been with," she said, laughing. "Don't get me wrong, I love it. But sometimes I feel like it might be unfair to you, having to witness it. You would tell me—or him—if it bothered you, right? I know you've said it didn't bother you before, but I just want to be certain," she asked, her tone thoughtful as she looked up at him.

"Let me explain it this way so you'll understand and feel more at ease. Since Ren has come into our lives, I've realized the depth of your sexual appetite. I always knew you had a higher libido than I did—frankly, I haven't wanted sex this much since meeting you—but it still pales in comparison to what I see you share with Ren."

"I always want you in my bed, but not necessarily for sex. I just want to be close to you. Yet when you're there, clearly wanting sex, it's hard to resist you. With Ren here, I'm content because I know you're fulfilled, he's satisfied, and I'm getting what I need from both of you."

"I do feel better," she said with a smile, reassured. She hesitated, her finger tracing tiny circles on his chest, before asking, "Did you guys talk at all about our future together as a trio?"

Kasey chuckled. "That's all we talked about. I couldn't get Ren to stop. He's deliriously happy at the thought of having kids and us forming a big family. The only way I could shut him up was to put something in his mouth." He glanced at

Julia, a broad smile playing on his lips, clearly pleased with his own crude joke.

"Kasey!" Julia laughed, hugging him tightly. "That was naughty. I like it. We're definitely a bad influence on you." She leaned back to meet his eyes. "I know Ren is thrilled, but what about you? I know you're happy being with me and Ren, but how do you feel about the children part? Did I throw you off with that? I need to know you're not just going along with it to please me. I don't want you feeling pressured. I could have children with Ren, and we'd still be a family."

"You did catch me off guard with the timing," Kasey admitted, "but it's not like I didn't know you'd want a family eventually. I'd love to have kids with you. My only concern is whether I'll be a good parent. What if I overcompensate for my past and end up raising a spoiled, entitled kid? Then I remember—I have the two of you to make sure that doesn't happen."

He paused, his voice softening. "Sometimes I still have to remind myself I don't have to tackle big issues alone anymore. I've got you both. As a team, we could absolutely manage raising a family. I'm not worried about it now. We're ready whenever you are. But… I'd like a little time to travel as a trio first. I want to show you the world."

***

Baby, you have no idea how happy you've made me. And I absolutely want you to show me the world. I can't imagine anything I'd want more than to travel with both of you."

After a quiet moment, she said softly, "You should head back; he'll miss you." Her luminous azure eyes gazed up at him, and her tight embrace betrayed her true feelings.

"Ren will be fine; he's a big boy. If he misses me, he knows where to find me—just like you do. How about I stay here with you? I know how much you love sleeping outdoors."

Grabbing another throw, he settled in beside her.

"I'm so lucky to have you," she murmured, snuggling close. "I love you."

***

On the group's final full day together, Julia planned a leisurely beach day, with a few hours set aside for creative input between Giles, Nigel, and Ren.

The lazy morning began later than usual, with no one—even Haruto—making an appearance until nearly ten. Julia and Kasey slept until nine-thirty, then took a quiet stroll along the shore, hand in hand, their thoughts on the future they were building together. When they returned, they found the rest of the group gathering on the deck, cups of tea or coffee in hand, their sun-kissed faces content.

Ren, freshly showered and with his damp hair pulled back in a ponytail, sat with Giles and Nigel, deep in discussion about the new line. Nearby, Haruto perked up considerably when Kasey suggested continuing their Tai Chi routine. He eagerly agreed, with Akira joining in, while Will opted to capture the moment from the sidelines, snapping photos from the sand.

The day unfolded at a relaxed pace, with everyone engrossed in their own activities—some packing, some swimming, some sunbathing—all while indulging in an array of leftovers throughout the day.

Amid the extended karaoke session, a movie screening, and animated conversations, the night stretched on, each moment cherished as their departure loomed.

The next day, as the vacation drew to a close, a flurry of packing and heartfelt goodbyes filled the morning. Julia watched Akira bid an emotional farewell to Will on the beach, their embrace brimming with unspoken feelings. Tears welled in her eyes as she hugged Giles and Nigel, already missing them. Gunther surprised her with a tight hug that lifted her off the ground, its intensity catching her off guard. Nearby, Haruto and Kasey exchanged low bows, cementing their newfound friendship.

At three in the afternoon, Carl escorted the group to the airport while Charley followed Julia, Kasey, and Ren back to New York in the utility vehicle. The trio chose to rent a car for the ride home, preferring the privacy to talk freely, while Charley remained close behind. Julia stretched out in the back seat, her excitement bubbling over as she recounted the week's events and shared how satisfied she was with how everything had turned out. As she and Ren discussed ideas for the new line and the brothers' creative input, Kasey found his mind wandering. His thoughts lingered on a future filled with Julia, Ren, and children, a life that felt more real and attainable than ever before.

***

Returning to the office, Ren dedicated his days to the upcoming launch of the new fashion line, tentatively slated for the first week of November. He expanded his team by hiring skilled seamstresses and enlisting talented fashion students as interns, all working together to bring his creative vision to life. Hours were spent in virtual meetings with Giles, meticulously dissecting his 70s-inspired designs, exchanging ideas, and refining sketches. As the pace accelerated and the team geared up for the launch of Hawthorne-Masters, Ren returned home each night exhausted but filled with an overwhelming sense of satisfaction and accomplishment.

The team's momentum surged further when Rex joined the project after a particularly lucrative lunch with Julia and Ren. Julia, more confident in Ren's commitment to her, handled Rex's obvious attraction to him with newfound ease, feeling secure in the bond they shared.

573

Despite Ren's demanding work schedule, Julia found moments to spice up his day, surprising him with steamy encounters in his office—bent over his desk, straddling him on his couch, and in his bathroom. The interludes offered him much-needed stress relief and added a thrilling edge to her day.

At home, Julia, Kasey, and Ren found their rhythm as a trio, adopting a flexible sleep schedule to ensure everyone's needs were met.

***

Two weeks after Julia proposed the idea of Vice President of New Acquisitions for Kasey, the board approved it. The next day, she took him out to lunch to share the news and celebrate, needing time away from the office to arrange a special surprise for him.

"So, what's the big news, sweetheart?" Kasey asked eagerly as they waited for their entrees.

With a radiant smile and excitement in her voice, Julia, trying to sound professional, revealed, "Based solely on your exceptional merits and the invaluable contributions you've made, as of today, you're the new Vice President of New Acquisitions. It's long-overdue recognition for your dedication and hard work."

She gave his hand a squeeze and continued, "I've never seen the board agree so quickly to a senior position like this. Rick and Jack were your biggest supporters—there was absolutely no pushback. This role gives you the authority to make the decisions you've already been handling without needing my sign-off.

"I see this as a temporary position for about a year. After that, the role of President is yours when I fully step into the position of CEO. I can't do both effectively. I'm planning to ask Henry to assist me like he did my father, and you'll be getting your own assistant to handle all the tedious stuff. Like

Ren said, you should only be focusing on strategic work—not bullshit, and you shouldn't be babysitting me anymore.

"Congratulations, Mr. Vice President! How's it feel?"

"It feels great, but I enjoy babysitting you," Kasey said with a warm smile. "Thank you, Julia."

"Oh no," she interrupted, shaking her head. "Don't thank me. I told you—you earned this. Thank *you* for doing the job you do every day without any thought of reward. This past year, I couldn't have done my job properly without you. You picked up the slack when I couldn't function. Nothing suffered because of your unwavering support of me and my role.

"I want you right beside me as I truly take the reins of this company. You have so many skills I don't possess, and they're exactly what I need to make us an unbeatable team."

Grateful and touched, Kasey accepted the new role with humility. Placing his hand on top of hers, he said, "I'll be right by your side in whatever you need. I will always be on your team." He squeezed her hand, his loving eyes sparkling with happiness, knowing they were not only united in their commitment to each other but also in their shared vision for the company's future.

***

Shortly after Julia and Kasey arrived back at work, Ren strolled in with an air of effortless confidence. He made his way to Kasey's couch, settling comfortably with a grin. "Congratulations, Mr. VP. How's it feel?" he asked, spreading his legs, one ankle resting on the opposite knee, and draping his arms casually over the back and arm of the couch.

"Thanks, it feels really good. By the way, I understand you might have had a hand in this," Kasey replied, glancing at Ren while continuing to pack a box. "Julia mentioned you suggested I shouldn't be burdened with so much bullshit work, as she put it."

"I think that's exactly how I put it," Ren laughed.

"Thanks. It's always nice to realize I have two allies in my corner now. It still takes some getting used to."

"Well, get used to it," Ren affirmed. "You have two people who care about you, appreciate everything you do, and want the best for you. You deserve this promotion. Julia just needed to see it."

Kasey glanced toward Julia's office. "Did you see what she did? She had a desk made to match hers and had it delivered while we were at lunch."

"I know. It was delivered to my workroom last night, just waiting for you to go to lunch."

Kasey smiled at the thought of the two of them collaborating on surprises for him. "This will be my assistant's office. She said if I don't like working alongside her, I can get my own office, but I'm pretty sure that's not what she'd want. I don't mind, though; I work so closely with her, I might as well be here," he explained, noting the thoughtful arrangement of the desks facing each other.

"She really wants to keep you close, huh?" Ren said with a knowing smile, observing the setup.

A pleased expression crossed Kasey's face as he continued clearing out his desk. "Help me with this—grab the door," he said, motioning toward Julia's office as he picked up a box. Ren grabbed his laptop and followed him inside.

"Where's Julia?"

"She's in a meeting."

"Well, I just stopped by to congratulate you. I'd better get back. I'll see you later, Mr. Vice President," Ren said, giving Kasey an affectionate pat on the back before leaving.

***

September 24th arrived, bringing Julia's excitement for Kasey's twenty-eighth birthday the next day. She and Ren had planned for Kasey to spend all day Sunday with Ren, saving her gift for his actual birthday on Monday.

Kasey's special day with Ren began with a morning run, followed by a steamy shower together and then a trip to the shooting range. Ren enjoyed himself as much as Kasey, both of them reveling in the thrill of firing the Jericho handgun.

Afterward, they strolled through Kasey's neighborhood, exploring local shops and soaking in the lively atmosphere. The day culminated in dinner at a cozy bistro, where they tucked themselves away at a quiet table in the back, immersed in conversation.

During the meal, Ren presented Kasey with a special gift: a limited-edition watch inspired by Spike Spiegel from *Cowboy Bebop*. The metallic navy piece featured subtle yellow accents, reflecting Spike's iconic attire. The back was engraved with a silhouette of Spike, while the crown bore an etching of a rose— a nod to Julia's significance in the story. Kasey was thrilled, immediately slipping the watch onto his wrist alongside his ID bracelet.

"Thank you, Ren. I love it," Kasey said, his handsome face glowing with love and gratitude. "I've had the best day with you. We definitely have to go to the firing range again—you were amazing." His cheeks flushed a rosy hue as he bashfully added, glancing down before looking back at Ren, "Not gonna lie, you looked pretty hot holding the Jericho."

Under the table, Ren gave Kasey's knee a firm squeeze, his smoldering gaze making Kasey catch his breath and quicken his heartbeat. Leaning forward, Ren whispered, "Not as hot as you are with that gun strapped to your chest under your jacket, Spike." He had mentioned earlier how jealous he was of Kasey's concealed carry license.

Kasey's face lit up. "Seems like we both have a thing for guns. After the launch, we should all take a few days and go to the ranch. You'd love target shooting in the great outdoors—it's beautiful there. Julia hasn't been back since the funeral. I think it's time we helped her through that."

"Wow, it's been that long? I didn't know that," Ren said thoughtfully. Then, with his characteristic cheerfulness, he added, "We'll definitely get her to go when the time comes. She can't resist either one of us if we ask her nicely. And with both of us there to stand by her, she'll get through it."

He flashed a devilish grin as he handed the waitress his card and changed the subject. "Hey, this birthday is not over yet. I have something I'm dying to give you when we get home. Let's get out of here."

Arriving home a short time later, Julia greeted them at the door, listened to a brief summary of their day, and kissed them both goodnight. She then retired to her room, giving them ample time to finish their birthday date together and enjoy each other's company, knowing tomorrow would be her turn.

***

The following morning, Ren and Kasey headed to the office, leaving Julia behind to diligently orchestrate her birthday surprise. Alice and her son arrived to help transform Kasey's training room into a traditional Japanese tea room. They cleared the floor and strategically placed shoji screens along the walls. Once they finished, a delivery arrived with the final items needed for the transformation.

In the center of the room, they positioned a long, low wooden table on tatami mats, surrounded by cushions. The table was set with traditional tea utensils, bowls, scoops, and containers. A beautiful ikebana arrangement of phalaenopsis orchids in an organic honey bamboo container added a touch of elegance in one corner. Soft, diffused light emanating from paper lanterns would provide gentle illumination, complemented by the flickering glow of candles Julia chose to enhance the ambiance, avoiding harsh shadows.

At three in the afternoon, consultant Mei arrived, ready to guide Julia in the tea ceremony and transform them both into beautiful geisha. Accompanying Mei was a kitsuke-shi, tasked with dressing them in their kimonos and later performing traditional music on the shamisen. Mei expertly applied Julia's long, sleek, black wig and makeup. The wig was styled in a half-up, half-down fashion, which was then adorned with elegant Ogi Kanzashi ornaments, their fan-shaped designs adding a touch of sophistication, and Darari Kanzashi, with their long, cascading elements enhancing the intricate beauty of her look and adding a touch of sparkle and sound to the hairstyle. Julia's makeup was flawlessly applied, opting for a pale look instead of the traditional white, giving her classic geisha appearance a unique twist—resembling a manga goddess.

Prompted by Julia, Ren ensured Kasey was home promptly at six. They waited eagerly at the door of the brownstone, anticipation buzzing for the surprise within. Following instructions, they rang the doorbell, and Mei greeted them with a respectful bow, welcoming them inside in Japanese. They took off their shoes and stepped inside, where they were enveloped by the serene melody of the shamisen, the delicate scent of incense, and the soft glow of lanterns and candles scattered throughout the living room and kitchen, leading to the tea room. Julia stood before them, a shy smile gracing her lips as she bowed, embodying the essence of a geisha, ready to immerse herself and her partners in a world of refined rituals.

Julia gently slipped Kasey's suit jacket off his shoulders, replacing it with a stunning kimono, while Mei did the same for Ren. Speaking softly to Kasey in Japanese, Julia gestured towards the transformed room, inviting him to step inside. The new shoji screens, adorned with intricate crane paintings, captivated Kasey as he crossed the threshold. Mei had entered before them, turning on the video camera set up discreetly in one corner, to capture Kasey's gift for posterity.

As Julia glided into the room, the soft rustling of her silk kimono and the delicate tap of her wooden sandals filled the air. The tatami-mat floor beneath her accentuated her deliberate and graceful movements, each step carrying an air of poise and sophistication. The notes of the shamisen intertwined with the rhythmic flow of the ceremony, creating a serene atmosphere that transported everyone present into a harmonious blend of tradition and elegance.

Before the service began, Julia offered traditional snacks Mei had brought to complement the bitterness of the matcha. There was Kuri Wagashi, a seasonal delicacy during the fall, made with sweetened chestnuts and shaped like tiny pumpkins; Momiji Manju, maple-leaf shaped cakes filled with sweet red bean paste; and Sweet Potato Wagashi, shaped in cubes.

Anticipation brimmed as Julia skillfully began the intricate steps of the tea ceremony. She cleaned the utensils, emphasizing cleanliness and mindfulness. The precision in her movements, from preparing the matcha to serving it with the utmost care, showcased her deep respect for the tradition and her devotion to Kasey in learning it.

Ren exchanged looks of amazement with Kasey at how meticulous Julia's attention to detail was. He marveled at her dedication: from instruction on the tea ceremony and Japanese lessons at lunchtime for weeks to the meticulous preparation of the training room and the flawless execution of her attire, makeup, and demeanor.

Kasey couldn't tear his eyes away from Julia—entranced by her beauty, grace, her earnest attempts at speaking Japanese, and her unwavering commitment to the role. If she encountered any difficulty, Mei seamlessly stepped in to assist, resulting in an unforgettable birthday surprise for Kasey.

At the conclusion of the three-hour ceremony, Mei and Julia respectfully bowed, and Mei stepped out of the room. Ren helped her and the dresser gather their belongings, escorted them out, and quietly slipped away to his room, leaving Julia and Kasey to enjoy their evening alone.

"Kissu mii," she whispered, her lips curling into a playful smile as she asked for a kiss.

"My love, you take my breath away. I can't mess up your makeup yet. I'd like a picture of us, please," he requested, stepping to the door and calling Ren, asking him to bring his camera to take pictures of them. Kasey didn't want just selfies; he wanted a full portrait of them to enlarge and hang in his training room.

After taking photos of the three of them individually, as couples, and together, Ren asked Kasey for a quick picture of him with the katana. Julia liked the picture so much she took more of Kasey and Ren together with the magnificent sword, looking like powerful shoguns.

With the photos finished, Ren quietly slipped out, leaving Kasey and Julia wrapped in each other's arms in the serene tea room.

Looking deep into her eyes, Kasey whispered, "You were simply flawless tonight. It's incredible how you mastered the tea ceremony, even picked up some Japanese, and orchestrated all this for me," his words of praise and gratitude tickling her ear. Careful not to disturb her makeup, he pressed a tender kiss to her neck.

"Could we sleep in here tonight? I could bring the mats in and put them under the pillows, he asked softly.

With a grin and a nod, she agreed, and he left to fetch the mats and a blanket while she pushed the table to the side. Carefully arranging the thick training mats underneath the pillows and spreading out the blanket, he selected music on his phone reminiscent of what the musician had played and blew out a few of the candles leaving the room in a soft glow, setting the scene.

"Julia?" he whispered, pulling her close and nuzzling her neck.

"Yes, baby?" she murmured.

"Do you think we could video me undressing you? From where the camera is, it wouldn't be too revealing—" Julia interrupted, "It sounds hot to me, let's do it."

"Wait, there's something else."

"Anything, baby, it's your birthday."

"I know we said we would save role-playing for the three of us, but just this once, could we play out a fantasy of mine? You put so much effort into all this, and I can't tell you how much I love it." With a downward glance, his piercing blue-gray eyes looking out from under his hair, his lips curled up in one corner, he asked, "Could you speak Japanese and call me Danna-sama?"

"What does it mean?" she asked, curious and eager to see what he had in mind.

"Well, when Ren asked to take a picture with the katana and said he felt like an ancient shogun with his kimono on, I just got the image of a shogun with his geisha making love for the first time in this setting. Danna-sama was a way geishas referred to their patrons. It meant husband or master. And I want to call you O-hime-sama; it means princess. It was a way a shogun might show his high level of respect for her."

Julia gave Kasey her sexiest grin and whispered," Asobou ka?" The phrase she used as Misty, "Shall we play?"

Both love and lust flashed in Kasey's expression. He gave her hand a tender kiss. Then, he took care to make sure the camera was pointed in the exact direction to get the view of what he wanted. And before he left, he slid the katana into the sash of his kimono. He left the room with instructions for her to turn the camera on and walk to her spot.

When he stepped into the room, she bowed deeply as her face turned slightly to the side, shyly avoiding eye contact. As she gracefully rose, she said sweetly, "O-tanjoubi omedetou, Danna-sama. Aishiteru," which translated to "Happy birthday, husband. I love you."

Her expression of complete and utter love stirred deep emotions in him, choking his voice as he replied, "Aishiteru, O-hime-sama." Gently lifting her face with his fingers, his lips tenderly grazed hers.

He stood back as she slowly and gracefully slid the sword out of his sash and placed it gently on the table.

With utmost care, he removed the larger ornaments and combs from her hair and slowly undressed her; each garment respectfully placed on the table until only her blue silk nagajuban remained.

He pulled her close, his voice low and husky in her ear. "Should I turn off the camera?" he whispered. "Absolutely not," she replied seductively. "I want to watch you make love to me, Danna-sama."

He eased her gently onto the pillows. As she watched him undress completely, she was surprised to see him slip back into his kimono before lying beside her.

She surrendered to Kasey's fantasy, letting him make love to her with a newfound passion. As he whispered in Japanese, his confidence soared, imagining himself as a powerful shogun and her, his cherished geisha.

Their R-rated shogun and geisha fantasy, during which he lovingly kept Julia's naked body hidden beneath his kimono while making love to her, was everything he could have wanted. With the soft glow of red lanterns and their distance from the camera, the filmed encounter felt like an intimate scene straight out of a love story.

Unexpectedly, Kasey pulled Julia onto his lap as he settled back on his heels. He draped his kimono over her, but she guided his hand downward, revealing her breasts while keeping the rest of her hidden. She remained still in his lap, his presence deep within her, letting his hands and mouth explore her body for the camera. When his fingers slipped between her legs, teasing slow circles in her slick, swollen flesh, she began to move, her soft moans quickly turning into shameless cries of pleasure. Julia's breasts swayed with every motion, her sweet sounds spilling freely from her lips.

As she cried out, "Aishiteru, Danna-sama," her body trembled in climax, sending Kasey over the edge seconds later. The camera captured it all—an unforgettable addition to his birthday celebration. Once they caught their breath, Kasey eagerly reviewed the footage, pulling Julia into his arms, her body nestled snugly within his kimono. Satisfied and more aroused than ever, Kasey turned off the camera, then consumed her with wild abandon, reminiscent of their first night together. Every touch, every kiss, was infused with his overwhelming love and gratitude for the gift she had given him.

***

Ren came down the next morning to find a naked Julia, barely covered by the blanket, her wig askew and makeup smudged, alongside Kasey still in his kimono, both blissfully asleep, exhausted from their passionate night. Grinning mischievously, he snapped a quick photo, sending it to their phones before waking them.

Leaning against the door frame, he gently roused the pair. "Julia, Spike, time to rise and shine. We're gonna be late."

Dazed, Julia sat up quickly, adjusting her crooked wig as she mumbled, "You go in now. Tell Charley to come get us at twelve. And tell Barbara too, please." She fell back into Kasey's embrace, snuggling into him as he closed his eyes. Amazed he didn't even budge for work, Ren chuckled softly and backed away, realizing their influence on him.

By ten o'clock, Kasey lovingly kissed Julia awake, "Good morning, O-hime-sama," he whispered in her ear. "We need to get up and shower."

"Morning, Danna-sama, she murmured, still groggy, but blissfully happy. "That was some spell we had going last night. Baby, you were on fire. I came twice, and you didn't even use the vibrator." Kasey smiled, blushing at her praise.

"That was the best birthday I've ever experienced. Between you and Ren, I feel so loved and cared for. I will never forget how beautiful you were last night and how much work and love you put into your gift. Thank you, Julia. You fill my life with so much happiness."

"You are very welcome. I'm thrilled you enjoyed my gift; I did put my heart into it. And last night wasn't just good for you. I had the best time. I would love to be your O-hime-sama again. I felt so different trying to be delicate and refined in the kimono, but once it came off—"

Kasey interrupted, "You were the Julia I know and love desperately."

She gazed at him, seeing love and appreciation in his eyes, and smiled. "I need to lose this wig," she chuckled, scratching her head, "you can't possibly take me seriously looking like this."

"You look absolutely adorable. Now let's get moving. Don't forget you have a meeting," he urged, helping her to her feet.

***

"So, that was one hell of a birthday present, huh?' Ren said as he took a seat on the couch in Julia and Kasey's office.

Kasey smiled, "She outdid herself. It amazes me how much thought and effort she puts into expressing her love. It was one of the sweetest things anyone has ever done for me. And afterward wasn't too shabby either," he said, a crooked smile forming as he dipped his head slightly, and looked out from under his hair. "I think we might leave the tea room there permanently. It looks beautiful. I can move my training room to the fourth floor. We could use the tea room as a dining room... and for other activities," he suggested playfully. "It was inspirational."

Ren laughed, "Looked like you were certainly inspired. Jules was stunningly beautiful last night, and this morning, she was a hot mess. Speaking of, where is she?"

"She had a meeting with legal; we barely made it in time. I have never been late for anything in my life. She can be a handful with that; no time management at all," he said. "It was my own fault. I should have woken her sooner. I know better. She moves like a snail sometimes. That's her only fault, and it's not even all that bad, so I guess I'll just learn to live with it," he said with a smile. "She's worth it."

"You're not wrong there," Ren grinned, wholeheartedly agreeing.

"By the way, thanks for the picture,' Kasey grinned. "With the earlier ones you took, it's a real before-and-after shot. I loved it. Not so sure Julia will," he chuckled. With his eyes crinkling at the corners and a sly grin, he added, "She even let me video us. She called me Danna-sama, and I called her O-hime-sama."

Wrapping his arm around Kasey's shoulder and drawing him close, he whispered, "Ahh, the gift that keeps on giving. Lucky you. I can't imagine anything hotter. I might ask Julia if I could borrow it for my next night alone. Porn starring my two favorite people." He gave Kasey a quick bite on the neck and said, "I'd better stop thinking about it, or I might have to drag you into the bathroom. Too late—it's got a mind of its own,' Ren laughed, both of them eyeing his obvious hard-on.

"Jesus, Ren, you're insatiable,' Kasey said, turning and heading toward the bathroom. "But since I'm in a really good mood and you need to get back to work and focus," he looked back over his shoulder and said in a low husky voice, "Come with me."

A few minutes later, they opened the door to find Julia smiling, perched on the corner of her desk.

"That was not exactly discreet, Mr. Cortland," Julia playfully scolded, bringing a rosy hue to his cheeks. She turned to Ren, "You are such a bad influence, sir, because I know Kasey was not the one to instigate the encounter."

"Well, you're partially wrong. We both got turned on talking about your little video, and Spike here graciously offered to handle the raging boner I was sporting."

"Well, then, I can't blame either of you... it's an extremely hot video if I do say so myself. Maybe we should all watch it together tonight and fuck like bunnies all over that tea room."

"Enough sex talk, or the two of us will be out of commission again," Kasey said, guiding a grinning Ren to the door. "Back to work, we'll pick this up where we left off tonight."

"As for you," he said, turning back to Julia with a grin, 'let me help you off that desk. We've got work to do."

***

Chapter 23: The Launch of Hawthorne-Masters

In the final week of September and throughout October, the brownstone buzzed with activity as extensive renovations transformed its interior. Ren's domain now occupied a spacious suite on the third floor. His dark wood king-size platform bed, complete with built-in side tables, dominated the bedroom, its crisp white sheets, pillows, and duvet all trimmed in navy. A beautifully carved table beneath the window held a bonsai tree—a gift from Julia and Kasey. Named Yamato, meaning "great harmony" by Kasey, it symbolized the unity Ren had brought to them all since moving in. They had brought their bonsai home at the end of the summer season, and now one resided in each of their rooms. A sleek electric fireplace occupied one wall, a request from Julia so they could make love in front of the fire, with a sheepskin rug already spread across the floor.

Ren's bedroom featured a lavish bathroom with a state-of-the-art Japanese bidet and an expansive walk-in shower, spacious enough to accommodate all three of them. The shower boasted dual rain shower heads and jets positioned on three sides for a luxurious experience. In a cozy corner of his new sitting room, a drafting table stood equipped with pens, pencils, and office essentials, ready for moments of inspiration. A generously sized dressing room provided ample space for his extensive wardrobe, shoes, boots, watches, and accessories.

A beautifully decorated guest suite was also located on the same floor.

The training room found its new home on the fourth floor, while the tea room downstairs underwent further modifications. Its traditional aesthetics were enhanced with a unique touch—a discreet twin futon hidden behind a shoji screen, reserved for those "inspirational nights."

A room on the fourth floor for Alice was also completed, leaving two empty rooms and the training room on the same floor. The apartment downstairs was updated for security, with a bedroom set up, the kitchen stocked with utensils, dishware, and small appliances, and a command center in the living room equipped with security cameras covering the entire property, including feeds from the shore house.

Julia's new bedroom and dressing room were meticulously crafted to her exact specifications, the result of a collaborative effort with Ren during a lazy Sunday afternoon. At the heart of the design was her king-size bed, nestled beneath a beautifully carved light wood canopy adorned with twinkling lights. Sheer curtains could be drawn shut around the bed's natural wood frame, crafted from tree branches, creating a magical and romantic cocoon. The bed was dressed in luxurious white sheets and plush, fluffy pillows, accented by a collection of smaller slate blue throw pillows. Adjacent to the bed, an oversized slate blue chaise lounge and matching chair with delicate white pillows offered a serene retreat. Above the intricately carved mantel of her fireplace hung a framed portrait of a cherished memory—the selfie Ren had taken of the three of them on Kasey's birthday night. For the first time,

Julia's room reflected her happiness, featuring a palette completely free of gray or black.

***

Two days before the painters were scheduled to begin, Kasey joined Ren and Julia in the tea room for dinner, holding his mother's cherished scrapbook close to his chest. Placing it carefully on the table, he admitted, "I'm ready to share memories of my mother with you both. This is all I have of her that truly holds meaning for me. I keep some of her jewelry in a safe deposit box, but none of that means as much to me as this." His face and gray eyes betrayed a rare, deep vulnerability.

"Baby, come sit between us and tell us all about her," Julia urged, patting the space beside her. As they ate, Kasey carefully turned the pages of the scrapbook, recounting the stories behind each photo. His deep love for his mother radiated with every word. As they neared the end of the book, Julia offered quiet support, her hand resting on his thigh, silently encouraging him to continue. When Kasey's resolve wavered near the final pages, Ren and Julia wrapped their arms around him, holding him close and giving him the strength to finish.

Turning to Julia, Kasey confessed, "I'm sure you noticed my mom called me 'sweetheart.' I hope it's okay that I call you that. It was special to me, and I wanted to share it with you. It meant a lot when you said you liked it. Unlike Ren, I'm not good at pet names or nicknames." Soft chuckles filled the room as Ren rubbed Kasey's back.

Julia leaned into him and replied, "I love that you call me 'sweetheart,' and now that I know why, it means even more. Maybe you could show us the picture you'd like to have enlarged. We can take care of that soon and hang our portraits side by side." She smiled warmly as she spoke.

"I was thinking—what if we made one of the spare rooms on the fourth floor into a meditation room? We could hang

591

the portraits there and sit with them whenever we felt the need," Kasey suggested.

"That's a wonderful idea, baby. I love it," Julia said, her excitement evident. "We could do a few pictures."

"We could even hang one of your grandmother's, Ren, and add a Buddhist shrine if you'd like. I know you were close to her," Kasey suggested gently.

"That's really thoughtful of you. I'd love that—it would be perfect for meditation." Taking Kasey's hand, Ren added sincerely, "I'm so glad you felt comfortable enough to show us this, Spike. Let's bring your mom into our lives. And maybe soon, you'll feel ready to start sharing more of the good times you had with her. If it gets too emotional, we're here to help you through it."

Kasey hesitated for a moment, his voice soft as he admitted, "I've never really talked about her before because... I wasn't sure I could handle it. The emotional toll was too much, and I wasn't ready to share how attached I was to her— or what losing her did to me. It hurt so much; I didn't think I could make it through."

Julia reached for his hand, squeezing it gently as she leaned into him. "I'm so proud of you. This was a big step," she said softly, brushing a stray strand of hair back from his face before leaning in to kiss him.

Kasey smiled gratefully, glancing at them both before admitting, "I know it's supposed to be my night alone, but I was wondering if maybe we could all sleep together. I think I could use some of that support tonight."

"Of course we can. You didn't think we'd let you sleep alone tonight, did you?" Ren replied warmly, placing a reassuring hand on Kasey's shoulder. Lightening the mood, he teased, "I was even willing to give up my time with Jules for you—but this is much better. And I promise to keep my weapon holstered if that's what you need." With a playful jab to Kasey's side, Ren chuckled, easing the moment into something lighter—full of love, care, and just the right touch of humor.

As they settled into bed that night, Kasey nestled between his partners, their warm embrace making him feel wholly content, supported, and deeply loved.

***

While Kasey and Julia juggled brownstone renovations and office responsibilities, Ren concentrated on his demanding workload, preparing their debut collection. He passed his design sketches and Julia's specific requests to his ex-boss, Nick Galloway, who stepped in to oversee most of the renovations. With expert contractors and reliable vendors at his disposal, Nick ensured everything moved along smoothly, pushing to complete the work as quickly as possible. The only delay was the intricately carved canopy for Julia's bed, which required a little extra cash to motivate the artist to finish within three weeks.

During days of heavy construction, when the plumbing and electricity were disrupted, the three of them retreated to Julia's condo to escape the chaos. Ren, visiting her condo for the first time, fell in love with the city's energy and the building's amenities, especially the gym with its sauna and running track. He and Kasey made full use of the facilities during their stay.

One night, Ren persuaded them to check out a local bar, where they enjoyed good food, drinks, and lively music. He and Julia danced late into the night, but Ren's enthusiasm for beer got the better of him. By the time Kasey suggested it was time to head home, he was both amused and a little concerned by just how many pints Ren had polished off.

***

593

At work, Rex, as expected, contributed a wealth of creative inspiration. His playful flirtation with Ren was lighthearted rather than predatory, and neither Julia nor Kasey felt threatened by it. Instead, Rex and Ren developed a productive partnership and friendship, with Rex helping to add the finishing touches to some of Ren's more urban pieces while Ren concentrated on his 70s collection with Giles.

The show was set for a Thursday night in November, just before the anniversary of her family's tragedy. Driven by a determination to prove herself and honor her father's memory, Julia insisted on a date before the anniversary. She aimed to quickly establish the fashion house's success, envisioning a future where she could freely embrace her relationships.

Twice, Raven Black visited Masters Inc. for sneak previews and interviews. Both times, she maintained a flirtatious demeanor with Ren but stayed within respectful boundaries, much to Julia's relief. Recognizing Raven's value in generating publicity and adhering to the adage "Keep your friends close and enemies closer," Julia enlisted her help in organizing the guest list and seating for the show. Raven's extensive network proved invaluable, and though Julia hesitated to admit it, she appreciated Raven's assistance. Additionally, Raven worked seamlessly with Derrick, who seemed to be nursing a budding crush on her.

***

As the runway show approached, weariness and pressure weighed heavily on the trio, evident as they lounged on the couch in their living room, barely focused on the show they were watching.

Ren, feeling pressure on multiple fronts, fretted over the impending judgment of his creative vision and his responsibility to ensure the debut's success. With Jack, Rick, and most of the other board members from Colorado flying in for the event, he didn't want to let anyone down, least of all Julia. Kasey spent a generous amount of time reassuring both Ren and Julia that the launch would go smoothly and be a success.

By ten o'clock, Ren and Julia were nestled in bed, and for the first time since they started sharing one, he told Julia he was simply too tired for sex. "Baby girl," he murmured as she snuggled against him, her head finding its place on his chest, her leg intertwining with his. "I'm utterly spent. Not even your charms could get me going tonight; I can barely keep my eyes open." He kissed the top of her head. "Goodnight, I love you."

With a soft sigh, she responded, "I was gonna say the same thing. Night, babe, I love you too." In a matter of minutes, they were both sound asleep.

***

Julia began the day with excitement, knowing she would soon see the entire group from vacation, including Akira, whose presence would undoubtedly make Will happy. She was also thrilled that Micki and James were flying in a day early and staying for a couple of days. Nigel, Giles, and the rest of the vacation crew arrived three days before the show to prepare with Ren, once again enjoying Julia's hospitality by staying at her condo. Akira was invited to stay at the newly finished brownstone with Will.

The four designers and Julia convened the following day for a trial run of the show, noting any adjustments needed before the upcoming event. They also managed the ever-changing seat arrangements as last-minute ticket requests flooded in, leaving only standing room available—a promising indicator of high demand.

Carl coordinated with Kasey to ensure extra security personnel were in place for the event and arranged transportation for Julia's guests staying at her condo. While

Nigel, Haruto, Giles, and Gunther stayed at the condo, Micki and James were set to lodge at the brownstone along with Will and Akira.

Ren and Rex worked late into the night at the condo after long days in the workroom with Nigel and Giles. The soft hum of sewing machines filled the air, accompanied by the occasional clink of glasses as Gunther moved around like a mother hen, refilling drinks, serving snacks, and ensuring the older men didn't overdo it. Alongside Haruto, they meticulously adjusted the fit of each piece, with Haruto's tailoring expertise proving invaluable as he tweaked seams and hems to achieve flawless silhouettes for the models. Despite the pressure, the group found joy in their time together, treating it as a bonding experience.

The young duo listened intently as Giles regaled them with stories of his and Nigel's early days in the 70s—tales of grueling deadlines, wild parties, and the camaraderie that kept them going. Giles's voice was animated, his laughter contagious as he worked, and even Nigel chimed in now and then with his usual understated wit. Each story left the fledgling designers inspired by the passion and determination of the generation before them.

During this time, Julia and Kasey deeply missed Ren's presence at home, acutely aware of how much quieter it was without him. Since he often chose to sleep at the condo, too tired to return home, they decided it was best to give him the space he needed to focus on the show, trusting that he would seek them out when he was ready.

Micki and James finally arrived, providing a welcome distraction for Julia from the launch and missing Ren. She delighted in giving them a tour of the extensively renovated brownstone, her pride evident as she walked them through each carefully designed space. Showing them her new bedroom suite and the beautifully decorated, spacious dressing room, she felt a deep sense of accomplishment. "I never imagined it would turn out this perfect," she admitted, a small smile playing on her lips.

When they stepped into Ren's bedroom, Julia paused briefly, taking in the room that was so distinctly *him*. A pang of longing stirred within her, but she quickly tucked it away, forcing a neutral expression. Micki, however, caught the flicker of emotion and gave Julia a knowing smirk, her silence speaking volumes.

In the meditation room, Micki and James exchanged knowing glances when they saw the picture of Kasey and his mother displayed beside Julia's family portrait. Micki brushed her fingers across the frame, a soft smile spreading across her face. "He's come so far, hasn't he?" she said quietly. Julia nodded, her heart swelling with pride, knowing how much that photo symbolized Kasey's journey.

***

The evening before the show, everyone gathered at the brownstone for a sushi meal in the tranquil tea room. After dinner, they lingered in the serene setting, engaging in small talk while watching highlights of Julia's tea ceremony triumph on Kasey's laptop. They marveled at her performance and appearance, the video briefly diverting everyone's attention from the looming runway showcase. At eight o'clock, Ren, Rex, Nigel, Giles, Haruto, and Gunther left for the venue to make last-minute adjustments to the décor and run a sound check with the DJ.

Julia and Kasey kissed Ren goodbye in the foyer, with Julia clinging to him tightly. She buried her face in his shoulder, breathing in his familiar scent as if to hold onto a piece of him for the long night ahead.

"We both miss you," she whispered in his ear. "I can't wait for you to be back home."

Ren kissed the top of her head before stepping back, his dark eyes warm as he briefly touched Kasey's arm. "Just one more night, baby girl. I'll be home with you both tomorrow. I have to go. Love you both," he said before bounding down the steps and heading to the car.

"Come on, sweetheart, let's get you inside where it's warm," Kasey said gently, wrapping an arm around her shoulders and guiding her back inside.

***

Ren curated stunning looks for Julia and Micki from the designer who had previously loaned her clothes, securing the pieces in exchange for coveted seats at the show. Will's outfit—baggy black trousers with tapered legs, a striped dress shirt under a gray wool vest, an open knee-length brown jacket, and black-and-white pointed-toe loafers with thick black soles—was also styled by Ren. The ensemble transformed him, a bold departure from his usual mismatched baggy clothes and sneakers. It drew unanimous approval, especially from Akira, who turned heads in her signature blend of cutting-edge Tokyo fashion, effortlessly chic and completely her own.

Kasey and James, alongside Nigel and Haruto, opted for sleek, modernized versions of Hawthorne Apparel's signature suits. Each cut and detail radiated classic sophistication, making them look every bit the refined gentlemen. Giles and Gunther, by contrast, embraced their creative edge, pairing tailored legacy suits with vibrant silk t-shirts and high-top sneakers, blending the old with the bold. Ren and Rex stole the spotlight, showcasing their own visionary creations, a perfect preview of what was to come on the runway.

***

The day of the show was a whirlwind of activity. Ren, Rex, and the brothers arrived early at the venue, fine-tuning every detail and coordinating the models with the music during the

598

final dress rehearsal. Back at the brownstone, Julia and Kasey spent the morning with Akira, Will, Micki, and James, joined by Gunther and Haruto, savoring the quiet moments of calm before the storm.

As the afternoon turned into evening, the air buzzed with anticipation as everyone readied themselves for the event. Excitement surged through the brownstone as final touches were made, outfits were perfected, and nerves gave way to exhilaration.

Arriving together in a sleek stretch limo outside the venue, they were met with a frenzy of photographers and reporters clamoring for interviews. Julia, exuding bold sophistication, wore an Alexander McQueen-inspired ensemble: a tailored cropped jacket with sharp, exaggerated shoulders over a fitted black leather skirt that hit mid-thigh. Paired with sleek over-the-knee boots and a minimalist choker, her look was daring yet refined, perfectly embodying the edgy vision of Masters Inc.

Graciously fielding questions and posing for pictures, Julia radiated star power, her presence commanding the spotlight. Micki marveled at the attention, whispering, "This is unreal," while Akira snapped photo after photo on her phone, capturing every detail for her Instagram feed.

The security team, led by Carl and Charley, was impeccably coordinated, their sleek black suits and turtlenecks a nod to Archer's iconic style—personally chosen by Julia, of course. They managed the crowd with precision, ensuring the group's safety while exuding effortless cool that perfectly complemented the glamour of the evening.

Kasey and Julia slipped backstage to offer silent yet meaningful support to Ren and the brothers before the show began. The scene backstage was chaotic as models hurriedly changed into the designers' creations, makeup artists meticulously applied finishing touches, and hairstylists sculpted both classic and avant-garde looks. The air buzzed with electric energy, each moment building toward the unveiling of Hawthorne-Masters' vision on the runway.

Positioning themselves discreetly, they observed Ren effortlessly commanding the chaos, his authoritative presence ensuring every detail met his exacting standards. The seasoned calm of Giles and Nigel provided a steadying anchor amidst the frenzy, their quiet confidence lending an air of civility to the storm—a perfect embodiment of the British mantra, "Keep calm and carry on."

When Ren finally caught sight of them, their bright smiles and Julia's encouraging thumbs-up drew a grateful grin from him. He mouthed "Thank you" before swiftly redirecting his attention to adjusting a model's outfit with precision.

Julia and Kasey exchanged smiles and waves with a focused Nigel and Giles before slipping out to take their seats.

***

As the lights dimmed in the converted warehouse—an industrial chic venue with exposed brick walls, metal beams, and a high ceiling laced with hanging Edison bulbs—anticipation crackled like static in the air. The diverse crowd, an eclectic mix of celebrities draped in couture, YouTube fashionistas snapping selfies, and industry insiders with sharp, appraising eyes, leaned forward in their seats. All waited breathlessly for the designs about to claim the runway.

In the coveted front row, Julia and Kasey sat poised, the perfect picture of effortless sophistication. Beside them, Raven chatted animatedly, her glossy black hair catching the glow of the dim lights, flanked by Haruto, Rick, and Jack, each dressed impeccably for the occasion. Just behind them, Micki, James, Will, and Akira sat in the second row, wide-eyed and starstruck. Akira snapped photo after photo, her phone capturing the buzz and glamour of the moment for her feed.

The runway stretched long and sleek, elevated just enough to command attention. Behind it, a jaw-dropping backdrop blended the glittering Manhattan skyline with graffiti-splashed walls, their neon colors glowing faintly in the moody light. On the opposite side, the luminous London skyline shimmered, anchored by a vintage street lamp that cast a golden glow over the scene—a nostalgic nod to the view Julia and Kasey had shared from the London Eye.

Music throbbed through the space, a masterfully curated mix of sleek electronic beats intertwined with urban street sounds—car horns, distant voices, the echo of subway brakes—all perfectly timed to heighten the drama. Spotlights snapped into place, carving a blazing path down the runway, as the crowd collectively held its breath for the show to begin.

As Julia and Kasey watched the show unfold, they held hands tightly, their excitement radiating between them. The lights dimmed, and the music shifted to sleek, elegant tones reminiscent of a Bond movie, setting the stage for the opening designs.

The crowd erupted into applause as confident models strutted down the runway, their every move captured in a flurry of flashbulbs and camera clicks, a dazzling blur of light and motion. The show opened with a series of impeccably crafted suits in wool, silk, and cashmere, their rich textures showcasing the sophistication of Hawthorne-Masters. Navy, charcoal, and deep burgundy dominated the palette, accented by bold patterns like pinstripes and subtle checks. Accessories elevated each look: polished cuff links, pocket squares in striking contrasts, sleek leather briefcases, and timeless watches gleaming under the spotlights.

Then, the atmosphere shifted. Urban beats pulsed through the venue as a graffiti artist took center stage, spraying the words *Hawthorne-Masters* in vivid strokes across the New York backdrop. Models emerged clad in distressed jeans, bomber jackets, hoodies, and graphic tees, the earthy tones of olive, brown, and gray punctuated by bold pops of electric blue, crimson, and neon accents. Accessories brought the streetwear edge to life: beanies, snapbacks, chunky sneakers, layered chains, bracelets, and statement rings that glinted under the dramatic lighting.

The two styles converged in a striking finale. One model paired a tailored blazer with a graphic tee and distressed jeans, while another donned a classic suit offset by chunky sneakers and a heavy layered chain. The seamless blend of high fashion and street style drew audible gasps of admiration from the audience, a testament to the collection's versatility and daring spirit.

At the climactic conclusion, the music morphed into a pulsating medley of disco beats as lights danced in vibrant, multicolored patterns across the venue. Ren and Giles's reinterpreted casual 70s creations took the stage, their bold and nostalgic designs accompanied by two couples dancing off to the side. The infectious thump of Donna Summer's *"I Feel Love"* filled the air, drawing thunderous applause and prompting much of the crowd to stand and move to the irresistible beat. The energy became electric as the DJ, sensing the moment, kept the music going while Ren sent the models down the runway for another stroll, the audience dancing alongside in joyous abandon.

Julia stood swaying to the rhythm, wrapped in Kasey's arms, a serene smile on her lips as she took in the fully engaged crowd. The atmosphere buzzed with a contagious joy that felt like magic—a celebration of art, passion, and connection.

As the show ended on that extraordinary high note, Ren, Rex, Giles, and Nigel stepped forward to take their bows alongside the models who had brought their vision to life. The applause was deafening, a wave of adoration that washed over them. Ren felt a rush of exhilaration; the culmination of countless hours of hard work and unrelenting passion crystallized in this breathtaking moment. Rex, unable to contain himself, jumped around with his hands in the air before pulling Ren, Nigel, and Giles into a tight, exuberant hug.

Nigel, ever the seasoned professional, allowed himself a rare, broad smile of satisfaction, lifting his hand in a royal wave to the crowd as the weight of their achievement settled in. Giles, glowing with pride, locked eyes with Gunther in the audience, blowing him a kiss before turning to shower the crowd with playful air kisses, his beaming expression a testament to the joy of the evening.

Julia and Kasey joined in, enthusiastically clapping and cheering, their pride evident as they watched Ren bask in the glow of well-deserved congratulations. His face radiated pure bliss, the culmination of months of effort and passion reflected in the adoring crowd's response.

Rick and Jack, buoyed by the enthusiastic reception, took turns enveloping Julia in bear hugs, offering heartfelt congratulations to her before moving on to Ren and the other designers. After spending a lively hour mingling with guests at the venue, Julia, Ren, and their entourage retreated to her condo to celebrate in style.

Rex, Raven, and a group of their close friends joined in, toasting to success with an open bar, flowing champagne, and trays of elegantly arranged hors d'oeuvres served by attentive staff. With the arrival of Jack, Rick, and the other board members, the condo was soon filled to capacity, laughter and chatter spilling out onto the spacious balcony. Though the board members' visit was brief, their effusive praise left no doubt—they were genuinely thrilled by the show's overwhelming success.

When the board members left, and the party reached its peak, Ren grabbed Julia's hand and led her into one of the bedrooms, locking the door behind them.

"Ren, there are so many people—what if someone saw us coming in here?" she asked, glancing toward the door as he guided her to an overstuffed chair in the corner, its tufted arms exactly what he wanted. He didn't answer, just pulled her close, his touch rough, his kisses demanding.

"You're so fucking hot, baby. I missed you so much. I need you right now," he growled, his voice thick with desire. His lips claimed her neck, leaving a bruise as his hands roamed her body. Spinning her around, he bent her over the arm of the chair without hesitation. Julia barely had time to catch her breath before she felt him tug her panties down, his hands firm and impatient.

Ren dropped his pants and spit into his palm, rubbing it on the tip of his erection before thrusting into her with one hard stroke.

"Oh God, Ren!" she cried out, her voice catching as he drove into her hard and fast. Her face burned, her nails digging into the plush arm of the chair as his hand twisted in her hair, pulling her head back while keeping her pinned beneath him.

"I missed you too," she groaned, gasping as he pushed harder, his strength lifting her hips off the chair and her feet off the floor.

Grunting, "Oh yeah," as he came, Ren collapsed briefly against her back, his breath ragged in her ear.

Straightening up, he slapped her ass hard enough to sting. "Thanks, baby, I needed that," he muttered, yanking up his pants and heading for the door without another glance.

Julia stood there, slick between her legs, her panties around her ankles, stunned. Her mind raced as she realized she'd just seen a side of Ren she'd never encountered before—drunk, dismissive Ren.

As much as she hated seeing Ren drunk, Julia couldn't deny how much his bad-boy side thrilled her, making their rough encounter far more exciting than it should have been. She cleaned herself up and made her way back to the party, finding Kasey already watching Ren closely.

When he noticed her, Kasey walked over. "I think Ren's a little drunk. We should keep an eye on him."

"He's more than a little drunk," she replied with a smirk. "He just pulled me into my bedroom and was… well, a bit rough. I'm sure he's just excited and relieved the show was a hit, but yeah, we should definitely keep an eye on him."

Kasey's brow furrowed as he studied her. "He wasn't too rough, was he?"

"No, baby. Nothing I couldn't handle," Julia reassured him, placing a hand on his arm. "But I did see a different side of him."

Kasey leaned in, kissing her softly. "I'll watch him, don't worry. Go mingle—this is your night, too. You helped bring your company a big success tonight. Congratulations, sweetheart."

"Thank you. I wish my dad was here to see this," Julia said, her voice soft with emotion. "I'm so grateful to everyone involved. Because of them, I didn't let him down. I accomplished what I set out to do. I'm very happy." She hugged Kasey tightly before sending him off to check on Ren while she mingled and basked in their success.

The party continued for another hour, the attendees reveling in the show's triumph. Laughter echoed through the condo as the crowd grew looser, with many ending up drunk, high, or both. Kasey eventually pulled Ren aside, his voice low but firm as he gently suggested slowing down while guests were still around. Sensing Kasey's concern, Ren agreed and begrudgingly switched to water.

At one point, Micki cornered Julia, her tone both amused and a little exasperated. "Ren's drinking really dulls his sweet, gentle side," she noted, glancing toward the increasingly animated designer. Ren, loud and flirtatious, had just sealed his celebration with an open-mouth kiss on Rex in front of everyone. While most thought it was hilarious, Rex's flustered expression said otherwise, his confused feelings clearly a casualty of the evening's antics.

As the party wound down, Julia and Kasey ushered the brownstone's overnight guests to their rooms, carefully wrangling their decidedly drunk partner along the way. After bidding goodnight to the condo's remaining guests, they finally headed home, ready for some much-needed rest after a night of triumph and chaos.

***

Instead of passing out, Ren found himself too wired to sleep, his excitement overwhelming any chance of rest. After hours of tossing and turning—and several cups of coffee— Ren, now sober and brimming with energy, reached for his phone to dive into the reviews. When he couldn't contain himself any longer, he barged into Kasey's room, rousing the still-exhausted pair.

"Jules, Spike, look at these reviews!" he exclaimed, his voice alive with childlike glee as he plopped down on the bed.

Julia groaned softly, burying her face in the pillow, while Kasey blinked sleepily at the glowing screen Ren shoved between them.

Still groggy, they listened as Ren read the glowing reviews aloud, one after another.

"Congratulations, Ren. You did it," Julia praised, her voice warm with pride as she sat up and rubbed her eyes. Her heart swelled, knowing how much this moment meant to him.

"We did it," Ren corrected, his tone sincere as he looked at both of them. "I couldn't have done it without you. Your support and encouragement meant everything."

Julia smiled, leaning against Kasey, who nodded in agreement.

Ren's grin widened as he added, "I'm thrilled for Giles and Nigel too—the reviews on their updated suits are fantastic. Listen to this," he said, reading aloud a review that hailed the brothers as a prime example that age is no barrier to creativity.

Julia laughed softly, watching Ren's excitement. "Did you manage to get any sleep at all?" she asked, already knowing the answer as he continued scrolling, eyes alight with joy.

"A little, I think," Ren mumbled, rubbing his eyes. "I'm just too excited to sleep."

"Would you like me to make you some breakfast? Are you hungry?" Kasey asked warmly, happy to see Ren so ecstatic.

"No, thanks, Spike. I couldn't eat right now," Ren replied with a grin. "I'm sorry I woke you, but I couldn't wait to share the good news. You guys should go back to sleep."

As he started to get up, Julia tugged him back between her and Kasey. "Don't be silly. We want to celebrate with you," she said, her voice soft but insistent. "Tell us all about the reviews and who you talked to last night, if you can remember," she teased. "There was so much going on, I couldn't keep up with it all. Spill, babe—we're listening." She snuggled closer, resting her head against his shoulder.

For the next hour, Julia and Kasey listened with warm smiles as Ren bubbled over with stories, his joy pouring out in every word. It didn't take long to realize he had no idea just how drunk he had been the night before, his exuberance masking any memory of his wilder moments.

Kasey slipped out of bed to shower and check on their guests, leaving Julia and Ren lying in each other's arms. Physically exhausted but mentally energized by their success, they basked in the quiet intimacy of the moment. As they talked, Ren absentmindedly toyed with the tiny bow on Julia's nightie, his leg brushing slowly against hers.

"Do you want to have a little celebratory sex before we go downstairs?" Julia suggested coyly, her tone playful and knowing.

Ren grinned, his expression equal parts amused and apologetic. "I'd love nothing more, but I'm afraid not every part of me is up to it. I drank way too much last night, and honestly? I'm exhausted. I might not even be able to finish."

Julia smirked, her brow arching. "You certainly had no problem finishing at the condo. It seems the bad boy in you takes center stage when you drink beer."

Ren frowned, a flicker of confusion crossing his face. "We had sex at the condo? During the party?"

"Yes, Ren," she said, raising an amused brow. "You don't remember? You pulled me into my bedroom, bent me over the chair, did me while pulling my hair, and left me with a smack on the ass and a 'Thanks, babe, I needed that.'" Her tone remained light despite the rough encounter, her teasing clear.

A slow wave of realization and regret spread across his face. "Shit, I did do that, didn't I?" He sighed heavily, his voice tinged with worry. "Damn, I didn't hurt you—or do anything else stupid last night, did I?"

Julia reached up, brushing her fingers through his hair with a reassuring smile. "No, you didn't hurt me. Though I wonder what it says about me that I found it kind of hot," she admitted with a small laugh. "But I am a little concerned about your drinking. I know we were celebrating, but you did give Rex an open-mouth kiss in front of everyone. I'm sure that was a little… confusing for him."

Ren listened, embarrassment coloring his face as he processed the idea of being so drunk he couldn't remember his encounter with Julia—or the kiss with Rex.

"I'm so sorry, Jules, for my behavior last night. I crossed a line I shouldn't have. I'll call Rex later and apologize. I wouldn't want to ruin our friendship. I really like him. That was stupid of me."

"Don't beat yourself up, babe. Just maybe… less drinking, more smoking when we party. At least if you overindulge with smoking, you just fall asleep."

She pulled him close, brushing her lips against his. "In case you don't remember, I told you last night—I'm so proud of you. The launch couldn't have gone better. You're a hit, babe, and I love you."

"I love you too, Jules," Ren said, his grin softening. "I'm sorry I was a douchebag last night. I don't deserve you." His smile turned mischievous as he added, "How about I make it up to you? My mouth is still fully functioning." He started moving down her body with a wicked gleam in his eyes.

Julia laughed, catching his face in her hands. "Maybe we should wait until Kasey leaves—show a little respect," she teased, her tone light and playful.

"Okay by me," he replied with a sly grin, his hand already wandering under the covers, his fingers sliding between her legs.

"That's not holding off," she giggled, her breath catching as he touched her.

The bathroom door opened, and Kasey stepped out, his hair still damp. He took one look at the pair and quipped, "I was sure I'd be walking into some kind of sex right now… surprising."

"We're just trying to be respectful—we were waiting until you left," Ren said with a grin that was anything but innocent.

"Well, thanks for the consideration, but it's not necessary," Kasey replied with a wink. "I don't mind watching."

Julia laughed as Kasey walked out of the room, shaking her head with a smirk. "He's impossible," she murmured, turning her gaze back to Ren. "But you… you're incorrigible." Her words were teasing, but her tone was inviting, her fingers curling in his hair as he moved lower.

Ren wasted no time picking up where he left off, diving face-first between her legs. Julia's soft giggles turned to seductive moans, her body arching as her fingers tightened in his hair. The way she responded drove Ren wild, his adrenaline now pumping. Before she knew it, he was inside her, their bodies moving together with an unrelenting intensity that left no room for anything else but each other.

***

Chapter 24: Drunk Ren and Jealousy

As Friday dawned, the group eagerly anticipated a long weekend together, planning to stay at the beach house through late Sunday to celebrate their success. Julia orchestrated the getaway, ensuring they could all spend quality time together.

Most traveled by helicopter, except Akira and Will, who opted for a road trip in Will's car. Carl and Charley arrived ahead of them, ensuring the luggage was ready and waiting. The reunion felt seamless, as though no time had passed, with everyone effortlessly slipping back into vacation mode.

"Ren, Nigel, and Giles chatted excitedly in the living room about the show's success, basking in the accolades, while Gunther sat nearby, quietly beaming with pride. The sound of waves breaking on the shore mingled with their laughter, a soothing backdrop to their conversation. Kasey and Haruto practiced Tai Chi on the deck, sheltered from the cold November wind but invigorated by the salty air, their synchronized movements framed by the early morning light. Haruto paused mid-stance to comment softly to Kasey, 'The ocean always feels alive this time of year, doesn't it?"

Sleeping arrangements were quickly sorted: Julia, Ren, and Kasey would share a room; Will and Akira took the spare, and Micki and James settled upstairs. Giles, Gunther, Nigel, and Haruto each kept their previous rooms.

***

With Micki and James in attendance, the dance party and karaoke that night were off the charts. Once Haruto had called it a night and Nigel followed suit, Giles and Gunther lingered, captivated by the lively dynamics of the close-knit group. They exchanged amused glances, marveling at Julia and Micki's open display of affection and the seductive way they danced together.

As they moved seamlessly into a playful routine with Will and James, Giles leaned over to Kasey, his grin mischievous. "If I were thirty years younger, I'd be right out there between those two lovely women. Bloody hell, that's some sexy dancing. I take it she's quite close to Micki and James?"

Kasey chuckled. "Micki's been Julia's best friend since they were kids. Julia and James had a thing in college, but they quickly realized Micki and James were a better match. The three of them have stayed incredibly tight ever since." He shot Giles a sly smile, adding, "Their bond is solid, and it keeps life... interesting."

"Indeed... our little Ms. Masters is quite the fascinating character," Giles mused. His gaze fixed on Julia dancing provocatively, sandwiched between James and Micki, the trio's shared history evident in their easy connection. "I'd be quite possessive if she were my partner," he admitted, watching Julia's playful interaction with James as Micki walked off to get a drink.

"I only felt possessive when I was deciding whether to start a relationship with her," Kasey replied. "But once we became a couple—and now a trio—I trust her completely. I

612

also knew exactly what I was signing up for with Julia. She's extroverted, affectionate, and tactile. I can't and wouldn't want to stop her from being herself. That bond with Micki and James? It's not something I'd ever want to change. They're good people who've stood by her through thick and thin. It's just their way of showing affection, and I don't mind. Ren, though? He's a lot like Julia—jealous and maybe a little possessive." Kasey chuckled, his tone light but knowing.

"Oh, I saw her with Ren and Akira, and she pointed out Raven Black to me at the after-party. Quite the complicated little love life she has," Giles remarked, his eyes flicking to Ren, whose intense gaze followed Julia as she danced with James. "Looks like Ren might need a bit of reassurance. She's quite the little provocateur, isn't she?" he added, watching Julia's every move.

"She definitely can be," Kasey smirked, his gaze shifting to Ren, who was nursing his beer. "He's just adjusting. Excuse me—I'd better douse that fire before it spreads." Rising from his seat, Kasey crossed the room to where Ren stood by the kitchen island.

"What's going on? You look a little upset. It's been an exhausting twenty-four hours, and you haven't really slept. Maybe you—"

Ren cut him off. "Doesn't it bother you at all when he's all over her? Worse—when she's all over him?" He glanced at Kasey, then continued without waiting for an answer. "I'm sorry, but it bothers me—more than it should, judging by that look on your face," he admitted, his voice tinged with frustration.

"Ren, she's just being herself," Kasey said gently. "She's had a long-standing relationship with Micki and James, and honestly, we're the ones who upset their apple cart. They just need time to adjust to her new situation. Think about it—they didn't want to stop... I asked them to. Then you showed up, and she completely changed to include you. Could you give her up so easily if you were James, after all those years of being with her?

"She loves you, she's loyal, and she'd never hurt you. If it's really bothering you, talk to her. I'm positive she has no idea this is upsetting you." He rubbed Ren's back reassuringly.

"I'm going to bed. I'm probably just overtired. I don't want to stop the fun to say goodnight, so just let everyone know I'll see them in the morning." Placing a hand behind Kasey's head, he pulled him close, resting his forehead against Kasey's as he grumbled, "You're always the level-headed one. You're right—I'm just being overly sensitive. Goodnight." With a quick peck, he grabbed his beer and headed up the stairs.

"Quite adept at putting out fires, aren't you? That was expertly done," Giles remarked with a smile as Kasey returned to his seat.

"Mmm, I'm not so sure," Kasey replied, sensing Ren's lingering mood. "Sometimes, I think I'm getting practice for kids. It's like wrangling toddlers—or teenagers."

Just then, Julia plopped down in Kasey's lap, her hair slightly tousled from dancing.

"Where's Ren? Did he go to bed without saying goodnight?" she asked, scanning the room.

"He was exhausted. He didn't want to interrupt the fun. He told me to tell you he'll see you in the morning," Kasey said with a warm smile.

"Are you sure everything's okay? I'm gonna go check on him. If he's asleep, I'll be right back, but if he's awake..." She giggled and slipped off Kasey's lap. "I doubt I'll make it out of the room."

She headed for the stairs, and Kasey turned to Giles, shaking his head with a bemused smile.

As the laughter and music continued around him, Kasey's smile faded slightly. He couldn't help but hope Ren had cooled off enough to talk things through with Julia. The last thing they needed was more friction after such an exhausting day.

***

Julia quietly opened the bedroom door, stepping inside and closing it softly behind her.

As her eyes adjusted to the dim light, she spotted Ren lying on his back, arms folded behind his head, propped up against the pillows. His empty beer bottle rested on the side table.

"Finally done grinding against James? Spike and I aren't enough for you?" His tone dripped with bitterness and accusation.

"Ren?!" Julia froze, stunned. "I don't like how you just spoke to me. That was mean and uncalled for," she said, her voice trembling with emotion. "Apologize."

Ren said nothing, his gaze locked on her with the defiance of a petulant child. When it was clear he wasn't going to respond, she turned sharply on her heel and stormed out, slamming the door behind her.

Tears welled in her eyes, but she quickly drew in a deep breath, forcing herself to regain control. Everyone was still occupied downstairs, so she slipped out the front door and walked slowly down the long driveway, the chilly November wind biting against her skin.

Halfway to the guard shack, she saw Carl approaching, his expression shifting to surprise at the sight of her out alone.

"Would you mind if I sat here with you for a bit? There are so many people in the house," Julia said, her teeth chattering slightly from the cold. She had left without a coat and was beginning to feel the chill.

"Not at all. Is everything alright?" Carl asked gently. "Come inside; it's warm in here."

"I just needed some time away from everyone." Her voice wavered under the weight of her fatigue and Ren's hurtful words. Tears threatened to surface again, but she quickly regained her composure. "I'm sorry for bothering you," she added softly.

"You're not bothering me," Carl said firmly. "But does anyone know where you are? Or am I about to get a frantic call from Kasey asking if I've seen you?"

Julia started to speak, but Carl nodded toward the driveway. "Never mind—that looks like him now." Standing just outside the guardhouse with the door open, Carl had a clear view as Kasey strode toward them.

"Hey, Carl. Where is she?" Kasey called out as he approached the guardhouse. Carl pointed inside before stepping away discreetly.

Kasey slipped off his jacket and draped it over Julia's shoulders. "What happened? I went upstairs to bed, and Ren was beside himself over something he said to you. He wouldn't tell me exactly, but I've got a pretty good idea."

Julia opened her mouth to respond but broke into tears instead. Kasey slipped an arm around her and spoke softly. "Put the jacket on and come with me. Everyone's gone to bed. Let's go talk on the deck and let Carl get back to work."

Taking her hand, he led her toward the house. She followed hesitantly, feeling comforted by his steady presence but still weighed down by the night's events.

"Night, Carl. Sorry about that," Julia said over her shoulder.

"No worries, Jules," Carl replied with a wave as he stepped back inside.

Halfway up the driveway, Julia recounted Ren's words, her emotions still raw. "He asked me if I was done grinding on James and if you and Ren weren't enough for me." It felt like he was calling me a slut. His tone was so derogatory and mean," she said, her voice trembling with hurt.

Kasey spoke gently. "He didn't mean it, Julia. He's exhausted—and probably drunk. I know that's no excuse, but think about how you felt when Raven touched him. James's touch is a lot more intimate than Raven's. Ren is jealous, just like you were." He paused, letting his words sink in.

"Granted, he shouldn't have said it, but can you see how it might feel for him? Watching the woman he loves being so close with another man—even if it's James? In a way, **that's** even harder for Ren because he knows you've been with James for years, and there's real history and deep feelings there."

"I was just dancing like I always do," Julia said softly, beginning to understand Ren's perspective but still deeply hurt.

As they reached the circular driveway in front of the house, Ren stepped outside, his expression stricken. "Can I talk to Jules alone?"

"I'll be inside if you need me to referee," Kasey replied with a small smile. "Just remember, you love each other."

Julia and Ren stood in silence for a long moment before she finally spoke, her voice trembling. "You insinuated I'm a slut, Ren. It hurt as much as if you'd slapped me. I'm not a—"

Ren pulled her into his arms, cutting her off, his voice heavy with regret. "I'm sorry. I didn't mean it to sound like that. I'm just so jealous. I can't stand the thought of you with anyone besides me and Spike—even if it's James. Watching you two together made me crazy, and I should've talked to you instead of going up alone.

"I lay there, picturing you with him, and it felt like a gut punch. By the time you came in, I'd worked myself into a frenzy and took it all out on you. I didn't think—I just wanted you to feel as awful as I did. I'm an idiot and a jealous asshole, and you bring out such strong emotions in me."

He held her tighter, his chest tight with guilt. "Please forgive me. I'm sorry I hurt you. I love you, Jules—more than anything."

Ren stepped back, his voice barely above a whisper. "I'll sleep on the deck tonight; give you some space."

She didn't respond, prompting Ren to plead, "Say something. Tell me to go to hell—anything. Please, just talk to me."

Julia looked up, her tearful eyes heavy with sadness. "It wasn't just what you said—it was how you said it that hurt. You should've talked to me. I honestly didn't know it would upset you so much.

"I forgive you, but I need some space. Please go upstairs. I like sleeping outside, and if Kasey's awake, tell him he doesn't need to come down. I'd really rather be alone tonight. Let's go inside—I'm exhausted and cold. We can talk more tomorrow."

Ren opened the door, and she stepped inside, with him following close behind. As she headed for the deck, sniffling, Ren called out softly, "I love you, Jules. I'm so sorry," his nerves fraying as he watched her retreat.

"Night, Ren. We'll talk in the morning," she replied, her voice weary.

They parted ways for the night, their connection bent but not broken.

Ren walked into the bedroom to find Kasey lying on the bed, scrolling through his phone. Seeing the anguish on Ren's face and Julia nowhere in sight, Kasey got up immediately and went to him.

Ren rested his head on Kasey's shoulder, and Kasey wrapped him in a comforting embrace.

"I've ruined everything. I don't know what made me say that to her. What the hell is wrong with me?"

"Nothing's wrong with you. Don't be silly. She might be mad for a bit, but she loves you. You didn't ruin anything. Just give her time," Kasey reassured him. "Where is she?"

Ren met Kasey's gaze. "Sleeping on the deck. She can't even be in the same room as me." His voice cracked. "I feel awful."

"That's it. Get into bed. You're exhausted, and being in this condition isn't helping. Get some sleep—we'll tackle this in the morning. She's not going anywhere," Kasey insisted.

Ren went into the bathroom to wash his face while Kasey stood by the window, watching Julia make her way to the water's edge, a blanket pulled tightly around her shoulders. When Ren came out, Kasey decided not to mention it, knowing it would only upset him more.

"Lie down. Let me rub your shoulders—you'll feel better," Kasey said softly, his voice low and comforting.

"Thanks, Spike. You're the best," Ren muttered into his pillow as Kasey's strong hands worked to ease his tension. Within minutes, Ren was sound asleep.

Kasey glanced back out the window, spotting Julia's solitary figure on the sand, gently rocking back and forth. Just as he considered going to her, he saw Micki crossing the sand. She sat beside Julia, wrapping her arms and another blanket around her.

Relieved, Kasey returned to bed, exhaustion finally catching up with him.

***

"I thought you went to bed," Julia said softly as Micki sat down beside her.

"I heard you and Ren. You guys were right below our room. I'm sorry we caused trouble. Things got a bit out of hand tonight with all the celebrating." Micki offered a small, apologetic smile as she took Julia's hand. "You know, things stopping between the three of us hit James pretty hard. He'd gotten used to us all being together a few times a year, and he misses you, ya little shit. He got a little more playful than he should've."

"It wasn't James' fault—I was encouraging him," Julia admitted.

"What did Ren say to you? I didn't catch everything— something about you being a slut? He didn't actually say that, did he?"

"I said it felt like he was calling me a slut. His exact words were, 'You done grinding against James? Kasey and I aren't enough for you?'"

"Oh, that wasn't cool," Micki said gently.

"I was disregarding his feelings, but I swear, Micki, the way he said it was so harsh. I never thought he could be like that. He's always so sweet and loving. Maybe I'm overreacting—he's apologized repeatedly, and I believe he regrets it, but it stung like a slap."

Micki pulled Julia into a tight hug. "You told me yourself—Ren hasn't slept well in days with the show and all, and neither have you. Let's chalk it up to exhaustion and too much celebrating. And let's face it, kiddo, he's not Kasey. He's more high-strung, and now we know he's extremely jealous—

just like someone else I know. Cut the boy some slack. He sounded utterly devastated. It must've wrecked him to know you wouldn't share a room with him."

"It looked like it did," Julia admitted, her voice tinged with sadness.

"Just one thing—you might need to have a little talk with him about his drinking. Between last night and tonight, he acted and sounded like someone with a bad case of beer balls. Hopefully, it's not going to be a problem."

Micki kissed Julia on the head. "C'mon, it's late, it's cold, and you need sleep. Let's go in. Let him wake up to you. Let him off the hook. I bet he'll never say something like that again."

"Thanks. You always know what to say to help me out," Julia said as they crossed the cold sand. Then she paused. "Wait—does James know about this?"

"Are you kidding? James was asleep before his head hit the pillow," Micki chuckled softly.

"Please, please don't tell him. I don't want him feeling awkward around Ren," Julia pleaded.

"My lips are sealed, kiddo. Promise. I'll see you in the morning."

***

Julia slipped quietly into the bedroom making her way to Kasey's side of the bed. He greeted her with a sleepy smile, "I was hoping you come up, get in."

"Could I sleep in the middle? she whispered softly.

"Of course," he replied, making room for her as she settled between them.

"He's genuinely sorry, Julia. He was a mess when he came in," Kasey reassured her.

"I know. I realized I was just trying to punish him, and I don't want to. That's just mean, and two wrongs don't make a right. Has he ever gotten mad at you?" she asked, curious.

"No, we've never had a disagreement."

"I think we should have a talk with him about his drinking. I think part of this was jealousy, but a part of it was because he was tired and drinking like last night."

"I already decided to have a talk with him. I didn't like what I saw either. Don't worry, sweetheart, we'll work this out." Kasey kissed her neck as he spooned her. "Try and get some sleep."

As she lay there, watching Ren sleep peacefully beside her, a wave of tenderness washed over her. She thought back to the moment Rick called her "darlin'" in the office and how shattered she'd felt. Ren hadn't just comforted her—he'd made sure she was seen, heard, and protected. From the moment they'd met, he'd always been that way: considerate, attentive, and endlessly patient.

Even now, despite the harshness of his words earlier, she knew it came from a place of love—flawed but genuine. All she wanted now was to reconcile, to remind him of how deeply he mattered to her.

***

The next morning, Kasey was already downstairs when Julia woke, but Ren was still fast asleep beside her. She got up quietly to use the bathroom, then slipped back into bed, her cool body a stark contrast to his warmth.

Ren stirred, his eyes slowly opening to find Julia's gaze locked on him. "I'm so sorry," he whispered, his voice thick with emotion.

Without a word, she leaned in and kissed him, her tenderness conveying forgiveness. Ren pulled her close, their connection rekindling in a way that was both profound and loving—the kind of intimacy that only comes with making up.

As they lay tangled together, Julia broke the silence. "I want to apologize. I was being disrespectful to you last night. I should've known better." She hesitated before continuing. "It's just... Micki, James, and I have been a trio of sorts for years, and I fell into old habits. I've been intimately connected to James off and on since I was eighteen.

"I love him, but not the way I love you. We were truly friends with benefits. I never shared much about my dating past with you, but after being hurt by a man I loved enough to live with, I gave up on love. I didn't look for relationships—I looked for fun and sex.

"When I was in a dating lull, or when I needed that loving connection, I turned to James and Micki. We had threesomes a few times a year. I'd be lying if I said I won't miss that closeness, but I'm willing to give it up for you and Kasey."

However, after you and Kasey, I love Micki. In some ways, I love her as much or even more. We're bonded. I can understand you not wanting me to touch or be touched by James, but I can't agree to that with Micki. We've been inseparable since we were young girls. I stopped sleeping with James because Kasey asked me to, but I still make out and fool around a little with Micki when we have dance parties. I don't want to give up that part of our friendship."

She paused, letting her words sink in before continuing. "James and I crossed the line last night. We were both drunk and high, and I know that's no excuse, but I also know James misses me—and I miss him too. This is the longest we've gone without sleeping together in seven years. It's like a breakup neither of us wanted, but I want Kasey and you more."

"This relationship with you and Kasey is a real learning experience for me. Now that I know how much it bothers you,

I won't encourage it again. James has never made a move I didn't signal first. Last night, I forgot myself, and I'm truly sorry."

Julia fixed her earnest gaze on him, her sincerity clear in every word.

"You're sweet for apologizing, but I'll never forgive myself for treating you the way I did," Ren confessed. "I need to rein in my jealousy and remember that you love me—and that's all that matters.

"You're right about you and James. I know it would torture me to suddenly lose that closeness if I were him. I didn't fully understand the depth of your bond or how long you've been connected. As for Micki," he smiled, "I actually really enjoy watching the two of you. But James is different. I can't share you with another man—other than Spike, obviously."

He took a deep breath, his tone softening. "I guess I could handle the dance parties, knowing I get to feel up Micki and sleep with you at the end of the night. She does have a great rack."

Julia gave him a side-eye, but her lips twitched in spite of herself as he chuckled softly and kissed her head, his embrace tightening.

"Baby, I'd be lost without you," he said earnestly.

"I'm not going anywhere, Ren. This is exactly where I want to be."

***

Coming downstairs, hand in hand, Ren and Julia were met with Kasey's reassuring smile. He felt a quiet sense of relief, knowing their rift had been mended and their relationship was back on track. The rest of the day, Ren and Julia were inseparable, their determination to reaffirm their bond unmistakable. Yet, the awareness of how deeply their actions affected one another lingered.

***

Later, during a run, Kasey diplomatically broached the subject of Ren's drinking. "You nearly lost more than you were willing to risk, Ren. That's not like you," he said, his tone calm but firm.

Ren stopped, turning to face Kasey. "I'm so sorry I acted like such a douchebag these last two days. I don't normally drink to excess, but I guess when I do, I lose all my manners. It won't happen again.

"I can't believe I was rough and dismissive with Julia physically and then hurt her even worse emotionally. I was an idiot. I'm giving you permission right now to punch me in the face if you ever see me getting out of hand again."

"Don't be ridiculous. I would never hit you," Kasey said with a smile. "But I will pull you aside and let you know if you're being a douchebag—your word. And I'll keep an eye out if you're drinking too much. I don't want to see you do something you'll regret later."

"I promise, I'm sticking to wine for now—if I drink at all. Beer seems to bring out a side of me I don't like. My behavior as a boyfriend these last 24 hours has been less than stellar.

"I also want to apologize to you for kissing Rex the way I did. One, I don't even remember it, which is shameful in itself; two, it wasn't fair to Rex; and three, I disrespected you and Julia. I'm really sorry, Spike."

Ren's voice softened, and for a moment, he looked down at his feet, ashamed. Kasey noticed the way his hands fidgeted nervously as if searching for something to ground him.

Kasey rested a hand on Ren's shoulder. "Just like Julia, I forgive you. But I'll be keeping an eye on you, cowboy."

The touch, the smile, and the nickname instantly let Ren know things were back on track with both his partners.

"Come on, let's finish this run and forget all this craziness," Kasey said, turning and jogging slowly as he waited for Ren. The cool November air nipped at their skin, and the crunch of leaves beneath their shoes filled the quiet space between them.

"Thanks, buddy. I love you too," Ren said, grinning as he sprinted past. Kasey laughed, his breath misting in the air, and raced him all the way back to the house.

That evening, the karaoke and dance party took on a decidedly less sexual tone, with everyone showing more restrained behavior. On the dance floor, Julia made a conscious effort to dial it back, subtly redirecting James's playful energy with a teasing smile or a step back, keeping things light. As she'd explained to Ren, James followed her cues, blissfully unaware of the previous night's turmoil.

***

On Sunday morning, Kasey followed his usual routine, rising early with plans for a quick run before Tai Chi with Haruto. As he hydrated at the kitchen island, he idly scrolled through the news on his phone. Suddenly, his thumb froze over the screen, his stomach dropping at a tabloid headline:

Creative Director of New Fashion House in Secret Same-Sex Relationship with Boss's Boyfriend.

"His breath hitched as he opened the article, his heart pounding. Grainy photos filled the screen-shots of Ren kissing him on the beach house deck, both of them running shirtless on the beach and standing close in the water, talking. They were clearly taken from a telescopic lens on a boat anchored offshore."

626

His chest tightened as he scrolled through the invasive shots, each one twisting a private moment into something salacious. The photos, paired with the text, left little room for innocent interpretation.

The article didn't hold back. It speculated about their living arrangement, insinuating that Julia was either a beard or oblivious to their "secret romance." Worse, it hinted that Ren's new position as Creative Director was less about merit and more about favoritism stemming from their supposed affair.

A wave of anger and protectiveness surged through Kasey. This wasn't just an attack on Ren—it was an attack on all of them. He could already imagine how it might spiral, threatening Ren's reputation, Julia's image, and the careful balance they'd built together.

As the weight of the situation settled over him, Kasey set his phone down with a steadying breath. They needed to see this, but he had to think carefully about how to break the news.

"That didn't sound good," Giles remarked, raising an eyebrow as he strode into the kitchen with Gunther in tow.

"We have a problem," Kasey said, spinning around to face him. His expression was grim, urgency crackling in his tone.

"What's happened?" Giles asked sharply.

Without a word, Kasey held up his phone, showing him the damning article. Giles's face darkened as he scanned the screen, and a string of expletives burst forth. "Bollocks! They waited until after the debut to pull this stunt. Bloody hell!"

"I need to let Julia and Ren know," Kasey said, already moving toward the stairs.

Kasey took the steps two at a time, his heart pounding in his chest. He pushed open the bedroom door, the early-morning light slicing through the curtains. Julia stirred at the sound, and he crossed the room to her side of the bed.

"Julia, Ren, wake up," he urged, brushing Julia's arm gently to rouse her.

"What's up, baby? It's still early," Julia mumbled, her voice thick with sleep as she shifted beneath the covers.

"We have a problem. You both need to get up—now," he said firmly.

Julia blinked rapidly, brushing the hair out of her eyes as she sat up, her grogginess giving way to alarm.

"What's wrong?" she asked, her gaze locking on Kasey.

Ren rolled over, propping himself up on one elbow, his eyes narrowing on Kasey.

"We've been outed," Kasey explained, his words clipped. "There's an article in a tabloid. They have pictures of Ren and me kissing on the deck. The story implies you're either a beard for us or completely clueless." His voice cracked under the weight of frustration and simmering anger.

Julia's eyes widened in disbelief. "Let me see," she said, her voice calm despite the storm of thoughts racing through her mind—legal battles, damage control, and the inevitable fallout with the board. Kasey handed her the phone.

Ren, meanwhile, was already spiraling. "What the fuck? Who would go through this much trouble? They've obviously been holding these pictures for a while. Are we being stalked without even knowing it?"

Julia placed a steadying hand on Ren's chest, her touch firm but soothing. "Calm down, babe. Let's not panic." She exhaled slowly, her voice carrying the edge of authority. "We need to tackle this strategically."

Her gaze flicked to Kasey. "Get Dante on the line while I get dressed. Legal needs to start digging into this now. Is Carl on duty today? We'll need to talk to him. We need a private investigator immediately to find out who's behind this and who took those photos." She handed the phone back to Kasey with a crisp nod before turning to Ren.

"Check social media. See how far this has gotten and track who's saying what. If anyone asks, it's 'no comment' for now. We need to figure out who's with us and who isn't."

Julia rolled out of bed like a woman on a mission, her cool composure a stark contrast to the fire in her eyes. Outside of her love life, Julia was a focused beast when threatened, and nothing about this situation would be left to chance.

She paused at the dresser, pulling out clothes with deliberate efficiency. "I have a suspicion about who's behind this," she said, her tone steel-edged as she glanced back over her shoulder.

***

"Who do you think is behind this?" Giles asked as they gathered around the kitchen island, tension thick in the air.

Julia crossed her arms tightly over her chest, her frustration simmering beneath the surface. "Over a year ago, at a Cattlemen's dinner, a militant group of animal rights protesters tried to throw blood on me and my father. Kasey stopped the guy, and he ended up drenching another protester instead. The group got a lot of bad press and disavowed the guy, making him look like an ass.

"But he wasn't done," she continued, her voice edged with anger. "He started sending threatening letters to me and Kasey. We forwarded them to the FBI, and he was threatened with jail time. I think it's him—he's fixated on ruining my reputation. He doesn't give a damn about Ren and Kasey; he wants to hurt me. And what better way than making it look like I gave Ren the job because he was sleeping with my boyfriend?"

"You never told me you were getting threatening letters," Micki said, her concern deepening as she leaned forward.

Julia exhaled heavily, her shoulders sagging slightly. "After the plane crash, there were some really cruel ones," she admitted. "I didn't want to deal with it; it was too painful. Kasey handled it for me."

She paused, her gaze dropping to the counter as if the memories were too heavy to hold. "My father and the company have been getting hate mail for years—it comes with the territory in the cattle industry. I didn't think much of it at first."

"We hadn't heard from him in a while. I thought he'd given up, but I guess this is what he's been planning."

Kasey's phone buzzed, and he glanced at the screen. "It's Dante, Julia. Do you want to take this on the deck?"

"No, thanks. I'll go upstairs—this might take a while," she said, taking the phone and making her way upstairs without another word.

"What bad timing," Will muttered, shaking his head.

"Not for him," Kasey said bitterly. "He knew this would be the perfect time to hit Julia where it hurts. He's banking on bad publicity derailing the fashion house's debut."

"Is there anything we can do to help?" James asked, his voice laced with concern.

"Thanks, but this is Julia's wheelhouse—lawyers and private detectives. Right now, all we can do is wait and see how bad the fallout is before making any moves."

"Spike, the story's already been picked up by the *Daily News* and the *New York Post*," Ren called out, his tone flat with frustration.

"Damn it, it's out now." Kasey let out a sharp breath, his jaw tightening. "That was fast."

His words hung in the air as Julia came downstairs, fury radiating off her. "That didn't take long," Kasey muttered, meeting her glare.

"I had to end my call with Dante when Rick called," Julia began, her voice laced with fury. "He wanted to know if the story was true and said the board would like to talk to me. He spoke to me like I was a child. If those goddamn idiots think they're going to push me around because my father isn't here, they'd better think again. I'll take every one of those sons of bitches down, including my godfather. It's time to remind them who owns this company—and it's not any of them. Where the hell is their support?"

"You go girl—show 'em who's boss," Micki said, her tone bright and unflinching, always ready to bolster Julia's confidence.

"Fuckin' right I'm the boss. I think they've forgotten that," Julia shot back, her gaze snapping to Giles, Nigel, and Haruto. They stood frozen; their shock mingled with a quiet admiration for her shift in demeanor.

"I apologize for the language—it'll probably get worse before it gets better—but this is how I need to fight with this bunch of cowboys," Julia said, her chin lifting defiantly.

"No, no, darling, don't apologize," Nigel interjected with a wave of his hand. "Do what you need to do to fight your battle. The wankers deserve everything they get for not supporting you three immediately."

Julia and Kasey spent the rest of the day in crisis mode, meticulously planning her next steps. Every detail was scrutinized, every scenario considered.

James and Ren manned the phones, fielding an onslaught of calls from reporters with a unified, unwavering response: "No comment at this time."

Meanwhile, Giles, Nigel, and Haruto gathered in the library to draft a statement of support for Julia and Ren should the need arise. The three men, deeply upset by the situation, worked with quiet determination, their concern for their young partners evident in every carefully chosen word.

Julia received a less patronizing call from Jack, who informed her that the board would convene the next day at eleven o'clock to discuss strategy and her response to the story. Though Jack's tone was more sympathetic than Rick's, it wasn't enough to temper Julia's frustration. Her voice, sharp with anger, echoed through the house as she vented about the situation.

Despite being told it would be a closed-door meeting, Julia made her stance clear: Ren and Kasey would attend. "They're directly involved," she'd snapped, her voice carrying down the stairs. "That's not up for negotiation."

***

Julia kept her emotions tightly in check, unwilling to let the weight of the day cast a shadow over the evening with her guests. Kasey stayed close to Ren, offering quiet reassurances, though Ren's unease about the fashion house debut and the potential fallout from the bad press was evident in the tension lining his face.

The mood was subdued, but James's early barbecue dinner brought a measure of comfort. They gathered around the table, breaking into small groups for quiet conversation while a movie played softly in the background. The gentle rhythm of voices and shared laughter offered a brief reprieve from the storm swirling outside their sanctuary.

Micki nudged Julia, nodding toward the beach where Will and Akira sat wrapped in blankets.

"Are they seriously on the sand in this cold?" Micki asked with a grin as Will draped a blanket over their shoulders and leaned in to say something to Akira.

Julia chuckled softly. "He's spent more time with her than with us." She paused, her smile warming. "It's strange, but I'm glad for him. He looks happy, and they seem to really enjoy each other's company."

"I'm happy for him too," Julia said with a small smile. "I just wish she lived closer so they could spend more time together. Who knows? Maybe someday she'll spend some time here in the States. It'd give them a real chance to let this relationship grow."

James approached, slipping his arm around Julia's waist and pulling her gently against his side. "If there's anything we can do to help, even if it means sticking around a little longer for moral support, just say the word. Honestly, if you can prove this is a vendetta against you, it might flip the narrative in your favor. The LGBTQ+ community would rally behind you, and with big names like Nigel, Giles, Raven, and Rex on your side, that kind of backing could turn this into a win." He hugged her warmly. "You've got this, Jules. Your dumbass board just needs reminding that you hold all the cards."

Julia hugged him back, her smile widening. "Thank you, James. I do hold all the cards. Now I just need to play them right."

Across the room, Ren observed the interaction intently, his thoughts churning as he tried to reframe what he was seeing. Julia's easy connection with James tugged at something in him he wasn't used to feeling.

Noticing the tension in Ren's expression, Kasey draped an arm around his shoulders and leaned in. "You alright?"

Ren sighed, his voice low. "Yeah… I'm trying to focus on the best-friend vibe between them and not let my mind go anywhere else. But it's hard. I like James—he's a good guy—but damn, Spike, jealousy hits different. I've never felt this before. How do you deal with it?"

Kasey's arm tightened, his tone gentle but firm. "I remind myself of what we've been through—what Julia went through to be with me. The things she said after I hurt her by being with you? That was raw, honest love. She loves me, Ren. She loves you too. And she would never betray that.

She's open about her feelings, about everything. If something's bothering her, she tells us. If you're worried, just talk to her. Don't let it fester. You don't have to fight it alone."

Ren's shoulders relaxed slightly as Kasey rested his head briefly against his. "Thanks, Spike. You always know how to pull me back from the edge."

Kasey smiled softly. "That's what we do, Ren. We've got each other."

***

At seven o'clock, it was time to start saying goodbye to her guests.

"Just remember, dear—keep calm and carry on," Giles said with a warm smile as he embraced Julia tightly. "I have no doubt you'll make those cowboys rue the day they underestimated you. We'll be sending good vibes from across the pond."

Nigel, Giles, Gunther, Haruto, and Akira followed with their goodbyes, each offering words of encouragement before they were driven to the airport. As they parted, Nigel clasped

Julia's hand firmly. "Keep us up to date once we land, darling. We'll be anxiously waiting to hear how things unfold."

Two hours later, Micki hugged Julia goodbye, reluctant to leave. "Are you sure you wouldn't like us to stay a few more days? I hate leaving with all this craziness going on."

Julia smiled, touched by the offer. "Thank you, but there's nothing you can do here that you can't do from home. You can support me over the phone, and James needs to get back to work."

Micki sighed, clearly unconvinced. "Fine, but keep me in the loop. I'll be worried about you. And don't forget—give those guys hell. Like James said, you hold all the cards. Time to make Buck proud. This isn't just about the fashion house; this is the real test of leadership—making a room full of your father's friends realize you're the boss now."

Julia's eyes softened, and she wrapped Micki in a tight hug. "Thank you for always being here for me, no matter what. You always know what to say to make me feel better. I love you."

"Ride or die, kiddo," Micki whispered, her voice thick with emotion as she kissed Julia's cheek.

***

Back in the city by eleven, with everyone else en route to their own homes, Julia, Ren, and Kasey sat silently in the living room. A movie flickered on the screen, but none of them paid it any mind. Each was lost in their thoughts, the weight of the impending board meeting pressing heavily on their minds.

That night, Julia chose to sleep alone, craving the solitude to clear her head and get a good night's rest. But before dawn, wide awake and buzzing with adrenaline, she slipped into bed between Ren and Kasey.

"My adrenaline's off the charts," she purred in Ren's ear, pressing against Kasey with a teasing smile. "I need to burn off some of this energy. Anybody wanna help me with that?"

Ren's hand was already trailing over her body as she giggled, her invitation clearly accepted.

After a restful night—and an even more invigorating morning—Julia felt ready to face the board and whatever challenges awaited her.

***

Overnight, the story had exploded across media platforms, all circling the same pressing question: Why hadn't Julia, Ren, or Masters Inc. confirmed or denied the allegations? Conservative voices, bolstered by random street interviews in Colorado, called for Julia's dismissal from the board, citing her personal life and claiming Ren's position was due to favoritism rather than merit.

Julia's frustration mounted with every passing hour as it became glaringly clear—there was no support from her board, neither personal nor public.

Amid the media frenzy, it was no surprise when a reporter appeared at Ren's father's doorstep seeking a statement. Standing beside Ren's mother, Mr. Ito remained composed, firmly asserting his son's right to privacy. He didn't hold back, openly criticizing Masters Inc. for failing to support Ren and Julia, especially given their recent successes.

Ren had ensured his mother knew about the launch, and she had quietly shared the news with his father. However, Ren had no idea that his father, who had remained distant for nearly a year, would publicly defend him—or that he even knew Kasey was back in his son's life.

Worn down by the emotional roller coaster of the past few days, Ren broke down when Kasey showed him his father's statement. Tears streamed down his face as a wave of emotions surged through him. Their relationship, he had believed, was too fractured to repair. Yet here was his father, resolute, standing up for him in the face of public scrutiny.

For the first time in months, Ren felt a glimmer of hope. His father had his back, even after everything that had passed between them. It wasn't just a statement of support—it was a crack in the wall dividing them.

***

Chapter 25: I Am the Boss

At the office, curious glances followed the trio—a determined Julia flanked by Kasey and Ren—as they stepped off the elevator and entered her and Kasey's office together.

"That was a bit awkward," Ren remarked as they settled onto the couch.

"That's funny," Julia said with a grin, "I imagined us doing a slow-motion superhero walk," which made both Kasey and Ren smile.

A few minutes later, Derrick buzzed Ren to inform him of numerous interview and statement requests requiring his attention.

"Do you need any help with what you're planning to say to the board?" Kasey offered.

"No, thank you, baby, I've got this. Ren, have Derrick let the press know that a statement will be coming from me this afternoon. Also, I need you to buy me something to wear for the press statement—just pick something off the rack at Neiman Marcus and have it sent over. I've changed my mind;

I don't want to wear a skirt. Get something with a tapered leg that I can wear with my Louboutin."

"No problem. I'll make sure you look powerful and confident," Ren assured her.

"Kasey, any updates from the investigator?"

"Not yet; he's tracking the pictures and the seller. All we need is the name to prove this was a vendetta."

"Also, make sure Carl and Charley are outside with us for the press. All right, give me some time alone. Don't look so worried, babe—I'll fix this," she reassured Ren with a quick kiss, ignoring any prying eyes.

Before heading to the boardroom, with Kasey and Ren in the outer office along with Barbara and the secretaries listening, Julia belted out Sia's "Unstoppable," pumping her confidence to the max. As they headed to the boardroom, Ren stood tall, imagining Julia's "superhero slow-mo" walk and feeling confident in her ability to "fix this."

***

At eleven o'clock, the three of them stood outside the imposing boardroom entrance. Radiating confidence, Julia turned to them with a determined look. "This is how I defend myself and the people I love," she declared, her tone steely.

As Julia swung open the door, the room fell silent. Ren and Kasey found seats in the back while she strode purposefully to the head of the long conference table, fixing her gaze on everyone present.

"Jules," Rick attempted to speak.

Julia cut him off with a sharp glance. "Nope, no interruptions," she declared firmly. Standing tall, she placed her hands on the back of the chair in front of her, her knuckles whitening as she gripped it. "As CEO, majority stockholder, and—let's not forget—owner of this company, I'll be doing the talking. I'll try to keep this professional, but I can't guarantee it—I'm pretty damn pissed." She paused, her grip tightening momentarily before she released it, allowing a hint of her Western twang to edge into her voice as she gathered herself to continue.

"Rick, any questions or objections you or the board may have about my personal life are irrelevant." Julia leaned forward, planting her hands firmly on the table, her fingers splayed wide as if trying to hold back a rising tide of frustration. "It's baffling why any of you feel entitled to question me about my personal life when the first thing you should have done was look for ways to protect me, protect our Vice President and our Creative Director, and most of all, protect our company."

She straightened, crossing her arms as she began pacing slowly behind her chair, the sharp click of her stiletto heels on the polished floor punctuating the silence in the room with each deliberate step. "If it had been Buck being harassed, you would have circled the wagons and stood with him. Would any of you have dared to question Buck about something personal? Not a chance, and let's be real—we all know why." Julia paused, turning to face them again, uncrossing her arms as she pointed a finger at Rick. "He would have told you to stay the fuck out of his private life, or he would have beaten your ass."

Julia let the weight of her words hang in the air for a moment, then relaxed her stance, her voice lowering but not losing its edge. "Since I'm not likely to get physical with any of you, let me tell you what I will do instead. But first, let me make one thing clear: negative publicity is fleeting. Handle it right, and it burns itself out. Mishandle it, and you fuel the flames. Your lack of support, evidenced by the absence of a statement backing the three of us, implies disapproval. Your first instinct should have been to protect me and, in turn, protect our company. This reaction is unacceptable.

Summoning me here like a scolded child implies I did something wrong. And for what? A verbal spanking? I'm the boss. Let me repeat that, in case any of you missed it: I am the boss."

As she delivered those words, Julia straightened to her full height, her gaze sweeping across the room, daring anyone to challenge her. She placed both hands firmly on the table, leaning in just enough to make her authority impossible to ignore.

"I have ironclad contracts in place safeguarding my interests. Any infighting you cause by undermining me in any way will only hurt the company—and, for most of you, your only source of income. Not me. I could take steps to dissolve this company today, and it would take every dime you have to stop me. I own the Double O outright. Do you comprehend how much I'm worth? That ranch alone is valued at over four hundred million, and it's all mine, boys. Plus, I'm the majority stockholder in this company. I'm prepared to tie your sorry asses up in litigation 'til you're bankrupt or buried."

Rick attempted to interrupt, "Jules—"

"I'm not finished, Rick," Julia shot back, her eyes narrowing into a cold, piercing stare that silenced him instantly. "Ren just handed this company a lucrative new business, and you all approved his credentials when I hired him. Clearly, he knows what he's doing—our launch was extremely well-received, and most of you were there to see it. Kasey has busted his ass harder for this company than any of you ever did." Her tone grew scathing. "And this is how you repay them and me?" She slammed her hand on the table with a force that made the wood vibrate, punctuating her words with undeniable finality. "With no support? Thinking you can treat me like a child instead of your boss? Do not mistake my personal affection for any of you as a sign of weakness—that would be a deadly mistake on your part. You all seem to forget who raised and taught me everything he knew."

Julia leaned forward slightly, her gaze unwavering as she prepared to deliver her next words with the weight of authority. "Let me spell it out for you so there's no misunderstanding. This is the truth, and it'll be coming out later when I address the media: Kasey, Ren, and I do live together; we are domestic partners. We love each other and intend to build a life together. Get used to it. And if any of you think you can take a misguided moral stance with me..." She chuckled contemptuously and smirked, crossing her arms with confident defiance. "Think again. I grew up with all but two of you. I saw the shady things you did—the unhinged drinking, brawling, womanizing—all of it. Plus, none of you know this, but when I became President of Acquisitions, Buck sat me down and handed me an insurance policy in case something like this ever happened. He gave me the lowdown on each and every one of you. Everyone," she said, turning to look directly at Rick. "I know where all the bodies are buried, boys. I have enough information on each one of you knuckleheads to end a marriage or two and definitely send the tax man to your door. Buck had no intention of using that information against his closest friends, but he figured if you were disloyal enough to try and mess with me, he would help me take you down. He always was one step ahead of you."

Adding insult to injury, Julia continued, "Furthermore, we're certain this invasion of our privacy was perpetrated by the same militant activist at the Cattlemen's Dinner who tried to assault Buck and me. He's been harassing Kasey and me for months. You were all aware of the letters. We're waiting for proof from a private investigator to confirm it's him. Instead of supporting the man who has protected your company's owner and CEO—multiple times—including the attempted mugging—you show him no loyalty." She paused, her hands gripping the table as if anchoring herself, her knuckles turning white with the force of her hold. "So, if you still wanna disrespect me and disregard the loyalty I deserve, I'll dissolve this company. I'll take the Masters name and start a new one. I'll sell most of the Double O and leave the cattle industry behind, leaving each one of you scrambling. I have nothing left to prove to myself or to you." Julia straightened, releasing her grip, and looked out over the room, shaking her head slowly, her voice heavy with disappointment. "After everything my father did to make you all wealthy men... you're not only bad businessmen, but even worse friends. Buck would be profoundly disappointed in every one of you."

With a stern warning and an ultimatum, Julia concluded, "You have exactly two hours to decide where your loyalties lie. Either issue a statement supporting the three of us, or I will unleash holy hell on every one of you. This will start with my statement to the media, announcing company restructuring— and it won't be me leaving. We already have notable figures and communities ready to stand and support us the moment my statement goes out. It's just a real shame it wasn't my own board."

She started for the door, her heels clicking sharply against the floor, each step a clear signal of her unyielding resolve. "I'm leaving, and I don't want to hear a damn thing from any of you unless it's an apology. You have two hours. Decide wisely, you dumbass cowboys."

With that, she turned on her heel, her movements precise and controlled, and walked out, Kasey and Ren falling in step behind her. As the door closed behind her, she couldn't help but smile at the ensuing chaos. Walking toward the elevator, she smirked, "And that's how you throw the fear of God into assholes who fuck with you."

"Holy shit, Jules, that was so badass. Now that was a verbal spanking," Ren exclaimed, still reeling from what he had just witnessed, his eyes wide with admiration. Kasey smiled and nodded in agreement with a knowing look. He had seen Julia in action before in the boardroom, though never in such a personal context. As the elevator doors opened, Jack emerged from the boardroom, the echoes of heated arguments trailing behind him until the door shut again.

"Jules, could I have a word, please? Kasey, Ren, this involves you too," Jack said, addressing the trio. "The board has, unsurprisingly, unanimously decided to issue a statement of support. You can write it however you feel is best for you and the company. And... I owe y'all an apology for not pushing harder for immediate action to support you."

Then, with a hint of amusement, he added, "You've got those boys sweating bullets. That move was pure Buck, little lady. He'd be proud. You're a lot like him—a real fighter when challenged. And don't be too hard on Rick; you know how he can be. He'll come around. I suppose we all need to stop seeing you as the little tomboy tagging along and sitting on our laps and start seeing you as the incredibly competent CEO you've become."

He paused briefly, continuing thoughtfully, "I'm not gonna lie, Jules, I find your lifestyle a little weird. But it's your life, your choice. I knew about Kasey back when your dad had him checked out. I remember how Buck reacted when he found out. He didn't understand it either, but he always said he trusted your judgment. He liked Kasey a lot; he made that clear more than once. If your dad thought Kasey was a man good enough for his daughter, who am I to judge? Just know, I've got your back, always."

"Thank you, Jack. Your support means the world to me," she replied warmly, embracing him.

"I better get back in there before they tear each other apart. They're already hitting the bottle," Jack joked, heading back into the fray. "You really got 'em all worked up."

Julia smiled with relief. "One problem down, now let's tackle the next. I could use some help drafting this statement," she said, stepping into the elevator.

"Are you sure you need help? That was one hell of a statement you just made," Kasey remarked proudly. "You really brought the room to its knees."

"Once James reminded me I hold all the cards—the stock, the ranch, and the fucking money—they were easy. Plus, I pulled out Buck's insurance policy. That was guaranteed to shut them the fuck up and hopefully keep them in line. Sorry, I'm still worked up," she said with a smile, her eyes sparkling and her cheeks flushed.

"Don't apologize; you're so powerful and sexy right now," Ren said, awed by Julia.

"Focus, babe. We still have work to do," she said with a determined chuckle as the doors opened, and they headed for her office.

***

Kasey and Julia settled in to craft her statement while Ren concentrated on perfecting her outfit. Midway through their task, they received the awaited call: the detective had successfully traced the photos back to the protester who had clashed with Kasey. Armed with this crucial information, drafting her statement became less daunting.

She reached out to Jack, requesting that he come to her office. "Would you mind delivering the company statement before I address the issue myself? Here's what we'd like you to say." Jack reviewed the prepared statement and responded,

"Not a problem at all. I'll gladly stand alongside you, representing the board."

"Excellent. I've decided to bring the press into the lobby—it's too cold outside, and I'd rather not shiver. We'll set up a podium, and my security team will handle the press. We're about to grab some lunch—would you like us to order something for you?" Julia offered.

"No, thanks, Jules. I'm gonna have a private talk with Rick, see if I can get him to come apologize."

"It's not necessary, Jack. I don't want you to have to force him. He doesn't have to agree with my choices, but he does have to respect my position. I'll meet you outside in an hour."

***

As Julia exited the elevator, the flash of cameras momentarily blinded her as she made her way to the podium beside Jack. His imposing presence in a suit, polished boots, and Stetson brought memories of Buck flooding back. For a brief moment, she felt her father's spirit strengthening her resolve.

"Good afternoon, I'm Jack Dorsey, a senior board member of Masters Inc.," he announced, the flashbulbs going off once more. "We would like to take this opportunity to address recent allegations involving our CEO, Julia Masters, our VP of New Acquisitions, Kasey Cortland, and our Creative Director for Hawthorne-Masters, Ren Ito."

"While it's our company policy not to delve into the private lives of our employees, we stand firmly behind them. Their personal lives are just that—personal. Furthermore, we want to clarify that this exposé is a result of targeted harassment against Ms. Masters and Mr. Cortland by a former member of a radical animal rights group. He had been stalking them both since Mr. Cortland intervened to protect Ms. Masters and her late father a year ago. Only hours ago, the perpetrator was apprehended, which prompted our decision to remain silent until now."

Julia and Kasey had skillfully positioned the board to appear supportive from the very start.

Jack asserted firmly, "Here at Masters Inc., we denounce all forms of violence and harassment and will take legal action to prevent any further incidents. Thank you. Ms. Masters would like to say a few words at this time."

As camera flashes illuminated the room, Jack stepped aside, allowing Julia to command the spotlight, with Ren and Kasey flanking her. She exuded strength and confidence in her short black asymmetrical jacket with silver buttons, a white textured t-shirt, matching tapered trousers, and 4-inch Louboutins—an outfit that made her feel every bit the formidable leader she was.

"Good afternoon, everyone. Thank you for being here today. I'll keep this brief," Julia began, stepping forward with a confident posture, her gaze sweeping the room before briefly glancing at her notes. "In our modern world, the invasion of personal information into the public domain presents a constant challenge, especially for those in the public eye." She paused, glancing up at the cameras before continuing. "Privacy seems to be a forgotten concept, with boundaries frequently breached. For anyone in influential positions, what should truly matter are their capabilities as professionals and leaders— their work ethic, intelligence, and how they treat their colleagues." Julia's tone grew firmer as she placed a hand on the podium, leaning slightly forward. "Personal relationships should not be subject to public scrutiny."

She paused, then straightened up. "Unfortunately, the persistent intrusion of paparazzi and gossip mongers continues to violate our privacy, both at home with our families and during leisure moments. This behavior is unacceptable and needs to be addressed. I understand that change won't happen overnight, so I feel compelled to set the record straight to prevent future speculation."

She looked directly at the reporters, a soft smile crossing her face as she spoke. "Kasey Cortland and Ren Ito are not only my life partners—but also partners to each other. We share our lives and our home. It's disheartening that this information has been disclosed at this time in a way aimed at tarnishing our reputations and damaging our brand. Following the successful launch of our new fashion house, Hawthorne-Masters, Mr. Ito has admirably fulfilled the position he was hired for. The dynamics of my personal relationships concern only myself and my partners."

Julia raised her chin slightly, her voice carrying a note of defiance. "Respect for diverse lifestyles is fundamental, particularly when they involve consenting adults. We mustn't forget the principle of 'live and let live.'"

She paused, letting the words sink in, then added with a slight nod. "As Captain Holt from Brooklyn Nine-Nine aptly put it, 'Every time someone steps up and says who they are, the world becomes a better and more interesting place.' Well," she smiled warmly, reaching out to take each of their hands in hers, "this is who we are."

"Thank you for your time," she concluded, squeezing their hands gently. Amid the flurry of flashing bulbs and the clamor of reporters hungry for details, Julia smiled as she walked toward the elevators hand in hand with Kasey and Ren, stepping away from the intense spotlight.

***

"It's all out there now," Julia said, grinning. She turned to Jack, who left with them. "Thank you, Jack, for your support. I won't forget it," she said as she hugged him.

"I'm glad I could be here for you. You let me know if you need anything else. We'll touch base after you take some time and decompress. Goodbye, Kasey, Ren," he said as he shook their hands. "You better take good care of this little lady, or you'll have me to answer to."

Sinking into the couch in her office, Julia kicked off her shoes. She rested her head on Kasey's lap, and Ren took her feet in his hands, gently massaging them as she spoke. "We need to touch base with Giles, Nigel, and Haruto—let them know what's happening and thank them for their statement of support."

The three of them sat quietly talking for the next half hour before their phones started buzzing. Julia got a text from Raven that simply said, "Sorry," while Ren got one from Rex that read, "Lucky you." Marisol even texted Kasey, telling him how thrilled she was for him and asking him to stop by soon and introduce his partners. The rest of the day was spent fielding calls, texts, and requests for interviews. Most of the messages were positive, but a few still clung to outdated notions of love, marriage, and what constitutes a family.

One surprising call came from Ren's father, who, while not apologizing for past actions, expressed pride in Ren's success, leaving Ren tearful at the unexpected sentiment. A later conversation with his mother revealed his father's quiet remorse for their estrangement. It remained unspoken but acknowledged, and Ren accepted it, understanding this was his father's way of expressing regret.

****

On the way home, Julia fell asleep on Kasey's shoulder in the car, exhaustion evident from the adrenaline rush of the last twenty-four hours. "Oh shit," she muttered as she woke up to the sight of reporters gathered outside their brownstone—a first for them. However, Charley and Carl swiftly ushered them indoors, shielding them from the chaos.

"What a crazy day," Julia mumbled to herself as she trudged toward her bedroom, her energy completely drained. "I'm sorry, but I am totally tapped out. I feel like I just fought a battle, and I could sleep for a week," she said wearily.

"You did, baby, and you won. And I— we couldn't be prouder," Ren said, trailing after her. "Aren't you hungry? Can we get you anything?"

"I'm more tired than anything else," she replied, kicking off her shoes and shedding her pants as she headed straight for bed. Peeling off her blouse and dropping it onto the floor, she slipped under the covers. "I'm gonna say goodnight now, in case I sleep through."

Ren leaned in to give her a kiss, while Kasey, gathering her clothes and neatly placing them on a chair, settled beside her on the bed.

"You were absolutely incredible today. You never cease to amaze me. Get some rest—you know where to find us if you wake up later," he whispered, planting a kiss on her forehead as she settled in for a much-needed rest.

Later that night, she quietly made her way to Kasey's bedroom, a contented smile gracing her lips as she slipped between them, relieved that she no longer had to conceal her love for either of them.

***

Chapter 26: The Rule Of Three

The next day at work brought a flood of interview requests and messages of support that felt endless. Amid the chaos, Julia, Kasey, and Ren sat for a brief interview with Raven on her podcast *Shadows and Stilettos*. During the interview, they shared how they met, their plans for the future of Hawthorne-Masters, and their journey as a committed trio. Julia and Ren did most of the talking while Kasey briefly recounted how he and Ren had met at boarding school.

Julia expressed how helpless they'd felt when something so personal was taken from them, emphasizing the pain of being outed without their consent. "It was never our choice. It was never a decision we made. To have that taken from us... it's like losing a part of yourself before you were even ready to let it go." Her words resonated deeply, capturing the vulnerability they'd endured. Ren caught her gaze, a subtle but understanding nod passing between them as Kasey stayed quiet, offering her space to express the frustration that they all felt.

As the interview continued, Julia couldn't help but reflect on how far they'd come—how far she had come; from the girl who had once stood in her father's shadow to the woman now standing firm in her own light, leading a life she never imagined possible.

It took a week for the frenzy to finally subside, allowing life to return to some semblance of normal—just in time for Julia to face the anniversary of the loss of her family. As much as she wanted to let the world move forward, she couldn't shake the thought that loomed over her—the anniversary. It had been a year, but the pain felt as fresh as the first day. The grief, the anger, the loss, all waiting for her in silence. It would come soon, and she wasn't sure if she was ready for it.

Opting for a low-key observance, Julia, along with Kasey, Ren, and Will, retreated to the serene refuge of the ranch for Thanksgiving— a welcome break from the media's prying eyes. Since the funeral, Julia had avoided the ranch; the memories were too raw to face. When Kasey first suggested going there, Julia hesitated, unsure if she would find any comfort in a place so steeped in her family's history.

Ren gently expressed his eagerness to see where she grew up, subtly encouraging her. Micki, James, and Will all added their voices to the conversation over time, each letting her know—without pressure—that it was time to confront her past. Knowing she would have all the emotional support she needed, Julia agreed—it was time to reconcile with the place she once called home. To make the occasion even more special, she arranged for Akira to fly in, eager for her to spend time with Will and get to know everyone better.

Months after the funeral, at Julia's request, Micki and a few of Lily's close friends had cleared out the main house, sorting through the remnants of a life once lived. Some items were carefully stored away; others donated to charity. Though the space felt emptier without the familiar objects that once filled it, stepping through the door stirred deep, unspoken emotions. The walls—now bare—seemed to hum with echoes of the past, a mix of comfort and pain.

With Kasey and Ren offering steady support and soft words of reassurance, Julia gradually found herself reconnecting with the place. The ranch, once a symbol of loss, began to transform into a space of healing.

Accompanied by Micki, James, and Will, Julia and Kasey introduced Ren and Akira to the joys of ranch life. They spent their days on horseback, riding through the vast expanse of land—hooves kicking up dust as they galloped across sun-dappled fields, the air rich with the scent of pine and wildflowers. Wide, open skies and rolling hills stretched endlessly before them, a reminder of the boundless beauty surrounding them. Each ride deepened their connection, the stories shared, and the laughter exchanged, weaving them closer together until the day seemed to stretch on forever.

Their nights were filled with the warmth of friendship, the living room echoing with laughter and the crackle of the fireplace. The air was alive with the cheerful chatter of card games, the competitive edge of board games, and the playful energy of video games. Julia, Micki, and James took it upon themselves to teach everyone some Western line dances, their boots tapping out a rhythmic beat on the wooden floor. To everyone's surprise, they even managed to coax the usually reserved Kasey into joining in, much to the group's delight.

During the day, while the men indulged in target shooting, their competitive spirits emerging as they aimed at distant targets, Julia, Micki, and Akira relaxed nearby. They shared stories over mugs of hot chocolate by the fire pit, the conversation flowing easily, punctuated by bursts of laughter and the occasional serious reflection. It was during one of these peaceful moments, as they watched the men from a distance, that Akira casually mentioned she was considering moving to America to be closer to Will. Her words hung in the air, quiet but full of meaning, a testament to the deepening connections at the ranch.

On the Saturday after Thanksgiving, Micki asked Julia to dress up and join her and Akira at the winery to check out a new offering—a plan that conveniently took Julia away from the ranch for a couple of hours.

Upon their return, they chatted animatedly as they walked through the front door. Micki excused herself, announcing she needed to use the bathroom, while Akira mentioned she was heading to the kitchen for something to drink.

As Julia rounded the corner into the living room, she was greeted by a breathtaking sight—like something straight out of a romantic movie. The room glowed with the soft flicker of countless candles, casting a warm golden light over everything. Exquisite floral arrangements featuring her favorite flower—star-gazer lilies—adorned every surface, filling the air with a delicate, intoxicating fragrance.

Standing before the roaring fireplace in formal attire were Kasey and Ren, both looking impossibly handsome. The firelight flickered against their faces, softening their features as they smiled warmly at her.

"What's going on?" Julia asked softly, her voice laced with confusion and surprise. Her gaze darted between Kasey and the scene unfolding before her, her heart racing. Kasey gently took her hand, his touch reassuring, and led her to the couch. As she sat, he smoothly dropped to one knee in front of her, a gesture so sincere it took her breath away. Julia's heart fluttered as she looked into his eyes, her mind replaying their journey from the moment they first met to this very instant. She felt an overwhelming sense of gratitude and love, the weight of the moment sinking in. Committing to Kasey, to their shared future, meant embracing everything they had dreamed of together.

"Julia, you are the love of my life," Kasey said, his voice steady but thick with emotion. "I can't imagine a day without you, nor would I ever want to. You fill my world with so much love, so much happiness. I'm grateful for you every single day. I want nothing more than to spend the rest of my life with you and Ren, building our family together."

With those heartfelt words, he reached into his pocket and pulled out a ring box, opening it to reveal a stunning 4-carat, emerald-cut, flawless pink diamond set in a vintage platinum band. The light from the nearby candles danced off the facets of the gem, making it seem almost ethereal. "I love you, Julia, with all my heart," he continued, his gaze never leaving hers. "Will you commit to me as I have committed to you?"

Tears of joy streamed down her face, her heart swelling with emotion. She nodded, unable to form words at first, then whispered, "Yes, Kasey, I'm fully committed to you. I love you, baby, and I can't imagine my life without you." She leaned forward, pulling him into a tender kiss, the salt from her tears mingling with the softness of his lips, sealing the moment. Julia couldn't help but think of how much Kasey had changed. From the quiet, guarded man she'd first met to the one who now radiated happiness and contentment, ready to build a future with her. Her love had brought him out of the shadows, and it filled her with pride to see him so fulfilled.

As Kasey rose to his feet, Ren followed suit, lowering himself onto one knee and gently clasping Julia's hand. As she looked at him, memories of their journey together flooded her mind. The connection they shared had only grown stronger, and now, committing to Ren felt like the natural continuation of the love that had already transformed her life.

"Jules, you are my everything," he declared with heartfelt sincerity. "The love we share, the bond we've formed with Kasey, is unlike anything I've ever known. All I want is to journey through life with you and Kasey by my side as a family." His voice unwavering, he continued, "It would bring me immeasurable joy if you would honor me with your commitment, just as I commit myself to you." With deep emotion, he offered her his ring, two smaller, emerald-shaped, white diamonds that, when combined with Kasey's, formed a single band, the pink diamond nestled between the two white ones, symbolizing the three of them and their intertwined destinies.

Overwhelmed with emotion, Julia's tears spoke volumes as she whispered, "Yes, Ren. I'm wholeheartedly committed to you. I love you." Their lips met in a deep, passionate kiss, a testament to the depth of their shared affection. As Kasey offered her a handkerchief, their closest friends emerged from the shadows, showering them with applause and cheers. Will, grinning from ear to ear, shoved a video camera in their faces to capture the celebration.

Amid the jubilation of this unexpected yet deeply cherished moment, Julia cried happy tears while Kasey and Ren hugged and kissed, a silent reminder of their commitment to each other.

"Oh my God, did you guys plan this together?" Julia marveled, her heart brimming with happiness.

"It was all Kasey and Ren's doing. I just whisked you away to give them time to prepare," Micki explained with a wide smile. Watching Julia's eyes light up, a quiet sense of pride and joy swelled in Micki's chest. She had always hoped Julia would find her happiness, and seeing it realized in such a perfect way made her heart swell. "You're truly something else, Julia Masters. You didn't just get a man to put a ring on it—you got two."

"It's not like I didn't think this would happen someday, but you both caught me off guard in the most wonderful way. My ring is absolutely gorgeous," Julia said, her heart swelling with love as she showed the ring to Micki and Akira.

Enveloped in the joy and excitement of the moment, Julia realized that the ranch, once a place of sorrow, had now transformed into the happy backdrop for a beautiful new chapter in her life.

"I'm thrilled you chose the ranch for this," Julia beamed, her eyes sparkling with gratitude. "You've given me a new cherished memory. I'll never forget getting engaged here, and when the time comes, it'll be the perfect setting for our commitment ceremony." She grinned, a playful twinkle in her eye. "I know you didn't think you'd get away without having a big party. This cowgirl is wearing the big dress and having all our friends and family celebrate with us."

"That's right," Micki chimed in, her voice full of excitement, "I'm not missing out on being my best girl's maid of honor."

"Whatever you want, sweetheart. We're all in," Kasey said as he and Ren wrapped Julia in a loving hug.

Later that evening, Ren shared the engagement news with his parents, who welcomed Julia with open arms. His mother beamed, exchanging pleasantries with Kasey in Japanese, the shared joy deepening their bond. His father, ever stoic, didn't speak directly to Kasey, but there was a brief moment—an almost reluctant nod in Kasey's direction—that carried more weight than words. Ren noticed it, and while he knew real change wouldn't come overnight, he felt a flicker of hope. His father was trying, and that was something.

The trio shared their news with Nigel, Giles, and Gunther. Nigel was the first to react, his voice booming with excitement over the speaker. "Ah, my dear girl, we knew this was coming!"

Giles chimed in next, his tone warm with a hint of teasing, "Looks like we'll need to plan another visit—this wedding won't plan itself!" Gunther, ever the pragmatist, joked, "You know the villa is still yours for the honeymoon, right? Don't make us offer a third time." Laughter filled the line, their joy effortlessly bridging the miles between them.

Akira called Haruto, and Kasey took the phone, accepting Haruto's excited congratulations.

Julia stepped away to call Jack, her heart pounding as she nervously asked him to walk her down the aisle. There was a pause on the other end, and for a brief moment, she feared he might not want to. But then his voice came through, warm and filled with pride. "I'd be honored, Jules. Couldn't be happier for you." Julia smiled, her heart swelling with affection, reflecting on all the times Jack had supported her. This felt like a full circle—a bond between them that had only deepened over the years.

Later, as they settled into bed, their bodies intertwined as seamlessly as their hearts, each of them knowing they'd found their bliss. As they drifted off to sleep, Julia's head resting gently on Ren's chest, with Kasey spooning her from behind, the truth settled deep within them: together, they embodied the essence of the rule of three—stronger, more complete, and utterly fulfilled.

***

Thank you for joining Julia, Kasey, and Ren on their journey in *The Rule of Three: A Tale of Love, Lust, and Polyamory.* Their story doesn't end here—there's more to come as their lives, love, and relationships continue to evolve.

Stay tuned for the next installment in the *Rule of Three* series, where their journey will take even more unexpected twists and turns.